About the author

Jeffery Deaver is the bestselling author of eighteen suspense novels, including *The Bone Collector*, which was made into a feature film by Universal Pictures. He has been nominated for four Edgar Awards from the Mystery Writers of America and an Anthony Award, is a two-time recipient of the Ellery Queen Readers Award for Best Short Story of the Year and recently won the WHSmith Thumping Good Read Award. He lives in California and Virginia.

Visit his website at www.jefferydeaver.com

The Bone Collector
Praying for Sleep

Jeffery Deaver

CORONET BOOKS
Hodder & Stoughton

The Bone Collector copyright © 1997 by Jeffery Deaver
Praying for Sleep copyright © 1994 by Jeffery Deaver

The Bone Collector first published in Great Britain in 1997 by Hodder &
Stoughton
Praying for Sleep first published in USA in 1994 by Viking Penguin
First published in Great Britain in 1994 by Hodder & Stoughton

This paperback omnibus edition published in 2003 by Hodder &
Stoughton
A division of Hodder Headline

A Coronet paperback

10 9 8 7 6 5 4 3 2 1

A CIP catalogue record for this title
is available from the British Library

ISBN 0 340 83076 X

Printed and bound in Great Britain by
Mackays of Chatham plc, Chatham, Kent

Hodder & Stoughton
A division of Hodder Headline
338 Euston Road
London NW1 3BH

The Bone Collector

For my family, Dee, Danny, Julie, Ethel
and Nelson . . . Apples don't fall far.

And for Diana too.

1
KING FOR A DAY

"The present in New York is so powerful
that the past is lost."

John Jay Chapman

ONE

S he wanted only to sleep.

The plane had touched down two hours late and there'd been a marathon wait for the luggage. And *then* the car service had messed up; the limo'd left an hour ago. So now they were waiting for a cab.

She stood in the line of passengers, her lean body listing against the weight of her laptop computer. John rattled on about interest rates and new ways of restructuring the deal but all she could think was: Friday night, 10:30. I wanna pull on my sweats and hit the hay.

Gazing at the endless stream of Yellow Cabs. Something about the color and the similarity of the cars reminded her of insects. And she shivered with the creepy-crawly feeling she remembered from her childhood in the mountains when she and her brother'd find a gut-killed badger or kick over a red-ant nest and gaze at the wet mass of squirming bodies and legs.

T.J. Colfax shuffled forward as the cab pulled up and squealed to a stop.

The cabbie popped the trunk but stayed in the car. They had to load their own luggage, which ticked John off. He was used to people doing things for him. Tammie Jean didn't care; she was still occasionally surprised to find that she had a secretary to type and file for her. She tossed her suitcase in, closed the trunk and climbed inside.

John got in after her, slammed the door and mopped his pudgy face and balding scalp as if the effort of pitching his suitbag in the trunk had exhausted him.

"First stop East Seventy-second," John muttered through the divider.

"Then the Upper West Side," T.J. added. The Plexiglas between the front and back seats was badly scuffed and she could hardly see the driver.

The cab shot away from the curb and was soon cruising down the expressway toward Manhattan.

"Look," John said, "that's why all the crowds."

He was pointing at a billboard welcoming delegates to the UN peace conference, which was starting on Monday. There were going to be ten thousand visitors in town. T.J. gazed up at the bill-board—blacks and whites and Asians, waving and smiling. There was something wrong about the artwork, though. The proportions and the colors were off. And the faces all seemed pasty.

T.J. muttered, "Body snatchers."

They sped along the broad expressway, which glared an uneasy yellow under the highway lights. Past the old Navy Yard, past the Brooklyn piers.

John finally stopped talking and pulled out his Texas Instruments, started crunching some numbers. T.J. sat back in the seat, looking at the steamy sidewalks and sullen faces of people sitting on the brownstone stoops overlooking the highway. They seemed half-comatose in the heat.

It was hot in the cab too and T.J. reached for the button to lower the window. She wasn't surprised to find that it didn't work. She reached across John. His was broken too. It was then that she noticed that the door locks were missing.

The door handles too.

Her hand slid over the door, feeling for the nub of the handle. Nothing—it was as if someone had cut it off with a hacksaw.

"What?" John asked.

"Well, the doors . . . How do we open them?"

John was looking from one to the other when the sign for the Midtown Tunnel came and went.

"Hey!" John rapped on the divider. "You missed the turn. Where're you going?"

"Maybe he's going to take the Queensboro," T.J. suggested. The bridge meant a longer route but avoided the tunnel's toll. She sat forward and tapped on the Plexiglas, using her ring.

"Are you taking the bridge?"

He ignored them.

"Hey!"

And a moment later they sped past the Queensboro turnoff.

"Shit," John cried. "Where're you taking us? Harlem. I'll bet he's taking us to Harlem."

T.J. looked out the window. A car was moving parallel to them, passing slowly. She banged on the window hard.

"Help!" she shouted. "Please . . ."

The car's driver glanced at her once, then again, frowning. He slowed and pulled behind them but with a hard jolt the cab skidded down an exit ramp into Queens, turned into an alley and sped through a deserted warehouse district. They must've been going sixty miles an hour.

"What're you *doing*?"

T.J. banged on the divider. "Slow down. Where are?—

"Oh, God, no," John muttered. "Look."

The driver had pulled on a ski mask.

"What do you want?" T.J. shouted.

"Money? We'll give you money."

Still, silence from the front of the cab.

T.J. ripped open her Targus bag and pulled out her black laptop. She reared back and slammed the corner of the computer into the window. The glass held though the sound of the bang seemed to scare the hell out of the driver. The cab swerved and nearly hit the brick wall of the building they were speeding past.

"Money! How much? I can give you a lot of money!" John sputtered, tears dripping down his fat cheeks.

T.J. rammed the window again with the laptop. The screen flew off under the force of the blow but the window remained intact.

She tried once more and the body of the computer split open and fell from her hands.

"Oh, shit . . ."

They both pitched forward violently as the cab skidded to a stop in a dingy, unlit cul-de-sac.

The driver climbed out of the cab, a small pistol in his hand.

"Please, no," she pleaded.

He walked to the back of the cab and leaned down, peering into the greasy glass. He stood there for a long time, as she and John scooted backwards, against the opposite door, their sweating bodies pressed together.

The driver cupped his hands against the glare from the streetlights and looked at them closely.

A sudden crack resonated through the air, and T.J. flinched. John gave a short scream.

In the distance, behind the driver, the sky filled with red and blue fiery streaks. More pops and whistles. He turned and gazed up as a huge, orange spider spread over the city.

Fireworks, T.J. recalled reading in the *Times*. A present from the mayor and the UN secretary-general for the conference delegates, welcoming them to the greatest city on earth.

The driver turned back to the cab. With a loud snap he pulled up on the latch and slowly opened the door.

———

The call was anonymous. As usual.

So there was no way of checking back to see *which* vacant lot the RP meant. Central had radioed, *"He said Thirty-seven near Eleven. That's all."*

Reporting parties weren't known for Triple A directions to crime scenes.

Already sweating though it was just nine in the morning, Amelia Sachs pushed through a stand of tall grass. She was walking the strip search—what the Crime Scene people called it—an S-shaped pattern. Nothing. She bent her head to the speaker/mike pinned to her navy-blue uniform blouse.

"Portable 5885. Can't find anything, Central. You have a further-to?"

Through crisp static the dispatcher replied, "Nothing more on location, 5885. But one thing . . . the RP said he hoped the vic was dead. K."

"Say again, Central."

"The RP said he hoped the victim was dead. For his sake. K."

"K."

Hoped the vic was dead?

Sachs struggled over a wilted chain-link and searched another empty lot. Nothing.

She wanted to quit. Call in a 10-90, unfounded report, and go back to the Deuce, which was her regular beat. Her knees hurt and she was hot as stew in this lousy August weather. She wanted to slip into the Port Authority, hang with the kids and have a tall can of Arizona iced tea. Then, at 11:30—just a couple of hours away—she'd clean out her locker at Midtown South and head downtown for the training session.

But she didn't—couldn't—blow off the call. She kept going: along the hot sidewalk, through the gap between two abandoned tenements, through another vegetation-filled field.

Her long index finger pushed into her flattop uniform cap, through the layers of long red hair piled high on her head. She scratched compulsively then reached up underneath the cap and scratched some more. Sweat ran down her forehead and tickled and she dug into her eyebrow too.

Thinking: My last two hours on the street. I can live with it.

As Sachs stepped farther into the brush she felt the first uneasiness of the morning.

Somebody's watching me.

The hot wind rustled the dry brush and cars and trucks sped noisily to and from the Lincoln Tunnel. She thought what Patrol officers often did: This city is so damn loud somebody could come up right behind me, knife-range away, and I'd never know it.

Or line up iron sights on my back . . .

She spun around quickly.

Nothing but leaves and rusting machinery and trash.

Climbing a pile of stones, wincing. Amelia Sachs, thirty-one—a *mere* thirty-one, her mother would say—was plagued by arthritis. Inherited from her grandfather as clearly as she'd received her mother's willowy build and her father's good looks and career (the red hair was anybody's guess). Another jolt of pain as she eased through a tall curtain of dying bushes. She was fortunate to stop herself one pace from a sheer thirty-foot drop.

Below her was a gloomy canyon—cut deep into the bedrock of the West Side. Through it ran the Amtrak roadbed for trains bound north.

She squinted, looking at the floor of the canyon, not far from the railroad bed.

What *is* that?

A circle of overturned earth, a small tree branch sticking out of the top? It looked like—

Oh, my good Lord . . .

She shivered at the sight. Felt the nausea rise, prickling her skin like a wave of flame. She managed to step on that tiny part inside her that wanted to turn away and pretend she hadn't seen this.

He hoped the victim was dead. For his sake.

She ran toward an iron ladder that led down from the sidewalk to the roadbed. She reached for the railing but stopped just in time. Shit. The perp might've escaped, this way. If she touched it she might screw up any prints he'd left. Okay, we do it the hard way. Breathing deeply to dull the pain in her joints, she began climbing down the rock face itself, slipping her issue shoes—polished like silver for the first day of her new assignment—into crevices cut in the stone. She jumped the last four feet to the roadbed and ran to the grave.

"Oh, man . . ."

It wasn't a branch sticking out of the ground; it was a hand. The body'd been buried vertical and the dirt piled on until just the forearm, wrist and hand protruded. She stared at the ring finger; all the flesh had been whittled away and a woman's diamond cocktail ring had been replaced on the bloody, stripped bone.

Sachs dropped to her knees and began to dig.

Dirt flying under her dog-paddling hands, she noticed that the uncut fingers were splayed, stretched beyond where they could normally bend. Which told her that the vic had been alive when the last shovelful of dirt was spooned onto the face.

And maybe still was.

Sachs dug furiously into the loosely packed earth, cutting her hand on a bottle shard, her dark blood mixing into the darker earth. And then she came to the hair and a forehead below it, a cyanotic bluish-gray from the lack of oxygen. Digging further until she could see the dull eyes and the mouth, which had twisted into a horrible grin as the vic had tried in the last few seconds to stay above the rising tide of black earth.

It wasn't a woman. Despite the ring. He was a heavyset man in his fifties. As dead as the soil he floated in.

Backing away, she couldn't take her eyes off his and nearly stumbled over a railroad track. She could think of absolutely nothing for a full minute. Except what it must've been like to die that way.

Then: Come *on*, honey. You got yourself a homicide crime scene and you're first officer.

You know what to do.

ADAPT

A is for Arrest a known perp.

D is for Detain material witnesses and suspects.

A is for Assess the crime scene.

P is for . . .

What was *P* again?

She lowered her head to the mike. "Portable 5885 to Central. Further-to. I've got a 10-29 by the train tracks at Three-eight and Eleven. Homicide, K. Need detectives, CS, bus and tour doctor. K."

"Roger, 5885. Perp in custody, K?"

"No perp."

"Five-eight-eight-five, K."

Sachs stared at the finger, the one whittled down to the bone. The incongruous ring. The eyes. And the grin . . . oh, that fucking grin. A shudder ripped through her body. Amelia Sachs had swum among snakes in summer-camp rivers and had boasted truthfully she'd have no problem bungee-jumping from a hundred-foot bridge. But let her think of confinement . . . think of being trapped, immobile, and the panic attack'd grab her like an electric shock. Which was why Sachs walked fast when she walked and why she drove cars like light itself.

When you move they can't getcha . . .

She heard a sound and cocked her head.

A rumble, deep, getting louder.

Scraps of paper blowing along the roadbed of the tracks. Dust dervishes swirling about her like angry ghosts.

Then a low wail . . .

Five-foot-nine Patrol Officer Amelia Sachs found herself facing down a thirty-ton Amtrak locomotive, the red, white and blue slab of steel approaching at a determined ten miles an hour.

"Hold up, there!" she shouted.

The engineer ignored her.

Sachs jogged onto the roadbed and planted herself right in the middle of the track, spread her stance and waved her arms, signaling him to stop. The locomotive squealed to a halt. The engineer stuck his head out the window.

"You can't go through here," she told him.

He asked her what she meant. She thought he looked woefully young to be driving such a big train.

"It's a crime scene. Please shut off the engine."

"Lady, I don't see any crimes."

But Sachs wasn't listening. She was looking up at a gap in the chain-link on the west side of the train viaduct, at the top, near Eleventh Avenue.

That would have been one way to get the body here without being seen—parking on Eleventh and dragging the body through the narrow alley to the cliff. On Thirty-seventh, the cross street, he could be spotted from two dozen apartment windows.

"That train, sir. Just leave it right there."

"I can't leave it here."

"Please shut off the engine."

"We don't shut off the engines of trains like this. They run all the time."

"And call the dispatcher. Or somebody. Have them stop the southbound trains too."

"We can't do that."

"Now, sir. I've got the number of that vehicle of yours."

"Vehicle?"

"I'd suggest you do it immediately," Sachs barked.

"What're you going to do, lady? Gimme a ticket?"

But Amelia Sachs was once again climbing back up the stone walls, her poor joints creaking, her lips tasting limestone dust, clay and her own sweat. She jogged to the alley she'd noticed from the roadbed and then turned around, studying Eleventh Avenue and the Javits Center across it. The hall was bustling with crowds—spectators and press. A huge banner proclaimed, *Welcome UN Delegates!* But earlier this morning, when the street was deserted, the perp could easily have found a parking space along here and carried the body to the tracks undetected. Sachs strode to Eleventh, surveyed the six-lane avenue, which was jammed with traffic.

Let's do it.

She waded into the sea of cars and trucks and stopped the north-bound lanes cold. Several drivers tried end runs and she had to issue two citations and finally drag trash cans out into the middle of the street as a barricade to make sure the good residents did their civic duty.

Sachs had finally remembered the next of the first officer's ADAPT rules.

P is for Protect the crime scene.

The sound of angry horns began to fill the hazy morning sky, soon supplemented by the drivers' angrier shouts. A short time later she heard the sirens join the cacophony as the first of the emergency vehicles arrived.

Forty minutes later, the scene was swarming with uniforms and investigators, dozens of them—a lot more than a hit in Hell's Kitchen, however gruesome the cause of death, seemed to warrant. But, Sachs learned from another cop, this was a hot case, a media groper—the vic was one of two passengers who'd arrived at JFK last night, gotten into a cab and headed for the city. They'd never arrived at their homes.

"CNN's watching," the uniform whispered.

So Amelia Sachs wasn't surprised to see blond Vince Peretti, chief of the Central Investigation and Resource Division, which oversaw the crime scene unit, climb over the top of the embankment and pause as he brushed dust from his thousand-dollar suit.

She was, however, surprised to see him notice her and gesture her over, a faint smile on his clean-cut face. It occurred to her she was about to receive a nod of gratitude for her *Cliffhanger* routine. Saved the fingerprints on *that* ladder, boys. Maybe even a commendation. In the last hour of the last day of Patrol. Going out in a blaze of glory.

He looked her up and down. "Patrolwoman, you're nc rookie, are you? I'm safe in making that assumption."

"I'm sorry, sir?"

"You're not a rookie, I assume."

She wasn't, not technically, though she had only three years' service under her belt, unlike most of the other Patrol officers her age; they had nine or ten years in. Sachs had foundered for a few years before attending the academy. "I'm not sure what you're asking."

He looked exasperated and the smile vanished. "You were first officer?"

"Yessir."

"Why'd you close down Eleventh Avenue? What were you *thinking* of?"

She looked along the broad street, which was still blocked by her trash-can barricade. She'd gotten used to the honking but realized now it was really quite loud; the line of cars extended for miles.

"Sir, the first officer's job is to arrest a perp, detain any witnesses, protect—"

"I know the ADAPT rule, officer. You closed the street tc protect the crime scene?"

"Yessir. I didn't think the perp would park on the cross street. He could be seen too easily from those apartments See, there? Eleventh seemed like a better choice."

"Well, it was a wrong choice. There were no footprints on *that* side of the tracks, and two sets going to the ladder that leads up to Thirty-seven."

"I closed Thirty-seven too."

"That's my point. That's all that needed to be closed. And the train?" he asked. "Why'd you stop that?"

"Well, sir. I thought that a train going through the scene might disturb evidence. Or something."

"Or *something*, officer?"

"I didn't express myself very well, sir. I meant—"

"What about Newark Airport?"

"Yessir." She looked around for help. There were officers nearby but they were busily ignoring the dressing-down. "What exactly about Newark?"

"Why didn't you shut that down too?"

Oh, wonderful. A schoolmarm. Her Julia Roberts lips grew taut but she said reasonably, "Sir, in my judgment, it seemed likely that—"

"The New York Thruway would've been a good choice too. And the Jersey Pike and Long Island Expressway. I-70, all the way to St Louis. Those are likely means of escape."

She lowered her head slightly and stared back at Peretti. The two of them were exactly the same height, though his heels were higher.

"I've gotten calls from the commissioner," he continued, "the head of the Port Authority, the UN secretary-general's office, the head of that expo—" He nodded toward the Javits Center. "We've fucked up the conference schedule, a U.S. senator's speech and traffic on the entire West Side. The train tracks were fifty feet from the vic and the street you closed was a good two-hundred feet away and thirty above. I mean, even Hurricane Eva didn't fuck up Amtrak's Northeast Corridor like this."

"I just thought—"

Peretti smiled. Because Sachs was a beautiful woman— her "foundering" before attending the academy had involved steady assignments for the Chantelle Modeling Agency on Madison Avenue—the cop chose to forgive her.

"Patrolwoman Sachs"—he glanced at the name tag on her chest, flattened chastely by the American Body Armor vest— "an object lesson. Crime scene work is a balance. It'd be nice if we could cordon off the whole city after every homicide and detain about three million people. But we can't do that. I say this constructively. For your edification."

"Actually, sir," she said brusquely, "I'm transferring out of Patrol. Effective as of noon today."

He nodded, smiled cheerfully. "Then, enough said. But for the record, it *was* your decision to stop the train and close the street."

"Yessir, it was," she said smartly. "No mistake about that."

He jotted this into a black watch book with slashing strokes of his sweaty pen.

Oh, please . . .

"Now, remove those garbage cans. You direct traffic until the street's clear again. You hear me?"

Without a yessir or nosir or any other acknowledgment she wandered to Eleventh Avenue and slowly began removing the garbage cans. Every single driver who passed her scowled or muttered something. Sachs glanced at her watch.

An hour to go.

I can live with it.

TWO

With a terse flutter of wings the peregrine dropped onto the window ledge. The light outside, midmorning, was brilliant and the air looked fiercely hot.

"There you are," the man whispered. Then cocked his head at the sound of the buzzer of the door downstairs.

"Is that him?" he shouted toward the stairs. "Is it?"

Lincoln Rhyme heard nothing in response and turned back to the window. The bird's head swiveled, a fast, jerky movement that the falcon nevertheless made elegant. Rhyme observed that its talons were bloody. A piece of yellow flesh dangled from the black nutshell beak. It extended a short neck and eased to the nest in movements reminiscent not of a bird's but a snake's. The falcon dropped the meat into the upturned mouth of the fuzzy blue hatchling. I'm looking, Rhyme thought, at the only living creature in New York City with no predator. Except maybe God Himself.

He heard the footsteps come up the stairs slowly.

"Was that him?" he asked Thom.

The young man answered, "No."

"Who was it? The doorbell rang, didn't it?"

Thom's eyes went to the window. "The bird's back. Look, bloodstains on your windowsill. Can you see them?"

The female falcon inched into view. Blue-gray like a fish, iridescent. Her head scanned the sky.

"They're always together. Do they mate for life?" Thom wondered aloud. "Like geese?"

Rhyme's eyes returned to Thom, who was bent forward at

his trim, youthful waist, gazing at the nest through the spattered window.

"Who was it?" Rhyme repeated. The young man was stalling now and it irritated Rhyme.

"A visitor."

"A visitor? Ha." Rhyme snorted. He tried to recall when his last *visitor* had been here. It must have been three months ago. Who'd it been? That reporter maybe or some distant cousin. Well, Peter Taylor, one of Rhyme's spinal cord specialists. And Blaine had been here several times. But she of course was not a *vis-i-tor*.

"It's freezing," Thom complained. His reaction was to open the window. Immediate gratification. Youth.

"Don't open the window," Rhyme ordered. "And tell me who the hell's here."

"It's freezing."

"You'll disturb the bird. You can turn the air conditioner down. *I'll* turn it down."

"We were here first," Thom said, further lifting the huge pane of window. "The birds moved in with full knowledge of you." The falcons glanced toward the noise, glaring. But then they always glared. They remained on the ledge, lording over their domain of anemic ginkgo trees and alternate-side-of-the-street parkers.

Rhyme repeated. "Who *is* it?"

"Lon Sellitto."

"Lon?"

What was he doing here?

Thom examined the room. "The place is a mess."

Rhyme didn't like the fuss of cleaning. He didn't like the bustle, the noise of the vacuum—which he found particularly irritating. He was content here, as it was. This room, which he called his office, was on the second floor of his Gothic townhouse on the Upper West Side of the city, overlooking Central Park. The room was large, twenty-by-twenty, and virtually every one of those feet was occupied. Sometimes he closed his eyes, playing a game, and tried to detect the smell of the different objects in the room here. The thousands of books and magazines, the Tower of Pisa stacks of photocopies, the hot transistors of the TV, the dust-frosted lightbulbs, the cork bulletin boards. Vinyl, peroxide, latex, upholstery.

Three different kinds of single-malt Scotch.

Falcon shit.

"I don't want to see him. Tell him I'm busy."

"And a young cop. Ernie Banks. No, he was a baseball player, right? You really should let me clean. You never notice how filthy someplace is till people come to call."

"Come to call? My, that sounds quaint. Victorian. How does *this* sound? Tell 'em to get the hell out. How's that for fin-desiècle etiquette?"

A mess . . .

Thom was speaking of the room but Rhyme supposed he meant his boss too.

Rhyme's hair was black and thick as a twenty-year-old's—though he was twice that age—but the strands were wild and bushy, desperately in need of a wash and cut. His face sprouted a dirty-looking three days' growth of black beard and he'd wakened with an incessant tickle in his ear, which meant that those hairs needed trimming as well. Rhyme's nails were long, finger and toe, and he'd been wearing the same clothes for a week—polka-dotted pajamas, god-awful ugly. His eyes were narrow, deep brown, and set in a face that Blaine had told him on a number of occasions, passionate and otherwise, was handsome.

"They want to talk to you," Thom continued. "They say it's very important."

"Well, bully for them."

"You haven't seen Lon for nearly a year."

"Why does that mean I want to see him now? Have you scared off the bird? I'll be pissed if you have."

"It's important, Lincoln."

"*Very* important, I recall you saying. Where's that doctor? He might've called. I was dozing earlier. And you were out."

"You've been awake since six A.M."

"No." He paused. "I woke up, yes. But then I dozed off. I was sound asleep. Did you check messages?"

Thom said, "Yes. Nothing from him."

"He said he'd be here midmorning."

"And it's just past eleven. Maybe we'll hold off notifying air-sea rescue. What do you say?"

"Have you been on the phone?" Rhyme asked abruptly. "Maybe he tried to call while you were on."

"I was talking to—"

"Did I say anything?" Rhyme asked. "Now you're angry. I didn't say you shouldn't be making phone calls. You can do that. You've always been able to do that. My point is just that he might've called while you were on the line."

"No, your point this morning is to be a shit."

"There you go. You know, they have this thing—call waiting. You can get two calls at once. I wish we had that. What does my old friend Lon want? And *his* friend the baseball player?"

"Ask them."

"I'm asking *you*."

"They want to see you. That's all I know."

"About something vay-ree im-por-tant."

"Lincoln." Thom sighed. The good-looking young man ran his hand through his blond hair. He wore tan slacks and a white shirt, with a blue floral tie, immaculately knotted. When he'd hired Thom a year ago Rhyme had said he could wear jeans and T-shirts if he wanted. But he'd been dressed impeccably every day since. Rhyme didn't know why it contributed to the decision to keep the young man on, but it had. None of Thom's predecessors had lasted more than six weeks. The number of those who quit was exactly equal to the firees.

"All right, what did you tell them?"

"I told them to give me a few minutes to make sure you were decent then they could come up. Briefly."

"You did that. Without asking me. Thank you very much."

Thom retreated a few steps and called down the narrow stairway to the first floor, "Come on, gentlemen."

"They told you something, didn't they?" Rhyme said. "You're holding out on me."

Thom didn't answer and Rhyme watched the two men approach. As they entered the room Rhyme spoke first. He said to Thom, "Close the curtain. You've already upset the birds way too much."

Which really meant only that he'd had enough of the sputtering sunlight.

——————

Mute.

With the foul, sticky tape on her mouth she couldn't speak a word and that made her feel more helpless than the metal handcuffs tight on her wrists. Than the grip of his short, strong fingers on her biceps.

The taxi driver, still in his ski mask, led her down the grimy, wet corridor, past rows of ducts and piping. They were in the basement of an office building. She had no idea where.

If I could talk to him . . .

T.J. Colfax was a player, the bitch of Morgan Stanley's third floor. A negotiator.

Money? You want money? I'll get you money, lots of it, boy. Bushels. She thought this a dozen times, trying to catch his eye, as if she could actually force the words into his thoughts.

Pleeeeeeeeease, she begged silently, and began thinking about the mechanics of cashing in her 401(k) and giving him her retirement fund. *Oh, please . . .*

She remembered last night: The man turning back from the fireworks, dragging them from the cab, handcuffing them. He'd thrown them into the trunk and they'd begun driving again. First over rough cobblestones and broken asphalt then smooth roads then rough again. She heard the whir of wheels on a bridge. More turns, more rough roads. Finally, the cab stopped and the driver got out and seemed to open a gate or some doors. He drove into a garage, she thought. All the sounds of the city were cut off and the car's bubbling exhaust rose in volume, reverberating off close walls.

Then the cab trunk opened and the man pulled her out. He yanked the diamond ring off her finger and pocketed it. Then he led her past walls of spooky faces, faded paintings of blank eyes staring at her, a butcher, a devil, three sorrowful children—painted on the crumbling plaster. Dragged her down into a moldy basement and dumped her on the floor. He clopped upstairs, leaving her in the dark, surrounded by a sickening smell—rotting flesh, garbage. There she'd lain for hours, sleeping a little, crying a lot. She'd wakened abruptly at a loud sound. A sharp explosion. Nearby. Then more troubled sleep.

A half hour ago he'd come for her again. Led her to the trunk and they'd driven for another twenty minutes. Here. Wherever *here* was.

They now walked into a dim basement room. In the center was a thick black pipe; he handcuffed her to it then gripped her feet and pulled them out straight in front of her, propping her in a sitting position. He crouched and tied her legs together with thin rope—it took several minutes; he was wearing leather gloves. Then he rose and gazed at her for a long moment, bent down and tore her blouse open. He walked around behind her and she gasped, feeling his hands on her shoulder, probing, squeezing her shoulder blades.

Crying, pleading through the tape.

Knowing what was coming.

The hands moved down, along her arms, and then under them and around the front of her body. But he didn't touch her breasts. No, as the hands spidered across her skin they seemed to be searching for her ribs. He prodded them and stroked. T.J. shivered and tried to pull away. He gripped her tight and caressed some more, pressing hard, feeling the give of the bone.

He stood. She heard receding footsteps. For a long moment there was silence except for the groans of air conditioners and elevators. Then she barked a frightened grunt at a sound right behind her. A repetitive noise. *Wsssh. Wsssh.* Very familiar but something she couldn't place. She tried to turn to see what he was doing but couldn't. What was it? Listening to the rhythmic sound, over and over and over. It took her right back to her mother's house.

Wsssh. Wsssh.

Saturday morning in the small bungalow in Bedford, Tennessee. It was the only day her mother didn't work and she devoted most of it to housecleaning. T.J. would wake up to a hot sun and stumble downstairs to help her. *Wsssh.* As she cried at this memory she listened to the sound and wondered why on earth he was sweeping the floor and with such careful, precise strokes of the broom.

———

He saw surprise and discomfort on their faces.

Something you don't find very often with New York City homicide cops.

Lon Sellitto and young Banks (Jerry, not Ernie) sat where Rhyme gestured with his bush-crowned head: twin dusty, uncomfortable rattan chairs.

Rhyme had changed considerably since Sellitto had last been here and the detective didn't hide his shock very well. Banks had no benchmark against which to judge what he was seeing but he was shocked nonetheless. The sloppy room, the vagrant gazing at them suspiciously. The smell too certainly— the visceral aroma surrounding the creature Lincoln Rhyme now was.

He immensely regretted letting them up.

"Why didn't you call first, Lon?"

"You would've told us not to come."

True.

Thom crested the stairs and Rhyme preempted him. "No, Thom, we won't be needing you." He'd remembered that the young man always asked guests if they wanted something to drink or eat.

Such a goddamn Martha Stewart.

Silence for a moment. Large, rumpled Sellitto—a twenty-year vet—glanced down into a box beside the bed and started to speak. Whatever he'd been about to say was cut off by the sight of disposable adult diapers.

Jerry Banks said, "I read your book, sir." The young cop had a bad hand when it came to shaving, lots of nicks. And what a charming cowlick in his hair! My good Lord, he can't be more than twelve. The more worn the world gets, Rhyme reflected, the younger its inhabitants seem to be.

"Which one?"

"Well, your crime scene manual, of course. But I meant the picture book. The one a couple years ago."

"There were words too. It was *mostly* words, in fact. Did you read them?"

"Oh, well, sure," Banks said quickly.

A huge stack of remaindered volumes of *The Scenes of the Crime* sat against one wall of his room.

"I didn't know you and Lon were friends," Banks added.

"Ah, Lon didn't trot out the yearbook? Show you the pictures? Strip his sleeve and show his scars and say these wounds I had with Lincoln Rhyme?"

Sellitto wasn't smiling. Well, I can give him even less to smile about if he likes. The senior detective was digging through his attaché case. And what does he have in *there*?

"How long were you partnered?" Banks asked, making conversation.

"There's a verb for you," Rhyme said. And looked at the clock.

"We weren't partners," Sellitto said. "I was Homicide, he was head of IRD."

"Oh," Banks said, even more impressed. Running the Central Investigation and Resource Division was one of the most prestigious jobs in the department.

"Yeah," Rhyme said, looking out the window, as if his doctor might be arriving via falcon. "The two musketeers."

In a patient voice, which infuriated Rhyme, Sellitto said, "Seven years, off and on, we worked together."

"And good years they were," Rhyme intoned.

Thom scowled but Sellitto missed the irony. Or more likely ignored it. He said, "We have a problem, Lincoln. We need some help."

Snap. The stack of papers landed on the bedside table.

"Some help?" The laugh exploded from the narrow nose Blaine had always suspected was the product of a surgeon's vision though it was not. She also thought his lips were too perfect (Add a scar, she'd once joked and during one of their fights she nearly had). And why, he wondered, does her voluptuous apparition keep rising today? He'd wakened thinking about his ex and had felt compelled to write her a letter, which was on the computer screen at that moment. He now saved the document on the disk. Silence filled the room as he entered the commands with a single finger.

"Lincoln?" Sellitto asked.

"Yessir. Some help. From me. I heard."

Banks kept an inappropriate smile on his face while he shuffled his butt uneasily in the chair.

"I've got an appointment in, well, any minute now," Rhyme said.

"An appointment."

"A doctor."

"Really?" Banks asked, probably to murder the silence that loomed again.

Sellitto, not sure where the conversation was going, asked, "And how've you been?"

Banks and Sellitto hadn't asked about his health when they'd arrived. It was a question people tended to avoid when they saw Lincoln Rhyme. The answer risked being a very complicated, and almost certainly an unpleasant, one.

He said simply, "I've been fine, thanks. And you? Betty?"

"We're divorced," Sellitto said quickly.

"Really?"

"She got the house and I got half a kid." The chunky cop said this with forced cheer, as if he'd used the line before, and Rhyme supposed there was a painful story behind the breakup. One he had no desire to hear. Still, he wasn't surprised that the marriage had tanked. Sellitto was a workhorse. He was one of the hundred or so first-grade detectives on the force and had been for years—he got the grade when they were handed out for merit not just time served. He'd worked close to eighty hours a week. Rhyme hadn't even known he was married for the first few months they'd worked together.

"Where you living now?" Rhyme asked, hoping a nice social conversation would tucker them out and send them on their way.

"Brooklyn. The Heights. I walk to work sometimes. You know those diets I was always on? The trick's not dieting. It's exercise."

He didn't look any fatter or thinner than the Lon Sellitto of three and a half years ago. Or the Sellitto of fifteen years ago for that matter.

"So," collegiate Banks said, "a doctor, you were saying. For a . . ."

"A new form of treatment?" Rhyme finished the dwindling question. "Exactly."

"Good luck."

"Thank you *so* much."

It was 11:36 A.M. Well past midmorning. Tardiness is inexcusable in a man of medicine.

He watched Bank's eyes twice scan his legs. He caught the pimply boy a second time and wasn't surprised to see the detective blush.

"So," Rhyme said. "I'm afraid I don't really have time to help you."

"But he's not here yet, right, the doctor?" asked Lon Sellitto in the same bulletproof tone he'd used to puncture homicide suspects' cover stories.

Thom appeared at the doorway with a coffeepot.

Prick, Rhyme mouthed.

"Lincoln forgot to offer you gentlemen something."

"Thom treats me like a child."

"If the bootie fits," the aide retorted.

"All right," Rhyme snapped. "Have some coffee. I'll have some mother's milk."

"Too early," Thom said. "The bar isn't open." And weathered Rhyme's glowering face quite well.

Again Bank's eyes browsed Rhyme's body. Maybe he'd been expecting just skin and bones. But the atrophying had stopped not long after the accident and his first physical therapists had exhausted him with exercise. Thom too, who may have been a prick at times and an old mother hen at others, was a damn good PT. He put Rhyme through passive ROM exercises every day. Taking meticulous notes on the goniometry—measurements of the range of motion that he applied to each joint in Rhyme's body. Carefully checking the spasticity as he kept the arms and legs in a constant cycle of abduction and adduction. ROM work wasn't a miracle but it built up some tone, cut down on debilitating contractures and kept the blood flowing. For someone whose muscular activities had been limited to his shoulders, head and left ring finger for three and a half years, Lincoln Rhyme wasn't in such bad shape.

The young detective looked away from the complicated black ECU control sitting by Rhyme's finger, hardwired to another controller, sprouting conduit and cables, which ran to the computer and a wall panel.

A quad's life is wires, a therapist had told Rhyme a long time ago. The rich ones, at least. The lucky ones.

Sellitto said, "There was a murder early this morning on the West Side."

"We've had reports of some homeless men and women disappearing over the past month," Banks said. "At first we thought it might be one of them. But it wasn't," he added dramatically. "The vic was one of those people last night."

Rhyme trained a blank expression on the young man with the dotted face. "Those *people*?"

"He doesn't watch the news," Thom said. "If you're talking about the kidnapping he hasn't heard."

"You don't watch the news?" Sellitto laughed. "You're the SOB read four papers a day and recorded the local news to watch when he got home. Blaine told me you called her Katie Couric one night when you were making love."

"I only read literature now," Rhyme said pompously, and falsely.

Thom added, "'Literature is news that stays news.'"

Rhyme ignored him.

Sellitto said, "Man and woman coming back from business on the Coast. Got into a Yellow Cab at JFK. Never made it home."

"There was a report about eleven-thirty. This cab was driving down the BQE in Queens. White male and female passenger in the back seat. Looked like they were trying to break a window out. Pounding on the glass. Nobody got tags or medallion."

"This witness—who saw the cab. Any look at the driver?"

"No."

"The woman passenger?"

"No sign of her."

Eleven forty-one. Rhyme was furious with Dr William Berger. "Nasty business," he muttered absently.

Sellitto exhaled long and loud.

"Go on, go on," Rhyme said.

"He was wearing her ring," Banks said.

"*Who* was wearing *what*?"

"The vic. They found this morning. He was wearing the woman's ring. The other passenger's."

"You're sure it was hers?"

"Had her initials inside."

"So you've got an unsub," Rhyme continued, "who wants you to know he's got the woman and she's still alive."

"What's an unsub?" Thom asked.

When Rhyme ignored him Sellitto said, "Unknown subject."

"But you know how he got it to fit?" Banks asked, a little wide-eyed for Rhyme's taste. "Her ring?"

"I give up."

"Cut the skin off the guy's finger. All of it. Down to the bone."

Rhyme gave a faint smile. "Ah, he's a smart one, isn't he?"

"Why's that smart?"

"To make sure nobody came by and took the ring. It was bloody, right?"

"A mess."

"Hard to see the ring in the first place. Then AIDS, hepatitis. Even if somebody noticed, a lot of folks'd take a pass on that trophy. What's her name, Lon?"

The older detective nodded to his partner, who flipped open his watchbook.

"Tammie Jean Colfax. She goes by T.J. Twenty-eight. Works for Morgan Stanley."

Rhyme observed that Banks too wore a ring. A school ring of some sort. The boy was too polished to be just a high-school and academy grad. No whiff of army about him. Wouldn't be surprised if the jewelry bore the name Yale. A homicide detective? What was the world coming to?

The young cop cupped his coffee in hands that shook sporadically. With a minuscule gesture of his own ring finger on the Everest & Jennings ECU panel, to which his left hand was strapped, Rhyme clicked through several settings, turning the AC down. He tended not to waste controls on things like heating and air conditioning; he reserved it for necessities like lights, the computer and his page-turning frame. But when the room got too cold his nose ran. And *that's* fucking torture for a quad.

"No ransom note?" Rhyme asked.

"Nothing."

"You're the case officer?" Rhyme asked Sellitto.

"Under Jim Polling. Yeah. And we want you to review the CS report."

Another laugh. "Me? I haven't looked at a crime scene report in three years. What could I possibly tell you?"

"You could tell us tons, Linc."

"Who's head of IRD now?"

"Vince Peretti."

"The congressman's boy," Rhyme recalled. "Have him review it."

A moment's hesitation. "We'd rather have you."

"Who's we?"

"The chief. Yours truly."

"And how," Rhyme asked, smiling like a schoolgirl, "does Captain Peretti feel about this vote of no confidence?"

Sellitto stood and paced through the room, glancing down at the stacks of magazines. *Forensic Science Review.* Harding & Boyle Scientific Equipment Company catalog. *The New Scotland Yard Forensic Investigation Annual. American College of Forensic Examiners Journal. Report of the American Society of Crime Lab Directors.* CRC Press *Forensics. Journal of the International Institute of Forensic Science.*

"Look at them," Rhyme said. "The subscriptions lapsed ages ago. And they're all dusty."

"*Everything* in here's fucking dusty, Linc. Why don't you get off your lazy ass and clean this pigsty up?"

Banks looked horrified. Rhyme squelched the burst of laughter that felt alien inside him. His guard had slipped and irritation had dissolved into amusement. He momentarily regretted that he and Sellitto had drifted apart. Then he shot the feeling dead. He grumbled, "I can't help you. Sorry."

"We've got the peace conference starting on Monday. We—"

"What conference?"

"At the UN. Ambassadors, heads of state. There'll be ten thousand dignitaries in town. You heard about that thing in London two days ago?"

"*Thing?*" Rhyme repeated caustically.

"Somebody tried to bomb the hotel where UNESCO was meeting. The mayor's scared shitless somebody's going to move on the conference here. He doesn't want ugly *Post* headlines."

"There's also the little problem," Rhyme said astringently,

"that Miss Tammie Jean might not be enjoying her tri home either."

"Jerry, tell him some details. Whet his appetite."

Banks turned his attention from Rhyme's legs to hi bed, which was—Rhyme readily admitted—by far the mor interesting of the two. Especially the control panel. It looke like something off the space shuttle and cost just abou as much. "Ten hours after they're snatched we find th male passenger—John Ulbrecht—shot and buried alive i the Amtrak roadbed near Thirty-seventh and Eleventh. Wel we find him dead. He'd *been* buried alive. Bullet was a .32. Banks looked up and added, "The Honda Accord of slugs."

Meaning there'd be no wily deductions about the unsu from exotic weaponry. This Banks seems smart, Rhym thought, and all he suffers from is youth, which he migh or might not outgrow. Lincoln Rhyme believed he himself ha never been young.

"Rifling on the slug?" Rhyme asked.

"Six lands and grooves, left twist."

"So he's got himself a Colt," Rhyme said and glanced ove the crime scene diagram again.

"You said 'he,'" the young detective continued. "Actuall it's 'they.'"

"What?"

"Unsubs. There're two of them. There were two sets o footprints between the grave and the base of an iron ladde leading up to the street," Banks said, pointing to the C diagram.

"Any prints on the ladder?"

"None. It was wiped. Did a good job of it. The footprint go to the grave and back to the ladder. Anyway, there *ha* to be two of 'em to schlepp the vic. He weighed over tw hundred pounds. One man couldn't've done it."

"Keep going."

"They got him to the grave, dropped him in, shot hir and buried him, went back to the ladder, climbed it an vanished."

"Shot him in the grave?" Rhyme inquired.

"Yep. There was no blood trail anywhere around the ladde or the path to the grave."

Rhyme found himself mildly interested. But he said, "What do you need me for?"

Sellitto grinned ragged yellow teeth. "We got ourselves a mystery, Linc. A buncha PE that doesn't make any fucking sense at all."

"So?" It was a rare crime scene when every bit of physical evidence made sense.

"Naw, this is real weird. Read the report. Please. I'll put it here. How's this thing work?" Sellitto looked at Thom, who fitted the report in the page-turning frame.

"I don't have time, Lon," Rhyme protested.

"That's quite a contraption," Banks offered, looking at the frame. Rhyme didn't respond. He glanced at the first page then read it carefully. Moved his ring finger a precise millimeter to the left. A rubber wand turned the page.

Reading. Thinking: Well, this *is* odd.

"Who was in charge of the scene?"

"Peretti himself. When he heard the vic was one of the taxi people he came down and took over."

Rhyme continued to read. For a minute the unimaginative words of cop writing held his interest. Then the doorbell rang and his heart galloped with a great shudder. His eyes slipped to Thom. They were cold and made clear that the time for banter was over. Thom nodded and went downstairs immediately.

All thoughts of cabdrivers and PE and kidnapped bankers vanished from the sweeping mind of Lincoln Rhyme.

"It's Dr Berger," Thom announced over the intercom.

At last. At long last.

"Well, I'm sorry, Lon. I'll have to ask you to leave. It was good seeing you again." A smile. "Interesting case, this one is."

Sellitto hesitated then rose. "But will you read through the report, Lincoln? Tell us what you think?"

Rhyme said, "You bet," then leaned his head back against the pillow. Quads like Rhyme, who had full head-and-neck movement, could activate a dozen controls just by three-dimensional movements of the head. But Rhyme shunned headrests. There were so few sensuous pleasures left to him that he was unwilling to abdicate the comfort of nestling his head against his two-hundred-dollar down pillow. The visitors had tired him out. Not even noon, and all he wanted to do wa sleep. His neck muscles throbbed in agony.

When Sellitto and Banks were at the door Rhyme said "Lon, wait."

The detective turned.

"One thing you should know. You've only found half th crime scene. The important one is the other one—the primary scene. His house. That's where he'll be. And it'll be hard a hell to find."

"Why do you think there's another scene?"

"Because he didn't shoot the vic at the grave. He shot him there—at the primary scene. And that's probably where he' got the woman. It'll be underground or in a very deserted par of city. Or both . . . Because, Banks"—Rhyme preempted the young detective's question—"he wouldn't risk shooting someone and holding a captive there unless it was quiet and private."

"Maybe he used a silencer."

"No traces of rubber or cotton baffling on the slug," Rhyme snapped.

"But how could the man've been shot there?" Banks countered. "I mean, there wasn't any blood spatter at the scene."

"I assume the victim was shot in the face," Rhyme announced.

"Well, yes," Banks answered, putting a stupid smile on hi own. "How'd you know?"

"Very painful, very incapacitating, very little blood with a .32 Rarely lethal if you miss the brain. With the vic in that shape the unsub could lead him around wherever he wanted. I say unsub singular because there's only one of them."

A pause. "But . . . there were two sets of prints," Banks nearly whispered, as if he were defusing a land mine.

Rhyme sighed. "The soles're identical. They were left by the same man making the trip twice. To fool us. And the prints going north are the same depth as the prints going south. S he wasn't carrying a two-hundred-pound load one way and not the other. Was the vic barefoot?"

Banks flipped through his notes. "Socks."

"Okay, then the perp was wearing the vic's shoes for his clever little stroll to the ladder and back."

"If he didn't come down the ladder how *did* he get to the grave?"

"He led the man along the train tracks themselves. Probably from the north."

"There're no other ladders to the roadbed for blocks in either direction."

"But there *are* tunnels running parallel to the tracks," Rhyme continued. "They hook up with the basements of some of the old warehouses along Eleventh Avenue. A gangster during Prohibition—Owney Madden—had them dug so he could slip shipments of bootleg whisky onto New York Central trains going up to Albany and Bridgeport."

"But why not just bury the vic near the tunnel? Why risk being seen schlepping the guy all the way to the overpass?"

Impatient now. "You *do* get what he's telling us, don't you?"

Banks started to speak then shook his head.

"He *had* to put the body where it'd be seen," Rhyme said. "He needed someone to find it. That's why he left the hand in the air. He's *waving* at us. To get our attention. Sorry, you may have only one unsub but he's plenty smart enough for two. There's an access door to a tunnel somewhere nearby. Get down there and dust it for prints. There won't be any. But you'll have to do it just the same. The press, you know. When the story starts coming out . . . Well, good luck, gentlemen. Now, you'll have to excuse me. Lon?"

"Yes?"

"Don't forget about the primary crime scene. Whatever happens, you'll have to find it. And fast."

"Thanks, Linc. Just read the report."

Rhyme said of course he would and observed that they believed the lie. Completely.

THREE

He had the best bedside manner Rhyme had ever encountered. And if anyone had had experience with bedside manners it was Lincoln Rhyme. He'd once calculated he'd seen seventy-eight degreed, card-carrying doctors in the past three and a half years.

"Nice view," Berger said, gazing out the window.

"Isn't it? Beautiful."

Though because of the height of the bed Rhyme could see nothing except a hazy sky sizzling over Central Park. That—and the birds—had been the essence of his view since he'd moved here from his last rehab hospital two and half years ago. He kept the shades drawn most of the time.

Thom was busy rolling his boss—the maneuver helped keep his lungs clear—and then catheterizing Rhyme's bladder, which had to be done every five or six hours. After spinal cord trauma, sphincters can be stuck open or they can be stuck closed. Rhyme was fortunate that his got jammed closed—fortunate, that is, provided someone was around to open up the uncooperative little tube with a catheter and K-Y jelly four times a day.

Dr Berger observed this procedure clinically and Rhyme paid no heed to the lack of privacy. One of the first things crips get over is modesty. While there's sometimes a halfhearted effort at draping—shrouding the body when cleaning, evacuating and examining—serious crips, real crips, *macho* crips don't care. At Rhyme's first rehab center, after a patient had gone to a party or been on a date the night before, all the wardmates would wheel over to his bed to check the patient's urine output, which was the barometer of how successful the outing had been. One time Rhyme earned his fellow crips' undying admiration by registering a staggering 1430 cc's.

He said to Berger, "Check out the ledge, doctor. I have my own guardian angels."

"Well. Hawks?"

"Peregrine falcons. Usually they nest higher. I don't know why they picked me to live with."

Berger glanced at the birds then turned away from the window, let the curtain fall back. The aviary didn't interest him. He wasn't a large man but he looked fit, a runner, Rhyme guessed. He seemed to be in his late forties but the black hair didn't have a trace of gray in it and he was as good-looking as any news anchor.

"That's quite a bed."

"You like it?"

The bed was a Clinitron, a huge rectangular slab. It was an air-fluidized support bed and contained nearly a ton of silicone-coated glass beads. Pressurized air flowed through the beads, which supported Rhyme's body. If he had been able to feel, it would have felt as if he was floating.

Berger was sipping the coffee that Rhyme had ordered Thom to fetch and that the young man had brought, rolling his eyes, whispering, "Aren't we suddenly social?" before retreating.

The doctor asked Rhyme, "You were a policeman, you were telling me."

"Yes. I was head of forensics for the NYPD."

"Were you shot?"

"Nope. Searching a crime scene. Some workmen'd found a body at a subway-stop construction site. It was a young patrolman who'd disappeared six months before—we had a serial killer shooting cops. I got a request to work the case personally and when I was searching it a beam collapsed. I was buried for about four hours."

"Someone was actually going around murdering policemen?"

"Killed three and wounded another one. The perp was a cop himself. Dan Shepherd. A sergeant working Patrol."

Berger glanced at the pink scar on Rhyme's neck. The

telltale insignia of quadriplegia—the entrance wound for the ventilator tube that remains embedded in the throat for months after the accident. Sometimes for years, sometimes forever. But Rhyme had—thanks to his own mulish nature and his therapists' herculean efforts—weaned himself off the ventilator. He now had a pair of lungs on him that he bet could keep him underwater for five minutes.

"So, a cervical trauma."

"C4."

"Ah, yes."

C4 is the demilitarized zone of spinal cord injuries. An SCI above the fourth cervical vertebra might very well have killed him. Below C4 he would have regained some use of his arms and hands, if not his legs. But trauma to the infamous fourth kept him alive though virtually a total quadriplegic. He'd lost the use of his legs and arms. His abdominal and intercostal muscles were mostly gone and he was breathing primarily from his diaphragm. He could move his head and neck, his shoulders slightly. The only fluke was that the crushing oak beam had spared a single, minuscule strand of motor neuron. Which allowed him to move his left ring finger.

Rhyme spared the doctor the soap opera of the year following the accident. The month of skull traction: tongs gripping holes drilled into his head and pulling his spine straight. Twelve weeks of the halo device—the plastic bib and steel scaffolding around his head to keep the neck immobile. To keep his lungs pumping, a large ventilator for a year then a phrenic nerve stimulator. The catheters. The surgery. The paralytic ileus, the stress ulcers, hypotension and bradycardia, bedsores turning into decubitus ulcers, contractures as the muscle tissue began to shrink and threatened to steal away the precious mobility of his finger, the infuriating phantom pain—burns and aches in extremities that could feel no sensation.

He did, however, tell Berger about the latest wrinkle. "Autonomic dysreflexia."

The problem had been occurring more often recently. Pounding heartbeat, off-the-charts blood pressure, raging headaches. It could be brought on by something as simple as constipation. He explained that nothing could be done to prevent it except avoiding stress and physical constriction.

Rhyme's SCI specialist, Dr Peter Taylor, had become concerned with the frequency of the attacks. The last one—a month ago—was so severe that Taylor'd given Thom instructions in how to treat the condition without waiting for medical help and insisted that the aide program the doctor's number into the phone's speed dialer. Taylor had warned that a severe enough bout could lead to a heart attack or stroke.

Berger took in the facts with some sympathy then said, 'Before I got into my present line I specialized in geriatric orthopedics. Mostly hip and joint replacements. I don't know much neurology. What about chances for recovery?"

"None, the condition's permanent," Rhyme said, perhaps a little too quickly. He added, "You understand my problem, don't you, doctor?"

"I think so. But I'd like to hear it in your words."

Shaking his head to clear a renegade strand of hair, Rhyme said, "Everyone has the right to kill himself."

Berger said, "I think I'd disagree with that. In most societies you may have the power but *not* the right. There's a difference."

Rhyme exhaled a bitter laugh. "I'm not much of a philosopher. But I don't even have the power. That's why I need you."

Lincoln Rhyme had asked four doctors to kill him. They'd all refused. He'd said, okay, he'd do it himself and simply stopped eating. But the process of wasting himself to death became pure torture. It left him violently stomach-sick and racked with unbearable headaches. He couldn't sleep. So he'd given up on that and, during the course of a hugely awkward conversation, asked Thom to kill him. The young man had grown tearful—the only time he'd shown that much emotion—and said he wished he could. He'd sit by and watch Rhyme die, he'd refuse to revive him. But he wouldn't actually kill him.

Then, a miracle. If you could call it that.

After *The Scenes of the Crime* had come out, reporters had appeared to interview him. One article—in *The New York Times*—contained this stark quotation from author Rhyme:

"No, I'm not planning any more books. The fact is, my next big project is killing myself. It's quite a challenge.

I've been looking for someone to help me for the past six months."

That screeching-stop line got the attention of the NYPD counseling service and several people from Rhyme's past, most notably Blaine (who told him he was nuts to consider it, he had to quit thinking only about himself—just like when they'd been together—and, now that she was here, she thought she should mention that she was remarrying).

The quotation also caught the attention of William Berger, who'd called unexpectedly one night from Seattle. After a few moments of pleasant conversation Berger explained that he'd read the article about Rhyme. Then a hollow pause and he'd asked, "Ever hear of the Lethe Society?"

Rhyme had. It was a pro-euthanasia group he'd been trying to track down for months. It was far more aggressive than Safe Passage or the Hemlock Society. "Our volunteers are wanted for questioning in dozens of assisted suicides throughout the country," Berger explained. "We have to keep a low profile."

He said he wanted to follow up on Rhyme's request. Berger refused to act quickly and they'd had several conversations over the past seven or eight months. Today was their first meeting.

"There's no way you can pass, by yourself?"

Pass . . .

"Short of Gene Harrod's approach, no. And even that's a little iffy."

Harrod was young man in Boston, a quad, who decided he wanted to kill himself. Unable to find anyone to help him he finally committed suicide the only way he was able to. With the little control he had he set a fire in his apartment and when it was blazing drove his wheelchair into it, setting himself aflame. He died of third-degree burns.

The case often raised by right-to-deathers as an example of the tragedy that anti-euthanasia laws can cause.

Berger was familiar with the case and shook his head sympathetically. "No, that's no way for anyone to die." He assayed Rhyme's body, the wires, the control panels. "What are your mechanical skills?"

Rhyme explained about the ECUs—the E&J controller that

his ring finger operated, the sip-and-puff control for his mouth, the chin joysticks, and the computer dictation unit that could type out words on the screen as he spoke them.

"But everything has to be set up by someone else?" Berger asked. "For instance, someone would have to go to the store, buy a gun, mount it, rig the trigger and hook it up to your controller?"

"Yes."

Making that person guilty of a conspiracy to commit murder, as well as manslaughter.

"What about your equipment?" Rhyme asked. "It's effective?"

"Equipment?"

"What you use? To, uhm, do the deed?"

"It's very effective. I've never had a patient complain."

Rhyme blinked and Berger laughed. Rhyme joined him. If you can't laugh about death what can you laugh about?

"Take a look."

"You have it with you?" Hope blossomed in Rhyme's heart. It was the first time he'd felt that warm sensation in years.

The doctor opened his attaché case and—rather ceremonially, Rhyme thought—set out a bottle of brandy. A small bottle of pills. A plastic bag and a rubber band.

"What's the drug?"

"Seconal. Nobody prescribes it anymore. In the old days suicide was a lot easier. These babies'd do the trick, no question. Now, it's almost impossible to kill yourself with modern tranquilizers. Halcion, Librium, Dalmane, Xanax . . . You may sleep for a long time but you're going to wake up eventually."

"And the bag?"

"Ah, the bag." Berger picked it up. "That's the emblem of the Lethe Society. Unofficially, of course—it's not like we have a logo. If the pills and the brandy aren't enough then we use the bag. Over the head, with a rubber band around the neck. We add a little ice inside because it gets pretty hot after a few minutes."

Rhyme couldn't take his eyes off the trio of implements. The bag, thick plastic, like a painter's drop cloth. The brandy was cheap, he observed, and the drugs generic.

"This's a nice house," Berger said, looking around. "Central Park West . . . Do you live on disability?"

"Some. I've also done consulting for the police and the FBI. After the accident . . . the construction company that was doing the excavating settled for three million. They swore there was no liability but there's apparently a rule of law that a quadriplegic automatically wins any lawsuits against construction companies, no matter who was at fault. At least if the plaintiff comes to court and drools."

"And you wrote that book, right?"

"I get some money from that. Not a lot. It was a 'better-seller.' Not a best-seller."

Berger picked up a copy of *The Scenes of the Crime*, flipped through it. "Famous crime scenes. Look at all this." He laughed. "There are, what, forty, fifty scenes?"

"Fifty-one."

Rhyme had revisited—in his mind and imagination, since he'd written it after the accident—as many old crime scenes in New York City as he could recall. Some solved, some not. He'd written about the Old Brewery, the notorious tenement in Five Points, where thirteen unrelated murders were recorded on a single night in 1839. About Charles Aubridge Deacon, who murdered his mother on July 13, 1863, during the Civil War draft riots, claiming former slaves had killed her and fueling the rampage against blacks. About architect Stanford White's love-triangle murder atop the original Madison Square Garden and about Judge Crater's disappearance. About George Metesky, the mad bomber of the '50s, and Murph the Surf, who boosted the Star of India diamond.

"Nineteenth-century building supplies, underground streams, butler's schools," Berger recited, flipping through the book, "gay baths, Chinatown whorehouses, Russian Orthodox churches . . . How d'you learn all this about the city?"

Rhyme shrugged. In his years as head of IRD he'd studied as much about the city as he had about forensics. Its history, politics, geology, sociology, infrastructure. He said, "Criminalistics doesn't exist in a vacuum. The more you know about your environment, the better you can apply—"

Just as he heard the enthusiasm creep into his voice he stopped abruptly.

Furious with himself that he'd been foxed so easily.

"Nice try, Dr Berger," Rhyme said stiffly.

"Ah, come on. Call me Bill. Please."

Rhyme wasn't going to be derailed. "I've heard it before. Take a big, clean, smooth piece of paper and write down all the reasons why I should kill myself. And then take another big, clean smooth piece of paper and write all the reasons why I shouldn't. Words like *productive, useful, interesting, challenging* come to mind. Big words. Ten-dollar words. They don't mean shit to me. Besides, I couldn't pick up a fucking pencil to save my soul."

"Lincoln," Berger continued kindly, "I have to make sure you're the appropriate candidate for the program."

"'Candidate'? 'Program'? Ah, the tyranny of euphemism," Rhyme said bitterly. "Doctor, I've made up my mind. I'd like to do it today. Now, as a matter of fact."

"Why today?"

Rhyme's eyes had returned to the bottles and the bag. He whispered, "Why not? What's today? August twenty-third? That's as good a day to die as any."

The doctor tapped his narrow lips. "I *have* to spend some time talking to you, Lincoln. If I'm convinced that you really want to go ahead—"

"I do," Rhyme said, noting as he often did how weak our words sound without the body gestures to accompany them. He wanted desperately to lay his hand on Berger's arm or lift his palms beseechingly.

Without asking if he could, Berger pulled out a packet of Marlboros and lit a cigarette. He took a folding metal ashtray from his pocket and opened it up. Crossed his thin legs. He looked like a foppish frat boy at an Ivy League smoker. "Lincoln, you understand the problem here, don't you?"

Sure, he understood. It was the very reason why Berger was here and why one of Rhyme's own doctors hadn't "done the deed." Hastening an inevitable death was one thing; nearly one-third of practicing doctors who treated terminal patients had prescribed or administered fatal doses of drugs. Most prosecutors turned a blind eye toward them unless a doctor flaunted it—like Kevorkian.

But a quad? A hemi? A para? A crip? Oh, that was different.

Lincoln Rhyme was forty years old. He'd been weaned off the ventilator. Barring some insidious gene in the Rhyme stock, there was no medical reason why he couldn't live to eighty.

Berger added, "Let me be blunt, Lincoln. I also have to be sure this isn't a setup."

"Setup?"

"Prosecutors. I've been entrapped before."

Rhyme laughed. "The New York attorney general's a busy man. He's not going to wire a crip to bag himself a euthanasist."

Glancing absently at the crime scene report.

> . . . ten feet southwest of victim, found in a cluster on a small pile of white sand: a ball of fiber, approximately six centimeters in diameter, off-white in color. The fiber was sampled in the energy-dispersive X-ray unit and found to consist of $A_2 B_5$ (Si, $A_8 O_{22}$ (OH)$_2$. No source was indicated and the fibers could not be individuated. Sample sent to FBI PERT office for analysis.

"I just have to be careful," Berger continued. "This is my whole professional life now. I gave up orthopedics completely. Anyway, it's more than a job. I've decided to devote my life to helping others end theirs."

> Adjacent to this fiber, approximately three inches away were found two scraps of paper. One was common newsprint, with the words "three P.M." printed in Times Roman type, in ink consistent with that used in commercial newspapers. The other scrap appeared to be the corner of a page from a book with the page number "823" printed on it. The typeface was Garamond and the paper was calendared. ALS and subsequent ninhydrin analysis reveal no latent friction-ridge prints on either . . . Individuation was not possible.

Several things nagged Rhyme. The fiber, for one. Why hadn't Peretti caught on as to what it was? It was so obvious.

And why was this PE—the newspaper scraps and the fiber—all clustered together? Something was wrong here.

"Lincoln?"

"Sorry."

"I was saying . . . You're not a burn victim in unbearable pain. You're not homeless. You've got money, you've got talent. Your police consulting . . . that helps a lot of people. If you want one, you could have a, yes, *productive* life ahead of you. A long life."

"Long, yes. That's the problem. A long life." He was tired of being on good behavior. He snapped, "But I don't *want* a long life. It's as simple as that."

Berger said slowly, "If there's the slightest chance you might've regretted your decision, well, see, *I'm* the one who'd have to live with it. Not you."

"Who's ever certain about something like this?"

Eyes slipping back to the report.

> *An iron bolt was found on top of the scraps of paper. It was a hex bolt, bead-stamped with the letters "CE". Two inches long, clock-wise twist, $^{15}/_{16}$" in diameter.*

"I've got a busy schedule for the next few days," Berger said, looking at his watch. It was a Rolex; well, death has always been lucrative. "Let's take an hour or so now. Talk for a while, then have a cooling-off day and I'll come back."

Something was nagging at Rhyme. An infuriating itch—the curse of all quads—though in this case it was an intellectual itch. The kind that had plagued Rhyme all his life.

"Say, doctor, I wonder if you could do me a favor. That report there. Could you flip through it? See if you could find a picture of a bolt."

Berger hesitated. "A picture?"

"A Polaroid. It'll be glued in somewhere toward the back. The turning frame takes too long."

Berger lifted the report out of the frame and turned the pages for Rhyme.

"There. Stop."

As he gazed at the photo a twinge of urgency pricked at him. Oh, not here, not now. *Please, no.*

"I'm sorry, could you flip back to the page where we were?"

Berger did.

Rhyme said nothing and read carefully.

The paper scraps . . .

Three P.M. . . . page 823.

Rhyme's heart was pounding, sweat popped out on his head. He heard a frantic buzzing in his ears.

Here's a headline for the tabloids. MAN DIES DURING TALK WITH DEATH DOC . . .

Berger blinked. "Lincoln? Are you all right?" The man's canny eyes examined Rhyme carefully.

As casually as he could, Rhyme said, "You know, doctor, I'm sorry. But there's something I've got to take care of."

Berger nodded slowly, uncertainly. "Affairs aren't in order after all?"

Smiling. Nonchalant. "I'm just wondering if I could ask you to come back in a few hours."

Careful here. If he senses *purpose* he'll mark you down non-suicidal, take his bottles and his plastic bag and fly back to Starbucks land.

Opening a date book, Berger said, "The rest of the day isn't good. Then tomorrow . . . No. I'm afraid Monday's the earliest. Day after tomorrow."

Rhyme hesitated. Lord . . . His soul's desire was finally within his grasp, what he'd dreamed of every day for the past year. Yes or no?

Decide.

Finally, Rhyme heard himself say, "All right. Monday." Plastering a hopeless smile on his face.

"What exactly's the problem?"

"A man I used to work with. He asked for some advice. I wasn't paying as much attention to it as I should have. I have to call him."

No, it wasn't dysreflexia at all—or an anxiety attack.

Lincoln Rhyme was feeling something he hadn't felt in years. He was in one big fucking hurry.

"Could I ask you to send Thom up here? I think he's downstairs in the kitchen."

"Yes, of course. I'd be happy to."

Rhyme could see something odd in Berger's eyes. What was it? Caution? Maybe. It almost seemed like disappointment. But there was no time to think about it now. As the doctor's footsteps receded down the stairs Rhyme shouted in a booming baritone, "Thom? Thom!"

"What?" the young man's voice called.

"Call Lon. Get him back here. Now!"

Rhyme glanced at the clock. It was after noon. They had less than three hours.

FOUR

"The crime scene was staged," Lincoln Rhyme said.

Lon Sellitto had tossed his jacket off, revealing a savagely wrinkled shirt. He now leaned back, arms crossed, against a table strewn with papers and books.

Jerry Banks was back too and his pale-blue eyes were on Rhyme's; the bed and its control panel no longer interested him.

Sellitto frowned. "But what story's the unsub tryin' to sell us?"

At crime scenes, especially homicides, perps often monkeyed with PE to lead investigators astray. Some were clever about it but most weren't. Like the husband who beat his wife to death then tried to make it look like a robbery—though he only thought to steal *her* jewelry, leaving his gold bracelets and diamond pinkie ring on his dresser.

"That's what's so interesting," Rhyme continued. "It's not about what happened, Lon. It's what's *going to* happen."

Sellitto the skeptic asked, "What makes you think so?"

"The scraps of paper. They mean three o'clock today."

"Today?"

"Look!" Nodding toward the report, an impatient jerk of his head.

"That one scrap says three P.P.," Banks pointed out. "But the other's a page number. Why do you think it means today?"

"It's *not* a page number." Rhyme lifted an eyebrow. They still didn't get it. "Logic! The only reason to leave clues was to tell us something. If that's the case then 823 has to be something more than just a page number because there's no clue as to what book it's from. Well, if it's not a page number what is it?"

Silence.

Exasperated, Rhyme snapped, "It's a *date*! Eight twenty-three. August twenty-third. Something's going to happen at three P.M. today. Now, the ball of fiber? It's asbestos."

"Asbestos?" Sellitto asked.

"In the report? The formula? It's hornblende. Silicon dioxide. That *is* asbestos. Why Peretti sent it to the FBI is beyond me. So. We have asbestos on a railbed where there shouldn't be any. And we've got an iron bolt with decaying oxidation on the head but none on the threads. That means it's been bolted someplace for a long time and just recently removed."

"Maybe it was overturned in the dirt," Banks offered. "When he was digging the grave?"

Rhyme said, "No. In Midtown the bedrock's close to the surface, which means so are the aquifers. All the soil from Thirty-fourth Street up to Harlem contains enough moisture to oxidize iron within a few days. It'd be completely rusted, not just the head, if it'd been buried. No, it was unbolted from someplace, carried to the scene and left there. And that sand . . . Come on, what's white sand doing on a train roadbed in Midtown Manhattan? The soil composition there is loam, silt, granite, hardpan and soft clay."

Banks started to speak but Rhyme cut him off abruptly. "And what were these things doing all clustered together? Oh, he's telling us something, our unsub. You bet he is. Banks, what about the access door?"

"You were right," the young man said. "They found one about a hundred feet north of the grave. Broken open from the inside. You were also right about the prints. Zip. And no tire tracks or trace evidence either."

A lock of dirty asbestos, a bolt, a torn newspaper . . .

"The scene?" Rhyme asked. "Intact?"

"Released."

Lincoln Rhyme, the crip with the killer lungs, exhaled a loud hiss of air, disgusted. "Who made *that* mistake?"

"I don't know," Sellitto said lamely. "Watch commander probably."

It was Peretti, Rhyme understood. "Then you're stuck with what you've got."

Whatever clues as to who the kidnapper was and what he had in mind were either in the report or gone forever, trampled under the feet of cops and spectators and railroad workers. Spadework—canvassing the neighborhood around the scene, interviewing witnesses, cultivating leads, traditional *detective* work—was done leisurely. But crime scenes themselves had to be worked "like mad lightning," Rhyme would command his officers in IRD. And he'd fired more than a few CSU techs who hadn't moved fast enough for his taste.

"Peretti ran the scene himself?" he asked.

"Peretti and a full complement."

"Full complement?" Rhyme asked wryly. "What's a *full complement*?"

Sellitto looked at Banks, who said, "Four techs from Photo, four from Latents. Eight searchers. ME tour doctor."

"*Eight* crime scene searchers?"

There's a bell curve in processing a crime scene. Two officers are considered the most efficient for a single homicide. By yourself you can miss things; three and up you tend to miss more things. Lincoln Rhyme had always searched scenes alone. He let the Latents people do the print work and Photo do the snap-shooting and videoing. But he always walked the grid by himself.

Peretti. Rhyme had hired the young man, son of a wealthy politico, six, seven years ago and he'd proved a good, by-the-book CS detective. Crime Scene is considered a plum and there's always a long waiting list to get into the unit. Rhyme took perverse pleasure in thinning the ranks of applicants by offering them a look at the family album—a collection of particularly gruesome crime-scene photos. Some officers would blanch, some would snicker. Some handed the book back, eyebrows raised, as if asking, So what? And those were the ones that Lincoln Rhyme would hire. Peretti'd been one of them.

Sellitto had asked a question. Rhyme found the detective looking at him. He repeated, "You'll work with us on this, won't you, Lincoln?"

"Work with you?" He coughed a laugh. "I can't, Lon. No.

I'm just spitting out a few ideas for you. You've got it. Run with it. Thom, get me Berger." He was now regretting the decision to postpone his tête-à-tête with the death doctor. Maybe it wasn't too late. He couldn't bear the thought of waiting another day or two of his *passing*. And Monday . . . He didn't want to die on Monday. It seemed common.

"Say please."

"Thom!"

"All right," the young aide said, hands raised in surrender.

Rhyme glanced at the spot on his bedside table where the bottle, the pills and the plastic bag had sat—so very close, but like everything else in this life wholly out of Lincoln Rhyme's reach.

Sellitto made a phone call, cocked his head as the call was answered. He identified himself. The clock on the wall clicked to twelve-thirty.

"Yessir." The detective's voice sank into a respectful whisper. The mayor, Rhyme guessed. "About the kidnapping at Kennedy. I've been talking to Lincoln Rhyme . . . Yessir, he has some thoughts on it." The detective wandered to the window, staring blankly at the falcon and trying to explain the inexplicable to the man running the most mysterious city on earth. He hung up and turned to Rhyme.

"He and the chief both want you, Linc. They asked specifically. Wilson himself."

Rhyme laughed. "Lon, look around the room. Look at *me*! Does it seem like I could run a case?"

"Not a normal case, no. But this isn't a very normal one now, is it?"

"I'm sorry. I just don't have time. That doctor. The treatment. Thom, did you call him?"

"Haven't yet. Will in just a minute."

"Now! Do it now!"

Thom looked at Sellitto. Walked to the door, stepped outside. Rhyme knew he wasn't going to call. Bugger the world.

Banks touched a dot of razor scar and blurted, "Just give us some thoughts. Please. This unsub, you said he—"

Sellitto waved him silent. He kept his eyes on Rhyme.

Oh, you prick, Rhyme thought. The old silence. How we

hate it and hurry to fill it. How many witnesses and suspects had caved under hot, thick silences just like this. Well, he and Sellitto *had* been a good team. Rhyme knew evidence and Lon Sellitto knew people.

The two musketeers. And if there was a third it was the purity of unsmiling science.

The detective's eyes dipped to the crime scene report. "Lincoln. What do you think's going to happen today at three?"

"I don't have any idea," Rhyme pronounced.

"Don'tcha?"

Cheap, Lon. I'll get you for that.

Finally, Rhyme said. "He's going to kill her—the woman in the taxi. And in some real bad way, I guarantee you. Something that'll rival getting buried alive."

"Jesus," Thom whispered from the doorway.

Why couldn't they just leave him alone? Would it do any good to tell them about the agony he felt in his neck and shoulders? Or about the phantom pain—far weaker and far eerier—roaming through his alien body? About the exhaustion he felt from the daily struggle to do, well, everything? About the most overwhelming fatigue of all—from having to rely on someone else?

Maybe he could tell them about the mosquito that'd gotten into the room last night and strafed his head for an hour; Rhyme grew dizzy with fatigue nodding it away until the insect finally landed on his ear, where Rhyme let it stab him—since that was a place he could rub against the pillow for relief from the itch.

Sellitto lifted an eyebrow.

"Today," Rhyme sighed. "One day. That's it."

"Thanks, Linc. We owe you." Sellitto pulled up a chair next to the bed. Nodded Banks to do the same. "Now. Gimme your thoughts. What's this asshole's game?"

Rhyme said, "Not so fast. I don't work alone."

"Fair enough. Who d'you want on board?"

"A tech from IRD. Whoever's the best in the lab. I want him here with the basic equipment. And we better get some tactical boys. Emergency Services. Oh, and I want some phones," Rhyme instructed, glancing at the Scotch on his dresser. He remembered the brandy Berger had in his kit. No way was he going out on cheap crap like that. His *Final Exit* number would be courtesy of either sixteen-year-old Lagavulin or opulent Macallan aged for decades. Or—why not?—both.

Banks pulled out his own cellular phone. "What kind of lines? Just—"

"Landlines."

"In here?"

"Of course not," Rhyme barked.

Sellitto said, "He means he wants people to make calls. From the Big Building."

"Oh."

"Call downtown," Sellitto ordered. "Have 'em give us three or four dispatchers."

"Lon," Rhyme asked, "who's doing the spadework on the death this morning?"

Banks stifled a laugh. "The Hardy Boys."

A glare from Rhyme took the smile off his face. "Detectives Bedding and Saul, sir," the boy added quickly.

But then Sellitto grinned too. "The Hardy Boys. Everybody calls 'em that. You don't know 'em, Linc. They're from the Homicide Task Force downtown."

"They look kind of alike is the thing," Banks explained. "And, well, their delivery is a little funny."

"I don't want comedians."

"No, they're good," Sellitto said. "The best canvassers we got. You know that beast 'napped that eight-year-old girl in Queens last year? Bedding and Saul did the canvass. Interviewed the entire 'hood—took twenty-two *hundred* statements. It was 'causa them we saved her. When we heard the vic this morning was the passenger from JFK, Chief Wilson himself put 'em on board."

"What're they doing now?"

"Witnesses mostly. Around the train tracks. And sniffing around about the driver and the cab."

Rhyme yelled to Thom in the hallway, "Did you call Berger? No, of course you didn't. The word 'insubordination' mean anything to you? At least make yourself useful. Bring that crime scene report closer and start turning the pages." He nodded toward the turning frame. "That damn thing's an Edsel."

"Aren't we in a sunny mood today?" the aide spat back.

"Hold it up *higher*. I'm getting glare."

He read for a minute. Then looked up.

Sellitto was on the phone but Rhyme interrupted him. "Whatever happens at three today, if we can find where he's talking about, it's going to be a crime scene. I'll need someone to work it."

"Good," Sellitto said. "I'll call Peretti. Toss him a bone. I know his nose'll be out of joint 'cause we're tiptoeing around him."

Rhyme grunted. "Did I ask for Peretti?"

"But he's the IRD golden boy," Banks said.

"I don't want him," Rhyme muttered. "There's somebody else I want."

Sellitto and Banks exchanged glances. The older detective smiled, brushing pointlessly at his wrinkled shirt. "Whoever you want, Linc, you got him. Remember, you're king for a day."

———

Staring at the dim eye.

T.J. Colfax, dark-haired refugee from the hills of Eastern Tennessee, NYU Business School grad, quick-as-a-whip currency trader, had just swum out of a deep dream. Her tangled hair stuck to her cheeks, sweat crawling in veins down her face and neck and chest.

She found herself looking into the black eye—a hole in a rusty pipe, about six inches across, from which a small access plate had been removed.

She sucked mildewy air through her nose—her mouth was still taped shut. Tasting plastic, the hot adhesive. Bitter.

And John? she wondered. Where was he? Refusing to think about the loud crack she'd heard last night in the basement. She'd grown up in Eastern Tennessee and knew what gunshots sounded like.

Please, she prayed for her boss. Let him be all right.

Stay calm, she raged to herself. You fucking start to cry again, you remember what happened. In the basement, after the gunshot, she'd lost it completely, breaking down, sobbing in panic, and had nearly suffocated.

Right. Calm.

Look at the black eye in the pipe. Pretend it's winking at you. The eye of your guardian angel.

T.J. sat on the floor, surrounded by a hundred pipes and ducts and snakes of conduit and wires. Hotter than her brother's diner, hotter than the back seat of Jule Whelan's Nova ten years ago. Water dripped, stalactites drooped from the ancient girders above her head. A half-dozen tiny yellow bulbs were the only illumination. Above her head—directly above—was a sign. She couldn't read it clearly, though she caught the red border. At the end of whatever the message might have been was a fat exclamation point.

She struggled once more but the cuffs held her tight, pinching against the bone. From her throat rose a desperate cry, an animal's cry. But the thick tape on her mouth and the insistent churning of machinery swallowed up the sound; no one could've heard her.

The black eye continued to stare. You'll save me, won't you? she thought.

Suddenly the silence was broken by a clanging slam, an iron bell, far away. Like a ship's door slamming shut. The noise came from the hole in the pipe. From her friendly eye.

She jerked the cuffs against the pipe and tried to stand. But she couldn't move more than a few inches.

Okay, don't panic. Just relax. You'll be all right.

It was then that she happened to see the sign above her head. In her jockeying for slack she'd straightened up slightly and moved her head to the side. This gave her an oblique view of the words.

Oh, no. Oh, Jesus in my heart . . .

The tears began again.

She imagined her mother, her hair pulled back from her round face, wearing her cornflower-blue housedress, whispering, "Be all raht, honey love. Doan' you worry."

But she didn't believe the words.

She believed what the sign said.

> *Extreme Danger! Superheated steam under High Pressure. Do not remove plate from pipe. Call Consolidated Edison for access. Extreme danger!*

The black eye gaped at her, the eye that opened into the heart of the steam pipe. It stared directly at the pink flesh of her chest. From somewhere deep inside the pipe came another clink of metal on metal, workers hammering, tightening old joints.

As Tammie Jean Colfax cried and cried she heard another clink. Then a distant groan, very faint. And it seemed to her, through her tears, that the black eye finally winked.

FIVE

"Here's the situation," Lincoln Rhyme announced. "We've got a kidnap victim and a three P.M. deadline."

"No ransom demands"—Sellitto supplemented Rhyme's synopsis, then turned aside to answer his chirping phone.

"Jerry," Rhyme said to Banks, "brief them about the scene this morning."

There were more people hovering in Lincoln Rhyme's dark room than in recent memory. Oh, after the accident friends had sometimes stopped by unannounced (the odds were pretty good that Rhyme'd be home of course) but he'd discouraged that. And he'd stopped returning phone calls too, growing more and more reclusive, drifting into solitude. He'd spend his hours writing his book and, when he was uninspired to write another one, reading. And when that grew tedious there were rental movies and pay-per-view and music. And then he'd given up TV and the stereo and spent hours staring at the art prints the aide had dutifully taped up on the wall opposite the bed. Finally they too had come down.

Solitude.

It was all he craved, and oh how he missed it now.

Pacing, looking tense, was compact Jim Polling. Lon Sellitto was the case officer but an incident like this needed a captain on board and Polling had volunteered for the job. The case was a time bomb and could nuke careers in a heartbeat so the chief and the dep coms were happy to have him intercept the flak. They'd be practicing the fine art of distancing and when the Betacams rolled their press conferences would be peppered with words like *delegated* and *assigned* and *taking the advice of* and they'd be fast to glance at Polling when it came time to field the hardball questions. Rhyme couldn't imagine why any cop in the world would volunteer to head up a case like this one.

But Polling was an odd one. The little man had pummeled his way through Midtown North Precinct as one of the city's most successful, and notorious, homicide detectives. Known for his bad temper, he'd gotten into serious trouble when he'd killed an unarmed suspect. But he'd managed, amazingly, to pull his career together by getting a conviction in the Shepherd case—the cop-serial-killer case, the one in which Rhyme'd been injured. Promoted to captain after that very public collar, Polling went through one of those embarrassing midlife changes—giving up blue jeans and Sears suits for Brooks Brothers (today he wore navy-blue Calvin Klein casual) and began his dogged climb toward a plush corner office high in One Police Plaza.

Another officer leaned against a nearby table. Crew-cut, rangy Bo Haumann was a captain and head of the Emergency Services Unit. NYPD's SWAT team.

Banks finished his synopsis just as Sellitto pushed disconnect and folded his phone. "The Hardy Boys."

"Anything more on the cab?" Polling asked.

"Nothing. They're still beating bushes."

"Any sign she was fucking somebody she shouldn't've been?" Polling asked. "Maybe a psycho boyfriend?"

"Naw, no boyfriends. Just dated a few guys casually. No stalkers, it looks like."

"And still no ransom calls?" Rhyme asked.

"No."

The doorbell rang. Thom went to answer it.

Rhyme looked toward the approaching voices.

A moment later the aide escorted a uniformed police officer up the stairs. She appeared very young from a distance but as she drew closer he could see she was probably thirty or so. She was tall and had that sullen, equine beauty of women gazing out from the pages of fashion magazines.

We see others as we see ourselves and since the accident Lincoln Rhyme rarely thought of people in terms of their bodies. He observed her height, trim hips, fiery red hair.

Somebody else'd weigh those features and say, What a knockout. But for Rhyme that thought didn't occur to him. What did register was the look in her eyes.

Not the surprise—obviously, nobody'd warned he was a crip—but something else. An expression he'd never seen before. It was as if his condition was putting her at ease. The exact opposite of how most people reacted. As she walked into the room she was relaxing.

"Officer Sachs?" Rhyme asked.

"Yessir," she said, catching herself just as she was about to extend a hand. "Detective Rhyme."

Sellitto introduced her to Polling and Haumann. She'd know about the latter two, by reputation if nothing else, and now her eyes grew cautious once more.

She took in the room, the dust, the gloominess. Glanced at one of the art posters. It was partially unrolled, lying under a table. *Nighthawks*, by Edward Hopper. The lonely people in a diner late at night. That one had been the last to come down.

Rhyme briefly explained about the 3:00 P.M. deadline. Sachs nodded calmly but Rhyme could see the flicker of what?— fear? disgust?—in her eyes.

Jerry Banks, fingers encumbered by a class ring but not a wedding band, was attracted immediately by the lamp of her beauty and offered her a particular smile. But Sachs's single glance in response made clear that no matches were being made here. And probably never would be.

Polling said, "Maybe it's a trap. We find the place he's leading us to, walk in and there's a bomb."

"I doubt it," Sellitto said, shrugging. "Why go to all this trouble? If you want to kill cops all you gotta do is find one and fucking shoot him."

Awkward silence for a moment as Polling looked quickly from Sellitto to Rhyme. The collective thought registered that it was on the Shepherd case that Rhyme had been injured.

But faux pas meant nothing to Lincoln Rhyme. He continued, "I agree with Lon. But I'd tell any Search and Surveillance or HRT teams to keep an eye out for ambush. Our boy seems to be writing his own rules."

Sachs looked again at the poster of the Hopper painting. Rhyme followed her gaze. Maybe the people in the diner really weren't lonely, he reflected. Come to think of it, they all looked pretty damn content.

"We've got two types of physical evidence here," Rhyme continued. "Standard PE. What the unsub didn't mean to leave behind. Hair, fibers, fingerprints, maybe blood, shoeprints. If we can find enough of it—and if we're lucky—that'll lead us to the primary crime scene. That's where he lives."

"Or his hidey-hole," Sellitto offered. "Something temporary."

"A safe house?" Rhyme mused, nodding. "Bet you're right, Lon. He needs someplace to operate out of." He continued, "Then there's the planted evidence. Apart from the scraps of paper—which tell us the time and date—we've got the bolt, the wad of asbestos and the sand."

"A fucking scavenger hunt," Haumann growled and ran a hand through his slick buzz cut. He looked just like the drill sergeant Rhyme recalled he'd been.

"So I can tell the brass there's a chance of getting the vic in time?" Polling asked.

"I think so, yes."

The captain made a call and wandered to the corner of the room as he talked. When he hung up he grunted, "The mayor. The chief's with 'im. There's gonna to be a press conference in an hour and I gotta be there to make sure their dicks're in their pants and their flies're zipped. Anything more I can tell the big boys?"

Sellitto glanced at Rhyme, who shook his head.

"Not yet," the detective said.

Polling gave Sellitto his cellular phone number and left, literally jogging out the door.

A moment later a skinny, balding man in his thirties ambled up the stairs. Mel Cooper was as goofy-looking as ever, the nerdy neighbor in a sitcom. He was followed by two younger cops carrying a steamer trunk and two suitcases that seemed to weigh a thousand pounds each. The officers deposited their heavy loads and left.

"Mel."

"Detective." Cooper walked up to Rhyme and gripped his useless right hand. The only physical contact today with any of his guests, Rhyme noted. He and Cooper had worked together for years. With degrees in organic chemistry, math and physics, Cooper was an expert both in identification—friction-ridge prints, DNA and forensic reconstruction—and in PE analysis.

"How's the world's foremost criminalist?" Cooper asked him.

Rhyme scoffed good-naturedly. The title had been bestowed on him by the press some years ago, after the surprising news that the FBI had selected him—a city cop—as adviser in putting together PERT, their Physical Evidence Response Team. Not satisfied with "forensic scientist" or "forensic specialist," reporters dubbed Rhyme a "criminalist."

The word had actually been around for years, first applied in the United States to the legendary Paul Leland Kirk, who ran the UC Berkeley School of Criminology. The school, the first in the country, had been founded by the even more legendary Chief August Vollmer. The handle had recently become chic, and when techs around the country sidled up to blondes at cocktail parties now they described themselves as criminalists, not forensic scientists.

"Everybody's nightmare," Cooper said, "you get into a cab and turns out there's a psycho behind the wheel. And the whole world's watching the Big Apple 'causa that conference. Wondered if they might not bring you out of retirement for this one."

"How's your mother?" Rhyme asked.

"Still complaining about every ache and pain. Still healthier than me."

Cooper lived with the elderly woman in the Queens bungalow where he'd been born. His passion was ballroom dancing—the tango his speciality. Cop gossip being what it is, there'd been speculation around IRD as to the man's sexual preference. Rhyme had had no interest in his employees' personal lives but had been as surprised as everyone else to finally meet Greta, Cooper's steady girlfriend, a stunning Scandinavian who taught advanced mathematics at Columbia.

Cooper opened the large trunk, which was padded with velvet. He lifted out parts for three large microscopes and began assembling them.

"Oh, house current." He glanced at the outlets, disappointed. He pushed his metal-rimmed glasses up on his nose.

"That's because it's a house, Mel."

"I assumed you lived in a lab. Wouldn't have been surprised."

Rhyme stared at the instruments, gray and black, battered. Similar to the ones he'd lived with for over fifteen years. A standard compound microscope, a phase-contrast 'scope, and a polarized-light model. Cooper opened the suitcases, which contained a Mr Wizard assortment of bottles and jars and scientific instruments. In a flash, words came back to Rhyme, words that had once been part of his daily vocabulary. EDTA vacuum blood-collection tubes, acetic acid, orthotolidine, luminol reagent, Magna-Brush, Ruhemann's purple phenomenon . . .

The skinny man looked around the room. "Looks just like your office used to, Lincoln. How do you *find* anything? Say, I need some room here."

"Thom." Rhyme moved his head toward the least cluttered table. They moved aside magazines and papers and books, revealing a tabletop Rhyme had not seen in a year.

Sellitto gazed at the crime scene report. "Whatta we call the unsub? We don't have a case number yet."

Rhyme glanced at Banks. "Pick a number. Any number."

Banks suggested, "The page number. Well, the date, I mean."

"Unsub 823. Good as any."

Sellitto jotted this on the report.

"Uhm, excuse me? Detective Rhyme?"

It was the patrolwoman who'd spoken. Rhyme turned to her.

"I was supposed to be at the Big Building at noon." Coptalk for One Police Plaza.

"Officer Sachs . . ." He'd forgotten about her momentarily. "You were first officer this morning? At that homicide by the railroad tracks."

"That's right, I took the call." When she spoke, she spoke to Thom.

"I'm *here*, officer," Rhyme reminded sternly, barely controlling his temper. "Over here." It infuriated him when people talked to him through others, through *healthy* people.

Her head swiveled quickly and he saw the lesson had been learned. "Yessir," she said, a soft tone in her voice but ice in her eyes.

"I'm decommissioned. Just call me Lincoln."

"Would you just get it over with, please?"

"How's that?" he asked.

"The reason why you brought me here. I'm sorry. I wasn't thinking. If you want a written apology I'll do it. Only, I'm late for my new assignment and I haven't had a chance to call my commander."

"Apology?" Rhyme asked.

"The thing is, I didn't have any real crime scene experience. I was sort of flying by the seat of my pants."

"What are you talking about?"

"Stopping the trains and closing Eleventh Avenue. It was *my* fault the senator missed his speech in New Jersey and that some of the senior UN people didn't make it in from Newark Airport in time for their meetings."

Rhyme was chuckling. "Do you know who I am?"

"Well, I've heard of you of course. I thought you . . ."

"Were dead?" Rhyme asked.

"No. I didn't mean that." Though she had. She continued quickly, "We all used your book in the academy. But we don't hear about you. Personally, I mean . . ." She looked up at the wall and said stiffly, "In my judgment, as first officer, I thought it was best to stop the train and close the street to protect the scene. And that's what I did. Sir."

"Call me Lincoln. And you're . . ."

"I—"

"Your first name?"

"Amelia."

"Amelia. After the aviatrix?"

"Nosir. A family name."

"Amelia, I don't want an apology. You were right and Vince Peretti was wrong."

Sellitto stirred at this indiscretion but Lincoln Rhyme didn't care. He was, after all, one of the few people in the world who could stay flat on his ass when the president of the United States himself walked into the room. He continued, "Peretti worked the scene like the mayor was looking over his shoulder and that's the A-number-one way to screw it up. He had too many people, he was dead wrong to let the trains and traffic move and he should never have released the scene as early as he did. If we'd kept the tracks secure, who knows, we might've just found a credit card receipt with a name on it. Or a big beautiful thumbprint."

"That may be," Sellitto said delicately. "But let's just keep it to ourselves." Giving silent orders, his eyes swiveling toward Sachs and Cooper and young Jerry Banks.

Rhyme snorted an irreverent laugh. Then turned back to Sachs, whom he caught, like Banks that morning, staring at his legs and body under the apricot-colored blanket. He said to her, "I asked you here to work the next crime scene for us."

"What?" No speaking through interpreters this time.

"Work for us," he said shortly. "The next crime scene."

"But"—she laughed—"I'm not IRD. I'm Patrol. I've never done CS work."

"This is an unusual case. As Detective Sellitto himself'll tell you. It's real *weird*. Right, Lon? True, if it was a classic scene, I wouldn't want you. But we need a fresh pair of eyes on this one."

She glanced at Sellitto, who said nothing. "I just . . . I'd be no good at it. I'm sure."

"All right," Rhyme said patiently. "The truth?"

She nodded.

"I need somebody who's got the balls to stop a train in its tracks to protect a scene and to put up with the heat afterwards."

"Thank you for the opportunity, sir. Lincoln. But—"

Rhyme said shortly, "Lon."

"Officer," the detective grunted to Sachs, "you're not being given any options here. You've been assigned to this case to assist at the crime scene."

"Sir, I have to protest. I'm transferring out of Patrol. Today. I've got a medical transfer. Effective an hour ago."

"Medical?" Rhyme inquired.

She hesitated, glancing unwilling at his legs again. "I have arthritis."

"Do you?" Rhyme asked.

"Chronic arthritis."

"I'm sorry to hear that."

She continued quickly, "I only took that call this morning because someone was home sick. I didn't plan on it."

"Yes, well, I had other plans too," Lincoln Rhyme said. "Now, let's look at some evidence."

SIX

"The bolt."

Remembering the classic crime scene rule: Analyze the most unusual evidence first.

Thom turned the plastic bag over and over in his hands as Rhyme studied the metal rod, half rusted, half not. Dull. Worn.

"You're sure about the prints? You tried small-particle reagent? That's the best for PE exposed to the elements."

"Yup," Mel Cooper confirmed.

"Thom," Rhyme ordered, "get this hair out of my eyes! Comb it back. I told you to comb it back this morning."

The aide sighed and brushed at the tangled black strands. "Watch it," he whispered ominously to his boss and Rhyme jerked his head dismissively, mussing his hair further. Amelia Sachs sat sullenly in the corner. Her legs rested under the chair in a sprinter's starting position and, sure enough, she looked like she was just waiting for the gun.

Rhyme turned back to the bolt.

When he headed IRD, Rhyme had started assembling databases. Like the federal auto-paint-chip index or the BATF's tobacco files. He'd set up a bullet-standards file, fibers, cloth, tires, shoes, tools, motor oil, transmission fluid. He'd spent hundreds of hours compiling lists, indexed and cross-referenced.

Even during Rhyme's obsessive tenure, though, IRD had never gotten around to cataloging hardware. He wondered why not and he was angry at himself for not taking the time to do it and angrier still at Vince Peretti for not thinking of it either.

"We need to call every bolt manufacturer and jobber in he Northeast. No, in the *country*. Ask if they make a model ike this and who they sell to. Fax a description and picture of the bolt to our dispatchers at Communications."

"Hell, there could be a million of them," Banks said. "Every Ace Hardware and Sears in the country."

"I don't think so," Rhyme responded. "It's got to be a viable clue. He wouldn't have left it if it was useless. There's a limited source of these bolts. I bet you."

Sellitto made a call and looked up a few minutes later. "I've got you dispatchers, Lincoln. Four of them. Where do we get a list of manufacturers?"

"Get a patrolman down to Forty-second Street," Rhyme replied. "Public Library. They have corporate directories there. Until we get one, have the dispatchers start working through the Business-to-Business Yellow Pages."

Sellitto repeated this into the phone.

Rhyme glanced at the clock. It was one-thirty.

"Now, the asbestos."

For an instant, the word glowed in his mind. He felt a jolt—in places where no jolts could be felt. What was familiar about asbestos? Something he'd read or heard about—recently, it seemed, though Lincoln Rhyme no longer trusted his sense of time. When you lie on your back frozen in place month after month after month, time slows to near-death. He might be thinking of something he'd read two years ago.

"What do we know about asbestos?" he mused. No one answered but that didn't matter; he answered himself. As he referred to do anyway. Asbestos was a complex molecule, silicate polymer. It doesn't burn because, like glass, it's already oxidized.

When he'd run crime scenes of old murders—working with forensic anthropologists and odontologists—Rhyme often found himself in asbestos-insulated buildings. He remembered the peculiar taste of the face masks they'd had to wear during the excavation. In fact, he now recalled, it'd been during an asbestos-removal cleanup at the City Hall subway stop three and a half years ago that crews found the body of one of the policemen murdered by Dan Shepherd dumped in a generator room. As Rhyme had bent down over it slowly to lift a fiber from the officer's light-blue blouse, he'd heard the crack and groan of the oak beam. The mask had probably saved him from choking to death on the dust and dirt that caved in around him.

"Maybe he's got her at a cleanup site," Sellitto said.

"Could be," Rhyme agreed.

Sellitto ordered his young assistant, "Call EPA and city Environmental. Find out if there're any sites where cleanup's going on right now."

The detective made the call.

"Bo," Rhyme asked Haumann, "you have teams to deploy?"

"Ready to roll," the ESU commander confirmed. "Though I gotta tell you, we've got over half the force tied up with this UN thing. They're on loan to the Secret Service and UN security."

"Got some EPA info here." Banks gestured to Haumann and they retired to a corner of the room. They moved aside several stacks of books. As Haumann unfurled one of ESU's tactical maps of New York something clattered to the floor.

Banks jumped. "Jesus."

From the angle where he lay, Rhyme couldn't see what had fallen. Haumann hesitated then bent down and retrieved the bleached piece of spinal column and replaced it on the table.

Rhyme felt several pairs of eyes on him but he said nothing about the bone. Haumann leaned over the map, as Banks, on the phone, fed him information about asbestos-cleanup sites. The commander marked them in grease pencil. There appeared to be a lot of them, scattered all over the five boroughs of the city. It was discouraging.

"We have to narrow it down more. Let's see, the sand," Rhyme said to Cooper. "'Scope it. Tell me what you think."

Sellitto handed the evidence envelope to the tech, who poured the contents out onto an enamel examination tray. The glistening powder left a small cloud of dust. There was also a stone, worn smooth, which slid into the center of the pile.

Lincoln Rhyme's throat caught. Not at what he saw—he didn't yet know *what* he was looking at—but at the flawed nerve impulse that shot from his brain and died halfway to his useless right arm, urging it to grab a pencil and to probe. The first time in a year or so he'd felt that urge. It nearly brought tears into his eyes and his only solace was the memory of the tiny bottle of Seconal and the plastic bag that Dr Berger carried with him—images that hovered like a saving angel over the room.

He cleared his throat. "Print it!"

"What?" Cooper asked.

"The stone."

Sellitto looked at him inquiringly.

"The rock doesn't belong there," Rhyme said. "Apples and oranges. I want to know why. Print it."

Using porcelain-tipped forceps, Cooper picked up the stone and examined it. He slipped on goggles and hit the rock with a beam from a PoliLight—a power pack the size of a car battery with a light wand attached.

"Nothing," Cooper said.

"VMD?"

Vacuum metal deposition is the Cadillac of techniques for raising latent prints on nonporous surfaces. It evaporates gold or zinc in a vacuum chamber containing the object to be tested; the metal coats the latent print, making the whorls and peaks very visible.

But Cooper didn't have a VMD with him.

"What *do* you have?" asked Rhyme, not pleased.

"Sudan black, stabilized physical developer, iodine, amido black, DFO and gentian violet, Magna-Brush."

He'd also brought ninhydrin for raising prints on porous surfaces and a Super Glue frame for smooth surfaces. Rhyme recalled the stunning news that had swept the forensic community some years ago: A technician working in a U.S. Army forensic lab in Japan had used Super Glue to fix a broken camera and found to his amazement that the fumes from the adhesive raised latent fingerprints better than most chemicals made for that purpose.

This was the method Cooper now used. With forceps he set the rock in a small glass box and put a dab of glue on the hot plate inside. A few minutes later he lifted the rock out.

"We've got something," he said. He dusted it with long-wavelength UV powder and hit it with the beam from the

PoliLight wand. A print was clearly visible. Dead center. Cooper photographed it with Polaroid CU-5, a 1:1 camera. He showed the picture to Rhyme.

"Hold it closer." Rhyme squinted as he examined it. "Yes! He rolled it."

Rolling prints—rocking a finger onto a surface—produced an impression different from one made by picking up an object. It was a subtle difference—in the width of the friction ridges at various points on the pattern—but one that Rhyme now recognized clearly.

"And look, what's that?" he mused. "That line." There was a faint crescent mark above the print itself.

"It looks almost like—"

"Yep," Rhyme said, "her fingernail. You wouldn't normally get that. But I'll bet he tipped the stone just to make sure it got picked up. It left an oil impression. Like a friction ridge."

"Why would he do that?" Sachs asked.

Once more miffed that nobody seemed to be picking up these points as fast as he was, Rhyme explained tersely, "He's telling us two things. First, he's making sure we know the victim's a woman. In case we didn't make the connection between her and the body this morning."

"Why do that?" Banks asked.

"To up the ante," Rhyme said. "Make us sweat more. He's let us know there's a woman at risk. He's valuated the victims—just like we all do—even though we claim we don't." Rhyme happened to glance at Sachs's hands. He was surprised to see that, for such a beautiful woman, *her* fingers were a mess. Four ended in fleshy Band-Aids and several others were chewed to the quick. The cuticle of one was caked with brown blood. He noticed too the red inflammation of the skin beneath her eyebrows, from plucking them, he assumed. And a scratch mark beside her ear. All self-destructive habits. There're a million ways to do yourself in besides pills and Armagnac.

Rhyme announced, "The other thing he's telling us I already warned you about. He knows evidence. He's saying, Don't bother with regular forensic PE. I won't be leaving any. That's what *he* thinks of course. But we'll find something. You bet we will." Suddenly Rhyme frowned. "The map! We need the map. Thom!"

The aide blurted, "What map?"

"You *know* what map I mean."

Thom sighed. "Not a clue, Lincoln."

Glancing out the window and speaking half to himself, Rhyme mused, "The railroad underpass, the bootleg tunnels and access doors, the asbestos—those're all old. He likes *historical* New York. I want the Randel map."

"Which is where?"

"The research files for my book. Where else?"

Thom dug through folders and pulled out a photocopy of a long, horizontal map of Manhattan. "This?"

"*That, yes!*"

It was the Randel Survey, drawn in 1811 for the commissioners of the city to plan out the grid of streets in Manhattan. The map had been printed horizontally, with Battery Park, south, to the left and Harlem, north, to the right. Laid out this way, the island resembled the body of a dog leaping, its narrow head lifted for an attack.

"Pin it up there. Good."

As the aide did, Rhyme blurted, "Thom, we're going to deputize you. Give him a shiny badge or something, Lon."

"Lincoln," he muttered.

"We need you. Come on. Haven't you always wanted to be Sam Spade or Kojak?"

"Only Judy Garland," the aide replied.

"Jessica Fletcher then! You'll be writing the profile. Come on now, get out that Mont Blanc you're always letting stick vainly out of your shirt pocket."

The young man rolled his eyes as he lifted his Parker pen and took a dusty yellow pad from a stack under one of the tables.

"No, I've got a better idea," Rhyme announced. "Put up one of those posters. Those art posters. Tape it up backwards and write on the back in marker. Write big now. So I can see it."

Thom selected a Monet lily pads and mounted it to the wall.

"On the top," the criminalist ordered, "write 'Unsub

823.' Then four columns. 'Appearance. Residence. Vehicle. Other.' Beautiful. Now, let's start. What do we know about him?"

Sellitto said, "Vehicle . . . He's got a Yellow Cab."

"Right. And under 'Other' add that he knows CS—crime scene—procedures."

"Which," Sellitto added, "maybe means he's had his turn in the barrel."

"How's that?" Thom asked.

"He might have a record," the detective explained.

Banks said, "Should we add that he's armed with a .32 Colt?"

"Fuck yes," his boss confirmed.

Rhyme contributed, "And he knows FRs. . . ."

"What?" Thom asked.

"Friction ridges—fingerprints. That's what they are, you know, ridges on our hands and feet to give us traction. And put down that he's probably working out of a safe house. Good job, Thom. Look at him. He's a born law enforcer."

Thom glowered and stepped away from the wall, brushing at his shirt, which had picked up a stringy cobweb from the wall.

"There we go, folks," Sellitto said. "Our first look at Mr 823."

Rhyme turned to Mel Cooper. "Now, the sand. What can we tell about it?"

Cooper lifted the goggles onto his pale forehead. He poured a sample onto a slide and slipped it under the polarized-light 'scope. He adjusted dials.

"Hmm. This is curious. No birefringence."

Polarizing microscopes show birefringence—the double refraction of crystals and fibers and some other materials. Seashore sand birefringes dramatically.

"So it isn't sand," Rhyme muttered. "It's something ground up. . . .Can you individuate it?"

Individuation . . . The goal of the criminalist. Most physical evidence can be *identified*. But even if you know what it is there are usually hundreds or thousands of sources it might have come from. *Individuated* evidence is something that could have come from only one source or a very limited number of sources. A fingerprint, a DNA profile, a paint chip that fits into a missing spot on the perp's car like a jigsaw-puzzle piece.

"Maybe," the tech responded, "if I can figure out *what* it is."

"Ground glass?" Rhyme suggested.

Glass is essentially melted sand but the glassmaking process alters the crystalline structure. You don't get birefringence with ground glass. Cooper examined the sample closely.

"No, I don't think it's glass. I don't know what it is. I wish I had an EDX here."

A popular crime lab tool was a scanning electron microscope married to an energy-dispersive X-ray unit; it determined what elements were in trace samples found at crime scenes.

"Get him one," Rhyme ordered Sellitto, then looked around the room. "We need more equipment. I want a vacuum metal fingerprint unit too. And a GC-MS." A gas chromatograph broke down substances into their component elements, and mass photospectrometry used light to identify each one of them. These instruments let criminalists test an unknown sample as small as one millionth of a gram and compare it against a database of a hundred thousand known substances, cataloged by identity *and* name brand.

Sellitto phoned the wish list in to the CSU lab.

"But we can't wait for the fancy toys, Mel. You'll have to do it the old-fashioned way. Tell me more about our phony sand."

"It's mixed with a little dirt. There's loam, flecks of quartz, feldspar and mica. But minimal leaf and decomposed-plant fragments. Flecks here of what could be bentonite."

"Bentonite." Rhyme was pleased. "That's a volcanic ash that builders use in slurry when they're digging foundations in watery areas of the city where the bedrock's deep. It prevents cave-ins. So we're looking for a developed area that's on or near the water, probably south of Thirty-fourth Street. North of that the bed-rock's much closer to the surface and they don't need slurry."

Cooper moved the slide. "If I had to guess, I'd say this is mostly calcium. Wait, something fibrous here."

The knob turned and Rhyme would've paid anything to be looking through that eyepiece. Flashed back to all the evenings he'd spent with his face pressed against the gray sponge rubber, watching fibers or flecks of humus or blood cells or metal shavings swim into and out of focus.

"Here's something else. A larger granule. Three layers. One similar to horn, then two layers of calcium. Slightly different colors. The other one's translucent."

"Three layers?" Rhyme spat out angrily. "Hell, it's a seashell!" He felt furious with himself. He should have thought of that.

"Yep, that's it." Cooper was nodding. "Oyster, I think."

The oyster beds around the city were mostly off the coasts of Long Island and New Jersey. Rhyme had hoped that the unsub would limit the geographic area of the search to Manhattan—where the victim that morning was found. He muttered, "If he's opening up the whole metro area the search'll be hopeless."

Cooper said, "I'm looking at something else. I think it's lime. But very old. Granular."

"Concrete maybe?" Rhyme suggested.

"Possibly. Yes. I don't get the shells then," Cooper added reflectively. "Around New York the oyster beds're full of vegetation and mud. This is mixed with concrete and there's virtually no vegetable matter at all."

Rhyme barked suddenly. "Edges! What are the edges of the shell like, Mel?"

The tech gazed into the eyepiece. "Fractured, not worn. This's been pulverized by dry pressure. Not eroded by water."

Rhyme's eyes slipped over the Randel map, scanning right and left. Focusing on the leaping dog's rump.

"Got it!" he cried.

In 1913 F. W. Woolworth built the sixty-story structure that still bears his name, terracotta-clad, covered with gargoyles and Gothic sculpture. For sixteen years it was the world's tallest building. Because the bedrock in that part of Manhattan was more than a hundred feet below Broadway, workmen had to dig deep shafts to anchor the building. It wasn't long after the groundbreaking that workmen discovered the remains of Manhattan industrialist Talbott Soames, who'd been kidnapped in 1906. The man's body was found buried in a thick bed of what looked like white sand but was really ground oyster shells, a fact the tabloids had a hey-day with, noting the obese tycoon's obsession with rich food. The shells were so common along the lower eastern tip of Manhattan they'd been used for landfill. They were what had given Pearl Street its name.

"She's downtown somewhere," Rhyme announced. "Probably the east side. And maybe near Pearl. She'll be underground, about five to fifteen feet down. Maybe a construction site, maybe a basement. An old building or tunnel."

"Cross-check the EPA diagram, Jerry," Sellitto instructed. "Where they're doing asbestos cleanup."

"Along Pearl? Nothing." The young officer held up the map he and Haumann were working from. "There're three-dozen cleanup sites—in Midtown, Harlem and the Bronx. But nothing downtown."

Asbestos . . . asbestos . . ." Rhyme mused again. *What* was so familiar about it?

It was 2:05 P.M.

"Bo, we've got to move. Get your people down there and start a search. All the buildings along Pearl Street. Water Street too."

"Man," the cop sighed, "that's beaucoup buildings." He started for the door.

Rhyme said to Sellitto, "Lon, you better go too. This's going to be a photo finish. They'll need all the searchers they can get. Amelia, I want you down there too."

"Look, I've been thinking—"

"Officer," Sellitto snapped, "you got your orders."

A faint glower crossed her beautiful face.

Rhyme said to Cooper, "Mel, you drive over here in a bus?"

"An RRV," he answered.

The city's big crime scene buses were large vans—filled

with instruments and evidence-collection supplies, better equipped than the entire labs of many small towns. But when Rhyme was running IRD he'd ordered smaller crime scene vehicles—station wagons basically—containing the essential collection-and-analysis equipment. The Rapid Response Vehicles looked placid but Rhyme had bullied Transportation into getting them fitted with turbocharged Police Interceptor engines. They often beat Patrol's squad cars to the scene; on more than one occasion the first officer was a seasoned crime scene tech. Which is every prosecutor's dream.

"Give Amelia the keys."

Cooper handed them to Sachs, who stared briefly at Rhyme then wheeled and hurried down the stairs. Even her footsteps sounded angry.

"All right, Lon. What's on your mind?"

Sellitto glanced at the empty hallway and walked up close to Rhyme. "You really want P.D. for this?"

"P.D.?"

"I mean her. Sachs. P.D.'s a nickname."

"For what?"

"Don't say it around her. Ticks her off. Her dad was a beat cop for forty years. So they call her the Portable's Daughter."

"You don't think I should've picked her?"

"Naw, I don't. Why d'you want her?"

"Because she climbed down a thirty-foot embankment so she wouldn't contaminate the scene. She closed a major avenue and an Amtrak line. That's initiative."

"Come on, Linc. I know a dozen CS cops'd do something like that."

"Well, she's the one I wanted." And Rhyme gave Sellitto a grave look, reminding him, subtly but without debate, what the terms of this bargain had been.

"All I'll say is," the detective muttered, "I just talked to Polling. Peretti's fucking outa joint about being flanked and if—no, I'll say *when*—the brass finds out somebody from Patrol's walking the grid at the scene, there'll be fucking trouble."

"Probably," Rhyme said softly, gazing at the profile poster, "but I have a feeling that's going to be the least of our trouble today."

And let his weary head ease back into the thick down pillow.

SEVEN

The station wagon raced toward the dark, sooty canyons of Wall Street, downtown New York.

Amelia Sachs's fingers danced lightly on the steering wheel as she tried to imagine where T.J. Colfax might be held captive. Finding her seemed hopeless. The approaching financial district had never looked so enormous, so full of alleys, so filled with manholes and doorways and buildings peppered with black windows.

So many places to hide a hostage.

In her mind she saw the hand sticking out of the grave beside the railroad tracks. The diamond ring sitting on the bloody bone of a finger. Sachs recognized the type of jewelry. She called them consolation rings—the sort lonely rich girls bought themselves. The sort she'd be wearing if she were rich.

Speeding south, dodging bicycle messengers and cabs.

Even on this glaring afternoon, under a choked sun, this was a spooky part of town. The buildings cast grim shadows and were coated with grime dark as dried blood.

Sachs took a turn at forty, skidding on the spongy asphalt, and punched the pedal to bring the station wagon back up to sixty.

Excellent engine, she thought. And decided to see how well the wagon handled at seventy.

Years before, while her old man slept—he worked the three-to-eleven watch usually—teenage Amie Sachs would palm the keys to his Camaro and tell her mother Rose she was going shopping, did she want anything from the Fort Hamilton pork store? And before her mother could say, "No, but you take

UNSUB 823			
Appearance	Residence	Vehicle	Other
	• Prob. has safe house	• Yellow Cab	• knows CS proc. • possibly has record • knows FR prints • gun = .32 Colt

the train, you're not driving," the girl would disappear out the door, fire up the car and race west.

Coming home three hours later, pork-less, Amie would sneak up the stairs to be confronted by a mother frantic and angry, who—to her daughter's amusement—would lecture her about the risks of getting pregnant and how that would ruin her chances to use her beautiful face to make a million dollars at modeling. And when finally the woman learned that her daughter wasn't sleeping around but was merely driving a hundred m.p.h. on Long Island highways, she grew frantic and angry and would lecture the girl about smashing up her beautiful face and ruining her chances to make a million dollars at modeling.

Things grew even worse when she got her driver's license.

Sachs now sliced between two double-parked trucks, hoping that neither a passenger nor a driver would open his door. In a Doppler whisper she was past them.

When you move they can't getcha. . . .

Lon Sellitto kneaded his rotund face with blunt fingertips and paid no attention to the Indy 500 driving. He talked with his partner about the case like an accountant discussing a balance sheet. As for Banks, though, he was no longer stealing infatuated glances at Sachs's eyes and lips and had taken to checking the speedometer every minute or so.

They skidded in a frantic turn past the Brooklyn Bridge. She thought again of the woman captive, picturing T.J.'s long, elegant nails, while she tapped her own picked fingers on the wheel. She saw again in her mind the image that refused to go away: the white birch branch of a hand, sticking up out of the moist grave. The single bloody bone.

"He's kind of loony," she blurted suddenly, to change the direction of her thoughts.

"Who?" Sellitto asked.

"Rhyme."

Banks added, "Ask me, he looks like Howard Hughes's kid brother."

"Yeah, well, that surprised me," the older detective admitted. "Wasn't looking too good. Used to be a handsome guy. But, well, you know. After what he's been through. How come if you drive like this, Sachs, you're a portable?"

"Where I got assigned. They didn't ask, they *told* me." Just like you did, she reflected. "Was he really as good as that?"

"Rhyme? Better. Most CSU guys in New York handle two hundred bodies a year. Tops. Rhyme did double that. Even when he was running IRD. Take Peretti, he's a good man but he gets out once every two weeks or so and only on media cases. You're not hearing this from me, officer."

"Nosir."

"But Rhyme'd run the scenes himself. And when he wasn't running scenes he'd be out walking around."

"Doing what?"

"Just walking around. Looking at stuff. He walked miles. All over the city. Buying things, picking up things, *collecting* things."

"What kinds of things?"

"Evidence standards. Dirt, food, magazines, hubcaps, shoes, medical books, drugs, plants . . . You name it, he'd find it and catalog it. You know—so when some PE came in he'd have a better idea where the perp might've been or what he'd been doing. You'd page him and he'd be in Harlem or the Lower East Side or Hell's Kitchen."

"Police in his blood?"

"Naw. Father was some kind of scientist at a national laboratory or something."

"Is that what Rhyme studied? Science?"

"Yeah. Went to school at Champaign-Urbana, got a coupla fancy degrees. Chemistry and history. Which I have no idea why. His folks're gone since I knew him. That'd be, hell, coming on fifteen years now. And he doesn't have any brothers or sisters. He grew up in Illinois. That's why the name, Lincoln."

She wanted to ask if he was, or had been, married but didn't. She settled for: "Is he really that much of a . . ."

"You can say it, officer."

"A shit?"

Banks laughed.

Sellitto said, "My ma had this expression. She said somebody was 'of a mind.' Well, that describes Rhyme. He's of a mind. One time this dumb-ass tech sprayed luminol—that's a blood reagent—on a fingerprint, instead of ninhydrin. Ruined the print. Rhyme fired him on the spot. Another time a cop took a leak at a scene and flushed the toilet. Man, Rhyme went ballistic, told him to get his ass down to the basement and bring back whatever was in the sewer trap." Sellitto laughed. "The cop, he had rank, he said, 'I'm not doing that, I'm a lieutenant.' And Rhyme said, 'Got news, You're a plumber now.' I could go on and on. Fuck, officer, you doing eighty?"

They streaked past the Big Building and she thought, achingly, That's where I oughta be right now. Meeting fellow information officers, sitting through the training session, soaking up the air conditioning.

She steered expertly around a taxi that was oozing through a red light.

Jesus, this is hot. Dust hot, stink hot, gas hot. The ugly hours of the city. Tempers spurted like gray water shooting from hydrants up in Harlem. Two Christmases ago, she and her boyfriend had an abbreviated holiday celebration—from 11:00 P.M. to midnight, the only mutual free time their watches allowed—in the four-degree night. She and Nick, sitting at Rockefeller Center, outside, near the skating rink, drinking coffee and brandy. They'd agreed they'd rather have a week of cold than a single hot August day.

Finally, streaking down Pearl she spotted Haumann's command post. Leaving eight-foot skid marks, Sachs put the RRV into a slot between his car and an EMS bus.

"Damn, you drive good." Sellitto climbed out. For some reason Sachs was delighted to notice Jerry Banks's sweaty fingerprints remained prominently on the window when he pushed the rear door open.

EMS officers and Patrol uniforms were everywhere, fifty or sixty of them. And more were on their way. It seemed as if the entire attention of Police Plaza was focused on downtown New York. Sachs found herself thinking idly that if anybody wanted to try an assassination or to take over Gracie Mansion or a consulate, this'd be the time to do it.

Haumann trotted up to the station wagon. He said to Sellitto, "We're doing door-to-door, seeing about construction along Pearl. Nobody knows anything about asbestos work and nobody's heard any calls for help."

Sachs started to climb out but Haumann said, "No, officer. Your orders're to stay here with the CS vehicle."

She got out anyway.

"Yessir. Who exactly said that?"

"Detective Rhyme. I just talked to him. You're supposed to call in to Central when you're at the CP."

Haumann was walking away. Sellitto and Banks hurried toward the command post.

"Detective Sellitto," Sachs called.

He turned. She said, "Excuse me, detective. The thing is, who's my watch commander? Who'm I reporting to?"

He said shortly, "You're reporting to Rhyme."

She laughed. "But I can't be *reporting* to him."

Sellitto gazed at her blankly.

"I mean, aren't there liability issues or something? Jurisdiction? He's a *civilian*. I need somebody, a shield, to report to."

Sellitto said evenly, "Officer, listen up. We're *all* reporting to Lincoln Rhyme. I don't care whether he's a civilian or he's the chief or he's the fucking Caped Crusader. Got that?"

"But—"

"You wanna complain, do it in writing and do it tomorrow."

And he was gone. Sachs stared after him for a moment then returned to the front seat of the wagon and called in to Central that she was 10–84 at the scene. Awaiting instructions.

She laughed grimly as the woman reported, "Ten-four, Portable 5885. Be advised. Detective Rhyme will be in touch shortly, K."

Detective Rhyme.

"Ten-four, K," Sachs responded and looked in the back of the wagon, wondering idly what was in the black suitcases.

Two-forty P.M.

The phone rang in Rhyme's townhouse. Thom answered. "It's a dispatcher from headquarters."

"Put 'em through."

The speakerphone burst to life. "Detective Rhyme, you don't remember me but I worked at IRD when you were there. Civilian. Did phone detail then. Emma Rollins."

"Of course. How're the youngsters, Emma?" Rhyme had a memory of a large, cheerful black woman, supporting five children with two jobs. He recalled her blunt finger stabbing buttons so hard she once actually broke one of the government-issue phones.

"Jeremy's starting college in a couple weeks and Dora's still acting, or she thinks she is. The little ones're doing just fine."

"Lon Sellitto recruited you, did he?"

"Nosir. I heard you were working on the case and I booted some child back to 911. Emma's taking this job, I told her."

"What've you got for us?"

"We're working out of a directory of companies making bolts. And a book that lists places wholesaling them. Here's what we found. It was the letters did it. The ones stamped on the bolt. The *CE*. They're made special for Con Ed."

Hell. Of course.

"They're marked that way because they're a different size than most bolts this company sells—fifteen-sixteenths of an inch, and a lot more threads than most other bolts. That'd be Michigan Tool and Die in Detroit. They use 'em in old pipes only in New York. Ones made sixty, seventy years ago. The way the parts of the pipe fit together they have to be real close seals. Fit closer'n a bride and groom on their wedding night's what the man told me. Trying to make me blush."

"Emma, I love you. You stay on call, will you?"

"You bet I will."

"Thom!" Rhyme shouted. "This phone isn't going to work. I need to make calls myself. That voice-activation thing in the computer. Can I use it?"

"You never ordered it."

"I didn't?"

"No."

"Well, I need it."

"Well, we don't have it."

"Do *something*. I want to be able to make calls."

"I think there's a manual ECU somewhere." Thom dug through a box against the wall. He found a small electronic console and plugged one end into the phone and the other into a stalk control that mounted next to Rhyme's cheek.

"That's too awkward!"

"Well, it's all we've got. If we'd hooked up the infrared above your eyebrow like I suggested, you could've been making phone-sex calls for the past two years."

"Too many fucking wires," Rhyme spat out.

His neck spasmed suddenly and knocked the controller out of reach. "Fuck."

Suddenly this minute task—not to mention their mission—seemed impossible to Lincoln Rhyme. He was exhausted, his neck hurt, his head. His eyes particularly. They stung and—this was *more* painful to him—he felt a chip of urge to rub the backs of his fingers across his closed lids. A tiny gesture of relief, something the rest of the world did every day.

Thom replaced the joystick. Rhyme summoned patience from somewhere and asked his aide, "How does it work?"

"There's the screen. See it on the controller? Just move the stick till it's on a number, wait one second and it's programmed in. Then do the next number the same way. When you've got all seven, push the stick here to dial."

He snapped, "It's not working."

"Just practice."

"We don't have time!"

Thom snarled, "I've been answering the phone for you way too long."

"All right," Rhyme said, lowering his voice—his way of apology. "I'll practice later. Could you please get me Con Ed? And I need to speak to a supervisor."

The rope hurt and the cuffs hurt but it was the noise that scared her the most.

Tammie Jean Colfax felt all the sweat in her body run down her face and chest and arms as she struggled to saw the handcuff links back and forth on the rusty bolt. Her wrists were numb but it seemed to her that she was wearing through some of the chain.

She paused, exhausted, and twitched her arms this way and that to keep a cramp at bay. She listened again. It was, she thought, the sound of workmen tightening bolts and hammering parts into place. Final taps of hammers. She imagined they were just finishing up their job on the pipe and thinking of going home.

Don't go, she cried to herself. Don't leave me. As long as the men were there, working, she was safe.

A final bang, then ringing silence.

Git on outa thayr, girl. G'on.

Mamma . . .

T.J. cried for several minutes, thinking of her family back in Eastern Tennessee. Her nostrils clogged but as she began to choke she blew her nose violently, felt an explosion of tears and mucus. Then she was breathing again. It gave her confidence. Strength. She began to saw once more.

"I appreciate the urgency, detective. But I don't know how I can help you. We use bolts all over the city. Oil lines, gas lines . . ."

"All right," Rhyme said tersely and asked the Con Ed supervisor at the company's headquarters on Fourteenth Street, "Do you insulate wiring with asbestos?"

A hesitation.

"We've cleaned up ninety percent of that," the woman said defensively. "Ninety-*five*."

People could be so irritating. "I understand that. I just need to know if there's still any asbestos used for insulation."

"No," she said adamantly. "Well, never for electricity. Just the steam and that's the smallest percentage of our service."

Steam!

It was the least-known and the scariest of the city's utilities. Con Ed heated water to 1,000 degrees then shot it through a hundred-mile network of pipes running under Manhattan. The blistering steam itself was superheated—about 380 degrees—and rocketed through the city at seventy-five miles an hour.

Rhyme now recalled an article in the paper. "Didn't you have a break in the line last week?"

"Yessir. But there was no asbestos leak. That site had been cleaned years ago."

"But there *is* asbestos around some of your pipes in the system downtown?"

She hesitated. "Well . . ."

"Where was the break?" Rhyme continued quickly.

"Broadway. A block north of Chambers."

"Wasn't there an article in the *Times* about it?"

"I don't know. Maybe. Yes."

"And did the article mention asbestos?"

"It did," she admitted, "but it just said that in the past asbestos contamination'd been a problem."

"The pipe that broke, was it . . . does it cross Pearl Street farther south?"

"Well, let me see. Yes, it does. At Hanover Street. On the north side."

He pictured T.J. Colfax, the woman with the thin fingers and long nails, about to die.

"And the steam's going back on at three?"

"That's right. Any minute now."

"It can't!" Rhyme shouted. "Somebody's tampered with the line. You can't turn that steam back on!"

Cooper looked up uneasily from his microscope.

The supervisor said, "Well, I don't know . . ."

Rhyme barked to Thom, "Call Lon, tell him she's in a basement at Hanover and Pearl. The north side." He told him about the steam. "Get the fire department there too. Heat-protective outfits."

Rhyme shouted into the speakerphone. "Call the work crews! Now! They can't turn that steam back on. They can't!" He repeated the words absently, detesting his exquisite imagination, which showed, in an endless loop, the woman's flesh growing pink then red then splitting apart under the fierce clouds of sputtering white steam.

In the station wagon the radio crackled. It was three minutes to three by Sachs's watch. She answered the call.

"Portable 5885, K—"

"Forget the officialese, Amelia," Rhyme said. "We don't have time."

"I—"

"We think we know where she is. Hanover and Pearl."

She glanced over her shoulder and saw dozens of ESU officers running flat-out toward an old building.

"Do you want me to—"

"They'll look for her. You have to get ready to work the scene."

"But I can help—"

"No. I want you to go to the back of the station wagon. There's a suitcase in it labeled zero two. Take it with you. And in a small black case there's a PoliLight. You saw one in my room. Mel was using it. Take that too. In the suitcase marked zero three you'll find a headset and stalk mike. Plug it into your Motorola and get over to the building where the officers are. Call me back when you're rigged. Channel thirty-seven. I'll be on a landline but you'll be patched through to me."

Channel thirty-seven. The special ops citywide frequency. The priority frequency.

"What?—" she asked. But the dead radio did not respond.

She had a long black halogen flashlight on her utility belt so she left the bulky twelve-volter in the back of the wagon and grabbed the PoliLight and the heavy suitcase. It must have weighed fifty pounds. Just what my damn joints need. She adjusted her grip and, teeth clamped together against the pain, hurried toward the intersection.

Sellitto, breathless, ran to the building. Banks joined them.

"You hear?" the older detective asked. Sachs nodded.

"This is it?" she asked.

Sellitto nodded toward the alley. "He had to take her in this way, The lobby's got a guard station." They now trotted down the shadowy, cobblestoned canyon, steaming hot, smelling of piss and garbage. Battered blue Dumpsters sat nearby.

"There," Sellitto shouted. "Those doors."

The cops fanned out, running. Three of the four doors were locked tight from the inside.

The fourth had been jimmied open and was now chained shut. The chain and lock were new.

"This's it!" Sellitto reached for the door, hesitated. Thinking probably about fingerprints. Then he grabbed the handle and yanked. It opened a few inches but the chain held tight. He sent three of the uniforms around to the front to get into the basement from the inside. One cop worked a cobblestone loose from the alley floor and began pounding on the door handle. A half-dozen blows, a dozen. He winced as his hand struck the door; blood gushed from a torn finger.

A fireman ran up with a Halligan tool—a combination pickax and crowbar. He rammed the end into the chain and ripped the padlock open. Sellitto looked at Sachs expectantly. She gazed back.

"Well, go, officer!" he barked.

"What?"

"Didn't he tell you?"

"Who?"

"Rhyme."

Hell, she'd forgotten to plug in the headset. She fumbled it, finally got it plugged in. Heard: "Amelia, where—"

"I'm here."

"Are you at the building?"

"Yes."

"Go inside. They shut the steam off but I don't know if it was in time. Take a medic and one ESU trooper. Go to the boiler room. You'll probably see her right away, the Colfax woman. Walk to her but not directly, not in a straight line from the door to her. I don't want you to disturb any footprints he might've left. Understand?"

"Yes." She nodded emphatically, not thinking that he couldn't see her. Gesturing the medic and an Emergency Services trooper after her, Sachs stepped forward into the murky corridor, shadows everywhere, the groan of machinery, dripping water.

"Amelia," Rhyme said.

"Yes."

"We were talking about ambush before. From what I know about him now I don't think that's the case. He's not there, Amelia. That would be illogical. But keep your shooting hand free."

Illogical.

"Okay."

"Now go! Fast."

EIGHT

A murky cavern. Hot, black, damp.

The three of them moved quickly down the filthy hallway toward the only doorway Sachs could see. A sign said BOILER ROOM. She was behind the ESU officer, who wore full body armor and helmet. The medic was in the rear.

Her right knuckles and shoulder throbbed from the weight of the suitcase. She shifted it to her left hand, nearly dropped it and readjusted her grip. They continued to the door.

There, the SWAT officer pushed inside and swung his machine gun around the dimly lit room. A flashlight was attached to the barrel and it cast a line of pale light in the shreds of steam. Sachs smelled moisture, mold. And another scent, loathsome.

Click. "Amelia?" The staticky burst of Rhyme's voice scared the absolute hell out of her. "Where are you, Amelia?"

With a shaking hand she turned down the volume.

"Inside," she gasped.

"Is she alive?"

Sachs rocked on her feet, staring at the sight. She squinted, not sure at first what she was seeing. Then she understood.

"Oh, no." Whispering. Feeling the nausea.

The sickening boiled-meat smell wafted around her. But that wasn't the worst of it. Neither was the sight of the woman's skin, bright red, almost orange, peeling off in huge scales. The face completely stripped of skin. No, what brought the dread home was the angle of T.J. Colfax's body, the impossible twisting of her limbs and torso as she'd tried to get away from the spray of ravaging heat.

He hoped the vic was dead. For his sake. . . .

"Is she alive?" Rhyme repeated.

"No," Sachs whispered. "I don't see how . . . No."

"Is the room secure?"

Sachs glanced at the officer, who'd heard the transmission and nodded.

"Scene secure."

Rhyme told her, "I want the ESU trooper out then you and the medic go check on her."

Sachs gagged once on the smell and forced herself to control the reflex. She and the medic walked in an oblique path to the pipe. He bent unemotionally forward and felt the woman's neck. He shook his head.

"Amelia?" Rhyme asked.

Her second body in the line of duty. Both in one day.

The medic said, "DCDS."

Sachs nodded, said formally into the mike, "We have a deceased, confirmed dead at the scene."

"Scalded to death?" Rhyme asked.

"Looks like it."

"Tied to the wall?"

"A pipe. Handcuffed, hands behind. Feet tied with clothesline. Duct-tape gag. He opened the steam pipe. She was only a couple of feet from it. God."

Rhyme continued, "Back the medic out the way you came. To the door. Watch where you put your feet."

She did this, staring at the body. How could the skin be so red? Like a boiled crab shell.

"All right, Amelia. You're going to work the scene. Open the suitcase."

She said nothing. Kept staring.

"Amelia, are you at the door? . . . Amelia?"

"*What?*" she shouted.

"Are you at the door?"

His voice was so fucking calm. So different from the snide, demanding voice of the man she remembered in the bedroom. Calm . . . and something else. She didn't know what.

"Yes, I'm at the door. You know, this is crazy."

"Utterly insane," Rhyme agreed, almost cheerfully. "Is the suitcase open?"

She flipped up the lid and glanced inside. Pliers and forceps, a flex mirror on a handle, cotton balls, eyedroppers, pinking sheers, pipettes, spatulas, scalpels . . .

What *is* all this?

. . . a Dustbuster, cheesecloth, envelopes, sifting screens, brushes, scissors, plastic and paper bags, metal cans, bottles— 5 percent nitric acid, ninhydrin, silicone, iodide, friction-ridge-printing supplies.

Impossible. Into the mike she said, "I don't think you believed me, detective. I really *don't* know anything about CS work."

Eyes on the woman's ruined body. Water dripped off her peeled nose. A bit of white—bone—showed through the cheek. And her face was drawn into a anguished grin. Just like the vic that morning.

"I believed you, Amelia," he said dismissively. "Now, the case is open?" He was calm and he sounded . . . what? Yes, *that* was the tone. Seductive. He sounds like a lover.

I hate him, she thought. It's wrong to hate a cripple. But I fucking hate him.

"You're in the basement, right?"

"Yessir."

"Listen, you've got to call me Lincoln. We're going to know each other very well by the time this is over."

Which is gonna be about sixty minutes, tops.

"You'll find some rubber bands in the suitcase, if I'm not mistaken."

"I see some."

"Put them around your shoes. Where the ball of your foot is. If there's any confusion as to footprints you'll know which ones are yours."

"Okay, done."

"Take some evidence bags and envelopes. Put a dozen of each in your pocket. Can you use chopsticks?"

"What did you say?"

"You live in the city, right? You ever go to Mott Street? For General Tsao's chicken? Cold noddles with sesame paste?"

Her gorge rose at the talk of food. She refused to glance at the woman dangling in front of her.

"I can use chopsticks," she said icily.

"Look in the suitcase. I'm not sure you'll find them. They kept them there when I was running scenes."

"I don't see any."

"Well, you'll find some pencils. Put those in your pocket. Now you're going to walk a grid. Cover every inch. Are you ready?"

"Yes."

"First tell me what you see."

"One big room. Maybe twenty by thirty. Full of rusted pipes. Cracked concrete floor. Walls're brick. Mold."

"Any boxes? Anything on the floor?"

"No, it's empty. Except for the pipes, oil tanks, the boiler. There's the sand—the shells, a pile of it spilling out of a crack in the wall. And there's some gray stuff too—"

"'Stuff'?" he jumped. "I don't recognize that word. What's '*stuff*'?"

A burst of anger tore through her. She calmed and said, "It's the asbestos but not wadded up like this morning. It's in crumbling sheets."

"Good. Now, the first sweep. You're looking for footprints and any staged clues that he's left for us."

"You think he left more?"

"Oh, I'll betcha," Rhyme said. "Put on the goggles and use the PoliLight. Keep it low. Grid the room. Every inch. Get going. You know how to walk a grid?"

"Yes."

"How?"

She bristled. "I don't need to be tested."

"Ah, humor me. How?"

"Back and forth in one direction, then back and forth in the perpendicular direction."

"Each step, no more than one foot in length."

She hadn't known that. "I know," she said.

"Go ahead."

The PoliLight flashed on with an eerie, otherworldy glow. She knew it was something called an ALS—alternative light source—and that it made fingerprints and semen and blood and some shoeprints fluoresce. The brilliant bile-green light made shadows dance and jump and more than once she nearly drew down on a dark form that turned out to be a mere phantom of darkness.

"Amelia?" Rhyme's voice was sharp. She jumped again.

"Yes? What?"

"Do you see any footprints?"

She continued to stare at the floor. "I, uh, no. I see streaks in the dust. Or something." She cringed at the careless word. But Rhyme, unlike Peretti that morning, paid no attention. He said, "So. He swept up afterwards."

She was surprised. "Yeah, that's it! Broom marks. How'd you know?"

Rhyme laughed—a jarring sound to Sachs in this rank tomb—and he said, "He was smart enough to cover his tracks this morning; no reason to stop now. Oh, he's good, this boy is. But we're good too. Keep going."

Sachs bent over, her joints on fire, and began the search. She covered every square foot of the floor. "Nothing here. Nothing at all."

He picked up on the note of finality in her voice. "You've only just started, Amelia. Crime scenes are three-dimensional. Remember that. What you mean is there's nothing on the floor. Now search the walls. Start with the spot farthest away from the steam and cover every inch."

She slowly circled the horrible marionette in the center of the room. She thought of a Maypole game she'd played at some Brooklyn street feast when she was six or seven, as her father proudly took home movies. Circling slowly. It was an empty room and yet there were a thousand different places to search.

Hopeless . . . Impossible.

But it wasn't. On a ledge, about six feet above the floor, she found the next set of clues. She barked a fast laugh. "Got something here."

"In a cluster?"

"Yes. A big splinter of dark wood."

"Chopsticks."

"What?" she asked.

"The pencils. Use them to pick it up. Is it wet?"

"Everything in here's wet."

"Sure, it would be. The steam. Put it in a paper evidence bag.

Plastic keeps the moisture in and in this heat bacteria'll destroy the trace evidence. What else is there?" he asked eagerly.

"It's, I don't know, hairs, I think. Short, trimmed. A little pile of them."

"Loose or attached to skin?"

"Loose."

"There's a role of two-inch tape in the suitcase. 3M. Pick them up with that."

Sachs lifted most of the hairs, placed them in a paper envelope. She studied the ledge around the hairs. "I see some stains. Looks like rust or blood." She thought to hit the spot with the PoliLight. "They're fluorescing."

"Can you do a presumptive blood test?"

"No."

"Let's just assume it's blood. Could it be the victim's?"

"Doesn't seem to be. It's too far away and there's no trail to her body."

"Does it lead anywhere?"

"Looks like it. To a brick in the wall. It's loose. No prints on it. I'm going to move it aside. I—oh, Jesus!" Sachs gasped and stumbled back a foot or two, nearly fell.

"What?" Rhyme asked.

She eased forward, staring in disbelief.

"Amelia. Talk to me."

"It's a bone. A bloody bone."

"Human?"

"I don't know," she answered. "How would I . . . ? I don't know."

"Recent kill?"

"Looks like it. About two inches long and two in diameter. There's blood and flesh on it. It's been sawn off. Jesus. Who the fuck'd do something—"

"Don't get rattled."

"What if he got it from another victim?"

"Then we better find 'im pretty damn soon, Amelia. Bag it. Plastic for the bone."

As she did this, he asked, "Any other staged clues?" He sounded concerned.

"No."

"That's all? Hairs, a bone and a splinter of wood. He's no making it very easy, is he?"

"Should I bring it back to your . . . office?"

Rhyme was laughing. "He'd like us to call it quits. Bu no. We're not through yet. Let's find out a little more abou Unsub 823."

"But there's nothing here."

"Oh, yes there is, Amelia. There's his address and his phone number and his description and his hopes and aspirations They're all around you."

She was furious at his professor's tone and remaine silent.

"You have the flashlight?"

"I've got my issue halogen—"

"No," he grumbled. "Issue lights are too narrow. You nee the twelve-volt broad beam."

"Well, I didn't bring it," she snapped. "Should I go bacl and get it?"

"No time. Check out the pipes."

She searched for ten minutes, climbing up to the ceil ing, and with the powerful light she illuminated spots tha perhaps hadn't been lit in fifty years. "No, I don't se a thing."

"Go back to the door. Hurry."

She hesitated and returned.

"Okay, I'm here."

"Now. Close your eyes. What do you smell?"

"Smell? Did you say smell?" Was he crazy?

"Always smell the air at a crime scene. It can tell you hundred things."

She kept her eyes wide and breathed in. She said, "Well, don't *know* what I smell."

"That's not an acceptable answer."

She exhaled in exasperation and hoped the hiss was comin through his telephone loud and clear. She jammed her lid closed, inhaled, fought the nausea again. "Mold, mustiness The smell of hot water from the steam."

"You don't know where it's from. Just describe it."

"Hot water. The woman's perfume."

"Are you sure it's hers?"

"Well, no."

"Are you wearing any?"

"No."

"How 'bout aftershave? The medic? The ESU officer?"

"I don't think so. No."

"Describe it."

"Dry. Like gin."

"Take a guess, man's aftershave or woman's perfume."

What had Nick worn? Arrid Extra Dry.

"I don't know," she said. "Man's."

"Walk to the body."

She glanced once at the pipe then down to the floor.

"I—"

"Do it," Lincoln Rhyme said.

She did. The peeling skin was like black-and-red birch.

"Smell her neck."

"It's all . . . I mean, there isn't much skin left."

"I'm sorry, Amelia, but you have to do it. We have to see if it's her perfume."

She did, inhaled. Gagged, nearly vomited.

I'm going to puke, she thought. Just like Nick and me that night at Pancho's, done in by those damn frozen daiquiris. Two hard-ass cops, swigging down sissy drinks with blue plastic swordfish swimming in them.

"Do you smell the perfume?"

Here it comes . . . Gagging again.

No. No! She closed her eyes, concentrated on her aching joints. The most painful one—her knee. And, miraculously, the wave of nausea passed. "It's not her perfume."

"Good. So maybe our boy's vain enough to wear a lot of aftershave. That could be a social-class indicator. Or maybe he wants to cover up some of the smell he might've left. Garlic, cigars, fish, whisky. We'll have to see. Now, Amelia, listen carefully."

"What?"

"I want you to be him."

Oh. Psychoshit. Just what I need.

"I really don't think we have time for this."

"There's never enough time in crime scene work," Rhyme continued soothingly. "But that doesn't stop us. Just get into

his head. You've been thinking the way we think. I want you
to think the way he does."

"Well, how do I do that?"

"Use your imagination. That's why God gave us one. Now
you're him. You've got her cuffed and gagged. You take her
into the room there. You cuff her to the pipe. You scare her.
You're enjoying this."

"How do you know he's enjoying it?"

"*You're* enjoying it. Not *him*. How do I know? Because
nobody goes to this much trouble to do something they don't
enjoy. Now, you know your way around. You've been here
before."

"Why d'you think that?"

"You had to check it out earlier—to find a deserted place
with a feeder pipe from the steam system. And to get the clues
he left by the train tracks."

Sachs was mesmerized by his fluid, low voice. She forgot
completely that his body was destroyed. "Oh. Right."

"You take the steam-pipe cover off. What are you thinking?"

"I don't know. That I want to get it over with. Get
out."

But the words were hardly out of her mouth before she
thought: Wrong. And she wasn't surprised when she heard
Rhyme's tongue click in her headset. "Do you really?"
he asked.

"No. I want to make it last."

"Yes! I think that's exactly what you want. You're thinking about what the steam will do to her. What else do
you feel?"

"I . . ."

A thought formed in her mind, vague. She saw the woman
screaming, crying, calling for help. Saw something else . . .
some*one* else. Him, she thought. Unsub 823. But what about
him? She was close to understanding. What . . . *what*? But
suddenly the thought vanished. Gone.

"I don't know," she whispered.

"Do you feel any urgency? Or are you pretty cool about
what you're doing?"

"I'm in a hurry. I have to leave. The cops could be here at
any minute. But I still . . ."

"What?"

"Shhhh," she ordered, and scanned the room again, looking or whatever had put the seed of the vanished thought in er mind.

The room was swimming, a black, starry night. Swirls f darkness and distant, jaundiced lights. Lord, don't let ne faint!

Maybe he—

There! That's it. Sachs's eyes were following the steam ipe. She was looking at another access plate in a shadowy lcove of the room. It would have been a better hiding place or the girl—you couldn't see it from the doorway if you were valking past—and the second plate had only four bolts on it, ot eight, like the one he chose.

Why not that pipe?

Then she understood.

"He doesn't want . . . *I* don't want to leave just yet because want to keep an eye on her."

"Why do you think that?" he inquired, echoing her own vords just moments before.

"There's another pipe I could've chained her to but I picked ne one that was in the open."

"So you could see her?"

"I think so."

"Why?"

"Maybe to make sure she can't get away. Maybe to make ure the gag's tight . . . I don't know."

"Good, Amelia. But what does it *mean*? How can we *use* nat fact?"

Sachs looked around the room for the place where he'd ave the best view of the girl without being seen. It turned ut to be a shadowy spot between two large heating-oil anks.

"Yes!" she said excitedly, looking at the floor. "He was ere." Forgetting the role-playing. "He swept up."

She scanned the area with the bile glow of the PoliLight and.

"No footprints," she said, disappointed. But as she lifted ne light to shut it off, a smudge glowed on one of the anks.

"I've got a print!" she announced.

"A print?"

"You get a better view of the girl if you lean forward and support yourself on a tank. That's what he did, I'm sure. Only it's weird, Lincoln. It's . . . deformed. His hand." She shivered, looking at the monstrous palm.

"In the suitcase there's an aerosol bottle labeled DFO. It's a fluorescent stain. Spray that on the print, hit the PoliLight and shoot the image with the one-to-one Polaroid."

She told him when she'd finished this and he said, "Now Dustbust the floor between the tanks. If we're lucky he scratched off a hair or chewed a fingernail."

My habits, Sachs thought. It was one of the things that had finally ruined her modeling career—the bloody nail, the worried eyebrow. She'd tried and tried and tried to stop. Finally gave up, discouraged, bewildered that a tiny habit could change the direction of your life so dramatically.

"Bag the vacuum filter."

"In paper?"

"Yes, paper. Now, the body, Amelia."

"What?"

"Well, you've *got* to process the body."

Her heart sank. Somebody else, please. Have somebody else do it. She said, "Not until the ME's finished. That's the rule."

"No rules today, Amelia. We're making up our own. The medical examiner'll get her after us."

Sachs approached the woman.

"You know the routine?"

"Yes." She stepped close to the destroyed body.

Then froze. Hands inches from the victim's skin.

I can't do it. She shuddered. Told herself to keep going. But she couldn't; the muscles weren't responding.

"Sachs? You there?"

She couldn't answer.

I can't do this . . . It was as simple as that. Impossible. I *can't.*

"Sachs?"

And then she looked into herself and, somehow, saw her father, in uniform, stooping low on the hot, pitted sidewalk of West Forty-second Street, sliding his arm around a scabby drunk to help him home. Then was seeing her Nick as he laughed and drank beer in a Bronx tavern with a hijacker who'd kill him in a second if he knew the young cop was working undercover. The two men in her life, doing what they had to do.

"Amelia?"

These two images bobbed in her thoughts, and why they calmed her, or where that calm came from, she couldn't begin to guess. "I'm here," she said to Lincoln Rhyme and went about her business as she'd been taught. Taking the nail scrapings, combing the hair—pubic and head. Telling Rhyme what she did as she did it.

Ignoring the dull orbs of eyes . . .

Ignoring the crimson flesh.

Trying to ignore the smell.

"Get her clothing," Rhyme said. "Cut off everything. Put a sheet of newsprint under them first to pick up any trace that falls off."

"Should I check the pockets?"

"No, we'll do that here. Wrap them up in the paper."

Sachs cut the blouse and skirt off, the panties. She reached out for what she thought was the woman's bra, dangling from her chest. It felt curious, disintegrating in her fingers. Then, like a slap she realized what she held and she gave a short scream. It wasn't cloth, it was skin.

"Amelia? Are you all right?"

"Yes!" she gasped. "I'm fine."

"Describe the restraints."

"Duct tape for the gag, two inches wide. Standard-issue cuffs for hands, clothesline for the feet."

"PoliLight her body. He might've touched her with his bare hands. Look for prints."

She did. "Nothing."

"Okay. Now cut the clothesline—but not through the knot. Bag it. In plastic."

Sachs did. Then Rhyme said, "We need the cuffs."

"Okay. I've got a cuff key."

"No, Amelia. Don't open them."

"What?"

"The cuff lock mechanism is one of the best ways to pick up trace from the perp."

"Well, how'm I supposed to get them off without a key?" She laughed.

"There's a razor saw in the suitcase."

"You want me to cut off the cuffs?"

There was a pause. Rhyme said, "No, not the cuffs, Amelia."

"Well, what *do* you want me to . . . Oh, you can't be serious. Her *hands*?"

"You have to." He was irritated at her reluctance.

Okay, that's it. Sellitto and Polling've picked a nutcase for a partner. Maybe *their* careers're tanking but I'm not going down with them.

"Forget it."

"Amelia, it's just another way to collect evidence."

Why did he sound so reasonable? She thought desperately for excuses. "They'll get blood all over them if I cut—"

"Her heart's not beating. Besides," he added like a TV chef, "the blood'll be cooked into a solid."

The gorge rising again.

"Go on, Amelia. Go to the suitcase. Get the saw. In the lid." He added a frosty, "Please."

"Why'd you have me scrape under her nails? I could've just brought you back her hands!"

"Amelia, we need the cuffs. We have to open them here and we can't wait for the ME. It has to be done."

She walked back to the doorway. Unsnapped the thongs, lifted the wicked-looking saw from the case. She stared at the woman, frozen in her tortured pose in the center of the vile room.

"Amelia? *Amelia?*"

Outside, they sky was still clogged with stagnant, yellow air and the buildings nearby were covered with soot like charred bones. But Sachs had never been so glad to be out in the city air as now. The CU suitcase in one hand, the razor saw in the other; the headset dangling dead around her neck. Sachs ignored the huge crowd of cops and spectators staring at her and walked straight toward the station wagon.

As she passed Sellitto she handed him the saw without pausing, practically tossed it to him. "If he wants it done that badly tell him he can damn well walk down here and do it himself."

2

LOCARD'S PRINCIPLE

*In real life, you only get one shot at the
homicide crime scene.*

Vernon J. Geberth,
Lieutenant Commander (Ret.)
New York Police Department

NINE

I've got myself into a situation here, sir."

The man across the desk looked like a TV show's idea of a big-city deputy police commissioner. Which happened to be his rank. White hair, a temperate jowl, gold-rimmed glasses, posture to die for.

"Now what's the problem, officer?"

Dep. Com. Randolph C. Eckert looked down his long nose with a gaze that Sachs recognized immediately; his nod to equality was to be as stern with the female officers as with the male ones.

"I've got a complaint, sir," she said stiffly. "You heard about that taxi kidnapping case?"

He nodded. "Ah, has *that* got the city in double dutch."

She believed that was a schoolchild's game of jump rope but wouldn't presume to correct a deputy commissioner.

"That damn UN conference," he continued, "and the whole world's watching. It's unfair. People don't talk about crime in Washington. Or Detroit. Well, Detroit they do. Say, Chicago. Never. No, it's New York that people thump on. Richmond, Virginia, had more murders per capital than we did last year. I looked it up. And I'd rather parachute unarmed into Central Harlem than drive windows-up through South East D.C. any day."

"Yessir."

"Understand they found that girl dead. It was on all the news. Those reporters."

"Downtown. Just now."

"Now that's a pity."

"Yessir."

"They just killed her? Like that? No ransom demand or anything?"

"I didn't hear about any ransom."

"What's this complaint?"

"I was first officer in a related homicide this morning."

"You're Patrol?" Eckert asked.

"I *was* Patrol. I was supposed to be transferring to Public Affairs today at noon. For a training session." She lifted her hands, tipped with flesh-colored Band-Aids, and dropped them in her lap. "But they shanghaied me."

"Who?"

"Detective Lon Sellitto, sir. And Captain Haumann. And Lincoln Rhyme."

"Rhyme?"

"Yessir."

"Not the fellow was in charge of IRD a few years ago?"

"Yessir. That's him."

"I thought he was dead."

Egos like that will never die.

"Very much alive, sir."

The dep com was looking out his window. "He's not on the force anymore. What's he doing involved in this?"

"Consultant, I guess. It's Lon Sellitto's case. Captain Polling's overseeing it. I've been waiting for this reassignment for eight months. But they've got me working crime scene. I've never *done* crime scene. It doesn't make any sense and frankly I resent being assigned to a job I've had no training for."

"Crime scene?"

"Rhyme ordered me to run the whole scene. By myself."

Eckert didn't understand this. The words weren't registering. "Why is a civilian ordering uniformed officers to do *anything*?"

"My point, sir." She set the hook. "I mean, I'll help up to a point. But I'm just not prepared to dismember victims . . ."

"What?"

She blinked as if surprised he hadn't heard. She explained about the handcuffs.

"Lord in heaven, what the hell're they thinking of? Pardon my French. Don't they know the whole country's watching.

It's been on CNN all day, this kidnapping. Cutting off her hands? Say, you're Herman Sachs's daughter."

"That's right."

"Good officer. *Excellent* officer. I gave him one of his commendations. The man was what a beat cop ought to be. Midtown South, right?"

"Hell's Kitchen. My beat."

My *former* beat.

"Herman Sachs probably prevented more crime than the entire detective division solves in a year. Just calming everything down, you know."

"That was Pop. Sure."

"Her hands?" Eckert snorted. "The girl's family'll sue us. As soon as they find out about it. They sue us for everything. There's a rapist suing us now 'cause he got shot in the leg coming at an officer with a knife. His lawyer's got this theory he's calling the 'least deadly alternative.' Instead of shooting, we're supposed to taze them or use Mace. Or ask them politely, I don't know. I better give the chief and the mayor a heads-up on this one. I'll make some calls, officer." He looked at a wall clock. It was a little after four. "Your watch over for the day?"

"I have to report back to Lincoln Rhyme's house. That's where we're working out of." She thought of the hacksaw. She said coolly, "His bedroom really. That's our CP."

"A civilian's bedroom is your command post?"

"I'd appreciate anything you can do, sir. I've waited a long time for that transfer."

"Cut her hands off. My good Lord."

She stood and walked to the door and out into one of the corridors that would soon be her new assignment. The feeling of relief took only a little longer to arrive than she'd expected.

He stood at the bottle-glass window, watching a pack of wild dogs prowl though the lot across the street.

He was on the first floor of this old building, a marble-clad Federal dating to the early 1800s. Surrounded by vacant lots and tenements—some abandoned, some occupied by paying tenants though most by squatters—this old mansion had been empty for years.

The bone collector took the piece of emery paper in his hand once more and continued to rub. He looked down at his handiwork. Then out the window again.

His hands, in their circular motion, precise. The tiny scrap of sandpaper whispering, *shhhhh, shhhhh* . . . Like a mother hushing her child.

A decade ago, the days of promise in New York, some crazy artist had moved in here. He'd filled the dank, two-storey place with broken and rusting antiques. Wrought-iron grilles, hunks of crown molding and framed squares of spidered stained glass, scabby columns. Some of the artist's work remained on the walls. Frescoes on the old plaster: murals, never completed, of workers, children, angst-ridden lovers. Round, emotionless faces—the man's motif—stared blankly, as if the souls had been nipped out of their smooth bodies.

The painter was never very successful, even after the most ironclad of marketing ideas—his own suicide—and the bank foreclosed on the building several years ago.

Shhhhh . . .

The bone collector had stumbled across the place last year and he'd known immediately that this was home. The desolation of the neighborhood was certainly important to him—it was obviously practical. But there was another appeal, more personal: the lot across the street. During some excavation several years ago a backhoe had unearthed a load of human bones. It turned out this had been one of the city's old cemeteries. Newspaper articles about it suggested the graves might contain the remains not only of Federal and Colonial New Yorkers but Manate and Lenape Indians as well.

He now set aside what he'd been smoothing with the emery paper—a carpal, the delicate palm bone—and picked up the wrist, which he'd carefully detached from the radius and ulna last night just before leaving for Kennedy Airport to collect the first victims. It had been drying for over a week and most of the flesh was gone but it still took some effort to separate the elaborate cluster of bones. They snapped apart with faint plops, like fish breaking the surface of a lake.

Oh, the constables, they were a lot better than he'd anticipated. He'd been watching them search along Pearl Street, wondering if they'd ever figure out where he'd left the woman from the airport. Astonished when they suddenly ran toward the right building. He'd guessed it would take two or three victims until they got a feel for the clues. They hadn't saved her of course. But they might have. A minute or two earlier would have made all the difference.

As with so much in life.

The navicular, the lunate, the hamate, the capitate . . . the bones, intertwined like a Greek puzzle ring, came apart under his strong fingers. He picked bits of flesh and tendon off them. He selected the greater multangulum—at the base of where the thumb had once been—and began to sand once more.

Shhhhh, shhhhhhh.

The bone collector squinted as he looked outside and imagined he saw a man standing beside one of the old graves. It *must* have been his imagination because the man wore a bowler hat and was dressed in mustard-colored gabardine. He rested some dark roses beside the tombstone and then turned away from it, dodging the horses and carriages on his way to the elegantly arched bridge over the Collect Pond outlet at Canal Street. Who'd he been visiting? Parents? A brother? Family who'd died of consumption or in one of the terrible influenza epidemics that'd been ravaging the city recently—

Recently?

No, not recently of course. A hundred years ago—*that's* what he meant.

He squinted and looked again. No sign of the carriages or the horses. Or the man with the bowler hat. Though they'd seemed as real as flesh and blood.

However real *they* are.

Shhhhh, shhhhhh.

It was intruding again, the past. He was seeing things that'd happened *before*, that had happened *then*, as if they were now. He could control it. He *knew* he could.

But as he gazed out the window he realized that of course there was no before or after. Not for him. He drifted back and forth through time, a day, five years, a hundred years or two, like a dried leaf on a windy day.

He looked at his watch. It was time to leave.

Setting the bone on the mantel, he washed his hands carefully—like a surgeon. Then for five minutes he ran a pet-hair roller over his clothes to pick up any bone dust or dirt or body hairs that might lead the constables to him.

He walked into the carriage house past the half-finished painting of a moon-faced butcher in a bloody white apron. The bone collector started to get into the taxi but then changed his mind. Unpredictability is the best defense. This time he'd take the carriage . . . the *sedan*, the Ford. He started it, he drove into the street, closed and locked the garage door behind him.

No before or after . . .

As he passed the cemetery the pack of dogs glanced up at the Ford then returned to scuffling through the brush, looking for rats and nosing madly for water in the unbearable heat.

No then or now . . .

He took the ski mask and gloves from his pocket, set them on the seat beside him as he sped out of the old neighborhood. The bone collector was going hunting.

TEN

Something had changed about the room but she couldn't quite decide what.

Lincoln Rhyme saw it in her eyes.

"We missed you, Amelia," he said coyly. "Errands?"

She looked away from him. "Apparently nobody'd told my new commander I wouldn't be showing up for work today. I thought somebody ought to."

"Ah, yes."

She was gazing at the wall, slowly figuring it out. In addition to the basic instruments that Mel Cooper had brought with him, there was now a scanning electron microscope fitted with the X-ray unit, flotation and hot-stage 'scope setups for testing glass, a comparison microscope, a density-gradient tube for soil testing and a hundred beakers, jars and bottles of chemicals.

And in the middle of the room, Cooper's pride—the computerized gas chromatograph and mass spectrometer. Along with another computer, on-line with Cooper's own terminal at the IRD lab.

Sachs stepped over the thick cables snaking downstairs—house current worked, yes, but the amperage was too taxed for the bedroom outlets alone. And in that slight sidestep, an elegant, practiced maneuver, Rhyme observed how truly beautiful she was. Certainly the most beautiful woman he'd ever seen in the police department ranks.

For a brief instant he found her immeasurably appealing. People said that sex was all in the mind and Rhyme knew that this was true. Cutting the cord didn't stop the urge. He remembered, still with a faint crunch of horror, a night six months after the accident. He and Blaine had tried. Just to see what happened, they'd disclaimed, trying to be casual. No big deal.

But it *had* been a big deal. Sex is a messy business to start with and when you add catheters and bags to the equation you need a lot of stamina and humor and a better foundation than they'd had. Mostly, though, what killed the moment, and killed it fast, was her face. He saw in Blaine Chapman Rhyme's tough, game smile that she was doing it from pity and that stabbed him in the heart. He filed for divorce two weeks later. Blaine had protested but she signed the papers on the first go-round.

Sellitto and Banks had returned and were organizing the evidence Sachs had collected. She looked on, mildly interested.

Rhyme said to her, "The Latents Unit only found eight other recent partials and they belong to the two maintenance men in the building."

"Oh."

He nodded broadly. "Only *eight*!"

"He's complimenting you," Thom explained. "Enjoy it. That's the most you'll ever get out of him."

"No translations needed, please and thank you, Thom."

She responded, "I'm happy I could help." Pleasant as could be.

Well, what was *this*? Rhyme had fully expected her to storm into his room and fling the evidence bags onto his bed. Maybe the saw itself or even the plastic bag containing the vic's severed hands. He'd been looking forward to a real knock-down, drag-out; people rarely take the gloves off when they fight with a crip. He'd been thinking of that look in her eyes when she'd met him, perhaps evidence of some ambiguous kinship between them.

But no, he saw now he was wrong. Amelia Sachs was like everybody else—patting him on the head and looking for the nearest exit.

With a snap, his heart turned to ice. When he spoke it was to a cobweb high on the far wall. "We've been talking about the deadline for the next victim, officer. There doesn't seem to be specific time."

"What we think," Sellitto continued, "whatever this prick's got planned for the next one is something ongoing. He doesn't know exactly when the time of death will be. Lincoln thought maybe he's buried some poor SOB someplace where there's not much air."

Sachs's eye narrowed slightly at this. Rhyme noticed it. Burial alive. If you've got to have a phobia, that's as good as any.

They were interrupted by two men in gray suits who climbed the stairs and walked into the bedroom as if they lived here.

"We knocked," one of them said.

"We rang the bell," said the other.

"No answer."

They were in their forties, one taller than the other but both with the same sandy-colored hair. They bore identical smiles and before the Brooklyn drawl destroyed the image Rhyme had thought: Hayseed farm boys. One had an honest-to-God dusting of freckles along the bridge of his pale nose.

"Gentlemen."

Sellitto introduced the Hardy Boys: Detectives Bedding and Saul, the spadework team. Their skill was canvassing—interviewing people who live near a crime scene for wits and leads. It was a fine art but one that Rhyme had never learned, had no desire to. He was content to unearth hard facts and hand them off to officers like these, who, armed with the data, became living lie detectors who could shred perps' best cover stories. Neither of them seemed to think it was the least bit weird to be reporting to a bedridden civilian.

Saul, the taller of them, the freckle, said, "We've found thirty-six—"

"—eight, if you count a couple of crack-heads. Which he doesn't. I do."

"—subjects. Interviewed all of them. Haven't had much luck."

"Most of 'em blind, deaf, amnesiacs. You know, the usual."

"No sign of the taxi. Combed the West Side. Zero. Zip."

Bedding: "But tell them the good news."

"We found a wit."

"A witness?" Banks asked eagerly. "Fan-tastic."

Rhyme, considerably less enthusiastic, said, "Go on."

"'Round the TOD this morning at the train tracks."

"He saw a man walk down Eleventh Avenue, turn—"

"'Suddenly,' he said," added no-freckle Bedding.

"—And go through an alley that led to the train underpass. He just stood there for a while—"

"Looking down."

Rhyme was troubled by this. "That doesn't sound like our boy. He's too smart to risk being seen like that."

"But—" Saul continued, raising a finger and glancing at his partner.

"There was only one window in the whole 'hood you could see the place from."

"Which is where our wit happened to be standing."

"Up early, bless his heart."

Before he remembered he was angry with her Rhyme asked, "Well, Amelia, how's it feel?"

"I'm sorry?" Her attention returned from the window.

"To be right," Rhyme said. "You pegged Eleventh Avenue. Not Thirty-seventh."

She didn't know how to respond but Rhyme turned immediately back to the twins. "Description?"

"Our wit couldn't say much."

"Was on the sauce. Already."

"He said it was a smallish guy. No hair color. Race—"

"Probably white."

"Wearing?" Rhyme asked.

"Something dark. Best he could say."

"And doing what?" Sellitto asked.

"I quote. 'He just like stood there, looking down. I thought he gonna jump. You know, in front of a train. Looked at his watch a couple times.'"

"And then finally left. Said he kept looking around. Like he didn't want to be seen."

What had he been doing? Rhyme wondered. Watching the victim die? Or was this before he planted the body, checking to see if the roadbed was deserted?

Sellitto asked, "Walked or drove?"

"Walked. We checked every parking lot—"

"And garage."

"—in the neighborhood. But that's near the convention center so you got parking coming out your ears. There're so many lots the attendants stand in the street with orange flags and wave cars in."

"And 'causa the expo half of them were full by seven. We got a list of about nine hundred tags."

Sellitto shook his head. "Follow up on it—"

"It's delegated," said Bedding.

"—but I betcha this's one unsub who ain't putting cars in lots," the detective continued. "Or getting parking tickets."

Rhyme nodded his agreement and asked, "The building at Pearl Street?"

One, or both, of the twins said, "That's next on our list. We're on our way."

Rhyme caught Sachs checking her watch, which sat on her white wrist near her ruddy fingers. He instructed Thom to add these new characteristics of the unsub to the profile chart.

"You want to interview that guy?" Banks asked. "The one by the railroad?"

"No. I don't trust witnesses," Rhyme said bombastically. "I want to get back to work." He glanced at Mel Cooper. "Hairs, blood, bone, and a sliver of wood. The bone first," Rhyme instructed.

Morgen . . .

Young Monelle Gerger opened her eyes and slowly sat up in the sagging bed. In her two years in east Greenwich Village she'd never gotten used to morning.

Her round, twenty-one-year-old body eased forward and she got a blast of unrelenting August sunlight in her bleary eyes. *"Mein Gott . . ."*

She'd left the club at five, home at six, made love with Brian until seven . . .

What time was it now?

Early morning, she was sure.

She squinted at the clock. Oh. Four-thirty in the afternoon. Not so *früh morgens* after all.

Coffee or laundry?

It was around this time of day that she'd wander over to

Dojo's for a veggie-burger breakfast and three cups of their tough coffee. There she'd meet people she knew, clubbies like herself—downtown people.

But she'd let a lot of things go lately, the domestic things. And so now she pulled on two baggy T-shirts to hide her chubby figure and jeans, hung five or six chains around her neck and grabbed the laundry basket, tossed the Wisk onto it.

Monelle undid the three dead bolts barring the door. She hefted the laundry basket and walked down the dark staircase of the residence hall. At the basement level she paused.

Irgendwas stimmt hier nicht.

Feeling uneasy, Monelle looked around the deserted stairway, the murky corridors.

What's different?

The light, that's it! The bulbs in the hall're burned out. No—she looked closely—they were *missing.* Fucking kids'll steal anything. She'd moved in here, the Deutsche Haus—because it was supposedly a haven for German artists and musicians. It turned out to be just another filthy, way-overpriced East Village walk-up, like all the other tenements around here. The only difference was that she could bitch to the manager in her native tongue.

She continued through the basement door into the incinerator room, which was so dark she had to grope her way along the wall to make sure she didn't trip over the junk on the floor.

Pushing open the door, she stepped into the corridor that led to the laundry room.

A shuffling. A skitter.

She turned quickly and saw nothing but motionless shadows. All she heard was the sound of traffic, the groans of an old, old building.

Through the dimness. Past stacks of boxes and discarded chairs and tables. Under wires caked with greasy dust. Monelle continued toward the laundry room. No bulbs here either. She was uneasy, recalling something that hadn't occurred to her for years. Walking with her father down a narrow alley off Lange Strasse, near the Obermain Brücke, on their way to the zoo. She must have been five or six. Her father had suddenly gripped her by the shoulder and pointed to the bridge and told her matter-of-factly that a hungry troll lived underneath it. When they crossed it on their way home, he warned, they'd have to walk quickly. She now felt a ripple of panic rise up her spine to her crew-cut blonde hair.

Stupid. Trolls . . .

She continued down the dank corridor, listening to the humming of some electrical equipment. Far off she heard a song by the feuding brothers in Oasis.

The laundry room was dark.

Well, if *those* bulbs were gone, that was it. She'd go upstairs, and pound on Herr Neischen's door until he came running. She'd given him hell for the broken latches on the front and back doors and for the beer-guzzling kids he never kicked off the front stoop. She'd give him hell for the missing bulbs too.

She reached inside and flicked the switch.

Brilliant white light. Three large bulbs glowed like suns, revealing a room that was filthy but empty. Monelle strode up to the bank of four machines and dumped the whites in one, the colors in the next. She counted out quarters, dropped them into slots and shoved the levers forward.

Nothing.

Monelle jiggled the lever. Then hit the machine itself. No response.

"Shit. This *gottverdammte* building."

Then she saw the power cord. Some idiot had unplugged the machines. She knew who. Neischen had a twelve-year-old son who was responsible for most of the carnage around the building. When she'd complained about something last year the little shit'd tried to kick her.

She picked up the cord and crouched, reaching behind the machine to find the outlet. She plugged it in.

And felt the man's breath on her neck.

Nein!

He was sandwiched between the wall and the back of the washer. Barking a fast scream, she caught a glimpse of ski mask and dark clothes then his hand clamped down on her arm like an animal's jaw. She was off balance and he easily jerked her forward. She tumbled to the floor, hitting her face on the rough concrete, and swallowed the scream forming in her throat.

He was on her in an instant, pinning her arms to the concrete, slapping a piece of thick gray tape over her mouth.

Hilfe!

Nein, bitte nicht.

Bitte nicht.

He wasn't large but he was strong. He easily rolled her over onto her stomach and she heard the ratcheting of the handcuffs closing on her wrists.

Then he stood up. For a long moment, no sound but the drip of water, the rasp of Monelle's breath, the click of a small motor somewhere in the basement.

Waiting for the hands to touch her body, to tear off her clothes. She heard him walk to the doorway to make sure they were alone.

Oh, he had complete privacy, she knew, furious with herself; she was one of the few residents who used the laundry room. Most of them avoided it because it was so deserted, so close to the back doors and windows, so far away from help.

He returned and rolled her over onto her back. Whispered something she couldn't make out. Then: "Hanna."

Hanna? It's a mistake! He thinks I'm somebody else. She shook her head broadly, trying to make him understand this.

But then, looking at his eyes, she stopped. Even though he wore a ski mask, it was clear that something was wrong. He was upset. He scanned her body, shaking his head. He closed his gloved fingers around her big arms. Squeezed her thick shoulders, grabbed a pinch of fat. She shivered in pain.

That's what she saw: disappointment. He'd caught her and now he wasn't sure he wanted her after all.

He reached into his pocket and slowly withdrew his hand. The click of the knife opening was like an electric shock. It started a jag of sobbing.

Nein, nein, nein!

A hiss of breath escaped from his teeth like wind through winter trees. He crouched over her, debating.

"Hanna," he whispered. "What am I going to do?"

Then, suddenly, he made a decision. He put the knife away and yanked her to her feet then led her out to the corridor and through the rear door—the one with the broken lock she'd been hounding Herr Neischen for weeks to fix.

ELEVEN

A criminalist is a renaissance man.

He's got to know botany, geology, ballistics, medicine, chemistry, literature, engineering. If he knows facts—that ash with a high strontium content probably came from a highway flare, that *faca* is Portuguese for "knife," that Ethiopian diners use no utensils and eat with their right hands exclusively, that a slug with five land-and-groove rifling marks, right twist, could not have been fired by a Colt pistol—if he knows these things he may just make the connection that places an unsub at the crime scene.

One subject all criminalists know is anatomy. And this was certainly a specialty of Lincoln Rhyme's, for he had spent the past three and a half years enmeshed in the quirky logic of bone and nerve.

He now glanced at the evidence bag from the steam room, dangling in Jerry Bank's hand, and announced, "Leg bone. Not human. So it's not from the next vic."

It was a ring of bone about two inches around, sawn through evenly. There was blood in the tracks left by the saw blade.

"A medium-sized animal," Rhyme continued. "Large dog, sheep, goat. It'd support, I'd guess, a hundred to a hundred fifty pounds of weight. Let's make sure the blood's from an animal though. Still could be the vic's."

Perps had been known to beat or stab people to death with bones. Rhyme himself had had three such cases; the weapons had been a beef knuckle bone, a deer's leg bone, and in one disturbing case the victim's own ulna.

Mel Cooper ran a gel-diffusion test for blood origin.

UNSUB 823			
Appearance	Residence	Vehicle	Other
• Caucasian male, slight build • Dark clothing	• Prob. has safe house	• Yellow Cab	• knows CS proc. • possibly has record • knows FR prints • gun = .32 Colt

"We'll have to wait a bit for the results," Cooper explained apologetically.

"Amelia," Rhyme said, "maybe you could help us here. Use the eye loupe and look the bone over carefully. Tell us what you see."

"Not the microscope?" she asked. He thought she'd protest but she stepped forward to the bone, peered at it with curiosity.

"Too much magnification," Rhyme explained.

She put on the goggles and bent over the white enamel tray. Cooper turned on a gooseneck lamp.

"The cutting marks," Rhyme said. "Is it hacked up or are they even?"

"They're pretty even."

"A power saw."

Rhyme wondered if the animal had been alive when he'd done this.

"See anything unusual?"

She pored over the bone for a moment, muttered, "I don't know. I don't think so. It just looks like a hunk of bone."

It was then that Thom walked past and glanced at the tray. "That's your clue? That's funny."

"Funny," Rhyme said. "*Funny*?"

Sellitto asked, "You got a theory?"

"No theory." He bent down and smelled it. "It's osso bucco."

"What?"

"Veal shank. I made it for you once, Lincoln. Osso bucco. Braised veal shank." He looked at Sachs and grimaced. "He said it needed more salt."

"Goddamn!" Sellitto cried. "He bought it at a grocery store!"

"If we're lucky," Rhyme said, "he bought it at *his* grocery store."

Cooper confirmed that the precipitin test showed negative for human blood on the samples Sachs had collected. "Probably bovine," he said.

"But what's he trying to tell us?" Banks asked.

Rhyme had no idea. "Let's keep going. Oh, anything on the chain and padlock?"

Cooper glanced at the hardware in a crisp plastic bag. "Nobody name-stamps chain anymore. So we're out of luck there. The lock's a Secure-Pro middle-of-the-line model. It isn't very secure and definitely not professional. How long d'it take to break it?"

"Three whole seconds," Sellitto said.

"See. No serial numbers and it's sold in every hardware and variety store in the country."

"Key or combination?" Rhyme asked.

"Combination."

"Call the manufacturer. Ask them if we take it apart and reconstruct the combination from the tumblers, will that tell us which shipment it was in and where it went to?"

Banks whistled. "Man, that's a long shot."

Rhyme's glare sent a ferocious blush across his face. "And the enthusiasm in your voice, detective, tells me you're just the one to handle the job."

"Yessir"—the young man held up his cellular phone defensively—"I'm on it."

Rhyme asked, "Is that blood on the chain?"

Sellitto said, "One of our boys. Cut himself pretty bad trying to break the lock off."

"So it's contaminated." Rhyme scowled.

"He was trying to save her," Sachs said to him.

"I understand. That was good of him. It's still contaminated." Rhyme glanced back at the table beside Cooper. "Prints?"

Cooper said he'd checked it and found only Sellitto's on the links.

"All right, the splinter of wood Amelia found. Check for prints."

"I did," Sachs said quickly. "At the scene."

P.D., Rhyme reflected. She didn't seem to be the nickname sort. Beautiful people rarely were.

"Let's try the heavy guns, just to be sure," Rhyme said and instructed Cooper, "Use DFO or ninhydrin. Then hit it with the nit-yag."

"The what?" Banks asked.

"A neodymium:yttrium aluminum garnet laser."

The tech spritzed the splinter with liquid from a plastic spray bottle and trained the laser beam on the wood. He slipped on tinted goggles and examined it carefully. "Nothing."

He shut off the light and examined the splinter closely. It was about six inches long, dark wood. There were black smears on it, like tar, and it was impregnated with dirt. He held it with forceps.

"I know Lincoln likes the chopstick approach," Cooper said, "but I always ask for a fork when I go to Ming Wa's."

"You could be crushing the cells," the criminalist grumbled.

"I *could* be but I'm not," Cooper responded.

"What kind of wood?" Rhyme wondered. "Want to run an spodogram?"

"No, it's oak. No question."

"Saw or plane marks?" Rhyme leaned forward. Suddenly his neck spasmed and the cramp that bolted through the muscles was unbearable. He gasped, closed his eyes and twisted his neck, stretching. He felt Thom's strong hands massaging the muscles. The pain finally faded.

"Lincoln?" Sellitto asked. "You okay?"

Rhyme breathed deeply. "Fine. It's nothing."

"Here." Cooper brought the piece of wood over to the bed, lowered the magnifying goggles over Rhyme's eyes.

Rhyme examined the specimen. "Cut in the direction of the grain with a frame saw. There're big variations in the cuts. So I'd guess it was a post or beam milled over a hundred years ago. Steam saw probably. Hold it closer, Mel. I want to smell it."

He held the splinter under Rhyme's nose.

"Creosote—coal-tar distillation. Used for weather-proofing wood before lumber companies started pressure-treating. Piers, docks, railroad ties."

"Maybe we've got a train buff here," Sellitto said. "Remember the tracks this morning."

"Could be." Rhyme ordered, "Check for cellular compression, Mel."

The tech examined the splinter under the compound microscope. "It's compressed all right. But *with* the grain. Not against it. Not a railroad tie. This is from a post or column. Weight-bearing."

A bone . . . an old wooden post . . .

"I see dirt embedded in the wood. That tell us anything?"

Cooper set a large pad of newsprint on the table, tore the cover off. He held the splinter over the pad and brushed some dirt from cracks in the wood. He examined the speckles lying on the white paper—a reverse constellation.

"You have enough for a density-gradient test?" Rhyme asked.

In a D-G test, dirt is poured into a tube containing liquids of different specific gravities. The soil separates and each particle hangs suspended according to its own gravity. Rhyme had established a very extensive library of density-gradient profiles for dirt from all over the five boroughs. Unfortunately the test only worked with a fair amount of soil; Cooper didn't think they had enough. "We could try it but we'd have to use the entire sample. And if it didn't work we wouldn't have anything left for other tests."

Rhyme instructed him to do a visual then analyze it in the GC-MS—the chromatograph-spectrometer.

The technician brushed some dirt onto a slide. He gazed at it for a few minutes under the compound microscope. "This is strange, Lincoln. It's topsoil. With an unusually high level of vegetation in it. But it's in a curious form. Very deteriorated, very decomposed." He looked up and Rhyme noticed the dark lines under his eyes from the eyepieces. He remembered that after hours of lab work the marks were quite pronounced and that occasionally a forensic tech would emerge from the IRD lab only to be greeted by a chorus of *Rocky Raccoon*.

"Burn it," Rhyme ordered.

Cooper mounted a sample in the GC-MS unit. The machine rumbled to life and there was a hiss. "A minute or two."

"While we're waiting," Rhyme said, "the bone . . . I keep wondering about the bone. 'Scope it, Mel."

Cooper carefully set the bone onto the examination stage of the compound microscope. He went over it carefully. "Whoa, got something here."

"What?"

"Very small. Transparent. Hand me the hemostat," Cooper said to Sachs, nodding at a pair of gripper tweezers. She handed them to him and he carefully probed in the marrow of the bone. He lifted something out.

"A tiny piece of regenerated cellulose," Cooper announced.

"Cellophane," Rhyme said. "Tell me more."

"Stretch and pinch marks. I'd say he didn't leave it intentionally; there are no cut edges. It's not inconsistent with heavy-duty cello," Cooper said.

"'Not inconsistent.'" Rhyme scowled. "I don't like his hedges."

"We *have* to hedge, Lincoln," Cooper said, cheerfully.

"'Associate with.' 'Suggest.' I particularly hate 'not inconsistent.'"

"Very versatile," Cooper said. "The boldest I'll be is that it's probably commerical butcher or grocery store cellophane. Not Saran Wrap. Definitely not generic-brand wrap."

Jerry Banks walked inside from the hallway. "Bad news. The Secure-Pro company doesn't keep any records on combinations. A machine sets them at random."

"Ah."

"But interesting . . . they said they get calls from the police all the time about their products and you're the first one who's ever thought of tracing a lock through the combination."

"How 'interesting' can it be if it's a dead end?" Rhyme grumbled and turned to Mel Cooper, who was shaking his head as he stared at the GC-MS computer. "What?"

"Got that soil sample result. But I'm afraid the machine might be on the fritz. The nitrogen's off the charts. We should run it again, use more sample this time."

Rhyme instructed him to go ahead. His eyes turned back to the bone. "Mel, how recent was the kill?"

He examined some scrapings under the electron microscope.

"Minimal bacteria clusters. Bambi here was recently deceased, looks like. Or just out of the fridge about eight hours."

"So our perp just bought it," Rhyme said.

"Or a month ago and froze it," Sellitto suggested.

"No," Cooper said. "It hasn't been frozen. There's no evidence of tissue damage from ice crystals. And it hasn't been refrigerated that long. It's not desiccated; modern refrigerators dehydrate food."

"It's a good lead," Rhyme said. "Let's get to work on it."

"'Get to work'?" Sachs laughed. "Are you saying we call

up all the grocery stores in the city and find out who sold veal bones yesterday?"

"No," Rhyme countered. "In the past *two* days."

"You want the Hardy Boys?"

"Let them keep doing what they're doing. Call Emma, down-town, if she's still working. And if she isn't get her back to the office with the other dispatchers and put them on overtime. Get her a list of every grocery chain in town. I'll bet our boy isn't buying groceries for a family of four so have Emma limit the list to customers buying five items or less."

"Warrants?" Banks asked.

"Anybody balks, we'll get a warrant," Sellitto said. "But let's try without. Who knows? Some citizens might actually cooperate. I'm told it happens."

"But how are the stores going to know who bought veal shanks?" Sachs asked. She was no longer as aloof as she had been. There was an edge in her voice. Rhyme wondered if her frustration might be a sympton of what he himself had often felt—the burdensome weight of the evidence. The essential problem for the criminalist is not that there's too little evidence but that there's too much.

"Checkout scanners," Rhyme said. "They record purchases on computer. For inventory and restocking. Go ahead, Banks. I see something just crossed your mind. Speak up. I won't send you to Siberia this time."

"Well, only the chains have scanners, sir," the young detective offered. "There're hundreds of independents and butcher shops that don't."

"Good point. But I think he wouldn't go to a small shop. Anonymity's important to him. He'll be doing his buying at big stores. Impersonal."

Sellitto called Communications and explained to Emma what they needed.

"Let's get a polarized shot of the cellophane," Rhyme said to Cooper.

The technician put the minuscule fragment in a polarizing 'scope, then fitted the Polaroid camera to the eyepiece and took a shot. It was a colorful picture, a rainbow with gray streaks through it. Rhyme examined it. This pattern told them nothing by itself but it could be compared with other cello samples to see if they came from a common source.

Rhyme had a thought. "Lon, get a dozen Emergency Service officers over here. On the double."

"Here?" Sellitto asked.

"We're going to put an operation together."

"You're sure about that?" the detective asked.

"Yes! I want them now."

"All right." He nodded to Banks, who made the call to Haumann.

"Now, what about the other planted clue—those hairs Amelia found?"

Cooper poked through them with a probe then mounted several in the phase-contrast microscope. This instrument shot two light sources at a single subject, the second beam delayed slightly—out of phase—so the sample was both illuminated and set off by shadow.

"It's not human," Cooper said. "I'll tell you that right now. And they're guard hairs, not down."

Hairs from the animal's coat, he meant.

"What kind? Dog?"

"Veal calf?" Banks suggested, once again youthfully enthusiastic.

"Check the scales," Rhyme ordered. Meaning the microscopic flakes that make up the outer sheath of a strand of hair.

Cooper typed on his computer keyboard and a few seconds later thumbnail images of scaly rods popped onto the screen. "This is thanks to you, Lincoln. Remember the database?"

At IRD Rhyme had compiled a huge collection of micrographs of different types of hair. "I do, yes, Mel. But they were in three-ring binders when I saw 'em last. How'd you get them on the computer?"

"ScanMaster of course. JPEG compressed."

Jay-peg? What was that? In a few years technology had soared beyond Rhyme. Amazing . . .

And as Cooper examined the images, Lincoln Rhyme wondered again what he'd been wondering all day—the question that kept floating to the surface: Why the clues? The human creature is so astonishing but count on it before anything else to be just that—a creature. A laughing animal, a dangerous one, a clever one, a scared one, but always acting for a *reason*—a motive that will move the beast toward its desires. Scientist Lincoln Rhyme didn't believe in chance, or randomness, or frivolity. Even psychopaths had their own logic, twisted though it may have been, and he knew there was a reason Unsub 823 spoke to them only in this cryptic way.

Cooper called, "Got it. Rodent. Probably a rat. And the hairs were shaved off."

"That's a hell of a clue," Banks said. "There's a million rats in the city. That doesn't pin down anyplace. What's the point of telling us that?"

Sellitto closed his eyes momentarily and muttered something under his breath. Sachs didn't notice the look. She glanced at Rhyme curiously. He was surprised that she hadn't figured out what the kidnapper's message was but he said nothing. He saw no reason to share this horrifying bit of knowledge with anyone else for the time being.

———

James Schneider's seventh victim, or eighth, should you choose to number poor, angelic little Maggie O'Connor among them, was the wife of a hardworking immigrant, who had established the family's modest habitation near Hester Street on the Lower East Side of the City.

It was thanks to the courage of this unfortunate woman that the constables and the police discovered the identity of the criminal. Hanna Goldschmidt was of German–Jewish extraction and was held in high esteem by the close-knit community in which she, her husband and their six children (one had died at birth) lived.

The bone collector drove through the streets slowly, careful to remain under the speed limit though he knew perfectly well that the traffic cops in New York wouldn't stop you for something as minor as speeding.

He paused at a light and glanced up at another UN billboard. His eyes took in the bland, smiling faces—like the eerie faces painted on the walls of the mansion—and then looked beyond it, at the city around him. He was, occasionally, surprised to look up and find the buildings so massive, the stone cornices o high aloft, the glass so smooth, the cars so sleek, the people o scrubbed. The city he knew was dark, low, smoky, smelling f sweat and mud. Horses would trample you, roving gangs f hoodlums—some as young as ten or eleven—would knock ou on the head with a shillelagh or sap and make off vith your pocket watch and billfold . . . *This* was the bone collector's city.

Sometimes, though, he found himself just like this—driving spiffy silver Taurus XL along a smooth asphalt road, listening o WNYC and irritated, like all New Yorkers, when he missed green light, wondering why the hell didn't the city let you nake right turns on red.

He cocked his head, heard several thumps from the trunk f the car. But there was so much ambient noise that no one vould hear Hanna's protests.

The light changed.

It is, of course, exceptional even in these enlightened times or a woman to venture forth into the city streets in the evening, naccompanied by a gentlemen; and in those days it was more xceptional still. Yet on this unfortunate night Hanna had no hoice but to quit her abode for a brief time. Her youngest had a fever, and, with her husband praying devoutly at a nearby ynagogue, she issued forth into the night to secure a poultice or the child's fiery forehead. As she closed the door she said o her eldest daughter,—

"Lock tight the bolt behind me. I shall return soon."

But, alas, she would not be true to those words. For only moments later she chanced to encounter James Schneider.

The bone collector looked around at the shabby streets ere. This area—near where he'd buried the first victim— vas Hell's Kitchen, on the West Side of the city, once the astion of Irish gangs, now populated more and more with oung professionals, ad agencies, photo studios and stylish estaurants.

He smelled manure and wasn't the least surprised when uddenly a horse reared in front of him.

Then he noticed that the animal wasn't an apparition from he 1800s but was being hitched to one of the hansom cabs hat cruised Central Park charging very twentieth-century fees. Their stables were located here.

He laughed to himself. Though it was a hollow sound.

One can only speculate as to what occurred, for there were no witnesses. But we can picture the horror all too clearly. The villain drew the struggling woman into an alley and stabbed her with a dagger, his cruel intent not to kill but to subdue, as was his wont. But such was the strength in good Mrs Goldschmidt's soul, thinking as she surely was of her fledglings back in the nest, that she surprised the monster by assaulting him ferociously:—she struck him repeatedly about the face and ripped hair from his head.

She freed herself momentarily and from her mouth issued an horrendous scream. The cowardly Schneider struck her several times more and fled.

The brave woman staggered to the sidewalk and collapsed where she died in the arms of a constable who had responded to the alarm neighbors had raised.

This story appeared in a book, which was with the bone collector now, resting in his hip pocket. *Crime in Old New York.* He couldn't explain his overwhelming attraction to the slim volume. If he had to describe his relation to this book he would have to say he was addicted to it. Seventy-five years old and still in remarkable shape, a bookbinding jewel. It was his good-luck charm and his talisman. He'd found it at a small branch of the public library and committed one of the few larcenies of his life by slipping it into his raincoat one day and strolling out of the building.

He'd read the chapter on Schneider a hundred times and virtually had it memorized.

Driving slowly. They were almost there.

When Hanna's poor, weeping husband huddled over her lifeless body, he looked upon her face:—one last time before she was taken to the funeral home (for in the Jewish faith it is dictated that the dead must be interred as quickly as possible). And he noticed upon her porcelain cheek a bruise in the shape of a curious emblem. It was a round symbol and appeared to be a crescent moon and a cluster of what might be taken to be stars hovering over the same.

The constable exclaimed that this must have been an imprint made by the ring of the heinous butcher himself when he struck the poor victim. Detectives enlisted the aid of an artist and he sketched a picture of the impression. (The good reader is referred to plate XXII.) Rounds were made of jewelers in the city, and several names and addresses were secured of men who had bought such rings in the recent past. Two of the gentlemen purchasing these rings were beyond suspicion, being as they were a deacon of a church and another a learned professor at a fine university. Yet the third was a man of whom the constables had long harbored suspicion of nefarious activity. To wit:—one James Schneider.

This gentleman had at one time been influential in several benevolent organizations in the city of Manhattan: the Consumptives' Assistance League and the Pensioners' Welfare Society, most notably. He had come under the eye of the constabulary when several elderly charges from said groups vanished not long after Schneider paid them calls. He was never charged with any offense but soon after the investigations, he dropped from sight.

In the aftermath of Hanna Goldschmidt's heinous murder, a still search of the dubious haunts of the city revealed no abode where Schneider might be found. The constables posted broadsides throughout the down-town and River-front areas, setting forth the description of the villain, but he could not be apprehended;—a true tragedy, to be sure, in light of the carnage that was soon to befall the city at his vile hands.

The streets were clear. The bone collector drove into the alley. He opened the warehouse door and drove down a wooden ramp into a long tunnel.

After making sure the place was deserted, he walked to the back of the car. He opened the trunk and pulled Hanna out. She was fleshy, fat, like a bag of limp mulch. He grew angry again and he carried her roughly down another wide tunnel. Traffic from the West Side Highway sped over them. He listened to her wheezing and was just reaching out to loosen the gag when he felt her shudder and go completely limp. Gasping for breath with the effort of carrying her, he rested her on the floor of the tunnel and eased the tape off her mouth. Air dribbled in weakly. Had she just fainted? He listened to her heart. It seemed to be beating fine.

He cut the clothesline binding her ankles, leaned forward

and whispered, "Hanna, *kommen Sie mit mir mit*, Hanna Goldschmidt . . ."

"*Nein*," she muttered, her voice trailing to silence.

He leaned closer, lightly slapped her face. "Hanna, you must come with me."

And she screamed: "*Mein Name ist nicht Hanna!*" Then kicked him square in the jaw.

A burst of yellow light flashed through his head and he leapt sideways two or three feet, trying to keep his balance. Hanna sprang up, raced blindly down a dark corridor. But he was after her fast. He tackled her before she'd gotten ten yards away. She fell hard; he did too, grunting as he lost his breath.

He lay on his side for a minute, consumed with pain, struggling to breathe, gripping her T-shirts as she thrashed. Lying on her back, hands still cuffed, the girl used the only weapon she had—one of her feet, which she lifted in the air and brought down hard onto his hand. A spike of pain shot through him and his glove flew off. She lifted her strong leg again and only her bad aim saved him from her heel, which slammed so hard into the ground it would've broken bones if she'd connected.

"*So nicht!*" he growled madly and grabbed her by the throat with his bare hand and squeezed until she squirmed and whined and then stopped squirming and whining. She trembled several times and went still.

When he listened to her heart the beating was very faint. No tricks this time. He snatched up his glove, pulled it on and dragged her back through the tunnel to the post. Bound her feet once more and put a new piece of tape on her mouth. As she came to, his hand was straying over her body. She gasped at first and shrank away as he caressed the flesh behind her ear. Her elbow, her jaw. There weren't many other places he wanted to touch her. She was so *padded* . . . it disgusted him.

Yet *beneath* the skin . . . He gripped her leg firmly. Her wide eyes stared as he fumbled in his pocket and the knife appeared. Without a moment's hesitation he cut through her skin down to the yellow-white bone. She screamed through the tape, a manic wail, and kicked hard but he held her tight. Enjoying this, Hanna? The girl sobbed and groaned loudly. So he had to lower his ear to her leg to hear the delicious sound of the tip of the blade scraping back and forth on the bone. *Skrisssss.*

Then he took her arm.

They locked eyes for a moment and as she shook her head pathetically, begging in silence. His gaze dropped to her pudgy forearm and again the cut was deep. Her whole body went rigid with the pain. Another wild, muted scream. Again he lowered his head like a musician, listening to the sound of the blade scraping the ulna. Back and forth. *Skrissss, skrisssss* . . . It was some moments later that he realized she'd fainted.

Finally he pried himself away and returned to the car. He planted the next clues then took the broom from the trunk and carefully swept over their footsteps. He drove up the ramp, parked, left the engine running and climbed out once more, carefully sweeping away the tire tracks.

He paused and looked back down the tunnel. Staring at her, just staring. Suddenly a rare smile crossed the bone collector's lips. He was surprised that the first of the guests had already shown up. A dozen pairs of tiny red eyes, two dozen, then three . . . It seemed they were gazing at Hanna's bloody flesh with curiosity . . . and what might have been hunger. Though that could have been his imagination; Lord knew, it was vivid enough.

TWELVE

Mel, go through the Colfax woman's clothes. Amelia, would you help him?"

She offered him another pleasant nod, the sort meant for polite society. Rhyme realized he was really quite angry with her.

At the tech's direction she pulled on latex gloves, gently opened the clothing and ran a horsehair brush through the garments, above large sheets of clean newsprint. Tiny flecks fell out. Cooper picked them up on tape and examined them through the compound 'scope.

"Not much," he reported. "The steam took care of most of the trace. I see a little soil. Not enough to D-G. Wait . . . Excellent. I've got a couple of fibers. Look at these. . . ."

Well, I can't, Rhyme thought angrily.

"Navy blue, acrylic-and-wool blend, I'd guess. It isn't coarse enough to be carpet and it's not lobed. So it's clothing."

"In this heat he's not going to be wearing thick socks or a sweater. Ski mask?"

"That'd be my bet," Cooper said.

Rhyme reflected, "So he's serious about giving us a chance to save them. If he was bent on killing, it wouldn't matter if they saw him or not."

Silletto added, "Also means the asshole thinks he can get away. Doesn't have suicide on his mind. Might just give us some bargaining power if he's got hostages when we nail him."

"I like that optimism of yours, Lon," Rhyme said.

Thom answered the buzzer and a moment later Jim Polling climbed the stairs, looking disheveled and harried. Well, shuttling between press conferences, the mayor's office and the federal building would do that to you.

"Too bad about the trout," Sellitto called to him. Then explained to Rhyme, "Jimmy here's one of those *real* fishermen. Ties his own flies and everything. Me, I go out on a party boat with a six-pack and I'm happy."

"We'll nail this fucker then worry about the fish," Polling said, helping himself to the coffee Thom had left by the window. He looked outside and blinked in surprise to find two large birds staring at him. He turned back to Rhyme and explained that because of the kidnapping he'd had to postpone a fishing trip to Vermont. Rhyme had never fished—never had the time or inclination for any hobbies—but he found he envied Polling. The serenity of fishing appealed to him. It was a sport you could practice in solitude. Crip sports tended to be in-your-face athletics. Competitive. Proving things to the world . . . and to yourself. Wheelchair basketball, tennis, marathons. Rhyme decided if he had to have a sport it'd be fishing. Though casting a line with a single finger was probably beyond modern technology.

Polling said, "The press is calling him a serial kidnapper."

If the bootie fits, Rhyme reflected.

"And the mayor's going nuts. Wants to call in the feds. I talked the chief into sitting tight on that one. But we can't lose another vic."

"We'll do our best," Rhyme said caustically.

Polling sipped the black coffee and stepped close to the bed. "You okay, Lincoln?"

Rhyme said, "Fine."

Polling appraised him for a moment longer then nodded to Sellitto. "Brief me. We got another press conference in a half hour. You see the last one? Hear what that reporter asked? What did we think the vic's family felt about her being scalded to death?"

Banks shook his head. "Man."

"I nearly decked the fucker," Polling said.

Three and a half years ago, Rhyme recalled, during the cop-killer investigation, the captain had smashed a news crew's videocam when the reporter wondered if Polling was being too aggressive in his investigations just because the suspect, Dan Shepherd, was a member of the force.

Polling and Sellitto retired to a corner of Rhyme's room and the detective filled him in. When the captain descended the stairs this time, Rhyme noticed, he wasn't half as buoyant as he had been.

"Okay," Cooper announced. "We've got a hair. It was in her pocket."

"The whole shaft?" Rhyme asked, without much hope, and was not surprised when Cooper sighed. "Sorry. No bulb."

Without a bulb attached, hair isn't individuated evidence; it's merely class evidence. You can't run a DNA test and link it to a specific person. Still, it has good probative value. The famous Canadian Mounties study a few years ago concluded that if a hair found at the scene matches a suspect's hair the odds are around 4,500 to 1 that he's the one who left it. The problem with hair, though, is that you can't deduce much about the person it belonged to. Sex is almost impossible to determine, and race can't be reliably established. Age can be estimated only with infant hair. Color is deceptive because of wide pigmentation variations and cosmetic dyes, and since everybody loses dozens of hairs every day you can't even tell if the suspect is going bald.

"Check it against the vic's. Do a scale count and medulla pigmentation comparison," Rhyme ordered.

A moment later Cooper looked up from the 'scope. "It's not hers, the Colfax woman's."

"Description?" asked Rhyme.

"Light brown. No kink so I'd say not Negroid. Pigmentation suggests it's not Mongoloid."

"So Caucasian," Rhyme said, nodding at the chart on the wall. "Confirms what the wit said. Head or body hair?"

"There's little diameter variation and a uniform pigment distribution. It's head hair."

"Length?"

"Three centimeters."

Thom asked if he should add to the profile that the kidnapper had brown hair.

Rhyme said no. "We'll wait for some corroboration. Just

write down that we know he wears a ski mask, navy blue. Fingernail scrapings, Mel?"

Cooper examined the trace but found nothing useful.

"The print you found. The one on the wall. Let's take a look at it. Could you show it to me, Amelia?"

Sachs hesitated then carried the Polaroid over to him.

"Your monster," Rhyme said. It was a large deformed palm, indeed grotesque, not with the elegant swirls and bifurcations of friction ridges but a mottled pattern of tiny lines.

"It's a wonderful picture—you're a virtual Edward Weston, Amelia. But unfortunately it's not a hand. Those aren't ridges. It's a glove. Leather. Old. Right, Mel?"

The technician nodded.

"Thom, write down that he has an old pair of gloves." Rhyme said to the others, "We're starting to get some ideas about him. He's not leaving *his* FR prints at the scene. But he is leaving glove prints. If we find the glove in his possession we can still place him at the scene. He's smart. But not brilliant."

Sachs asked, "And what do brilliant criminals wear?"

"Cotton-lined suede," Rhyme said. Then asked, "Where's the filter? From the vacuum?"

The technician emptied the cone filter—like one from a coffee-maker—onto a sheet of white paper.

Trace evidence . . .

DAs and reporters and juries loved obvious clues. Bloody gloves, knives, recently fired guns, love letters, semen and fingerprints. But Lincoln Rhyme's favorite evidence was trace—the dust and effluence at crime scenes, so easily overlooked by perps.

But the vacuum had captured nothing helpful.

"All right," Rhyme said, "let's move on. Let's look at the handcuffs."

Sachs stiffened as Cooper opened the plastic bag and slid the cuffs out onto a sheet of newsprint. There was, as Rhyme had predicted, minimal blood. The tour doctor from the medical examiner's office had done the honors with the razor saw, after an NYPD lawyer had faxed a release to the ME.

Cooper examined the cuffs carefully. "Boyd & Keller. Bottom of the line. No serial number." He sprayed the chrome with DFO and hit the PoliLight. "No prints, just a smudge from the glove."

"Let's open them up."

Cooper used a generic cuff key to click them open. With a lens-cleaning air puffer he blew into the mechanism.

"You're still mad at me, Amelia," Rhyme said. "About the hands."

The question caught her off guard. "I wasn't mad," she said after a moment. "I thought it was unprofessional. What you were suggesting."

"Do you know who Edmond Locard was?"

She shook her head.

"A Frenchman. Born in 1877. He founded the University of Lyons' Institute of Criminalistics. He came up with the one rule I lived by when I ran IRD. Locard's Exchange Principle. He thought that whenever two human beings come into contact, something from one is exchanged to the other, and vice versa. Maybe dust, blood, skin cells, dirt, fibers, metallic residue. It might be tough to find exactly what's been exchanged, and even harder to figure out what it means. But an exchange *does* occur—and because of that we can catch our unsubs."

This bit of history didn't interest her in the least.

"You're lucky," Mel Cooper said to Sachs, not looking up. "He was going to have you and the medic do a spot autopsy and examine the contents of her stomach."

"It would've been helpful," Rhyme said, avoiding her eyes.

"I talked him out of it," Cooper said.

"Autopsy," Sachs said, sighing, as if nothing about Rhyme could surprise her.

Why, she isn't even *here*, he thought angrily. Her mind's a thousand miles away.

"Ah," Cooper said. "Found something. I think it's a bit of the glove."

Cooper mounted a fleck on the compound microscope. Examined it.

"Leather. Reddish-colored. Polished on one side."

"Red, that's good," Sellitto said. To Sachs he explained, "The wilder their clothes, the easier it is to find the perp. They don't teach you that at the academy, bet. Sometime

I'll tell you 'bout the time we collared Jimmy Plaid, from the Gambino crew. You remember that, Jerry?"

"You could spot those pants a mile away," the young detective said.

Cooper continued, "The leather's desiccated. Not much oil in the grain. You were right too about them being old."

"What kind of animal?"

"I'd say kidskin. High quality."

"If they were new it might mean he was rich," Rhyme grumbled. "But since they're old he might've found them on the street or bought them secondhand. No snappy deductions from 823's accessorizing, looks like. Okay. Thom, just add to the profile that the gloves are reddish kidskin. What else do we have?"

"He wears aftershave," Sachs reminded him.

"Forgot that. Good. Maybe to cover up another scent. Unsubs do that sometimes. Write it down, Thom. What did it smell like again, Amelia? You described it."

"Dry. Like gin."

"What about the clothesline?" Rhyme asked.

Cooper examined it. "I've seen this before. Plastic. Several dozen interior filaments composed of six to ten different plastic types and one—no, two—metallic filaments."

"I want a manufacturer and source."

Cooper shook his head. "Impossible. Too generic."

"Damn," Rhyme muttered. "And the knot?"

"Now *that's* unusual. Very efficient. See how it loops around twice? PVC is the hardest cord to tie and this knot ain't going anywhere."

"They have a knot file downtown?"

"No."

Inexcusable, he thought.

"Sir?"

Rhyme turned to Banks.

"I do some sailing . . ."

"Out of Westport," Rhyme said.

"Well, as a matter of fact, yeah. How'd you know?"

If there were a forensic test for location of origin Jerry Banks would turn up positive for Connecticut. "Lucky guess."

"It isn't nautical. I don't recognize it."

"That's good to know. Hang it up there." Rhyme nodded toward the wall, next to the Polaroid of the cellophane and the Monet poster. "We'll get to it later."

The doorbell rang and Thom disappeared to answer it. Rhyme had a bad moment thinking that perhaps it was Dr Berger returning to tell him he was no longer interested in helping him with their "project."

But the heavy thud of boots told Rhyme who had come a-calling.

The Emergency Services officers, all large, all somber, dressed in combat gear, entered the room politely and nodded to Sellitto and Banks. They were men of action and Rhyme bet that behind the twenty still eyes were ten very bad reactions to the sight of a man laid up forever on his back.

"Gentlemen, you've heard about the kidnapping last night and the death of the victim this afternoon." He continued through the affirmative muttering, "Our unsub has another victim. We have a lead in the case and I need you to hit locations around the city and secure evidence. Immediately and simultaneously. One man, one location."

"You mean," one mustachioed officer asked uncertainly, "no backup."

"You won't need it."

"All due respect, sir, I'm not inclined to go into any tactical situation without backup. A partner at least."

"I don't think there'll be any firefights. The targets are the major chain grocery stores in town."

"Grocery stores?"

"Not every store. Just one of every chain. J&G's, ShopRite, Food Warehouse . . ."

"What exactly are we going to do?"

"Buy veal shanks."

"What?"

"One package at each store. I'm afraid I'll have to ask you to pay from your own pocket, gentlemen. But the city'll reimburse you. Oh, and we need them ASAP."

She lay on her side, immobile.

Her eyes had grown accustomed to the dimness of the old

tunnel and she could see the little fuckers moving closer. One in particular she kept her eyes on.

Monelle's leg stung like a bitch but most of the pain was in her arm, from where he'd cut deep into her skin. Because it was cuffed behind her she couldn't see the wound, didn't know how much she'd bled. But it must have been a lot; she was very faint and could feel the sticky ooze all over her arms and side.

The sound of scratching—needlish claws on concrete. The gray-brown lumps rustling in the shadows. The rats continued to twitch their way toward her. There must have been a hundred of them.

She forced herself to stay completely still and kept her eyes on the big black one. Schwarzie, she called him. He was in the front, moving back and forth, studying her.

Monelle Gerger had been around the world twice by the time she was nineteen. She'd hitched through Sri Lanka and Cambodia and Pakistan. Through Nebraska, where women stared at her eyebrow rings and braless boobs with contempt. Through Iran, where men stared at her bare arms like dogs in heat. She'd slept in city parks in Guatemala City and spent three days with rebel forces in Nicaragua after getting lost on the way to a wildlife refuge.

But she'd never been so scared as now.

Mein Gott.

And what scared her the most was what she was about to do to herself.

One rat ran close, a small one, its brown body zipping forward, backing up, moving forward again a few inches. Rats were scary, she decided, because they were more like reptiles than rodents. A snaky nose and snaky tail. And those fucking red eyes.

Behind him was Schwarzie, the size of a small cat. He rose up on his haunches and stared at what fascinated him. Watching. Waiting.

Then the little one attacked. Scurrying on his four needlish feet, ignoring her muffled scream, he darted fast and straight. Quick as a roach he tore a bite from her cut leg. The wound stung like fire. Monelle squealed—in pain, yes, but from anger too. I don't fucking want *you*! She slammed her heel into his back with a dull crunch. He quivered once and lay still.

Another one raced up to her neck, ripped away a bite then leapt back, staring at her, twitching his nose as if he were running his tongue around his little rat mouth, savoring her flavor.

Dieser Schmerz . . .

She shivered as the searing burn radiated from the bite. *Dieser Schmerz!* The pain! Monelle forced herself to lie still again.

The tiny attacker poised for another run but suddenly he twitched and turned away. Monelle saw why. Schwarzie was finally easing to the front of the pack. He was coming after what he wanted.

Good, good.

He was the one she'd been waiting for. Because he hadn't seemed interested in the blood or her flesh; he'd padded up close twenty minutes before, fascinated by the silver tape across her mouth.

The smaller rat scurried back into the swarming bodies as Schwarzie eased forward, on his obscenely tiny feet. Paused. Then advanced again. Six feet, five.

Then three.

She remained completely still. Breathing as shallowly as she dared, afraid the inhalation would scare him off.

Schwarzie paused. Padded forward again. Then stopped. Two feet away from her head.

Don't move a muscle.

His back was humped high and his lips kept retracting over his brown and yellow teeth. He moved another foot closer and stopped, eyes darting. Sat up, rubbed his clawed paws together, eased forward again.

Monelle Gerger played dead.

Another six inches. *Vorwärts!*

Come on!

Then he was at her face. She smelled garbage and oil on his body, feces, rotten meat. He sniffed and she felt the unbearable tickle of whiskers on her nose as his tiny teeth emerged from his mouth and began to chew the tape.

For five minutes he gnawed around her mouth. Once another

rat scooted in, sank his teeth into her ankle. She closed her eyes to the pain and tried to ignore it. Schwarzie chased him away then stood in the shadows studying her.

Vorwärts, Schwarzie! Come on!

Slowly he padded back to her. Tears running down her cheek, Monelle reluctantly lowered her mouth to him.

Chewing, chewing . . .

Come on!

She felt his vile, hot breath in her mouth as he broke through the tape and began to rip off larger chunks of the shiny plastic. He pulled the pieces from his mouth and squeezed them greedily in his front claws.

Big enough now? she wondered.

It would have to be. She couldn't take any more.

Slowly she lifted her head up, one millimeter at a time. Schwarzie blinked and leaned forward, curiously.

Monelle spread her jaws and heard the wonderful sound of the ripping tape. She sucked air deep into her lungs. She could breathe again!

And she could shout for help.

"*Bitte, helfen Sie mir!*" Please help me.

Schwarzie backed away, startled by her ragged howl, dropping his precious silver tape. But he didn't go very far. He stopped and turned back, rose on his pudgy haunches.

Ignoring his black, humped body she kicked the post she was tied to. Dust and dirt floated down like gray snow but the wood didn't give a bit. She screamed until her throat burned.

"*Bitte.* Help me!"

The sticky rush of traffic swallowed the sound.

Stillness for a moment. Then Schwarzie started toward her again. He wasn't alone this time. The slimy pack followed his lead. Twitching, nervous. But drawn steadily by the tempting smell of her blood.

———

Bone and wood, wood and bone.

"Mel, what do you have there?" Rhyme was nodding toward the computer attached to the chromatograph-spectrometer. Cooper had once more retested the dirt they'd found in the splinter of wood.

"It's still nitrogen-rich. Off the charts."

Three separate tests, the results all the same. A diagnostic check of the unit showed it was working fine. Cooper reflected and said, "That much nitrogen—maybe a firearms or ammunition manufacturer."

"That'd be Connecticut, not Manhattan." Rhyme looked at the clock. 6:30. How fast time had raced past today. How slowly it had moved for the past three and a half years. He felt as if he'd been awake for days and days.

The young detective pored over the map of Manhattan, moving aside the pale vertebra that had fallen to the floor earlier.

The disk had been left here by Rhyme's SCI specialist, Peter Taylor. An early appointment with the man. The doctor had examined him expertly then sat back in the rustling rattan chair and pulled something out of his pocket.

"Show-and-tell time," the doctor had said.

Rhyme had glanced at Taylor's open hand.

"This's a fourth cervical vertebra. Just like the one in your neck. The one that broke. See the little tails on the end?" The doctor turned it over and over for a moment then asked, "What do you think of when you see it?"

Rhyme respected Taylor—who didn't treat him like a child or a moron or a major inconvenience—but that day he hadn't been in the mood to play the inspiration game. He hadn't answered.

Taylor continued anyway, "Some of my patients think it looks like a stingray. Some say it's a spaceship. Or an airplane. Or a truck. Whenever I ask that question people usually compare it to something big. Nobody ever says, 'Oh, a hunk of calcium and magnesium.' See, they don't like the idea that something so insignificant has made their lives pure hell."

Rhyme had glanced back at the doctor skeptically but the placid, gray-haired medico was an old hand at SCI patients and he said kindly, "Don't tune me out, Lincoln."

Taylor had held the disk up close to Rhyme's face. "You're thinking it's unfair this little thing causing you so much grief. But forget that. *Forget* it. I want you to remember what it was like before the accident. The good and bad in your life. Happiness, sadness . . . You can feel that again." The doctor's face had grown still. "But frankly all I see now is somebody who's given up."

Taylor had left the vertebra on the bedside table. Accidentally, it seemed. But then Rhyme realized the act was calculated. Over the past months while Rhyme was trying to decide whether or not to kill himself he'd stared at the tiny disk. It became an blem for Taylor's argument—the pro-living argument. But in the end that side lost; the doctor's words, as valid as they might be, couldn't overcome the burden of pain and heartache and exhaustion Lincoln Rhyme felt day after day after day.

He now looked away from the disk—to Amelia Sachs— and said, "I want you to think about the scene again."

"I told you everything I saw."

"Not *saw*, I want to know what you felt."

Rhyme remembered the thousands of times he'd run crime scenes. Sometimes a miracle would happen. He'd be looking around and somehow ideas about the unsub would come to him. He couldn't explain how. The behaviorists talked about profiling as if they'd invented it. But criminalists had been profiling for hundreds of years. Walk the grid, walk where *he's* walked, find what *he's* left behind, figure out what *he's* taken with him—and you'll come away from the scene with a profile as clear as a portrait.

"Tell me," he prodded. "What did you feel?"

"Uneasy. Tense. Hot." She shrugged. "I don't know. I really don't. Sorry."

If he'd been mobile Rhyme would have leapt from the bed, grabbed her shoulders and shaken her. Shouted: *But you know what I'm talking about! I know you do. Why won't you work with me? . . . Why are you ignoring me?*

Then he understood something. . . .That she *was* there, in the steamy basement. Hovering over T.J.'s ruined body. Smelling the vile smell. He saw it in the way her thumb flicked a bloody cuticle, he saw it in the way she maintained the no-man's-land of politeness between the two of them. She detested being in that vile basement, and she hated him for reminding her that part of her was still there.

"You're walking through the room," he said.

"I really don't think I can be any more help."

"Play along," he said, forcing his temper down. He smiled. "Tell me what you thought."

Her face went still and she said, "It's . . . just thoughts. Impressions everybody'd have."

"But *you* were there. *Everybody* wasn't. Tell us."

"It was scary or something . . ." She seemed to regret the clumsy word.

Unprofessional

"I felt—"

"Somebody watching you?" he asked.

This surprised her. "Yes. That's exactly it."

Rhyme had felt it himself. Many times. He'd felt it three and a half years ago, bending down over the decomposing body of the young policeman, picking a fiber off the uniform. He'd been *positive* that someone was nearby. But there was no one—just a large oak beam that chose that moment to groan and splinter and come crashing down on the fulcrum of Lincoln Rhyme's fourth cervical vertebra with the weight of the earth.

"What else did you think, Amelia?"

She wasn't resisting anymore. Her lips were relaxed, her eyes drifting over the curled *Nighthawks* poster—the diners, lonely or contentedly alone. She said, "Well, I remember saying to myself, 'Man, this place is old.' It was like those pictures you see of turn-of-the-century factories and things. And I—"

"Wait," Rhyme barked. "Let's think about that. Old . . ."

His eyes strayed to the Randel Survey map. He'd commented before on the unsub's interest in historical New York. The building where T.J. Colfax had died was old too. And so was the tunnel for the railroad where they'd found the first body. The New York Central trains used to run aboveground. There'd been so many crossing fatalities that Eleventh Avenue had earned the name Death Avenue and the railroad had finally been forced to move the tracks belowground.

"And Pearl Street," he mused to himself, "was a major byway in early New York. Why's he so interested in old things?" He asked Sellitto, "Is Terry Dobyns still with us?"

"Oh, the shrink? Yeah. We worked a case last year. Come

to think of it, he asked about you. Said he called you a couple times and you never—"

"Right, right, right," Rhyme said. "Get him over here. I want his thoughts on 823's patterns. Now, Amelia, what else did you think?"

She shrugged but far too nonchalantly. "Nothing."

"No?"

And where *did* she keep her feelings? he wondered, recalling something Blaine had said once, seeing a gorgeous woman walking down Fifth Avenue: *The more beautiful the package, the harder it is to unwrap.*

"I don't know . . . All right, I remember one thing I thought. But it doesn't mean anything. It's not, like a professional observation."

Professional . . .

It's a bitch when you set your own standards, ain't it, Amelia?

"Let's hear it," he said to her.

"When you were having me pretend to be him? And I found where he stood to look back at her?"

"Keep going."

"Well, I thought . . ." For a moment it seemed that tears threatened to fill her beautiful eyes. They were iridescent blue, he noticed. Instantly she controlled herself. "I wondered, did she have a dog. The Colfax woman."

"A dog? Why'd you wonder that?"

She hesitated a moment then said, "This friend of mine . . . a few years ago. We were talking about getting a dog when, well, if we moved in together. I always wanted one. A collie. It was funny. That was the kind my friend wanted too. Even before we knew each other."

"A dog." Rhyme's heart popped like beetles on a summer screen door. "And?"

"I thought that woman—"

"T.J.," Rhyme said.

"T.J.," Sachs continued. "I just thought how sad it was—if she had any pets she wouldn't be coming home to them and playing with them anymore. I didn't think about her boyfriends or husbands. I thought about pets."

"But why *that* thought? Dogs, pets. Why?"

"I don't know why."

Silence.

Finally she said, "I suppose seeing her tied up there . . . And I was thinking how he stood to the side to watch her. Just standing between the oil tanks. It was like he was watching an animal in a pen."

Rhyme glanced at the sine waves on the GC-MS computer screen.

Animals . . .

Nitrogen . . .

"Shit!" Rhyme blurted.

Heads turned toward him.

"It's shit." Staring at the screen.

"Yes, of course!" Cooper said, replastering his strands of hair. "All the nitrogen. It's manure. And it's old manure at that."

Suddenly Lincoln Rhyme had one of those moments he'd reflected on earlier. The thought just burst into his mind. The image was of lambs.

Sellitto asked, "Lincoln, you okay?"

A lamb, sauntering down the street.

It was like he was watching an animal . . .

"Thom," Sellitto was saying, "is he all right?"

. . . in a pen.

Rhyme could picture the carefree animal. A bell around its neck, a dozen others behind.

"Lincoln," Thom said urgently. "You're sweating. Are you all right?"

"Shhhhh," the criminalist ordered.

He felt the tickle running down his face. Inspiration and heart failure; the symptoms are oddly similar. Think, think . . .

Bones, wooden posts and manure . . .

"Yes!" he whispered. A Judas lamb, leading the flock to slaughter.

"Stockyards," Rhyme announced to the room. "She's being held in a stockyard."

THIRTEEN

"There are no stockyards in Manhattan."

"The *past*, Lon," Rhyme reminded him. "Old things turn on him. Get his juices flowing. We should think of *old* stockyards. The older the better."

In researching his book, Rhyme had read about a murder that gentleman mobster Owney Madden was accused of committing: gunning down a rival bootlegger outside his Hell's Kitchen townhouse. Madden was never convicted—not for this particular murder, at any rate. He took the stand and, in his melodious British-accented voice, lectured the courtroom about betrayal. "This entire case has been trumped up by my rivals, who are speaking lies about me. Your honor, do you know what they remind me of? In my neighborhood, in Hell's Kitchen, the flocks of lambs were led through the streets from the stockyards to the slaughterhouses on Forty-second Street. And you know who led them? Not a dog, not a man. But one of theirs. A Judas lamb with a bell around its neck. He'd lead the flock up that ramp. But then he'd stop and the rest of them would go on inside. I'm an innocent lamb and those witnesses against me, they're the Judases."

Rhyme continued. "Call the library, Banks. They must have a historian."

The young detective flipped open his cellular phone and called. His voice dropped a tone or two as he spoke. After he explained what they needed he stopped speaking and gazed at the map of the city.

"Well?" Rhyme asked.

"They're finding someone. They've got—" He lowered his

UNSUB 823			
Appearance	Residence	Vehicle	Other
• Caucasian male, slight build • Dark clothing • Old gloves, reddish kidskin • Aftershave; to cover up other scent? • Ski mask? Navy blue?	• Prob. has safe house	• Yellow Cab	• knows CS proc. • possibly has record • knows FR prints • gun = .32 Colt • Ties vics w/ unusual knots • "Old" appeals to him

head as someone answered and the young man repeated his request. He started nodding and announced to the room, "I've got two locations . . . no, three."

"Who is it?" Rhyme barked. "Who're you talking to?"

"The curator of the city archives . . . He says there've been three major stockyard areas in Manhattan. One on the West Side, around Sixtieth Street . . . One in Harlem in the 1930s or '40s. And on the Lower East Side during the Revolution."

"We need addresses, Banks. Addresses!"

Listening.

"He's not sure."

"Why can't he look it up? Tell him to look it up!"

Banks responded, "He heard you, sir . . . He says, in what? Look them up in what? They didn't have Yellow Pages back then. He's looking at old—"

"Demographic maps of commercial neighborhoods without street names," Rhyme groused. "Obviously. Have him *guess*."

"That's what he's doing. He's guessing."

Rhyme called, "Well, we need him to guess *fast*."

Banks listened, nodding.

"What, what, what, *what*?"

"Around Sixtieth Street and Tenth," the young officer said. A moment later: "Lexington near the Harlem River . . . And then . . . where the Delancey farm was. Is that near Delancey Street?—"

"Of *course* it is. From Little Italy all the way to the East River. Lots of territory. *Miles*. Can't he narrow it down?"

"Around Catherine Street. Lafayette . . . Walker. He's not sure."

"Near the courthouses," Sellitto said and told Banks, "Get Haumann's teams moving. Divide 'em up. Hit all three neighborhoods."

The young detective made the call, then looked up. "What now?"

"We wait," Rhyme said.

Sellitto muttered, "I fucking hate waiting."

Sachs asked Rhyme, "Can I use your phone."

Rhyme nodded toward the one on his bedside table.

She hesitated. "You have one in there?" She pointed to the hallway.

Rhyme nodded.

With perfect posture she walked out of the bedroom. In the hallway mirror he could see her, solemn, making the precious phone call. Who? he wondered. Boyfriend, husband? Day-care center? Why had she hesitated before mentioning her "friend" when she told them about the collie? There was a story behind that, Rhyme bet.

Whomever she was calling wasn't there. He noticed her eyes turn to dark-blue pebbles when there was no answer. She looked up and caught Rhyme gazing at her in the dusty glass. She turned her back. The phone slipped to the cradle and she returned to his room.

There was silence for a full five minutes. Rhyme lacked the mechanism most people have for bleeding off tension. He'd been a manic pacer when he was mobile, drove the officers in IRD crazy. Now, his eyes energetically scanned the Randel map of the city as Sachs dug beneath her Patrol cap and scratched at her scalp. Invisible Mel Cooper cataloged evidence, calm as a surgeon.

All but one of the people in the room jumped inordinately when Sellitto's phone brayed. He listened; his face broke into a grin.

"Got it!" One of Haumann's squads is at Eleventh and Sixtieth. They can hear a woman's screams coming from somewhere around there. They dunno where for sure. They're doing a door-to-door."

"Get your running shoes on," Rhyme ordered Sachs.

He saw her face sag. She glanced at Rhyme's phone, as if it might be ringing with a reprieve call from the governor at any minute. Then a look at Sellitto, who was poring over the ESU tactical map of the West Side.

"Amelia," Rhyme said, "we lost one. That's too bad. But we don't have to lose any more."

"If you saw her," she whispered. "If you only saw what he did to her—"

"Oh, but I have, Amelia," he said evenly, his eyes relentless and challenging. "I've seen what happened to T.J. I've seen what happens to bodies left in hot trunks for a month. I've seen what a pound of C4 does to arms and legs and faces. I worked the Happy Land social club fire. Over eighty people burned to death. We took Polaroids of the vics' faces, or what was left of them, for their families to identify—because there's no way in hell a human being could walk past those rows of bodies and stay sane. Except us. We didn't have any choice." He inhaled against the excruciating pain that swept through his neck. "See, if you're going to get by in this business, Amelia . . . If you're going to get by in *life*, you're going to have to learn to give up the dead."

One by one the others in the room had stopped what they were doing and were looking at the two of them.

No pleasantries now from Amelia Sachs. No polite smiles. She tried for a moment to make her gaze cryptic. But it was transparent as glass. Her fury at him—out of proportion to his comment—roiled through her, her long face folded under the dark energy. She swept aside a lock of lazy red hair and snatched the headset from the table. At the top of the stairs she paused and looked at him with a withering glance, reminding Rhyme that there was nothing colder than a beautiful woman's cold smile.

And for some reason he found himself thinking: Welcome back, Amelia.

"Whatcha got? You got goodies, you got a story, you got pictures?"

The Scruff sat in a bar on the East Side of Manhattan, Third Avenue—which is to the city what strip malls are to the 'burbs. This was a dingy tavern, soon to be rockin' with Yuppies on the make. But now it was the refuge of badly dressed locals, eating suppers of questionable fish and limp salads.

The lean man, skin like knotty ebony, wore a very white shirt and a very green suit. He leaned closer to the Scruff. "You got news, you got secret codes, you got letters? You got shit?"

"Man. Ha."

"You're not laughing when you say ha," said Fred Dellray, really D'Ellret but that had been generations ago. He was six foot four, rarely smiled despite the Jabberwocky banter, and was a star special agent in the Manhattan office of the FBI.

"No, man. I'm not laughing."

"So what've you *got?*" Dellray squeezed the end of a cigarette, which perched over his left ear.

"It takes time, man." The Scruff, a short man, scratched his greasy hair.

"But you ain't got time. Time is precious, time is fleeing, and time is one thing you. Ain't. Got."

Dellray put his huge hand under the table, on which sat two coffees, and squeezed the Scruff's thigh until he whined.

Six months ago the skinny little guy had been caught trying to sell automatic M-16s to a couple of right-wing crazies, who—whether they actually were or not—also happened to be under-cover BATF agents.

The feds hadn't wanted the Scruff himself of course, the greasy little wild-eyed *thing*. They wanted whoever was supplying the guns. ATF swam upstream a ways but no great busts were forthcoming and so they gave him to Dellray, the Bureau's Número Uno snitch handler, to see if he might be some use. So far, though, he'd proved to be just an irritating, mousy little skel who didn't, apparently, have news, secret codes or even shit for the feds.

"The only way we're dropping down a charge, any charge, is you give us something beautiful and sticky. Are we all together on that?"

"I don't have nothing for youse guys right *now* is what I'm saying. Just *now*."

"Not true, not true. You gotchaself somethin'. I can see it in your face. You're knowing something, mon."

A bus pulled up outside, with a hiss of brake air. A crowd of Pakistanis climbed from the open door.

"Man, that fucking UN conference," the Scruff muttered. "What the fuck they coming here for? This city's too crowded already. All them foreigners."

"'Fucking conference.' You little skel, you little turd," Dellray snapped. "Whatcha got against world peace?"

"Nothin'."

"Now, tell me something good."

"I don't know nothin' good."

"Who you talking to here?" Dellray grinning devilishly. "I'm the Chameleon. I can smile'n be happy or I can frown and play squeezie."

"No, man, no," the Scruff squealed. "Shit, that hurts. Cut it out."

The bartender looked over at them and a short glance from Dellray sent him back to polishing polished glasses.

"All right, maybe I know one thing. But I need help. I need—"

"Squeezie time again."

"Fuck you, man. Just fuck you!"

"Oh, that's mighty smart dialogue," Dellray shot back. "You sound like in those bad movies, you know, the bad guy and the good guy finally meet. Like Stallone and somebody. And all they can say to each other is, 'Fuck you, man.' 'No, fuck you.' 'No, fuck *you*.' Now, you're gonna tell me something useful. Are we all together on that?"

And just stared at the Scruff until he gave up.

"Okay, here's what it is. I'm trusting you, man. I'm—"

"Yeah, yeah, yeah. Whatcha got?"

"I was talking to Jackie, you know Jackie?"

"I know Jackie."

"An' he was telling me."

"What was he telling you?"

"He was telling me he heard anything anybody got coming in or going out this week, don't do it the airports."

"So what was coming in or going out? More 16s?"

"I told you, man, there wasn't nothing *I* had. I'm telling you what Jackie—"

"Told you."

"Right, man. Just in general, you know?" The Scruff turned big brown eyes on Dellray. "Would I lie to you?"

"Don't ever lose your dignity," the agent warned solemnly, pointing a stern finger at the Scruff's chest. "Now what's this about airports. Which one? Kennedy, La Guardia?"

"I don't know. All I know is word's up that some-body was gonna be at a airport here. Somebody who was pretty bad."

"Gimme a name."

"Don't got a name."

"Where's Jackie?"

"Dunno. South Africa, I think. Maybe Liberia."

"What's all this *mean*?" Dellray squeezed his cigarette again.

"I guess just there was a chance something was going down, you know, so nobody should be having shipments coming in then."

"You guess." The Scruff cringed but Dellray wasn't thinking about tormenting the little man any longer. He was hearing alarm bells: Jackie—an arms broker both Bureaus had known about for a year—might have heard something from one of his clients, soldiers in Africa and Central Europe and militia cells in America, about some terrorist hit at the airports. Dellray normally wouldn't've thought anything about this, except for that kidnapping at JFK last night. He hadn't paid much attention to it—it was NYPD's case. But now he was also thinking about that botched fragging at the UNESCO meeting in London the other day.

"Yo boy dint tell you anything more?"

"No, man. Nothing more. Hey, I'm hungry. Can we eat somethin'?"

"Remember what I told you about dignity? Quit moaning." Dellray stood up. "I gotta make a call."

The RRV skidded to a stop on Sixtieth Street.

Sachs snagged the crime-scene suitcase, the PoliLight and the big twelve-volt flashlight.

"Did you get her in time?" Sachs called to an ESU trooper. "Is she all right?"

No one answered at first. Then she heard the screams.

"What's going on?" she muttered, running breathless up to the large door, which had been battered in by Emergency Services. It opened onto a wide driveway that descended underneath an abandoned brick building. "She's still *there*?"

"That's right."

"Why?" demanded a shocked Amelia Sachs.

"They told us not to go in."

"Not to go in? She's screaming. Can't you hear her?"

An ESU cop said, "They told us to wait for you."

They. No, not *they* at all. Lincoln Rhyme. That son of a bitch.

"We were supposed to find her," the officer said. "*You're* supposed to go in."

She clicked the headset on. "Rhyme!" she barked. "Are you there?"

No answer . . . You goddamn coward.

Give up the dead . . . Sonofabitch! As furious as she'd been storming down the stairs in his townhouse a few minutes ago, she was twice as angry now.

Sachs glanced behind her and noticed a medic standing beside an EMS bus.

"You, come with me."

He took a step forward and saw her draw her weapon. He stopped.

"Whoa, time out," the medic said. "I don't have to go in until the area's secure."

"Now! Move!" She spun around and he must have seen more muzzle than he wanted. He grimaced and hurried after her.

From underground they heard: "Aiiiii! *Hilfe!*" Then sobbing.

Jesus. Sachs started to run toward the looming doorway, twelve feet high, smoky blackness inside.

She heard in her head: *You're him, Amelia. What are you thinking?*

Go away, she said silently.

But Lincoln Rhyme didn't go away.

You're a killer and a kidnapper, Amelia. Where would you walk, what would you touch?

Forget it! I'm going to save her. Hell with the crime scene . . .

"*Mein Gott!* Pleece! Some-von, Pleece help!"

Go, Sachs shouted to herself. Sprint! He's not in here. You're safe. Get her, go . . .

She picked up the pace, her utility belt clanking as she ran. Then, twenty feet down the tunnel, she pulled up. Debating. She didn't like which side won.

"Oh, fuck," she spat out. She set down the suitcase and opened it up. She blurted to the medic, "You, what's your name?"

The uneasy young man answered, "Tad Walsh. I mean, what's going on?" He glanced down into the murk.

"Oh . . . *Bitte, helfen Sie mir!*"

"Cover me," Sachs whispered.

"Cover you? Wait a minute, I don't do that."

"Take the gun, all right?"

"What'm I supposed to cover you *from*?"

Thrusting the automatic into his hand, she dropped to he knees. "Safety's off. Be careful."

She grabbed two rubber bands and slipped them ove her shoes. Taking the pistol back she ordered him to d the same.

With unsteady hands he slipped the bands on.

"I'm just thinking—"

"Quiet. He could still be here."

"Wait a minute now, ma'am," the medic whispered. "Thi ain't in my job description."

"It's not in mine either. Hold the light." She handed hi the flashlight.

"But if he's here he's probably gonna shoot at the light. mean, that's what *I'd* shoot at."

"Then hold it up high. Over my shoulder. I'll go in fron If anybody gets shot it'll be me."

"Then whatta I do?" Tad sounded like a teenager.

"I myself'd run like hell," Sachs muttered. "Now follow m And keep that beam steady."

Lugging the black CS suitcase in her left hand, holding he weapon in front of her, she gazed at the floor as they move into the darkness. She saw the familiar broom marks agai just like at the other scene.

"*Bitte nicht, bitte nicht, bitte . . .*" There was a brief scream then silence.

"What the hell's going on down there?" Tad whispered.

"Shhhh," Sachs hissed.

They walked slowly. Sachs blew on her fingers gripping th Glock—to dry the slick sweat—and carefully eyed the randor targets of wooden pillars, shadows and discarded machiner picked out by the flashlight held unsteadily in Tad's hand.

She found no footprints.

Of course not. He's smart.

But we're smart too, she heard Lincoln Rhyme say in h thoughts. And she told him to shut up.

Slower now.

Five more feet. A pause. Then moving slowly forward. Trying to ignore the girl's moans. She felt it again—that sensation of being watched, the slippery crawl of the iron sights tracking you. The body armor, she reflected, wouldn't stop a full-metal jacket. Half the bad guys used Black Talons anyway—so a leg or arm shot would kill you just as efficiently as a chest hit. And a lot more painfully. Nick had told her how one of those bullets could open up a human body; one of his partners, hit by two of the vicious slugs, had died in his arms.

Above and behind . . .

Thinking of him, she remembered one night, lying against Nick's solid chest, gazing at the silhouette of his handsome Italian face on her pillow as he told her about hostage-rescue entry—"Somebody inside wants to nail you when you go in they'll do it from above and behind . . ."

"Shit." She dropped to a crouch, spinning around and aiming the Glock toward the ceiling, ready to empty the entire clip.

"What?" Tad whispered, cowering. "*What?*"

The emptiness gaped at her.

"Nothing." And breathed deeply, stood up.

"Don't *do* that."

There was a gurgling noise ahead of them.

"Jesus," came Tad's high voice again. "I hate this."

This guy's a pussy, she thought. *I know that 'cause he's saying everything I want to.*

She stopped. "Shine the light up there. Ahead."

"Oh, my everloving . . ."

Sachs finally understood the hairs she'd found at the last scene. She remembered the look that had passed between Sellitto and Rhyme. He'd known then what the unsub had planned. He'd known this was what was happening to her—and *still* he'd told ESU to wait. She hated him that much more.

In front of them a pudgy girl lolled on the floor, in a pool of blood. She glanced toward the light with glazed eyes and passed out. Just as a huge black rat—big as a housecat—crawled up onto her belly and moved toward the girl's fleshy throat. He bared its dingy teeth to take a bite from the girl's chin.

Sachs smoothly lifted the chunky black Glock, her left palm circling under the butt for support. She aimed carefully.

Shooting is breathing.

Inhale, out. Squeeze.

Sachs fired her weapon for the first time in the line of duty. Four shots. The huge black rat standing on the girl's chest exploded. She hit one more on the floor behind and another one that, panicking, raced toward Sachs and the medic. The others vanished silently, fast as water on sand.

"Jesus," the medic said. "You could've hit the girl."

"From thirty feet?" Sachs snorted. "Not hardly."

The radio burst to life and Haumann asked if they were under fire.

"Negative," Sachs replied. "Just shooing a few rats."

"Roger, K."

She took the flashlight from the medic and shining it low, started forward.

"It's all right, miss," Sachs called. "You'll be all right."

The girl's eyes opened, head flipping from side to side.

"*Bitte, bitte . . .*"

She was very pale. Her blue eyes clung to Sachs, as if she was afraid to look away. "*Bitte, bitte . . .* Pleece . . ." Her voice rose to a wild keening and she began to sob and thrash in terror as the medic pressed bandages on her wounds.

Sachs cradled her bloody blond head, whispering, "You'll be all right, honey, you'll be all right, you'll be all right. . . ."

FOURTEEN

The office, high above downtown Manhattan, looked out over Jersey. The crap in the air made the sunset absolutely beautiful.

"We gotta."

"We can't."

"Gotta," Fred Dellray repeated and sipped his coffee—even worse than in the restaurant where the Scruff and he'd been sitting not long before. "Take it away from 'em. They'll live with it."

"It's a local case," responded the FBI's assistant special agent in charge of the Manhattan office. The ASAC was a meticulous man who could never work undercover—because when you saw him you thought, Oh, look, an FBI agent.

"It's not local. They're *treating* it local. But it's a big case."

"We're down eighty men because of the UN thing."

"And this's related to it," Dellray said. "I'm positive."

"Then we'll tell UN Security. Let everybody . . . Oh, don't give me that look."

"UN Security? UN *Security*? Say, you ever heara the words oxy-moron? . . . Billy, you see that picture? Of the scene this morning? The hand comin' outa the dirt, and all the skin cut offa that finger? That's a sick fuck out there."

"NYPD's keeping us informed," the ASAC said smartly. "We've got Behavioral on call if they want."

"Oh, Jesus Christ on the merry cross. 'Behavioral on call'? We gotta catch this ripper, Billy. *Catch* him. Not figger out his tick-tocky workings."

"Tell me what your snitch said again."

Dellray knew a crack in a rock when he saw one. Wasn't going to let it seal up again. Rapid fire now: about the Scruff and Jackie in Johannesburg or Monrovia and the hushed word throughout the illicit arms trade that something was going down at a New York airport this week so stay clear. "It's *him*," Dellray said. "Gotta be."

"NYPD's got a task force together."

"Not Anti-Terror. I made calls. Nobody at A-T there knows zippo about it. To NYPD it's 'dead tourists equal bad public relations.' I want this case, Billy." And Fred Dellray said the one word he'd never uttered in his eight years of undercover work. "Please."

"What grounds're you talking?"

"Oh-oh, bullshit question," Dellray said, stroking his index finger like a scolding teacher. "Lessee. We got ourselves that spiffy new anti-terrorism bill. But that's not enough for you, you want jurisdiction? I'll give you jurisdiction. A Port Authority felony. Kidnapping. I can fucking argue that this prick's driving a taxi so he's affecting interstate commerce. We don't want to play *those* games, do we, Billy?"

"You're not listening, Dellray. I can recite the U.S. Code in my sleep, thank you. I want to know if we're going to take over, what we tell people and make *everybody* happy. 'Cause remember, after this unsub's bagged and tagged we're going to have to keep working with NYPD. I'm not going to send my big brother to beat up their big brother even though I can. Anytime I want. Lon Sellitto's running the case and he's a good man."

"A lieutenant?" Dellray snorted. He tugged the cigarette out from behind his ear and held it under his nostrils for a moment.

"Jim Polling's in charge."

Dellray reared back with mock horror. "Polling? Little Adolph? The 'You-have-the-right-to-remain-silent-'cause-I'ma-hit-you-upside-the-motherfuckin'-head' Polling? *Him*?"

The ASAC had no response for that. He said, "Sellitto's good. A real workhorse. I've been with him on two OC task forces."

"That unsub's grabbing bodies right and left and this here boy's betting he's going to work his way up."

"Meaning?"

"We got senators in town. We got congressmen, we got heads of state. I think these folk he's grabbing now're just for practice."

"*You* been talking to Behavioral and not telling me?"

"It's what I smell." Dellray couldn't resist touching his lean nose.

The ASAC blew air from his clean-shaven-federal-agent cheeks. "Who's the CI?"

Dellray had trouble thinking of the Scruff as a confidential informant, which sounded like something out of a Dashiell Hammett novel. Most *CI*s were skels, short for skeletons, meaning scrawny, disgusting little hustlers. Which fit the Scruff to a T.

"He's a tick," Dellray admitted. "But Jackie, this guy he heard it from's solid."

"I know you want it, Fred. I understand." The ASAC said this with some sympathy. Because he knew exactly what was behind Dellray's request.

Even as a boy in Brooklyn, Dellray had wanted to be a cop. It hadn't mattered much to him what kind of cop as long as he could spent twenty-four hours a day doing it. But soon after joining the Bureau he found his calling—undercover work.

Teamed with his straight man and guardian angel Toby Dolittle, Dellray was responsible for sending a large number of perps away for a very long time—the sentences totaled close to a thousand years. ("They kin call us the Millennium Team, Toby-o," he declared to his partner once.) The clue to Dellray's success was his nickname: "the Chameleon." Bestowed after—in the space of twenty-four hours—he played a brain-dead cluckhead in a Harlem crack house and a Haitian dignitary at a dinner in the Panamanian consulate, complete with diagonal red ribbon on his chest and impenetrable accent. The two of them were regularly loaned out to ATF or DEA and, occasionally, city police departments. Drugs and guns were their specialty though they had a minor in 'jacked merchandise.

The irony of undercover work is that the better you are, the earlier the retirement. Word gets around and the big boys, the perps worth going after, become harder to fox. Dolittle and Dellray found themselves working less in the field and more as handlers of informants and other undercover agents. And while it wasn't Dellray's first choice—nothing excited him like the street—it still got him out of the office more often than most SAs in the Bureau. It had never occurred to him to request a transfer.

Until two years ago—a warm April morning in New York. Dellray was just about to leave the office to catch a plane at La Guardia when he got a phone call from the assistant director of the Bureau in Washington. The FBI is a nest of hierarchy and Dellray couldn't imagine why the big man himself was calling. Until he heard the AD's somber voice break the news that Toby Dolittle, along with an assistant U.S. attorney from Manhattan, had been on the ground floor of the Oklahoma City federal building that morning, preparing for the deposition session that Dellray himself was just about to depart for.

Their bodies were being flown back to New York the next day.

Which was the same day that Dellray put in the first of his RFT-2230 forms, requesting a transfer to the Bureau's Anti-Terror Division.

The bombing had been the crime of crimes to Fred Dellray, who, when no one was looking, devoured books on politics and philosophy. He believed there was nothing essentially unAmerican about greed or lust—hey, those qualities were encouraged everywhere from Wall Street to Capitol Hill. And if people stepped over the border of legality, Dellray was pleased to track them down—but he never did so with personal animosity. But to murder people for their beliefs—hell, to murder children before they even knew *what* they believed— my God, that was a stab at the heart of the country. Sitting in his two-room, sparsely furnished Brooklyn apartment after Toby's funeral, Dellray decided that this was the kind of crime he wanted a crack at.

But unfortunately the Chameleon's reputation preceded him. The Bureau's best undercover agent was now their best handler, running agents and CIs throughout the East Coast. His bosses simply couldn't afford to let him go to one of the more quiescent departments of the FBI. Dellray was a minor legend, personally responsible for some of the Bureau's greatest recent successes. So it was with considerable regret that his persistent requests were turned down.

The ASAC was well aware of this history and he now added a sincere, "I wish I could help out, Fred. I'm sorry."

But all Dellray heard in these words was the rock cracking a little further. And so the Chameleon pulled a persona off the rack and stared down his boss. He wished he still had his fake gold tooth. Street man Dellray was a tough hombre with one mother-fucker of a mean stare. And in that look was the unmistakable message anybody on the street would know instinctively: I done for you, now you do for me.

Finally the smarmy ASAC said lamely, "It's just that we need *something*."

"Somethin'?"

"A hook," the ASAC said. "We don't have a hook."

A reason to take the case away from NYPD, he meant.

Politics, politics, polifuckingtics.

Dellray lowered his head but the eyes, brown as polish, didn't waver a millimeter from the ASAC. "He cut the skin off that vic's finger this morning, Billy. Clean down to the bone. Then buried him alive."

Two scrubbed, federal-agent hands met beneath a crisp jaw. The ASAC said slowly, "Here's a thought. There's a deputy commissioner at NYPD. Name's Eckert. You know him? He's a friend of mine."

The girl lay on her back on a stretcher, eyes closed, conscious but groggy. Still pale. An IV of glucose ran into her arm. Now that she'd been rehydrated she was coherent and surprisingly calm, all things considered.

Sachs walked back to the gates of hell and stood looking down into the black doorway. She clicked on the radio and called Lincoln Rhyme. This time he answered.

"How's the scene look?" Rhyme asked casually.

Her answer was a curt: "We got her out. If you're interested."

"Ah, good. How is she?"

"Not good."

"But alive, right."

"Barely."

"You're upset because of the rats, aren't you, Amelia?"

She didn't answer.

"Because I didn't let Bo's men get her right away. Are you there, Amelia?"

"I'm here."

"There are five contaminants of crime scenes," Rhyme explained. She noticed he'd gone into his low, seductive tone again. "The weather, the victim's family, the suspect, souvenir hunters. The last is the worst. Guess what it is?"

"You tell me."

"Other cops. If I'd let ESU in they could've destroyed all the trace. You know how to handle a scene now. And I'll bet you preserved everything just fine."

Sachs needed to say, "I don't think she'll ever be the same after this. The rats were all over her."

"Yes, I imagine they were. That's their nature."

Their nature . . .

"But five minutes or ten wasn't going to make any difference. She—"

Click.

She shut off the radio and walked to Walsh, the medic.

"I want to interview her. Is she too groggy?"

"Not yet. We gave her locals—to stitch the lacerations and the bites. She'll want some Demerol in a half hour or so."

Sachs smiled and crouched down beside her. "Hi, how you doing?"

The girl, fat but very pretty, nodded.

"Can I ask you some questions?"

"Yes, pleece. I want you get him."

Sellitto arrived and ambled up to them. He smiled down at the girl, who gazed at him blankly. He proffered a badge she had no interest in and identified himself.

"You all right, miss?"

The girl shrugged.

Sweating fiercely in the muggy heat, Sellitto nodded Sachs aside. "Polling been here?"

"Haven't seen him. Maybe he's at Lincoln's."

"No, I just called there. He's gotta get to City Hall pronto."

"What's the problem?"

Sellitto lowered his voice, his doughy face twisted up. "A fuckup—our transmissions're supposed to be secure. But those fucking reporters, somebody's got an unscrambler or something. They heard we didn't go in right away to get her." He nodded toward the girl.

"Well, we *didn't*," Sachs said harshly. "Rhyme told ESU to wait until I got here."

The detective winced. "Man, I hope they don't have *that* on tape. We need Polling for damage control." He nodded to the girl. "Interviewed her yet?"

"No. Just about to." With some regret Sachs clicked on the radio and heard Rhyme's urgent voice.

". . . you there? This goddamn thing doesn't—"

"I'm here," Sachs said coolly.

"What happened?"

"Interference, I guess. I'm with the vic."

The girl blinked at the exchange and Sachs smiled. "I'm not talking to myself." Gestured toward the mike. "Police headquarters. What's your name?"

"Monelle. Monelle Gerger." She looked at her bitten arm, pulled up a dressing and examined a wound.

"Interview her fast," Rhyme instructed, "then work the scene."

Hand covering the microphone stalk, Sachs whispered fiercely to Sellitto, "This man is a pain in the ass to work for. Sir."

"Humor him, officer."

"Amelia!" Rhyme barked. "Answer me!"

"We're interviewing her, all right?" she snapped.

Sellitto asked, "Can you tell us what happened?"

Monelle began to talk, a disjointed story about being in the laundry room of a residence hall in the East Village. He'd been hiding, waiting for her.

"What residence hall?" Sellitto asked.

"The Deutsche Haus. It's, you know, mostly German expatriates and students."

"What happened then?" Sellitto continued. Sachs noted that

although the big detective appeared gruffer, more ornery than Rhyme, he was really the more compassionate of the two.

"He threwed me in the trunk of car and drove here."

"Did you get a look at him?"

The woman closed her eyes. Sachs repeated the question and Monelle said she hadn't; he was, as Rhyme had guessed, wearing a navy-blue ski mask.

"*Und* gloves."

"Describe them."

They were dark. She didn't remember what color.

"Any unusual characteristics? The kidnapper?"

"No. He was white. I could tell that."

"Did you see the license plate of the taxi?" Sellitto asked.

"*Was?*" the girl asked, drifting into her native tongue.

"Did you see—"

Sachs jumped as Rhyme interrupted: "*Das Nummernschild.*"

Thinking: How the hell does he *know* all this? She repeated the word and the girl shook her head no then squinted. "What you mean, taxi?"

"Wasn't he driving a Yellow Cab?"

"Taxicab? *Nein.* No. It was regular car."

"Hear that, Lincoln?"

"Yup. Our boy's got another set of wheels. And he put her in the trunk so it's not a station wagon or hatchback."

Sachs repeated this. The girl nodded. "Like a sedan."

"Any idea of the make or color?" Sellitto continued.

Monelle answered, "Light, I think. Maybe silver or gray. Or that, you know, what is it? Light brown."

"Beige?"

She nodded.

"Maybe beige," Sachs added for Rhyme's benefit.

Sellitto asked, "Was there anything in the trunk? Anything at all? Tools, clothes, suitcases?"

Monelle said there wasn't. It was empty.

Rhyme had a question. "What did it smell like? The trunk."

Sachs relayed the query.

"I don't know."

"Oil and grease?"

"No. It smelled . . . clean."

"So maybe a new car," Rhyme reflected.

Monelle dissolved into tears for a moment. Then shook her head. Sachs took her hand and, finally, she continued. "We drove for long time. *Seemed* like long time."

"You're doing fine, honey," Sachs said.

Rhyme's voice interrupted. "Tell her to strip."

"What?"

"Take her clothes off."

"I will not."

"Have the medics give her a robe. We need her clothes, Amelia."

"But," Sachs whispered, "she's crying."

"Please," Rhyme said urgently. "It's important."

Sellitto nodded and Sachs, tight-lipped, explained to the girl about the clothes and was surprised when Monelle nodded. She was, it turned out, eager to get out of the bloody garments anyway. Giving her privacy, Sellitto walked away, to confer with Bo Haumann. Monelle put on a gown the medic offered her and one of the plain-clothes detectives covered her with his sportscoat. Sachs bagged the jeans and T-shirts.

"Got them," Sachs said into the radio.

"Now she's got to walk the scene with you," Rhyme said.

"What?"

"But make sure she's behind you. So she doesn't contaminate any PE."

Sachs looked at the young woman, huddling on a gurney beside the two EMS buses.

"She's in no shape to do that. He cut her. All the way to the bone. So she'd bleed and the rats'd get her."

"Is she mobile?"

"Probably. But you know what she's just been through?"

"She can give you the route they walked. She can tell you where he stood."

"She's going to the ER. She lost a lot of blood."

A hesitation. He said pleasantly, "Just ask her."

But his joviality was fake and Sachs heard just impatience. She could tell that Rhyme was a man who wasn't used to coddling people, who didn't *have* to. He was someone used to having his own way.

He persisted, "Just once around the grid."

You can go fuck yourself, Lincoln Rhyme.

"It's—"

"Important. I know."

Nothing from the other end of the line.

She was looking at Monelle. Then she heard a voice, no, *her* voice say to the girl, "I'm going down there to look for evidence. Will you come with me?"

The girl's eyes nailed Sachs deep in her heart. Tears burst. "No, no, no. I am not doing that. *Bitte nicht, oh, bitte nicht . . .*"

Sachs nodded, squeezed the woman's arm. She began to speak into the mike, steeling herself for his reaction, but Rhyme surprised her by saying, "All right, Amelia. Let it go. Just ask her what happened when they arrived."

The girl explained how she'd kicked him and escaped into an adjoining tunnel.

"I kick him again," she said with some satisfaction. "Knock off his glove. Then he get all pissed and strangle me. He—"

"Without the glove on?" Rhyme blurted.

Sachs repeated the question and Monelle said, "Yes."

"Prints, excellent!" Rhyme shouted, his voice distorting in the mike. "When did it happen? How long ago?"

Monelle guessed about an hour and a half.

"Hell," Rhyme muttered. "Prints on skin last an hour, ninety minutes, tops. Can you print skin, Amelia?"

"I never have before."

"Well, you're about to. But fast. In the CS suitcase there'll be a packet labeled Kromekote. Pull out a card."

She found a stack of glossy five-by-seven cards, similar to photographic paper.

"Got it. Do I dust her neck?"

"No. Press the card, glossy side down, against her skin where she thinks he touched her. Press for about three seconds."

Sachs did this, as Monelle stoically gazed at the sky. Then, as Rhyme instructed, she dusted the card with metallic powder, using a puffy Magna-Brush.

"Well?" Rhyme asked eagerly.

"It's no good. A shape of a finger. But no visible ridges. Should I pitch it?"

"Never throw away *anything* at a crime scene, Sachs," he lectured sternly. "Bring it back. I want to see it anyway."

"One thing, I am thinking I forget," said Monelle. "He touch me."

"You mean he molested you?" Sachs asked gently. "Rape?"

"No, no. Not in a sex way. He touch my shoulder, face, behind my ear. Elbow. He squeezed me. I don't know why."

"You hear that, Lincoln? He touched her. But it didn't seem like he was getting off on it."

"Yes."

"*Und* . . . And one thing I am forgetting," Monelle said. "He spoke German. Not good. Like he only study it in school. And he call me Hanna."

"Called her what?"

"Hanna," Sachs repeated into the mike. "Do you know why?" she asked the girl.

"No. But that's all he call me. He seemed to like saying the name."

"Did you get that, Lincoln."

"Yes, I did. Now do the scene. Time's awasting."

As Sachs stood, Monelle suddenly reached up and gripped her wrist.

"Miss . . . Sachs. You are German?"

She smiled and answered, "A long time ago. A couple generations."

Monelle nodded. She pressed Sachs's palm to her cheek. "*Vielen Dank*. Thank you, Miss Sachs. *Danke schön*."

FIFTEEN

The three ESU halogens clicked to light, bringing an eerie tide of white glare to the grim tunnel.

Alone now at the scene Sachs gazed at the floor for a moment. Something had changed. What?

She drew her weapon again, dropped into a crouch. "He's here," she whispered, stepping behind one of the posts.

"What?" Rhyme asked.

"He's come back. There were some dead rats here. They're gone."

She heard Rhyme's laughter.

"What's so funny?"

"No, Amelia. Their friends took the bodies away."

"Their friends?"

"Had a case up in Harlem once. Dismembered, decomposed body. A lot of the bones were hidden in a big circle around the torso. The skull was in an oil drum, toes underneath piles of leaves . . . Had the borough in an uproar. The press was talking about Satanists, serial killers. Guess who the perp turned out to be?"

"No idea," she said stiffly.

"The vic himself. It was a suicide. Raccoons, rats and squirrels made off with the remains. Like trophies. Nobody knows why but they love their souvenirs. Now, where are you?"

"At the foot of the ramp."

"What do you see?"

"A wide tunnel. Two side tunnels, narrower. Flat ceiling, supported by wooden posts. The posts're all battered and nicked. The floor's old concrete, covered with dirt."

		UNSUB 823	
Appearance	Residence	Vehicle	Other
• Caucasian male, slight build • Dark clothing • Old gloves, reddish kidskin • Aftershave; to cover up other scent? • Ski mask? Navy blue? • Gloves are dark	• Prob. has safe house	• Yellow Cab • Recent model sedan • Lt. gray, silver, biege	• knows CS proc. • possibly has record • knows FR prints • gun = .32 Colt • Ties vics w/ unusual knots • "Old" appeals to him • Called one vic "Hanna" • Knows basic German

"And manure?"

"Looks like it. In the center, right in front of me's the post she was tied to."

"Windows?"

"None. No doors either." She looked over the wide tunnel, the floor disappearing into a black universe a thousand miles away. She felt the crawl of hopelessness. "It's too big! There's too much space to cover."

"Amelia, relax."

"I'll never find *anything* here."

"I know it seems overwhelming. But just keep in mind that there're only three types of PE that we're concerned about. Objects, body materials and impressions. That's all. It's less daunting if you think of it that way.

Easy for you to say.

"And the scene isn't as big as it looks. Just concentrate on the places they walked. Go to the post."

Sachs walked the path. Staring down.

The ESU lights were brilliant but they also made the shadows starker, revealing a dozen places the kidnapper could hide. A chill trickled down her spine. Stay close, Lincoln, she thought reluctantly. I'm pissed, sure, but I wanna hear you. Breathe or something.

She paused, shone the PoliLight over the ground.

"Is it all swept?" he asked.

"Yes. Just like before."

The body armor chafed her breasts despite the sports bra and undershirt and as hot as it was outside it was unbearable down here. Her skin prickled and she felt a ravenous desire to scratch under her vest.

"I'm at the post."

"Vacuum the area for trace."

Sachs ran the Dustbuster. Hating the noise. It covered up any sound of approaching footsteps, guns cocking, knives being drawn. Involuntarily she looked behind her once, twice. Nearly dropped the vacuum as her hand strayed to her gun.

Sachs looked at the impression in the dust of where Monelle's body had lain. *I'm him. I'm dragging her along. She kicks me. I stumble . . .*

Monelle could have kicked in only one direction, away from

the ramp. The unsub didn't fall, she'd said. Which meant he must've landed on his feet. Sachs walked a yard or two into the gloom.

"Bingo!" Sachs shouted.

"What? Tell me?"

"Footprints. He missed a spot sweeping up."

"Not hers?"

"No. She was wearing running shoes. These are smooth soles. Like dress shoes. Two good prints. We'll know what size feet he's got."

"No, they won't tell us that. Soles can be larger or smaller than the uppers. But it may tell us something. In the CS bag there's an electrostatic printer. It's a small box with a wand on it. There'll be some sheets of acetate next to it. Separate the paper, lay the acetate on the print and run the wand over it."

She found the device and made two images of the prints. Carefully slipped them into a paper envelope.

Sachs returned to the post. "And here's a bit of straw from the broom."

"From?—"

"Sorry," Sachs said quickly. "We don't know where it's from. A bit of straw. I'm picking it up and bagging it."

Getting good with these pencils. Hey, Lincoln, you son of a bitch, know what I'm doing to celebrate my permanent retirement from crime scene detail? I'm going out for Chinese.

The ESU halogens didn't reach into the side tunnel where Monelle had run. Sachs paused at the day-night line then plunged forward into the shadows. The flashlight beam swept the floor in front of her.

"Talk to me, Amelia."

"There isn't much to see. He swept up here too. Jesus, he thinks of everything."

"What *do* you see?"

"Just marks in the dust."

I tackle her, I bring her down. I'm mad. Furious. I try to strangle her.

Sachs stared at the ground.

"Here's something—knee prints! When he was strangling her he must have straddled her waist. He left knee prints and he missed them when he swept."

"Electrostatic them."

She did, quicker this time. Getting the hang of the equipment. She was slipping the print into the envelope when something caught her eye. Another mark in the dust.

What is that?

"Lincoln . . . I'm looking at the spot where . . . it looks like the glove fell here. When they were struggling."

She clicked on the PoliLight. And couldn't believe what she saw.

"A print. I've got a fingerprint!"

"What?" Rhyme asked, incredulous. "It's not hers?"

"Nope, couldn't be. I can see the dust where she was lying. Her hands were cuffed the whole time. It's where he picked up the glove. He probably thought he'd swept here but missed it. It's a big, fat beautiful one!"

"Stain it, light it and shoot the son of a bitch on the one-to-one."

It took her only two tries to get a crisp Polaroid. She felt like she'd found a hundred-dollar bill in the street.

"Vacuum the area and then go back to the post. Walk the grid," he told her.

She slowly walked the floor, back and forth. One foot at a time.

"Don't forget to look up," he reminded her. "I once caught an unsub because of a single hair on the ceiling. He'd loaded a .357 round in a true .38 and the blowback pasted a hair from his hand on the crown molding."

"I'm looking. It's a tile ceiling. Dirty. Nothing else. Nowhere to stash anything. No ledges or doorways."

"Where're the staged clues?" he asked.

"I don't see anything."

Back and forth. Five minutes passed. Six, seven.

"Maybe he didn't leave any this time," Sachs suggested. "Maybe Monelle's the last."

"No," Rhyme said with certainty.

Then behind one of the wooden pillars a flash caught her eye.

"Here's something in the corner . . . Yep. Here they are."

"Shoot it 'fore you touch it."

She took a photograph and then picked up a wad of white cloth with the pencils. "Women's underwear. Wet."

"Semen?"

"I don't know," she said. Wondering if he was going to ask her to smell it.

Rhyme ordered, "Try the PoliLight. Proteins will fluoresce."

She fetched the light, turned it on. It illuminated the cloth but the liquid didn't glow. "No."

"Bag it. In plastic. What else?" he asked eagerly.

"A leaf. Long, thin, pointed at one end."

It had been cut sometime ago and was dry and turning brown.

She heard Rhyme sigh in frustration. "There're about eight thousand varieties of deciduous vegetation in Manhattan," he explained. "Not very helpful. What's underneath the leaf?"

Why does he think there's anything there?

But there was. A scrap of newsprint. Blank on one side, the other was printed with a drawing of the phases of the moon.

"The moon?" Rhyme mused. "Any prints? Spray it with ninhydrin and scan it fast with the light."

A blast of the PoliLight revealed nothing.

"That's all."

Silence for a moment. "What're the clues sitting on?"

"Oh, I don't know."

"You *have* to know."

"Well, the ground," she answered testily. "Dirt." What else would they be sitting on?

"Is it like all the rest of the dirt around there?"

"Yes." Then she looked closely. Hell, it was different. "Well, not exactly. It's a different color."

Was he *always* right?

Rhyme instructed, "Bag it. In paper."

As she scooped up the grains he said, "Amelia?"

"Yeah?"

"He's not there," Rhyme said reassuringly.

"I guess."

"I heard something in your voice."

"I'm fine," she said shortly. "I'm smelling the air. I smell blood. Mold and mildew. And the aftershave again."

"The same as before?"

"Yes."

"Where's it coming from?"

Sniffing the air, Sachs walked in a spiral, the Maypole again, until she came to another wooden post.

"Here. It's strongest right here."

"What's 'here,' Amelia? You're my legs *and* my eyes, remember."

"One of these wooden columns. Like the kind she was tied to. About fifteen feet away."

"So he might have rested against it. Any prints?"

She sprayed it with ninhydrin and shone the light on it.

"No. But the smell's very strong."

"Sample a portion of the post where it's the strongest. There's a Moto Tool in the case. Black. A portable drill. Take a sampling bit—it's like a hollow drill bit—and mount it in the tool. There's something called a chuck. It's a—"

"I own a drill press," she said tersely.

"Oh," Rhyme said.

She drilled a piece of the post out, then flicked sweat from her forehead. "Bag it in plastic?" she asked. He told her yes. She felt faint, lowered her head and caught her breath. No fucking air in here.

"Anything else?" Rhyme asked.

"Nothing that I can see."

"I'm proud of you, Amelia. Come on back and bring your treasures with you."

SIXTEEN

"C areful," Rhyme barked.

"I'm an expert at this."

"Is it new or old?"

"Shhh," Thom said.

"Oh, for Christ's sake. The blade, is it old or new?"

"Don't breathe . . . Ah, there we go. Smooth as a baby's butt."

The procedure was not forensic but cosmetic.

Thom was giving Rhyme his first shave in a week. He had also washed his hair and combed it straight back.

A half hour before, waiting for Sachs and the evidence to arrive, Rhyme had sent Cooper out of the room while Thom slicked up a catheter with K-Y and wielded the tube. After that business had been completed Thom had looked at him and said, "You look like shit. You realize that?"

"I don't care. Why would I care?"

Realizing suddenly that he did.

"How 'bout a shave?" the young man had asked.

"We don't have time."

Rhyme's real concern was that if Dr Berger saw him groomed he'd be less inclined to go ahead with the suicide. A disheveled patient is a despondent patient.

"And a wash."

"No."

"We've got company now, Lincoln."

Finally Rhyme had grumbled, "All right."

"And let's lose those pajamas, what do you say?"

"There's nothing wrong with them."

But that meant all right too.

Now, scrubbed and shaved, dressed in jeans and a white shirt, Rhyme ignored the mirror his aide held in front of him.

"Take that away."

"Remarkable improvement."

Lincoln Rhyme snorted derisively. "I'm going for a walk until they get back," he announced and settled his head back into the pillow. Mel Cooper turned to him with a perplexed expression.

"In his head," Thom explained.

"Your head?"

"I imagine it," Rhyme continued.

"That's quite a trick," Cooper said.

"I can walk through any neighborhood I want and never get mugged. Hike in the mountains and never get tired. *Climb* a mountain if I want. Go window-shopping on Fifth Avenue. Of course the things I see aren't necessarily there. But so what? Neither are the stars."

"How's that?" Cooper asked.

"The starlight we see is thousands or millions of years old. By the time it gets to Earth the stars themselves've moved. They're not where we see them." Rhyme sighed as the exhaustion flooded over him. "I suppose some of them have already burned out and disappeared." He closed his eyes.

———

"He's making it harder."

"Not necessarily," Rhyme answered Lon Sellitto.

Sellitto, Banks and Sachs had just returned from the stockyard scene.

"Underwear, the moon and a plant," cheerfully pessimistic Jerry Banks said. "That's not exactly a road map."

"Dirt too," Rhyme reminded, ever appreciative of soil.

"Have any idea what they mean?" Sellitto asked.

"Not yet," Rhyme said.

"Where's Polling?" Sellitto muttered. "He *still* hasn't answered his page."

"Haven't seen him," Rhyme said.

A figure appeared in the doorway.

"As I live and breathe," rumbled the stranger's smooth baritone.

Rhyme nodded the lanky man inside. He was somber-looking but his lean face suddenly cracked into a warm smile, as it tended to do at odd moments. Terry Dobyns was the sum total of the NYPD's behavioral science department. He'd studied with the FBI behaviorists down at Quantico and had degrees in forensic science and psychology.

The psychologist loved opera and touch football and when Lincoln Rhyme had awakened in the hospital after the accident three years ago Dobyns had been sitting beside him listening to *Aida* on a Walkman. He'd then spent the next three hours conducting what turned out to be the first of many counseling sessions about Rhyme's injury.

"Now what's this I recall the textbooks sayin' 'bout people who don't return phone calls?"

"Analyze me later, Terry. You hear about our unsub?"

"A bit," Dobyns said, looking Rhyme over. He wasn't an M.D. but he knew physiology. "You all right, Lincoln? Looking a little peaked."

"I'm getting a bit of a workout today," Rhyme admitted. "And I could use a nap. You know what a lazy SOB I am."

"Yeah, right. You're the man'd call me at three in the morning with some question about a perp and couldn't understand why I was in the sack. So what's up? You fishin' for a profile?"

"Whatever you can tell us'll help."

Sellitto briefed Dobyns, who—as Rhyme recalled from the days they worked together—never took notes but managed to retain everything he heard inside a head crowned with dark-red hair.

The psychologist paced in front of the wall chart, glancing up at it occasionally as he listened to the detective's rumbling voice.

He held up a finger, interrupting Sellitto. "The victims, the victims . . . They've all been found underground. Buried, in a basement, in the stockyard tunnel."

"Right," Rhyme confirmed.

"Go on."

Sellitto continued, explaining about the rescue of Monelle Gerger.

"Fine, all right," Dobyns said absently. Then braked to a halt and turned to the wall again. He spread his legs and, hands on hips, gazed at the sparse facts about Unsub 823. "Tell me more about this idea of yours, Lincoln. That he likes old things."

"I don't know what to make of it. So far his clues have something to do with historical New York. Building materials from the turn of the century, the stockyards, the steam system."

Dobyns stepped forward suddenly and tapped the profile. "Hanna. Tell me about Hanna."

"Amelia?" Rhyme asked.

She told Dobyns how the unsub had referred to Monelle Gerger as Hanna for no apparent reason. "She said he seemed to like saying the name. And speaking to her in German."

"And he took a bit of a chance to 'nap her, didn't he?" Dobyns noted. "The cab, at the airport—that was safe for him. But hiding in a laundry room . . . He must've been real motivated to snatch somebody German."

Dobyns twined some ruddy hair around a lengthy finger and flopped down in one of the squeaky rattan chairs, stretched his feet out in front of him.

"Okay, try this on for size. The underground . . . that's the key. It tells me he's somebody who's hiding something and when I hear that I start thinking hysteria."

"He's not acting hysterical," Sellitto said. "He's pretty damn calm and calculating."

"Not hysteria in that sense. It's a category of mental disorders. The condition manifests when something traumatic happens in a patient's life and the subconscious *converts* that trauma into something else. It's an attempt to protect the patient. With traditional conversion hysteria you see physical symptoms—nausea, pain, paralysis. But I think here we're dealing with a related problem. Dissociation—that's what we call it when the reaction to the trauma affects the mind, not the physical body. Hysterical amnesia, fugue states. And multiple personalities."

"Jekyll and Hyde?" Mel Cooper played straight man this time, beating Banks to the punch.

"Well, I don't think he's got true multiple personalities," Dobyns continued. "That's a very rare diagnosis and the classic mult pers is young and has a lower IQ than your boy." He nodded at the profile chart. "He's slick and he's smart. Clearly an organized offender." Dobyns stared out the window for a moment. "This is interesting, Lincoln. I think your unsub pulls on his other personality when it suits him—when he wants to kill—and that's important."

"Why?"

"Two reasons. First, it tells us something about his main personality. He's someone who's been trained—maybe at his job, maybe his upbringing—to help people, not hurt them. A priest, a counselor, politician, social worker. And, two, I think it means he's found himself a blueprint. If you can find out what it is, maybe you can get a lead to him."

"What kind of blueprint?"

"He may have wanted to kill for a long time. But he didn't act until he found himself a role model. Maybe from a book or movie. Or somebody he actually knows. It's someone he can identify with, someone whose own crimes in effect give him permission to kill. Now, I'm going out on a limb here—"

"Climb," Rhyme said. "Climb."

"His obsession with history tells me that his personality is a character from the past."

"Real life?"

"That I couldn't say. Maybe fictional, maybe not. Hanna, whoever she is, figures in the story somewhere. Germany too. Or German Americans."

"Any idea what might've set him off?"

"Freud felt it was caused by—what else?—sexual conflict at the Oedipal stage. Nowadays, the consensus is that developmental glitches're only one cause—any trauma can trigger it. And it doesn't have to be a single event. It could be a personality flaw, a long series of personal or professional disappointments. Hard to say." His eyes glowed as they gazed at the profile. "But I sure hope you bag him alive, Lincoln. I'd love the chance to get him on the couch for a few hours."

"Thom, are you writing this down?"

"Yes, bwana."

"But one question," Rhyme began.

Dobyns whirled around. "I'd say it's *the* question, Lincoln: Why is he leaving the clues? Right?"

"Yep. Why the clues?"

"Think about what he's done . . . He's talking to you. Not rambling incoherently like Son of Sam or the Zodiac killer. He's not schizophrenic. He's communicating—in *your* language. The language of forensics. Why?" More pacing, eyes flipping over the chart. "All I can think of is that he wants to share the guilt. See, it's hard for him to kill. It becomes easier if he makes us accomplices. If we don't save the vics in time their deaths are partly *our* fault."

"But that's good, isn't it?" Rhyme asked. "It means he'll keep giving us clues that are solvable. Otherwise, if the puzzle's too hard, he's not sharing the burden."

"Well, that's true," Dobyns said, smiling no longer. "But there's another factor at work too."

Sellitto supplied the answer. "Serial activity escalates."

"Right," Dobyns confirmed.

"How can he strike more often?" Banks muttered. "Every three hours isn't fast enough?"

"Oh, he'll find a way," the psychologist continued. "Most likely, he'll probably start targeting multiple victims." The psychologist's eyes narrowed. "Say, you all right, Lincoln?"

There were beads of sweat on the criminalist's forehead and he'd been squinting his eyes hard. "Just tired. A lot of excitement for an old crip."

"One last thing. The profile of the victims's vital in serial crimes. But here we've got different sexes, ages and economic classes. All white but he's been preying in a predominantly white pool so that's not statistically significant. With what we know so far we can't figure out why he's taken these particular people. If you can, you might just get ahead of him."

"Thanks, Terry," Rhyme said. "Stick around for a while."

"Sure, Lincoln. If you'd like."

Rhyme ordered, "Let's look at the PE from the stockyard scene. What've we got? The underwear?"

Mel Cooper assembled the bags that Sachs had brought back from the scene. He glanced at the one containing the underwear. "Katrina Fashion's D'Amore line," he announced. "One hundred percent cotton, elastic band. Cloth made in the U.S. They were cut and sewn in Taiwan."

"You can tell that just by looking at them?" Sachs asked, incredulous.

"Naw, I was reading," he answered, pointing at the label.

"Oh."

The cops laughed.

"He's telling us he's got another woman then?" Sachs asked.

"Probably," Rhyme said.

Cooper opened the bag. "Don't know what the liquid is. I'll do a chromatograph."

Rhyme asked Thom to hold up the scrap of paper with the phases of the moon on it. He studied it closely. A scrap like this was wonderful individuated evidence. You could fit it to the sheet it'd been torn from and link the two as closely as fingerprints. The problem here of course was that they had no original piece of paper. He wondered if they'd ever find it. The unsub might have destroyed it once he'd torn this bit out. Yet Lincoln Rhyme preferred to think not. He liked to picture it somewhere. Just waiting to be found. The way he always pictured source evidence: the automobile the paint chip had scraped off of, the finger that had lost the nail, the gun barrel that had discharged the rifled slug found in the victim's body. These sources—always close to the unsub—took on personalities of their own in Rhyme's mind. They could be imperious or cruel.

Or mysterious.

Phases of the moon.

Rhyme asked Dobyns if their unsub could be driven to act cyclically.

"No. The moon isn't in a major phase right now. We're four days past new."

"So the moons mean something else."

"If they're even moons in the first place," Sachs said. Pleased with herself, and rightly so, Rhyme thought. He said, "Good point, Amelia. Maybe he's talking about circles. About ink. About paper. About geometry. The planetarium . . ."

Rhyme realized that she was staring at him. Maybe just realizing now that he'd shaved and his hair was combed, his clothes changed.

And what was her mood now? he wondered. Angry at him, or disengaged? He couldn't tell. At the moment Amelia Sachs was as cryptic as Unsub 823.

The beeping of the fax machine sounded in the hallway. Thom went to get it and returned a moment later with two sheets of paper.

"It's from Emma Rollins," he announced. He held the sheets up for Rhyme to see.

"Our grocery scanner survey. Eleven stores in Manhattan sold veal shanks to customers buying fewer than five items in the last two days." He started to write on the poster then glanced at Rhyme. "The names of the stores?"

"Of course. We'll need them for cross-referencing later."

Thom wrote them down on the profile chart.

B'way & 82nd,
  ShopRite
B'way & 96th,
  Anderson Foods
Greenwich & Bank,
  ShopRite
2nd Ave., 72nd-73rd,
  Grocery World
Battery Park City,
  J&G's Emporium
1709 2nd Ave.,
  Anderson Foods
34th & Lex.,
  Food Warehouse
8th Ave. & 24th,
  ShopRite
Houston & Lafayette,
  ShopRite
6th Ave. & Houston,
  J&G's Emporium
Greenwich & Franklin,
  Grocery World

"That narrows it down," Sachs said, "to the entire city."

"Patience," said restless Lincoln Rhyme.

Mel Cooper was examining the straw that Sachs had found. "Nothing unique here." He tossed it aside.

"Is it new?" Rhyme asked. If it was they might cross-reference stores that had sold brooms and veal shanks on the same day.

But Cooper said, "Thought of that. It's six months old or older." He began shaking the trace evidence in the German girl's clothing out over a piece of newsprint.

"Several things here," he said, poring over the sheet. "Dirt."

"Enough for a density-gradient?"

"Nope. Just dust really. Probably from the scene."

Cooper looked over the rest of the effluence he'd brushed off the bloodstained clothing.

"Brick dust. Why's there so much brick?"

"From the rats I shot. The wall was brick."

"You shot them? At the scene?" Rhyme winced.

Sachs said defensively, "Well, yes. They were all over her."

He was angry but he let it go. Adding just, "All *kinds* of contaminants from gunfire. Lead, arsenic, carbon, silver."

"And here . . . another bit of reddish leather. From the glove. And . . . We've got another fiber. A different one."

Criminalists love fibers. This was a tiny gray tuft barely visible to the naked eye.

"Excellent," Rhyme announced. "And what else?"

"And here's the photo of the scene," Sachs said, "and the fingerprints. The one from her throat and from where he picked up the glove." She held them up.

"Good," Rhyme said, looking them over carefully.

There was a sheen of reluctant triumph on her face—the rush of winning, which is the flip side of hating yourself for being unprofessional.

Rhyme was studying the Polaroids of the prints when he heard footsteps on the stairs and Jim Polling arrived. He entered the room, did a double-take at the spiffed-up Lincoln Rhyme and strode to Sellitto.

"I was just at the scene," he said. "You saved the vic. Great job, guys." He nodded toward Sachs to show the noun included her too. "But the prick's 'napped another one?"

"Or's about to," Rhyme muttered, gazing at the prints.

"We're working on the clues right now," Banks said.

"Jim, I've been trying to track you down," Sellitto said. "I tried the mayor's office."

"I was with the chief. He had to fucking beg for some extra searchers. Got another fifty men pulled off UN security detail."

"Captain, there's something we got to talk about. We gotta problem. Something happened at the last scene . . ."

A voice as yet unheard from boomed through the room, "Problem? Who got a *problem*? We don't got no problems here, do we? None ay-tall."

Rhyme looked up at the tall, thin man in the doorway. He was jet black and wore a ridiculous green suit and shoes that shone like brown mirrors. Rhyme's heart plummeted. "Dellray."

"Lincoln Rhyme. New York's own Ironside. Hey, Lon. And Jim Polling, how's it hangin', buddy?"

Behind Dellray were a half-dozen other men and a woman. Rhyme knew in a heartbeat why the federal agents were here. Dellray scanned the officers in the room, his attention alighting momentarily on Sachs then flying away.

"What do you want?" Polling asked.

Dellray said, "Haven't you guessed, gemmuns. You're outa business. We closin' you up. Yessir. Just like a bookie."

SEVENTEEN

O ne of us.

That's how Dellray was looking at Lincoln Rhyme as he walked around the bed. Some people did this. Paralysis was a club and they crashed the party with jokes, nods, winks. You know I love you, man, 'cause I'm makin' funna you.

Lincoln Rhyme had learned that this attitude got tiring very, very quickly.

"Lookit that," Dellray said, poking at the Clinitron. "That's something outa *Star Trek*. Commander Riker, get your ass in the shuttle."

"Go away, Dellray," Polling said. "It's our case."

"And how's dis here patient doing, Dr Crusher?"

The captain was stepping forward, a rooster the lanky FBI agent towered over. "Dellray, you listening? Go away."

"Man, I'ma get me one of those, Rhyme. Lay my ass down in it, watcha game. Seriously, Lincoln, how you doin'? Been a few years."

"Did they knock?" Rhyme asked Thom.

"No, they didn't knock."

"You didn't knock," Rhyme said. "So may I suggest that you leave?"

"Gotta warrant," Dellray murmured, flicking papers in his breast pocket.

Amelia Sachs's right index fingernail worried her thumb, which was on the verge of bleeding.

Dellray looked around the room. He was clearly impressed at their impromptu lab but strangled the feeling fast. "We're taking over. Sorry."

UNSUB 823			
Appearance	Residence	Vehicle	Other
• Caucasian male, slight build • Dark clothing • Old gloves, reddish kidskin • Aftershave; to cover up other scent? • Ski mask? Navy blue? • Gloves are dark	• Prob. has safe house • Located near; B'way & 82nd, ShopRite B'way & 96th Anderson Foods Greenwich & Bank ShopRite 2nd Ave., 72nd-73rd, Grocery World Battery Park City, J&G's Emporium 1709 2nd Ave., Anderson Foods 34th & Lex., Food Warehouse 8th Ave. & 24th, ShopRite Houston & Lafayette, ShopRite 6th Ave. & Houston, J&G's Emporium Greenwich & Franklin, Grocery World	• Yellow Cab • Recent model sedan • Lt. gray, silver, biege	• knows CS proc. • possibly has record • knows FR prints • gun = .32 Colt • Ties vics w/ unusual knots • "Old" appeals to him • Called one vic "Hanna" • Knows basic German • Underground appeals to him • Dual personalities • Maybe priest, soc. worker, counselor

In twenty years of policing, Rhyme had never seen a peremptory takeover like this.

"Fuck this, Dellray," Sellitto began, "you passed on the case."

The agent swiveled his glossy black face around until he was looking down at the detective.

"Passed? Passed? I never got no ring-a-ling about it. D'jou call me?"

"No."

"Then who dropped the dime?"

"Well . . ." Sellitto, surprised, glanced at Polling, who said, "You got an advisory. That's all we've gotta send you." On the defensive now too.

"An advisory. Yeah. And, hey, how 'xactly was that delivered? Would that have been by Pony *Ex*-press? Book-rate mail? Tell me, Jim, what's the good of an overnight advisory when there's an ongoing operation?"

Polling said, "We didn't see the need."

"We?" Dellray asked quickly. Like a surgeon spotting a microscopic tumor.

"*I* didn't see the need," Polling snapped. "I told the mayor to keep it a local operation. We've got it under control. Now fuck off, Dellray."

"And you thought you could wrap it up in time for the eleven o'clock news."

Rhyme was startled when Polling shouted, "What we thought was none of your goddamn business. It's our fucking case." He knew about the captain's legendary temper but he'd never seen it in action.

"Ac-tu-ally, it's ou-ur fuck-ing case now." Dellray strolled past the table that held Cooper's equipment.

Rhyme said, "Don't do this, Fred. We're getting a handle on this guy. Work with us but don't take it away. This unsub isn't like anything you've ever seen."

Dellray smiled. "Let's see, what's the latest I hear about this 'fuck-ing' case? That you've got a civvy doin' the 'rensics." The agent forewent a glance at the Clinitron bed. "You got a portable doing crime scene. You got soldiers out buying groceries."

"Evidence standards, Frederick," Rhyme reminded stridently. "That's SOP."

Dellray looked disappointed. "But ESU, Lincoln? All those taxpayer dollars. Then there's cutting up people like *Texas Chainsaw . . .*"

How had *that* news got out? Everyone was sworn to secrecy on the dismemberment issue.

"And whatsis I hear 'bout Haumann's boys found the vic but dint go in and save her right away? Channel Five had a Big Ear mike on it. Got her screaming for a good five minutes 'fore you sent somebody in." He glanced at Sellitto with a wry grin. "Lon, my man, would that've been the *problem* you were just talking about?"

They'd come so far, Rhyme was thinking. They *were* getting a feel for him, starting to learn the unsub's language. Starting to see him. With a burst of surprise he understood that he was once again doing what he loved. After all these years. And now somebody was going to take it away from him. Anger rippled inside him.

"Take the case, Fred," Rhyme grumbled. "But don't cut us out. Don't do it."

"You lost two vics," Dellray reminded.

"We lost *one*," Sellitto corrected, looking uneasily at Polling, who was still fuming. "Nothing we coulda done about the first. He was a calling card."

Dobyns, arms crossed, merely observed the argument. But Jerry Banks leapt in. "We've got his routine down now. We aren't going to lose any more."

"You are if ESU's gonna sit around listenin' to vics scream their heads off."

Sellitto said, "It was my—"

"*My* decision," Rhyme sang out. "Mine."

"But you're civvy, Lincoln. So it couldn't have been your decision. It mighta been your *suggestion*. It mighta been your *recommendation*. But I don't think it was your decision."

Dellray's attention had turned to Sachs again. His eyes on her, he said to Rhyme, "You told Peretti not to run the scene? That's mighty curious, Lincoln. Why'd you go and do something like that?"

Rhyme said, "I'm better than he is."

"Peretti's not a happy boy scout. Nosir. He and I had a chin wag with Eckert."

Eckert? The dep com? How was he involved?

And with one glance at Sachs, at the evasive blue eyes, framed by strands of mussed red hair, he knew how.

Rhyme nailed her with a look, which she promptly avoided, and he said to Dellray, "Let's see . . . Peretti? Wasn't he the one opened up traffic on the spot where the unsub'd stood to watch the first vic? Wasn't he the one released the scene before we'd had a chance to pick up any serious trace? The scene my own Sachs here had the foresight to seal off. *My* Sachs had it right and Vince Peretti and everybody *else* had it wrong. Yes, she did."

She was gazing at her thumb, a look that bespoke seeing a familiar sight, and slipped a Kleenex from her pocket, wrapped it around the bloody digit.

Dellray summarized, "You shoulda called us at the beginning."

"Just get out," Polling muttered. Something snapped in his eyes and his voice rose. "Get the hell out!" he screamed.

Even cool Dellray blinked and eased back as the spittle flew from the captain's mouth.

Rhyme frowned at Polling. There was a chance they might salvage something of the case but not if Polling had a tantrum. "Jim . . ."

The captain ignored him. "Out!" he shouted again. "You are not taking over our case!" And startling everyone in the room, Polling leapt forward, grabbed the agent by his green lapels and shoved him against the wall. After a moment of stunned silence Dellray simply pushed the captain back with his fingertips and took out a cellular phone. He offered it to Polling.

"Call the mayor. Or Chief Wilson."

Polling eased instinctively away from Dellray—a short man putting some distance between himself and a tall one. "You want the case, you fucking got it." The captain strode to the stairs and then down them. The front door slammed.

"Jesus, Fred," Sellitto said, "work with us. We can nail this scumbag."

"We need the Bureau's A-T," said Dellray, now sounding like reason itself. "You're not set up for the terrorist angle."

"What terrorist angle?" Rhyme asked.

"The UN peace conference. Snitch o' mine said word was up that something was gonna go down at the airport. Where he snatched the vics."

"I wouldn't profile him as a terrorist," Dobyns said. "Whatever's going on inside him's psychologically motivated. It's not ideological."

"Well, fact is, Quantico and us're pegging him one way. 'Preciate that you feel different. But this's how we're handling it."

Rhyme gave up. Fatigue was spiriting him away. He wished Sellitto and his scar-faced assistant had never shown up this morning. He wished he'd never met Amelia Sachs. Wished he wasn't wearing the ridiculous crisp white shirt, which felt stiff at his neck and felt like nothing below it.

He realized that Dellray was speaking to him.

"I'm sorry?" Rhyme cocked a muscular eyebrow.

Dellray asked, "I mean, *couldn't* politics be a motive too?"

"Motive doesn't interest me," Rhyme said. "Evidence interests me."

Dellray glanced again at Cooper's table. "So. The case's ours. We all together on that?"

"What're our options?" Sellitto asked.

"You back us up with searchers. Or you can drop out altogether. That's about all that's left. We'll take the PE now, you don't mind."

Banks hesitated.

"Give 'em it," Sellitto ordered.

The young cop picked up the evidence bags from the most recent scene, slipped them into a large plastic bag. Dellray held his hands out. Banks glanced at the lean fingers and tossed the bag onto the table, walking back to the far side of the room—the cop side. Lincoln Rhyme was a demilitarized zone between them and Amelia Sachs stood riveted at the foot of Rhyme's bed.

Dellray said to her, "Officer Sachs?"

After a pause, her eyes on Rhyme, she responded, "Yes?"

"Commissioner Eckert wants ya t'come with us for debriefing 'bout the crime scenes. He said something about starting your new assignment on Monday."

She nodded.

Dellray turned to Rhyme and said sincerely, "Don'tcha worry, Lincoln. We're gonna git him. Next you hear, his head gonna be on a stake at the gates to the city."

He nodded to his fellow agents, who packed up the evidence and headed downstairs. From the hallway Dellray called to Sachs, "You coming, officer?"

She stood with her hands together, like a schoolgirl at a party she regretted she'd come to.

"In a minute."

Dellray vanished down the stairs.

"Those pricks," Banks muttered, flinging his watchbook onto the table. "Can you believe that?"

Sachs rocked on her heels.

"Better get going, Amelia," Rhyme said. "Your carriage awaits."

"Lincoln." Walking closer to the bed.

"It's all right," he said. "You did what you had to do."

"I have no business doing CS work," she blurted. "I never wanted to."

"And you won't be doing it anymore. That works out well, doesn't it?"

She started to walk to the door then turned and blurted, "You don't care about anything but the evidence, do you?"

Sellitto and Banks stirred but she ignored them.

"Say, Thom, could you show Amelia out?"

Sachs continued, "This is all just a game to you, isn't it? Monelle—"

"Who?"

Her eyes flared, "There! See? You don't even remember her name. Monelle Gerger. The girl in the tunnel . . . she was just a part of the puzzle to you. There were rats crawling all over her and you said, 'That's their nature'? That's their *nature*? She's never going to be the same again and all you cared about was your precious evidence."

"In living victims," he droned, lecturing, "rodent wounds are always superficial. As soon as the first li'l critter drooled on her she needed rabies vaccine. What did a few more bites matter?"

"Why don't we ask her opinion?" Sachs's smile was different now. It had turned pernicious, like those of the nurses and therapy aides who hated crips. They walked around rehab wards with smiles like this. Well, he hadn't been happy with the polite Amelia Sachs; he'd wanted the feisty one . . .

"Answer me something, Rhyme. Why did you really want me?"

"Thom, our guest has overstayed her welcome. Would you—?"

"Lincoln," the aide began.

"Thom," Rhyme snapped, "believe I asked you to do something."

"Because I don't know shit," Sachs blurted. "That's why! You didn't want a real CS tech because then you wouldn't be in charge. But me . . . you can send me here, send me there. I'll do exactly what you want, and I won't bitch and moan."

"Ah, the troops mutiny . . ." Rhyme said, lifting his eyes to the ceiling.

"But I'm not one of the troops. I never wanted this in the first place."

"I didn't want it either. But here we are. In bed together. Well, one of us." And he knew his cold smile was far, far icier than any she could muster.

"Why, you're just a spoiled brat, Rhyme."

"Hey, officer, time out here," Sellitto barked.

But she kept going. "You can't walk your crime scenes anymore and I'm sorry about that. But you're risking an investigation just to massage your ego and I say fuck that." She grabbed her Patrol hat and stormed out of the room.

He expected to hear a slamming door from downstairs, maybe breaking glass. But there was a faint click and then silence.

As Jerry Banks retrieved his watchbook and thumbed through it with more concentration than was needed, Sellitto said, "Lincoln, I'm sorry. I—"

"Nothing to it," Rhyme said, yawning excessively in the false hope that it would calm his stinging heart. "Nothing at all."

The cops stood beside the half-empty table for a few moments, difficult silence, then Cooper said, "Better get packed up." He hefted a black 'scope case onto the table and began to unscrew an eyepiece with the loving care of a musician disassembling his saxophone.

"Well, Thom," Rhyme said, "it's after sunset. You know what that tells me? Bar's open."

Their war room was impressive. It beat Lincoln Rhyme's bedroom hands down.

Half a floor at the federal building, three dozen agents, computers and electronic panels out of some Tom Clancy movie. The agents looked like lawyers or investment bankers. White shirts, ties. *Crisp* was the word that came to mind. And Amelia Sachs in the center, conspicuous in her navy-blue uniform, soiled with rat blood, dust and grainy shit from cattle dead a hundred years.

She was no longer shaking from her blowup with Rhyme and though her mind kept reeling with a hundred things she wanted to say, wished she *had* said, she forced herself to concentrate on what was happening around her.

A tall agent in an immaculate gray suit was conferring with Dellray—two large men, heads down, solemn. She believed he was the special agent in charge of the Manhattan office, Thomas Perkins, but she didn't know for certain; a Patrol officer has as much contact with the FBI as a dry cleaner or insurance salesman does. He seemed humorless, efficient, and kept glancing at a large map of Manhattan pinned to the wall. Perkins nodded several times as Dellray briefed him then he stepped up to a fiber-board table filled with manila folders, looked over the agents and began to speak.

"If I could have your attention . . . I've just been in communication with the director and the AG in Washington. You've all heard about the Kennedy Airport unsub by now. It's an unusual profile. Kidnapping, absent a sexual element, is rarely the basis for serial activity. In fact this's the first unsub of the sort we've had in the Southern District. In light of the possible connection with the events at the UN this week we're coordinating with headquarters, Quantico and the secretary-general's office. We've been told to be completely proactive on this case. It's getting prioritization at the highest level."

The SAC glanced at Dellray, who said, "We've taken over the case from the NYPD but we'll be using them for backup and personpower. We have the crime scene officer here to brief us on the scenes." Dellray sounded completely different here. Not a shred of Superfly.

"Have you vouchered the PE?" Perkins asked Sachs.

Sachs admitted that she hadn't. "We were working on saving the vics."

The SAC was troubled by this. At trial, otherwise solid cases tanked regularly because of slipups in recording the chain of custody of the physical evidence. It was the first thing the perps' defense lawyers wailed on.

"Make sure you do that before you leave."

"Yessir."

What a look on Rhyme's face when he guessed I bitched to Eckert and got them shut down. What a look . . .

My Sachs figured it out, my Sachs preserved the scene.

She worried a nail again. Stop it, she told herself, as she always did, and continued to dig into the flesh. The pain felt good. That's what the therapists never understood.

The SAC said, "Agent Dellray? Could you brief the room as regards the approach we'll be taking."

Dellray looked from the SAC to the other agents and continued, "At this moment we have field agents hitting every major terrorist cell in the city and pursuing whatever leads we can find that'll get us to the unsub's residence. *All* CIs, *all* undercover agents. It'll mean compromising some existing operations but we've decided it's worth the risk.

"Our job here is to be rapid response. You'll break out into groups of six agents each and be ready to move on any lead. You'll have complete hostage-rescue and barricade-entry support."

"Sir," Sachs said.

Perkins looked up, frowning. Apparently one didn't interrupt briefings until the approved Q&A break. "Yes, what is it, officer?"

"Well, I'm just wondering, sir. What about the victim?"

"Who, that German girl? You think we should interview her again?"

"No, sir. I meant the *next* victim."

Perkins responded, "Oh, we'll certainly stay cognizant of the fact that there may be other targets."

Sachs continued, "He's got one now."

"He does?" The SAC glanced at Dellray, who shrugged. Perkins asked Sachs, "How do you know?"

"Well, I don't exactly know, sir. But he left clues at the last scene and he wouldn't've done that if he didn't have another vic. Or was just about to snatch one."

"Noted, officer," the SAC continued. "We're going to mobilize as fast as we can to make sure nothing happens to them."

Dellray said to her, "We think it's best to focus on the beast himself."

"Detective Sachs—" Perkins began.

"I'm not a detective, sir. I'm assigned to Patrol."

"Yes, well," the SAC continued, looking at the stacks of files. "If you could just give us some of your bullet points, that would be helpful."

Thirty agents watching her. Two women among them.

"Just tell us whatcha saw," Dellray said, gripping an unlit cigarette between prominent teeth.

She gave them a synopsis of her searches of the crime scenes and the conclusions Rhyme and Terry Dobyns had come to. Most of the agents were troubled by the unsub's curious MO.

"Like a goddamn game," an agent muttered.

One asked if the clues had any political messages they could decipher.

"Well, sir, we really don't think he's a terrorist," Sachs persisted.

Perkins turned his high-powered attention toward her. "Let me ask you, officer, you concede he's smart, this unsub?"

"Very smart."

"Couldn't he be double-bluffing?"

"How do you mean?"

"You . . . I should say the NYPD's thinking is that he's just a nutcase. I mean, a criminal personality. But isn't it possible he's smart enough to make you *think* that. When something else's going on."

"Like what?"

"Take those clues he left. Couldn't they be diversions?"

"No, sir, they're directions," Sachs said. "Leading us to the vics."

"I understand that," quick Thomas Perkins said. "But by doing that he's also leading us *away* from other targets, right?"

She hadn't considered that. "I suppose it's possible."

"And Chief Wilson's been pulling men off UN security detail right and left to work the kidnapping. This unsub might be keeping everyone distracted, which leaves him free for his real mission."

Sachs remembered that she'd had a similar thought herself earlier in the day, watching all the searchers along Pearl Street. "And that'd be the UN?"

"We think so," Dellray said. "The perps behind the UNESCO bombing attempt in London might want to try again."

Meaning Rhyme was going off in the completely wrong direction. It eased the weight of her guilt somewhat.

"Now, officer, could you itemize the evidence for us?" Perkins asked.

Dellray gave her an inventory sheet of everything she'd found and she went through it item by item. As she spoke Sachs was aware of bustling activity around her—some agents taking calls, some standing and whispering to other agents, some taking notes. But when, glancing down at the sheet, she added, "Then I picked up this fingerprint of his at the last scene," she realized that the room had fallen utterly silent. She looked up. Every face in the office was staring at her in what could pass for shock—if federal agents were capable of that.

She glanced helplessly at Dellray, who cocked his head, "You saying you gotchaself a print?"

"Well, yes. His glove fell off in a struggle with the last vic and when he picked it up he brushed against the floor."

"Where is it?" Dellray asked quickly.

"Jesus," one agent called. "Why didn't you *say* anything?"

"Well, I—"

"Find it, find it!" somebody else called.

A murmur ran through the room.

Her hands shaking, Sachs dug through the evidence bags

and handed Dellray the Polaroid of the fingerprint. He held it up, looked carefully. Showed it to someone who, she guessed, was a friction-ridge expert. "Good," the agent offered. "It's definitely A-grade."

Sachs knew that prints were rated A, B and C, the lower category being unacceptable to most law enforcement agencies. But whatever pride she felt in her evidence-gathering skills was crushed by their collective dismay that she hadn't mentioned it before this.

Then everything started to happen at once. Dellray handed off to an agent who jogged to an elaborate computer in the corner of the office and rested the Polaroid on a large, curved bed of something called an Opti-Scan. Another agent turned on the computer and started typing in commands as Dellray snatched up the phone. He tapped his foot impatiently and then lowered his head as, somewhere, the call was answered.

"Ginnie, S'Dellray. This's gonna be a true-blue pain but I needya to shut down all AFIS Northeast Region requests and give the one I'm sending priority . . . I got Perkins here. He'll okay it and if that ain't enough I'll call the man in Washington himself. . . . It's the UN thing."

Sachs knew the Bureau's Automated Fingerprint Identification System was used by police departments throughout the country. That's what Dellray would be braking to a halt at the moment.

The agent at the computer said, "It's scanned. We're transmitting now."

"How long's it gonna take?"

"Ten, fifteen minutes."

Dellray pressed his dusty fingers together. "Please, please, please."

All around her was a cyclone of activity. Sachs heard voices talking about weapons, helicopters, vehicles, anti-terror negotiators. Phone calls, clattering keyboards, maps unrolling, pistols being checked.

Perkins was on the phone, talking to the hostage-rescue people, or the director, or the mayor. Maybe the president. Who knew? Sachs said to Dellray, "I didn't know the print was that big a deal."

"S'always a big deal. Least, with AFIS now it is. Used to

be you dusted for prints mostly for show. Let the vics and the press know you were doing *something*."

"You're kidding."

"Naw, not a bit. Take New York City. You do a cold search—that's when you don't have any suspects—you do a cold search manually, it'd take a tech fifty years to go through all the print cards. No foolin'. An automated search? Fifteen minutes. Used to be you'd ID a suspect maybe two, three percent of the time. Now we're running close to twenty, twenty-two percent. Oh, yup, prints're golden. Dincha tell Rhyme about it?"

"He knew, sure."

"And he didn't get all hands on board? My oh my, the man's slipping."

"Say, officer," SAC Perkins called, holding his hand over the phone, "I'll ask you to complete those chain-of-custody cards now. I want to get the PE off to PERT."

The Physical Evidence Response Team. Sachs remembered that Lincoln Rhyme had been the one the feds hired to help put it together.

"I'll do that. Sure."

"Mallory, Kemple, take that PE to an office and get our guest some COC cards. You have a pen, officer?"

"Yes, I do."

She followed the two men into a small office, clicking her ballpoint nervously while they hunted down and returned with a pack of federal-issue chain-of-custody cards. She sat down and broke the package open.

The voice behind her was the hip Dellray, the persona that seemed the eagerest to break out. In the car on the way here someone had referred to him as the Chameleon and she was beginning to see why.

"We call Perkins the Big Dict. Nyup—not 'dick' like you're thinking. 'Dict' like *dictionary*. But don' worry over him. He's smarter'n an agent sandwich. And better'n that he's pulled strings all the way to D.C., which is where strings gotta be pulled in cases like this." Dellray ran his cigarette beneath his nose as if it were a fine cigar. "You know, officer, you're foxy smart doing whatch're doing."

"Which is?"

"Getting out of Major Crimes. You don't want it." The lean black face, glossy and wrinkled only about the eyes, seemed sincere for the first time since she'd met him. "Best thing you ever did, going into Public Affairs. You'll do some good there and it won't turn you to dust. That's what happens, you bet. This job turns you to dust."

One of the last victims of James Schneider's mad compulsion, a young man named Ortega, had come to Manhattan from Mexico City, where political unrest (the much-heralded populist uprising, which had begun the year before) had made commerce difficult at best. Yet the ambitious entrepreneur had been in the city no more than one week when be vanished from sight. It was learned that he was last seen in front of a West Side tavern and authorities immediately suspected that be was yet another victim of Schneider's. Sadly, this was discovered to be the case.

The bone collector cruised the streets for fifteen minutes around NYU, Washington Square. Plenty of people hanging out. But kids mostly. Students in summer school. Skateboarders. It was festive, weird. Singers, jugglers, acrobats. It reminded him of the "museums," down on the Bowery, popular in the 1800s. They weren't museums at all of course but arcades, teeming with burlesque shows, exhibits of freaks and daredevils, and vendors selling everything from French postcards to splinters of the True Cross.

He slowed once or twice but nobody wanted a cab, or could afford one. He turned south.

Schneider tied bricks to Señor Ortega's feet and rolled him under a pier into the Hudson River so the foul water and the fish might reduce his body to mere bone. The corpse was found two weeks after he had vanished and so it was never known whether or not the unfortunate victim was alive or had full use of his senses when he was thrown into the drink. Yet it is suspected that this was so. For Schneider cruelly shortened the rope so that Señor Ortega's face was inches below the surface of Davy Jones's locker;—his hands undoubtedly thrashed madly about as he gazed upward at the air that would have been his salvation.

The bone collector saw a sickly young man standing by the curb. AIDS, he thought. But your bones are healthy—and *so* prominent. Your bones'll last forever. . . . The man didn't want a cab and the taxi cruised past, the bone collector hungrily gazing at his thin frame in the rearview mirror.

He looked back to the street just in time to swerve around an elderly man who'd stepped off the curb, his thin arm raised to flag down the cab. The man leapt back, as best he could, and the cab skidded to a stop just past him.

The man opened the back door and leaned inside. "You should look where you're going." He said this instructionally. Not with anger.

"Sorry," the bone collector muttered contritely.

The elderly man hesitated for a moment, looked up the street but saw no other taxis. He climbed in.

The door slammed shut.

Thinking: Old and thin. The skin would ride on his bones like silk.

"So, where to?" he called.

"East Side."

"You got it," he said as he pulled on the ski mask and spun the wheel sharply right. The cab sped west.

3

THE PORTABLE'S
DAUGHTER

*Overturn, overturn, overturn! is the maxim of
New York.... The very bones of our ancestors
are not permitted to lie quiet a quarter of a century,
and one generation of men seem studious to remove
all relics of those which preceded them.*

Philip Hone, Mayor of New York, Diary, 1845

EIGHTEEN

H it me again, Lon."
Rhyme drank through a straw, Sellitto from a glass. Both took the smoky liquor neat. The detective sank down in the squeaky rattan chair and Rhyme decided he looked a little like Peter Lorre in *Casablanca*.

Terry Dobyns was gone—after offering some acerbic psychological insights about narcissism and those employed by the federal government. Jerry Banks had left too. Mel Cooper continued to painstakingly disassemble and pack up his equipment.

"This is good, Lincoln." Sellitto sipped his Scotch. "Goddamn. I can't afford this shit. How old's it?"

"I think that one's twenty."

The detective eyed the tawny liquor. "Hell, this was a woman, she'd be legal and then some."

"Tell me something, Lon: Polling? That little tantrum of his. What was that all about?"

"Little Jimmy?" Sellitto laughed. "He's in trouble now. He's the one ran interference to take Peretti off the case and keep it out of the feds' hands. Really went out on a limb. Asking for you too, that took some doing. There were noses outa joint over that. I don't mean you personally. Just a civilian in on a hot case like this."

"Polling asked for me? I thought it was the chief."

"Yeah, but it was Polling put the bug in his ear in the first place. He called soon as he heard there'd been a taking and there was some bogus PE on the scene."

And wanted me? Rhyme wondered. This was curious.

Rhyme hadn't had any contact with Polling over the past few years—not since the cop-killer case in which Rhyme had been hurt. It had been Polling who'd run the case and eventually collared Dan Shepherd.

"You seem surprised," Sellitto said.

"That he asked for me? I am. We weren't on the best of terms. Didn't used to be anyway."

"Why's that?"

"I 14-43'd him."

An NYPD complaint form.

"Five, six years ago, when he was a lieutenant, I found him interrogating a suspect right in the middle of a secure scene. Contaminated it. I blew my stack. Put in a report and it got cited at one of his IA reviews—the one where he popped the unarmed suspect."

"Well, I guess all's forgiven, 'cause he wanted you bad."

"Lon, make a phone call for me, would you?"

"Sure."

"No," Thom said, lifting the phone out of the detective's hand. "Make him do it himself."

"I didn't have time to learn how it works," Rhyme said, nodding toward the dialing ECU Thom had hooked up earlier.

"You didn't *spend* the time. Big difference. Who're you calling?"

"Berger."

"No, you're not," Thom said. "It's late."

"I've been reading clocks for a while now," Rhyme replied coolly. "Call him. He's staying at the Plaza."

"No."

"I asked you to call him."

"Here." The aide slapped a slip of paper down on the far edge of the table but Rhyme read it easily. God may have taken much from Lincoln Rhyme but He'd given him the eyesight of a young man. He went through the process of dialing with his cheek on the control stalk. It was easier than he'd thought but he purposely took a long time and muttered as he did it. Infuriatingly, Thom ignored him and went downstairs.

Berger wasn't in his hotel room. Rhyme disconnected, mad that he wasn't able to slam the phone down.

"Problem?" Sellitto asked.

"No," Rhyme grumbled.

Where is he? Rhyme thought testily. It *was* late. Berger ought to be at his hotel room by now. Rhyme was stabbed with an odd feeling—jealousy that *his* death doctor was out helping someone else die.

Sellitto suddenly chuckled softly. Rhyme looked up. The cop was eating a candy bar. He'd forgotten that junk food'd been the staple of the big man's diet when they were working together. "I was thinking. Remember Bennie Ponzo?"

"The OC Task Force ten, twelve years ago?"

"Yeah."

Rhyme had enjoyed organized-crime work. The perps were pros. The crime scenes challenging. And the vics were rarely innocent.

"Who was that?" Mel Cooper asked.

"Hitman outa Bay Ridge," Sellitto said. "Remember after we booked him, the candy sandwich?"

Rhyme laughed, nodding.

"What's the story?" Cooper asked.

Sellitto said, "Okay, we're down at Central Booking, Lincoln and me and a couple other guys. And Bennie, remember, he was a big guy, he was sitting all hunched over, feeling his stomach. All of a sudden he goes, 'Yo, I'm hungry, I wanna candy sandwich.' And we're like looking at each other and I go, 'What's a candy sandwich?'' And he looks at me like I'm from Mars and goes, 'What the fuck you think it is? Ya take a Hershey bar, ya put it between two slices of bread and ya eat it. That's a fucking candy sandwich.'"

They laughed. Sellitto held out the bar to Cooper, who shook his head, then to Rhyme, who felt a sudden impulse to take a bite. It'd been over a year since he'd had chocolate. He avoided food like that—sugar, candy. Troublesome food. The little things about life were the biggest burdens, the ones that saddened and exhausted you the most. Okay, you'll never scuba-dive or hike the Alps. So what? A lot of people don't. But everybody brushes their teeth. And goes to the dentist, gets a filling, takes the train home. Everybody picks a hunk of peanut from out behind a molar when nobody's looking.

Everybody except Lincoln Rhyme.

He shook his head to Sellitto and drank a long swallow of

Scotch. His eyes slid back to the computer screen, recalling the goodbye letter to Blaine he'd been composing when Sellitto and Banks had interrupted him that morning. There were some other letters he wanted to write as well.

The one he was putting off writing was to Pete Taylor, the spinal cord trauma specialist. Most of the time Taylor and Rhyme had talked not about the patient's condition but about death. The doctor was an ardent opponent of euthanasia. Rhyme felt he owed him a letter to explain why he'd decided to go ahead with the suicide.

And Amelia Sachs?

The Portable's Daughter would get a note too, he decided.

Crips are generous, crips are kind, crips are iron . . .

Crips are nothing if not forgiving.

> Dear Amelia:
> My Dear Amelia:
> Amelia:
> Dear Officer Sachs:
>
> Inasmuch as we have had the pleasure of working together, I would like to take this opportunity to state that although I consider you a betraying judas, I've forgiven you. Furthermore I wish you well in your future career as a kisser of the media's ass. . . .

"What's her story, Lon? Sachs."

"Aside from the fact she's got a ball-buster temper I didn't know about?"

"She married?"

"Naw. A face and bod like that, you'da thought some good-lookin' hunk woulda snagged her by now. But she doesn't even date. We heard she was going with somebody a few years ago but she never talks about it." He lowered his voice. "Lipstick lesbos's what the rumor is. But I don't know from that—*my* social life's picking up women at the laundromat on Saturday night. Hey, it works. What can I say?"

You'll have to learn to give up the dead. . . .

Rhyme was thinking about the look in her face when he'd said that to her. What was that all about? Then he grew angry with himself for spending any time thinking about her. And took a good slug of Scotch.

The doorbell rang, then footsteps on the stairs. Rhyme and Sellitto glanced toward the doorway. The sound was from the boots of a tall man, wearing city-issue jodhpurs and a blue helmet. One of NYPD's elite mounted police. He handed a bulky envelope to Sellitto and returned down the stairs.

The detective opened it. "Lookit what we got here." He poured the contents onto the table. Rhyme glanced up with irritation. Three or four dozen plastic evidence bags, all labeled. Each contained a patch of cellophane from the packages of veal shanks they'd sent ESU to buy.

"A note from Haumann." He read: "'To: L. Rhyme. L. Sellitto. From: B. Haumann, TSRF.'"

"What's 'at?" Cooper asked. The police department is a nest of initials and acronyms. RMP—remote mobile patrol—is a squad car. IED—improvised explosive device—is a bomb. But TSRF was a new one. Rhyme shrugged.

Sellitto continued to read, chuckling. "'Tactical Supermarket Response Force. Re: Veal shanks. Citywide search discovered forty-six subjects, all of which were apprehended and neutralized with minimal force. We read them their rights and have transported same to detention facility in the kitchen of Officer T. P. Giancarlo's mother. Upon completion of interrogation, a half-dozen suspects will be transferred to your custody. Heat at 350 for thirty minutes.'"

Rhyme laughed. Then sipped more Scotch, savoring the flavor. This was one thing he'd miss, the smoky breath of the liquor. (Though in the peace of senseless sleep, how could you miss anything? Just like evidence, take away the baseline standard and you have nothing to judge the loss against; you're safe for all eternity.)

Cooper fanned out some of the samples. "Forty-six samples of the cello. One from each chain and the major independents."

Rhyme gazed at the samples: The odds were good for class identification. Individuation of cellophane'd be a bitch—the scrap found on the veal bone clue wouldn't of course exactly match one of these. But, because parent companies buy identical supplies for all their stores, you might learn in which *chain* 823 bought the veal and narrow down the neighborhoods he might live in. Maybe he should call the Bureau's physical-evidence team and—

No, no. Remember: it's their *fuck-ing* case now.

Rhyme commanded Cooper, "Bundle them up and ship them to our federal brethren."

Rhyme tried shutting down his computer and hit the wrong button with his sometimes ornery ring finger. The speakerphone came on with a loud wail of squelch.

"Shit," Rhyme muttered darkly. "Fucking machinery."

Uneasy with Rhyme's sudden anger, Sellitto glanced at his glass and joked, "Hell, Linc, Scotch this good's supposed to make you mellow."

"Got news," Thom replied sourly. "He *is* mellow."

He parked close to the huge drainpipe.

Climbing from the cab he could smell the fetid water, slimy and ripe. They were in a cul-de-sac leading to the wide runoff pipe that ran from the West Side Highway down to the Hudson River. No one could see them here.

The bone collector walked to the back of the cab, enjoying the sight of his elderly captive. Just like he'd enjoyed staring at the girl he'd tied in front of the steam pipe. And the wiggling hand by the railroad tracks early this morning.

Gazing at the frightened eyes. The man was thinner than he'd thought. Grayer. Hair disheveled.

Old in the flesh but young in the bone . . .

The man cowered away from him, arms folded defensively across his narrow chest.

Opening the door, the bone collector pressed his pistol against the man's breastbone.

"Please," his captive whispered, his voice quavering. "I don't have much money but you can have it all. We can go to an ATM. I'll—"

"Get out."

"Please don't hurt me."

The bone collector gestured with his head. The frail man looked around miserably then scooted forward. He stood beside the car, cowering, his arms still crossed, shivering despite the relentless heat.

"Why are you doing this?"

The bone collector stepped back and fished the cuffs from his pocket. Because he wore the thick gloves it took a few seconds to find the chrome links. As he dug them out he thought he saw a four-rigger tacking up the Hudson. The opposing current here wasn't as strong as in the East River, where sailing ships had a hell of a time making their way from the East, Montgomery and Out Ward wharves north. He squinted. No, wait—it wasn't a sailboat, it was just a cabin cruiser, Yuppies lounging on the long front deck.

As he reached forward with the cuffs, the man grabbed his captor's shirt, gripped it hard. "Please. I was going to the hospital. That's why I flagged you down. I've been having chest pains."

"Shut up."

And the man suddenly reached for the bone collector's face, the liver-spotted hands gripping his neck and shoulder and squeezing hard. A jolt of pain radiated from the spot where the yellow nails dug into him. With a burst of temper, he pulled his victim's hands off and cuffed him roughly.

Slapping a piece of tape on the man's mouth, the bone collector dragged him down the gravel embankment toward the mouth of the pipe, four feet in diameter. He stopped, examined the old man.

It'd be so easy to take you down to the bone.

The bone . . . Touching it. Hearing it.

He lifted the man's hand. The terrified eyes gazed back, his lips trembling. The bone collector caressed the man's fingers, squeezed the phalanges between his own (wished he could take his glove off but didn't dare). Then he lifted the man's palm and pressed it hard against his own ear.

"What?—"

His left hand curled around his mystified captive's little finger and slowly pulled until he heard the deep *thonk* of brittle bone snapping. A satisfying sound. The man screamed, a muted cry stuttering through the tape. And slumped to the ground.

The bone collector pulled him upright and led the stumbling

man into the mouth of the pipe. He prodded the man forward.

They emerged underneath the old, rotting pier. It was a disgusting place, strewn with the decomposed bodies of animals and fish, trash on the wet rocks, a gray-green sludge of kelp. A mound of seaweed rose and fell in the water, humping like a fat lover. Despite the evening heat in the rest of the city, down here it was cold as a March day.

Señor Ortega . . .

He lowered the man into the river, cuffed him to a pier post, ratcheting the bracelet tight around his wrist again. The captive's grayish face was about three feet above the surface of the water. The bone collector walked carefully over the slick rocks to the drainpipe. He turned and paused for a moment, watching, watching. He hadn't cared much whether the constables found the others or not. Hanna, the woman in the taxi. But this one . . . The bone collector hoped they didn't find him in time. Indeed, that they didn't find him at all. So he could come back in a month or two and see if the clever river had scrubbed the skeleton clean.

Back on the gravel drive he pulled the mask off and left the clues to the next scene not far from where he'd parked. He was angry, furious at the constables, and so this time he hid the clues. And he also included a special surprise. Something he'd been saving for them. The bone collector returned to the taxi.

The breeze was gentle, carrying the fragrance of the sour river with it. And the rustle of grass and, as always in the city, the *shushhhh* of traffic.

Like emery paper on bone.

He stopped and listened to this sound, head cocked as he looked out over the billion lights of the buildings, stretching to the north like an oblong galaxy. It was then that a woman, running fast, emerged on a jogging path beside the drainpipe and nearly collided with him.

In purple shorts and top, the thin brunette danced out of his way. Gasping, she stopped, flicked sweat from her face. In good shape—taut muscles—but not pretty. A hook of a nose, broad lips, blotchy skin.

But beneath that . . .

"You're not supposed . . . You shouldn't park here. This's a jogging path . . ."

Her words fading and fear rising into her eyes, which flicked from his face to the taxi to the wad of ski mask in his hand.

She knew who he was. He smiled, noting her remarkably pronounced clavicle.

Her right ankle shifted slightly, ready to take her weight when she sprinted away. But he got her first. He ducked low, to tackle her, and when she gave a fast scream and dropped her arms to block him the bone collector straightened up fast from his feint and swung his elbow into her temple. There was a crack like a snapping belt.

She went down on the gravel, hard, and lay still. Horrified, the bone collector dropped to his knees and cradled her head. He moaned, "No, no, no . . ." Furious with himself for striking so hard, sick at heart that he might've broken what seemed to be a perfect skull beneath the tentacles of stringy hair and the unremarkable face.

Amelia Sachs finished another COC card and took a break. She paused, found a vending machine and bought a paper cup of vile coffee. She returned to the windowless office, looked over the evidence she'd gathered.

She felt a curious fondness for the macabre collection. Maybe because of what she'd gone through to collect it—her fiery joints ached and she still shuddered when she thought of the buried body at the first scene this morning, the bloody branch of a hand, and of T.J. Colfax's dangling flesh. Until today physical evidence hadn't meant anything to her. PE was boring lectures on drowsy spring afternoons at the academy. PE was math, it was charts and graphs, it was science. It was dead.

No, Amie Sachs was going to be a people cop. Walking beats, dissing back the dissers, outing druggies. Spreading respect for the law—like her father. Or pounding it into them. Like handsome Nick Carelli, a five-year vet, the star of Street Crimes, grinning at the world with his *yo-you-gotta-problem?* smile.

That's just who *she* was going to be.

She looked at the crisp brown leaf she'd found in the stockyard tunnel. One of the clues 823 had left for them. And here was the underwear too. She remembered that the feebies had snagged the PE before Cooper'd finished the test on the . . . what was that machine? The chromatograph? She wondered what the liquid soaking the cotton was.

But these thoughts led to Lincoln Rhyme and he was the one person she didn't want to think about just now.

She began to voucher the rest of the PE. Each COC card had a series of blank lines that would list the custodians of the evidence, in sequence, from the initial discovery at the scene all the way to trial. Sachs had transported evidence several times and her name had appeared on COC cards. But this was the first time *A. Sachs, NYPD 5885* had occupied the first slot.

Once again she lifted the plastic bag containing the leaf.

He'd actually touched it. *Him.* The man who'd killed T. J. Colfax. Who'd held Monelle Gerger's pudgy arm and cut deep into it. Who was out searching for another vic right now—if he hadn't already snatched one.

Who'd buried that poor man this morning, waving for mercy he never got.

She thought of Locard's Exchange Principle. People coming into contact, each transferring something to the other. Something big, something small. Most likely they didn't even know what.

Had something of 823 come off on this leaf? A cell of skin? A dot of sweat? It was a stunning thought. She felt a thrill of excitement, of fear as if the killer were right here, in this tiny airless room with her.

Back to the COC cards. For ten minutes she filled them out and was just finishing the last one when the door burst open, startling her. She spun around.

Fred Dellray stood in the doorway, his green jacket abandoned, his starched shirt rumpled. Fingers pinching the cigarette behind his ear. "Step inside a minute'r two, officer. It's payoff time. Thought you might wanna be there."

Sachs followed him down the short corridor, two steps behind his lope.

"The AFIS results're comin' in," Dellray said.

The war room was even busier than before. Jacketless agents

hovered over desks. They were armed with their on-duty weapons—the big Sig-Sauer and Smith & Wesson automatics, 10mm and .45s. A half-dozen agents were clustered around the computer terminal beside the Opti-Scan.

Sachs hadn't liked the way Dellray'd taken the case away from them, but she had to admit that beneath the slick-talking hipster Dellray was one hell of a good cop. Agents—young and old—would come up to him with questions and he'd patiently answer them. He'd yank a phone from the cradle and cajole or berate whoever was on the other end to get him what he needed. Sometimes, he'd look up across the bustling room and roar, "We gonna nail this prick-dick? Yep, you betcha we are." And the straight-arrows'd look at him uneasily but with the obvious thought in mind that if anybody could nail him it'd be Dellray.

"Here, it's coming in now," an agent called.

Dellray barked, "I want open lines to New York, Jersey and Connecticut DMVs. And Corrections and Parole. INS too. Tell 'em to stand by for an incoming ID request. Put everything else on hold."

Agents peeled off and began making phone calls.

The computer screen filled.

She couldn't believe that Dellray actually crossed his stickish fingers.

Utter silence throughout the room.

"Got him!" the agent at the keyboard shouted.

"Ain't no unsub anymore," Dellray sang melodically, bending over the screen. "Listen up, people. We gotta name: Victor Pietrs. Born here, 1948. His parents were from Belgrade. So, we got a Serbian connection. ID brought to us courtesy of New York D of C. Convictions for drugs, assault, one with a deadly. Two sentences served. Okay, listen to this— psychiatric history, committed three times on involuntary orders. Intake at Bellevue and Manhattan Psychiatric. Last release date three years ago. LKA Washington Heights."

He looked up. "Who's got the phone companies?"

Several agents raised their hands.

"Make the calls," Dellray ordered.

An interminable five minutes.

"Not there. No current New York Telephone listing."

"Nothing in Jersey," another agent echoed.

"Negative, Connecticut."

"Fuck-all," Dellray muttered. "Mix the names up. Try variations. An' lookit phone-service accounts canceled in the past year for nonpayment."

For several minutes voices rose and fell like the tide.

Dellray paced manically and Sachs understood why his frame was so scrawny.

Suddenly an agent shouted, "Found him!"

Everyone turned to look.

"I'm on with NY DMV," another agent called. "They've got him. It's coming through now. . . . He's a cabbie. Got a hack license."

"Why don' that s'prise me," Dellray muttered. "Shoulda thoughta that. Where's home sweet home?"

"Morningside Heights. A block from the river." The agent wrote down the address and held it aloft as Dellray swept past and took it. "Know the neighborhood. Pretty deserted. Lotta druggies."

Another agent typed the address into his computer terminal. "Okay, checking deeds . . . Property's an old house. A bank's got title. He must be renting."

"You want HRT?" one agent called across the bustling room. "I got Quantico on the line."

"No time," Dellray announced. "Use the field office SWAT. Get 'em suited up."

Sachs asked, "And what about the next victim?"

"What next victim?"

"He's already taken somebody. He knows we've had the clues for an hour or two. He'd've planted the vic awhile ago. He had to."

"No reports of anybody missing," the agent said. "And if he did snatch 'em they're probably at his house."

"No, they wouldn't be."

"Why not?"

"They'd pick up too much PE," she said. "Lincoln Rhyme said he has a safe house."

"Well, then we'll get him to tell us where they are."

Another agent said, "We can be real persuasive."

"Let's move it," Dellray called. "Yo, ever'body, let's thank

Officer Amelia Sachs here. She's the one found that print and lifted it."

She was blushing. Could feel it, hated it. But she couldn't help herself. As she glanced down she noticed strange lines on her shoes. Squinting, she realized she was still wearing the rubber bands.

When she looked up she saw a room full of unsmiling federal agents checking weapons and heading for the door as they glanced at her. The same way, she thought, lumberjacks look at logs.

NINETEEN

In 1911 a tragedy of massive dimension befell our fair city. On March 25, hundreds of industrious young women were hard at work in a garment factory, one of the many, known notoriously as "sweat-shops," in Greenwich Village in down-town Manhattan.

So enamored of profits were the owners of this company that they denied the poor girls in their employ even the rudimentary facilities that slaves might enjoy. They believed the laborers could not be trusted to make expeditious visits to the rest-room facilities and so kept the doors to the cutting and sewing rooms under lock and key.

The bone collector was driving back to his building. He passed a squad car but he kept his eyes forward and the constables never noticed him.

On the day in question a fire started on the eighth floor of the building and within minutes swept through the factory, from which the young employees tried to flee. They were unable to escape, however, owing to the chained state of the door. Many died on the spot and many more, some horribly afire, leapt into the air a hundred feet above the cobblestones and died from the collision with unyielding Mother Earth.

There numbered 146 victims of the Triangle Shirtwaist fire. The police, however, were confounded by the inability to locate one of the victims, a young woman, Esther Weinraub, whom several witnesses had seen leap in desperation from the eighth floor window. None of the other girls who similarly leapt survived the fall. Was it possible that she, miraculously, had? For when the bodies were laid out in the street for bereaved

*family members to identify, poor Miss Weinraub's was not to
be found.*

*Reports began to circulate of a ghoul, a man seen carting
off a large bundle from the scene of the fire. So incensed were
the constables that someone might violate the sacred remains
of an innocent young woman that they put on a still search
for the man.*

*After several weeks, their diligent efforts bore fruit. Two
residents of Greenwich Village reported seeing a man leaving
the scene of the fire and carrying a heavy bundle "like a
carpet" over his shoulder. The constables picked up his
trail and tracked him to the West Side of the city, where
they interviewed neighbors and learned that the man fit the
description of James Schneider, who was still at large.*

*They narrowed their search to a decrepit abode in an alley
in Hell's Kitchen, not far from the 60th Street stock-yards. As
they entered the alleyway they were greeted with a revolting
stench . . .*

He was now driving past the very site of the Triangle
fire itself—maybe he'd even been subconsciously prompted
to come here. The Asch Building—the ironic name of the
structure that had housed the doomed factory—was gone and
the site was now a part of NYU. *Then and now* . . . The bone
collector would not have been surprised to see white-bloused
working girls, trailing sparks and faint smoke, tumbling
gracefully to their deaths, falling around him like snow.

*Upon breaking into Schneider's habitation, the authorities
found a sight that sent even the most seasoned of them reeling
with horror. The body of wretched Esther Weinraub—(or what
remained of it)—was found in the basement. Schneider was
bent on completing the work of the tragic fire and was slowly
removing the woman's flesh through means too shocking to
recount here.*

*A search of this loathsome place revealed a secret room,
off the basement, filled with bones that had been stripped clean
of flesh.*

*Beneath Schneider's bed, a constable found a diary, in
which the madman chronicled his history of evil. "Bone"—
(Schneider wrote)—"is the ultimate core of a human being.
It alters not, deceives not, yields not. Once the facade of our*

*intemperate ways of the flesh, the flaws of the lesser Races
and the weaker gender, are burnt or boiled away, we are—
all of us—noble bone. Bone does not lie. It is immortal."*

The lunatic writings set forth a chronicle of gruesom
experimentation as he sought to ascertain the most effectiv
way of cleansing his victims of their flesh. He tried boiling th
bodies, burning them, rendering with lye, staking them out fo
animals, and immersing them in water.

But one method above all he favored for this macabre sport
"*It is best, I have concluded*"—(his diary continues)—"*simply
to bury the body in rich earth and let Nature do the tediou
work. This is the most time-consuming method but the leas
likely to arouse suspicion as the odors are kept to a minimum
I prefer to inter the individuals while still alive, though why
that might be I cannot say with any certainty.*"

In his heretofore secret room three more bodies wer
discovered in this very condition. The splayed hands an
agog faces of the poor victims attest that they were indee
alive when Schneider piled the last shovelful of dirt upon thei
tormented crowns.

It was these dark designs that prompted the journalists o
the day to christen Schneider with the name by which be wa
forever after known:—"*The Bone Collector.*"

He drove on, his mind returning to the woman in the trunk
Esther Weinraub. Her thin elbow, her collarbone delicate a
a bird's wing. He sped the cab forward, even risked runnin
two red lights. He couldn't wait much longer.

———

"I'm not tired," Rhyme snapped.

"Tired or not, you need to rest."

"No, I need another drink."

Black suitcases lined the wall, awaiting the help of officer
from the Twentieth Precinct to transport them back to the IRI
lab. Mel Cooper was carting a microscope case downstairs
Lon Sellitto was still sitting in the rattan chair but he wasn'
saying much. Just coming to the obvious conclusion tha
Lincoln Rhyme was not a mellow drunk at all.

Thom said, "I'm sure your blood pressure's up. You
need rest."

"I need a drink."

Goddamn you, Amelia Sachs, Rhyme thought. And didn't know why.

"You should give it up. Drinking's never been any good for you."

Well, I'm *am* giving it up, Rhyme responded silently. For good. Monday. And no twelve-step plan for me; it's a one-stepper.

"Pour me another drink," he ordered.

Not really wanting one.

"No."

"Pour me a drink *now*!" Rhyme snapped.

"No way."

"Lon, would you please pour me another drink?"

"I—"

Thom said, "He doesn't get any more. When he's in a mood like this he's insufferable and we're not going to put up with him."

"You're going to withhold something from me? I could fire you."

"Fire away."

"Crip abuse! I'll get you indicted. Arrest him, Lon."

"Lincoln," Sellitto said placatingly.

"Arrest him!"

The detective was taken aback by the viciousness of Rhyme's words.

"Hey, buddy, maybe you should go a little light," Sellitto said.

"Oh, Christ," Rhyme groaned. He started to moan loudly.

Sellitto blurted, "What is it?" Thom was silent, looking on cautiously.

"My liver." Rhyme's face broke into a cruel grin. "Cirrhosis probably."

Thom swung around, furious. "I will *not* put up with this crap. Okay?"

"No, It's not oh-kay—"

A woman's voice, from the doorway: "We don't have much time."

"—at all."

Amelia Sachs walked into the room, glanced at the empty

tables. Rhyme felt spittle on his lip. He was overwhelmed with fury. Because she saw the drool. Because he wore a crisp white shirt he'd changed into just for her. And because he wanted desperately to be alone, forever, alone in the dark of motionless peace—where he was king. Not king for a day. But king for eternity.

The spit tickled. He cramped his already sore neck muscles trying to wipe his lip dry. Thom deftly swiped a Kleenex from a box and dried his boss's mouth and chin.

"Officer Sachs," Thom said. "Welcome. A shining example of maturity. We aren't seeing much of *that* right at the moment."

She wasn't wearing her hat and her navy blouse was open at the collar. Her long red hair tumbled to her shoulders. Nobody'd have any trouble differentiating *that* hair under a comparison 'scope.

"Mel let me in," she said, nodding toward the stairs.

"Isn't it past your bedtime, Sachs?"

Thom tapped a shoulder. *Behave yourself*, the gesture meant.

"I was just at the federal building," she said to Sellitto.

"How are our tax dollars doing?"

"They've caught him."

"*What?*" Sellitto asked. "Just like that? Jesus. They know about it downtown?"

"Perkins called the mayor. The guy's a cabbie. He was born here but his father's Serbian. So they're thinking he's trying to get even with the UN, or something. Got a yellow sheet. Oh, and a history of mental problems too. Dellray and feebie SWAT're on their way there right now."

"How'd they do it?" Rhyme asked. "Betcha it was the fingerprint."

She nodded.

"I suspected that would figure prominently. And, tell me how concerned were they about the next victim?"

"They're concerned," she said evenly. "But mostly they want to nail the unsub."

"Well, that's *their* nature. And let me guess. They're figuring they'll sweat the location of the vic out of him after they take him down."

"You got it."

"That may take some doing," Rhyme said. "I'll venture that opinion without the benefit of our Dr Dobyns and the Behavioral mavens. So, a change of heart, Amelia? Why'd you come back?"

"Because whether Dellray collars him or not I don't think we have time to wait. To save the next vic, I mean."

"Oh, but we're dismantled, haven't you heard? Shut down, done gone outa business." Rhyme was looking in the dark computer screen, trying to see if his hair had stayed combed.

"You giving up?" she asked.

"Officer," Sellitto began, "even if we wanted to do somethin' we don't have any of the PE. That's the only link—"

"I've got it."

"What?"

"All of it. It's downstairs in the RRV."

The detective glanced out the window.

Sachs continued, "From last scene. From all the scenes."

"You have it?" Rhyme asked. "How?"

But Sellitto was laughing. "She 'jacked it, Lincoln. Gawdamn!"

"Dellray doesn't need it," Sachs pointed out. "Except for the trial. They've got the unsub, we'll save the victim. Works out nice, hm?"

"But Mel Cooper just left."

"Naw, he's downstairs. I asked him to wait." Sachs crossed her arms. She glanced at the clock. After eleven. "We don't have much time," she repeated.

His eyes too were on the clock. Lord, he was tired. Thom was right; he'd been awake longer than in years. But, he was surprised—no, *shocked*—to find, that, while he might have been furious or embarrassed or stabbed with heartless frustration today, the passing minutes had not lain like hot, unbearable weights on his soul. As they had for the past three and a half years.

"Well, church mice in heaven." Rhyme barked a laugh. "Thom? *Thom!* We need coffee. On the double. Sachs, get those cello samples to the lab along with the Polaroid of the bit Mel lifted from the veal bone. I want a polarization-comparison report in an hour. And none of this 'most probably' crap. I want an answer—*which* grocery chain did our unsub buy the veal bone at. And get that little shadow of yours back here, Lon. The one named after the baseball player."

The black vans sped through side streets.

This was a more circuitous route to the perp's location but Dellray knew what he was doing; anti-terror operations were supposed to avoid major city streets, which were often monitored by accomplices. Dellray, in the back of the lead van, tightened the Velcro strap on the body armor. They were less than ten minutes away.

He looked at the failing apartments, the trash-filled lots as they sped along. The last time he'd been in this decrepit neighborhood he'd been Rastafarian Peter Haile Thomas from Queens. He'd bought 137 pounds of cocaine from a shriveled little Puerto Rican, who decided at the last minute to 'jack his buyer. He took Dellray's buy-and-bust money and aimed a gun at Dellray's groin, pulling the trigger as calmly as if he were picking vegetables at the A&P. Click, click, click. Misfire. Toby Dolittle and the backup team took the fucker and his minders down before the scumbag found his other piece, leaving one shook-up Dellray to reflect on the irony of nearly getting killed because the perp truly bought the agent's performance—that he was a dealer not a cop.

"ETA, four minutes," the driver called.

For some reason Dellray's thoughts flipped to Lincoln Rhyme. He regretted he'd been such a shit when he took over the case. But there hadn't been much choice. Sellitto was a bulldog and Polling was a psycho—though Dellray could handle them. Rhyme was the one who made him uneasy. Sharp as a razor (hell, it *had* been his team that found Pietrs's print, even if they didn't jump on it as fast as they should've). In the old days, before his accident, you couldn't beat Rhyme if he didn't want to get beat. And you couldn't fool him either.

Now, Rhyme was a busted toy. It was a sad thing what could happen to a man, how you could die and still be alive. Dellray had walked into his room—his *bedroom*, no less—and hit him hard. Harder than he needed to.

Maybe he'd call. He could—

"Show time," the driver called, and Dellray forgot all about Lincoln Rhyme.

The vans turned onto the street where Pietrs lived. Most of the other streets they'd passed had been filled with sweating residents, clutching beer bottles and cigarettes, hoping for a breath or two of cool air. But this one was dark, empty.

The vans cruised slowly to a stop. Two dozen agents climbed out, in black tactical outfits, carrying their H&Ks equipped with muzzle lights and laser sights. Two homeless men stared at them; one quickly hid his bottle of Colt 44 malt liquor under his shirt.

Dellray gazed at a window in Pietrs's building; it gave off a faint yellow glow.

The driver backed the first van into a shadowy parking space and whispered to Dellray, "It's Perkins." Tapping his headset. "He's got the director on the horn. They want to know who's leading the assault."

"I am," snapped the Chameleon. He turned to his team. "I want surveillance across the street and in the alleys. Snipers, here, there and there. An' I want ever'body in place fi' minutes 'go. Are we all together on that?"

Down the stairs, the old wood creaking.

His arm around her, he guided the woman, half-conscious from the blow to her head, into the basement. At the foot of the stairs, he shoved her to the dirt floor and gazed down at her. Esther . . .

Her eyes rose to meet his. Hopeless, begging. He didn't notice. All he saw was her body. He began to remove her clothing, the purple jogging outfit. It was unthinkable that a woman would actually go outside in this day and age wearing what was no more than, well, undergarments. He hadn't thought that Esther Weinraub was a whore. She'd been a working girl, stitching shirts, five for a penny.

The bone collector observed how her collarbone showed at her throat. And where some other man might glance over her breasts and dark areolae *he* stared at the indentation at the manubrium and the ribs blossoming from it like spider's legs.

"What're you doing?" she asked, groggy from the blow to her head.

The bone collector looked her over carefully but what he saw wasn't a young, anorectic woman, nose too broad, lips too full, with skin like dirty sand. He saw beneath those imperfections the perfect beauty of her *structure*.

He caressed her temple, stroked it gently. Don't let it be cracked, please. . . .

She coughed and her nostrils flared—the fumes *were* very strong down here though he hardly noticed them anymore.

"Don't hurt me again," she whispered, her head lolling. "Just don't hurt me. Please."

He took the knife from his pocket and bent down, cut her underwear off. She looked down at her naked body.

"You want that?" she said breathlessly. "Okay, you can fuck me. Okay."

The pleasure of the flesh, he thought . . . it just doesn't come close.

He pulled her to her feet and madly she pushed away from him and began stumbling toward a small doorway in the corner of the basement. Not running, not really trying to escape. Just sobbing, reaching out a hand, weaving toward the door.

The bone collector watched her, entranced by her slow, pathetic gait.

The doorway, which had once opened onto a coal chute, now led to a narrow tunnel that connected to the basement of the abandoned building next door.

Esther struggled to the metal door and pulled it open. She climbed inside.

It was no more than a minute later that he heard the wailing scream. Followed by a breathless, wrenching, "God, no, no, no . . ." Other words too, lost in her boiling howls of terror.

Then she was coming back through the tunnel, moving faster now, whipping her hands around her, as if she was trying to shake off what she'd just seen.

Come to me, Esther.

Stumbling over the dirt floor, sobbing.

Come to me.

Running straight into his patient, waiting arms, which

wrapped around her. He squeezed the woman tight as a lover, felt that marvelous collarbone beneath his fingers, and slowly dragged the frantic woman back toward the tunnel doorway.

TWENTY

The phases of the moon, the leaf, the damp underwear, dirt. Their team was back in Rhyme's bedroom—all except Polling and Haumann; it was straining NYPD loyalty to bring captains in on what was, no two ways about it, an unauthorized operation.

"You G-C'd the liquid in the underwear, right, Mel?"

"Have to do it again. They shut us down before we got the results."

He blotted out a sample and injected it into the chromatograph. As he ran the machine Sachs jockeyed to look at the peaks and valleys of the profile appearing on the screen. Like a stock index. Rhyme realized she was standing close to him, as if she'd edged near when he wasn't looking. She spoke in a low voice. "I was . . ."

"Yes?"

"I was blunter than I meant to be. Before, I mean. I have a temper. I don't know where I got it from. But I have it."

"You were right," Rhyme said.

They easily held each other's eyes and Rhyme thought of the times he and Blaine had had serious discussions. As they talked they always focused on an object between them—one of the ceramic horses she collected, a book, a nearly empty bottle of Merlot or Chardonnay.

He said, "I work scenes differently than most criminalists. I needed somebody without any preconceived ideas. But I also needed somebody with a mind of her own."

The contradictory qualities we seek in that elusive perfect lover. Strength and vulnerability, in equal measures.

"When I talked to Commissioner Eckert," she said, "it was just to get my transfer through. That's all I wanted. It never occurred to me that word'd get back to the feds and they'd take the case away."

"I know that."

"I still let my temper go. I'm sorry for that."

"Don't backpedal, Sachs. I need somebody to tell me I'm a jerk when I act like one. Thom does. That's why I love him."

"Don't get sentimental on me, Lincoln," Thom called from across the room.

Rhyme continued, "Nobody else ever tells me to go to hell. They're always walking on eggshells. I hate it."

"It doesn't seem like there've been many people around here to say much of anything to you lately."

After a moment he said, "That's true."

On the screen of the chromatograph-spectrometer the peaks and valleys stopped moving and became one of nature's infinite signatures. *Mel* Cooper tapped on the computer keys and read the results. "Water, diesel oil, phosphate, sodium, trace minerals . . . No idea what it means."

What, Rhyme wondered, was the message? The underwear itself? The liquid? He said, "Let's move on. I want to see the dirt."

Sachs brought him the bag. It contained pinkish sand, laced with chunks of clay and pebbles.

"Bull's liver," he announced. "Rock-and-sand mixture. Found just above the bedrock in Manhattan. Sodium silicate mixed in?"

Cooper ran the chromatograph. "Yep. Plenty of it."

"Then we're looking for a downtown location within fifty yards of the water—" Rhyme laughed at the astonished gaze on Sachs's face. "It's not magic, Sachs. I've just done my homework, that's all. Contractors mix sodium silicate with bull's liver to stabilize the earth when they dig foundations in deep-bedrock areas near the water. That means it's got to be downtown. Now, let's take a look at the leaf."

She held up the bag.

"No clue what it is," Rhyme said. "I don't think I've ever seen one like that. Not in Manhattan."

"I've got a list of horticulture web sites," Cooper said, staring at his computer screen. "I'll do some surfing."

Rhyme himself had spent some time on-line, cruising the Internet. As it had with books, movies and posters, his interest in the cyberworld had eventually paled. Perhaps because so much of his own world was virtual, the net was, in the end, a forlorn place for Lincoln Rhyme.

Cooper's screen flicked and danced as he clicked on hyperlinks and disappeared deeper into the web. "I'm downloading some files. Should take ten, twenty minutes."

Rhyme said, "All right. The rest of the clues Sachs found . . . Not the planted ones. The others. They might tell us about where he's been. Let's look at our secret weapon, Mel."

"Secret weapon?" Sachs asked.

"The trace evidence."

Special Agent Fred Dellray had put together a ten-man entry operation. Two teams plus search and surveillance. The flak-jacketed agents stood in the bushes, sweating madly. Across the street, upstairs in an abandoned brownstone, the S&S team had their Big Ears and video infrareds trained on the perp's house.

The three snipers, with their big Remingtons strapped, loaded and locked, lay prone on rooftops. Their binoculared spotters crouched beside them like Lamaze coaches.

Dellray—wearing an FBI windbreaker and jeans instead of his Leprechaun-green outfit—listened through his clip-on ear-phone.

"Surveillance to Command. We've got infrared on the basement. Somebody moving down there."

"What'sa view like?" Dellray asked.

"No view. Windows're too dirty."

"He all by his humble self? Maybe got a vic with him?" Knowing somehow that Officer Sachs was probably right; that he'd already 'napped somebody else now.

"Can't tell. We've just got motion and heat."

Dellray had sent other officers around to the sides of the house. They reported in. "No sign of anyone on the first or second floor. Garage is locked."

"Snipers?" Dellray asked. "Report."

"Shooter One to Command. I've acquired on front door. Over."

The others were covering the hallway and a room on the first floor. "Loaded and locked," they radioed in.

Dellray drew his large automatic.

"Okay, we got paper," Dellray said. Meaning a warrant. They wouldn't have to knock. "Lessgo! Teams one and two, deploy, deploy, deploy."

The first team took out the front door with a battering ram while the second used the slightly more civilized approach of breaking in the back-door window and unlocking the dead bolt. They streamed inside, Dellray following the last of Team One's officers into the old, filthy house. The smell of rotting flesh was overwhelming and Dellray, no stranger to crime scenes, swallowed hard, struggling to keep from vomiting.

The second team secured the ground floor and then charged up the stairs toward the bedroom while the first sped down the basement stairs, boots thumping loudly on the old wood.

Dellray raced down into the foul-smelling basement. He heard a door being kicked in somewhere below and the shout of, "Don't move! Federal agents. Freeze, freeze, freeze!"

But when he reached the basement doorway he heard the same agent blurt in very different tone, "What the hell's this? Oh, Jesus."

"Fuck," another one called. "That's gross."

"Shit in a flaming pile," Dellray spat out, choking, as he stepped inside. Swallowing hard at the vile smell.

The man's body lay on the floor, leaching black fluid. Throat cut. His dead, glazed eyes stared at the ceiling but his torso seemed to be moving—swelling and shifting. Dellray shuddered; he'd never developed much immunity to the sight of insect infestation. The number of bugs and worms suggested the vic'd been dead for at least three days.

"Why'd we get positive on the infrared?" one agent asked.

Dellray pointed out the rat and mouse teeth marks along the vic's bloated leg and side. "They're around here someplace. We interrupted dinner hour."

"So what happened? One of the vics get *him*?"

"Watcha talkin' about?" Dellray snapped.

"Isn't that him?"

"No, it's not *him*," Dellray exploded, gazing at one particular wound on the corpse.

One of the team was frowning. "Naw, Dellray. This's the guy. We got mug shots. That's Pietrs."

"Of course it's fucking Pietrs. But he ain't the unsub. Don'tcha get it?"

"No? What do you mean?"

It was all clear to him now. "Sumvabitch."

Dellray's phone chirped and made him jump. He flipped it open, listened for a minute. "She did *what*? Oh, like I really need this too. . . . No, we don't have the fucking perp in fucking custody."

He jammed the OFF button, pointed an angry finger at two SWAT agents. "You're coming with me."

"What's up, Dellray?"

"We gonna pay ourselves a visit. And what ain't we gonna be when we do it?" The agents looked at each other, frowning. But Dellray supplied the answer. "We ain't gonna be very nice at all."

———

Mel Cooper shook contents of the envelopes out onto print. Examined the dust with an eye loupe. "Well, there's the brick dust. And some other kind of stone. Marble, I think."

He put a sample on the slide and examined it under the compound 'scope. "Yep, marble. Rose-colored."

"Was there any marble at the stockyard tunnel? Where you found the German girl?"

"None," Sachs responded.

Cooper suggested it might have come from Monelle's residence hall when Unsub 823 grabbed her.

"No, I know the block the Deutsche Haus is in. It's just a converted East Village tenement. The best stone you'd find there'd be polished granite. Maybe, just maybe, it's a fleck of his hidey-hole. Anything notable about it?"

"Chisel marks," Cooper said, bending over the 'scope.

"Ah, good. How clean?"

"Not very. Ragged."

"So an old steam stonecutter?"

"Yes, I'd guess."

"Write, Thom," Rhyme instructed, nodding at the poster. "There's marble in his safe house. And it's old."

"But why do we care about his safe house?" Banks asked, looking at his watch. "The feds'll be there by now."

"You can never have too much information, Banks. Remember that. Now, what else've we got?"

"Another bit of the glove. That red leather. And what's this?" he asked Sachs, holding up a plastic bag containing a plug of wood.

"The sample of the aftershave. Where he brushed up against a post."

"Should I run an olfactory profile?" Cooper wondered.

"Let me smell it first," Rhyme said.

Sachs brought the bag over to him. Inside was a tiny disk of wood. She opened it up and he inhaled the air.

"Brut. How could you miss it? Thom, add that our man uses drugstore cologne."

Cooper announced, "Here's that other hair." The technician mounted it in a comparison 'scope. "Very similar to the one we found earlier. Probably the same source. Oh, hell, Lincoln, for you, I'll say it *is* the same. Brown."

"Are the ends cut or fractured naturally?"

"Cut."

"Good, we're closing in on hair color," Rhyme said.

Thom wrote *brown* just as Sellitto said, "Don't write that!"

"What?"

"Obviously it's not brown," Rhyme continued.

"I thought—"

"It's anything *but* brown. Blond, sandy, black, red . . ."

The detective explained, "'S'an old trick. You go into an alley behind a barbershop, cop some hairs from the garbage. Drop 'em around the scene."

"Oh." Banks filed this somewhere in his enthusiastic brain.

Rhyme said, "Okay. The fiber."

Cooper mounted it in the polarizing 'scope. As he adjusted knobs he said, "Birefringence of .053."

Rhyme blurted, "Nylon 6. What's it look like, Mel?"

"Very coarse. Lobed cross-section. Light gray."

"Carpet."

"Right. I'll check the database." A moment later he looked up from the computer. "It's a Hampstead Textile 118B fiber."

Rhyme exhaled a disgusted sigh.

"What?" Sachs asked.

"The most common trunk liner used by U.S. automakers. Found in over two hundred different makes going back fifteen years. Hopeless . . . Mel, is there anything *on* the fiber? Use the SEM."

The tech cranked up the scanning electron microscope. The screen burst to life with an eerie blue-green glow. The strand of fiber looked like a huge rope.

"Got something here. Crystals. A lot of 'em. They use titanium dioxide to deluster shiny carpet. That might be it."

"Gas it. It's important."

"There's not enough here, Lincoln. I'd have to burn the whole fiber."

"So, burn it."

Sellitto said delicately, "Borrowing federal evidence is one thing. Destroying it? I don't know 'bout that, Lincoln. If there's a trial . . ."

"We have to."

"Oh, man," Banks said.

Sellitto nodded reluctantly and Cooper mounted the sample. The machine hissed. A moment later the screen flickered and columns appeared. "There, that's the long-chained polymer molecule. The nylon. But that small wave, that's something else. Chlorine, detergent . . . It's cleanser."

"Remember," Rhyme said, "the German girl said the car smelled clean. Find out what kind it is."

Cooper ran the information through a brand-name database. "Pfizer Chemicals makes it. It's sold under the name Tidi-Kleen by Baer Automotive Products in Teterboro."

"Perfect!" cried Lincoln Rhyme. "I know the company. They sell in bulk to fleets. Mostly rental-car companies. Our unsub's driving a rental."

"He wouldn't be crazy enough to drive a rental car to crime scenes, would he?" Banks asked.

"It's stolen," Rhyme muttered, as if the young man had asked what was two plus two. "And it'll have stolen tags on it. Is Emma still with us?"

"She's probably home by now."

"Wake her up and have her start canvassing Hertz, Avis, National, Budget for thefts."

"Will do," Sellitto said, though uneasily, perhaps smelling the faint stench of burned federal evidence wafting through the air.

"The footprints?" Sachs asked.

Rhyme looked over the electrostatic impressions she'd lifted.

"Unusual wear on the soles. See the rubbed-down portion on the outsides of each shoe at the ball of the foot?"

"Pigeon-toed?" Thom wondered aloud.

"Possibly but there's no corresponding heel wear, which you'd expect to see." Rhyme studied the prints. "What I think is, he's a reader."

"A reader?"

"Sit in a chair there," Rhyme said to Sachs. "And hunch over the table, pretend you're reading."

She sat, then looked up. "And?"

"Pretend you're turning pages."

She did, several times. Looked up again

"Keep going. You're reading *War and Peace*."

The pages kept turning, her head was bowed. After a moment, without thinking, she crossed her ankles. The outside edges of her shoes were the only part that met the floor.

Rhyme pointed this out. "Put *that* in the profile, Thom. But add a question mark. Now let's look at the friction ridges."

Sachs said she didn't have the good fingerprint, the one they'd ID'd the unsub with. "It's still at the federal building."

But Rhyme wasn't interested in that print. It was the other one, the Kromekote Sachs had lifted from the German girl's skin, he wanted to look at.

"Not scannable," Cooper announced. "Isn't even C grade. I wouldn't give an opinion about this if I had to."

Rhyme said, "I'm not interested in identity. I'm interested

in that line there." It was crescent-shaped and sat right in the middle of the pad of the finger.

"What is it?" Sachs asked.

"A scar, I think," Cooper said. "From an old cut. A bad one. Looks like it went all the way to the bone."

Rhyme thought back to other markings and defects he'd seen on skin over the years. In the days before jobs became mostly paper shuffling and computer keyboarding it was far easier to tell people's jobs by examining their hands: distorted finger pads from manual typewriters, punctures from sewing machines and cobbler's needles, indentations and ink stains from stenographers' and accountants' pens, paper cuts from printing presses, scars from die cutters, distinctive calluses from various types of manual labor. . . .

But a scar like this told them nothing.

Not yet at any rate. Not until they had a suspect whose hands they might examine.

"What else? The knee print. This is good. Give us an idea of what he's wearing. Hold it up, Sachs. Higher! Baggy slacks. It retained that deep crease there so it's natural fiber. In this weather, I'll bet cotton. Not wool. You don't see silk slacks much nowadays."

"Lightweight, not denim," Cooper said.

"Sports clothes," Rhyme concluded. "Add that to our profile, Thom."

Cooper looked back at the computer screen and typed some more. "No luck with the leaf. Doesn't match anything at the Smithsonian."

Rhyme stretched back into his pillow. How much time would they have? An hour? Two?

The moon. Dirt. Brine . . .

He glanced at Sachs who was standing by herself in the corner. Her head was down and her long red hair fell dramatically toward the floor. She was looking into an evidence bag, a frown on her face, lost in concentration. How many times had Rhyme himself stood in the same pose, trying to—

"A newspaper!" she cried, looking up. "Where's a newspaper?" Her eyes were frantic as she looked from table to table. "Today's paper?"

"What is it, Sachs?" Rhyme asked.

She grabbed *The New York Times* from Jerry Banks and leafed quickly through it.

"That liquid . . . in the underwear," she said to Rhyme. "Could it be salt water?"

"Salt water?" Cooper pored over the GC-MS chart. "Of course! Water and sodium and other minerals. And the oil, phosphates. It's polluted seawater."

Her eyes met Rhyme's and they said simultaneously, "High tide!"

She held up the paper, open to the weather map. It contained a phases-of-the-moon diagram identical to the one found at the scene. Below it was a tidal chart. "High tide's in forty minutes."

Rhyme's face curled in disgust. He was never angrier than when he was angry with himself. "He's going to drown the vic. They're under a pier downtown." He looked hopelessly at the map of Manhattan, with its miles of shoreline. "Sachs, time to play race-car driver again. You and Banks go west. Lon, why don't you take the East Side? Around the South Street Seaport. And Mel, figure out what the hell that leaf is!"

———

A fluke of wave slapped his sagging head.

William Everett opened his eyes and snorted the shivery water from his nose. It was icy cold and he felt his questionable heart stutter as it struggled to send warming blood through his body.

He almost fainted again, like when the son of a bitch'd broken his finger, he floated back to waking, his thoughts. Then on his late wife—and for some reason, on their travels. They'd been to Giza. And to Guatemala. Nepal. Teheran (one week before the embassy takeover).

Their Southeast China Airlines plane had lost one of two engines an hour out of Beijing and Evelyn had lowered her head, the crash position, preparing to die and staring at an article in the in-flight magazine. It warned that drinking hot tea right after a meal was dangerous for you. She told him about it afterwards, at the Raffles bar in Singapore, and they'd laughed hysterically until tears came to their eyes.

Thinking of the kidnapper's cold eyes. His teeth, the bulky gloves.

Now, in this horrid wet tomb the unbearable pain rolled up his arm and into his jaw.

Broken finger or heart attack? he wondered.

Maybe a little of both.

Everett closed his eyes until the pain subsided. He looked around him. The chamber where he was handcuffed was beneath a rotting pier. A lip of wood dipped from the edge toward the churning water, which was about six inches below the bottom of the rim. Lights from boats on the river and the industrial sites of Jersey reflected through the narrow slit. The water was up to his neck now and although the roof of the pier was several feet above his head the cuffs were extended as far as they'd go.

The pain swept up from his finger again and Everett's head roared with the agony and dipped toward the water as he passed out. A noseful of water and the racking cough that followed revived him.

Then the moon tugged the plane of water slightly higher and with a sodden gulp the chamber was sealed off from the river outside. The room went dark. He was aware of the sounds of groaning waves and his own moaning from the pain.

He knew he was dead, knew he couldn't keep his head above the greasy surface for more than a few minutes. He closed his eyes, pressed his face against the slick, black column.

TWENTY-ONE

"All the way downtown, Sachs," Rhyme's voice clattered from the radio.

She punched the accelerator of the RRV, red lights flashing, as they screamed downtown along the West Side Highway. Ice-cool, she goosed the wagon up to eighty.

"Okay, whoa," said Jerry Banks.

Counting down. Twenty-third Street, Twentieth, the skidding jog at the Fourteenth Street garbage-barge dock. As they roared through the Village, the meatpacking district, a semi pulled out of a side street directly into her path. Instead of braking she nudged the wagon over the center curb like a steeple-chaser, drawing breathless oaths from Banks and a wail from the air horn of the big White, which jackknifed spectacularly.

"Oops," said Amelia Sachs and swung back into the southbound lane. To Rhyme she added, "Say again. Missed that."

Rhyme's tinny voice popped through her earphones. "Downtown is all I can tell you. Until we figure out what the leaf means."

"We're coming up on Battery Park City."

"Twenty-five minutes to high tide," Banks called.

Maybe Dellray's team could get the exact location out of him. They could drag Mr 823 into an alley somewhere with a bag of apples. Nick had told her that was the way they talked perps into "cooperating." Whack 'em in the gut with a bag of fruit. Really painful. No marks. When she was growing up she wouldn't have thought cops did that. Now she knew different.

Banks tapped her shoulder. "There. A bunch of old piers."

UNSUB 823			
Appearance	**Residence**	**Vehicle**	**Other**
• Caucasian male, slight build • Dark clothing • Old gloves, reddish kidskin • Aftershave; to cover up other scent? • Ski mask? Navy blue? • Gloves are dark • Aftershave = Brut • Hair color not brown • Deep scar, index finger • Casual clothes	• Prob. has safe house • Located near; B'way & 82nd, ShopRite B'way & 96th Anderson Foods Greenwich & Bank ShopRite 2nd Ave., 72nd-73rd, Grocery World Battery Park City, J&G's Emporium 1709 2nd Ave., Anderson Foods 34th & Lex., Food Warehouse 8th Ave. & 24th, ShopRite Houston & Lafayette, ShopRite 6th Ave. & Houston, J&G's Emporium Greenwich & Franklin, Grocery World • Old building, pink marble	• Yellow Cab • Recent model sedan • Lt. gray, silver, biege	• knows CS proc. • possibly has record • knows FR prints • gun = .32 Colt • Ties vics w/ unusual knots • "Old" appeals to him • Called one vic "Hanna" • Knows basic German • Underground appeals to him • Dual personalities • Maybe priest, soc. worker, counselor • Unusual wear on shoes, reads a lot?

Rotten wood, filthy. Spooky places.

They skidded to a stop and climbed out, running toward the water.

"You there, Rhyme?"

"Talk to me, Sachs. Where are you?"

"A pier just north of Battery Park City."

"I just heard from Lon, on the East Side. He hasn't found anything."

"It's hopeless," she said. "There're a dozen piers. Then the whole promenade . . . And the fireboat house and ferry docks and the pier at Battery Park . . . We need ESU."

"We don't *have* ESU, Sachs. They're not on our side anymore."

Twenty minutes to high tide.

Her eyes darted along the waterfront. Her shoulders sagged with helplessness. Hand on her weapon, she sprinted to the river, Jerry Banks not far behind.

———

"Get me *something* on that leaf, Mel. A guess, anything. Wing it."

Fidgeting, Cooper looked from the microscope to the computer screen.

Eight thousand varieties of leafy plants in Manhattan.

"It doesn't fit the cell structure of *anything*."

"It's old," Rhyme said. "How old?"

Cooper looked at the leaf again. "Mummified. I'd put it at a hundred years, little less maybe."

"What's gone extinct in the last hundred years?"

"Plants don't go extinct in an ecosystem like Manhattan. They always show up again."

A ping in Rhyme's mind. He was close to remembering something. He both loved and hated this feeling. He might grab the thought like a slow pop-up fly. Or it might vanish completely, leaving him with only the sting of lost inspiration.

Sixteen minutes to high tide.

What *was* the thought? He grappled with it, closed his eyes . . .

Pier, he was thinking. The vic's under a pier.

What about it? *Think!*

Pier . . . ships . . . unloading . . . cargo.

Unloading cargo!

His eyes snapped open. "Mel, is it a crop?"

"Oh, hell. I've been looking at general-horticulture pages, not cultivated crops." He typed for what seemed like hours.

"Well?"

"Hold on, hold on . . . Here's a list of the encoded binaries." He scanned it. "Alfalfa, barley, beets, corn, oats, tobacco . . ."

"Tobacco! Try that."

Cooper double clicked his mouse and the image slowly unfurled on the screen.

"That's it!"

"The World Trade Towers," Rhyme announced. "The land from there north used to be tobacco plantations. Thom, the research for my book—I want the map from the 1740s. And that modern map Bo Haumann was using for the asbestos-cleanup sites. Put them up there on the wall, next to each other."

The aide found the old map in Rhyme's files. He taped them both onto the wall near his bed. Crudely drawn, the older map showed the northern part of the settled city—a cluster on the lower portion of the isle—covered with plantations. There were three commercial wharves along the river, which was then called not the Hudson but the West River. Rhyme glanced at the recent map of the city. The farmland was gone of course, as were the original wharves, but the contemporary map showed an abandoned wharf in the exact location of one of the tobacco exporter's old piers.

Rhyme strained forward, struggling to see the street name it was near. He was about to shout for Thom to come hold the map closer when, from downstairs, he heard a loud snap and the door crashed inward. Glass shattered.

Thom started down the stairs.

"I want to see him." The terse voice filled the hallway.

"Just a—" the aide began.

"No. Not in a minute, not in a hour. But right. Fucking. Now."

"Mel," Rhyme whispered, "ditch the evidence, shut the systems down."

"But—"

"Do it!"

Rhyme shook his head violently, dislodging the headset microphone. It fell onto the side of the Clinitron. Footsteps pounded up the stairs.

Thom did the best he could to stall but the visitors were three federal agents and two of the three were holding large guns. Slowly they backed him up the stairs.

Bless him, Mel Cooper pulled apart a compound microscope in five seconds flat and was calmly replacing the components with meticulous care as the FBI crested the stairs and stormed into Rhyme's room. The evidence bags were stuffed under a table and covered with *National Geographics*.

"Ah, Dellray," Rhyme asked. "Find our unsub, did you?"

"Why didn't you tell us?"

"Tell you what?"

"That the fingerprint was bogus."

"No one asked me."

"Bogus?" Cooper asked, mystified.

"Well, it was a real print," Rhyme said, as if it were obvious. "But it wasn't the unsub's. Our boy needed a taxi to catch his fish with. So he met—what *was* his name?"

"Victor Pietrs," Dellray muttered and gave the cabbie's history.

"Nice touch," Rhyme said with some genuine admiration. "Picked a Serb with a rap sheet and mental problems. Wonder how long he looked for a candidate. Anyway, 823 killed poor Mr Pietrs and stole his cab. Cut off his finger. He kept it and figured if we were getting too close he'd leave a nice obvious print at a scene to throw us off. I guess it worked."

Rhyme glanced at the clock. Fourteen minutes left.

"How'd you know?" Dellray glanced at the maps on Rhyme's wall but, thank God, wasn't interested in them.

"The print showed signs of dehydration and shriveling. Bet the body was a mess. And you found it in the basement? Am I right? Where our boy likes to stow his victims."

Dellray ignored him and nosed around the room like a giant terrier.

"Where you hidin' our evidence?"

"Evidence? I don't know what you're talking about. Say, did

you break my door? Last time you walked in without knocking. Now you just kicked it in."

"You know, Lincoln, I was thinking of apologizing to you for before—"

"That's big of you, Fred."

"But now I'm a inch away from collaring your ass."

Rhyme glanced down at the microphone headset, dangling on the floor. He imagined Sachs's voice bleating from the earphones.

"Gimme that evidence, Rhyme. You don't realize what kind of pissy-bad trouble you're in."

"Thom," Rhyme asked slowly, "Agent Dellray startled me and I dropped my Walkman headset. Could you hook it on the bedframe?"

The aide didn't miss a beat. He rested the mike next to Rhyme's head, out of Dellray's sight.

"Thank you," Rhyme said to Thom. Then added, "You know, I haven't had my bath yet. I think it's about time, wouldn't you say?"

"I've been wondering when you were going to ask," said Thom, with the ability of a natural-born actor.

"Come in, Rhyme. For Christ's sake. Where are you?"

Then she heard a voice in her headset. Thom's. It sounded stilted, exaggerated. Something was wrong.

"I've got the new sponge," the voice said.

"Looks like a good one," Rhyme answered.

"Rhyme?" Sachs blurted. "What the hell's going on?"

"Cost seventeen dollars. It ought to be good. I'm going to turn you over."

More voices sounded through the earphones but she couldn't make them out.

Sachs and Banks were jogging along the waterfront, peering over the wharves into the gray-brown water of the Hudson. She motioned to Banks to stop, leaned away from the cramp below her breastbone, spit into the river. Tried to catch her breath.

Through the headset she heard: ". . . won't take long. You'll have to excuse us, gentlemen."

". . . we'll just wait, you don't mind."

"I do mind," Rhyme said. "Can't I get a little privacy here?"

"Rhyme, can you hear me?" Sachs called desperately. What the hell was he doing?

"Nup. No privacy for them that steal evidence."

Dellray! He was in Rhyme's room. Well, that's the end of it. The vic's as good as dead.

"I want that evidence," the agent barked.

"Well, what you're going to *get* is a panoramic view of a man taking a sponge bath, Dellray."

Banks started to speak but she waved him quiet.

Some muttered words she couldn't hear.

The agent's angry shout.

Then Rhyme's calm voice again. ". . . You know, Dellray, I used to be a swimmer. Swam every day."

"We've got less than ten minutes," Sachs whispered. The water lapped calmly. Two placid boats cruised past.

Dellray muttered something.

"I'd go down to the Hudson River and swim. It was a lot cleaner then. The water, I mean."

A garbled transmission. He was breaking up.

". . . old pier. My favorite one's gone now. Used to be the home of the Hudson Dusters. That gang, you ever hear of them? In the 1890s. North of where Battery Park City is now. You look bored. Tired of looking at a crip's flabby ass? No? Suit yourself. That pier was between North Moore and Chambers. I'd dive in, swim around the piers . . ."

"North Moore and Chambers!" Sachs shouted. Spinning around. They'd missed it because they'd gone too far south. It was a quarter mile from where they were. She could see the brown scabby wood, a large drainpipe backing up with tidal water. How much time was left? Hardly any. There was no way they could save him.

She ripped the headset off and started sprinting to the car, Banks close behind.

"Can you swim?" she asked.

"Me? A lap or two at the Health and Racquet Club."

They'd never make it.

Sachs stopped suddenly, spun around in a fast circle, gazing at the deserted streets.

The water was nearly to his nose.

A small wave washed over William Everett's face just as he inhaled and the foul, salty liquid streamed into his throat. He began to choke, a deep, horrible sound. Racking. The water filled his lungs. He lost his grip on the pier piling and sank under the surface, stiffened and rose once more, then sank again.

No, Lord, no . . . please don't let—

He shook the cuffs, kicked hard, trying to get some play. As if some miracle might happen and his puny muscles could bend the huge bolt he was cuffed to.

Snorting water from his nose, swiping his head back and forth in panic. He cleared his lungs momentarily. Neck muscles on fire—as painful as his shattered finger—from bending his head back to find the faint layer of air just above his face.

He had a moment's respite.

Then another wave, slightly higher.

And that was it.

He couldn't fight anymore. Surrender. Join Evelyn, say good-bye . . .

And William Everett let go. He floated beneath the surface into the drecky water, full of junk and tendrils of seaweed.

Then jerked back in horror. No, no . . .

He was here. The kidnapper! He'd come back.

Everett kicked to the surface, sneezing more water, trying desperately to get away. The man shone a brilliant light into Everett's eyes and reached toward him with a knife.

No, no . . .

It wasn't enough to drown him, he had to slash him to death. Without thinking Everett kicked out toward him. But the kidnapper vanished under the water . . . and then, *snap*, Everett's hands were free.

The old man forgot his placid goodbyes and kicked like hell to the surface, sucking sour air through his nose and ripping the tape from his mouth. Gasping, spitting the foul water. His head banged solidly into the underside of the oak pier and he laughed out loud. "Oh, God, God, God . . ."

Then another face appeared . . . Also hooded, with another

blindingly bright lamp attached, and Everett could just make out the NYFD emblem on the man's wetsuit. They weren't knives the men held but metal cutters. One of them thrust a bitter rubber mouthpiece between Everett's lips and he inhaled a dazzling breath of oxygen.

The diver slipped his arm around him and together they swam to the lip of the pier.

"Take a deep breath, we'll be out in a minute."

He filled his narrow lungs to bursting and, eyes closed, sailed with the diver deep into the water, lit eerily by the man's yellow light. It was a short but harrowing trip, straight down then up again through cloudy, flecked water. Once he slipped out of the diver's hands and they separated momentarily. But William Everett took the glitch in stride. After this evening, a solo swim in the choppy Hudson River was a piece of cake.

She hadn't planned on taking a cab. The airport bus would've been fine.

But Pammy was wired from too little sleep—they'd both been up since five that morning—and she was getting restless. The little girl needed to be in bed soon, tucked away with her blanket and her bottle of Hawaiian Punch. Besides, Carole herself couldn't wait to get to Manhattan—she was just a skinny Midwest gal who'd never been farther east than Ohio in all her forty-one years, and she was dying for her first look at the Big Apple.

Carole collected her luggage and they started toward the exit. She checked to make sure she had everything they'd left Kate and Eddie's house with that afternoon.

Pammy, Pooh, purse, blanket, suitcase, yellow knapsack.

Everything accounted for.

Her friends had warned her about the city. "They'll hustle you," Eddie'd said. "Purse snatchers, pickpockets."

"And don't play those card games on the street," maternal Kate had added.

"I don't play cards in my *living* room," Carole reminded her, laughing. "Why'm I going to start playing on the streets of Manhattan?"

But she appreciated their concern. After all, here she was,

a widow with a three-year-old, heading to the toughest city on earth for the UN conference—more foreigners, hell, more *people* than she'd ever seen at one time.

Carole found a pay phone and called the residence hotel to check on their reservations. The night manager said the room was ready and waiting for them. He'd see them in forty-five minutes or so.

They walked through automatic doors and were socked breathless by the scalding summer air. Carole paused, looking around. Gripping Pammy firmly with one hand, the handle of the battered suitcase with the other. The heavy yellow knapsack was snug on her shoulder.

They joined the line of passengers waiting at the taxi starter's booth.

Carole glanced at a huge billboard across the highway. *Welcome U.N. Delegates!* it announced. The artwork was terrible, but she stared at it for a long moment; one of the men on the board looked like Ronnie.

For a time, after he died, two years ago, virtually everything reminded her of her handsome, crew-cut husband. She'd drive past McDonald's and remember that he liked Big Macs. Actors in movies who didn't look a thing like him might cock their heads the way he used to. She'd see a flyer for a lawn-mower sale and remember how much he loved to cut their tiny square of grass in Arlington Heights.

Then the tears would come. And she'd go back on Prozac or imipramine. She'd spend a week in bed. Reluctantly acquiesce in Kate's offer that she stay with her and Eddie for a night. Or a week. Or a month.

But no tears anymore. She was here to jump-start her life. The sorrow was behind her now.

Tossing her mass of dark-blond hair off her sweaty shoulders, Carole ushered Pammy forward and kicked the luggage ahead of them as the taxi queue moved up several places. She looked all around, trying to catch a glimpse of Manhattan. But she could see nothing except traffic and the tails of airplanes and a sea of people and cabs and cars. Steam rose like frantic ghosts from manholes and the night sky was black and yellow and hazy.

Well, she'd see the city soon enough, she guessed. She

hoped that Pammy was old enough to keep her first memory of the sight.

"How do you like our adventure so far, honey?"

"Adventure. I like adventures. I want some 'Waiin Punch. Can I please have some?"

Please . . . That was new. The three-year-old was learning all the keys and buttons. Carole laughed. "We'll get you some soon."

Finally they got their cab. The trunk popped open and Carole dumped the luggage inside, slammed the lid. They climbed into the back seat and closed the door.

Pammy, Pooh, purse . . .

The driver asked, "Where to?" And Carole gave him the address of the Midtown Residence Hotel, shouting through the Plexiglas divider.

The driver pulled into traffic. Carole sat back and settled Pammy on her lap.

"Will we go past the UN?" she called.

But the man was concentrating on changing lanes and didn't hear her.

"I'm here for the conference," she explained. "The UN conference."

Still no answer.

She wondered if he had trouble with English. Kate had warned her that the taxi drivers in New York were all foreigners. ("Taking American jobs," Eddie grumbled. "But don't get me started on *that*.") She couldn't see him clearly through the scuffed divider.

Maybe he just doesn't want to talk.

They swung onto another highway—and, suddenly, there it was in front of her, the jagged skyline of the city. Brilliant. Like the crystals that Kate and Eddie collected. A huge cluster of blue and gold and silver buildings in the middle of the island and another cluster way to the left. It was bigger than anything Carole had ever seen in her life and for a moment the island seemed like a massive ship.

"Look, Pammy, that's where we're going. Is that beeaaautiful or what?"

A moment later, though, the view was cut off as the driver turned off the expressway and made a fast turn at the bottom of the ramp. Then they were moving through hot, deserted streets, lined with dark brick buildings.

Carole leaned forward. "Is this the right way to the city?"

Again, no answer.

She rapped hard on the Plexiglas. "Are you going the right way? Answer me. *Answer me!*"

"Mommy, what's wrong?" Pammy said and started to cry.

"Where are you going?" Carole shouted.

But the man just kept driving—leisurely, stopping at all the red lights, never going over the speed limit. And when he pulled into the deserted parking lot behind a dark, abandoned factory he made sure he signaled properly.

Oh no . . . no!

He pulled on a ski mask and climbed from the cab. Walking to the back, he reached for the door. But he hesitated and his hand dropped. He leaned forward, face against the window, and tapped on the glass. Once, twice, three times. Getting the attention of lizards in the reptile room at a zoo. He stared at the mother and daughter for a long moment before he opened the door.

TWENTY-TWO

"H ow'd you do it, Sachs?"
Standing beside the pungent Hudson River, she spoke into her stalk mike. "I remembered seeing the fireboat station at Battery Park. They scrambled a couple divers and were at the pier in about three minutes. Man, you should've seen that boat move! I want to try one of those someday."

Rhyme explained to her about the fingerless cabbie.

"Son of a bitch!" she said, clicking her tongue in disgust. "The weasel tricked us all."

"Not all of us," Rhyme reminded her coyly.

"So Dellray knows I boosted the evidence. Is he looking for me?"

"He said he was heading back to the federal building. Probably to decide which one of us to collar first. How's the scene there, Sachs?"

"Pretty bad," she reported. "He parked on gravel—"

"So no footprints."

"But it's worse than that. The tide backed out of this big drainpipe and where he parked's underwater."

"Hell," Rhyme muttered. "No trace, no prints, no nothing. How's the vic?"

"Not so good. Exposure, broken finger. He's had heart problems. They're going to keep him in the hospital for a day or two."

"Can he tell us anything?"

Sachs walked over to Banks, who was interviewing William Everett.

"He wasn't big," the man said matter-of-factly, carefully

examining the splint the medic was putting on his hand. "And he wasn't really strong, not a muscle man. But he was stronger'n me. I grabbed him and he just pulled my hands away."

"Description?" Banks asked.

Everett recounted the dark clothes and ski mask. That was all he could remember.

"One thing I should tell you," Everett held up his bandaged hand. "He's got a mean streak. I grabbed him, like I said. I wasn't thinking—I just panicked. But he got real mad. That's when he busted my finger."

"Retaliation, hm?" Banks asked.

"I guess. But that's not the strange part."

"No?"

"The strange part is he listened to it."

The young detective had stopped writing. Looked at Sachs.

"He held my hand against his ear, real tight, and bent the finger until it broke. Like he was listening. And liking it."

"Did you hear that, Rhyme?"

"Yes. Thom's added it to our profile. I don't know what it means, though. We'll have to think about it."

"Any sign of the planted PE?"

"Not yet."

"Grid it, Sachs. Oh, and get the vic's—"

"Clothes? I've already asked him. I—Rhyme, you all right?" She heard a fit of coughing.

The transmission was shut off momentarily. He came back on a moment later. "You there, Rhyme? Everything okay?"

"Fine," he said quickly. "Get going. Walk the grid."

She surveyed the scene, lit starkly by the ESU halogens. It was so frustrating. He'd *been* here. He'd walked on the gravel just a few feet away. But whatever PE he'd inadvertently left behind was lying inches below the surface of the dim water. She covered the ground slowly. Back and forth.

"I can't see *anything*. The clues might've been washed away."

"No, he's too smart not to've taken the tide into account. They'll be on dry land somewhere."

"I've got an idea," she said suddenly. "Come on down here."

"What?"

"Work the scene with me, Rhyme."

Silence.

"Rhyme, did you hear me?"

"Are you talking to me?" he asked.

"You *look* like De Niro. You can't act as good as De Niro. You know? That scene from *Taxi Driver*?"

Rhyme didn't laugh. He said, "The line's 'Are you looking at me?' Not 'talking to me.'"

Sachs continued, unfazed, "Come on down. Work the scene with me."

"I'll spread my wings. No, better yet, I'll project myself there. Telepathy, you know."

"Quit joking. I'm serious."

"I—"

"We need you. I can't find the planted clues."

"But they'll be there. You just have to try a little harder."

"I've walked the entire grid twice."

"Then you've defined the perimeter too narrowly. Add another few feet and keep going. Eight twenty-three's not finished yet, not by a long shot."

"You're changing the subject. Come on down and help me."

"How?" Rhyme asked. "How'm I supposed to do that?"

"I had a friend who was challenged," she began. "And he—"

"You mean he was a *crip*," Rhyme corrected. Softly but firmly.

She continued, "His aide'd put him into this fancy wheel-chair every morning and he drove himself all over the place. To the movies, to—"

"Those chairs . . ." Rhyme's voice sounded hollow. "They don't work for me."

She stopped speaking.

He continued, "The problem's how I was injured. It'd be dangerous for me to be in a wheelchair. It could"—he hesitated—"make things worse."

"I'm sorry. I didn't know."

After a moment he said, "Of course you didn't."

Blew that one. Oh, boy. Brother . . .

But Rhyme didn't seem any the worse for her faux pas. His

voice was smooth, unemotional. "Listen, you've got to get on with the search. Our unsub's making it trickier. But it won't be impossible . . . Here's an idea. He's the underground man, right? Maybe he buried them."

She looked over the scene.

Maybe there . . . She saw a mound of earth and leaves in a patch of tall grass near the gravel. It didn't look right; the mound seemed too assembled.

Sachs crouched beside it, lowered her head and, using the pencils, began to clear away leaves.

She turned her face slightly to the left and found she was staring at a rearing head, bared fangs . . .

"Jesus Lord," she shouted, stumbling backwards, falling hard on her butt, scrambling to draw her weapon.

No . . .

Rhyme shouted, "You all right?"

Sachs drew a target and tried to steady the gun with very unsteady hands. Jerry Banks came running up, his own Glock drawn. He stopped. Sachs climbed to her feet, looking at what was in front of them.

"Man," Banks whispered.

"It's a snake—well, a snake's skeleton," Sachs told Rhyme. "A rattlesnake. Fuck." Holstered the Glock. "It's mounted on a board."

"A snake? Interesting." Rhyme sounded intrigued.

"Yeah, real interesting," she muttered. She pulled on latex gloves and lifted the coiled bones. She turned it over. "'Metamorphosis.'"

"What?"

"A label on the bottom. The name of the store it came from, I'd guess. 604 Broadway."

Rhyme said, "I'll have the Hardy Boys check it out. What've we got? Tell me the clues."

They were underneath the snake. In a Baggie. Her heart pounded as she crouched down over the bag.

"A book of matches," she said.

"Okay, maybe he's thinking arson. Anything printed on them?"

"Nope. But there's a smear of something. Like Vaseline. Only stinky."

"Good, Sachs—always smell evidence you're not sure about. Only be more precise."

She bent close. "Yuck."

"That's not precise."

"Sulfur maybe."

"Could be nitrate-based. Explosive. Tovex. Is it blue?"

"No, it's milky clear."

"Even if it could go bang I imagine it's a secondary explosive. They're the stable ones. Anything else?"

"Another scrap of paper. Something on it."

"What, Sachs? His name, his address, e-mail handle?"

"Looks like it's from a magazine. I can see a small black-and-white photo. Looks like part of a building but you can't see which one. And underneath that, all you can read is a date. May 20, 1906."

"Five, twenty, oh-six. I wonder if it's a code. Or an address. I'll have to think about it. Anything else?"

"Nope."

She heard him sigh. "All right, come on back, Sachs. What time is it? My God, almost one A.M. I haven't been up this late in years. Come on back and let's see what we have."

———

Of all the neighborhoods in Manhattan, the Lower East Side has remained the most unchanged over the course of the city's history.

Much of it's gone of course: The rolling pastoral fields. The solid mansions of John Hancock and early government luminaries. Der Kolek, the large freshwater lake (its Dutch name eventually corrupted to "The Collect," which more accurately described the grossly polluted pond). The notorious Five Points neighborhood—in the early 1800s the most dangerous square mile on earth—where a single tenement, like the decrepit Gates of Hell, might be the site of two or three hundred murders every year.

But thousands of the old buildings remained—tenements from the nineteenth century and Colonial frame houses and Federal brick townhomes from the prior, baroque meeting halls, several of the Egyptian-style public buildings constructed by order of the regally corrupt Congressman Fernando

Wood. Some were abandoned, their facades overgrown with weeds and floors cracked by persistent saplings. But many were still in use; this had been the land of Tammany Hall iniquity, of pushcarts and sweatshops, of the Henry Street Settlement house, Minsky's burlesque and the notorious Yiddish Gomorra—the Jewish Mafia. A neighborhood that gives birth to institutions like these does not die easily.

It was toward this neighborhood that the bone collector now piloted the taxi containing the thin woman and her young daughter.

Observing that the constabulary was on to him, James Schneider went once again to ground like the serpent that he was, seeking accommodations—it is speculated—in the cellars of the city's many tenant-houses (which the reader may perchance recognize as the still-prevalent "tenements"). And so he remained, quiescent for some months.

As he drove home, the bone collector saw around him not the Manhattan of the 1990s—the Korean delis, the dank bagel shops, the X-rated-video stores, the empty clothing boutiques—but a dreamy world of bowler-clad men, women in rustling crinoline, hems and cuffs filthy with street refuse. Hordes of buggies and wagons, the air filled with the sometimes pleasant, sometimes repulsive scent of methane.

But such was the foul, indefatigable drive within him to start his collection anew that he was soon forced from his lair to waylay yet another good citizen;—this, a young man newly arrived in town to attend university.

Driving through the notorious Eighteenth Ward, once the home of nearly fifty thousand people crammed into a thousand decrepit tenements. When most people thought of the nineteenth century they thought in sepia—because of old photographs. But this was wrong. Old Manhattan was the color of stone. With choking industrial smoke, paint prohibitively expensive and dim lighting, the city was many shades of gray and yellow.

Schneider snuck up behind the fellow and was about to strike when Fortune's conscience, at last, cried out. Two constables chanced upon the assault. They recognized Schneider and gave chase. The killer fled east, across that engineering marvel, the Manhattan Bridge, completed in 1909, two years before these events. But he stopped halfway across, seeing that three constables were approaching from Brooklyn, having heard the alarm raised by the whistles and pistol reports of their confederates from Manhattan.

Schneider, unarmed, as chance would have it, climbed onto the railing of the bridge as he was surrounded by the law. He shouted maniacal diatribes against the constables, condemning them for having ruined his life. His words grew ever madder. As the constabulary moved closer, he leapt from the rail into the River. A week later a pilot discovered his body on the shore of Welfare Island, near Hell Gate. There was little left, for the crabs and turtles had been diligently working to reduce Schneider to the very bone which he, in his madness, cherished.

He turned the taxi onto his deserted cobblestoned street, East Van Brevoort, and paused in front of the building. He checked the two filthy strings he'd run low across the doors to make certain that no one had entered. A sudden motion startled him and he heard the guttural snarling of the dogs again, their eyes yellow, teeth brown, bodies dotted with scars and sores. His hand strayed to his pistol but they suddenly turned and, yelping, charged after a cat or rat in the alley.

He saw no one on the hot sidewalks and opened the padlock securing the carriage-house door then climbed back inside the car and drove into the garage, parked beside his Taurus.

After the villain's death his effects were secured and perused by detectives. His diary showed that he had murdered eight good citizens of the city. Nor was he above grave robbery, for it was ascertained from his pages (if his claims be true) that he had violated several holy resting places in cemeteries around the city. None of his victims had accorded him the least affront;—nay, most were upstanding citizens, industrious and innocent. And yet he felt not a modicum of guilt. Indeed, he seems to have labored under the mad delusion that he was doing his victims a favor.

He paused, wiped sweat from his mouth. The ski mask itched. He dragged the woman and her daughter out of the trunk and through the garage. She was strong and fought hard. At last he managed to get the cuffs on them.

"You prick!" she howled. "Don't you dare touch my daughter. You touch her and I'll kill you."

He gripped her hard around the chest and taped her mouth. Then he did the little girl's too.

"Flesh withers and can be weak,"—(*the villain wrote in his ruthless yet steady hand*)—*"Bone is the strongest aspect of the body. As old as we may be in the flesh, we are always young in the bone. It is a noble goal I had, and it is beyond me why any-one might quarrel with it. I did a kindness to them all. They are immortal now. I freed them. I took them down to the bone."*

He dragged them into the basement and pushed the woman down hard on the floor, her daughter beside her. Tied their cuffs to the wall with clothesline. Then returned upstairs.

He lifted her yellow knapsack from the back of the cab, the suitcases from the trunk, and pushed through a bolt-studded wooden door into the main room of the building. He was about to toss them into a corner but found that, for some reason, he was curious about these particular captives. He sat down in front of one of the murals—a painting of a butcher, placidly holding a knife in one hand, a slab of beef in the other.

He examined the luggage tag. Carole Ganz. Carole with an *E*. Why the extra letter? he wondered. The suitcase contained nothing but clothes. He started through the knapsack. He found the cash right away. There must have been four or five thousand. He put it back in the zippered compartment.

There were a dozen child's toys: a doll, a tin of watercolors, a package of modeling clay, a Mr Potato Head kit. There were also an expensive Discman, a half-dozen CDs and a Sony travel clock radio.

He looked through some pictures. Photos of Carole and her girl. In most of the pictures the woman seemed very somber. In a few others, she seemed happier. There were no photos of Carole and her husband even though she wore a wedding ring. Many were of the mother and daughter with a couple— a heavyset woman wearing one of those old granny dresses and a bearded, balding man in a flannel shirt.

For a long time the bone collector gazed at a portrait of the little girl.

The fate of poor Maggie O'Connor, the young slip of a

girl, merely eight years of age, was particularly sad. It was her misfortune, the police speculate, that she stumbled across the path of James Schneider as he was disposing of one of his victims.

The girl, a resident of notorious "Hell's Kitchen," had come out to pluck horsehairs from one of the many dead animals found in that impoverished part of the city. It was the custom of youngsters to wind tail-hairs into bracelets and rings—the only trinkets such urchins might have to adorn themselves with.

Skin and bone, skin and bone.

He propped the photo on the mantelpiece, beside the small pile of bones he'd been working on that morning and some that he'd stolen from the store where he'd found the snake.

It is surmised that Schneider found young Maggie near his lair, witnessing the macabre spectacle of his murdering one of his victims. Whether he dispatched her quickly or slowly we cannot guess. But unlike his other victims, whose remains were ultimately discovered,—of frail, becurled Maggie O'Connor, nought was ever found.

The bone collector walked downstairs.

He ripped the tape off the mother's mouth and the woman gasped for air, eyed him with cold fury. "What do you want?" she rasped. *"What?"*

She wasn't as thin as Esther but, thank God, she was nothing at all like fat Hanna Goldschmidt. He could see so *much* of her soul. The narrow mandible, the clavicle. And, through the thin blue skirt, the hint of the innominate bone—a fusion of the ilium, the ischium, the pubis. Names like Roman gods.

The little girl squirmed. He leaned forward and placed his hand on her head. Skulls don't grow from a single piece of bone but from eight separate ones, and the crown rises up like the triangular slabs of the Astrodome roof. He touched the girl's occipital bone, the parietal bones of the cap of the skull. And two of his favorites, the sensuous bones around the eye sockets—the sphenoid and the ethmoid.

"Stop it!" Carole shook her head, furious. "Keep away from her."

"Shhhh," he said, holding his gloved finger to his lips. He

looked at the little girl, who cried and pressed close to her mother.

"Maggie O'Connor," he cooed, looking at the shape of the girl's face. "My little Maggie."

The woman glared at him.

"You were in the wrong place at the wrong time, child. What did you see me do?"

Young in the bone.

"What are you talking about?" Carole whispered.

He turned his attention to her.

The bone collector had always wondered about Maggie O'Connor's mother.

"Where's your husband?"

"He's dead," she spat out. Then glanced at the little girl and said more softly, "He was killed two years ago. Look, just let my daughter go. She can't tell them anything about you. Are you . . . listening to me? What are you doing?"

He gripped Carole's hands and lifted them.

He fondled the metacarpals of the wrists. The phalanges—the tiny fingers. Squeezing the bones.

"No, don't do that. I don't like that. Please!" Her voice crackled with panic.

He felt out of control and didn't like the sensation one bit. If he was going to succeed here, with the victims, with his plans, he had to fight down the encroaching lust—the madness was driving him further and further into the past, confusing the now with the then.

Before and after . . .

He needed all of his intelligence and craftiness to finish what he'd started.

And yet . . . yet . . .

She was *so* thin, she was so taut. He closed his eyes and imagined how a knife blade scraping over her tibia would sing like the bowing of an old violin.

His breathing was fast, he was sweating rivers.

When finally he opened his eyes he found he was looking at her sandals. He didn't have many foot bones in good condition. The homeless people he'd been preying on in the past months . . . well, they'd suffered from rickets and osteoporosis, their toes were impacted by badly fitting shoes.

"I'll make a deal with you," he heard himself saying.

She looked down at her daughter. Wriggled closer to her. "I'll make a deal. I'll let you go if you let me do something."

"What?" Carole whispered.

"Let me take your skin off."

She blinked.

He whispered, "Let me. Please? A foot. Just one of your feet. If you do that I'll let you go."

"What . . . ?"

"Down to the bone."

She gazed at him with horror. Swallowed.

What would it matter? he thought. She was so nearly there anyway, so thin, so angular. Yes, there was something different about her—different from the other victims.

He put the pistol away and took the knife out of his pocket. Opened it with a startling click.

She didn't move, her eyes slid to the little girl. Back to him.

"You'll let us go?"

He nodded. "You haven't seen my face. You don't know where this place is."

A long moment. She stared around her at the basement. She muttered a word. A name, he thought. Ron or Rob.

And with her eyes firmly on his, she extended her legs and pushed her feet toward him. He slipped her shoe off the right foot.

He took her toes. Kneaded the fragile twigs.

She leaned back, the cables of her tendons rising beautifully from her neck. Her eyes squeezed shut. He caressed her skin with the blade.

A firm grip on the knife.

She closed her eyes, inhaled and gave a faint whimper. "Go ahead," she whispered. And turned the girl's face away. Hugged her tightly.

The bone collector imagined her in a Victorian outfit, crinoline and black lace. He saw the three of them, sitting together at Delmonico's or strolling down Fifth Avenue. He saw little Maggie with them, dressed in frothy lace, rolling a hoop with a stick as they walked over the Canal bridge.

Then and now . . .

He nestled the stained blade in the arch of her foot.

"Mommy!" the girl screamed.

Something popped within him. For a moment he was overwhelmed with revulsion at what he was doing. At himself.

No! He couldn't do it. Not to *her*. Esther or Hanna, yes. Or the next one. But not her.

The bone collector shook his head sadly and touched her cheekbone with the back of his hand. He slapped the tape over Carole's mouth again and cut the cord binding her feet.

"Come on," he muttered.

She struggled fiercely but he gripped her head hard and pinched her nostrils till she passed out. Then he hefted her over his shoulder and started up the stairs, carefully lifting the bag that sat nearby. Very carefully. It was not the sort of thing he wanted to drop. Up the stairs. Pausing only once, to look at young, curly-haired Maggie O'Connor, sitting in the dirt, looking hopelessly up at him.

TWENTY-THREE

He snagged them both in front of Rhyme's townhouse. Quick as the coiled snake that Jerry Banks was carrying at his side like a souvenir from Santa Fe.

Dellray and two agents stepped from an alley. He announced casually, "Got some news, honey dear. You're under arrest for the theft of evidence under custodial care of the U.S. government."

Lincoln Rhyme had been wrong. Dellray hadn't made it to the federal building after all. He'd been staking out Rhyme's digs.

Banks rolled his eyes. "Chill out, Dellray. We saved the vic."

"And a mighty good thing you did, sonny. If you hadn't we were gonna bring you up on homicide."

"But *we* saved 'im," Sachs said. "And you didn't."

"Thanks for that snappy recap, officer. Hold your wrists out."

"This is bullshit."

"Cuff this young lady," the Chameleon said dramatically to a burly agent beside him.

She began, "We found more clues, Agent Dellray. He's got another one. And I don't know how much time we have."

"Oh, and invite that thayre boy to ouah party too." Dellray nodded to Banks, who turned to the woman FBI agent approaching him and seemed to be thinking of decking her.

Dellray said a cheerful, "No, no, no. You don' wanna."

UNSUB 823			
Appearance	Residence	Vehicle	Other
• Caucasian male, slight build • Dark clothing • Old gloves, reddish kidskin • Aftershave; to cover up other scent? • Ski mask? Navy blue? • Gloves are dark • Aftershave = Brut • Hair color not brown • Deep scar, index finger • Casual clothes	• Prob. has safe house • Located near; B'way & 82nd, ShopRite B'way & 96th Anderson Foods Greenwich & Bank ShopRite 2nd Ave., 72nd-73rd, Grocery World Battery Park City, J&G's Emporium 1709 2nd Ave., Anderson Foods 34th & Lex., Food Warehouse 8th Ave. & 24th, ShopRite Houston & Lafayette, ShopRite 6th Ave. & Houston, J&G's Emporium Greenwich & Franklin, Grocery World • Old building, pink marble	• Yellow Cab • Recent model sedan • Lt. gray, silver, biege • Rental car; prob. stolen	• knows CS proc. • possibly has record • knows FR prints • gun = .32 Colt • Ties vics w/ unusual knots • "Old" appeals to him • Called one vic "Hanna" • Knows basic German • Underground appeals to him • Dual personalities • Maybe priest, soc. worker, counselor • Unusual wear on shoes, reads a lot? • Listened as he broke vic's finger

Banks reluctantly held out his hands.

Sachs, angry, offered the agent a cold smile. "How was your trip to Morningside Heights?"

"He still killed that cabbie. Our PERT boys're crawling over that house now like beetles on dung."

"And that's all they're going to find," Sachs said. "This unsub knows crime scenes better than you and I do."

"Downtown," Dellray announced, nodding at Sachs, who winced as the cuffs ratcheted tight around her wrists.

"We can save the next one too. If you—"

"You know what you got, Officer Sachs? Take a guess. You gotchaself the right to *re*-main silent. You got—"

"All right," the voice called from behind them. Sachs looked around and saw Jim Polling striding along the sidewalk. His slacks and dark sports shirt were rumpled. It looked as if he'd napped in them, though his bleary face suggested he hadn't slept in days. You could see a day's growth of beard and his sandy hair was an unruly mess.

Dellray blinked uneasily though it wasn't the cop he was troubled by but the tall physique of the U.S. attorney for the Southern District behind Polling. And bringing up the rear, SAC Perkins.

"Okay, Fred. Let 'em go." From the U.S. attorney.

In the modulated baritone of an FM disk jockey the Chameleon said, "She stole evidence, sir. She—"

"I just expedited some forensic analysis," Sachs said.

"Listen—" Dellray began.

"Nope," Polling said, completely in control now. No temper tantrums. "No, we're *not* listening." He turned to Sachs and barked, "But don't you try to be funny."

"Nosir. Sorry, sir."

The U.S. attorney said to Dellray. "Fred, you made a judgment call and it went south. Facts of life."

"It was a good lead," Dellray said.

"Well, we're changing the direction of the investigation," the U.S. attorney continued.

SAC Perkins said, "We've been conferencing with the director and with Behavioral. We've decided that Detectives Rhyme and Sellitto's positioning is the approach to pursue."

"But my snitch was clear that *something* was going down at the airport. That's not the sorta thing he'd be wishy about."

"It comes down to this, Fred," the U.S. attorney said bluntly. "*Whatever* the fucker's up to, it was Rhyme's team that saved the vics."

Dellray's lengthy fingers folded into an uncertain fist, opened again. "I appreciate that fact, sir. But—"

"Agent Dellray, this's a decision that has already been made."

The glossy black face—so energized at the federal building when he was marshaling his troops—was now somber, reserved. For the moment, the hipster was gone. "Yessir."

"This most recent hostage would've died if Detective Sachs here hadn't intervened," the U.S. attorney said.

"That'd be *Officer* Sachs," she corrected. "And it was mostly Lincoln Rhyme. I was his legman. So to speak."

"The case is going back to the city," the U.S. attorney announced. "The Bureau's A-T is to continue to handle terrorist-informant liaison but with reduced manpower. Anything they learn should be conveyed to Detectives Sellitto and Rhyme. Dellray, you're gonna put bodies at their disposal for any search-and-surveillance or hostage-rescue effort. Or anything else they might need. Got that?"

"Yessir."

"Good. You want to remove those handcuffs from these officers now?"

Dellray placidly unlocked the cuffs and slipped them into his pocket. He walked to a large van parked nearby. As Sachs picked up the evidence bag she saw him standing by himself at the edge of a pool of streetlight, his index finger lifted, stroking the cigarette behind his ear. She wasted a moment's sympathy on the fee-bie then turned and ran up the stairs, two at a time, after Jerry Banks and his rattlesnake.

"I have it figured out. Well, almost."

Sachs had just walked into Rhyme's room when he made this pronouncement. He was quite pleased with himself.

"Everything except the rattler and the glop."

She delivered the new evidence to Mel Cooper. The room

had been transformed yet again and the tables were covered with new vials and beakers and pillboxes and lab equipment and boxes. It wasn't much compared to the feds' headquarters but, to Amelia Sachs, it felt oddly like home.

"Tell me," she said.

"Tomorrow's Sunday . . . pardon me—today's Sunday. He's going to burn down a church."

"How do you figure?"

"The date."

"On the scrap of paper? What's it mean?"

"You ever hear of the anarchists?"

"Little Russians in trench coats carrying around those bombs that look like bowling balls?" Banks said.

"From the man who reads picture books," Rhyme commented dryly. "Your Saturday-morning-cartoon roots are showing, Banks. Anarchism was an old social movement calling for the abolition of government. One anarchist, Enrico Malatesta—his shtick was 'propaganda by deed.' Translated that means murder and mayhem. One of his followers, an American named Eugene Lockworthy, lived in New York. One Sunday morning he bolted the doors of a church on the Upper East Side just after the service began and set the place on fire. Killed eighteen parishioners."

"And that happened on May 20, 1906?" Sachs asked.

"Yep."

"I'm not going to ask how you figured that out."

Rhyme shrugged. "Obvious. Our unsub likes history, right? He gave us some matches so he's telling us he's planning arson. I just thought back to the city's famous fires—the Triangle Shirt-waist, Crystal Palace, the *General Slocum* excursion boat . . . I checked the dates—May twentieth was the First Methodist Church fire."

Sachs asked, "But where? Same location as that church?"

"Doubt it," Sellitto said. "There's a commercial high-rise there now. Eight twenty-three doesn't like new places. I've got a couple men on it just in case but we're sure he's going for a church."

"And we think," Rhyme added, "that he's going to wait till a service starts."

"Why?"

"For one thing, that's what Lockworthy did," Sellitto continued. "Also, we were thinking 'bout what Terry Dobyns was telling us—upping the ante. Going for multiple vics."

"So we've got a little more time. Until the service starts."

Rhyme looked up at the ceiling. "Now, how many churches are there in Manhattan?"

"Hundreds."

"That was rhetorical, Banks. I mean—let's keep looking over the clues. He'll have to narrow it down some."

Footsteps on the stair.

It was the twins once again.

"We passed Fred Dellray outside."

"He wasn't the least bit cordial."

"Or happy."

"Whoa, look at that." Saul—Rhyme believed it was Saul; he'd forgotten who had the freckles—nodded at the snake. "I've seen more of those in one night than I ever want to again."

"Snakes?" Rhyme asked.

"We were at Metamorphosis. It's a—"

"—very spooky place. Met the owner there. Weird guy. As you may've guessed."

"Long, long beard. Wish we hadn't gone at night," Bedding continued.

"They sell taxidermied bats and insects. You wouldn't believe some of the insects—"

"Five inches long."

"—and critters like that one." Saul nodded at the snake.

"Scorpions, a lot of scorpions."

"Anyway, they had a break-in a month ago and guess what got took? A rattler's skeleton."

"Reported?" Rhyme asked.

"Yep."

"But total value of the perped merch was only a hundred bucks or so. So Larceny wasn't like all-hands-on-board, you know."

"But tell them."

Saul nodded. "The snake wasn't the only thing missing. Whoever broke in took a couple dozen bones."

"Human bones?" Rhyme asked.

"Yep. That's what the owner thought was funny. Some of those insects—"

"Forget five inches, some of 'em were eight. Easy."

"—are worth three or four hundred. But all the perp boosted was the snake and some bones."

"Any particular ones?" Rhyme asked.

"An assortment. Like your Whitman's Sampler."

"His words, not ours."

"Mostly little ones. Hand and foot. And a rib, maybe two."

"The guy wasn't sure."

"Any CS report?"

"For 'jacked bones? Noooope."

The Hardy Boys departed once more, heading downtown to the last scene to start canvassing the neighborhood.

Rhyme wondered about the snake. Was it giving them a location? Did it relate to the First Methodist fire? If rattlers had been indigenous to Manhattan, urban development had long ago played Saint Patrick and purged the island of them. Was he making a play on the word *snake* or *rattler*?

Then Rhyme suddenly believed he understood. "The snake's for us."

"Us?" Banks laughed.

"It's a slap in the face."

"Whose face?"

"Everybody who's looking for him. I think it's a practical joke."

"I wasn't laughing very hard," Sachs said.

"Your expression *was* pretty funny." Banks grinned.

"I think we're better than he expected and he's not happy about it. He's mad and he's taking it out on us. Thom, add that to our profile, if you would. He's mocking us."

Sellitto's phone rang. He opened it and answered. "Emma darlin'. Whatcha got?" He nodded as he jotted notes. Then looked up and announced, "Rental-car thefts. Two Avises disappeared from their location in the Bronx in the past week, one in Midtown. They're out 'cause the colors're wrong: red, green and white. No Nationals. Four Hertz were 'jacked. Three in Manhattan—one from their downtown East Side location, from Midtown and from the Upper West Side. There were two green and—this could be it—one tan. But a silver Ford got boosted from White Plains. That's my vote."

"Agree," Rhyme announced. "White Plains."

"How do you know?" Sachs asked. "Monelle said it could've been either beige or silver."

"Because our boy's in the city," Rhyme explained, "and if he's going to boost something as obvious as a car he'll do it as far away from his safe house as he can. It's a Ford, you said?"

Sellitto asked Emma the question, then looked up. "Taurus. This year's model. Dark-gray interior. Tag's irrelevant."

Rhyme nodded. "The first thing he changed, the plates. Thank her and tell her to get some sleep. But not to wander too far from the phone."

"Got something here, Lincoln," Mel Cooper called.

"What's that?"

"The glop. I'm running it through the database of brand names now." He stared at the screen. "Cross-referencing . . . Let's see, the most likely match is Kink-Away. It's a retail hair straightener."

"Politically incorrect but helpful. That puts us up in Harlem, wouldn't you think? Narrows down the churches considerably."

Banks was looking through the religious-service directories of all three metro newspapers. "I count twenty-two."

"When's the earliest service?"

"Three have services at eight. Six at nine. One at nine-thirty. The rest at ten or eleven."

"He'll go for one of the first services. He's already giving us hours to find the place."

Sellitto said, "I've got Haumann getting the ESU boys together again."

"How 'bout Dellray?" Sachs said. She pictured the forlorn agent by himself on the street corner outside.

"What about him?" Sellitto muttered.

"Aw, let's cut him in. He wants a piece of this guy bad."

"Perkins said he was supposed to help," Banks offered.

"You really want him?" Sellitto asked, frowning.

Sachs was nodding. "Sure."

Rhyme agreed. "Okay, he can run the fed S&S teams. I

want a team on each church right away. All entrances. But they should stay way back. I don't want to spook him. Maybe we can nail him in the act."

Sellitto took a phone call. He looked up, eyes closed. "Jesus."

"Oh, no," Rhyme muttered.

The detective wiped his sweating face and nodded. "Central got a 9–1–1 from the night manager at this place? The Midtown Residence Hotel? Woman and her little girl called him from La Guardia, said they were just about to get a cab. That was a while ago; they never showed up. With all the news about the 'nappings he thought he should call. Her name's Carole Ganz. From Chicago."

"Hell," Banks muttered. "A little girl too? Oughta just pull all the cabs off the streets till we nail his butt."

Rhyme was drenched with weariness. His head raged. He remembered working a crime scene at a bomb factory. Nitroglycerin had bled out of some dynamite and seeped into an armchair Rhyme had to search for trace. Nitro gave you blinding headaches.

The screen of Cooper's computer flickered. "E-mail," he announced and called up the message. He read the fine type.

"They've polarized all the samples of cello that ESU collected. They think the scrap we found in the bone at the Pearl Street scene was from a ShopRite grocery store. It's closest to the cello they use."

"Good," Rhyme called. He nodded at the poster. "Cross off all the grocery stores but the ShopRites. What locations do we have?"

He watched Thom ink through the stores, leaving Four.

B'way & 82nd
Greenwich & Bank
8th Ave. & 24th
Houston & Lafayette

"That leaves us with the Upper West Side, West Village, Chelsea and the Lower East Side."

"But he could have gone anywhere to buy them."

"Oh, sure he could've, Sachs. He could've bought them in

White Plains when he was stealing the car. Or in Cleveland visiting his mother. But see, there's a point when unsubs feel comfortable in their deception and they stop bothering to cover their tracks. The stupid—or lazy—ones toss the smoking gun in the Dumpster behind their building and go on their merry way. The smarter ones drop it in a bucket of Spackle and pitch it into Hell Gate. The brilliant ones sneak into a refinery and vaporize it in a five-thousand-degree-centigrade furnace. Our unsub's smart, sure. But he's like every other perp in the history of the world. He's got limits. I'm betting he thinks we won't have the time or inclination to look for him or his safe house because we'll be concentrating on the planted clues. And of course he's dead wrong. This is *exactly* how we'll find him. Now, let's see if we can't get a little closer to his lair. Mel, anything in the vic's clothes from the last scene?"

But the tidal water had washed away virtually everything from William Everett's clothing.

"You say they fought, Sachs? The unsub and this Everett?"

"Wasn't much of a fight. Everett grabbed his shirt."

Rhyme clicked his tongue. "I must be getting tired. If I'd thought about it I would have had you scrape under his nails. Even if he was underwater that's one place—"

"Here you go," she said, holding up two small plastic bags.

"You scraped?"

She nodded.

"But why're there two bags?"

Holding up one bag then the other she said, "Left hand, right hand."

Mel Cooper broke into a laugh. "Even *you* never thought about separate bags for scraping, Lincoln. It's a great idea."

Rhyme grunted. "Differentiating the hands *might* have some marginal forensic value."

"Whoa," Cooper said, laughing still. "That means he thinks it's a brilliant idea and he's sorry he didn't think of it first."

The tech examined the scrapings. "Got some brick here."

"There was no brick anywhere around the drainpipe or the field," Sachs said.

"It's fragments. But there's something attached to it. I can't tell what."

Banks asked, "Could it've come from the stockyard tunnel? There was a lotta brick there, right?"

"All *that* came from Annie Oakley here," Rhyme said, nodding ruefully at Sachs. "No, remember, the unsub'd left before she pulled out her six-gun." Then he frowned, found himself straining forward. "Mel, I want to see that brick. In the 'scope. Is there any way?"

Cooper looked over Rhyme's computer. "I think we can rig something up." He ran a cable from the video-output port on the compound 'scope to his own computer and then dug into a large suitcase. He pulled out a long, thick gray wire. "This's a serial cable." He connected the two computers and transferred some software to Rhyme's Compaq. In five minutes, Rhyme, delighted, was seeing exactly what Cooper was looking at through the eyepiece.

The criminalist's eyes scanned the chunk of brick—hugely magnified. He laughed out loud. "He outfoxed himself. See those white blobs attached to the brick?"

"What are they?" Sellitto asked.

"Looks like glue," Cooper offered.

"Exactly. From a pet-hair roller. Perps who're real cautious use them to clean trace off themselves. But it backfired. Some bits of adhesive must've come off the roller and stuck to his clothes. So we *know* it's from his safe house. Held the brick in place until Everett picked it up under his fingernails."

"Does the brick tell us anything?" Sachs asked.

"It's old. And it's expensive—cheap brick was very porous because they mixed in filler. I'd guess his place is either institutional or built by someone wealthy. At least a hundred years old. Maybe older."

"Ah, here we go," Cooper said. "Another bit of glove, it looks like. If the damn things keep disintegrating we'll be down to his friction ridges before too long."

Rhyme's screen flashed and a moment later what he recognized as a tiny fleck of leather came on the screen. "Something's funny here," Cooper said.

"It's not red," Rhyme observed. "Like the other particle. This fleck's black. Run it through the microspectrophotometer."

Cooper ran the test and then tapped his computer screen.

"It's leather. But the dye is different. Maybe it's stained or faded."

Rhyme was leaning forward, straining, looking closely at the fleck on the screen when he realized he was in trouble. Serious trouble.

"Hey, you okay?" It was Sachs who'd spoken.

Rhyme didn't answer. His neck and jaw began to shiver violently. A feeling like panic rose from the crest of his shattered spine and moved up into his scalp. Then, as if a thermostat had clicked on, the chills and goose bumps vanished and he began to sweat. Perspiration poured from his face and tickled frantically.

"Thom!" he whispered. "Thom, it's happening."

Then he gasped as the headache seared through his face and spread along the walls of his skull. He jammed his teeth together, swayed his head, anything to stop the unbearable agony. But nothing worked. The light in the room flickered. The pain was so bad his reaction was to flee from it, to run flat-out on legs that hadn't moved in years.

"Lincoln!" Sellitto was shouting.

"His face," Sachs gasped, "it's bright red."

And his hands were pale as ivory. All of his body below the magic latitude at C4 was turning white. Rhyme's blood, on its phony, desperate mission to get to where it thought it was needed, surged into the tiny capillaries of his brain, expanding them, threatening to burst the delicate filaments.

As the attack grew worse Rhyme was aware of Thom over him, ripping the blankets off the Clinitron. He was aware of Sachs stepping forward, her radiant blue eyes narrowed in concern. The last thing he saw before the blackness was the falcon pushing off the ledge on his huge wings, startled by the sudden flurry of activity in the room, seeking easy oblivion in the hot air over the empty streets of the city.

TWENTY-FOUR

When Rhyme passed out, Sellitto got to the phone first. "Call 911 for EMS," Thom instructed. "Then hit that number there. Speed dial. It's Pete Taylor, our spinal cord specialist."

Sellitto made the calls.

Thom was shouting, "I'll need some help here. Somebody!"

Sachs was closest. She nodded, stepped up to Rhyme. The aide had grabbed the unconscious man under the arms and pulled him higher up in bed. He ripped open the shirt and prodded the pale chest, saying, "Everybody else, if you could just leave us."

Sellitto, Banks and Cooper hesitated for a moment then stepped through the doorway. Sellitto closed the door behind them.

A beige box appeared in the aide's hands. It had switches and dials on the top and sprouted a wire ending in a flat disk, which he placed over Rhyme's chest and taped down.

"Phrenic nerve stimulator. It'll keep him breathing." He clicked on the machine.

As Thom slipped a blood-pressure cuff onto Rhyme's alabaster-white arm, Sachs realized with a start that his body was virtually wrinkle-free. He was in his forties but his body was that of a twenty-five-year-old.

"Why's his face so red? It looks like he's going to explode."

"He is," Thom said matter-of-factly, yanking a doctor's kit from underneath the bedside table. He opened it then he continued to take the pressure. "Dysreflexia . . . All the stress today. Mental *and* physical. He's not used to it."

"He kept saying he was tired."

"I know. And I wasn't paying careful enough attention. Shhhh. I have to listen." He plugged the stethoscope into his ears, inflated the cuff and let the air out slowly. Staring at his watch. His hands were rock-steady. "Shit. Diastolic's one twenty-five. Shit."

Father in heaven, Sachs thought. He's going to stroke out.

Thom nodded at the black bag. "Find the bottle of nifedipine. And open up one of those syringes." As she searched, Thom yanked down Rhyme's pajamas and grabbed a catheter from beside the bed, tore open its plastic wrapper too. He smeared the end with K-Y jelly and lifted Rhyme's pale penis, inserting the catheter gently but quickly into the tip.

"This's part of the problem. Bowel and urinary pressure can trigger an attack. He's been drinking way more than he should today."

She opened the hypodermic but said, "I don't know how to do the needle."

"I'll do it." He looked up at her. "Could I ask . . . would you mind doing this? I don't want the tube to get a kink in it."

"Okay. Sure."

"You want gloves?"

She pulled on a pair and carefully took Rhyme's penis in her left hand. She held the tube in her right. It had been a long, long time since she'd held a man here. The skin was soft and she thought how strange it was that this center of a man's being is, most of the time, as delicate as silk.

Thom expertly injected the drug.

"Come on, Lincoln . . ."

A siren sounded in the distance.

"They're almost here," she said glancing out the window.

"If we don't bring him back now there's nothing they can do."

"How long does it take the drug to work?"

Thom stared at the unresponsive Rhyme, said, "It should've by now. But too high a dose and he goes into shock." The aide bent down and lifted an eyelid. The blue pupil was glazed, unfocused.

"This isn't good." He took the pressure again. "One fifty. Christ."

"It'll kill him," she said.

"Oh. That's not the problem."

"What?" a shocked Amelia Sachs whispered.

"He doesn't mind dying." He looked at her briefly as if surprised she hadn't figured this out. "He just doesn't want to be any more paralyzed than he already is." He prepared another injection. "He may already've had one. A stroke, I mean. *That's* what terrifies him."

Thom leaned forward and injected more of the drug.

The siren was closer now. Honking too. Cars would be blocking the ambulance's way, in no hurry to pull aside— one of the things that infuriated Sachs about the city.

"You can take the catheter out now."

She carefully extracted the tube. "Should I . . ." Nodding toward the urine bag.

Thom managed a weak smile. "That's my job."

Several minutes passed. The ambulance seemed to make no progress then a voice crackled over a speaker and gradually the siren grew closer.

Suddenly Rhyme stirred. His head shook slightly. Then it lolled back and forth, pressed into the pillow. His skin lost some of its florid tone.

"Lincoln, can you hear me?"

He moaned, "Thom . . ."

Rhyme was shivering violently. Thom covered him with a sheet.

Sachs found herself smoothing Rhyme's mussed hair. She took a tissue and wiped his forehead.

Footsteps pounded on the stairs and two burly EMS medics appeared, radios crackling. They hurried into the room, took Rhyme's blood pressure and checked the nerve stimulator. A moment later Dr Peter Taylor burst into the room.

"Peter," Thom said. "Dysreflexia."

"Pressure?"

"It's down. But it was bad. Crested at one fifty."

The doctor winced.

Thom introduced Taylor to the EMS techs. They seemed pleased an expert was there and stepped back as Taylor walked over to the bedside.

"Doctor," Rhyme said groggily.

"Let's look at those eyes." Taylor shone a light into Rhyme's pupils. Sachs scanned the doctor's face for a reaction and was troubled by his frown.

"Don't need the nerve stimulator," Rhyme whispered.

"You and your lungs, right?" the doctor asked wryly. "Well, let's keep it going for a little while, why don't we? Just till we see what exactly's going on here." He glanced at Sachs. "Maybe you could wait downstairs."

Taylor leaned close and Rhyme noticed the beads of sweat dotting the doctor's scalp under his thin hair.

The man's deft hands lifted a lid and gazed again into one pupil, then the next. He rigged up the sphygmomanometer and took Rhyme's blood pressure, his eyes distant with that concentration of medicos lost in their minute, vital tasks.

"Approaching normal," he announced. "How's the urine?"

"Eleven hundred cc's," Thom said.

Taylor glowered. "Been neglecting things? Or just drinking to excess?"

Rhyme glowered right back. "We were distracted, doctor. It's been a busy night."

Taylor followed Rhyme's nod and glanced around the room, surprised, as if someone had just sneaked the equipment in when he wasn't looking. "What's all this?"

"They hauled me out of retirement."

Taylor's perplexed frown grew into a smile. "About time. I've been after you for months to do something with your life. Now, what's the bowel situation?"

Thom said, "Probably twelve hours, fourteen."

"Careless of you," Taylor chided.

"It wasn't *his* fault," Rhyme snapped. "I've had a roomful of people here all day."

"I don't want to hear excuses," the doctor shot back. This was Pete Taylor, who never spoke *through* anyone when he talked to Rhyme and never let his bullying patient bully him.

"We better take care of things." He pulled on surgical gloves, leaned over Rhyme's torso. His fingers began manipulating the abdomen to trick the numb intestines into doing their work. Thom lifted the blankets and got the disposable diapers.

A moment later the job was done and Thom cleaned his boss.

Taylor said suddenly, "So you've given up that nonsense, I hope?" Studying Rhyme closely.

That nonsense . . .

He'd meant the suicide. With a glance at Thom, Rhyme said, "Haven't thought about that for a while."

"Good." Taylor looked over the instruments on the table. "This is what you ought to be doing. Maybe the department'll put you back on the payroll."

"Don't think I could pass the physical."

"How's the head?"

"'A dozen sledgehammers' comes close to describing it. My neck too. Had two bad cramps so far today."

Taylor walked behind the Clinitron, pressed his fingers on either side of Rhyme's spine, where—Rhyme supposed, though he'd never seen the spot of course—there were prominent incision scars from the operations he'd had over the years. Taylor gave Rhyme an expert massage, digging deep into the taut straps of muscle in his shoulders and neck. The pain slowly vanished.

He felt the doctor's thumbs pause at what he guessed was the shattered vertebra.

The spaceship, the stingray . . .

"Someday they'll fix this," Taylor said. "Someday, it'll be no worse than breaking your leg. You listen to me. I predict it."

Fifteen minutes later Peter Taylor came down the stairs and joined the cops on the sidewalk.

"Is he all right?" Amelia Sachs asked anxiously.

"The pressure's down. He needs rest mostly."

The doctor, a plain-looking man, suddenly realized he was talking to a very beautiful woman. He smoothed his thinning gray hair and cast a discreet glance at her willowy figure. His eyes then went to the squad cars in front of the townhouse and he asked, "What's the case he's helping you with?"

Sellitto demurred, as all detectives will in the face of that question from civilians. But Sachs had guessed Taylor and Rhyme were close so she said, "The kidnappings? Have you heard about them?"

"The taxi-driver case? It's on all the news. Good for him. Work is the best thing that could happen to him. He needs friends and he needs purpose."

Thom appeared at the top of the stairs. "He said thanks, Pete. Well, he didn't actually say thanks. But he meant it. You know how he is."

"Level with me," Taylor asked, voice lower now, conspiratorial. "Is he still planning on talking to them?"

And when Thom said, "No, he's not," something in his tone told Sachs that he was lying. She didn't know about what or what significance it might have. But it rankled.

Planning on talking to them?

In any case Taylor seemed not to pick up on the aide's deceit. He said, "I'll come back tomorrow, see how he's doing."

Thom said he'd appreciate it and Taylor slung his bag over his shoulder and started up the sidewalk. The aide gestured to Sellitto. "He'd like to talk to you for a minute." The detective climbed the stairs quickly. He disappeared into the room and a few minutes later he and Thom walked outside. Sellitto, solemn himself now, glanced at her. "Your turn." And nodded toward the stairs.

———

Rhyme lay in the massive bed, hair mussed, face no longer red, hands no longer ivory. The room smelled ripe, visceral. There were clean sheets on the bed and his clothes had been changed again. This time the pajamas were as green as Dellray's suit.

"Those are the ugliest PJs I've ever seen," she said. "Your ex gave them to you, didn't she?"

"How'd you guess? An anniversary present . . . Sorry for the scare," he said, looking away from her. He seemed suddenly timid and that upset her. She thought of her father in the pre-op room at Sloan-Kettering before they took him down to the exploratory surgery he never awoke from. Weakness can be more frightening than threat.

"Sorry?" she asked ominously. "No more of that shit, Rhyme."

He appraised her for a minute then said, "You two'll do fine."

"We two?"

"You and Lon. Mel too of course. And Jim Polling."

"What do you mean?"

"I'm retiring."

"You're *what?*"

"Too taxing for the old system, I'm afraid."

"But you can't quit." She waved at the Monet poster. "Look at everything we've found about 823. We're so close."

"So you don't need me. All you need is a little luck."

"Luck? It took years to get Bundy. And what about the Zodiac killer? And the Werewolf?"

"We've got good information here. Hard information. You'll come up with some good leads. You'll nail him, Sachs. Your swan song before they lap you up into Public Affairs. I've got a feeling Unsub 823's getting cocky; they might even collar him at the church."

"You look fine," she said after a moment. Though he didn't.

Rhyme laughed. Then the smile faded. "I'm very tired. And I hurt. Hell, I think I hurt in places the docs'll say I *can't* hurt."

"Do what I do. Take a nap."

He tried to snort a derisive laugh but he sounded weak. She hated seeing him this way. He coughed briefly, glanced down at the nerve stimulator, and grimaced, as if he was embarrassed that he depended on the machine. "Sachs . . . I don't suppose we'll be working together again. I just wanted to say that you've got a good career ahead of you, you make the right choices."

"Well, I'll come back and see you after we snag his bad ass."

"I'd like that. I'm glad you were first officer yesterday morning. There's nobody else I'd rather've walked the grid with."

"I—"

"Lincoln," a voice said. She turned to see a man in the doorway. He looked around the room curiously, taking in all the equipment.

"Been some excitement around here, looks like."

"Doctor," Rhyme said. His face blossoming into a smile. "Please come in."

He stepped into the room. "I got Thom's message. Emergency, he said?"

"Dr William Berger, this is Amelia Sachs."

But Sachs could see she'd already ceased to exist in Lincoln Rhyme's universe. Whatever else was left to be said—and she felt there were some things, maybe many things—would have to wait. She walked through the door. Thom, who stood in the large hallway outside, closed the door behind her and, ever proper, paused, nodding for her to precede him.

As Sachs walked out into the steamy night she heard a voice from nearby. "Excuse me."

She turned and found Dr Peter Taylor standing by himself under a ginkgo tree. "Can I talk to you for a minute?"

Sachs followed Taylor up the sidewalk a few doors.

"Yes?" she asked. He leaned against a stone wall and gave another self-conscious swipe at his hair. Sachs recalled how many times she'd intimidated men with a single word or glance. She thought, as she often did: What a useless power beauty is.

"You're his friend, right?" the doctor asked her. "I mean, you work with him but you're a friend too."

"Sure. I guess I am."

"That man who just went inside. Do you know who he is?"

"Berger, I think. He's a doctor."

"Did he say where he was from?"

"No."

Taylor looked up at Rhyme's bedroom window for a moment. He asked, "You know the Lethe Society?"

"No, oh, wait . . . It's a euthanasia group, right?"

Taylor nodded. "I know all of Lincoln's doctors. And I've never heard of Berger. I was just thinking maybe he's with them."

"What?"

Is he still talking to them . . .

So *that's* what the conversation was about.

She felt weightless from the shock. "Has he . . . has he seriously talked about this before?"

"Oh, yes." Taylor sighed, gazed into the smoky night sky. "Oh, yes." Then glanced at her name badge. "Officer Sachs, I've spent hours trying to talk him out of it. Days. But I've also worked with quads for years and I know how stubborn they are. Maybe he'd listen to you. Just a few words. I was thinking . . . Could you?—"

"Oh, goddamn it, Rhyme," she muttered and started down the sidewalk at a run, leaving the doctor in midsentence.

She got to the front door of the townhouse just as Thom was closing it. She pushed past him. "Forgot my watchbook."

"Your?—"

"Be right back."

"You can't go up there. He's with his doctor."

"I'll just be a second."

She was at the landing before Thom started after her.

He must have known it was a scam because he took the stairs two at a time. But she had a good lead and had shoved open Rhyme's door before the aide got to the top of the stairs.

She pushed in, startling both Rhyme and the doctor, who was leaning against the table, arms crossed. She closed the door and locked it. Thom began pounding. Berger turned toward her with a frown of curiosity on his face.

"Sachs," Rhyme blurted.

"I have to talk to you."

"What about?"

"About you."

"Later."

"How much later, Rhyme?" she asked sarcastically. "Tomorrow? Next week?"

"What do you mean?"

"You want me to schedule a meeting for, maybe, a week from Wednesday? Will you be able to make it then? Will you be *around*?"

"Sachs—"

"I want to talk to you. Alone."

"No."

"Then we'll do it the hard way." She stepped up to Berger. "You're under arrest. The charge is attempted assisted suicide." And the handcuffs flashed, click, click, snapping onto his wrists in a silver blur.

She guessed the building was a church.

Carole Ganz lay in the basement, on the floor. A single shaft of cold, oblique light fell on the wall, illuminating a shabby picture of Jesus and a stack of mildewy Golden Book Bible stories. A half-dozen tiny chairs—for Sunday-school students, she guessed—were nested in the middle of the room.

The cuffs were still on and so was the gag. He'd also tied her to a pipe near the wall with a four-foot-long piece of clothesline.

On a tall table nearby she could see the top of a large glass jug.

If she could knock it off she might use a piece of glass to cut the clothesline. The table seemed out of reach but she rolled over onto her side and started to squirm, like a caterpillar, toward it.

This reminded her of Pammy when she was an infant, rolling on the bed between herself and Ron; she thought of her baby, alone in that horrible basement, and started to cry.

Pammy, Pooh, purse.

For a moment, for a brief moment, she weakened. Wished she'd never left Chicago.

No, stop thinking that way! Quit feeling sorry for yourself! This was the absolute right thing to do. You did it for Ron. And for yourself too. He'd be proud of you. Kate had told her that a thousand times, and she believed it.

Struggling once more. She moved a foot closer to the table.

Groggy, couldn't think straight.

Her throat stung from the terrible thirst. And the mold and mildew in the air.

She crawled a little farther then lay on her side, catching her breath, staring up at the table. It seemed hopeless. What's the use? she thought.

Wondering what was going through Pammy's mind.

You fucker! thought Carole. I'll *kill* you for this!

She squirmed, trying to move farther along the floor. But instead, she lost her balance and rolled onto her back. She gasped, knowing what was coming. No! With a loud pop, her wrist snapped. She screamed through the gag. Blacked out. When she came to a moment later she was overwhelmed with nausea.

No, no, no . . . If she vomited she'd die. With the gag on, that would be it.

Fight it down! Fight it. Come on. You can do it. Here I go . . . She retched once. Then again.

No! Control it.

Rising in her throat.

Control . . .

Control it. . . .

And she did. Breathing through her nose, concentrating on Kate and Eddie and Pammy, on the yellow knapsack containing all her precious possessions. Seeing it, picturing it from every angle. Her whole life was in there. Her *new* life.

Ron, I don't want to blow it. I came here for you, honey . . .

She closed her eyes. Thought: Breathe deep. In, out.

Finally, the nausea subsided. And a moment later she was feeling better and, though she was crying in pain from the snapped wrist, she managed to continue to caterpillar her way toward the table, one foot. Two.

She felt a thump as her head collided with the table leg. She'd just managed to connect with it and couldn't move any farther. She swung her head back and forth and jostled the table hard. She heard the bottle slosh as it shifted on the tabletop. She looked up.

A bit of the jug was showing beyond the edge of the table. Carole drew back her head and hit the table leg one last time.

No! She'd knocked the leg out of reach. The jug teetered for a moment but stayed upright. Carole strained to get more slack from the clothesline but couldn't.

Damn. Oh, damn! As she gazed hopelessly up at the filthy bottle she realized it was filled with a liquid and something floated inside. What *is* that?

She scrunched her way back toward the wall a foot or two and looked up.

It seemed like a lightbulb inside. No, not a whole bulb, just the filament and the base, screwed into a socket. A wire ran from the socket out of the jug to one of those timers that turn the lights on and off when you're away on vacation. It looked like—

A bomb! Now she recognized the faintest whiff of gasoline.

No, no . . .

Carole began to squirm away from the table as fast as she could, sobbing in desperation. There was a filing cabinet by the wall. It'd give her some protection. She drew her legs up then felt a chill of panic and unwound them furiously. The motion knocked her off balance. She realized, to her horror, that she was rolling onto her back once more. Oh, stop. Don't . . . She stayed poised, perfectly still, for a long moment, quivering as she tried to shift her weight forward. But then she continued to roll, collapsing onto her cuffed hand, her shattered wrist taking the weight of her body. There was a moment of incredible pain and, mercifully, she fainted once more.

TWENTY-FIVE

"**N**o way, Rhyme. You can't do it."

Berger looked on uneasily. Rhyme supposed that in this line of work he'd seen all sorts of hysterical scenarios played out at moments like this. The biggest problem Berger'd have wasn't those wanting to die but those who wanted everyone else to live.

Thom pounded on the door.

"Thom," Rhyme called. "It's all right. You can leave us." Then to Sachs: "We've said our farewells. You and me. It's bad form to ruin a perfect exit."

"You can't do this."

Who'd blown the whistle? Pete Taylor maybe. The doctor must've guessed that he and Thom were lying.

Rhyme saw her eyes slip to the three items on the table. The gifts of the Magi. The brandy, the pills and the plastic bag. Also a rubber band, similar to the ones Sachs still wore on her shoes. (How many times had he come home from a crime scene to find Blaine staring at the bands on his shoes, horrified? "Everybody'll think my husband can't afford new shoes. He's keeping the soles on with rubber bands. *Honestly*, Lincoln!")

"Sachs, take the cuffs off the good doctor here. I'll have to ask you to leave one last time."

She barked a fast laugh. "Excuse me. This's a crime in New York. The DA could bootstrap it into murder, he wanted to."

Berger said, "I'm just having a conversation with a patient."

"That's why the charge's only attempt. So far. Maybe we

should run your name and prints through NCIC. See what we come up with."

"Lincoln," Berger said quickly, alarmed. "I can't—"

"We'll get it worked out," Rhyme said. "Sachs, please."

Feet apart, hands on trim hips, her gorgeous face imperious. "Let's go," she barked to the doctor.

"Sachs, you have no idea how important this is."

"I won't let you kill yourself."

"Let me?" Rhyme snapped. "*Let* me? And why exactly do I need your permission?"

Berger said, "Miss . . . Officer Sachs, it's his decision and it's completely consensual. Lincoln's more informed than most of the patients I deal with."

"Patients? Victims, you mean."

"Sachs!" Rhyme blurted, trying to keep the desperation from his voice. "It's taken me a year to find someone to help me."

"Maybe because it's wrong. Ever consider that? Why now, Rhyme? Right in the middle of the case?"

"If I have another attack and a stroke, I might lose all ability to communicate. I could be conscious for forty years and completely unable to move. And if I'm not brain-dead, nobody in the universe is going to pull the plug. At least now I'm still able to communicate my decisions."

"But why?" she blurted.

"Why not?" Rhyme answered. "Tell me. Why not?"

"Well . . ." It seemed as if the arguments against suicide were so obvious she was having trouble articulating them. "Because . . ."

"Because *why*, Sachs?"

"For one thing, it's cowardly."

Rhyme laughed. "Do you want to debate it, Sachs? *Do* you? Fair enough. 'Cowardly,' you say. That leads us to Sir Thomas Browne: 'When life is more terrible than death, it's the truest valor to live.' Courage in the face of insurmountable adversity . . . A classic argument in favor of living. But if that's true then why anesthetize patients before surgery? Why sell aspirin? Why fix broken arms? Why is Prozac the most prescribed medicine in America? Sorry, but there's nothing intrinsically good about pain."

"But you're not in pain."

"And how do you define pain, Sachs? Maybe the absence of all feeling can be pain too."

"You can contribute so much. Look at all you know. All the forensics, all the history."

"The social-contribution argument. That's a popular one." He glanced at Berger but the medico remained silent. Rhyme saw his interest dip to the bone sitting on the table—the pale disk of spinal column. He picked it up, kneaded it in his cuffed hands. He was a former orthopedics man, Rhyme recalled.

He continued to Sachs, "But who says we should contribute anything to life? Besides, the corollary is I might contribute something bad. I might cause some harm too. To myself or someone else."

"That's what life is."

Rhyme smiled. "But I'm choosing death, not life."

Sachs looked uneasy as she thought hard. "It's just . . . death isn't natural. Life is."

"No? Freud'd disagree with you. He gave up on the pleasure principle and came to feel that there was another force—a nonerotic primary aggression, he called it. Working to unbind the connections we build in life. Our own destruction's a perfectly natural force. Everything dies; what's more natural than that?"

Again she worried a portion of her scalp.

"All right," she said. "Life's more of a challenge to you than most people. But I thought . . . everything I've seen about you tells me you're somebody who likes challenges."

"Challenges? Let me tell you about challenges. I was on a ventilator for a year. See the tracheostomy scar on my neck? Well, through positive-pressure breathing exercises—and the greatest willpower I could muster—I managed to get off the machine. In fact I've got lungs like nobody's business. They're as strong as yours. In a C4 quad that's one for the books, Sachs. It consumed my life for eight months. Do you understand what I'm saying? Eight months just to handle a basic animal function. I'm not talking about painting the Sistine Chapel or playing the violin. I'm talking about fucking *breathing*."

"But you could get better. Next year, they might find a cure."

"No. Not next year. Not in ten years."

"You don't know that. They must be doing research—"

"Sure they are. Want to know what? I'm an expert. Transplanting embryonic nerve tissue onto damaged tissue to promote axonal regeneration." These words tripped easily from his handsome lips. "No significant effect. Some doctors are chemically treating the affected areas to create an environment where cells can regenerate. No significant effect— not in advanced species. Lower forms of life show pretty good success. If I were a frog I'd be walking again. Well, hopping."

"So there *are* people working on it?" Sachs asked.

"Sure. But no one expects any breakthroughs for twenty, thirty years."

"If they were expected," she shot back, "then they wouldn't be breakthroughs, now would they?"

Rhyme laughed. She was good.

Sachs tossed the veil of red hair from her eyes and said, "Your career was law enforcement, remember. Suicide's illegal."

"It's a sin too," he responded. "The Dakota Indians believed that the ghosts of those who committed suicide had to drag around the tree they'd hanged themselves from for all eternity. Did that stop suicide? Nope. They just used small trees."

"Tell you what, Rhyme. Here's my last argument." She nodded at Berger, grabbed the cuff chain. "I'm taking him in and booking him. Refute *that* one."

"Lincoln," Berger said uneasily, panic in his eyes.

Sachs took the doctor by the shoulder and led him to the door. "No," he said. "Please. Don't do this."

As Sachs opened the door Rhyme called out, "Sachs, before you do that answer me something."

She paused. One hand on the knob.

"One question."

She looked back.

"Have you ever wanted to? Kill yourself?"

She unlocked the door with a loud snap.

He said, "Answer me!"

Sachs didn't open the door. She stood with her back to him. "No. Never."

"Are you happy with your life?"

"As much as anybody."

"You're never depressed?"

"I didn't say that. I said I've never wanted to kill myself."

"You like to drive, you were telling me. People who like to drive like to drive fast. You do, don't you?"

"Yes. Sometimes."

"What's the fastest you've done?"

"I don't know."

"Over eighty?"

A dismissing smile. "Yes."

"Over a hundred?"

She gestured upward with her thumb.

"One ten? One twenty?" he asked, smiling in astonishment.

"Clocked at 168."

"My, Sachs, you *are* impressive. Well, driving that fast, didn't you think that maybe, just maybe, something might happen. A rod or axle or something would break, a tire would blow, a spot of oil on the road?"

"It was pretty safe. I'm not crazy."

"*Pretty* safe. But driving as fast as a small plane, well, that's not *completely* safe, now, is it?"

"You're leading the witness."

"No, I'm not. Stay with me. You drive that fast, you have to accept that you could have an accident and die, right?"

"Maybe," she conceded.

Berger, cuffed hands in front of him, looked on nervously, as he kneaded the pale yellow disk of spinal column.

"So you've moved close to that line, right? Ah, you know what I'm talking about. I know you do—the line between the *risk* of dying and the *certainty* of dying. See, Sachs, if you carry the dead around with you it's a very short step over that line. A short step to joining them."

She lowered her head and her face went completely still, as the curtain of hair obscured her eyes.

"Giving up the dead," he whispered, praying she wouldn't leave with Berger, knowing he was so very close to pushing her over the edge. "I touched a nerve there. How much of you wants to follow the dead? More than a little, Sachs. Oh, much more than a little."

She was hesitating. He knew he was near her heart.

She turned angrily to Berger, gripped him by the cuffs. "Come on." Pushed through the door.

Rhyme called, "You know what I'm saying, don't you?"

Again she stopped.

"Sometimes . . . things happen, Sachs. Sometimes you just can't be what you ought to be, you can't have what you ought to have. And life changes. Maybe just a little, maybe a lot. And at some point it just isn't worth the fight to try to fix what went wrong."

He watched them standing, motionless, in the doorway. The room was utterly silent. She turned and looked back at him.

"Death cures loneliness," Rhyme continued. "It cures tension. It cures the itch." Just like she'd glanced at his legs earlier he now gave a fast look at her torn fingers.

She released Berger's cuffs and walked to the window. Tears glistened on her cheeks in the yellow radiance from the street-lights outside.

"Sachs, I'm tired," he said earnestly. "I can't tell you how tired I am. You know how hard life is to start with. Pile on a whole mountainful of . . . burdens. Washing, eating, crapping, making phone calls, buttoning shirts, scratching your nose . . . Then pile on a thousand more. And more after that."

He fell silent. After a long moment she said, "I'll make a deal with you."

"What's that?"

She nodded toward the poster. "Eight twenty-three's got that mother and her little girl . . . Help us save them. Just them. If you do that I'll give him an hour alone with you." She glanced at Berger. "Provided he gets the hell out of town afterwards."

Rhyme shook his head. "Sachs, if I have a stroke, if I can't communicate . . ."

"If that happens," she said evenly, "even if you can't say a word, the deal still holds. I'll make sure you have one hour together." She crossed her arms, spread her feet again, in what was now Rhyme's favorite image of Amelia Sachs. He wished he could've seen her on the railroad tracks that morning, stopping the train. She said, "That's the best I'll do."

A moment passed. Rhyme nodded. "Okay. It's a deal." To Berger he said, "Monday?"

"Okay, Lincoln. Fair enough." Berger, still shaken, watched Sachs cautiously as she unlocked the cuffs. Afraid, it seemed, that she might change her mind. When he was free he walked quickly to the door. He realized he was still holding the vertebra and returned, set it—almost reverently—next to Rhyme on the crime scene report for the first murder that morning.

———

"Happier'n hogs in red Virginia mud," Sachs remarked, slouching in the squeaky rattan chair. Meaning Sellitto and Polling, after she'd told them that Rhyme had agreed to remain on the case for another day.

"Polling particularly," she said. "I thought the little guy was going to hug me. Don't tell him I called him that. How are you feeling? You look better." She sipped some Scotch and set the glass back on the bedside table, beside Rhyme's tumbler.

"Not bad."

Thom was changing the bedclothes. "You were sweating like a fountain," he said.

"But only above my neck," Rhyme pointed out. "Sweating, I mean."

"That right?" Sachs asked.

"Yep. That's how it works. Thermostat's busted below that. I never need any axial deodorant."

"Axial?"

"Pit," Rhyme snorted. "*Armpit*. My first aide never said armpit. He'd say, 'I'm going to elevate you by your axials, Lincoln.' Oh, and: 'If you feel like regurgitating go right ahead, Lincoln.' He called himself a 'caregiver.' The word was actually on his résumé. I have no idea why I hired him. We're very superstitious, Sachs. We think calling something by a different name is going to change it. Unsub. Perpetrator. But that aide, he was just a nurse who was up to his own armpits in piss 'n' puke. Right, Thom? Nothing to be ashamed of. It's an honorable profession. Messy but honorable."

"I thrive on mess. That's why I work for you."

"What're you, Thom? An aide or a caregiver?"

"I'm a saint."

"Ha, fast with the comebacks. And fast with the needle too. He brought me back from the dead. Done it more than once."

Rhyme was suddenly pierced with a fear that Sachs had seen him naked. Eyes fixed firmly on the unsub profile, he asked, 'Say, do I owe you some thanks too, Sachs? Did you play Clara Barton here?" He uneasily waited for her answer, didn't know how he could look at her again if she had.

"Nup," Thom answered. "Saved you all by my lonesome. Didn't want any of these sensitive souls repulsed by the sight of your baggy rear end."

Thank you, Thom, he thought. Then barked, "Now go away. We have to talk about the case. Sachs and me."

"You need some sleep."

"Of course I do. But we still need to talk about the case. Good night, good night."

After Thom left, Sachs poured some Macallan in a glass. She lowered her head and inhaled the smoky vapors.

"Who snitched?" Rhyme asked. "Pete?"

"Who?" she asked.

"Dr Taylor, the SCI man."

She hesitated long enough for him to know that Taylor was the one. She said finally, "He cares about you."

"Of course he does. That's the problem—I want him to care a little *less*. Does he know about Berger?"

"He suspects."

Rhyme grimaced. "Look, tell him that Berger's just an old friend. He . . . what?"

Sachs exhaled slowly, as if shooting cigarette smoke through her pursed lips. "You not only want me to let you kill yourself you want me to lie to the one person who could talk you out of it."

"He couldn't talk me out of it," Rhyme responded.

"Then why do you want me to lie?"

He laughed. "Let's just keep Dr Taylor in the dark for a few more days."

"All right," she said. "Jesus, you're a tough person to deal with."

He examined her closely. "Why don't you tell me about it."

"About what?"

"Who's the dead? That you haven't given up?"

"There's plenty of them."

"Such as?"

"Read the newspaper."

"Come on, Sachs."

She shook her head, stared down at her Scotch with a faint smile on her lips. "No, I don't think so."

He put her silence down to reluctance about having an intimate conversation with someone she'd known only for one day. Which seemed ironic, considering she sat next to a dozen catheters, a tube of K-Y jelly and a box of Depends. Still he wasn't going to push it and said nothing more. So he was surprised when she suddenly looked up and blurted, "It's just . . . It's just . . . Oh, *hell*." And as the sobbing began she lifted her hands to her face, spilling a good two inches of Scotland's best all over the parquet.

TWENTY-SIX

"I can't believe I'm telling you this." She sat huddled in the deep chair, legs drawn up, issue shoes kicked off. The tears were gone though her face was as ruddy as her hair.

"Go on," he encouraged.

"That guy I told you about? We were going to get an apartment together."

"Oh, with the collie. You didn't say it was a guy. Your boyfriend?"

The secret lover? Rhyme wondered.

"He *was* my boyfriend."

"I was thinking maybe it was your father you'd lost."

"Naw. Pop did pass away—three years ago. Cancer. But we knew it was coming. If that prepares you for it I guess we were prepared. But Nick . . ."

"He was killed?" Rhyme asked softly.

But she didn't answer. "Nick Carelli. One of us. A cop. Detective, third. Worked Street Crimes."

The name was familiar. Rhyme said nothing and let her continue.

"We lived together for a while. Talked about getting married." She paused, seemed to be lining up her thoughts like targets at a shooting range. "He worked undercover. So we were pretty secret about our relationship. He couldn't let word get around on the street that his gal was a cop." She cleared her throat. "It's hard to explain. See, we had this . . . thing between us. It was . . . it hasn't happened for me very often. Hell, it *never* happened before Nick. We clicked in some really deep way. He knew I had to be a cop and that wasn't a problem for him. Same with me and his working undercover. That kind of . . . wave-length. You know, where you just completely understand someone? You ever felt what I'm talking about? With your wife?"

Rhyme smiled faintly. "I did. Yes. But not with Blaine, my wife." And that was all he wanted to say on the subject. "How'd you meet?" he asked.

"The assignments lectures at the academy. Where somebody gets up and they tell you a little about what their division does. Nick was lecturing on undercover work. He asked me out on the spot. Our first date was at Rodman's Neck."

"The gun range?"

She nodded, sniffing. "Afterwards, we went to his mom's in Brooklyn and had pasta and a bottle of Chianti. She pinched me hard and said I was too skinny to have babies. Made me eat two cannoli. We went back to my place and he stayed over that night. Quite a first date, huh? From then on we saw each other all the time. It was gonna work, Rhyme. I felt it. It was gonna work just fine."

Rhyme said, "What happened?"

"He was . . ."

Another bolstering hit of old liquor. "He was on the take is what happened. The whole time I knew him."

"He was?"

"Crooked. Oh, way crooked. I never had a clue. Not a single goddamn clue. He socked it away in banks around the city. He dusted close to two hundred thousand."

Lincoln was silent a moment. "I'm sorry, Sachs. Drugs?"

"No. Merch, mostly. Appliances, TVs. 'Jackings. They called it the Brooklyn Connection. The papers did."

Rhyme was nodding. "That's why I remember it. There were a dozen of them in the ring, right? All cops?"

"Mostly. A few ICC people too."

"What happened to him? Nick?"

"You know what happens when cops bust cops. They beat the crap out of him. Said he resisted but I know he didn't. Broke three ribs, a couple fingers, smashed his face all up. Pleaded guilty but he still got twenty to thirty."

"For hijacking?" Rhyme was astonished.

"He worked a couple of the jobs himself. Pistol-whipped

one driver, took a shot at another one. Just to scare him. I *know* it was just to scare him. But the judge threw him away." She closed her eyes, pressed her lips together hard.

"When he got collared, Internal Affairs went after him like they were in heat. They checked pen registers. We were real careful about calling each other. He said perps sometimes tapped his line. But there were some calls to my place. IA came after me too. So Nick just cut me off. I mean, he *had* to. Otherwise I would've gone down with him. You know IA— it's always a goddamn witch-hunt."

"What happened?"

"To convince them that I wasn't anything to him . . . Well, he said some things about me." She swallowed, her eyes fixed on the floor. "At the IA inquest they wanted to know about me. Nick said, 'Oh, P.D. Sachs? I just fucked her a few times. Turned out she was lousy. So I dumped her.'" She tilted her head back and mopped tears with her sleeve. "The nickname? P.D."

"Lon told me."

She frowned. "Did he tell you what it means?"

"The Portable's Daughter. After your father."

She smiled wanly. "That's how it started. But that's not how it ended up. At the inquest Nick said I was such a lousy fuck it really stood for 'Pussy Diver' 'cause I probably liked girls better. Guess how fast *that* went through the department."

"It's a low common denominator out there, Sachs."

She took a deep breath. "I saw him in court toward the end of the inquest. He looked at me once and . . . I can't even describe what was in his eyes. Just pure heartbreak. Oh, he did it to protect me. But still . . . You were right, you know. About the lonely stuff."

"I didn't mean—"

"No," she said, unsmiling. "I hit you, you hit me. That was fair. And you were right. I hate being alone. I *want* to go out, I *want* to meet somebody. But after Nick I lost my taste for sex." Sachs gave a sour laugh. "Everybody thinks looking like me's wonderful. I could have my pick of guys, right? Bullshit. The only ones with the balls to ask me out're the ones who want to screw all the time. So I just gave up. It's easier by myself. I hate it, but it's easier."

At last Rhyme understood her reaction at seeing him for the first time. She was at ease with him because here was a man who was no threat to her. No sexual come-ons. Someone she wouldn't have to fend off. And perhaps a certain camaraderie too—as if they were both missing the same, crucial gene.

"You know," he joked, "you and me, we ought to get together and *not* have an affair."

She laughed. "So tell me about your wife. How long were you married?"

"Seven years. Six before the accident, one after."

"And she left you?"

"Nope. I left her. I didn't want her to feel guilty about it."

"Good of you."

"I'd have driven her out eventually. I'm a prick. You've only seen my good side." After a moment he asked, "This thing with Nick . . . it have anything to do with why you're leaving Patrol?"

"No. Well, yes."

"Gunshy?"

Finally she nodded. "Life on the street's different now. That's what did it to Nick, you know. What turned him. It's not like it was when Pop was walking his beat. Things were better then."

"You mean it's not like the *stories* your dad told you."

"Maybe," she conceded. Sachs slumped the chair. "The arthritis? That's true but it's not as serious as I pretend it is."

"I know," Rhyme said.

"You know? How?"

"I just looked at the evidence and drew some conclusions."

"Is that why you've been on my case all day? You knew I was faking?"

"I've been on your case," he said, "because you're better than you think you are."

She gave him a screwy look.

"Ah, Sachs, you remind me of me."

"I do?"

"Let me tell you a story. I'd been on crime scene detail maybe a year when we got a call from Homicide there was a guy found dead in an alley in Greenwich Village. All the sergeants were out and so I got elected to run the scene. I was twenty-six years old, remember. I go up there and check it out and it turns out the dead guy's the head of the City Health and Human Services. Now, what's he got all around him but a load of Polaroids? You should've seen some of those snaps—he'd been to one of those S&M clubs off Washington Street. Oh, and I forgot to mention, when they found him he was dressed in a stunning little black minidress and fishnet stockings.

"So, I secure the scene. All of a sudden a captain shows up and starts to cross the tape. I know he's planning to have those pictures disappear on the way to the evidence room but I was so naive I didn't care much about the pictures—I was just worried about somebody walking through the scene."

"P is for Protect the crime scene."

Rhyme chuckled. "So I didn't let him in. While he was standing at the tape screaming at me a dep com tried an end run. I told him no. *He* started screaming at me. The scene stays virgin till IRD's through with it, I told them. Guess who finally showed up?"

"The mayor?"

"Well, deputy mayor."

"And you held 'em all off?"

"Nobody got into that scene except Latents and Photography. Of course my payback was spending six months printing floaters. But we nailed the perp with some trace and a print off one of those Polaroids—happened to be the same snap the *Post* used on page one, as a matter of fact. Just like what you did yesterday morning, Sachs. Closing off the tracks and Eleventh Avenue."

"I didn't think about it," she said. "I just did it. Why're you looking at me that way?"

"Come on, Sachs. You *know* where you ought to be. On the street. Patrol, Major Crimes, IRD, doesn't matter . . . But Public Affairs? You'll rot there. It's a good job for some people but not you. Don't give up so fast."

"Oh, and you're *not* giving up? What about Berger?"

"Things're a little different with me."

Her glance questioned, They are? And she went prowling for a Kleenex. When she returned to the chair she asked, "You don't carry any corpses around with you?"

"I have in my day. They're all buried now."

"Tell me."

"Really, there's nothing—"

"Not true. I can tell. Come on—I showed you mine."

He felt an odd chill. He knew it wasn't dysreflexia. His smile faded.

"Rhyme, go on," she persisted. "I'd like to hear."

"Well, there was a case a few years ago," he said, "I made a mistake. A bad mistake."

"Tell me." She poured them each another finger of the Scotch.

"It was a domestic murder-suicide call. Husband and wife in a Chinatown apartment. He shot her, killed himself. I didn't have much time for the scene; I worked it fast. And I committed a classic error—I'd made up my mind about what I was going to find before I started looking. I found some fibers that I couldn't place but I assumed that the husband and wife'd tracked them in. I found the bullet fragments but didn't check them against the gun we found at the scene. I noticed the blowback pattern but didn't grid it to double-check the exact position of the gun. I did the search, signed off and went back to the office."

"What happened?"

"The scene had been staged. It was really a burglary-murder. And the perp had never left the apartment."

"What? He was still there?"

"After I left he crawled out from under the bed and started shooting. He killed one forensic tech and wounded an assistant ME. He got out on the street and there was a shootout with a couple of portables who'd heard the 10–13. The perp was shot up—he died later—but he killed one of the cops and wounded the other. He also shot up a family that'd just come out of a Chinese restaurant across the street. Used one of the kids as a shield."

"Oh, my God."

"Colin Stanton was the father's name. He wasn't hurt at all and he'd been an army medic—EMS said he probably could've saved his wife or one or both of the kids if he'd tried to stop the bleeding but he panicked and froze. He just stood there, watching them all die in front of him."

"Jesus, Rhyme. But it wasn't your fault. You—"

"Let me finish. That wasn't the end of it."

"No?"

"The husband went back home—upstate New York. Had a breakdown and went into a mental hospital for a while. He tried to kill himself. They put him under a suicide watch. First he tried to cut his wrist with a piece of paper—a magazine cover. Then he sneaked into the library and found a water glass in the librarian's bathroom, shattered it and slashed his wrists. They stitched him up okay and kept him in the mental hospital for another year or so. Finally they released him. A month or so after he was out he tried again. Used a knife." Rhyme added coolly, "That time it worked."

He'd learned about Stanton's death in an obituary faxed from the Albany County coroner to NYPD Public Affairs. Someone there had sent it to Rhyme via interoffice mail with a Post-It attached: *FYI—thought you'd be interested*, the officer had written.

"There was an IA investigation. Professional incompetence. They slapped my wrist. I think they should've fired me."

She sighed and closed her eyes for a moment. "And you're telling me you don't feel guilty about that?"

"Not anymore."

"I don't believe you."

"I served my time, Sachs. I lived with those bodies for a while. But I gave 'em up. If I hadn't, how could I have kept on working?"

After a long moment she said, "When I was eighteen I got a ticket. Speeding. I was doing ninety in a forty zone."

"Well."

"Dad said he'd front me the money for the fine but I'd have to pay him back. With interest. But you know what else he told me? He said he would've tanned my hide for running a red light or reckless driving. But going fast he understood. He told me, 'I know how you feel, honey. When you move they can't getcha.'" Sachs said to Rhyme, "If I couldn't drive, if I couldn't move, then maybe I'd do it too. Kill myself."

"I used to walk everywhere," Rhyme said. "I never did drive much. Haven't owned a car in twenty years. What kind do you have?"

"Nothing a snooty Manhattanite like you'd drive. A Chevy. Camaro. It was my father's."

"Who gave you the drill press. For working on cars, I assume?"

She nodded. "And a torque wrench. And spark-gap set. And my first set of ratcheting sockets—my thirteenth-birthday present." Laughing softly. "That Chevy, it's a wobbly-knob car. You know what that is? An American car. The radio and vents and light switches are all loose and cheesy. But the suspension's like a rock, it's light as an egg crate and I'll take on a BMW any day."

"And I'll be you have."

"Once or twice."

"Cars are status in the crip world," Rhyme explained. "We'd sit—or lie—around the ward in rehab and talk about what we could get out of our insurance companies. Wheelchair vans were the top of the heap. Next are hand-control cars. Which wouldn't do me any good of course." He squinted, testing his supple memory. "I haven't been in a car in years. I can't remember the last time."

"Got an idea," Sachs said suddenly. "Before your friend— Dr Berger—comes back, let me take you for a ride. Or is that a problem? Sitting up? You were saying that wheelchairs don't work for you."

"Well, no, wheelchairs're a problem. But a car? I think that'd be okay." He laughed. "A hundred and sixty-eight? Miles per hour?"

"That was a special day," Sachs said, nodding at the memory. "Good conditions. And no highway patrol."

The phone buzzed and Rhyme answered it himself. It was Lon Sellitto.

"We got S&S on all the target churches in Harlem. Dellray's in charge of that—man's become a true believer, Lincoln. You wouldn't recognize him. Oh, and I've got thirty portables and a ton of UN security cruising for any other churches we might've missed. If he doesn't show up, we're going to do a sweep of all of them at seven-thirty. Just in case he snuck in without us seeing him. I think we're going to nail him, Linc," the detective said, suspiciously enthusiastic for a New York City homicide cop.

"Okay, Lon, I'll send Amelia up to your CP around eight."
They hung up.

Thom knocked on the door before coming into the room.
As if he'd catch us in a compromising position, Rhyme
laughed to himself.

"No more excuses," he said testily. "Bed. Now."

It was after 3:00 A.M. and Rhyme had left exhaustion far
behind long ago. He was floating somewhere else. Above his
body. He wondered if he'd start to hallucinate.

"Yes, mother," he said. "Officer Sachs's staying over,
Thom. Could you get her a blanket, please?"

"What did you say?" Thom turned to face him.

"A blanket."

"No, after that," the aide said. "That word?"

"I don't know. 'Please'?"

Thom's eyes went wide with alarm. "Are you all right?
You want me to get Pete Taylor back here? The head of
Columbia-Presbyterian? The surgeon general?"

"See how this son of a bitch torments me?" Rhyme
said to Sachs. "He never knows how close he comes to
getting fired."

"A wake-up call for when?"

"Six-thirty should be fine," Rhyme said.

When he was gone, Rhyme asked, "Hey, Sachs, you like
music?"

"Love it."

"What kind?"

"Oldies, doo-wop, Motown . . . How 'bout you? You seem
like a classical kind of guy."

"See that closet there?"

"This one?"

"No, no, the other one. To the right. Open it up."

She did and gasped in amazement. The closet was a small
room filled with close to a thousand CDs.

"It's like Tower Records."

"That stereo, see it on the shelf?"

She ran her hand over the dusty black Harmon Kardon.

"It cost more than my first car," Rhyme said. "I don't use
it anymore."

"Why not?"

He didn't answer but said instead, "Put something on. Is it plugged in? It is? Good. Pick something."

A moment later she stepped out of the closet and walked over to the couch as Levi Stubbs and the Four Tops started singing about love.

It had been a year since there'd been a note of music in this room, Rhyme estimated. Silently he tried to answer Sachs's question about why he'd stopped listening. He couldn't.

Sachs lifted files and books off the couch. Lay back on it and thumbed through a copy of *Scenes of the Crime*.

"Can I have one?" she asked.

"Take ten."

"Will you . . ." Her voice braked to a halt.

"Sign it for you?" He laughed. She joined him. "How 'bout if I put my thumbprint on it? Graphoanalysts'll never give you more than an eighty-five percent probability of a handwriting match. But a thumbprint? Any friction-ridge expert'll certify it's mine."

He watched her read the first chapter. Her eyes drooped. She closed the book.

"Will you do something for me?" she asked.

"What?"

"Read to me. Something from the book. When Nick and I were together . . ." Her voice faded.

"What?"

"When we were together, a lot of times Nick'd read out loud before we went to sleep. Books, the paper, magazines . . . It's one of the things I miss the most."

"I'm a terrible reader," Rhyme confessed. "I sound like I'm reciting crime scene reports. But I've got this memory . . . It's pretty good. How 'bout if I just tell you about some scenes?"

"Would you?" She turned her back, pulled her navy blouse off and unstrapped the thin American Body Armor vest, tossed it aside. Beneath it she wore a mesh T-shirt and under that a sports bra. She pulled the blouse back on and lay on the couch, pulling the blanket over her, and curled up on her side, closed her eyes.

With the environmental-control unit Rhyme dimmed the lights.

"I always found the sites of death fascinating," he began. "They're like shrines. We're a lot more interested in where people bought the big one than where they were born. Take John Kennedy. A thousand people a day visit the Texas Book Depository in Dallas. How many you think make pilgrimages to some obstetrics ward in Boston?"

Rhyme nestled his head in the luxurious softness of the pillow. "Is this boring you?"

"No," she said. "Please don't stop."

"You know what I've always wondered about, Sachs?"

"Tell me."

"It's fascinated me for years—Calvary. Two thousand years ago. Now, *there's* a crime scene I'd like to've worked. I know what you're going to say: But we know the perps. Well, do we? All we really know is what the witnesses tell us. Remember what I say—never trust a wit. Maybe those Bible accounts aren't what happened at all. Where's the *proof*? The PE. The nails, blood, sweat, the spear, the cross, the vinegar. Sandal prints and friction ridges."

Rhyme turned his head slightly to the left and he continued to talk about crime scenes and evidence until Sachs's chest rose and fell steadily and faint strands of her fiery red hair blew back and forth under her shallow breath. With his left index finger he flipped through the ESU control and shut off the light. He too was soon asleep.

———

A faint light of dawn was in the sky.

Awakening, Carole Ganz could see it through the chicken-wire-impregnated glass above her head. Pammy. Oh, baby . . . Then she thought of Ron. And all her possessions sitting in that terrible basement. The money, the yellow knapsack . . .

Mostly, though, she was thinking about Pammy.

Something had wakened her from a light, troubled sleep. What was it?

The pain from her wrist? It throbbed horribly. She adjusted herself slightly. She—

The tubular howl of a pipe organ and a rising chorus of voices filled the room again.

That's what had wakened her. Music. A crashing wave

of music. The church wasn't abandoned. There were people around! She laughed to herself. Somebody would—

And that was when she remembered the bomb.

Carole peered around the filing cabinet. It was still there, teetering on the edge of the table. It had the crude look of real bombs and murder weapons—not the slick, shiny gadgets you see in movies. Sloppy tape, badly stripped wires, dirty gasoline . . . Maybe it's a dud, she thought. In the daylight it didn't look so dangerous.

Another burst of music. It came from directly over her head. Accompanied by a shuffling of footsteps. A door closed. Creaks and groans as people moved around the old, dry wood floors. Plumes of dust fell from the joists.

The soaring voices were cut off in mid-passage. A moment later they started singing again.

Carole banged with her feet but the floor was concrete, the walls brick. She tried to scream but the sound was swallowed by the gag. The rehearsal continued, the solemn, vigorous music rattling through the basement.

After ten minutes Carole collapsed on the floor in exhaustion. Her eyes were drawn back to the bomb again. Now the light was better and she could see the timer clearly.

Carole squinted. The timer!

It wasn't a dud at all. The arrow was set for 6:15 A.M. The dial showed the time was now 5:30.

Squirming her way farther behind the filing cabinet, Carole began to kick the metal sides with her knee. But whatever faint noises the blows made immediately vanished in the booming, mournful rendition of "Swing Low, Sweet Chariot" filling the church basement from above.

4
DOWN TO THE BONE

"This only is denied the Gods: the power to remake the past."

Aristotle

TWENTY-SEVEN

He awoke to a scent. As he often did.

And—as on many mornings—he didn't at first open his eyes but just remained in his half-seated position, trying to figure out what the unfamiliar smell might be:

The gassy scent of dawn air? The dew on the oil-slick streets? Damp plaster? He tried to detect the scent of Amelia Sachs but could not.

His thoughts skipped over her and continued. What *was* it?

Cleanser? No.

A chemical from Cooper's impromptu lab?

No, he recognized all of those.

It was . . . Ah, yes . . . marking pen.

Now he could open his eyes and—after a glance at sleeping Sachs to make certain she hadn't deserted him—found himself gazing at the Monet poster on the wall. That's where the smell was coming from. The hot, humid air of this August morning had wilted the paper and brought the scent out.

- knows CS proc.
- possibly has record
- knows FR prints
- gun = .32 Colt
- Ties vics w/ unusual knots
- "Old" appeals to him
- Called one vic "Hanna"
- Knows basic German
- Underground appeals to him

UNSUB 823			
Appearance	**Residence**	**Vehicle**	**Other**
• Caucasian male, slight build • Dark clothing • Old gloves, reddish kidskin • Aftershave; to cover up other scent? • Ski mask? Navy blue? • Gloves are dark • Aftershave = Brut • Hair color not brown • Deep scar, index finger • Casual clothes • Gloves faded? Stained?	• Prob. has safe house • Located near; B'way & 82nd, ShopRite Greenwich & Bank, ShopRite 8th Ave. & 24th ShopRite Houston & Lafayette, ShopRite • Old building, pink marble • At least 100 years old, prob. mansion or institutional	• Yellow Cab • Recent model sedan • Lt. gray, silver, biege • Rental car; prob. stolen • Hertz, silver Taurus, this year's model	• knows CS proc. • possibly has record • knows FR prints • gun = .32 Colt • Ties vics w/ unusual knots • "Old" appeals to him • Called one vic "Hanna" • Knows basic German • Underground appeals to him • Dual personalities • Maybe priest, soc. worker, counselor • Unusual wear on shoes, reads a lot? • Listened as he broke vic's finger • Left snake as slap at investigators

The wall clock's pale numbers glowed: 5:45 A.M. His eyes returned to the poster. He couldn't see it clearly, just a ghostly pattern of pure white against a lesser white. But there was enough light from the dawn sky to make out most of the words.

- Dual personalities
- Maybe priest, soc. worker, counselor
- Unusual wear on shoes, reads a lot?
- Listened as he broke vic's finger
- Left snake as slap at investigators

The falcons were waking. He was aware of a flutter at the window. Rhyme's eyes skipped over the chart again. In his office at IRD he'd nailed up a dozen erasable marker boards and on them he'd keep a tally of the characteristics of the unsubs in major cases. He remembered: pacing, staring at them, wondering about the people they described.

Molecules of paint, mud, pollen, leaf . . .

- Old building, pink marble

Thinking about a clever jewel thief he and Lon had collared ten years ago. At Central Booking the perp had coyly said they'd never find the loot from the prior jobs but if they'd consider a plea he'd tell them where he'd hidden it. Rhyme had responded, "Well, we *have* been having some trouble figuring out where it is."

"I'm sure you have," the snide crook said.

"See," Rhyme continued, "we've narrowed it down to the stone wall in the coal bin of a Colonial farmhouse on the Connecticut River. About five miles north of Long Island Sound. I just can't tell whether the house is on the east bank or the west bank of the river."

When the story made the rounds the phrase everybody used to describe the expression on the perp's face was: You had to fucking be there.

Maybe it *is* magic, Sachs, he thought.

> • At least 100 years old,
> prob. mansion or
> institutional

He scanned the poster once again and closed his eyes, leaning back into his glorious pillow. It was then that he felt the jolt. Almost like a slap on his face. The shock rose to his scalp like spreading fire. Eyes wide, locked onto the poster.

> • "Old" appeals to him

"Sachs!" he cried. "Wake up!"

She stirred and sat up. "What? What's . . . ?"

Old, old, old . . .

"I made a mistake," he said tersely. "There's a problem."

She thought at first it was something medical and she leapt from the couch, reaching for Thom's medical bag.

"No, the clues, Sachs, the *clues* . . . I got it wrong." His breathing was rapid and he ground his teeth together as he thought.

She pulled her clothes on, sat back, her fingers disappearing automatically into her scalp, scratching. "What, Rhyme? What is it?"

"The church. It might not be in Harlem." He repeated, "I made a mistake."

Just like with the perp who killed Colin Stanton's family. In criminalistics you can nail down a hundred clues perfectly and it's the one you miss that gets people killed.

"What time is it?" she asked.

"Quarter to six, a little after. Get the newspaper. The church-services schedule."

Sachs found the paper, thumbed through it. Then looked up. "What're you thinking?"

"Eight twenty-three's obsessed with what's old. If he's after an old black church then he might not mean uptown. Philip Payton started the Afro-American Realty Company in Harlem in 1900. There were two other black settlements in the city. Downtown where the courthouses are now and San Juan Hill.

They're mostly white now but . . . Oh, what the hell was I thinking of?"

"Where's San Juan Hill?"

"Just north of Hell's Kitchen. On the West Side. It was named in honor of all the black soldiers who fought in the Spanish–American War."

She read through the paper.

"Downtown churches," she said. "Well, in Battery Park there's the Seamen's Institute. A chapel there. They have services. Trinity. Saint Paul's."

"That wasn't the black area. Farther north and east."

"A Presbyterian church in Chinatown."

"Any Baptist. Evangelical?"

"No, nothing in that area at all. There's—Oh, hell." With resignation in her eyes she sighed. "Oh, no."

Rhyme understood. "Sunrise service!"

She was nodding. "Holy Tabernacle Baptist . . . Oh, Rhyme, there's a gospel service starting at six. Fifty-ninth and Eleventh Avenue."

"That's San Juan Hill! Call them!"

She grabbed the phone and dialed the number. She stood, head down, fiercely plucking an eyebrow and shaking her head. "Answer, answer . . . Hell. It's a recording. The minister must be out of his office." She said into the receiver, "This is the New York Police Department. We have reason to believe there's a firebomb in your church. Evacuate as fast as possible." She hung up, pulled her shoes on.

"Go, Sachs. You've got to get there. Now!"

"Me?"

"We're closer than the nearest precinct. You can be there in ten minutes."

She jogged toward the door, slinging her utility belt around her waist.

"I'll call the precinct," he yelled as she leapt down the stairs, hair a red cloud around her head. "And Sachs, if you ever wanted to drive fast, do it now."

———

The RRV wagon skidded into 81st Street, speeding west.

Sachs burst into the intersection at Broadway, skidded hard

and whacked a *New York Post* vending machine, sending it through Zabar's window before she brought the wagon under control. She remembered all the crime scene equipment in the back. Rear-heavy vehicle, she thought; don't corner at fifty.

Then down Broadway. Brake at the intersections. Check left. Check right. Clear. Punch it!

She peeled off on Ninth Avenue at Lincoln Center and headed south. I'm only—

Oh, hell!

A mad stop on screaming tires.

The street was closed.

A row of blue sawhorses blocked Ninth for a street fair later that morning. A banner proclaimed, *Crafts and Delicacies of all Nations. Hand in hand, we are all one.*

Gaw . . . *damn* UN! She backed up a half block and got the wagon up to fifty before she slammed into the first sawhorse. Spreading portable aluminum tables and wooden display racks in her wake, she tore a swath through the deserted fair. Two blocks later the wagon broke through the southern barricade and she skidded west on Fifty-ninth, using far more of the sidewalk than she meant to.

There was the church, a hundred yards away.

Parishioners on the steps—parents, little girls in frilly white and pink dresses, young boys in dark suits and white shirts, their hair in gangsta knobs or fades.

And from a basement window, a small puff of gray smoke.

Sachs slammed the accelerator to the floor, the engine roaring.

Grabbing the radio. "RRV Two to Central, K?"

And in the instant it took her to glance down at the Motorola to make sure the volume was up, a big Mercedes slipped out of the alley directly into her path.

A fast glimpse of the family inside, eyes wide in horror, as the father slammed on the brakes.

Sachs instinctively spun the wheel hard to the left, putting the wagon into controlled skid. Come on, she was begging the tires, grip, grip, grip! But the oily asphalt was loose from the heat of the past few days and covered with dew. The wagon danced over the road like a hydrofoil.

The rear end met the Merc's front flat-on at fifty miles an hour. With an explosive boom the 560 sheared off the rear right side of the wagon. The black CS suitcases flew into the air, breaking open and strewing their contents along the street. Church-goers dove for cover from the splinters of glass and plastic and sheet metal.

The air bag popped and deflated, stunning Sachs. She covered her face as the wagon tumbled over a row of cars and through a newsstand then skidded to a stop upside down. Newspapers and plastic evidence bags floated to the ground like tiny paratroopers.

Held upside down by the harness, blinded by her hair, Sachs wiped blood from her torn forehead and lip and tried to pop the belt release. It held tight. Hot gasoline flowed into the car and trickled along her arm. She pulled a switchblade from her back pocket, flicked the knife open and cut the seat belt. Falling, she nearly skewered herself on the knife and lay, gasping, choking on the gas fumes.

Come on, girl, get out. Out!

The doors were jammed closed and there was no escape through the crushed rear end of the wagon. Sachs began kicking the windows. The glass wouldn't break. She drew her foot back and slammed it hard into the cracked windshield. No effect, except that she nearly sprained her ankle.

Her gun!

She slapped her hip; the gun had been torn from the holster and tossed somewhere inside the car. Feeling the hot drizzle of gasoline on her arm and shoulder, she searched frantically through the papers and CS equipment littering the ceiling of the station wagon.

Then she saw the clunky Glock near the dome light. She swept it up and aimed at the side window.

Go ahead. Backdrop's clear, no spectators yet.

Then she hesitated. Would the muzzle flash ignite the gas?

She held the gun as far away from her soaked uniform blouse as she could, debating. Then squeezed the trigger.

TWENTY-EIGHT

Five shots, a star pattern, and even then the honest General Motors glass held firm.

Three more blasts, deafening her in the confines of the wagon. But at least the gas didn't explode.

She began to kick again. Finally the window burst outward in a cascade of blue-green ice. Just as she rolled out the interior of the wagon exploded with a breathless *woosh*.

Stripping down to her T-shirt, she flung away her gas-soaked uniform blouse and bulletproof vest and tossed aside the head-set mike. Felt her ankle wobble but sprinted to the front door of the church, past the fleeing churchgoers and choir. The ground floor was filled with bubbling smoke. Nearby, a section of the floor rippled and steamed and then burst into flames.

The minister appeared suddenly, choking, tears streaming down his face. He was dragging an unconscious woman behind him. Sachs helped him get her to the door.

"Where's the basement?" she asked.

He coughed hard, shook his head.

"Where?" she cried, thinking of Carole Ganz and her little daughter. "The *basement*?"

"There. But . . ."

On the other side of the patch of burning floor.

Sachs could barely see it, the smoke was so thick. A wall collapsed in front of them, the old joists and posts behind it snapping and firing sparks and jets of hot gas, which hissed into the cloudy room. She hesitated, then started for the basement door.

The minister took her arm. "Wait." He opened a closet

and grabbed a fire extinguisher, yanked the arming pin. "Let's go."

Sachs shook her head. "Not you. Keep checking up here. Tell the fire department there's a police officer and another victim in the basement."

Sachs was sprinting now.

When you move . . .

She jumped over the fiery patch of floor. But because of the smoke she misjudged the distance to the wall; it was closer than she'd thought and she slammed into the wood paneling then fell backwards, rolling as her hair brushed the fire, some strands igniting. Gagging on the stink, she crushed the flames out and started to push herself to her feet. The floor, weakened by the flames beneath, broke under her weight and her face crashed into the oak. She felt the blaze in the basement lick her hands and arms as she yanked her hands back.

Rolling away from the edge she climbed to her feet and reached for the knob to the basement door. She stopped suddenly.

Come on, girl, think better! Feel a door before opening it. If it's too hot and you let oxygen into a superheated room it'll ignite and the backdraft'll fry your ass good. She touched the wood. It was scorching hot.

Then thought: But what the hell else can I do?

Spitting on her hand, she gripped the knob fast, twisting it open and releasing it just before the burn seared her palm.

The door burst open and a cloud of smoke and sparks shot outward.

"Anybody down there?" she called and started down.

The lower stairs were burning. She blasted them with a short burst of carbon dioxide and leapt into the murky basement. She broke through the second-to-last step, pitching forward. The extinguisher clattered to the floor as she grabbed the railing just in time to save her leg from snapping.

Pulling herself out of the broken step, Sachs squinted through the haze. The smoke wasn't as bad down here—it was rising—but the flames were raging all around her. The extinguisher had rolled under a burning table. Forget it! She ran through the smoke.

"Hello?" she shouted.

No answer.

Then remembered that Unsub 823 used duct tape; he liked his vics silent.

She kicked in a small doorway and looked inside the boiler room. There was a door leading outside but burning debris blocked it completely. Beside it stood the fuel tank, which was now surrounded by flames.

It won't explode, Sachs remembered from the academy—the lecture on arson. Fuel oil doesn't explode. Kick aside the debris and push the door open. Clear your escape route. *Then* go look for the woman and the girl.

She hesitated, watching the flames roll over the side of the oil tank.

It won't explode, it won't explode.

She started forward, edging toward the door.

It won't—

The tank suddenly puffed out like a heated soda can and split down the middle. The oil squirted into the air, igniting in a huge orange spume. A fiery pool formed on the floor and flowed toward Sachs.

Won't explode. Okay. But it burns pretty fucking well. She leapt back through the door, slammed it shut. So much for her escape route.

Backing toward the stairs, choking now, keeping low, looking for any signs of Carole and Maggie. Could 823 have changed the rules? Could he have given up on basements and put these vics in the church attic?

Crack.

A fast look upward. She saw a large oak beam, rippling with flames, start to fall.

With a scream Sachs leapt aside, but tripped and landed hard on her back, staring at the huge falling bar of wood streaking directly at her face and chest. Instinctively she held her hands up.

A huge bang as the beam landed on a child's Sunday-school chair. It stopped inches from Sachs's head. She crawled out from underneath and rolled to her feet.

Looking around the room, peering through the darkening smoke.

Hell no, she thought suddenly. I'm not losing another one.

Choking, Sachs turned back to the fire and staggered toward the one corner she hadn't checked.

As she jogged forward a leg shot out from behind a file cabinet and tripped her.

Hands flying outward, Sachs landed face down inches from a pool of burning oil. She rolled to her side, drawing her weapon and swinging it into the panicked face of a blond woman struggling to sit up.

Sachs pulled the gag off her mouth and the woman spit black mucus. She gagged for a moment, a deep, dying sound.

"Carole Ganz?"

She nodded.

"Your daughter?" Sachs cried.

"Not . . . here. My hands! The cuffs."

"No time. Come on." Sachs cut Carole's ankles free with her switchblade.

It was then that she saw, against the wall by the window, a melting plastic bag.

The planted clues! The ones that told where the little girl would be. She stepped toward it. But with a deafening bang the door to the boiler room cracked in half, spewing a six-inch tidal wave of burning oil over the floor, surrounding the bag, which disintegrated instantly.

Sachs stared for a moment and then heard the woman's scream. All the stairs were blazing now. Sachs knocked the fire extinguisher out from under the smoldering table. The handle and nozzle had melted away and the metal canister was too hot to grasp. With her knife she cut a patch off her uniform blouse and lifted the crackling extinguisher by its neck, flung it to the top of the burning stairs. It staggered for a moment, like an uncertain bowling pin, and then started down.

Sachs drew her Glock and when the red cylinder was halfway down, fired one round.

The extinguisher erupted in a huge booming explosion; pieces of red shrapnel from the casing hissed over their heads. The mushroom cloud of carbon dioxide and powder settled over the stairs and momentarily dampened most of the flames.

"Now, move!" Sachs shouted.

Together they took the steps two at a time, Sachs carrying

her own weight and half the woman's, and pushed through the doorway into the inferno on the first floor. They hugged the wall as they stumbled toward the exit, while above them stained-glass windows burst and rained hot shards— the colorful bodies of Jesus and matthew and Mary and God Himself—down upon the bent backs of the escaping women.

TWENTY-NINE

Forty minutes later, Sachs had been salved and bandaged and stitched and had sucked so much pure oxygen she felt like she was tripping. She sat beside Carole Ganz. They stared at what was left of the church. Which was virtually nothing.

Only two walls remained and, curiously, a portion of the third floor, jutting into space above a lunar landscape of ash and debris piled in the basement.

"Pammy, Pammy . . ." Carole moaned, then retched and spit. She took her own oxygen mask to her face, leaned back, weary and in pain.

Sachs examined another alcohol-soaked rag with which she was wiping the blood from her face. The rags had started out brown and were now merely pink. The wounds weren't serious—a cut on her forehead, swatches of second-degree burns on her arm and hand. Her lips were no longer flawless, however; the lower one had been cut deeply in the crash, the tear requiring three stitches.

Carole was suffering from smoke inhalation and a broken wrist. An impromptu cast covered her left wrist and she cradled it, head down, speaking through clenched teeth. Every breath was an alarming wheeze. "That son of a bitch." Coughing. "Why . . . Pammy? Why on earth? A three-year-old child!" She wiped angry tears with the back of her uninjured arm.

"Maybe he doesn't want to hurt her. So he just brought you to the church."

"No," she spat out angrily. "He doesn't care about her. He's sick! I saw the way he looked at her. I'm going to kill him. I'm going to fucking kill him." The harsh words dissolved into a harsher bout of coughing.

Sachs winced in pain. She'd unconsciously dug a nail into a burned fingertip. She pulled out her watchbook. "Can you tell me what happened?"

Between bouts of sobbing and throaty coughs, Carole told her the story of the kidnapping.

"You want me to call anybody?" Sachs asked. "Your husband?"

Carole didn't answer. She drew her knees up to her chin, hugged herself, wheezing roughly.

With her scalded right hand Sachs squeezed the woman's biceps and repeated the question.

"My husband . . ." She stared at Sachs with an eerie look. "My husband's dead."

"Oh, I'm sorry."

Carole grew groggy from the sedative and a woman medic helped her into the ambulance to get some rest. Sachs looked up and saw Lon Sellitto and Jerry Banks running toward her from the burned-out church.

"Jesus, officer." Sellitto was surveying the carnage in the street. "What about the girl?"

Sachs nodded. "He's still got her."

Banks said, "You okay?"

"Nothing serious." Sachs glanced toward the ambulance. "The vic, Carole, she doesn't have any money, no place to stay. She's in town to work for the UN. Think you could make some calls, detective? See if they could set her up for a while?"

"Sure," Sellitto said.

"And the planted clues?" Banks asked. He winced as he touched a bandage over his right eyebrow.

"Gone," Sachs said. "I saw them. In the basement. Couldn't get to them in time. Burned up and buried."

"Oh, man," Banks muttered. "What's going to happen to the little girl?"

What does he *think's* going to happen to her?

She walked back toward the wreck of the IRD wagon, found the headset. She pulled it on and was about to call in a patch request to Rhyme but hesitated then lifted off the mike. What could he tell her anyway? She looked at the church. How can you work a crime scene when there *is* no scene?

She was standing with her hands on her hips, staring out onto the smoldering hulk of the building, when she heard a sound she couldn't place. A whining, mechanical sound. She paid no attention to it until she was aware of Lon Sellitto pausing as he dusted ash off his wrinkled shirt. He said, "I don't believe it."

She turned toward the street.

A large black van was parked a block away. A hydraulic ramp was protruding off the side and something sat on it. She squinted. One of those bomb squad robots, it seemed. The ramp lowered to the sidewalk and the robot rolled off.

Then she laughed out loud.

The contraption turned toward them and started to move. The wheelchair reminded her of a Pontiac Firebird, candy-apple red. It was one of those electric models, small rear wheels, a large battery and motor mounted underneath.

Thom walked along beside it but Lincoln Rhyme himself was driving—in control, she observed wryly—via a straw that he held in his mouth. His movements were oddly graceful. Rhyme pulled up to her and stopped.

"All right, I lied," he said abruptly.

She exhaled a sigh. "About your back? When you said you couldn't use a wheelchair."

"I'm confessing I lied. You're going to be mad, Amelia. So be mad and get it over with."

"You ever notice when you're in a good mood you call me Sachs, when you're in a bad mood, you call me Amelia?"

"I'm not in a bad mood," he snapped.

"He really isn't," Thom agreed. "He just hates to get caught at anything." The aide nodded toward the impressive wheelchair. She glanced at the side. It was made by the Action Company, a Storm Arrow model. "He had this in the closet downstairs all the while he spun his pathetic little tale of woe. Oh, I let him have it for that."

"No annotations, Thom, thank you. I'm apologizing, all right? I. Am. Sorry."

"He's had it for years," Thom continued. "Learned the sip-'n'-puff cold. That's the straw control. He's really very good at it. By the way, he always calls *me* Thom. I *never* get preferential last-name treatment."

"I got tired of being stared at," Rhyme said matter-of-factly. "So I stopped going for joyrides." Then glanced at her torn lip. "Hurt?"

She touched her mouth, which was bent into a grin. "Stings like hell."

Rhyme glanced sideways. "And what happened to you, Banks? Shaving your forehead now?"

"Walked into a fire truck." The young man grinned and touched the bandage again.

"Rhyme," Sachs began, smiling no longer. "There's nothing here. He's got the little girl and I couldn't get to the planted PE in time."

"Ah, Sachs, there's always *something*. Have faith in the teachings of Monsieur Locard."

"I saw them burn up, the clues. And if there was anything left at all, it's all buried under tons of debris."

"Then we'll look for the clues he didn't mean to leave. We'll do this scene together, Sachs. You and me. Come on."

He gave two short breaths into the straw and started forward. They'd got ten feet nearer the church when she said suddenly, "Wait."

He braked to a stop.

"You're getting careless, Rhyme. Get some rubber bands on those wheels. Wouldn't want to confuse your prints with the unsub's."

———

"Where do we start?"

"We need a sample of the ash," Rhyme said. "There were some clean paint cans in the back of the wagon. See if you can find one."

She collected a can from the remains of the RRV.

"You know where the fire started?" Rhyme asked.

"Pretty much."

"Take a sample of ash—a pint or two—as close to the point of origin as you can get."

"Right," she said, climbing up on a five-foot-high wall of

brick—all that remained of the north side of the church. She peered down into the smoky pit at her feet.

A fire marshal called, "Hey, officer, we haven't secured the area yet. It's dangerous."

"Not as dangerous as the last time I was there," she answered. And holding the handle of the can in her teeth started down the wall.

Lincoln Rhyme watched her but he was really seeing himself, three and a half years ago, pull his suit jacket off and climb down into the construction site at the subway entrance near City Hall. "Sachs," Rhyme called. She turned. "Be careful. I saw what was left of the RRV. I don't want to lose you twice in one day."

She nodded and then disappeared over the edge of the wall.

After a few minutes Rhyme barked to Banks, "Where is she?"

"I don't know."

"What I'm saying is, could you go check on her?"

"Oh, sure." He walked to the wall, looked over.

"Well?" Rhyme asked.

"It's a mess."

"Of *course* it's a mess. Do you see her?"

"No."

"Sachs?" Rhyme shouted.

There was a long groan of wood then a crash. Dust rose.

"Sachs? Amelia?"

No answer.

Just as he was about to send ESU in after her they heard her voice. "Incoming."

"Jerry?" Rhyme called.

"Ready," the young detective called.

The can came flying up out of the basement. Banks caught it one-handed. Sachs climbed out of the basement, wiping her hands on her slacks, wincing.

"Okay?"

She nodded.

"Now, let's work the alley," Rhyme ordered. "There's traffic at all hours around here so he'd want the car off the street while he got her inside. That's where he parked. Used tha' door right there."

"How do you know?"

"There're two ways to open locked doors—without explos-ives, that is. Locks and hinges. This one'd be dead-bolted from the inside so he took the pins out of the hinges. See, he didn' bother to put them in very far again when he left."

They started at the door and worked their way to the back of the grim canyon, the smoldering building on their right. They moved a foot at a time, Sachs training the PoliLight on the cobblestones. "I want tire treads," Rhyme announced. "I want to know where his trunk was."

"Here," she said, examining the ground. "Treads. But I don' know whether these're the front or the rear tires. He might've backed in."

"Are they clear or fuzzy? The treadmarks?"

"A little fuzzy."

"Then those're the front." He laughed at her bewildered expression. "You're the automotive expert, Sachs. Next time you get in a car and start it see if you don't spin the wheel a little before you start moving. To see if the tires are pointed straight. The front treads're always fuzzier than the rear. Now, the stolen car was a '97 Ford Taurus. It measures 197.5 stem to stern, wheelbase 108.5. Approximately 45 inches from the center of the rear tire to the trunk. Measure that and vacuum."

"Come on, Rhyme. How'd you know that?"

"Looked it up this morning. You do the vic's clothing?"

"Yep. Nails and hair too. And, Rhyme, get this: the little girl's name is Pam but he called her Maggie. Just like he did with the German girl—he called her Hanna, remember?"

"You mean his other persona did," Rhyme said. "I wonder who the characters are in his little play."

"I'm going to vacuum around the door too," she announced. Rhyme watched her—face cut and hair uneven, singed short in spots. She vacuumed the base of the door and just as he was about to remind her that crime scenes were three-dimensional she ran the vacuum up and around the jamb.

"He probably looked inside before he took her in," she said, and began vacuuming the windowsills too.

Which would have been Rhyme's next order.

He listened to the whine of the Dustbuster. But second by second he was fading away. Into the past, some hours before.

"I'm—" Sachs began.

"Shhh," he said.

Like the walks he now took, like the concerts he now attended, like so many of the conversations he had, Rhyme was slipping deeper and deeper into his consciousness. And when he got to a particular place—even he had no idea where—he found he wasn't alone. He was picturing a short man wearing gloves, dark sports clothes, a ski mask. Climbing out of the silver Ford Taurus sedan, which smelled of cleanser and new car. The woman—Carole Ganz—was in the trunk, her child captive in an old building made of pink marble and expensive brick. He saw the man dragging the woman from the car.

Almost a memory, it was that clear.

Popping the hinges, pulling open the door, dragging her inside, tying her up. He started to leave but paused. He walked to a place where he could look back and see Carole clearly. Just like he'd stared down at the man he'd buried at the railroad tracks yesterday morning.

Just like he'd chained Tammie Jean Colfax to the pipe in the center of the room. So he could get a good look at her.

But why? Rhyme wondered. Why does he look? To make sure the vic can't escape? To make sure he hasn't left anything behind? To—

His eyes sprang open; the indistinct apparition of Unsub 823 vanished. "Sachs! Remember the Colfax scene? When you found the glove print?"

"Sure."

"You said he was watching her, that's the reason he chained her out in the open. But you didn't know why. Well, I figured it out. He watches the vics because he *has to*."

Because it's his nature.

"What do you mean?"

"Come on!"

Rhyme sipped twice into the straw control, which turned the Arrow wheelchair around. Then puffed hard and he started forward.

He wheeled to the sidewalk, sipped hard into the straw to stop. He squinted as he looked all around him. "He wants to see his victims. And I'm betting he wanted to see the parishioners too. From someplace he thought was safe. Where he didn't bother to sweep up afterwards."

He was gazing across the street at the only secluded vantage point on the block: the outdoor patio of a restaurant opposite the church.

"There! Sweep it clean, Sachs."

She nodded, slipped a new clip into her Glock, grabbed evidence bags, a pair of pencils and the Dustbuster. He saw her run across the street and work her way up the steps carefully, examining them. "He was here," she shouted. "There's a glove print. And the shoeprint—it's worn just like the other ones."

Yes! Rhyme thought. Oh, this felt good. The warm sun, the air, the spectators. And the excitement of the chase.

When you move they can't getcha.

Well, if *we* move faster, maybe we can.

Rhyme happened to glance at the crowd and saw that some people were staring at him. But far more were watching Amelia Sachs.

For fifteen minutes she pored over the scene and when she returned she held up a small evidence bag.

"What did you find, Sachs? His driver's license? His birth certificate?"

"Gold," she said, smiling. "I found some gold."

THIRTY

C ome on, people," Rhyme called. "We've got to move on this one. Before he gets the girl to the next scene. I mean *move*!"

Thom did a sitting transfer to get Rhyme from the Storm Arrow back into bed, perching him momentarily on a sliding board and then easing him back into the Clinitron. Sachs glanced at the wheelchair elevator that had been built into one of the bedroom closets—it was the one he hadn't wanted her to open when he was directing her to the stereo and CDs.

Rhyme lay still for a moment, breathing deeply from the exertion.

"The clues're gone," he reminded them. "There's no way we can figure out where the next scene is. So we're going for the big one—his safe house."

"You think you can find it?" Sellitto asked.

Do we have a choice? Rhyme thought, and said nothing.

Banks hurried up the stairs. He hadn't even stepped into the bedroom before Rhyme blurted, "What did they say? Tell me. *Tell* me."

Rhyme knew that the tiny fleck of gold that Sachs had found was beyond the capabilities of Mel Cooper's impromptu lab. He'd asked the young detective to speed it down to the FBI's regional PERT office and have it analyzed.

"They'll call us in the next half hour."

"Half *hour*?" Rhyme muttered. "Didn't they give it priority?"

"You bet they did. Dellray was there. You should've seen him. He ordered every other case put on hold and said if the metallurgy report wasn't in your hands ASAP there'd be one mean mother—you get the picture—reaming their—you get the rest of the picture."

"Rhyme," Sachs said, "there's something else the Ganz woman said that might be important. He told her he'd let her go if she agreed to let him flail her foot."

"Flail?"

"Cut the skin off it."

"*Flay*," Rhyme corrected.

"Oh. Anyway, he didn't do anything. She said it was—in the end—like he couldn't bring himself to cut her."

"Just like the first scene—the man by the railroad tracks," Sellitto offered.

"Interesting. . . ." Rhyme reflected, "I thought he'd cut the vic's finger to discourage anybody from stealing the ring. But maybe not. Look at his behavior: Cutting the finger off the cabbie and carrying it around. Cutting the German girl's arm and leg. Stealing the bones and the snake skeleton. Listening while he broke Everett's finger . . . There's something about the way he sees his victims. Something . . ."

"Anatomical?"

"Exactly, Sachs."

"Except the Ganz woman," Sellitto said.

"My point," Rhyme said. "He could've cut her and still kept her alive for us. But something stopped him. What?"

Sellitto said, "What's different about her? Can't be that she's a woman. Or she's from out of town. So was the German girl."

"Maybe he didn't want to hurt her in front of her daughter," Banks said.

"No," Rhyme said, laughing grimly, "compassion isn't his thing."

Sachs said suddenly, "But that *is* one thing different about her—she's a mother."

Rhyme considered this. "That could be it. Mother and daughter. It didn't carry enough weight for him to let them go. But it stopped him from torturing her. Thom, jot that down. With a question mark." He then asked Sachs, "Did she say anything else about the way he looked?"

Sachs flipped through her notebook.

"Same as before." She read. "Ski mask, slight build, black gloves, he—"

"*Black* gloves?" Rhyme looked at the chart on the wall. "Not red?"

"She said black. I asked her if she was sure."

"And that other bit of leather was black too, wasn't it, Mel? Maybe *that* was from the gloves. So what's the red leather from?"

Cooper shrugged. "I don't know but we found a couple pieces of it. So it's something close to him."

Rhyme looked over the evidence bags. "What else did we find?"

"The trace we vacuumed in the alley and by the doorway." Sachs tapped the filter over a sheet of newsprint and Cooper went over it with a loupe. "Plenty o' nothin'," he announced. "Mostly soil. Bits of minerals. Manhattan mica schist. Feldspar."

Which was found throughout the city.

"Keep going."

"Decomposed leaves. That's about it."

"How about the Ganz woman's clothes?"

Cooper and Sachs opened the newspaper and examined the trace.

"Mostly soil," Cooper said. "And a few bits of what look like stone."

"Where did he keep her at his safe house? Exactly?"

"On the floor in the basement. She said it was a dirt floor."

"Excellent!" Rhyme shouted. To Cooper: "Burn it. The soil."

Cooper placed a sample in the GC-MS. They waited impatiently for the results. Finally the computer screen blinked. The grid resembled a lunar landscape.

"All right, Lincoln. Interesting. I'm reading off-the-charts for tannin and—"

"Sodium carbonate?"

"Ain't he amazin'?" Cooper laughed. "How'd you know?"

"They were used in tanneries in the eighteenth and nineteenth centuries. The tannic acid cures the hide and the alkaline fixes it. So, his safe house is near the site of an old tannery."

He smiled. Couldn't help himself. He thought: You hear foot-steps, 823? That's us behind you.

His eyes slipped to the Randel Survey map. "Because of the smell no one wanted tanneries in their neighborhoods so the commissioners restricted them. I know there were some on the Lower East Side. And in West Greenwich Village—when it literally *was* a village, a suburb of the city. And then on the far West Side in the Fifties—near the stockyard tunnel where we found the German girl. Oh, and in Harlem in the early 1900s."

Rhyme glanced at the list of grocery stores—the locations of the ShopRites that sold veal shanks. "Chelsea's out. No tanning there. Harlem too—no *ShopRites* there. So, it's the West Village, Lower East Side or Midtown West Side—Hell's Kitchen again. Which he seems to like."

Only about ten square miles, Rhyme estimated cynically. He'd figured out on his first day on the job that it was easier to hide in Manhattan than in the North Woods.

"Let's keep going. What about the stone in Carole's clothes?"

Cooper was bent over the microscope. "Okay. Got it."

"Patch it in to me, Mel."

Rhyme's computer screen burst to life and he watched the flecks of stone and crystal, like brilliant asteroids.

"Move it around," Rhyme instructed. Three substances were bonded together.

"The one on the left is marble, pinkish," Cooper said. "Like what we found before. And in between, that gray stuff . . ."

"It's mortar. And the other is brownstone." Rhyme announced. "It's from a Federal-style building, like the 1812 City Hall. Only the front facade was marble; the rest was brownstone. They did it to save money. Well, they *did* it so the money appropriated for marble could find its way into various pockets. Now, what else do we have? The ash. Let's find the arson accelerant."

Cooper ran the ash sample through the GC-MS. He stared at the curve that appeared on the screen.

Newly refined gasoline, containing its manufacturer's dyes and additives, was unique and could be traced back to a single source, as long as different batches of gas weren't mixed together at the service station where the perp bought it. Cooper announced that the gasoline matched perfectly the brand sold by the Gas Exchange service stations.

Banks grabbed the Yellow Pages and flipped them open. "We've got six stations in Manhattan. Three downtown. One at Sixth Avenue and Houston. One on Delancey, 503 East. And one at Nineteenth and Eighth."

"Nineteenth's too far north," Rhyme said. He stared at the profile chart. "East Side or West. Which is it?"

Grocery stores, gasoline . . .

A lanky figure suddenly filled the doorway.

"I still invited to this here party?" Frederick Dellray asked.

"Depends," Rhyme countered. "You bearing gifts?"

"Ah got presents galore," the agent said, waving a folder emblazoned with the familiar disk of the FBI emblem.

"You *ever* knock, Dellray?" Sellitto asked.

"Got outa the habit, you know."

"Come on in," Rhyme said. "What've you got?"

"Dunno for sure. Doesn't make any sense to this boy. But then, whatta I know?"

Dellray read from the report for a moment then said, "We had Tony Farco at PERT—said 'Hey' to you by the way, Lincoln—analyze that bit of PE you found. Turns out it's gold leaf. Probably sixty to eighty years old. He found a few cellulose fibers attached so he thinks it's from a book."

"Of *course*! Gold topstain from a page," Rhyme said.

"Now he also found some particles of ink on it. He said, I'm quotin' the boy now: 'It's not inconsistent with the type of ink the New York Public Library uses to stamp the ends of their books.' Don't he talk funny?"

"A library book," Rhyme mused.

Amelia Sachs said, "A *red-leather-bound* library book."

Rhyme stared at her. "Right!" he shouted. "*That's* what the bits of red leather're from. Not the glove. It's a book he carries around with him. Could be his bible."

"Bible?" Dellray asked. "You thinkin' he's some kinda religious nutzo?"

"Not *the* Bible, Fred. Call the library again, Banks. Maybe that's how he wore down his shoes—in the reading room. I know, it's a long shot. But we don't have a lot of options here.

I want a list of all the antiquarian books stolen from Manhattan locations in the past year."

"Will do." The young man rubbed a shaving scar as he called the mayor at home and bluntly asked hizzoner to contact the director of the public library and tell them what they needed.

A half hour later the fax machine buzzed and spewed out two pages. Thom ripped the transmission out of the machine. "Whoa, readers sure have sticky fingers in this city," he said as he brought it to Rhyme.

Eighty-four books fifty years old or older had disappeared from the public library branches in the past twelve months, thirty-five of them in Manhattan.

Rhyme scanned the list. Dickens, Austen, Hemingway, Dreiser . . . Books about music, philosophy, wine, literary criticism, fairy tales. Their value was surprisingly low. Twenty, thirty dollars. He supposed that none of them were first editions but perhaps the thieves hadn't known that.

He continued to scan the list.

Nothing, nothing. Maybe—

And then he saw it.

Crime in Old New York, by Richard Wille Stephans, published by Bountiful Press in 1919. Its value was listed at sixty-five dollars, and it had been stolen from the Delancey Street branch of the New York Public Library nine months earlier. It was described as five by seven inches in size, bound in red kidskin, with marbleized endpapers, gilded edges.

"I want a copy of it. I don't care how. Get somebody to the Library of Congress if you have to."

Dellray said, "I'll take care of that one."

Grocery stores, gasoline, the library . . .

Rhyme had to make a decision. There were three hundred searchers available—cops and state troopers and federal agents—but they'd be spread microscopically thin if they had to search both the West and East sides of downtown New York.

Gazing at the profile chart.

Is your house in the West Village? Rhyme silently asked 823. Did you buy the gas and steal the book on the East Side to fox us? Or is that your real neighborhood? How clever are you? No, no, the question's not how clever you are but how clever you *think* you are. How confident were you that we'd never find those minuscule bits of yourself that M. Locard assures us you'd leave behind?

Finally Rhyme ordered, "Go with the Lower East. Forget the Village. Get everybody down there. All of Bo's troops, all of yours, Fred. Here's what you're looking for: A large Federal-style building, close to two hundred years old, rose-colored marble front, brownstone sides and back. May have been a mansion or a public building at one time. With a garage or carriage house attached. A Taurus sedan and a Yellow Cab coming and going for the past few weeks. More often in the last few days."

Rhyme glanced at Sachs.

Giving up the dead . . .

Sellitto and Dellray made their calls.

Sachs said to Rhyme, "I'm going too."

"I hadn't expected anything else."

When the door had closed downstairs he whispered, "Godspeed, Sachs. Godspeed."

THIRTY-ONE

Three squad cars cruised slowly through the streets of the Lower East Side. Two constables in each. Eyes searching.

And a moment later two black broughams appeared . . . two *sedans*, he meant. Unmarked, but their telltale searchlights next to the left side-view mirrors left no doubt who they were.

He'd known they were narrowing the search, of course, and that it was only a matter of time until they found his house. But he was shocked that they were this close. And he was particularly upset to see the cops get out and examine a silver Taurus parked on Canal Street.

How the hell had they found out about his carriage? He'd known that stealing a car was a huge risk but he thought it would take Hertz days to notice the missing vehicle. And even if they did he was sure the constables would never connect him with the theft. Oh, they were good.

One of the mean-eyed cops happened to glance at his cab.

Staring forward, the bone collector turned slowly onto Houston Street, lost himself in a crowd of other cabs. A half hour later, he'd ditched the taxi and the Hertz Taurus and had returned on foot to the mansion.

Young Maggie looked up at him.

She was scared, yes, but she'd stopped crying. He wondered if he should just keep her. Take himself a daughter. Raise her. The idea glowed within him for a moment or two then it faded.

UNSUB 823			
Appearance	**Residence**	**Vehicle**	**Other**
• Caucasian male, slight build • Dark clothing • Old gloves, reddish kidskin • Aftershave; to cover up other scent? • Ski mask? Navy blue? • Gloves are dark • Aftershave = Brut • Hair color not brown • Deep scar, index finger • Casual clothes • Gloves are black	• Prob. has safe house • Located near; B'way & 82nd, ShopRite Greenwich & Bank, ShopRite 8th Ave. & 24th ShopRite Houston & Lafayette, ShopRite • Old building, pink marble • At least 100 years old, prob. mansion or institutional • Federal-style building, Lower East Side	• Yellow Cab • Recent model sedan • Lt. gray, silver, biege • Rental car; prob. stolen • Hertz, silver Taurus, this year's model	• knows CS proc. • possibly has record • knows FR prints • gun = .32 Colt • Ties vics w/ unusual knots • "Old" appeals to him • Called one vic "Hanna" • Knows basic German • Underground appeals to him • Dual personalities • Maybe priest, soc. worker, counselor • Unusual wear on shoes, reads a lot? • Listened as he broke vic's finger • Left snake as slap at investigators • Wanted to flay vic's foot • Called one vic "Maggie" • Mother & child, special meaning to him? • Book "Crime in Old NY," his model?

No, there'd be too many questions. Also, there was something eerie about the way the girl was looking at him. She seemed older than her years. She'd always remember what he'd done. Oh, for a while she might think it had been a dream. But then someday the truth would come out. It always did. Repress what you will, someday the truth comes out.

No, he couldn't trust her any more than he trusted anyone else. Every human soul would let you down in the end. You could trust hate. You could trust bone. Everything else was betrayal.

He crouched beside Maggie and eased the tape off her mouth.

"Mommy!" she howled. "I want my mommy!"

He said nothing, just stood and looked down at her. At her delicate skull. At her twigs of arms.

She screamed like a siren.

He took off his glove. His fingers hovered over her for a moment. Then he caressed the soft hair on her head. (*"Fingerprints can be lifted from flesh, if taken within 90 minutes of contact [See KROMEKOTE], but no one has as yet successfully lifted and reconstructed friction-ridge prints from human hair."* Rhyme, *Physical Evidence*, 4th ed., Forensic Press, 1994.)

The bone collector slowly rose and walked upstairs, into the large living room of the building, past the paintings on the walls—the workers, the staring women and children. He cocked his head at a faint noise outside. Then louder—a clatter of metal. He grabbed his weapon and hurried to the back of the building. Unbolting the door he pushed it open suddenly, dropping into a two-handed shooting stance.

The pack of wild dogs glanced at him. They returned quickly to the trash can they'd knocked over. He slipped the gun into his pocket and returned to the living room.

He found himself next to the bottle-glass window again, looking out at the old graveyard. Oh, yes. There! There was the man again, wearing black, standing in the cemetery. In the distance the sky was spiked by the black masts of clipper ships and sloops docked in the East River along the Out Ward's shore.

The bone collector felt an overwhelming sense of sorrow.

He wondered if some tragedy had just occurred. Maybe the Great Fire of 1776 had just destroyed most of the buildings along Broadway. Or the yellow fever epidemic of 1795 had decimated the Irish community. Or the *General Slocum* excursion-boat fire in 1904 had killed killed over a thousand women and children, destroying the Lower East Side's German neighborhood.

Or maybe he was sensing tragedies soon to occur.

After a few minutes Maggie's screams grew quiet, replaced by the sounds of the old city, the roar of steam engines, the clang of bells, the pops of black-powder gunshots, the clop of hooves on resonant cobblestones.

He continued to stare, forgetting the constables who pursued him, forgetting Maggie, just watching the ghostly form stroll down the street.

Then and now.

His eyes remained focused out the window for a long moment, lost in a different time. And so he didn't notice the wild dogs, who'd pushed through the back door he'd left ajar. They looked at him through the doorway of the living room and paused only momentarily before turning around and loping quietly into the back of the building.

Noses lifted at the smells, ears pricked at the sounds of the strange place. Particularly the faint wailing that rose from somewhere beneath them.

———

It was a sign of their desperation that even the Hardy Boys split up.

Bedding was working a half-dozen blocks around Delancey, Saul was farther south. Sellitto and Banks each had their search areas, and the hundreds of other officers, FBI agents and troopers made the door-to-door rounds, asking about a slight man, a young child crying, a silver Ford Taurus, a deserted Federal-style building, fronted in rose marble, the rest of it dark brownstone.

Huh? What the hell you mean, Federal? . . . Seen a kid? You asking if I ever seen a kid on the Lower East? Yo, Jimmy, you ever see any kids 'round here? Like not in the last, what, sixty seconds?

Amelia Sachs was flexing her muscle. She insisted that she be on Sellitto's crew, the one hitting the ShopRite on East Houston that had sold Unsub 823 the veal chop. And the gas station that had sold him the gasoline. The library from which he'd stolen *Crime in Old New York*.

But they'd found no leads there and scattered like wolves smelling a dozen different scents. Each picked a chunk of neighborhood to call his or her own.

As Sachs gunned the engine of the new RRV and tried another block she felt the same frustration she'd known when working the crime scenes over the past several days: too damn much evidence, too much turf to cover. The hopelessness of it. Here, on the hot, damp streets, branching into a hundred other streets and alleys running past a thousand buildings—all old—finding the safe house seemed as impossible as finding that hair that Rhyme had told her about, pasted to the ceiling by the blowback from a .38 revolver.

She'd intended to hit every street but as time wore on and she thought of the child buried underground, near death, she began to search more quickly, speeding down streets, glancing right and left for the rosy-marble building. Doubt stabbed her. Had she missed the building in her haste? Or should she drive like lightning and cover more streets?

On and on. Another block, another. And still nothing.

After the villain's death his effects were secured and perused by detectives. His diary showed that he had murdered eight good citizens of the city. Nor was he above grave robbery, for it was ascertained from his pages (if his claims be true) that he had violated several holy resting places in cemeteries around the city. None of his victims had accorded him the least affront;—nay, most were upstanding citizens, industrious and innocent. And yet he felt not a modicum of guilt. Indeed, he seems to have labored under the mad delusion that he was doing his victims a favor.

Lincoln Rhyme's left ring finger twitched slightly and the

frame turned the onion-skin page of *Crime in Old New York*, which had been delivered by two federal officers ten minutes earlier, service expedited thanks to Fred Dellray's inimitable style.

> *"Flesh withers and can be weak,"*—*(the villain wrote in his ruthless yet steady hand)*—*"Bone is the strongest aspect of the body. As old as we may be in the flesh, we are always young in the bone. It is a noble goal I had, and it is beyond me why any-one might quarrel with it. I did a kindness to them all. They are immortal now. I freed them. I took them down to the bone."*

Terry Dobyns had been right. Chapter 10, "James Schneider: the 'Bone Collector,'" was a virtual blueprint for Unsub 823's behavior. The MOs were the same—fire, animals, water, boiling alive. Eight twenty-three prowled the same haunts Schneider had. He'd confused a German tourist with Hanna Goldschmidt, a turn-of-the-century immigrant, and had been drawn to a German residence hall to find a victim. And he'd called little Pammy Ganz by a different name too—Maggie. Apparently thinking she was the young O'Connor girl, one of Schneider's victims.

A very bad etching in the book, covered by tissue, showed a demonic James Schneider, sitting in a basement, examining a leg bone.

Rhyme stared at the Randel Survey map of the city.

Bones . . .

Rhyme was recalling a crime scene he'd run once. He'd been called to a construction site in lower Manhattan where some excavators had discovered a skull a few feet below the surface of a vacant lot. Rhyme saw immediately that the skull was very old and brought a forensic anthropologist into the case. They continued to dig and discovered a number of bones and skeletons.

A little research revealed that in 1741 there'd been a slave rebellion in Manhattan and a number of slaves—and militant white abolitionists—had been hanged on a small island in the Collect. The island became a popular site for hangings and several informal cemeteries and potter's fields sprang up in the area.

Where had the Collect been? Rhyme tried to recall. Near where Chinatown and the Lower East Side meet. But it was hard to say for certain because the pond had been filled in so long ago. It had been—

Yes! he thought, his heart thudding: The Collect had been filled in because it had grown so polluted the city commissioners considered it a major health risk. And among the main polluters were the tanneries on the eastern shore!

Pretty good with the dialer now, Rhyme didn't flub a single number and got put through to the mayor in the first try. Hizzoner, though, the man's personal secretary said, was at a brunch at the UN. But when Rhyme identified himself the secretary said, "One minute, sir," and in much less time than that he found himself on the line with a man who said, through a mouthful of food, "Talk to me, detective. How the fuck're we doing?"

———

"Five-eight-eight-five, K," Amelia Sachs said, answering the radio. Rhyme heard the edginess in her voice.

"Sachs."

"This isn't good," she told him. "We're not having any luck."

"I think I've got him."

"*What?*"

"The six-hundred block, East Van Brevoort. Near Chinatown."

"How'd you know?"

"The mayor put me in touch with the head of the Historical Society. There's an archaeologic dig down there. An old graveyard. Across the street from where a big tannery used to be. And there were some big Federal mansions in the area at one time. I think he's nearby."

"I'm rolling."

Through the speakerphone he heard a squeal of tires, then the siren cut in.

"I've called Lon and Haumann," he added. "They're on their way over now."

"Rhyme," her urgent voice cracked. "I'll get her out."

Ah, you've got a cop's good heart, Amelia, a *professional* heart, Rhyme thought. But you're still just a rookie. "Sachs?" he said.

"Yes?"

"I've been reading this book. Eight twenty-three's picked a bad one for this role model of his. Really bad."

She said nothing.

"What I'm saying is," he continued, "whether the girl's there or not, if you find him and he so much as flinches, you nail him."

"But we get him alive, he can lead us to her. We can—"

"No, Sachs. Listen to me. You take him out. Any sign he's going for a weapon, anything . . . you take him out."

Static clattered. Then he heard her steady voice, "I'm at Van Brevoort, Rhyme. You were right. Looks like his place."

Eighteen unmarkeds, two ESU vans and Amelia Sachs's RRV were clustered near a short, deserted street on the Lower East Side.

East Van Brevoort looked like it was in Sarajevo. The buildings were abandoned—two of them burned to the ground. On the east side of the street was a dilapidated hospital of some kind, its roof caved in. Next to it was a large hole in the ground, roped off, with a No Trespassing sign emblazoned with the County Court seal—the archaeologic dig Rhyme had mentioned. A scrawny dog had died and lay in the gutter, its corpse picked over by rats.

In the middle of the other side of the street was a marble-fronted townhouse, faintly pink, with an attached carriage house, marginally nicer than the other decrepit tenements along Van Brevoort.

Sellitto, Banks and Haumann stood beside the ESU van, as a dozen officers suited up in Kevlar and racked their M-16s. Sachs joined them and, without asking, tucked her hair under a helmet and started to vest up.

Sellitto said, "Sachs, you're not tactical."

Slapping the Velcro strap down, she stared at the detective, eyebrow lifted high, until he relented and said, "Okay. But you're rear guard. That's an order."

Haumann said, "You'll be Team Two."

"Yessir. I can live with that."

One ESU cop offered her an MP-5 machine gun. She thought about Nick—their date on the range at Rodman's Neck. They'd spent two hours practicing with automatic weapons, firing Z-patterns through doors, flip-reloading with taped banana clips and field-stripping M-16s to clear the sand jams that plagued the Colts. Nick loved the staccato clutter but Sachs didn't much like the messy firepower of the big weapons. She'd suggested a match between them with Glocks and had whupped him three straight at fifty feet. He laughed and kissed her hard as the last of her empty casings spun, ringing, onto the firing range.

"I'll just use my sidearm," she told the ESU officer.

The Hardy Boys ran up, crouching as if they were mindful of snipers.

"Here's what we've got. There's nobody around. Block is—"

"Completely empty."

"The windows of his building're all barred. A back entrance—"

"Leading into the alley. The door's open."

"Open?" Haumann asked, glancing at several of his officers.

Saul confirmed, "Not just unlocked but open."

"Booby traps?"

"Not that we could see. Which isn't to say—"

"There aren't any."

Sellitto asked, "Any vehicles in the alley?"

"Nope."

"Two front entrances. Main front door—"

"Which looks painted shut. The second's the carriage-house doors. Double, wide enough for two vehicles. There's a padlock and chain."

"But they're lying on the ground."

Haumann nodded, "So maybe he's inside."

"Maybe," Saul said, then added, "And tell him what we think we heard."

"Very faint. Could have been crying."

"Could have been screaming."

Sachs asked, "The little girl?"

"Maybe. But then it just stopped. How'd Rhyme figure this place?"

"You tell *me* how his mind works," Sellitto said.

Haumann called one of his commanders and issued a series of orders. A moment later two ESU vans pulled into the intersection and blocked the other end of the street.

"Team One, front door. Blow it with cutting charges. It's wood and it's old so keep the plastic down, okay? Team Two, into the alley. On my three, you go. Got it? Neutralize but we're assuming the girl's in there so check your backdrops 'fore you squeeze. Officer Sachs, you're sure you want to do this?"

A firm nod.

"Okay, boys and girls. Go get him."

THIRTY-TWO

Sachs and the five other officers of Team Two ran into the torrid alley, which had been blocked off by ESU trucks. Renegade weeds grew profusely through the cobblestones and cracked foundations and the desolation reminded Sachs of the train-track grave yesterday morning.

He hoped the victim was dead. For his sake . . .

Haumann had ordered troopers onto the roofs of the surrounding buildings, and she saw the muzzles of their black Colts bristling like antennae.

The team paused at the rear doorway. Her fellow cops glanced at Sachs as she checked the rubber bands over her shoes. Heard one of them whisper to another something about superstition.

Then she heard through her earphone:

"Team One leader at front door, charge mounted and armed. We are clear, K."

"Roger, Team One leader. Team Two?"

"Team Two, in position, K."

"Roger, Team Two leader. Both teams, dynamic entry. On my three."

Checked her weapon one last time.

"One . . ."

Her tongue touched a dot of sweat hanging from the swollen wound on her lip.

"Two . . ."

Okay, Rhyme, here we go . . .

"Three!"

The explosion was very sedate, a distant pop, and then

the teams were moving. Fast. She sprinted along behind the ESU troopers as they slipped inside and scattered, their muzzle-mounted flashlights crisscrossing the shafts of brilliant sunlight that streamed through the windows. Sachs found herself alone as the rest of the team dispersed, checking out armoires and closets and the shadows behind the grotesque statues the place was filled with.

She turned the corner. A pale face loomed. A knife . . .

A thud in her heart. Combat stance, gun up. She laid five pounds of pressure on the slick trigger before she realized she was staring at a painting on the wall. An eerie, moon-faced butcher, holding a knife in one hand, a slab of meat in the other.

Brother . . .

He picked a great place for home.

The ESU troops clopped upstairs, searching the first and second floors.

But Sachs was looking for something else.

She found the door leading down to the basement. Partly open. Okay. Halogen off. You've got to take a look first. But she remembered what Nick had said: never look around corners at head or chest level—that's where he's expecting you. Down on one knee. A deep breath. Go!

Nothing. Blackness.

Back to cover.

Listen . . .

At first she heard nothing. Then there was a definite scratching. A clatter. The sound of a fast breath or grunt.

He's there and he's digging his way out!

Into her mike she said, "I've got activity in the basement. Backup."

"*Roger.*"

But she couldn't wait. She thought of the little girl down there with him. And she started down the stairs. Paused and listened again. Then she realized she was standing with her body fully exposed from the waist down. She practically leapt down to the floor, dropped into a crouch in the darkness.

Breathe deep.

Now, do it!

The halogen in her left hand stabbed a brilliant rod of light through the room. The muzzle of her weapon targeted the center of the white disk as it swung left to right. Keep the beam down. He'd be at crotch level too. Remembering what Nick had told her: Perps don't fly.

Nothing. No sign of him.

"Officer Sachs?"

An ESU trooper was at the top of the stairs.

"Oh, no," she muttered, as her beam fell on Pammy Ganz, frozen in the corner of the basement.

"Don't move," she called to the trooper.

Inches away from the girl stood the pack of emaciated wild dogs, sniffing at her face, her fingers, her legs. The girl's wide eyes darted from one animal to the other. Her tiny chest rose and fell and tears streamed down her face. Her mouth was open and the dot of her pink tongue seemed glued to the right arc of her lip.

"Stay up there," she said to the ESU trooper. "Don't spook 'em."

Sachs drew targets but didn't fire. She could kill two or three but the others might panic and grab the girl. One was big enough to snap her neck with a single flip of its scarred, mangy head.

"Is he down there?" the ESU cop asked.

"Don't know. Get a medic here. To the top of the stairs. Nobody come down."

"Roger."

Her weapon sights floating from one animal to another, Sachs slowly started forward. One by one the dogs became aware of her and turned away from Pammy. The little girl was merely food; Sachs was a predator. They growled and snarled, front legs quivering as their hindquarters tensed, ready to jump.

"I'm ascared," Pammy said shrilly, drawing their attention again.

"Shhhh, honey," Sachs cooed. "Don't say anything. Be quiet."

"Mommy. I want my *mommy*!" Her abrasive howl set the dogs off. They danced in place, and swung their battered noses from right to left, growling.

"Easy, easy . . ."

Sachs moved to the left. The dogs were facing her now, glancing from her eyes to her outstretched hand and the gun. They separated into two packs. One stayed close to Pammy. The other moved around Sachs, trying to flank her.

She eased between the little girl and the three dogs closest to her.

The Glock swinging back and forth, a pendulum. Their black eyes on the black gun.

One dog, with a scabby yellow coat, snarled and stepped forward on Sachs's right.

The little girl was whimpering, "Mommy . . ."

Sachs moved slowly. She leaned down, clamped her hand on the child's sweatshirt and dragged Pammy behind her. The yellow dog moved closer.

"Shoo," Sachs said.

Closer still.

"Go away!"

The dogs behind the yellow one tensed as he bared cracked brown teeth.

"Get the fuck outa here!" Sachs snarled and slammed the barrel of the Glock onto his nose. The dog blinked in dismay, yelped, skittered up the stairs.

Pammy screamed, sending the others into a frenzy. They started fighting among themselves, a whirlwind of snapping teeth and slaver. A scarred Rottweiler tossed a dustmop of a mutt to the floor in front of Sachs. She stamped her foot beside the scrawny brown thing and he skittered to his feet, raced up the stairs. The others chased him like greyhounds after a rabbit.

Pammy began to sob. Sachs crouched beside her and swept the basement again with her light. No sign of the unsub.

"It's okay, honey. We'll have you home soon. You'll be all right. That man here? You remember him?"

She nodded.

"Did he leave?"

"I don't know. I want my mommy."

She heard the other officers call in. The first and second floors were secure. "The car and taxi?" Sachs asked. "Any sign?"

A trooper transmitted, "They're gone. He's probably left."

He's not there, Amelia. That would be illogical.

From the top of the stairs an officer called, "Basement secure?"

She said, "I'm going to check. Hold on."

"We're coming down."

"Negative on that," she said. "We've got a pretty clean crime scene here and I want to keep it that way. Just get a medic down here to check out the little girl."

The young medic, a sandy-haired man, walked down the stairs and crouched beside Pammy.

It was then that Sachs saw the trail leading into the back of the basement—to a low, black-painted metal door. She walked to it, avoiding the path itself to save the prints, and crouched down. The door was partly open and there seemed to be a tunnel on the other side, dark but not completely black, leading to another building.

An escape route. The son of a bitch.

With the knuckles of her left hand she pushed the door open wider. It didn't squeak. She peered into the tunnel. Faint light, twenty, thirty feet away. No moving shadows.

If Sachs saw anything in the dimness it was T.J.'s contorted body dangling from the black pipe, Monelle Gerger's round, limp body as the black rat crawled toward her throat.

"Portable 5885 to CP," Sachs said into her mike.

"Go ahead, K," Haumann's terse voice responded.

"I've got a tunnel leading to the building south of the Unsub's. Have somebody cover the doors and windows."

"Will do, K."

"I'm going in," she told him.

"The tunnel? We'll get you some backup, Sachs."

"Negative. I don't want the scene contaminated. Just have somebody keep an eye on the girl."

"Say again."

"No. No backup."

She clicked the light out and started crawling.

There'd been no courses in tunnel-rat work at the academy of course. But the things Nick had told her about securing a unfriendly scene came back to her. Weapon close to the body, not extended too far, where it could be knocked aside. Three steps—well, shuffles—forward, pause. Listen.

Two more steps. Pause. Listen. Four steps next time. Don't do anything predictable.

Hell, it's dark.

And what's that *smell*? She shivered in disgust at the hot, foul stink.

The claustrophobia wrapped around her like a cloud of oil smoke and she had to stop for a moment, concentrating on anything but the closeness of the walls. The panic slipped away but the smell was worse. She gagged.

Quiet, girl. Quiet!

Sachs controlled the reflex and kept going.

And what's that noise? Something electrical. A buzzing. Rising and falling.

Ten feet from the end of the tunnel. Through the doorway she could see a second large basement. Murky though not quite as dark as the one Pammy had been in. Light leached in through a greasy window. She saw motes of dust pedaling through the gloom.

No, no, girl, the gun's too far in front of you. One kick and it's gone. Close to your face. Keep your weight low and back! Use your arms to aim, ass for support.

Then she was at the doorway.

She gagged again, tried to stifle the sound.

Is he waiting for me, or not?

Head out, a fast look. You've got a helmet. It'll deflect anything but a full-metal or Teflon and remember he's shooting a .32. A girl gun.

All right. Think. Look which way first?

The *Patrolman's Guide* wasn't any help and Nick wasn't offering any advice at the moment. Flip a coin.

Left.

She stuck her head out fast, glancing to the left. Back into the tunnel.

She'd seen nothing. A blank wall, shadows.

If he's the other way he's seen me and's got good target positioning.

Okay, fuck. Just go. Fast.

When you move . . .

Sachs leapt.

. . . they can't getcha.

She hit the ground hard, rolling. Twisting around.

The figure was hidden in shadows against the wall to the right, under the window. Drawing a target she started to fire. Then froze.

Amelia Sachs gasped.

Oh, my God . . .

Her eyes were inexorably drawn to the woman's body, propped up against the wall.

From the waist up she was thin, with dark-brown hair, a gaunt face, small breasts, bony arms. Her skin was covered with swarms of flies—the buzzing Sachs had heard.

From the waist down, she was . . . nothing. Bloody hip bones, femur, the whip of her spine, feet . . . All the flesh had been dissolved in the repulsive bath she rested next to— a horrible stew, deep brown, chunks of flesh floating in it. Lye or acid of some sort. The fumes stung Sachs's eyes, while horror—and fury too—boiled in her heart.

Oh, you poor thing . . .

Sachs waved pointlessly at the flies that strafed the new intruder.

The woman's hands were relaxed, palms upward as if she were meditating. Eyes closed. A purple jogging outfit sat by her side.

She wasn't the only victim.

Another skeleton—completely stripped—lay beside a similar vat, older, empty of the terrible acid but coated with a dark sludge of blood and melted muscle. Its forearm and hand were missing. And beyond that was another one—this victim picked apart, the bones carefully scrubbed of all the flesh, cleaned, resting carefully on the floor. A stack of triple-ought sandpaper rested beside the skull. The elegant curve of the head shone like a trophy.

And then she heard it behind her.

A breath. Faint but unmistakable. The snap of air deep in a throat.

She spun around, furious at herself for her carelessness.

But the emptiness of the basement gaped back at her. She swept the light over the floor, which was stone and didn't show footprints as clearly as the dirt floor in 823's building next door.

Another inhalation.

Where was he? *Where*?

Sachs crouched further, sending the light sideways, up and down. . . .Nothing.

Where the fuck is he? Another tunnel? An exit to the street?

Looking at the floor again she spotted what she thought was a faint trail, leading into the shadows of the room. She moved along beside it.

Pause. Listen.

Breathing?

Yes. No.

Stupidly she spun around and looked at the dead woman once more.

Come *on*!

Eyes back again.

Moving along the floor.

Nothing. How can I hear him and not see him?

The wall ahead of her was solid. No doors or windows. She backed up, toward the skeletons.

From somewhere, Lincoln Rhyme's words came back. *"Crime scenes're three-dimensional."*

Sachs looked up suddenly, flashing the light in front of her. The huge Doberman's teeth shone back—dangling bits of gray flesh. Two feet away on a high ledge. He was waiting, like a wildcat, for her.

Neither of them moved for a moment. Absolutely frozen.

Then Sachs instinctively dropped her head and, before she could bring her weapon up, he launched himself toward her face. His teeth connected with the helmet. Gripping the strap in his mouth, he shook furiously, trying to break her neck as they fell backwards, onto the edge of an acid-filled pit. The pistol flew from her hand.

The dog kept his grip on her helmet while his hind legs galloped, his claws digging into her vest and belly and thighs. She hit him hard with her fists but it was like slugging wood; he didn't feel the blows at all.

Releasing the helmet, he reared back then lunged for her face. She flung her left arm over her eyes and, as he grabbed her forearm and she felt his teeth clamp down on her skin, she slipped the switchblade from her pocket and shoved the blade between his ribs. There was a yelp, a high sound, and he rolled off her, kept moving, speeding straight for the doorway.

Sachs snagged her pistol and was after him in an instant, scrabbling through the tunnel. She burst out to see the wounded animal sprinting straight toward Pammy and the medic, who stood frozen as the Doberman leapt into the air.

Sachs dropped into a crouch and squeezed off two rounds. One hit the back of the animal's head and the other streaked into the brick wall. The dog collapsed in a quivering pile at the medic's feet.

"Shots fired," she heard in her radio and a half-dozen troopers rushed down the stairs, pulled the dog away and deployed around the girl.

"It's all right!" Sachs shouted. "It was me!"

The team rose from their defensive positions.

Pammy was screaming, "Doggie dead . . . She made the doggie dead!"

Sachs holstered her weapon and hefted the girl onto her hip.

"Mommy!"

"You'll see your mommy soon," Sachs said. "We're going to call her right now."

Upstairs she set Pammy on the floor and turned to a young ESU officer standing nearby, "I lost my cuff key. Could you take those off her please? Open them over a piece of clean newspaper, wrap 'em up in the paper and put the whole thing in a plastic bag."

The officer rolled his eyes. "Listen, beautiful, go find yourself a rookie to order around." He started to walk away.

"Trooper," Bo Haumann barked, "you'll do what she says."

"Sir," he protested, "I'm ESU."

"Got news," Sachs muttered, "you're Crime Scene now."

Carole Ganz was lying on her back in a very beige bedroom, staring at the ceiling, thinking about the time a few weeks ago when she and Pammy and a bunch of friends were sitting around a campfire in Wisconsin at Kate and Eddie's place, talking, telling stories, singing songs.

Kate's voice wasn't so hot but Eddie could've been a pro. He could even play barre chords. He sang Carole King's "Tapestry" just for her and Carole sang along softly through her tears. Thinking that maybe, just maybe, she really was putting Ron's death behind her and getting on with her life.

She remembered Kate's voice from that night: "When you're angry, the only way to deal with it is to wrap up that anger and give it away. Give it to somebody else. Do you hear me? Don't keep it inside you. Give it away."

Well, she was angry now. Furious.

Some young kid—a mindless little shit—had taken her husband away, shot him in the back. And now some crazy man had taken her daughter. She wanted to explode. And it took all her willpower not to start flinging things against the wall and howling like a coyote.

She lay back on the bed and gingerly placed her shattered wrist on her belly. She'd taken a Demerol, which had eased the pain, but she hadn't been able to sleep. She'd done nothing but stay inside all day long, trying to get in touch with Kate and Eddie and waiting for news about Pammy.

She kept picturing Ron, kept picturing her anger, actually imagining herself packing it up in a box, wrapping it carefully, sealing it up . . .

And then the phone rang. She stared for a moment then yanked it off the cradle.

"Hello?"

Carole listened to the policewoman tell her that they'd found Pammy, that she was in the hospital but that she was okay. A moment later Pammy herself came on the phone and they were both crying and laughing at the same time.

Ten minutes later she was on her way to Manhattan Hospital, in the back seat of a black police sedan.

Carole practically sprinted down the corridor to Pammy's room and was surprised to be stopped by the police guard. So they hadn't caught the fucker yet? But was soon as she saw her daughter she forgot about him, forgot the terror in the taxi and the fiery basement. She threw her arms around her little girl.

"Oh, honey, I missed you! Are you okay? Really okay?"

"That lady, she killed a doggie—"

Carole turned and saw the tall, red-haired policewoman

standing nearby, the one who'd saved her from the church basement.

"—but it was all right because he was going to eat me."

Carole hugged Sachs. "I don't know what to say. . . .I just . . . Thank you, thank you."

"Pammy's fine," Sachs assured her. "Some scratches— nothing serious—and she's got a little cough."

"Mrs Ganz?" A young man walked into the room, carrying her suitcase and yellow knapsack. "I'm Detective Banks. We've got your things here."

"Oh, thank God."

"Is anything missing?" he asked her.

She looked through the knapsack carefully. It was all there. The money, Pammy's doll, the package of clay, the Mr Potato Head, the CDs, the clock radio . . . He hadn't taken anything. Wait. . . ."You know, I think there's a picture missing. I'm not sure. I thought I had more than these. But everything important's here."

The detective gave her a receipt to sign.

A young resident stepped into the room. He joked with Pammy about her Pooh bear as he took her blood pressure.

Carole asked him, "When can she leave?"

"Well, we'd like to keep her in for a few days. Just to make sure—"

"A few *days*? But she's fine."

"She's got a bit of bronchitis I want to keep an eye on. And . . ." He lowered his voice. "We're also going to bring in an abuse specialist. Just to make sure."

"But she was going to go with me tomorrow. To the UN ceremonies. I promised her."

The policewoman added, "It's easier to keep her guarded here. We don't know where the unsub—the kidnapper—is. We'll have an officer babysitting you too."

"Well, I guess. Can I stay with her for a while?"

"You bet," the resident said. "You can stay the night. We'll have a cot brought in."

Then Carole was alone with her daughter once more. She sat down on the bed and put her arm around the child's narrow shoulders. She had a bad moment remembering how *he*, that crazy man, had touched Pammy. How his eyes had looked when he'd asked if he could cut her own skin off . . . Carole shivered and began to cry.

It was Pammy who brought her back. "Mommy, tell me a story. . . . No, no, sing me something. Sing me the friend song. Pleeeeease?"

Calming down, Carole asked, "You want to hear that one, hm?"

"Yes!"

Carole hoisted the girl onto her lap and, in a reedy voice, started to sing "You've Got a Friend." Pammy sang snatches of it along with her.

It had been one of Ron's favorites and, in the past couple years, after he was gone, she hadn't been able to listen to more than a few bars without breaking into tears.

Today, she and Pammy finished it together, pretty much on key, dry-eyed and laughing.

THIRTY-THREE

Amelia Sachs finally made it home to her apartment i
Carroll Gardens, Brooklyn.

Exactly six blocks from her parents' house, where he
mother still lived. As soon as she walked in she hit the firs
speed-dial button on the kitchen phone.

"Mom. Me. I'm taking you to brunch at the Plaza. Wednes
day. That's my day off."

"What for? To celebrate your new assignment? How
Public Affairs? You didn't call."

A fast laugh. Sachs realized her mother had no idea wha
she'd been doing for the past day and a half.

"You been following the news, Mom?"

"Me? I'm Brokaw's secret admirer, you know that."

"You hear about this kidnapper the last few days?"

"Who hasn't? . . . What're you telling me, honey?"

"I've got the inside scoop."

And she told her astonished mother the story—about savin
the vics and about Lincoln Rhyme and, with some editing
about the crime scenes.

"Amie, your father'd be so proud."

"So, call in sick on Wednesday. The Plaza, OK?"

"Forget it, sweetheart. Save your money. I've got waffle
and Bob Evans in the freezer. You can come here."

"It's not that expensive, Mom."

"Not that much? It's a *fortune*."

"Well, hey," Sachs said, trying to sound spontaneous, "yo
like the Pink Teacup, don't you?"

A little place in the West Village that served up platter

of the best pancakes and eggs on the East Coast for next to nothing.

A pause.

"That might be nice."

This was a strategy Sachs had used successfully over the years.

"I've gotta get some rest, Mom. I'll call tomorrow."

"You work too hard. Amie, this case of yours . . . it wasn't dangerous, was it?"

"I was just doing the technical stuff, Mom. Crime scene. It doesn't get any safer than that."

"And they asked for *you* especially!" the woman said. Then repeated, "Your father'd be so proud."

They hung up and Sachs wandered into the bedroom, flopped down on the bed.

After she'd left Pammy's room Sachs had paid visits to the other two surviving victims of Unsub 823. Monelle Gerger, dotted with bandages and pumped full of anti-rabies serum, had been released and was returning to her family in Frankfurt "but just for rest of summer," she explained adamantly. "Not, you know, for good." And she'd pointing to her stereo and CD collection in the decrepit apartment in the Deutsche Haus by way of proving that no New World psycho was driving her permanently out of town.

William Everett was still in the hospital. The shattered finger was not a serious problem of course but his heart had been acting up again. Sachs was astonished to find that he'd owned a shop in Hell's Kitchen years ago and thought he might have known her father. "I knew all the beat cops," he said. She showed him her wallet picture of the man in his dress uniform. "I think so. Not sure. But I think so."

The calls had been social but Sachs had gone armed with her watchbook. Neither of the vics, though, had been able to tell her anything more about Unsub 823.

In her apartment now Sachs glanced out her window. She saw the ginkgoes and maples shiver in the sharp wind. She stripped off her uniform, scratched under her boobs—where it always itched like mad from being squooshed under the body armor. She pulled on a bathrobe.

Unsub 823 hadn't had much warning but it had been

enough. The safe house on Van Brevoort had been hosed completely. Even though the landlord said he'd moved in a long time ago—last January (with a phony ID, no one was very surprised to learn)—823 had left with everything he'd brought, trash included. After Sachs had worked the scene, NYPD Latents had descended and was dusting every surface in the place. So far the preliminary reports weren't encouraging.

. "Looks like he even wore gloves when he crapped," young Banks had reported to her.

A Mobile unit had found the taxi and the sedan. Unsub 823'd cleverly parked them near Avenue D and Ninth Street. Sellitto guessed it probably took a local gang seven or eight minutes to strip them down to their chassis. Any physical evidence the vehicles might've yielded was now in a dozen chop shops around the city.

Sachs turned on the tube and found the news. Nothing about the kidnappings. All the stories were about the opening ceremonies of the UN peace conference.

She stared at Bryant Gumbel, stared at the UN secretary-general, stared at some ambassador from the Middle East, stared far more intently than her interest warranted. She even studied the ads as if she were memorizing them.

Because there was something she definitely *didn't* want to think about: her bargain with Lincoln Rhyme.

The deal was clear. Now that the Carole and Pammy were safe, it was her turn to come through. To let him have his hour alone with Dr Berger.

Now *him*, Berger . . . She hadn't liked the look of the doctor at all. You could see one big fucking ego in his compact, athletic frame, his evasive eyes. His black hair perfectly combed. Expensive clothes. Why couldn't Rhyme have found someone like Kevorkian? He may have been quirky but at least seemed like a wise old grandfather?

Her lids closed.

Giving up the dead . . .

A bargain was a bargain. But goddammit, Rhyme . . .

Well, she couldn't let him go without one last try. He'd caught her off guard in his bedroom. She was flustered. Hadn't thought of any really good arguments. Monday. She had until tomorrow to try to convince him not to do it. Or at least to wait awhile. A month. Hell, a day.

What could she say to him? She'd jot down her arguments. Write a little speech.

Opening her eyes, she climbed out of bed to find a pen and some paper. I could—

Sachs froze, her breath whistling into her lungs like the wind outside.

He wore dark clothes, the ski mask and gloves black as oil.

Unsub 823 stood in the middle of her bedroom.

Her hand instinctively went toward the bedside table—her Glock and knife. But he was ready. The shovel swung fast and caught her on the side of her head. A yellow light exploded in her eyes.

She was on her hands and knees when the foot slammed into her rib cage and she collapsed to her stomach, struggling for breath. She felt her hands being cuffed behind her, a strip of duct tape slapped onto her mouth. Moving fast, efficiently. He rolled her onto her back; her robe fell open.

Kicking furiously, struggling madly to pull the cuffs apart.

Another blow to her stomach. She gagged and fell still as he reached for her. Gripped her at the armpits, dragged her out the back door and into the large private garden behind the apartment.

His eyes remained on her face, not even looking at her tits, her flat belly, her mound with its few red curls. She could easily have given that up to him if it would have saved her life.

But, no, Rhyme's diagnosis was right. It wasn't lust that drove 823. He had something else in mind. He dropped her willowy figure, face up, into a patch of black-eyed Susan and pachysandra, out of sight of the neighbors. He looked around, catching his breath. He picked up the shovel and plunged the blade into the dirt.

Amelia Sachs began to cry.

Rubbing the back of his head into the pillow.

Compulsive, a doctor had once told him after observing this behavior—an opinion Rhyme hadn't asked for. Or wanted.

His nestling, Rhyme reflected, was just a variation on Amelia Sachs's tearing her flesh with her own nails.

He stretched his neck muscles, rolling his head around, as he stared at the profile chart on the wall. Rhyme believed that the full story of the man's madness was here in front of him. In the black, swoopy handwriting—and the gaps between the words. But he couldn't see the story's ending. Not yet.

He looked over the clues again. There were only a few left unexplained.

The scar on the finger.

The knot.

The aftershave.

The scar was useless to them unless they had a suspect whose fingers they could examine. And there'd been no luck in identifying the knot—only preppy Banks's opinion that it wasn't nautical.

What about the cheap aftershave? Assuming that most unsubs wouldn't spritz themselves to go on a kidnapping spree, why had he worn it? Rhyme could only conclude again that he was trying to obscure another, a telltale scent. He ran through the possibilities: Food, liquor, chemicals, tobacco . . .

He felt eyes on him and looked to his right.

The black dots of the bony rattlesnake's eye sockets gazed toward the Clinitron. This was the one clue that was out of place. It had no purpose, except to taunt them.

Something occurred to him. Using the painstaking turning frame Rhyme slowly flipped back through *Crime in Old New York*. To the chapter on James Schneider. He found the paragraphs he'd remembered.

> *It has been suggested by a well-known physician of the mind (a practitioner of the discipline of "psychelogy," which has been much in the news of late) that James Schneider's ultimate intent had little to do with harming his victims. Rather—this learnéd doctor has suggested—the villain was seeking revenge against those that did him what he perceived to be harm: the city's constabulary, if not Society as a whole.*
>
> *Who can say where the source of this hate lay? Perhaps, like the Nile of old, its wellsprings were*

> *hidden to the world—and possibly even to the villain himself. Yet one reason may be found in a little-known fact: Young James Schneider, at the tender age of ten, saw his father dragged away by constables only to die in prison for a robbery which, it was later ascertained, he did not commit. Following this unfortunate arrest, the boy's mother fell into life on the street and abandoned her son, who grew up a ward of the state.*
>
> *Did the madman perchance commit these crimes to fling derision into the face of the very constabulary which had inadvertently destroyed his family?*
>
> *We will undoubtedly never know.*
>
> *Yet what does seem clear is that by mocking the ineffectualness of the protectors of its citizenry, James Schneider—the "bone collector"—was wreaking his vengeance upon the city itself as much as upon his innocent victims.*

Lincoln Rhyme lay back in his pillow and looked at the profile chart again.

Dirt is heavier than anything.

It's the earth itself, the dust of an iron core, and it doesn't kill by strangling the air from the lungs but by compressing the cells until they die from the panic of immobility.

Sachs wished that she *had* died. She prayed that she would. Fast. From fear or a heart attack. Before the first shovelful hit her face. She prayed for this harder than Lincoln Rhyme had prayed for his pills and liquor.

Lying in the grave the unsub had dug in her own backyard Sachs felt the progress of the rich earth, dense and wormy, moving along her body.

Sadistically, he was burying her slowly, casting only a shallow scoop at a time, scattering it carefully around her. He'd started with her feet. He was now up to her chest, the dirt slipping into her robe and around her breasts like a lover's fingers.

Heavier and heavier, compressing, binding her lungs; she could suck only an ounce or two of air at a time. He paused once or twice to look at her then continued.

He likes to watch . . .

Hands beneath her, neck straining to keep her head above the tide.

Then her chest was buried completely. Her shoulders, her throat. The cold earth rose to the hot skin of her face, packing around her head so she couldn't move. Finally he bent down and ripped the tape off her mouth. As Sachs tried to scream he spilled a handful of dirt into her face. She shivered, choked on the black earth. Ears ringing, hearing for some reason an old song from her infancy—"The Green Leaves of Summer," a song her father played over and over again on the hi-fi. Sorrowful, haunting. She closed her eyes. Everything was going black. Opened her mouth once and got another cup's worth of soil.

Giving up the dead . . .

And then she was under.

Completely quiet. Not choking or gasping—the earth was a perfect seal. She had no air in her lungs, couldn't make any sounds. Silence, except for the haunting melody and the growing roar in her ears.

Then the pressure on her face ceased as her body went numb, as numb as Lincoln Rhyme's. Her mind began to shut down.

Blackness, blackness. No words from her father. Nothing from Nick . . . No dreams of downshifting from five to four to goose the speedometer into three digits.

Blackness.

Giving up the . . .

The mass sinking down onto her, pushing, pushing. Seeing only one image: The hand rising out of the grave yesterday morning, waving for mercy. When no mercy would be given.

Waving for her to follow.

Rhyme, I'll miss you.

Giving up . . .

THIRTY-FOUR

Something struck her forehead. Hard. She felt the thump but no pain.

What, what? His shovel? A brick? Maybe in an instant of compassion 823'd decided that this slow death was more than anyone could bear and was striking for her throat to sever her veins.

Another blow, and another. She couldn't open her eyes, but she was aware of light growing around her. Colors. And air. She forced the mass of dirt from her mouth and sucked in tiny breaths, all she could manage. Began coughing in a loud bray, retching, spitting.

Her lids sprang open and through tearing eyes she found herself looking up at the muddy vision of Lon Sellitto, kneeling over her, beside two EMS medics, one of whom dug into her mouth with latex-clad fingers and pulled out more gunk, while the other readied an oxygen mask and green tank.

Sellitto and Banks continued to uncover her body, shoving the dirt away with their muscular hands. They pulled her up, leaving the robe behind like a shed skin. Sellitto, old divorcé that he was, looked chastely away from her body as he put his jacket around her shoulders. Young Jerry Banks did look of course but she loved him anyway.

"Did . . . you . . . ?" she wheezed, then surrendered to a racking cough.

Sellitto glanced expectantly at Banks, who was the more breathless of the two. He must've done the most running after the unsub. The young detective shook his head. "Got away."

Sitting up, she inhaled oxygen for a moment.

"How?" she wheezed. "How'd you know?"

"Rhyme," he answered. "Don't ask me how. He called in 10–13's for everybody on the team. When he heard we were okay he sent us over here ASAP."

Then the numbness left, snap, in a flash. And for the first time she realized what had nearly happened. She dropped the oxygen mask, backed away in panic, tears streaming, her panicky keening growing louder and louder. "No, no, no . . ."

Slapping her arms and thighs, frantic, trying to shake off the horror clinging to her like a teeming swarm of bees.

"Oh God oh God . . . No . . ."

"Sachs?" Banks asked, alarmed. "Hey, Sachs?"

The older detective waved his partner away. "It's okay." He kept his arm around her shoulders as she dropped to all fours and vomited violently, sobbing, sobbing, gripping the dirt desperately between her fingers as if she wanted to strangle it.

Finally Sachs calmed and sat back on her naked haunches. She began laughing, softly at first then louder and louder, hysterical, astonished to find that the skies had opened and it had been raining—huge hot summer drops—and she hadn't even realized it.

———

Arm around his shoulders. Face pressed against his. They stayed that way for a long moment.

"Sachs . . . Oh, Sachs."

She stepped away from the Clinitron and scooted an old armchair from the corner of the room. Sachs—wearing navy sweat-pants and a Hunter College T-shirt—flopped down into the chair and dangled her exquisite legs over the arm like a schoolgirl.

"Why us, Rhyme? Why'd he come after us?" Her voice was a raspy whisper from the dirt she'd swallowed.

"Because the people he kidnapped aren't the real victims. We are."

"Who's *we*?" she asked.

"I'm not sure. Society maybe. Or the city. Or the UN. Cops. I went back and reread his bible—the chapter on James

Schneider. Remember Terry's theory about why the unsub'd been leaving the clues?"

Sellitto said, "Sort of making us accessories. To share the guilt. Make it easier for him to kill."

Rhyme nodded but said, "I don't think that's the reason though. I think the clues were a way to attack *us*. Every dead vic was a loss for us."

In her old clothes, hair pulled back in a ponytail, Sachs looked more beautiful than any time in the past two days. But her eyes were tin. She'd be reliving every shovelful of dirt, he supposed, and Rhyme found the thought of her living burial so disturbing he had to look away.

"What's he got against us?" she asked.

"I don't know. Schneider's father was arrested by mistake and died in prison. Our unsub? Who knows why? I only care about evidence—"

"—not motives." Amelia Sachs finished the sentence.

"Why'd he start going after us directly?" Banks asked, nodding at Sachs.

"We found his hidey-hole and saved the little girl. I don't think he expected us so soon. Maybe he just got pissed. Lon, we need twenty-four-hour babysitters for all of us. He could've just taken off after we saved the kid but he stuck around to do some damage. You and Jerry, me, Cooper, Haumann, Polling, we're all on his list, betcha. Meanwhile, get Peretti's boys over to Sachs's. I'm sure he kept it clean but there might be something there. He left a lot faster than he'd planned to."

"I better get over there," Sachs said.

"No," Rhyme said.

"I have to work the scene."

"You have to get some rest," he ordered. "*That*'s what you have to do, Sachs. You don't mind my saying, you look lousy."

"Yeah, officer," Sellitto said. "'S an order. I told you to stand down for the rest of the day. We've got two hundred searchers looking for him. And Fred Dellray's got another hundred and twenty feebies."

"I got a crime scene in my own backyard and you're not gonna let me walk the grid?"

"That's it," Rhyme said, "in a nutshell."

Sellitto walked to the doorway. "Any problems with that, officer?"

"Nosir."

"Come on, Banks, we got work to do. You need a lift, Sachs? Or're they still trusting you with vehicles?"

"No thanks, got wheels downstairs," she said.

The two detectives left. Rhyme heard their voices echoing through the empty hall. Then the door closed and they were gone.

Rhyme realized the glaring overhead lights were on. He clicked through several commands and dimmed them.

Sachs stretched.

"Well," she said, just as Rhyme said, "So."

She glanced at the clock. "It's late."

"Sure is."

Rising, she walked to the table where her purse rested. She picked it up. Clicked it open, found her compact and examined her cut lip in the mirror.

"It doesn't look too bad," Rhyme said.

"Frankenstein," she said, prodding. "Why don't they use flesh-colored stitches?" She put the mirror away, slung the purse over her shoulder. "You moved the bed," she noticed. It was closer to the window.

"Thom did. I can look at the park. If I want to."

"Well, that's good."

She walked to the window. Looked down.

Oh, for Christ's sake, Rhyme thought to himself. Do it. What can happen? He blurted quickly, "You want to stay here? I mean, it's getting late. And Latents'll be dusting your place for hours."

He felt a mad bolt of anticipation deep within him. Well, kill *that*, he thought, furious with himself. Until her face blossomed into a smile. "I'd like that."

"Good." His jaw shivered from the adrenaline. "Wonderful. Thom!"

Listening to music, drinking some Scotch. Maybe he'd tell her more about famous crime scenes. The historian in him was also curious about her father, about police work in the '60s and '70s. About the infamous Midtown South Precinct in the old days.

Rhyme shouted, "Thom! Get some sheets. And a blanket. Thom! I don't know what the hell he's doing. *Thom*!"

Sachs started to say something but the aide appeared in the doorway and said testily, "One rude shout would've been enough, you know, Lincoln."

"Amelia's staying over again. Could you get some blankets and pillows for the couch?"

"No, not the couch again," she said. "It's like sleeping on rocks."

Rhyme was stabbed with a splinter of rejection. Thinking ruefully to himself: Been a few years since he'd felt *that* emotion. Resigned, he nonetheless smiled and said, "There's a bedroom downstairs. Thom can make it up for you."

But Sachs set down her purse. "That's okay, Thom. You don't have to."

"It's no bother."

"It's all right. Good night, Thom." She walked to the door.

"Well, I—"

She smiled.

"But—" he began, looking from her to Rhyme, who frowned, shook his head.

"Good *night*, Thom," she said firmly. "Watch your feet." And closed the door slowly, as he stepped back out of the way into the hall. It closed with a loud click.

Sachs kicked off her shoes, pulled off the sweats and T-shirt. She wore a lace bra and baggy cotton panties. She climbed into the Clinitron beside Rhyme, showing every bit of the authority beautiful women wield when it comes to climbing into bed with a man.

She wriggled down into the pellets and laughed. "This is one hell of a bed," she said, stretching like a cat. Eyes closed, Sachs asked, "You don't mind, do you?"

"I don't mind at all."

"Rhyme?"

"What?"

"Tell me more about your book, okay? Some more crime scenes?"

He started to describe a clever serial killer in Queens but in less than one minute she was asleep.

Rhyme glanced down and noted her breast against his chest, her knee resting on his thigh. A woman's hair was banked against his face for the first time in years. It tickled. He'd forgotten that this happened. For someone who lived so in the past, with such a good memory, he was surprised to find he couldn't exactly remember when he'd experienced this sensation last. What he could recall was an amalgam of evenings with Blaine, he supposed, before the accident. He *did* remember that he'd decided to endure the tickle, not push the strands away, so he wouldn't disturb his wife.

Now, of course, he couldn't brush away Sachs's hair if God Himself had asked. But he wouldn't think of moving it aside. Just the opposite; he wanted to prolong the sensation until the end of the universe.

THIRTY-FIVE

The next morning Lincoln Rhyme was alone again.

Thom had gone shopping and Mel Cooper was at the IRD lab downtown. Vince Peretti had completed the CS work at the mansion on Van Brevoort and at Sachs's. They'd found woefully few clues though Rhyme put the lack of PE down to the unsub's ingenuity, not Peretti's derivative talents.

Rhyme was awaiting the crime scene report. But both Dobyns and Sellitto believed that 823 had gone to ground—temporarily at least. There'd been no more attacks on the police and no other victims had been kidnapped in the past twelve hours.

Sachs's minder—a large Patrol officer from MTS—had accompanied her to an appointment with an ear, nose and throat man at a hospital in Brooklyn; the dirt had done quite a number on her throat. Rhyme himself had a bodyguard too—a uniform from the Twentieth Precinct, stationed in front of his townhouse—a friendly cop he'd known for years and with whom Rhyme enjoyed a running argument on the merits of Irish peat versus Scottish in the production of whisky.

Rhyme was in a great mood. He called downstairs on the intercom. "I'm expecting a doctor in a couple of hours. You can let him up."

The cop said he would.

Dr William Berger had assured Rhyme that today he'd be on time.

Rhyme leaned back in the pillow and realized he wasn't completely alone. On the windowsill, the falcons paced. Rarely skittish, they seemed uneasy. Another low front was

UNSUB 823

Appearance	Residence	Vehicle	Other
• Caucasian male, slight build	• Prob. has safe house	• Yellow Cab	• knows CS proc.
• Dark clothing	• Located near; Houston & Lafayette, ShopRite	• Recent model sedan	• possibly has record
• Old gloves, reddish kidskin		• Lt. gray, silver, biege	• knows FR prints
• Aftershave; to cover up other scent?	• Old building, pink marble	• Rental car; prob. stolen	• gun = .32 Colt
• Ski mask? Navy blue?	• At least 100 years old, prob. mansion or institutional	• Hertz, silver Taurus, this year's model	• Ties vics w/ unusual knots
• Gloves are dark			• "Old" appeals to him
• Aftershave = Brut	• Federal-style building, Lower East Side		• Called one vic "Hanna"
• Hair color not brown			• Knows basic German
• Deep scar, index finger	• Located near archaeologic dig		• Underground appeals to him
• Casual clothes			• Dual personalities
• Gloves are black			• Maybe priest, soc. worker, counselor
			• Unusual wear on shoes, reads a lot?
			• Listened as he broke vic's finger
			• Left snake as slap at investigators
			• Wanted to flay vic's foot
			• Called one vic "Maggie"
			• Mother & child, special meaning to him?
			• Book "Crime in Old NY," his model?
			• Bases crimes on James Schneider, the "Bone Collector"
			• Has hatred of police

approaching. Rhyme's window revealed a calm sky but he trusted the birds; they were infallible barometers.

He glanced at the clock on the wall. It was 11:00 A.M. Here he was, just like two days ago, awaiting Berger's arrival. That's life, he thought: postponement upon postponement but ultimately, with some luck, we get to where we're meant to be.

He watched television for twenty minutes, trolling for stories about the kidnappings. But all the stations were doing specials on the opening day of the UN conference. Rhyme found it boring and turned to a rerun of *Matlock*, flipped back to a gorgeous CNN reporter standing outside UN headquarters and then shut the damn set off.

The telephone rang and he went through the complicated gestures of answering it. "Hello."

There was a pause before a man's voice said, "Lincoln?"

"Yes?"

"Jim Polling. How you doin'?"

Rhyme realized that he hadn't seen much of the captain since early yesterday, except for the news conference last night, where he'd whispered prompts to the mayor and Chief Wilson.

"Okay. Any word on our unsub?" Rhyme asked.

"Nothing yet. But we'll get him." Another pause. "Hey, you alone?"

"Yep."

A longer pause.

"Okay if I stop by?"

"Sure."

"A half hour?"

"I'll be here," Rhyme said jovially.

He rested his head in the thick pillow and his eyes slipped to the knotted clothesline hanging beside the profile poster. Still no answer about the knot. It was—he laughed aloud at the joke—a loose end. He hated the idea of leaving the case without finding out what kind of knot it was. Then he remembered that Polling was a fisherman. Maybe he'd recognize—

Polling, Rhyme reflected.

James Polling . . .

Funny how the captain had insisted Rhyme handle the case. How he'd fought to keep him on it, rather than Peretti—who was the better choice, politically, for Polling. Remembering too how he'd lost his temper at Dellray when the feebie tried to strong-arm the investigation away from the NYPD.

Now that he thought about it, Polling's whole involvement in the case was a mystery. Eight twenty-three wasn't the kind of perp you took on voluntarily—even if you were looking for juicy cases to hang on your collar record. Too many chances to lose vics, too many opportunities for the press—and the brass—to snipe at you for fucking up.

Polling . . . Recalling how he'd breeze into Rhyme's bedroom, check out their progress and leave.

Sure, he was reporting to the mayor and the chief. But—the thought slipped unexpectedly into Rhyme's mind—was there someone *else* Polling was reporting back to?

Someone who wanted to keep tabs on the investigation? The unsub himself?

But how on earth could Polling have any connection with 823? It seemed—

And then it struck him.

Could Polling *be* the unsub?

Of course not. It was ridiculous. Laughable. Even apart from motive and means, there was the question of opportunity. The captain had been here, in Rhyme's room, when some of the kidnappings had occurred. . . .

Or had he?

Rhyme looked up at the profile chart.

Dark clothing and wrinkled cotton slacks. Polling'd been wearing dark sports clothes over the past several days. But so what? So did a lot of—

Downstairs a door opened and closed.

"Thom?"

No answer. The aide wasn't due back for hours.

"Lincoln?"

Oh, no. Hell. He started to dial on the ECU.

9–1–

With his chin he bumped the cursor to 2.

Footsteps on the stairs.

He tried to redial but in his desperation he knocked the joystick out of reach.

And Jim Polling walked into the room. Rhyme had counted on the babysitter's calling upstairs first. But of course a beat cop would let a police captain inside without thinking twice.

Polling's dark jacket was unbuttoned and Rhyme got a look at the automatic on his hip. He couldn't see if it was his issue weapon. But he knew that .32 Colts were on the NYPD list of approved personal weapons.

"Lincoln," Polling said. He was clearly uneasy, cautious. His eyes fell to the bleached bit of spinal cord.

"How you doing, Jim?"

"Not bad."

Polling the outdoorsman. Had the scar on the fingerprint been left by years of casting a fishing line? Or an accident with hunting a knife? Rhyme tried to look but Polling kept his hands jammed into his pockets. Was he holding something in there? A knife?

Polling certainly knew forensics and crime scenes—he knew how *not* to leave evidence.

The ski mask? If Polling was the unsub he'd have to wear the mask of course—because one of the vics might see him later. And the aftershave . . . what if the unsub hadn't *worn* the scent at all but had just carried a bottle with him and sprayed some at the scenes to make them *believe* he wore Brut? So when Polling showed up here, not wearing any, no one would suspect him.

"You're alone?" Polling asked.

"My assistant—"

"The cop downstairs said he wouldn't be back for a while."

Rhyme hesitated. "That's right."

Polling was slight but strong, sandy-haired. Terry Dobyns's words came back: Someone helpful, upstanding. A social worker, counselor, politician. Somebody helping other people.

Like a cop.

Rhyme wondered now if he was about to die. And to his shock he realized that he didn't want to. Not this way, not on somebody else's terms.

Polling walked to the bed.

Yet there was nothing he could do. He was at this man's complete mercy.

"Lincoln," Polling repeated gravely.

Their eyes met and the feeling of electrical connection went through them. Dry sparks. The captain looked quickly out the window. "You've been wondering, haven't you?"

"Wondering?"

"Why I wanted you on the case."

"I figured it was my personality."

This drew no smile from the captain.

"Why *did* you want me, Jim?"

The captain's fingers knitted together. Thin but strong. The hands of a fisherman, a sport that, yes, may be genteel but whose purpose is nonetheless to wrench a poor beast from his home and slice through its smooth belly with a thin knife.

"Four years ago, the Shepherd case. We were on it together."

Rhyme nodded.

"The workers found the body of that cop in the subway stop."

A groan, Rhyme recalled, like the sound of the *Tatanic* sinking in *A Night to Remember*. Then an explosion loud as a gunshot as the beam came down on his hapless neck, and dirt packed around his body.

"And you ran the scene. You yourself, like you always did."

"I did, yes."

"Did you know how we convicted Shepherd? We had a wit."

A witness? Rhyme hadn't heard that. After the accident he'd lost all track of the case, except for learning that Shepherd had been convicted and, three months later, stabbed to death on Riker's Island by an assailant who was never captured.

"An eyewitness," Polling continued. "He could place Shepherd at one of the victim's homes with the murder weapon." The captain stepped closer to the bed, crossed his arms. "We had the wit a day *before* we found the last body— the one in the subway. Before I put in the request that you run the scene."

"What're you saying, Jim?"

The captain's eyes rooted themselves to the floor. "We didn't need you. We didn't *need* your report."

Rhyme said nothing.

Polling nodded. "You understand what I'm saying? I wanted to nail that fuck Shepherd so bad. . . . I wanted an airtight case. And you know what a Lincoln Rhyme crime scene report does to defense lawyers. It scares the everlovin' shit out of them."

"But Shepherd would've been convicted even without my report from the subway scene."

"That's right, Lincoln. But it's worse than that. See, I got word from MTA Engineering that the site wasn't safe."

"The subway site. And you had me work the scene before they shored it up?"

"Shepherd was a cop-killer." Polling's face twisted up in disgust. "I wanted him so bad. I woulda done anything to nail him. But . . ." He lowered his head to his hands.

Rhyme said nothing. He heard the groan of the beam, the explosion of the breaking wood. Then the rustle of the dirt nestling around him. A curious, warm peace in his body while his heart stuttered with terror.

"Jim—"

"That's why I wanted you on this case, Lincoln. You see?" A miserable look crossed the captain's tough face; he stared at the disk of spinal column on the table. "I kept hearing these stories that your life was crap. You were wasting away here. Talking about killing yourself. I felt so fucking guilty. I wanted to try to give you some of your life back."

Rhyme said, "And you've been living with this for the last three and a half years."

"You know about me, Lincoln. *Everybody* knows about me. I collar somebody, he gives me any shit, he goes *down*. I get a hardon for some perp, I don't stop till the prick's bagged and tagged. I can't control it. I know I've fucked over people sometimes. But they were perps—or suspects, at least. They weren't my own, they weren't cops. What happened to you . . . that was a sin. It was just fucking wrong."

"I wasn't a rookie," Rhyme said. "I didn't *have* to work a scene I thought wasn't safe."

"But—"

"Bad time?" another voice said from the doorway.

Rhyme glanced up, expecting to see Berger. But it was Peter Taylor who'd come up the stairs. Rhyme recalled that he was coming by today to check on his patient after the dysreflexia attack. He supposed too that the doctor was planning to give him hell about Berger and the Lethe Society. He wasn't in the mood for that; he wanted time alone—to digest Polling's confession. At the moment it just sat there, numb as Rhyme's thigh. But he said, "Come on in, Peter."

"You've got a very funny security system, Lincoln. The guard asked if I was a doctor and he let me up. What? Do lawyers and accountants get booted?"

Rhyme laughed. "I'll only be a second." Rhyme turned back to Polling. "Fate, Jim. That's what happened to me. I was in the wrong place at the wrong time. It happens."

"Thanks, Lincoln." Polling put his hand on Rhyme's right shoulder and squeezed it gently.

Rhyme nodded and, to deflect the uneasy gratitude, introduced the men. "Jim, this is Pete Taylor, one of my doctors. And this is Jim Polling, we used to work together."

"Nice to meet you," Taylor said, sticking out his right hand. It was a broad gesture and Rhyme's eyes followed it, noticing for some reason the deep crescent scar on Taylor's right index finger.

"No!" Rhyme shouted.

"So you're a cop too." Taylor gripped Polling's hand tightly as he slid the knife, held firmly in his left hand, in and out of the captain's chest three times, navigating around the ribs with the delicacy of a surgeon. Undoubtedly so he wouldn't nick the precious bone.

THIRTY-SIX

In two long steps Taylor was beside the bed. He grabbed the ECU controller from beneath Rhyme's finger, flung it across the room.

Rhyme took a breath to shout. But the doctor said, "He's dead too. The constable." Nodding toward the door, meaning the bodyguard downstairs. Taylor stared with fascination as Polling thrashed like a spine-cracked animal, spraying his blood on the floor and walls.

"Jim!" Rhyme cried. "No, oh, no . . ."

The captain's hands curled over his ruined chest. A repugnant gurgling from his throat filled the room, accompanied by the mad thudding of his shoes on the floor as he died. Finally he quivered once violently and lay still. His glazed eyes, dotted with blood, stared at the ceiling.

Turning to the bed he kept his eyes on Lincoln Rhyme as he walked around it. Slowly circling, the knife in his hand. His breathing was hard.

"Who *are* you?" Rhyme gasped.

Silently Taylor stepped forward, put his fingers around Rhyme's arm, squeezed the bone several times, perhaps hard, perhaps not. His hand strayed to Rhyme's left ring finger. He lifted it off the ECU and caressed it with the dripping blade of the knife. Slipped the sharp point up under the nail.

Rhyme felt faint pain, a queasy sensation. Then harder. He gasped.

Then Taylor noticed something and froze. He gasped. Leaned forward. Staring at the copy of *Crime in Old New York* on the turning frame.

"That's how . . . You actually found it. . . .Oh, the constables should be proud to have you in their ranks, Lincoln Rhyme. I thought it'd be days before you got to the house. I thought Maggie'd be stripped down by the dogs by then."

"Why're you doing this?" Rhyme asked.

But Taylor didn't answer; he was examining Rhyme carefully, muttering, half to himself, "You didn't used to be this good, you know. In the old days. You missed a lot back then, didn't you? In the old days."

The old days . . . What did he mean?

He shook his balding head, gray hair—not brown—and glanced at a copy of Rhyme's forensic textbook. There was recognition in his eyes and slowly Rhyme began to understand.

"You read my book," the criminalist said. "You studied it. At the library, right? The public library branch near you?"

Eight twenty-three was, after all, a reader.

So he knew Rhyme's CS procedures. That's why he'd swept up so carefully, why he'd worn gloves touching even surfaces most criminals wouldn't't've thought would retain prints, why he'd sprayed the aftershave at the scene—he'd known exactly what Sachs would be looking for.

And of course the manual wasn't the only book he'd read.

Scenes of the Crime too. That's what had given him the idea for the planted clues—Old New York clues. Clues that only Lincoln Rhyme would be able to figure out.

Taylor picked up the disk of spinal column he'd given to Rhyme eight months ago. He kneaded it absently between his fingers. And Rhyme saw the gift, so touching back then, for the horrific preface that it was.

His eyes were unfocused, distant. Rhyme recalled he'd seen this before—when Taylor'd examined him over the past months. He'd put it down to a doctor's concentration but now knew it was madness. The control he'd been struggling to maintain was disappearing.

"Tell me," Rhyme asked. "Why?"

"Why?" Taylor whispered, moving his hand along Rhyme's leg, probing once more, knee, shin, ankle. "Because you were something remarkable, Rhyme. Unique. You were invulnerable."

"What do you mean?"

"How can you punish a man who wants to die? If you kill him you've done what he wants. So I had to make you want to live."

And the answer came to Rhyme finally.

The old days . . .

"It was fake, wasn't it?" he whispered. "That obituary from the Albany coroner. You wrote it yourself."

Colin Stanton. Dr Taylor was Colin Stanton.

The man whose family had been butchered in front of him on the streets of Chinatown. The man who stood paralyzed in front of the bodies of his wife and two children as they bled to death, and could not make the obscene choice about which of them to save.

You missed things. In the old days.

Now, too late, the final pieces fell into place.

His watching the victims: T.J. Colfax and Monelle and Carole Ganz. He'd risked capture to stand and stare at them— just as Stanton had stood over his family, watching as they died. He wanted revenge but he was a doctor, sworn never to take a life, and so in order to kill he had to become his spiritual ancestor—the bone collector, James Schneider, a nineteenth-century madman whose family had been destroyed by the police.

"After I got out of the mental hospital I came back to Manhattan. I read the inquest report about how you missed the killer at the crime scene, how he got out of the apartment. I knew I had to kill you. But I couldn't. I don't know why. . . .I kept waiting and waiting for something to happen. And then I found the book. James Schneider . . . He'd been through exactly what I had. He'd done it; I could too."

I took them down to the bone.

"The obituary," Rhyme said.

"Right. I wrote it myself on my computer. Faxed it to NYPD so they wouldn't suspect me. Then I became someone else. Dr Peter Taylor. I didn't realize until later why I picked that name. Can you figure it out?" Stanton's eyes strayed to the chart. "The answer's there."

Rhyme scanned the profile.

- Knows basic German.

"*Schneider*," Rhyme said, sighing. "It's German for 'tailor.'"

Stanton nodded. "I spent weeks at the library reading up on spinal cord trauma and then called you, claimed I'd been referred by Columbia SCI. I planned to kill you during the first appointment, cut your flesh off a strip at a time, let you bleed to death. It might've taken hours. Even days. But what happened?" His eyes grew wide. "I found out you wanted to kill *yourself*."

He leaned close to Rhyme. "Jesus, I still remember the first time I saw you. You son of a bitch. You *were* dead. And I knew what I had to do—I had to make you *want* to live. I had to give you purpose once more."

So it didn't matter whom he kidnapped. Anyone would do. "You didn't even care whether the victims lived or died."

"Of course not. All I wanted was to force *you* to try to save them."

"The knot," Rhyme asked, noticing the loop of clothesline hanging beside the poster. "It was a surgical suture?"

He nodded.

"Of course. And the scar on your finger?"

"My finger?" He frowned. "How did you . . . Her *neck*! You printed her neck, Hanna's. I *knew* that was possible. I didn't think about it." Angry with himself. "I broke a glass in the mental hospital library," Stanton continued. "To cut my wrist. I squeezed it till it broke." He madly traced the scar with his left index finger.

"The deaths," Rhyme said evenly, "your wife and children. It was an accident. A terrible accident, horrible. But it didn't happen on purpose. It was a mistake. I'm so sorry for you and for them."

In a sing-songy voice, Stanton chided, "Remember what you wrote? . . . in the preface of your textbook?" He recited perfectly, "'The criminalist knows that for every action there's a consequence. The presence of a perpetrator alters every crime scene, however subtly. It is because of this that we can identify and locate criminals and achieve justice.'" Stanton grabbed Rhyme's hair and tugged his head forward. They were inches apart. Rhyme could smell the madman's breath, see the lenses of sweat on the gray skin. "Well, I'm the consequence of *your* actions."

"What'll you accomplish? You kill me and I'm no worse off than I would've been."

"Oh, but I'm not going to kill you. Not yet."

Stanton released Rhyme's hair, backed away.

"You want to know what I'm going to do?" he whispered. "I'm going to kill your doctor, Berger. But not the way he's used to killing. Oh, no sleeping pills for him, no booze. We'll see how he likes death the old-fashioned way. Then your friend Sellitto. And Officer Sachs? Her too. She was lucky once. But I'll get her the next time. Another burial for her. And Thom too of course. He'll die right here in front of you. Work him down to the bone . . . Nice and slow." Stanton's breathing was fast. "Maybe we'll take care of him today. When's he due back?"

"*I* made the mistakes. It's my—" Rhyme suddenly coughed deeply. He cleared his throat, caught his breath. "It's *my* fault. Do whatever you want with me."

"No, it's all of you. It's—"

"Please. You can't—" Rhyme began to cough again. It turned into a violent racking. He managed to control it.

Stanton glanced at him.

"You *can't* hurt them. I'll do whatever—" Rhyme's voice seized. His head flew back, his eyes bulged.

And Lincoln Rhyme's breath stopped completely. His head thrashed, his shoulders shivered violently. The tendons in his neck tightened like steel cords.

"Rhyme!" Stanton cried.

Sputtering, saliva shooting from his lips, Rhyme trembled once, twice, an earthquake seemed to ripple through his entire limp body. His head fell back, blood trickled from the corner of his mouth.

"No!" Stanton shouted. Slamming his hands into Rhyme's chest. "You can't die!"

The doctor lifted Rhyme's lids, revealing only whites.

Stanton tore open Thom's medicine box and prepared a blood-pressure hypodermic, injected the drug. He yanked the pillow off the bed and pulled Rhyme flat. He tilted back Rhyme's lolling head, wiped the lips and placed his mouth on Rhyme's, breathing hard into the unresponsive lungs.

"No!" Stanton raged. "I won't let you die! You *can't!*"

No response.

Again. He checked the unmoving eyes.

"Come on! Come *on!*"

Another breath. Pounding on the still chest.

Then he backed up, frozen with panic and shock, staring, staring, watching the man die in front of him.

Finally he bent forward and one last time exhaled deeply into Rhyme's mouth.

And it was when Stanton turned his head and lowered his ear to listen for the faint sound of breath, any faint exhalation, that Rhyme's head shot forward like a striking snake. He closed his teeth on Stanton's neck, tearing through the carotid artery and gripping a portion of the man's own spine.

Down to . . .

Stanton screamed and scrabbled backwards, sliding Rhyme off the bed on top of him. Together they fell in a pile on the floor. The hot coppery blood gushed and gushed, filling Rhyme's mouth.

. . . the bone.

His lungs, his *killer* lungs, had already gone for a minute without air but he refused to loosen his grip now to gasp for breath, ignoring the searing pain from inside his cheek where he'd bit into the tender skin, bloodying it to give credence to his sham attack of dysreflexia. He growled in rage—seeing Amelia Sachs buried in dirt, seeing the steam spew over T.J. Colfax's body—and he shook his head, feeling the snap of bone and cartilage.

Pummeling Rhyme's chest, Stanton screamed again, kicking to get away from the monster that had socketed itself to him.

But Rhyme's grip was unbreakable. It was as if the spirits of all the dead muscles throughout his body had risen into his jaw.

Stanton clawed his way to the bedside table and managed to grab his knife. He jabbed it into Rhyme. Once, twice. But the only places he could reach were the criminalist's legs and arms. It's pain that incapacitates and pain was one thing to which Lincoln Rhyme was immune.

The vise of his jaws closed harder and Stanton's scream was cut off as his windpipe went. He plunged the knife deep into Rhyme's arm. It stopped when it hit bone. He started to draw it out to strike again but the madman's body froze then spasmed violently once, then again, and suddenly went completely limp.

Stanton collapsed to the floor, pulling Rhyme after him. The criminalist's head slammed onto the oak with a loud crack. Yet Rhyme wouldn't let go. He held tight and continued to crush the man's neck, shaking, tearing the flesh like a hungry lion crazed by blood and by the immeasurable satisfaction of a lust fulfilled.

5

WHEN YOU MOVE
THEY CAN'T GETCHA

"A physician's duty is not just to extend life,
it is to end suffering."

Dr Jack Kevorkian

THIRTY-SEVEN

It was nearly sunset when Amelia Sachs walked through his doorway.

She was no longer in sweats. Or uniform. She wore jeans and a forest-green blouse. Her beautiful face sported several scratches Rhyme didn't recognize, though given the events of the past three days he guessed the wounds weren't self-inflicted.

"Yuck," she said, walking around the portion of the floor where Stanton and Polling had died. It had been mopped with bleach—with the perp body-bagged, forensics became moot—but the pink island of stain was huge.

Rhyme watched Sachs pause and nod a cold greeting to Dr William Berger, who stood by the falcon window with his infamous briefcase at his side.

"So you got him, did you?" she asked, nodding at the bloodstain.

"Yeah," Rhyme said. "He's got."

"All by yourself?"

"It was hardly a fair fight," he offered. "I forced myself to hold back."

Outside, the liquid, ruddy light of the low sun ignited treetops and the marching line of elegant buildings along Fifth Avenue across the park.

Sachs glanced at Berger, who said, "Lincoln and I were just having a little talk."

"Were you?"

There was a long pause.

"Amelia," he began. "I'm going to go through with it. I've decided."

"I see." Her gorgeous lips, marred by the black lines of tiny stitches, tightened slightly. It was her only visible reaction. "You know, I hate it when you use my first name. I goddamn *hate* it."

How could he explain to her that *she* was largely the reason he was going ahead with his death? Waking that morning, with her beside him, he realized with a piquant sorrow that she would soon climb from the bed and dress and walk out the door—to her own life, to a *normal* life. Why, they were as doomed as lovers could be—if he dared even to think of them as lovers. It was only a matter of time until she met another Nick and fell in love. The 823 case was over, and without that binding them together, their lives would have to drift apart. Inevitable.

Oh, Stanton was smarter than he could've guessed. Rhyme *had* been drawn to the brink of the real world once again and, yes, he'd moved far over it.

Sachs, I lied: Sometimes you can't give up the dead. Sometimes you just have to go with them. . . .

Hands clenched, she walked to the window. "I tried to come up with a ballbuster of an argument to talk you out of it. You know, something real slick. But I couldn't. All I can say is, I just don't want you to do it."

"A deal's a deal, Sachs."

She looked at Berger. "Shit, Rhyme." Walking over to the bed, crouching down. She put her hand on his shoulder, brushed his hair off his forehead. "But will you do one thing for me?"

"What?"

"Give me a few hours."

"I'm not changing my mind."

"I understand. Just two hours. There's something you have to do first."

Rhyme looked at Berger, who said, "I can't stay much longer, Lincoln. My plane . . . If you want to wait a week I can come back. . . ."

"That's okay, doctor," Sachs said. "I'll help him do it."

"You?" the doctor asked cautiously.

Reluctantly she nodded. "Yes."

This wasn't *her* nature. Rhyme could see that clearly. But he

glanced into her blue eyes, which though tearful were remark‐
ably clear. He nodded. He said to Berger, "It's all right, doctor.
Could you just leave the—what's the euphemism of the day?"

"How's 'paraphernalia'?" Berger suggested.

"Could you just leave them there, on the table?"

"You're sure?" he asked Sachs.

She nodded again.

The doctor set the pills, brandy and plastic bag on the
bedside table. Then he rummaged through his briefcase. "I
don't have any rubber bands, I'm afraid. For the bag."

"That's all right," Sachs said, glancing down at her shoes.
"I've got some."

Then Berger stepped close to the bed, put his arm on
Rhyme's shoulder. "I wish you a peaceful self-deliverance,"
he said.

"Self-deliverance," Rhyme said wryly as Berger left. Then,
to Sachs: "Now. What's this I have to do?"

———

She took the turn at fifty, skidded hard, and slipped smoothly
up into fourth gear.

The wind blasted through the open windows and tossed their
hair behind them. The gusts were brutal but Amelia Sachs
wouldn't hear of driving with the windows up.

"That'd be un-Amurican," she announced, and broke the
100-mph mark.

When you move . . .

Rhyme had suggested it might be wiser to take their spin
on the NYPD training course but he wasn't surprised when
Sachs declared that that was a pussy run; she'd disposed of
it the first week at the academy. So they were out on Long
Island, their cover stories for the Nassau County police ready,
rehearsed and marginally credible.

"The thing above five-speeds is, top gear isn't the fastest.
That's a mileage gear. I don't give a shit about mileage." Then
she took his left hand and placed it on the round black knob,
encircled it with hers, downshifted.

The engine screamed and they shot up to 120, as trees and
houses streaked past and the uneasy horses grazing in the fields
stared at the black streak of Chevrolet.

"Isn't this the *best*, Rhyme?" she shouted. "Man, better than sex. Better than anything."

"I can feel the vibrations," he said. "I think I can. In my finger."

She smiled and he believed she squeezed his hand beneath hers. Finally, they ran out of deserted road, population loomed, and Sachs reluctantly slowed, turned around and pointed the nose of the car toward the hazy crescent of moon as it rose above the distant city, nearly invisible in the stew of hot August air.

"Let's try for one-fifty," she proposed. Lincoln Rhyme closed his eyes and lost himself in the sensation of wind and the perfume of freshly cut grass and the speed.

———

The night was the hottest of the month.

From Lincoln's Rhyme's new vantage point he could look down into the park and see the weirdos on the benches, the exhausted joggers, the families reclining around the smoke of dwindling barbecue fires like the survivors of a medieval battle. A few dog walkers unable to wait for the night's fever to break made their obligatory rounds, Baggies in hand.

Thom had put on a CD—Samuel Barber's elegiac Adagio for Strings. But Rhyme had snorted a derisive laugh, declared it a sorry cliché and ordered him to replace it with Gershwin.

Amelia Sachs climbed the stairs and walked into his bedroom, noticed him looking outside. "What do you see?" she asked.

"Hot people."

"And the birds? The falcons?"

"Ah, yes, they're there."

"Hot too?"

He examined the male. "I don't think so. Somehow, they seem above that sort of thing."

She set the bag on the foot of the bed and lifted out the contents, a bottle of expensive brandy. He'd reminded her of the Scotch but Sachs said she'd contribute the liquor. She set it next to the pills and the plastic bag. Looking like a breezy professional wife, home from Balducci's with piles of vegetables and seafood and too little time to whip them into dinner.

She'd also bought some ice, at Rhyme's request. He'd remembered what Berger had explained about the heat in the bag. She lifted the cap off the Courvoisier and poured herself a glass and filled his tumbler, arranged the straw toward his mouth.

"Where's Thom?" she asked him.

"Out."

"Does he know?"

"Yes."

They sipped the brandy.

"Do you want me to say anything to your wife?"

Rhyme considered it for a long moment, thinking: We have years to converse with someone, to blurt and rant, to explain our desires and anger and regrets—and oh how we squander those moments. Here he'd known Amelia Sachs all of three days and they'd bared their hearts far more than he and Blaine had done in nearly a decade.

"No," he said. "I've e-mailed her." A chuckle. "That's a comment on our times, I'd say."

More brandy, the astringent bite on his palate was dissipating. Growing smoother, duller, lighter.

Sachs leaned over the bed and tapped her glass to his.

"I have some money," Rhyme began. "I'm giving a lot of it to Blaine and to Thom. I—"

But she shushed him with a kiss to the forehead and shook her head.

A soft clatter of pebbles as she spilled the tiny Seconals into her hand.

Rhyme instinctively thought: The Dillie-Koppanyi color test reagent. Add 1 percent cobalt acetate in methanol to the suspect material followed by 5 percent isopropylamine in methanol. If the substance is a barbiturate the reagent turns a beautiful violet-blue color.

"How should we do it?" she asked, gazing at the pills. "I really don't know."

"Mix them in the booze," he suggested.

She dropped them in his tumbler. They dissolved quickly. How fragile they were. Like the dreams they induce.

She stirred the mixture with the straw. He glanced at her wounded nails but even that he couldn't be sorrowful for. This was *his* night and it was a night of joy.

Lincoln Rhyme had a sudden recollection of childhood in suburban Illinois. He never drank his milk and to get him to do so his mother bought straws coated on the inside with flavoring. Strawberry, chocolate. He hadn't thought about them until just this moment. It was a great invention, he remembered. He always looked forward to his afternoon milk.

Sachs pushed the straw close to his mouth. He took it between his lips. She put her hand on his arm.

Light or dark, music or silence, dreams or the meditation of dreamless sleep? What will I find?

He began to sip. The taste was really no different from straight liquor. A little more bitter maybe. It was like—

From downstairs came a huge pounding on the door. Hands and feet both, it seemed. Voices shouting too.

He lifted his lips away from the straw. Glanced into the dim stairwell.

She looked at him, frowning.

"Go see," he said to her.

She disappeared down the stairs and a moment later returned, looking unhappy. Lon Sellitto and Jerry Banks followed. Rhyme noticed that the young detective had done another butcher job on his face with a razor. He'd really have to get that under control.

Sellitto glanced at the bottle and the bag. His eyes swayed toward Sachs but she crossed her arms and held her own, silently ordering him to leave. This was not an issue of rank, the look told the detective, and what was happening here was none of his business. Sellitto's eyes acknowledged the message but he wasn't about to go anywhere just yet.

"Lincoln, I need to talk to you."

"Talk. But talk fast, Lon. We're busy."

The detective sat heavily in the noisy rattan chair. "An hour ago a bomb went off at the United Nations. Right next to the banquet hall. During the welcome dinner for the peace conference delegates."

"Six dead, fifty-four hurt," Banks added. "Twenty of them serious."

"My God," Sachs whispered.

"Tell him," Sellitto muttered.

Banks continued, "For the conference, the UN hired a bunch of temps. The perp was one of them—a receptionist. A half-dozen people saw her carrying a knapsack to work and putting it in a storeroom near the banquet hall. She left just before the bang. The bomb squad estimates we're looking at about two pounds of C4 or Semtex."

Sellitto said, "Linc, the bomb, it was a yellow knapsack, the wits said."

"Yellow?" Why was that familiar?

"UN human resources ID'd the receptionist as Carole Ganz."

"The mother," Rhyme and Sachs said simultaneously.

"Yeah. The woman you saved in the church. Only Ganz's an alias. Her real name's Charlotte Willoughby. She was married to a Ron Willoughby. Ring a bell?"

Rhyme said it didn't.

"It was in the news a couple years ago. He was an Army sergeant assigned to a UN peacekeeping force in Burma."

"Keep going," the criminalist said.

"Willoughby didn't want to go—thought an American soldier shouldn't be wearing a UN uniform and taking orders from anybody except the U.S. Army. It's a big right-wing issue nowadays. But he went anyway. Wasn't there a week before he's blown away by some little punk in Rangoon. Got shot in the back. Became a conservative martyr. Anti-Terror says his widow got recruited by an extremist group out in the Chicago burbs. Some U of C grads gone underground. Edward and Katherine Stone."

Banks took over the narrative. "The explosive was in a package of kid's modeling clay, along with some other toys. We think she was going to take the little girl with her so security at the banquet-hall entrance wouldn't think anything of the clay. But with Pammy in the hospital she didn't have her cover story so she gave up on the hall and just planted it in the storeroom. Did enough damage as it was."

"Rabbited?"

"Yep. Not a trace."

"What about the little girl," Sachs asked, "Pammy?"

"Gone. The woman checked her out of the hospital around the time of the bang. No sign of either of them."

Rhyme asked, "The cell?"

"The group in Chicago? They're gone too. Had a safe house in Wisconsin but it's been hosed. We don't know where they are."

"So *that* was the rumor Dellray's snitch heard." Rhyme laughed. "*Carole* was the one coming into the airport. Had nothing to do with Unsub 823."

He found Banks and Sellitto staring at him.

Oh, the old silent trick again.

"Forget it, Lon." Rhyme said, all too aware of the glass sitting inches from him, radiating a welcoming heat. "Impossible."

The older detective plucked his sweaty shirt away from his body, cringing. "God*damn* cold in here, Lincoln. Jesus. Look, just think about it. What'sa harm?"

"I can't help you."

Sellitto said, "There was a note. Carole wrote it and sent it to the secretary-general by interoffice envelope. Harping on world government, taking away American liberties. Some shit like that. Claimed credit for the UNESCO bombing in London too and said there'd be more. We've gotta get 'em, Linc."

Feeling his oats, scarface Banks said, "The secretary-general and the mayor both've asked for you. SAC Perkins too. And there'll be a call from the White House, you need any more persuading. We sure hope you don't, detective."

Rhyme didn't comment on the error regarding his rank.

"They've got the Bureau's PERT team ready to go. Fred Dellray's running the case and he asked—*respectfully*, yeah, he used that very word—he asked respectfully if you'd do the forensic work. And it's a virgin scene, except for getting the bodies and the wounded out."

"Then it's *not* virgin," Rhyme snapped. "It's extremely contaminated."

"All the more reason we need you," Banks ventured, adding "sir" to defuse Rhyme's glare.

Rhyme sighed, looked at the glass and the straw. Peace was so close to him just now. And pain too. Infinite sums of both.

He closed his eyes. Not a sound in the room.

Sellitto added, "It was just the woman herself, hey, wouldn't be that big a deal. But she's got her daughter with her, Lincoln. Underground, with a little girl? You know what that kid's life's going to be like?"

I'll get you for that too, Lon.

Rhyme nestled his head into the opulent pillow. Finally his eyes sprang open. He said, "There'd be some conditions."

"Name it, Linc."

"First of all," he said, "I don't work alone."

Rhyme looked toward Amelia Sachs.

She hesitated for a moment then smiled and stood, lifted the glass of tainted brandy out from under the straw. She opened the window wide and flung the tawny liquid into the ripe, hot air above the alley next to the townhouse, while, just feet away, the falcon looked up, glaring angrily at the motion of her arm, cocked his gray head, then turned back to feed his hungry youngster.

APPENDIX

Excerpts from: Glossary of Terms, Lincoln Rhyme, *Physical Evidence,* 4th ed., (New York, Forensic Press, 1994). Reprinted with permission.

Alternative light source (ALS): Any of several types of high-intensity lamps of varying wavelength and light color, used to visualize latent friction-ridge prints, and certain types of trace and biological evidence.

Automated Fingerprint Identification System (AFIS): One of several computerized systems for the scanning and storage of friction ridge prints.

Birefringence: The difference between two measures of refraction displayed by certain crystalline substances. Useful in identifying sand, fibers, and dirt.

Chain of custody (COC): A record of every person who has had possession of a piece of evidence from the moment of its collection at a crime scene to its introduction at trial.

COD: Cause of death.

Control samples: Physical evidence collected at a crime scene from known sources, used for comparison with evidence from an unknown source. For example, the victim's own blood and hair constitutes a control sample.

DCDS: Deceased, confirmed dead at scene.

Density-gradient testing (D-G): A technique for comparing soil samples to determine if they come from the same location. The test involves suspending dirt samples in tubes filled with liquids that have different density values.

DNA typing: Analyzing and charting the genetic structure within the cells of certain types of biological evidence (for example, blood, semen, hair) for the purpose of comparison with control samples from a known suspect. The process involves the isolation and comparison of fragments of DNA —deoxyribonucleic acid—the basic building block of the chromosome. Some types of DNA typing produce a mere likelihood that the evidence came from a suspect; other types are virtually conclusive, with the odds in the hundreds of millions that the evidence was from a particular individual. Also called "genetic typing," or—erroneously—"DNA fingerprinting" or "genetic fingerprinting."

Forensic anthropologist: A skeletal-remains expert, who aids crime scene investigators in evaluating and identifying remains and excavating grave sites.

Forensic odontologist: A dental expert also aids crime scene investigators in identifying victims through examination of dental remains and analysis of bite-mark evidence.

Friction ridges: The raised lines of skin on fingers, palms and the soles of feet, whose patterns are unique to each individual. Prints of friction ridges at crime scenes can be classified as 1) plastic (left in an impressionable substance such as putty); 2) evident (left by skin coated with a foreign substance like dust or blood), 3) latent (left by skin contaminated with bodily secretions such as grease or sweat and largely invisible).

Gas chromatograph/mass spectrometer (GC-MS): Two instruments used in forensic analysis to identify unknown substances such as drugs and trace evidence. They are often linked together. The gas chromatograph separates components in a substance and sends them to the mass spectrometer, which definitively identifies each of those components.

Grid: A common approach to searching for evidence whereby the searcher covers a crime scene back and forth in one direction (say, north–south) then covers the same scene in the perpendicular direction (east–west).

Gunshot residue (GSR): The material deposited on the hands and clothing of a person shooting a firearm, particularly barium and antimony. GSR remains on human skin for up to six hours if not removed intentionally by washing or inadvertently by excessive contact when a suspect is arrested and handcuffed (particularly if hands are cuffed behind back).

Identification of physical evidence: Determining the category or class of material that an item of evidence falls into. This is distinguishable from "individuation," which is determining the single source the item came from. For instance, a torn piece of paper can be *identified* as coated 40-lb. stock of the type often used in magazine printing. It can be *individuated* if the tear exactly matches a torn page in the July issue of *Vogue* found in the suspect's possession. Individuation, of course, has far more probative value than does identification.

Individuation of physical evidence: See "Identification of physical evidence."

Lividity: The purplish discoloring of portions of the skin of a deceased owing to the darkening and settling of the blood after death.

Locard's Exchange Principle: Formulated by Edmond Locard, a French criminalist, this theory holds that there is always an exchange of physical evidence between the perpetrator and the crime scene or his victim, however minute or difficult to detect that evidence might be.

Mass spectrometer: See "Gas chromatograph."

Ninhydrin: A chemical that visualizes latent friction-ridge prints on porous surfaces such as paper, cardboard, and wood.

Physical evidence (PE): In criminal law, PE refers to items or substances presented at trial to support the assertion by the defendant or the prosecution that a particular proposition is true. Physical evidence may comprise inanimate objects, body materials, or impressions.

Presumptive blood test: Any of a number of chemical techniques for determining if blood residue is present at a crime scene, even if it is not evident. Most common are tests using luminol and orthotolidine.

Scanning electron microscope (SEM): An instrument that fires electrons onto a specimen of evidence to be examined and projects the resulting image on a computer monitor. Magnification of 100,000X is possible with SEMs, compared with about 500X in the case of most optical microscopes. The SEM is often combined with an energy-dispersive X-ray unit (EDX), which can identify the elements in a sample at the same time the technician is viewing it.

Staging: A perpetrator's efforts to rearrange, add or remove evidence from a crime scene to make it appear that the crime he or she has committed did not occur or was committed by someone else.

Trace evidence: Bits of tiny, sometimes microscopic, substances such as dust, dirt, cellular material, and fibers.

Unsub: Unknown subject, that is, an unidentified suspect.

Vacuum-metal deposition (VMD): The most effective means for visualizing latent friction-ridge prints on smooth surfaces. Gold or zinc evaporated in a vacuum chamber, coats the object to be examined with a thin layer of metal, thereby making a print visible.

AUTHOR'S NOTE

I'm indebted to Peter A. Micheels, author of *The Detectives*, and E. W. Count, author of *Cop Talk*, whose books were not only wonderfully helpful in researching this one but great reads as well. Thanks to Pam Dorman, whose deft editorial touch is evident everywhere in this story. And of course thanks to my agent, Deborah Schneider . . . what would I do without ya? I'm grateful too to Nina Salter at Calmann-Lévy for her perceptive comments on an earlier draft of the book and to Karolyn Hutchinson at REP in Alexandria, Virginia, for invaluable help with wheelchairs and other equipment available for quadriplegics. And to Teddy Rosenbaum—a detective in her own right—for her fine copyediting job. Students of law enforcement may wonder about the structure of the NYPD and FBI as presented here; tweaking the organizational charts was my doing exclusively. Oh, yes—anyone interested in reading a copy of *Crime in Old New York* may have a little trouble finding one. The official story is that the book is a fictional creation, though I've also heard the rumor that the one copy in existence was recently stolen from the New York Public Library—by a person or persons unknown.

J.W.D.

Praying For Sleep

And can you, by no drift of conference,
Get from him why he puts on this confusion,
Grating so harshly all his days of quiet
With turbulent and dangerous lunacy?

Hamlet
William Shakespeare

1

Like a cradle, the hearse rocked him gently.

The old vehicle creaked along a country road, the asphalt cracked and root-humped. He believed the journey had so far taken several hours though he wouldn't have been surprised to find that they'd been on the road for days or weeks. At last he heard the squeal of bad brakes and was jostled by an abrupt turn. Then they were on a good road, a state road, and accelerating quickly.

He rubbed his face across a satiny label sewn inside the bag. He couldn't see the label in the darkness but he remembered the words elegantly stitched in black thread on yellow cloth.

Union Rubber Products
Trenton, NJ 08606
MADE IN USA

He caressed this label with his ample cheek and sucked air through the minuscule opening where the zipper hadn't completely seated. The smoothness of the hearse's transit suddenly troubled him. He felt he was falling straight down to hell, or maybe into a well where he'd be wedged immobile, head down, forever. . . .

This thought aroused a piercing fear of confinement and when it grew unbearable he craned his neck and drew back his thick lips. He gripped the inside of the zipper with lengthy teeth, yellow and gray as cat's claws, and with them he struggled to work the mechanism open. One inch, two, then several more. Cold, exhaust-scented air filled the bag. He inhaled greedily. The air diminished the bristle of claustrophobia. The men who took away the dead, he knew, called what he now lay in a "crash bag." But he couldn't recall these men ever taking away anyone dead from a crash. The dead ones died by leaping from the top of the stairwell in E Ward. They died from severed veins in their fat forearms. They died face down in toilets and they died like the man this afternoon—a strip of cloth wound round and round and round his neck.

But he couldn't recall a single crash.

His teeth rose from his lips again and he worked the zipper open further, eight inches, ten. His round shaved head emerged from the jagged opening. With his snarling lips and thick face he had the appearance of a bear—though one that was not only hairless but blue, for much of his head was dyed that color.

Finally able to look about he was disappointed to find that this wasn't a real hearse at all but merely a station wagon and it wasn't even black but tan. The back windows weren't shaded and he could see ghostly forms of trees, signs, power towers and barns as the wagon sped past—his view distorted by the misty darkness of the autumn evening.

In five minutes he began on the zipper again, angry that his arms were pinioned helpless by, he muttered in frustration, "damn good New Jersey rubber." He opened the crash bag another four inches.

He frowned. What was that *noise*?

Music! It came from the front seat, separated from the back by a black fiberboard divider. He generally liked music but certain melodies upset him greatly. The one he now heard, a country-western tune, for some reason set off within him bursts of uneasiness.

I hate this bag! he thought. It's too damn *tight*.

Then it occurred to him that he wasn't alone. That's it—the bag was filled with the souls of crashed and shattered bodies. The jumpers and the drowners and the wrist slitters.

He believed that these souls hated him, that they knew he was an impostor. They wanted to seal him up alive, forever, in this tight rubber bag. And with these thoughts came the evening's first burst of real panic—raw, liquid, cold. He tried to relax by using the breathing exercises he'd been taught but it was too late. Sweat popped out on his skin, tears formed in his eyes. He shoved his head viciously into the opening of the bag. He wrenched his hands up as far as they'd go and beat the thick rubber. He kicked with his bare feet. He slammed the bridge of his nose into the zipper, which snapped out of track and froze.

Michael Hrubek began to scream.

The music stopped, replaced by a mumble of confused voices. The hearse rippled sideways like an airplane in a crosswind.

Hrubek slammed his torso upward then fell back, again and again, trying to force his way out of the small opening, his massive neck muscles knotting into thick cables, his eyes bulging. He screamed and wept and screamed again. A tiny door in the black partition flew open and two wide eyes stared into the back of the vehicle. Surrendering to the fear Hrubek neither saw the attendant nor heard the man's hysterical shout, "Stop! Stop the car. Christ, *stop!*"

The station wagon careened onto the shoulder amid a staccato clatter of pebbles. A cloud of dust surrounded it, and the two attendants, wearing pastel green jumpsuits, leapt out and ran to the back of the hearse. One tore open the door. A small yellow light above Hrubek's face popped on, frightening him further and starting another jag of screaming.

"Shit, he's not dead," said the younger of the attendants.

"*Shit he's not dead?* It's an escape! Get back."

Hrubek screamed again and convulsed forward. His veins rose in deep clusters from his blue skull and neck, and straps of tendon quivered. Flecks of foam and blood filled the corner of his mouth. The belief, and hope, that he was having a stroke occurred simultaneously to each attendant.

"Settle down, you!" shouted the youthful one.

"You're just going to get in more trouble!" his partner said shrilly, and added with no threat or conviction whatsoever, "We've caught you now so just settle down. We're going to take you back."

Hrubek let go a huge scream. As if under the power of this sound alone the zipper gave way and metal teeth fired from the crash bag like shotgun pellets. Sobbing and gasping for air Hrubek leapt forward and rolled over the tailgate, crouching on the ground, naked except for his white boxer shorts. He ignored the attendants, who danced away from him, and rested his head against his own distorted reflection in the pitted chrome bumper of the hearse.

"All right, that's enough of that!" the younger attendant growled. When Hrubek said nothing but merely rubbed his cheek against the bumper and wept, the attendant lifted an oak branch twice the length of a baseball bat and waved it at him with some menace.

"No," the other attendant said to his partner, who nonetheless swung at the massive naked shoulders, as if taking on a fastball. The wood bounced off with hardly a sound and Hrubek seemed not to notice the blow. The attendant refreshed his grip. "Son of a bitch."

His partner's hand snagged the weapon. "No. That's not our job."

Hrubek stood, his chest heaving, and faced the attendants. They stepped back. But the huge man didn't advance. Exhausted, he studied the two men curiously for a moment and sank once more to the ground then scrabbled away, rolling into the grass by the road, oblivious to the cold autumn dew that lacquered his body. A whimper came from his fleshy throat.

The attendants eased toward the hearse. Without closing the back door they leapt inside and the wagon shot away, spraying Hrubek with stones and dirt. Numb, he didn't feel this pummeling and merely lay immobile on his side, gulping down cold air that smelled of dirt and shit and blood and grease. He watched the hearse vanish through a blue cloud of tire smoke, grateful that the men were gone and that they'd taken with them the terrible bag of New Jersey rubber filled with its ghostly occupants.

After a few minutes the panic became a stinging memory then a dark thought and then was nearly forgotten. Hrubek rose to his full six-foot, four-inch height and stood bald and blue as a Druid. He snatched up a handful of grass and wiped his mouth and chin. He studied the geography around him. The road was in the middle of a deep valley; bony ridges of rock rose up on either side of the wide asphalt. Behind him in the west—where the hearse had come from—the hospital was lost in darkness many miles away. Ahead lay the distant lights of houses.

Like an animal released from his captors, he circled in an awkward, cautious lope, uncertain of which direction to take.

Then, like an animal finding a scent, he turned toward the lights in the east and began to run, with an ominous grace and at a great speed.

2

Above them the sky had gone from resonant gunmetal to black.

"What's that? There?" The woman pointed to a cluster of stars above the distant line of alder and oak and occasional white birch that marked the end of their property.

The man sitting beside her stirred, setting his glass on the table. "I'm not sure."

"Cassiopeia, I'll bet." Her eyes lowered from the constellation to gaze into the large state park that was separated from their yard by the inky void of a dim New England lake.

"Could be."

They'd sat on this flagstone patio for an hour, warmed by a bottle of wine and by unusually congenial November air. A single candle in a blue fishnet holder lit their faces, and the scent of leaf decay, ripe and too sweet, floated about them. No neighbors lived within a half mile but they spoke in near whispers.

"Don't you sometimes," she asked slowly, "feel something of Mother around here still?"

He laughed. "You know what I always thought about ghosts? They'd have to be naked, wouldn't they? Clothes don't have souls."

She glanced toward him. His gray hair and tan slacks were the only aspects of him visible in the deepening night (and made him, she reflected, if anything, ghostlike). "I know there're no ghosts. That's not what I mean." She lifted the bottle of California's finest Chardonnay and poured herself more. She misjudged and the neck of the bottle rang loudly on her glass, startling them both.

Her husband's eyes remained on the stars as he asked, "Is some thing wrong?"

"No, nothing at all."

With long, ruddy and wrinkled hands Lisbonne Atcheson absently combed her short blond hair, shaping the strands but leaving them as unruly as before. She stretched her limber, forty-year-old body luxuriously and looked momentarily at the three-story colonial house rising behind them. After a moment she continued, "What I mean about Mother . . . It's tough to explain." But as a teacher of the Queen's language Lis was bound by the rule that difficulty of expression is no excuse for not expressing, and so she tried once more. "A 'presence.' *That's* what I mean."

On cue, the candle flickered in its cerulean holder.

"I rest my case." She nodded at the flame and they laughed. "What time is it?"

"Almost nine."

Lis slouched down into the lawn chair and pulled her knees up, tucking her long denim skirt around her legs. The tips of brown cowboy boots, tooled with gold vines, protruded from the hem. She gazed again at the stars and reflected that her mother would in fact have been a good candidate for ghosthood. She'd died just eight months ago, sitting in an antique rocking chair as she looked out over the patio where Lis and Owen now sat. The elderly woman had leaned forward suddenly as if recognizing a landmark and said, "Oh, of course," then died in a very peaceful second.

This house too would have been a good site for a haunting. The dark boxy structure contained more square footage than even a fertile eighteenth-century family might comfortably fill. It was sided with weather-stained cedar shakes, brown, scalish, rough. The trim was dark green. Once a Revolutionary War tavern, the house was divided into many small rooms connected by narrow hallways. Beams dotted with powder-post-beetle holes crisscrossed the ceilings, and Lis's father had claimed that several finger-size perforations in the walls and posts were from musket balls fired by rebel militia as they fought the British from room to room.

Hundreds of thousands of dollars had been sunk into the interior design of the house over the past fifty years but for some reason her parents had never properly wired the place; lamps with low-wattage bulbs were all that the circuits could bear. From the patio tonight these lights shone through the small squares of rippled panes like jaundiced eyes.

Lis, still thinking of her mother, said, "It was like the time near the end when she said, 'I just talked to your father and he said he was coming home soon.'" That conversation would have been a tricky one; the old man had been dead for two years at that point. "She *imagined* it, of course. But the feeling was real to her."

And their father? Lis wondered momentarily. No, L'Auberget *père* was probably not present in spirit. He'd dropped dead in a men's room in Heathrow Airport as he tugged angrily at a reluctant paper-towel dispenser.

"Superstition," Owen said.

"Well, in a way he *did* come home to her. She died a couple days later."

"Still."

"I guess I'm talking about what you feel when people are together again, people who knew someone who's gone."

Owen was tired of speaking about the spirits of the dead. He sipped his wine and told his wife he'd scheduled a business trip for Wednesday. He wondered if he could get a suit cleaned in time for his departure. "I'll be staying through Sunday, so if—"

"Wait. Did you hear something?" Lis turned quickly and looked at the dense mesh of lilacs that cut off their view of the back door of the house.

"No, I don't think I . . ." His voice faded and he held up a finger. He nodded. She couldn't see his expression but his posture seemed suddenly tense.

"There," she said. "There it was again."

It seemed like the snap of footsteps approaching the house from the driveway.

"That dog again?" Lis looked at Owen.

"The Busches'? No, he's penned in. I saw him when I went for my run. Deer probably."

Lis sighed. The local herd had feasted on over two hundred dollars in flower bulbs over the course of the summer, and just last week had stripped bare and killed a beautiful Japanese-maple sapling. She rose. "I'll give it a good scare."

"You want me to?"

"No. I want to call again anyway. Maybe I'll make some tea. Anything for you?"

"No."

She picked up the empty wine bottle and walked to the house, a fifty-foot trip along a path that wound through topiary, pungent boxwood and the bare, black lilac bushes. She passed a small reflecting pond in which floated several lily pads. Glancing down, she saw herself reflected, her face illuminated by the yellow lights from the first floor of the house. Lis had occasionally heard herself described as "plain" but had never taken this in a bad way. The word suggested a simplicity and resilience that were, to her, aspects of beauty. Looking into the water tonight she once again prodded her hair into place. Then a sharp gust of wind distorted her image in the water and she continued toward the house.

She heard nothing more of the mysterious noise and she relaxed. Ridgeton was among the safest towns in the state, a beautiful hamlet surrounded by wooded hills and fields that were filled with kelly-green grass, huge boulders, horses bred for running, picturesque sheep and cows. The town had been incorporated even before the thirteen states considered unionizing, and Ridgeton's evolution in the past three hundred years had been more in the ways of earthly convenience than economics or attitude. You could buy pizza by the slice and frozen yogurt, and you could rent Rototillers and videos but when all was said and done this was a walled village where the men were tied to the earth—they built on it, sold it and loaned against it—and the women marshaled children and food.

Ridgeton was a town that tragedy rarely touched and premeditated violence, never.

So tonight when Lis found that the kitchen door, latticed with squares of turquoise bottle glass, was wide open, she was more irritated than uneasy. She paused, the wine bottle in her hand slowly swinging to a stop. A faint trapezoid of amber light spread onto the lawn at Lis's feet.

She stepped around the thicket of lilacs and glanced into the driveway. No cars.

The wind, she concluded.

Stepping inside, she set the bottle on the butcher-block island and made a perfunctory search of the downstairs. No evidence of fat raccoons or curious skunks. She stood still for a moment listening for sounds within the house. Hearing nothing, Lis put the kettle on the stove then crouched to forage through the cabinet that contained the tea and coffee. Just as she placed her hand on the box of rose-hip tea, a shadow fell over her. She stood, gasping, and found herself looking into a pair of cautious hazel eyes.

The woman was about thirty-five. She had a black jacket over her arm and wore a loose-fitting white satin blouse, a short, shimmery skirt, and lace-up boots with short heels. Over her shoulder was a backpack.

Lis swallowed and found her hand quivering. The two women faced each other for a moment, silent. It was Lis who leaned forward quickly and embraced the younger woman. "Portia."

The woman unslung the backpack and dropped it on the island, next to the wine bottle.

"Hello, Lis."

There was a moment of thick silence. Lis said, "I didn't . . . I mean, I thought you were going to call when you got to the station. We'd pretty much decided you weren't coming. I called you and got your machine. Well, it's good to see you." She heard the nervous outpouring of her words and fell silent.

"I got a ride. Figured, why bother them?"

"It wouldn't have been a bother."

"Where were you guys? I looked upstairs."

Lis didn't speak for a moment but merely stared at the young woman's face, her blond hair—exactly Lis's shade—held back by a black headband. Portia frowned and repeated her question.

"Oh, we're out by the lake. It's a strange night, isn't it? Indian summer. In *November*. Have you eaten?"

"No, nothing. I had brunch at three. Lee stayed over last night and we slept late."

"Come on outside. Owen's out there. You'll have some wine."

"No, really. Nothing."

They headed back down the path, thick silence filling the short distance between them. Lis asked about the train ride.

"Late but it got here."

"Who'd you get a ride with?"

"Some guy. I think I went to high school with his son. He kept talking about Bobbie. Like I should know who Bobbie was if he didn't give me his last name."

"Bobbie Kelso. He's your age. His father's tall, bald?"

"I think," Portia said absently, looking out over the black lake.

Lis watched her eyes. "It's been so long since you've been here."

Portia gave a sound that might have been a laugh or a sniffle. They walked the rest of the way to the patio in silence.

"Welcome," Owen called, standing up. He kissed his sister-in-law's cheek. "We'd about given up on you."

"Yeah, well, one thing after another. Didn't get a chance to call. Sorry."

"No problem. We're flexible out here in the country. Have some wine."

"She got a ride with Irv Kelso," Lis said. Then she pointed to a lawn chair. "Sit down. I'll open another bottle. We've got a lot of catching up to do."

But Portia didn't sit. "No thanks. It's still early enough, isn't it? Why don't we get the dirty work over with?"

In the ensuing silence Lis looked from her sister to her husband then back again. "Well . . ."

Portia persisted, "Unless it'd be a hassle."

Owen shook his head. "Not really."

Lis hesitated. "You don't want to sit for a few minutes? We've got all tomorrow."

"Naw, let's just do it." She laughed. "Like the ad says."

Owen turned toward the younger woman. His face was in shadow and Lis couldn't see his expression. "If you want. Everything's in the den."

He led the way and Portia, with a glance at her older sister, followed.

Lis remained on the patio for a moment. She blew the candle out and picked it up. Then she too walked to the house, preceded by sparkling dew lifted off the grass and flung from the tips of her boots, while above her in the night sky Cassiopeia grew indistinct, then dark, then invisible behind a wedge of black cloud.

He walked along the gritty driveway, passing through pools of light beneath the antiquated, hoopy lamps sprouting from the uneven granite wall. From high above, a woman known to him only as Patient 223-81 keened breathlessly, mourning the loss of something only she understood.

He paused at a barred wooden door beside the loading dock. Into a silver plastic box—incongruous in this nearly medieval setting —the middle-aged man inserted a plastic card and flung the door open. Inside, a half dozen men and women, wearing white jackets or blue jumpsuits, glanced at him. Then they looked away uncomfortably.

A white-jacketed young doctor with nervous black hair and large lips stepped quickly to his side, whispering, "It's worse than we thought."

"Worse, Peter?" Dr. Ronald Adler asked vacantly as he stared at the gurney. "I don't know about that. I expect pretty bad."

He brushed his uncombed sandy-gray hair out of his eyes and touched a long finger to a thin, fleshy jowl as he looked down at the body. The corpse was huge and bald and had a time-smeared tattoo on the right biceps. A reddish discoloration encircled the massive neck. His back was as dark with sunken blood as his face was pale.

Adler motioned to the young doctor. "Let's go to my office. Why are all these people here? Shoo them out! My office. Now."

Vanishing through a narrow doorway the two men walked down the dim corridors, the only sounds their footsteps and a faint wail, which might have been either Patient 223-81 or the wind that gushed through the gaps in the building, which had been constructed a century ago. The walls of Adler's office were made from the same red granite used throughout the hospital but he was its director so the walls were paneled. Because this was a state hospital, however, the wormwood was fake and badly warped. The office seemed like that of a bail bondsman or an ambulance-chasing lawyer.

Adler flicked the light on and tossed his overcoat onto a button-studded couch. The summons tonight had found him between the legs of his wife and he'd leapt off the bed and dressed hastily. He noticed now that he'd forgotten his belt, and his slacks hung below his moderate belly. This embarrassed him and he quickly sat at his desk chair. He gazed momentarily at the phone as if perplexed it wasn't ringing.

To the young man, his assistant, Adler said, "Let's have it, doctor. Don't hover. Sit down and tell me."

"Details are pretty sketchy. He's built like Callaghan." Peter Grimes aimed his knobby hair toward the body in the loading dock. "We think he—"

Adler interrupted. "And *he* is . . . ?"

"The one who escaped? Michael Hrubek. Number 458-94."

"Go on." Adler fanned his fingers gingerly and Grimes placed a battered white file folder in front of the director.

"Hrubek, it seems—"

"He was the big fellow? Didn't think he was a troublemaker."

"Never was. Until today." Grimes kept retracting his lips like a fish chewing water and exposing little, even teeth. Adler found this repugnant and lowered his face to the file. The young doctor continued, "He shaved his head to look like Callaghan. Stole a razor to do it. Then he dyed his face blue. Broke a pen and mixed the ink with—" Adler's eyes swung to Grimes with a look of either anger or bewilderment. The young man said quickly, "Then he climbed into the freezer for an hour. Anybody else would've died. Just before the coroner's boys came by to pick up Callaghan, Hrubek hid the corpse and climbed into his body bag. The orderlies looked inside, saw a cold, blue body and—"

A barked laugh escaped from the director's thin lips, on which to his shock he detected the scent of his wife. The smile faded. "Blue? Incredible. Blue?"

Callaghan had died, Grimes explained, by strangulation. "He was blue when they found him this afternoon."

"Then he wasn't *blue* for long, my friend. As soon as they cut the sheet off him, he was *un*-blue. Didn't the fucking orderlies think of that?"

"Well," Peter Grimes said, and could think of nothing to add.

"Did he hurt the meat-wagon boys?" Adler asked. At some point tonight he'd have to total up how many people might sue the state as a result of the escape.

"Nope. They said they chased him but he disappeared."

"They chased him. I'm sure." Adler sighed sardonically, and turned back to the file. He motioned for Grimes to be quiet and began to read about Michael Hrubek.

DSM-III diagnosis: Paranoid schizophrenic . . . Monosymptomatic and delusional . . . Claims to have been committed in seventeen hospitals and escaped from seven of them. Unconfirmed.

Adler glanced up at his assistant. "Escaped from *seven* hospitals?" Before the young man could answer the question, to which there really was no answer, the director was reading once more.

. . . committed indefinitely pursuant to Section 403 of the State Mental Health Law. . . . Hallucinatory (auditory, nonvisual) . . . subject to severe panic attacks, during which Pt. may become psychotically violent. Pt.'s intelligence is average/above average. . . . Difficulty processing only the most abstract thought . . . Believes he is being persecuted and spied upon. Believes he is hated by others and gossiped about . . . Revenge and retribution, often in Biblical or historical contexts, seem to be integral parts of his delusion. . . . Particular animosity toward women . . .

Adler then read the intake resident's report about Hrubek's height, weight, strength, general good health and belligerence. His face remained impassive though his heart revved up a few beats and he thought with dread and clinical admiration, The son of a bitch is a killing animal. Jesus, Lord.

" 'Presently controlled by chlorpromazine hydrochloride, 3200 mgs./daily. P.O. in divided doses.' Is this for *real*, Peter?"

"Yes. I'm afraid so. Three grams of Thorazine."

"Fuck," Adler whispered.

"About which . . ." The assistant rocked against the desk with his thumbs pressed on a stack of books, the digits growing bright red under the pressure.

"Let's have it. All of it."

"He's been cheeking his meds."

Adler felt a bristle of heat course over his face. He whispered, "Tell me."

"There was a movie."

"A movie?"

Grimes clicked together two untrimmed nails. "An adventure film. And the hero pretended to take some drug or something—"

"You mean in the rec room? . . . *What* are you telling me?"

"An adventure film. But he didn't really take them. The pills. He pretended to but he cheeked them and spit 'em out later. Harrison Ford, I think. A lot of patients did that for a few days afterwards. I guess nobody thought Hrubek was that cognitively functional so they didn't watch him that closely. Or maybe it was Nick Nolte."

Adler exhaled slowly. "How long was he off the candy?"

"Four days. Well, make that five."

Flipping through his ordered mind Adler selected the *Psychopharmacology* file cabinet and peeked inside. Psychotic behavior in schizophrenics is controlled by antipsychotic medication. There's no physical addiction to Thorazine, as with narcotics, but going cold turkey off the drug would render Hrubek nauseous, dizzy, sweaty, and intensely nervous, all of which would increase the likelihood of panic attacks.

And panic was what made schizophrenics dangerous.

Off their Thorazine, patients like Hrubek sometimes fly into psychotic rages. Sometimes they murder.

Sometimes voices tell them what a good job they did with the knife or baseball bat and suggest that they go out and do it again.

Hrubek, Adler noted, would also experience severe insomnia. Which meant that the man would be wide awake for two or three days—ample opportunity to spread his mayhem about quite generously.

The moaning grew louder, filling the dim office. Adler's palms rose to his cheeks. Again he smelled his wife. Again he wished he could turn back the clock one hour. Again he wished he'd never heard of Michael Hrubek.

"How'd we find out about the Thorazine?"

"One of the orderlies," Grimes explained, chewing water again. "He found it under Hrubek's mattress."

"Who?"

"Stu Lowe."

"Who else knows? About him cheeking the candy?"

"Him, me, you. The chief nurse. Lowe told her."

"Oh, that's just great. Now listen to me. Tell Lowe . . . tell him it's his job if he ever repeats that. Not a single fucking word. Wait. . . ." A troubling thought occurred to Adler and he asked, "The morgue's in C Ward. How the hell did Hrubek have access to it?"

"I don't know."

"Well, find out."

"This all happened very fast, extremely fast," the flustered assistant blurted. "We don't have half the information we need. I'm getting files, calling people."

"*Don't* call people."

"I'm sorry?"

Adler snapped, "Don't call *anybody* about this without my okay."

"Well, the board . . ."

"Jesus, man, especially the board."

"I haven't yet," said Grimes quickly, wondering what had become of his cockiness.

"Good God!" Adler exploded. "You haven't called the police yet?"

"No, no. Of course not." This was a call he'd been about to make just as Adler arrived at the hospital. Grimes noticed with alarm how violently his own fingers were quivering. He wondered if he'd have a vagus-nerve lapse and faint. Or pee on his boss's floor.

"Let's think about this, shall we?" Adler mused. "He's sure to be wandering around out near . . . *Where* was it?"

"Stinson."

Adler repeated the name softly then touched the file under eight firm fingertips as if preventing it from rising into the inky stratosphere of his Victorian asylum office. His mood lifted slightly. "Who were the orderlies who schlepped the body from the morgue to the hearse?"

"Lowe was one. I think Frank Jessup was the other."

"Send 'em up to me." Forgetting his ill-fitting slacks Adler stood and walked to the grimy window. It hadn't been washed in six months. "You're responsible," Adler said sternly, "for keeping this absolutely quiet. Got it?"

"Yes sir," Grimes said automatically.

"And, goddamn it, find out how he got off E Ward."

"Yessir."

"If anyone . . . Tell the staff. If anyone leaks anything to the press they're fired. No police, no press. Send those boys up here. It's a hard job we've got here, isn't it? Don't you agree? Get me those orderlies. Now."

.   .   .

"Ronnie, are you feeling better?"

"I'm okay," the young heavyset man snapped. "So what? I mean, what're you going to *do* about it? *Honestly.*"

Dr. Richard Kohler felt the cheap bedsprings bouncing beneath Ronnie's weight as the patient scooted away from him, moving all the way to the headboard, as if Kohler were a molester. Ronnie's eyes flicked up and down suspiciously as he examined the man who'd been his father, brother, friend, tutor and physician for the past six months. He carefully studied the doctor's curly fringe of thinning hair, his bony face, narrow shoulders and thirty-one-inch waist. He seemed to be memorizing these features so he might have a good description in mind when he reported Kohler to the police.

"Are you uncomfortable, Ronnie?"

"I can't do it, I can't *do* it, doctor. I get too *scared*." He whined like a wrongly accused child. Then suddenly growing reasonable he said conversationally, "It's the can opener mostly."

"Was it the kitchen? All the work in the kitchen?"

"No no no," he whined. "The *can* opener. It's too *much*. I don't see why you don't *understand* it."

Kohler's body was racked by a yawn. He felt a painful longing for sleep. He'd been awake since 3:00 a.m. and had been here, at the halfway house, since 9:00. Kohler had helped the patients make breakfast and do the dishes. At 10:00 he shuttled four of them to part-time jobs, conferring with employers about his patients and mediating little disputes on their behalf.

The rest of the day he spent with the remaining five patients, who weren't employed or who had today, Sunday, off. The young men and women each had a psychotherapy session with Kohler and then returned to the mundane chores of running a household. They divided up into project groups that did what to healthy people were absurdly simple tasks: peeling potatoes and washing lettuce for dinner, cleaning windows and bathrooms, separating trash for recycling, reading aloud to each other. Some lowered their heads and completed their assignments with furrowed-brow determination. Others chewed their lips or plucked out eyebrows or cried or came close to hyperventilating from the challenge. Eventually the work got done.

Then, catastrophe.

Just before dinner, Ronnie had his attack. A patient standing beside him opened a can of tuna with the electric opener, and Ronnie fled screaming from the kitchen, triggering a chain reaction of hysteria in several other patients. Kohler had finally restored order and they sat down to dinner, Kohler with them. The food was eaten, dishes washed, the house straightened, games played, television programs hashed out (a *Cheers* rerun was the majority selection of the evening and the *M*A*S*H* minority abided grudgingly by the decision). Then meds were taken with juice, or the orange-flavored liquid Thorazine was chugged, and it was bedtime.

Kohler had found Ronnie hiding in the corner of his room.

"What would you like to do about the noise?" Kohler now asked.

"I don't *know*!" The patient's voice was dull as he chewed his tongue—an attempt to moisten a mouth painfully dry from his Proketazine.

Adaptation causes stress—the hardest thing for schizophrenics to cope with—and, Kohler reflected, Ronnie had plenty to adapt to here in the halfway house. He had to make decisions. To consider the likes and dislikes of the other people living with him. He had to plan ahead. The safety of the hospital was gone. Here he was confronted daily with these matters, and a downhearted Kohler could see the young man was losing the battle.

Outside, vaguely visible in the darkness, was a lawn that had been kept perfectly mowed by the patients all summer long and was now hand-stripped of every leaf that made the mistake of falling upon it. Kohler focused on the window and saw his haggard face in the black reflection, his eyes socketlike, his chin too narrow. He thought, for the thousandth time that year, about growing a beard to flesh out his features.

"Tomorrow," Kohler said to his unhappy patient, "we'll do something about it."

"Tomorrow? That's just *great*. I could be *dead* tomorrow, and so could *you*, mister. Don't forget it," snapped the patient—sneering at the man to whom he owed not only such peace of mind as he possessed but probably his life as well.

Even before he'd decided to attend medical school, Richard Kohler had learned not to take personal offense at anything schizophrenic patients said or did. If Ronnie's words troubled him at all, it was only because they offered a measure of the patient's relapse.

This was one of Kohler's clinical errors. The patient, involuntarily committed at Marsden State hospital, had responded well to his treatment there. After many trials to find a suitable medication and dosage Kohler began treating him with psychotherapy. He made excellent progress. When one of the halfway-house patients had improved enough to move into an apartment of her own, Kohler placed Ronnie here. Immediately, though, the stresses accompanying communal living had brought out the worst of Ronnie's illness and he'd regressed, growing sullen and defensive and paranoid.

"I don't trust you," Ronnie barked. "It's pretty fucking clear what's going on here and I don't like it one *bit*. And there's going to be a storm tonight. Electric storm, electric can opener. Get it? I mean, you tell me I can do *this*, I can do *that*. Well, it's bullshit!"

Into his perfect memory Kohler inserted a brief mental notation about Ronnie's use of the verb "can" and the source of his panic attack tonight. It was too late in the evening to do anything with this observation now but he'd review the young man's file tomorrow in his office at Marsden and write up a report then. He stretched and heard a deep bone pop. "Would you like to go back to the hospital, Ronnie?" he asked, though the doctor had already made this decision.

"That's what I'm *getting* at. There isn't that *racket* there."

"No, it's quieter."

"I think I'd like to go back, doctor. I *have* to go back," Ronnie said as if he were losing the argument. "There are reasons too numerous to list."

"We'll do it then. Tuesday. You get some sleep now."

Ronnie, still dressed, curled up on his side. Kohler insisted that he put on his pajamas and climb under the blankets properly, which he did without comment. He ordered Kohler to leave the light on, and did not say good night when the doctor left his room.

Kohler walked through the ground floor of the house, saying good night to the patients who were still awake and chatting with the night orderly who sat in the living room, watching television.

A breeze came through the open window and, enticed by it, Kohler stepped outside. The night was oddly warm for November. It reminded him of a particular fall evening during his last year of medical school at Duke. He recalled walking along the tarmac from the stairs of the United 737. That year the trip between La Guardia and Raleigh-Durham airports had been like a commute for him; he'd logged tens of thousands of miles between the two cities. The night he was thinking of was his return from New York after Thanksgiving vacation. He'd spent most of the holiday itself at Murray Hill Psychiatric Hospital in Manhattan and the Friday after it in his father's office, listening to the old man argue persuasively, then insist belligerently, that his son take up internal medicine— going so far as to condition his continuing financial support of the young man's education on his choice of specialty.

The next day, young Richard Kohler thanked his father for his hospitality, took an evening flight back to college and when school resumed on Monday was in the Bursar's Office at 9:00 a.m., applying for a student loan to allow him to continue his study of psychiatry.

Kohler again yawned painfully, picturing his home—a condominium a half hour from here. This was a rural area, where he could have afforded a very big house and plenty of property. But Kohler's goal had been to forsake land for convenience. No lawn mowing or landscaping or painting for him. He wanted a place to which he might escape, small and contained. Two bedrooms, two baths and a deck. Not that it didn't have elements of opulence—the condo contained one of the few cedar hottubs in this part of the state, several Kostabi and Hockney canvases and what was described as a "designer" kitchen ("But aren't all kitchens," he had slyly asked the real-estate broker, "designed by *somebody*?" and enjoyed her sycophantic laughter). The condo, which was on a hilltop and looked out over miles and miles of patchwork woods and farmland during the day and the sparkling lights of Boyleston at night, was—quite literally—Kohler's island of sanity in a most insane world.

Yet tonight he made his way back into the halfway house and climbed the creaking stairs to a room that measured ten by twelve feet and was outfitted only with a cot, a dresser and a metal mirror bolted to the wall.

He stripped off his suit jacket and loosened his tie then lay on the cot, kicking off his shoes. He looked out the window at a dull spray of stars then, lowering his eyes, saw a ridge of clouds in the west slicing the sky in half. The storm. He'd heard it was supposed to be a bad one. Although he himself liked the rain, he hoped there wouldn't be any thunder, which would terrify many of his patients. But this concern passed immediately from his mind as he closed his eyes. Sleep was all he could think of now. He could taste it. He felt the fatigue ache in his legs. He yawned cold tears into his eyes. And in less than sixty seconds he was asleep.

3

They signed their names a dozen times and became millionaires.

A hundred sheets of paper, filled with scrolly writing, peppered with words like *whereas* and *hereby*, sat on the desk before the two women. Affidavits, receipts, tax returns, releases, powers of attorney. Owen, stern and looking very much the lawyer, circulated each document and said, "Duly executed," every time a signature was scratched upon a sheet. He'd squeeze his notarial seal and sign his own name with a Mont Blanc and then check off another item on his closing sheet. Portia seemed amused at his severity and on the verge of needling him about it. Lis on the other hand—after six years of marriage—had grown used to her husband's playing Rumpole and paid little attention to his gravity.

"I feel," she said, "like a president signing a treaty."

The three of them were in the den, encircling the massive black mahogany desk that Lis's father had bought in Barcelona in the sixties. For this occasion—the closing of his estate—Lis had unearthed a shellacked découpage poster that she herself had made ten years ago. It had been a decoration for the party following the sale of her father's business and his retirement. On the left side of the canvas was pasted a photograph of his company's very first sign, a small hand-painted rectangle from the early fifties, which read, *L'Auberget et Fils Ltd.* Next to it was a glossy photo of the huge billboard that crowned the company when it was sold: *L'Auberget Liquor Importing, Inc.* Around the border was Lis's own diligent, stiff rendering of vines and grapes, done in purple and green marker. The years had turned the shellac coating a deep, sickly yellow.

Although the old man had never discussed the company with his daughters (there was no male heir; the *fils* was strictly for image), Lis—as executrix of the estate—had learned what an astonishing businessman her father had been. She knew from his frequent absences throughout her childhood that he'd been addicted to his job. But she'd never guessed, until their mother died and the money passed to her and Portia, exactly how much that hard work had amassed: nine million, plus this house, the Fifth Avenue co-op and a cottage outside of Lisbon.

Owen gathered up papers and put them into tidy bundles, labeling each with a yellow Post-it tag marked with his boxy writing.

"I'll have copies made for you, Portia."

"Keep them safe," Lis warned.

Portia tightened her mouth at the motherly tone and Lis winced, looking for a way to apologize. But before she could find the words, Owen lifted a bottle of champagne to the desk and opened it. He poured three glasses.

"Here's to . . ." Lis began and noticed the others gazing at her expectantly. She said the first thing into her mind. "Father and Mother."

Glasses chimed together.

"Practically speaking," Owen explained, "that's the end of the estate. Most of the transfers and disbursements've been made. We have one account still open. That's for the outstanding fees—the executrix, law firm and accountant. Oh, and for that other little matter." He looked at Lis. "Did you tell her?"

Lis shook her head.

Portia kept her eyes on Owen. "Tell me what?"

"We just got notice on Friday. You're going to be sued."

"What?"

"A challenge to the bequests."

"No! Who?"

"That problem with your father's will."

"What problem? There a fuck-up someplace?" Portia looked at Owen with amused suspicion.

"Not from me there wasn't. *I* didn't draft it. I'm talking about the problem with his school. Doesn't this ring a bell?"

Portia shook her head and Owen continued, explaining that when Andrew L'Auberget passed away he'd left his entire estate in trust for his wife. When she died the money went to the daughters, with a small bequest going to his alma mater, a private college in Massachusetts.

"Oh, bless me, for I have sinned," Portia whispered sarcastically and crossed herself. Their father had often reminisced—reverently and at great length—about his days at Kensington College.

"The bequest was for a thousand."

"So what? Let 'em have it."

Owen laughed. "Oh, but they don't want *that*. They want the million he was going to leave them originally."

"A *million*?"

"About a year before he died," Lis continued, "the school started admitting women. That was bad enough. But it also adopted a resolution banning gender and sexual-orientation discrimination. You must know all this, Portia." She turned to her husband. "Didn't you send her copies of the correspondence?"

"Please, Lis, a little credit. She's a beneficiary. She *had* to be copied."

"I probably got it. But, you know, if it's got a lawyer's letterhead on it and there's no check inside, who pays any attention?"

Lis started to speak but remained silent. Owen continued, "Your father did a codicil to his will, cutting his bequest to the school to a thousand. In protest."

"The old shit."

"Portia!"

"When he wrote the chancellor telling him about the change, he said he wasn't, I'm pretty much quoting, he wasn't *against* women and deviates. He was simply *for* tradition."

"I repeat, what a shit."

"The school's challenging the codicil."

"What do we do?"

"Basically, all we have to do is keep an amount equal to their original bequest in the estate account until it's settled. You don't have to worry. We'll win. But we still have to go through the formalities."

"Not worry?" Portia blurted. "It's a million dollars."

"Oh, they'll lose," Owen announced. "He *did* execute the codicil during that spell when he was taking Percodan pretty regularly and Lis *was* spending a lot of time at the house. That's what the school's lawyer's going to argue. Lack of capacity and undue influence by one of the other beneficiaries."

"Why do you say they won't win?"

Grim-faced, Lis sipped her champagne. "I don't want to hear this again."

Her husband smiled.

"I'm serious, Owen."

He said to his sister-in-law, "The lawyer for the school? I did a little investigating. Turns out he's been negotiating contracts on behalf of the school with a company his wife's got a major interest in. Big conflict of interest. And a felony, by the way. I'm going to offer him four or five to settle."

Lis said to Portia, "He makes it sound like a legal tactic. To me, it's blackmail."

"Of course it's blackmail," Portia said. "So? But you think this lawyer'll talk the school into settling?"

"He'll be . . . persuasive, I'm sure," Owen said. "Unless he wants an address change to the Bridewell Men's Colony."

"So basically, he's fucked." Portia laughed. She held up her glass. "Good job, attorney."

Owen tapped his glass to hers.

Portia drained her champagne and let Owen pour her more. To her sister she said, "I wouldn't get on this boy's bad side, Lis. He might do to you what he does unto others."

Owen's stony façade slipped and he laughed briefly.

Lis said, "I guess I just feel insulted. I didn't even *know* the school was getting any money in the will. I mean, can you imagine Father even *talking* to me about it? Undue influence? I say let them sue."

"Well, I say let our lawyer handle it." With her working-girl hair rimmed by the black lace headband Portia seemed miraculously transported back to six or seven—the age at which it first was clear that the sisters would be such different people. This process seemed to continue, by inches and miles, Lis sensed, even tonight.

Owen poured more Moët. "Never would've been a problem if your father'd kept his money to himself and his mouth shut. That's the moral: no good deed goes unpunished."

"Your services expensive, Owen?" Portia asked wryly.

"Never. At least not for beautiful women. It's in my retainer agreement."

Lis stepped between these two people, bound to her one by blood and one by law, and put her arms around Owen. "See why he's such a rainmaker?"

"Can't make much rain if he doesn't charge."

"I didn't say I'm free." Owen looked at Portia. "I just said I'm not expensive. You always have to pay for quality."

Lis walked to the stairway. "Portia, come here. I want to show you something."

The sisters left Owen stacking the papers and climbed upstairs. The silence again grew thick and Lis realized that it was her husband's presence that had made conversation possible between the sisters.

"Here we go." She stepped in front of Portia and then pushed open the door to a small bedroom, sweeping on the overhead light. *"Voilà."*

Portia was nodding as she studied the recently decorated room. Lis had spent a month on the place, making dozens of trips to Ralph Lauren and Laura Ashley for fabrics and wallpaper, to antique stores for furniture. She'd managed to find an old canopy bed that was virtually identical to the one that had been Portia's when this was her room years ago.

"What do you think?"

"Taking up interior decorating, are we?"

"That's the *same* curtain material. Amazing that I found it. Maybe a little yellower is all. Remember when we helped Mother sew them? I was, what?, fourteen. You were nine."

"I don't remember. Probably."

Lis looked at the woman's eyes.

"What a job," Portia offered, walking in a slow circle on the oval braided rug. "Incredible. Last time I was here it looked like an old closet. Mother'd just let it go to hell."

Then why don't you like it? Lis wondered silently.

She asked, "Remember Pooh?" and nodded at a mangy Steiff bear, whose glassy eyes stared vacantly at the corner of the room, where a shimmery cobweb had emerged since Lis had last cleaned the place, twenty-four hours ago.

Portia touched the bear's nose then stepped back to the door and crossed her arms.

"What's the matter?" Lis asked.

"It's just that I'm not sure I can stay."

"What do you mean?"

"I wasn't really planning on it."

"You're talking about *tonight*? Portia, really . . . It's too late to go."

"There're trains all night."

Lis's face grew hot. "I thought you'd be here for a couple of days."

"I know we talked about it. I . . . I guess I'd really rather just get the train back. I should've told you."

"You don't even call and say you'll be late. You don't even tell us you've gotten a ride. You just show up, get your money and leave?"

"Lis."

"But you can't just sit on a train for two hours and then turn around and go back. It's crazy." Lis walked to the bed. She reached for the bear then thought better of it. She sat on the chenille spread. "Portia, we haven't spoken in months. We've hardly said a damn word since last summer."

Portia finished her champagne and put the flute on the dresser. A questioning look started to cross her face.

"You *know* what I'm talking about," Lis said.

"Right now's tough for me to be away. Lee and I're going through a hard time."

"When'll be a *good* time?"

Portia waved her hands at the room. "I'm sorry you went to all this work. Maybe next week. A couple weeks. I'll come out earlier. Spend the day."

The silence was suddenly broken by Owen's voice, calling sharply for Lis. Startled, she looked toward the door then back to her lap and found that she'd picked up the bear after all. She stood abruptly, setting the toy back on the pillow.

"Lis," came Owen's urgent voice, "come down here."

"Coming." Then Lis turned to her sister. She said, "Let's talk about it," and before Portia could open her mouth to protest, walked out of the room.

"This smells of being whipped."

"Well, I'd guess."

Before the two men lay a sharp valley that rose fifty feet above them, filled with black rocks and tangles of vine and barkless branches, many dead and rotten. Moisture glittered on undergrowth like a million snake scales, and the dew stained their jumpsuits the same dark blue the uniforms turned when they worked the Piss 'n' Shit Ward.

"Look at that. How d'we even know it's his footprint?"

"Because it's size fourteen and he's barefoot. Who the hell's do you *think* it is? Now shut up."

The moon was fading behind clouds and in the growing darkness each man thought the scene before him was straight out of a horror film.

"Say, meaning to ask—you bumping uglies with Psaltz?"

"Adler's secretary?" Stuart Lowe snickered. "Like that'd be a real smart thing to do. I'm really thinking we should've bitched more. Didn't either of us *have* to come. We ain't cops."

The men were large—both muscular and tall—and sported crew cuts. Lowe, a blond. Frank Jessup was dark. They were easygoing and had neither hatred nor love for the troubled men and women under their care. Their job was a job and they were pleased to be paid decent money in an area that had little money for any work.

They were not, however, pleased about this assignment tonight.

"Was a honest mistake," Lowe muttered. "Who'd've guessed he'd do what he done?"

Jessup leaned against a pine tree and his nostrils flared at the aroma of turpentine. "How 'bout Mona? You fucking *her*?"

"Who?"

"Mona Cabrill. Mona the Moaner. The *nurse*. From D Ward."

"Oh. Right. No. Are you?"

"Not yet," Jessup said. "I myself'd slip her a dose of thiopental and jump her bones the minute she conked out."

Lowe grunted disagreeably. "Let's stay focused here, Frank."

"We'd hear him. Big fellow like that can't walk past without knocking something down. She didn't wear a bra last week. Tuesday. The head nurse sent her home to get one. But it was Tit City for a while."

There was a faint scent of campfire or woodstove smoke in the damp air. Lowe pressed a thick palm into each of his eye sockets while he examined exactly how scared he was. "My point is, they pay cops for this kind of stuff."

"Shhh," Jessup hissed abruptly. Lowe jumped, then—at the bark of laughter—hit his partner very hard on the arm. "You son of a bitch." They sparred for a moment, rougher than they meant to be because they were bleeding off tension. Then they started up the valley once more. The men were spooked, true, but it was more the setting than the escapee; both men knew Michael Hrubek. Lowe had supervised him for most of the four months the patient had been incarcerated at Marsden State hospital. Hrubek could be a real son of a bitch—sarcastic, picky, irritating—but he hadn't seemed particularly violent. Still, Lowe added, "I'm thinking we deep-six it and call the cops."

"We bring him back, we keep our jobs."

"They can't fire us for this. How was we to know?"

"They can't *fire* us?" Jessup snorted. "You're dreaming, boy. You and me're white men under forty. They can fire us 'cause they don't like the way we crap."

Lowe decided they should stop talking. They proceeded in silence thirty yards up the cold, suffocating valley before they noticed the motion. It was indistinct and might have been nothing more than a discarded grocery bag shifting in the breeze. But there was no breeze. Maybe a deer. But deer don't walk through the forest, humming singsong tunes to themselves. The orderlies glanced at each other and took stock of their weaponry—each had a container of Mace and a rubber truncheon. They adjusted their grips on the clubs and continued up the hill.

"He doesn't want to hurt anybody," Lowe announced, then added, "I've worked with him plenty."

"I'm pleased about that," Jessup whispered. "Shut the fuck up."

The moaning reminded Lowe, who was from Utah, of a leg-trapped coyote that wouldn't last the night. "It's getting louder," he said unnecessarily, and Frank Jessup was far too spooked by now to shush him again.

"It's a dog," Lowe suggested.

But it wasn't a dog. The sound came straight from the thick throat of Michael Hrubek, who with an astonishingly loud crash stumbled into the midst of the path twenty feet in front of the orderlies and froze like a fat statue.

Lowe, thinking of the many times he'd bathed and coddled and reasoned with Hrubek, suddenly felt himself the team leader. He stepped forward. "Hello, Michael. How are you?"

The response was mumbled.

Jessup called, "Hey, Mr. Michael! My fave patient! You all right?"

Except for muddy shorts Hrubek was naked. His face was out-landishly alien—with its blue tint, pursing lips and possessed eyes.

"Aren'tcha cold?" Lowe found the voice to say.

"You're Pinkerton agents, you fuckers."

"No, it's me. It's Frank. You remember me, Michael. From the hospital. And you know Stu here. We're the fuckin'-A orderlies from E Ward. You know *us*, man. Hey . . ." He laughed good-naturedly. "What are you doing without any clothes on?"

"What are you doing *hiding* in yours, fucker?" Hrubek retorted with a sneer.

Suddenly the reality of their mission struck Lowe with a jolt. My God, they weren't in the hospital. They weren't surrounded by fellow staffers. There was no telephone here, no psychiatric nurses nearby with two hundred milligrams of phenobarb. He grew weak with fear and when Hrubek gave a shout and fled up the valley, Jessup not far behind, Lowe remained where he was.

"Frank, hold up!" Lowe called.

But Jessup didn't wait, and reluctantly Lowe too started after the huge blue-white monster, who was leaping along the trail. Hrubek's voice echoed in the damp valley, begging not to be shot or tortured. Lowe caught up with Jessup and they ran side by side.

The orderlies crashed through the undergrowth, swinging their truncheons like machetes. Jessup panted, "Jesus, on these rocks! How can he run on these rocks?" A memory suddenly came to Lowe—the image of Hrubek standing behind the hospital's main building, his shoes around his neck, walking barefoot on gravel, over and over, muttering as if speaking to his feet and encouraging them to toughen up. That had been just last week.

"Frank," Lowe wheezed, "there's something funny about this. We oughta—"

And then they were flying.

Sailing through the black air. Trees and rocks tumbling upside down, over and over. With identical screams they plunged into the ravine that Hrubek had easily leapt over. The orderlies smacked against the rocks and branches on their way down and their spinning bodies slammed into the ground with vicious jolts. An icy cold began to radiate through Lowe's thigh and arm. They lay motionless in the gray ooze of the mud.

Jessup tasted blood. Lowe examined his bent fingers, attention to which flagged when he wiped the mud from his forearm and found that it wasn't mud at all but a wide, foot-long scrape where skin used to be. "Cocksucker," he wailed. "I'm gonna hurt that asshole bad, it's the last thing I do. Oh, shit. I'm bleeding to death. Oh, shit . . ." Lowe rolled into a sitting position and pressed the scrape, feeling in horror his own hot, torn flesh. Jessup was content to lie unmoving in the methane-scented mud and breathe a few cubic centimeters of air, the most his stunned lungs would accept. He gasped wetly. After a moment he was able to whisper, "I think—"

Lowe never found out what was on Jessup's mind because at that moment Hrubek strode into the middle of the ravine. He casually bent down, pushing Stuart Lowe aside, and plucked the men's tear-gas canisters from their belts, flinging them deep into the woods. He turned abruptly back to Lowe, who looked up into Hrubek's leering face and began to scream.

"Stop that!" Hrubek screamed in return. "Stop that *noise!*"

Lowe did, and using the advantage of Hrubek's own panic scrabbled away. Jessup's eyes closed and he began muttering incoherently.

Lowe lifted the truncheon.

"You're from Pinkerton," Hrubek barked. "*Pink*-er-ton. I'm in the *pink*, Mr. Fuckin'-A Orderly. Your arm looks pretty *pink* and *tend*-er. Nice try, but you shouldn't've come after me—I've got a *death* to at-*tend* to."

The rubber stick in Lowe's hand remained poised for a moment then with a gushing sound landed in the mud at his feet. He took off, running blindly through the woods, his courage suddenly as flimsy as the grass and saplings that bent beneath his pounding feet.

"Oh, don't leave me, Stu," Jessup cried into the mud at his lips. "I don't want to die alone."

Hrubek watched the disappearing form of Stuart Lowe then knelt on top of Jessup, pushing his head further into the ground. The orderly tasted dirt and grass, the flavor of which reminded him of his childhood. He began to cry.

"You dumb fucker," Hrubek said. Then he raged, "And I can't wear your *clothes* either." He poked sharply at the stitched label, *Marsden State Mental Health Facility*, on Jessup's jumpsuit. "What *good* are you?" He began to sing, " '*Good* night, ladies, good night, ladies, I'm going to see you cry. . . .' "

"Will you let me go, please, Michael?"

"You *found* me out, and what I'm doing has to be a surprise. 'Good night, laaaaaaadies, I'm going to see you *die*!' "

"I won't tell nobody, Michael. Please let me go. Oh, please. I got a wife."

"Oh, is she pret-ty? Do you fuck her *often*? Do you fuck her in unpleasant *ways*? Say, what's her address?"

"Please, Michael . . ."

"Sorry," Hrubek whispered and leaned down.

The orderly's scream was very loud and very brief. To Michael Hrubek's unbounded pleasure, it set in flight an exquisite owl, curiously golden in the ravine's blue light, which soared from a nearby oak tree and passed not five feet from the huge man's astounded face.

"*. . . repeating, the National Weather Service has issued an emergency storm warning for residents of Marsden, Cooper and Mahican counties. Winds in excess of eighty miles an hour, tornadoes and severe flooding in low-lying areas are expected. The Marsden River is already at flood level and expected to rise at least three more feet, cresting around one or two a.m. We'll bring you bulletins as more information is available. . . .*"

Portia found them in the den, leaning over the teak stereo cabinet, both grim.

Classical music resumed and Owen shut the radio off.

Portia asked what the problem was.

"Storm." He turned to look out the window. "The Marsden—it's one of the rivers that feed the lake."

"We were getting estimates on building up the shoreline," Lis said. "But we didn't think there'd be any flooding till the spring."

Lis left the den and walked into the large greenhouse, looking up at the sky, murky but still placid.

Her sister saw her troubled face and glanced at Owen.

"There's no foundation," he explained to her. "The greenhouse. Your parents built it right on the ground. If the yard floods—"

"It'll be the first to go," Lis said. Not to mention, she thought, what the fifty-foot oak tree, hovering overhead, might do to the thin glass panes of the greenhouse roof. She glanced at the brick wall beside her and absently straightened a stone gargoyle, who grinned mischievously as he stuck out his long, curly tongue. "Damn," she whispered.

"Are you sure it'll flood?" Portia asked. She sounded irritated—because, Lis supposed, her escape from the L'Auberget manse tonight was looking complicated.

"If it goes up three feet," Lis said, "it'll flood. It'll come right into the yard. It happened in the sixties, remember? Washed away the old porch. That was right here. Where we're standing."

Portia said she didn't recall.

Lis looked at the windows again, wishing they had time to put plywood on the roof and sides. They'd be lucky to build up the lakefront by two feet and tape half the windows before the storm hit. "So," she said, sighing, "we tape and sandbag."

Owen nodded.

Lis turned to her sister. "Portia, could I ask you to stay?"

The young woman said nothing. She seemed less irritated than daunted by a conspiracy to keep her there.

"We could really use your help."

Owen looked from one sister to the other, frowning. "Weren't you going to stay for a few days?"

"I'm really supposed to get back tonight."

Supposed? Lis wondered. And who had dictated that? The hard-times boyfriend? "I'll take you to the station tomorrow. First thing. You won't miss more than an hour of work."

Portia nodded. "Okay."

"Listen," Lis said sincerely, "I appreciate this."

She hurried outside to the garage, giving a short, silent prayer of thanks for the weather that would keep her sister here at least for the night. Suddenly, however, this benediction struck Lis as a token of bad luck and superstitiously she retracted it. She then went to work assembling shovels and tape and burlap bags.

4

"Three in two years." The tall man in the smart gray uniform rubbed his matching gray mustache and added, "They run away from you all here lickety-split."

Dr. Ronald Adler fiddled with his waistband. With a monumental sigh meant to put himself on the offensive he said, "Aren't there more valuable ways to use this time, Captain? Don? I'll bet there are."

The state trooper chuckled. "How come you didn't report it?"

"We reported Callaghan's, uhm, death," Adler said.

"You know what I'm saying, doctor."

"I thought we could get him back without any fuss."

"How exactly? By one orderly getting his arm exorcised around backwards and the other one crapping in his jumpsuit?"

"He is not essentially a dangerous man," Peter Grimes offered, incidentally reminding both Adler and the state trooper that he was in the room, a fact they had forgotten.

"Any competent staff member would've handled it differently. They were playing cowboy. They fell off the cliff and were injured."

"Fell. Uhm. You boys here tried a cover-up and that don't sit well with me."

"There's nothing to cover up. I don't call you every time Joe Patient wanders off the grounds."

"Don't go scratching me between the ears, Adler."

"We *almost* got him."

"Butcha didn't. Now what's he look like?"

"He's big," Grimes began before his voice froze in fear of careless adjectives.

"How the *hell* big? Come on, gemmuns. Time's awasting."

Adler gave the description then added, "He shaved his head and dyed his face blue. Don't ask, he just did. He has brown eyes, a wide face, dirty teeth, and he's twenty-seven years old."

Captain Don Haversham, a man twice Hrubek's age, jotted notes in even script. "Okay, we got a couple cars headed up to Stinson. I see that doesn't appeal to you, Adler, but it's gotta be done. Now tell me, how dangerous? Will he come jumping outta trees?"

"No, no," the director said, glancing at Grimes, who poked into his mushroom crown of black hair. Adler continued, "Hrubek, he's like—what would you say?—a big lovable dog. This escape, he's playing a game."

"Woof, woof," the captain said. "Seem to recall he was the one involved in that Indian Leap thing. That's not lovable, and that's not a dog."

Then why, Adler inquired, did the captain ask his opinion if the trooper'd already diagnosed Hrubek?

"I want to know if he's *still* dangerous after he's been in the care of you sawbones all these four months. I'd guess he is, though, what with that fellow you got on the slab tonight. Tell me, Hrubek, he taking his pills like a good boy?"

"Yes, he is," Adler said quickly. "But wait a minute. Callaghan was probably a suicide."

"Suicide?"

Grimes again looked toward his boss and tried to match round words and square facts.

"The coroner'll tell us for sure," Adler continued.

"I'm sure he will," Haversham said cheerfully. "Kind of a coincidence though, wouldn't you say? This Callaghan kills himself then your cuddle puppy Hrubek ske-daddles in his body bag?"

"Uhm." Adler pictured locking Haversham into the old hose

room with Billie Lind Prescott, who would, off his Stelazine, masturbate while howling at the top of his lungs for hour after hour after hour.

Grimes said, "The thing is . . ." and, as both men turned to him, stopped speaking.

Adler filled the void, "Young Peter was going to say that in the months Hrubek's been with us he's been a model patient. He sits quietly, doesn't bother anyone."

"He's like a vegetable."

A wet laugh burst from Haversham's throat. He said to Grimes, "Vegetable? Was a dog a minute ago. Must be getting worse. Tell me now, what kind of crazy is he exactly?"

"He's a paranoid schizophrenic."

"Schizo? Split personality? I seen that flick."

"No, not multiple personalities. Schizophrenic. It means he has delusions and can't cope with anxiety and stress."

"He stupid? A retard?"

The professional in Adler bristled at the word but he remained placid. "No. He's got a medium to high IQ. But he's not calculating."

The captain snickered. "He'd have to be kinda sorta calculating, wouldn't you think? To get clean away from a hospital for the criminally insane."

Adler's lips vanished momentarily as he turned them inward in contemplation. The taste of his wife returned and he wondered if he'd get an erection. He didn't, and he said to Haversham, "The escape was the fault of the orderlies. They'll be disciplined."

"Seems to me, they have been. At least the one with the broken arm."

"Listen, Don, can we do this one quietly?"

The captain grinned. "Why, scared of a little publicity, Mr. Three in Two Years?"

Adler paused then spoke in a low voice that barely broke above the ghostly wail that still filled the halls. "Now, listen to me, Captain. You quit jerking my chain. I've got close to a thousand of the most unfortunate people in the Northeast in my care and money to treat about one-quarter of 'em. I can—"

"All right now."

"—I can make some of their lives better and I can protect the general populace from them. I'm doing the fucking best I can with the fucking money I've got. Don't tell me that you haven't had troopers cut back too."

"Well, I have. That's a fact."

"If this escape becomes a big deal some prick of a reporter's going to run with it and then maybe there goes more money or maybe the state'll even look into closing down this place." Adler's arm swept toward the wards filled with his hapless charges—some asleep, some plotting, some howling, some floating through nightmares of madness or perhaps even dreaming dreams of sanity. "If that happens then half those people'll be wandering around outside and they're going to be *your* problem, not mine."

"Simmer down now, doc." Haversham, whose law-enforcement career like most senior officers' was informed more by his skills at self-preservation than detection, said, "Tell me the God's truth. You say a low-security patient wandered away, that's what I'll go with. But you tell me he's *dangerous*, it'll be a whole different ball game. What's it gonna be?"

Adler hiked up his waistband. He wondered if his wife was at home masturbating as ardently as Billie Lind Prescott. "Hrubek's half-comatose," Adler spoke directly into the eyes of Peter Grimes. The young assistant nodded numbly and added, "He's stumbling around in a daze like a gin-drunk fool," and wondered what on earth possessed him to say that.

"Okay," Haversham said with finality. "I'll send it out as a missing-patient notice. You got some fellow wandered off and you're worried about his welfare. That'll make sure it's not scanner-feed.

These boys and girls they call reporters round here won't even notice it, not with a storm gonna take off roofs."

"I appreciate this, Don."

"Now let me ask. You got some bucks to spend?"

"How's that?"

"There's somebody I'm thinking might be a help. But he ain't cheap."

"We're a state hospital," Adler said. "We don't have much money."

"That may be true. But one thing you *do* have is a escaped nutzo who happens to look like Attila the effing Hun. So, what about it? You gonna hear me out?"

"Oh, by all means, Captain. By all means."

A cold and anxious Michael Hrubek stood on broad, naked feet in the center of a large rectangle of ruined grass. His hands gripped the waistband of his muddy and dew-stained shorts, and he stared at the shabby building before him.

The small shop—taxidermy, trapping and hunting supplies— was surrounded by chicken wire suspended from rusted posts with Baggie twist ties. Much of the mesh was squashed to the ground in a way that for some reason depressed Hrubek profoundly.

He had run all the way from the site of the attack on the orderlies to this cluster of lights, ghostly in the fog: a truck stop, which contained this shop, a diner, a gas station and an antique store. Positive he was being pursued by the Secret Service, Hrubek wanted to keep moving. But, as he'd announced aloud to himself, a naked man'd be "too damn obvious. Make no mistake about that."

He'd then noticed a window in this outdoors shop and that had decided the matter.

He now stood in the exact spot where he'd been frozen in place for the past few minutes, gazing into the store at seven tiny animal skulls, boiled and bleached white as clouds.

Oh, look there. Look at that!

Seven was an important number in the cosmology of Michael Hrubek and he now leaned forward, counting them aloud, and enjoying the sound of the numbers in his mouth.

Seven skulls, seven letters, M-I-C-H-A-E-L.

Make no mistake, he thought. This is a special night.

Much of Hrubek's thinking was metaphoric and the image now occurred to him that he was waking up. He liked to sleep. He *loved* to sleep. Hours and hours in bed. His favorite position was on his side with his knees drawn up as far as his massive legs and thick chest and belly would allow. Most of his waking hours too were a type of sleep—a slippery succession of chaotic dreams, a jumble of disconnected faces and scenes that fished past him, products of both his troubled mind and various medications.

Awake!

He bent down and in the dirt at his feet wrote with his stubby finger: *i as I am AWakE tonIght. AWakE!*

He made his way around the store, noting a sign that said the owner was on vacation. He kicked in the side door and entered. Avoiding a tall black bear, mounted in a rearing position, he made a circuit of the shop. He inhaled deeply and smelled musk and boiled game flesh, his hands shaking with exhilaration. He noticed shelves containing clothing and he rummaged through the piles of shirts and coveralls until he found several items that more or less fit. Then socks, and finally an Irish-tweed cap that he liked very much. He placed it on his head.

"Very fashionable," he whispered, looking into a mirror.

Hrubek continued searching until he located a pair of engineer's boots and struggled to pull them on. They were tight but not painful. "John Worker," he muttered, running his hands over his clothes with approval. "John Worker." He poured cleaning fluid onto a rag and scrubbed hard at his face to remove the blue ink from his cheeks and forehead.

He solemnly placed the seven skulls into a green canvas backpack he found in the shop. Then, keeping a suspicious eye on the rearing bear, Hrubek crossed the floor to the sales counter, where he'd noticed a display of cellophane packs of beef jerky. He ripped them open with his teeth, one after another, and chewed down the salty meat, all eight packages.

He was about to leave when he glanced down, beneath the counter, and his face broke into a huge grin.

"A present from Jesus Cry-ist our Weeping Lord."

The pistol was a long-barreled Colt revolver. Hrubek lifted it to his face and smelled it and rubbed the cold blue metal on his cheek, grinning like a boy who'd just pocketed a ten-dollar bill. He put the gun in his backpack and, once more sizing up the bear, slipped from the door.

A wedge of light suddenly filled the grass, accompanied by the clatter of an aluminum door. Hrubek stepped quickly into a large open shed behind the shop and pulled the pistol from the backpack.

A man's voice cut through the night, "You left it out there, you go pick it up. It's rusted, I'll tan your hide, young man."

The man was speaking from a dingy but brightly lit one-story house from whose chimney drifted wood and trash smoke. It was about thirty yards from the shop.

A boy, about eight or nine, walked sullenly past the shed. Without looking inside he disappeared behind the shop. A moment later he started back toward the house, holding a long hammer close to his eyes, inspecting it and scratching hopelessly with his thumbnail at dots of rust.

A noise nearby startled Hrubek. A fat raccoon was in the shed, scuttling over the concrete floor. It hadn't seen him and was nosing obliviously among garbage bags. The boy had heard the scratching of claws on concrete and stopped. Holding the rusted hammer like a club he stepped to the shed door and peered into inky darkness.

Hrubek's heart began to pulsate violently as he wondered what to do if the boy confronted him. What *will* I *tell* him? I know—I will tell him that I am Will-*i-am* Tell. I will shoot him in the head, Hrubek said to himself, and tried to control his panicked breath. The raccoon paused cautiously as it heard the boy's footsteps. Its head turned and, seeing Hrubek, the animal tensed. Baring its fangs it panicked and leapt at the madman's leg. In a short portion of a second Hrubek lunged, seizing the big animal by the neck. Even before the needlelike claws lashed out, Hrubek snapped its spine with a quiet pop.

Nice try, he thought. No such luck.

The animal quivered once and died.

The boy stepped closer to the doorway and listened. When he heard nothing else he walked slowly back into the house. The back-yard spotlight was extinguished.

Hrubek calmed as he absently stroked the fur of the raccoon for a moment then arranged the animal very carefully on its stomach with its rear legs and tail spread out behind, its front paws reaching forward. Salivating with lust Hrubek picked up a screwdriver from a workbench and drove it deep into the back of the animal's skull. Then he extracted the tool and threw the limp corpse into the corner of the garage.

As he was about to leave he looked above his head and saw a row of six animal traps hanging from pegs.

Well, look at this. More presents . . . These'll slow 'em up, make no mistake!

Slipping three of the traps into his backpack, Hrubek stepped outside. He paused in the middle of a dusty patch behind the shop and smelled his hands. Mixed with the gasoline was a musky scent from the raccoon. He held his fingers close to his face and inhaled this smell on the wood-fire-laden air, deep, deep, so deep that his lungs hurt. As if the air overflowed into his groin, he went almost immediately erect. He guided his penis out of his overalls and stroked himself absently, using the slick blood from the screwdriver to lubricate the motion. Eyes closed, he swiveled his head sideways, keeping time with his right arm, feeling the pitch intensify, growing more and more dizzy as he hyperventilated.

He moaned an unearthly sound as he ejaculated, amply and hard, upon the dark earth.

Hrubek wiped his hands on the grass then he adjusted his Irish hat square on his head. Slipping into a stand of bushes he crouched down and made himself comfortable. There was only one more thing he needed right now and he knew in his heart God was about to send it to him.

Owen Atcheson pulled a large pile of burlap bags from a shelf in the greenhouse. They'd made good progress on the shoreline and had already built up one low-lying portion of lawn with several feet of sandbags. His muscles ached and he stretched hard, thinking of a meeting he had scheduled for tomorrow, his trip later in the week.

He glanced outside and saw Lis, beside the lakefront, filling bags with sand.

Moving silently down the aisle he passed plants whose names he neither knew nor cared to know. A timed watering valve clicked open and filled portions of the greenhouse with clouds of mist that obscured plants and the stone bas-reliefs that hung on the brick.

At the far end of the space he stopped. Portia looked up at him with her hazel eyes.

"I thought I saw you in here," he said.

"First aid." She pulled her skirt high, turning away from him and revealing on her thigh a small smear of blood a foot above the back of her knee.

"What happened?"

"Came down for a new roll of tape. I bent over and a fucking thorn got me in the ass. Part of it's still in there, I can feel it."

"Doesn't look too bad."

"Doesn't it? Hurts like hell." She turned around and looked him up and down then gave a short laugh. "You know, you look like a lord of the manor. Very medieval. Sort of like Sir Ralph Lauren."

Her voice seemed laced with mockery but immediately she smiled in a way that seemed to include him in a private joke. Her face contorted as she dug into the tiny wound with a fingernail lacquered red as the blood that dotted her skin.

Four silver rings were on each hand and a complicated spiral earring dangled from one lobe. The other was pierced by four silver hoops. Portia had refused Lis's offer of more practical clothing. She still wore her shimmering gold-and-silver skirt and loose blouse. The greenhouse was chill and it was clear to Owen that she wore no bra beneath the satiny white cloth. He scanned her figure briefly, reflecting that while his wife with her boyish figure might be called striking or handsome, her sister was a purely voluptuous creature. At times it amazed him that they shared the same genes.

"Let me look at it," he said.

Again, she turned her back and lifted her skirt. He clicked on a table lamp and shone it on her pale leg, then knelt to examine the wound.

"Would it really float away?" she asked. "The greenhouse?"

"Probably."

Portia smiled. "What would Lis do without her flowers? Do you have flood insurance?"

"No. The house is below flood level. They wouldn't write the policy."

"I don't imagine the rosebushes'd be covered anyway."

"It depends on the policy. That's a bargained risk."

"Once a lawyer always a lawyer," Portia said. He looked up but again could not tell if she was taunting him. She continued, "That porch Lis mentioned? On this part of the yard? I think she's wrong. I don't think it got washed away. I think Father tore it down to build Mother the greenhouse." Portia nodded toward a display of tall orange-red rosebushes. "Lis acts like it's a holy site. But Mother didn't even particularly want it."

"I thought that Ruth lived for her flowers."

"That's the way Lis tells it. But nope. It was Father who insisted. My own theory is that it was to keep her, let's say, occupied while he was away on business."

"Your mother's name and 'mischief' aren't words I'd ever put together." Owen dabbed away a dot of blood and peered into the wound.

"One never knows. Still waters and all. But then, was Father paranoid, or what?"

"I wouldn't know. I never liked him very much."

"Ooo, that hurts," she whispered as he probed, and lowered her head. "When we were young we had Sunday dinner on that old porch. Two p.m. sharp. Father rang a bell and we had to be there on the button. Roast, potatoes, green beans. We'd eat while he lectured about literature or business or space flights. Politics sometimes. Mostly he liked astronauts."

"It's really in there, the thorn. Just the tip. I can see it."

"Hurts like hell. Can you get it out?"

"I've got some tweezers." He pulled out a Swiss Army knife.

She dug into her pocket and handed him a Bic lighter. "Here." When he looked blank she laughed and said, "Sterilize it. Living in New York you learn to be careful about what you put into your body."

He took the lighter and ran a flame over the end of the tweezers.

"A Swiss Army knife," she said, watching him. "Does it have a corkscrew on it, and everything? Little scissors? A magnifying glass?"

"You know, Portia, sometimes it's hard to tell if you're making fun of somebody."

"It's probably my abrasive big-city attitude. It gets me into trouble sometimes. Don't take it personally." Portia fell silent and turned away, lowering her face to a rosebush. She inhaled deeply.

"I didn't know you smoked." He returned the lighter to her.

"I don't. Not cigarettes. And then, after we'd have our dessert, which was accompanied by . . . ?"

"I have no idea."

"Port."

Owen said he should have guessed.

"Do you like port, Owen?"

"No. I don't like port."

"Ow, Jesus, that hurts."

"Sorry."

He put his large hand on the front of Portia's thigh and held it firmly as he pressed the tiny blade of the tweezers against the base of the thorn. "Keep your hem up, so it doesn't get blood on it." She hiked her skirt slightly higher and he caught a fast view of the lace trim on red panties. He pressed harder with the tweezers.

Her eyes were closed and her teeth seated. "No, I can't stand port either but I *am* an expert on the subject. I paid attention during dear Father's dinnertime speeches. Nineteen seventeen was as good a year as the benchmark year. . . . Which was?" She raised a querying eyebrow. When he didn't respond she exhaled against the pain and said, "Why, 1963, of course. I thought all of you upper-crust gentlemen farmers knew that."

"I don't like to farm any more than I like port."

"Well, garden then." He felt her thigh quivering in his hand. He gripped it tighter. Portia continued, "A really good 1917 port has a bouquet that's reminiscent of tobacco. Sunday nights! After the port—and Father's lecture *about* port or NASA or lit-ra-ture or God knew what—and after our *bolos levados* and jam, we kids had nothing to do." She inhaled deeply, then asked, "Owen, I didn't really have to be here, did I? I could've signed everything in New York, had it notarized and mailed to you, right?"

He paused. "You could have, yes."

"So, what does she really want?"

"You're her sister."

"Does that mean I'm supposed to know why she asked me? Or does it mean she wants my company?"

"She hasn't seen much of you."

Portia laughed breathily. "You got that little sucker yet?"

"It's almost out." Owen glanced at the doorway at which his wife, if inclined to enter the greenhouse at this moment, would catch them at whatever it was that they were doing. He probed again with the tweezers, felt her shiver. She bit her lip and remained silent. Then he lifted out the thorn and stood.

Still holding her translucent skirt, Portia turned. Owen caught another flash of panties then held up the tweezers, the tip bright with her blood. "You'd think it'd be bigger," she said. "Thanks. You're a man of many talents."

"It's not too bad. Just a pinprick. But you should put something on it. Bactine. Peroxide."

"You have anything?"

"In the bathroom upstairs," he answered. "The one next to our bedroom."

She dabbed a Kleenex on the wound and examined the tissue. "Damn roses," Portia muttered, and dropping her hem she started toward the stairs.

5

He encircled her with his arms and pressed his mouth against hers. It was not a gentle kiss. Her fingers found his solid biceps and pulled him closer. Against his bare chest she rubbed her breasts, covered by only the thin cloth of her blouse.

I'm out of control, Owen thought. Out of goddamn control. He closed his eyes and kissed her again.

His tongue slipped between her lips and played with hers. She gripped his lower lip between her teeth and sucked it into her mouth. Then she hesitated and turned away, uneasy.

"No," he commanded. "Kiss me."

"What if she sees us?"

Owen shushed her, observing that her protest was halfhearted. It was as if the risk of being caught was part of her passion. Perhaps most of it.

His hands dropped to her blouse. She shuddered as a button popped off and fell at their feet but she gave no other resistance. The garment separated, and the backs of his hands brushed her exposed breasts.

"Are you—?" she began but he kissed her again and spread his large hand, so that a thumb and little finger each touched a nipple. His other hand curled around the white flesh of her back and pulled her closer.

His hand yanked her skirt high and stuffed the hem of the cloth into her waistband, exposing pale skin. She lifted her hips but he stroked her taut silk panties once and then didn't touch them again.

Instead he took her hand, unzipped his trousers and pulled himself out, closing her fingers around him roughly, silently instructing her to stroke, hard, so hard he was nearly in pain. When she flagged he ordered, "No, harder!"

And she did.

A moment later he stopped her, urgently gripping her shoulders and turning her around so that her back was to him. He rested his palm on the back of her hair and pushed her forward, then tugged the panties down. With both hands on her hips he entered her hard and instantly lost whatever self-restraint remained. He slammed against her. His hands clutched her breasts and he pulled her into him, her breath popping from her mouth in small bursts. He lowered his teeth to the back of her neck and closed them on the nape, biting hard, tasting sweat and perfume. She squirmed and pressed back against him, whimpering.

The sound triggered him. He slipped out and amid fierce spasms left a glistening stream down the inside of her thigh. He let his weight sag onto her back, gasping.

Then he was aware of motion and he realized that she'd been stroking herself all along. His hands slid around to her breasts once more and he pulled on her nipples. A few moments later he could feel her legs tense and, as she called his name in a high-pitched moan, once then again, her body shivered hard. She remained still for a moment then eased forward and rolled onto her back. He rested beside her, on his knees.

Inches apart, not touching.

As if words were wrong, as if words would give away this secret, he said nothing but leaned over and kissed her cheek in a formal, brotherly gesture. She squeezed his hand once.

Then Owen hefted his shovel and disappeared down the culvert, leaving his wife to lie like a trysting college girl beside the dark lake, on a neatly stacked row of sandbags.

·   ·   ·

Lis Atcheson watched the dull clouds overhead, and glanced uneasily at the house to see if Portia might have witnessed their exhibition.

The water lapped on rocks only feet from her head but seemed, despite the rising level, quite peaceful.

She breathed deeply a number of times and closed her eyes momentarily. What on earth had brought that on? she wondered. Owen was a man with an appetite stronger than hers, that was true, but he had a moodiness too; sex was the first thing to die when he turned sultry or preoccupied. It had been three or four weeks since he'd eased over to her side of the bed.

And the last time they'd found a more adventurous venue? The kitchen, the Cherokee, outdoors? Well, she couldn't remember. Months. Many months.

He'd come up to her ten minutes before, carrying a load of burlap bags from the greenhouse. Her back had been to him and she'd been bending down to muscle a sandbag into place on the levee when she heard the stack of empty bags fall nearby and felt his hands on her hips.

"Owen, *what* are you doing?" She laughed, and felt herself being pulled against him. He was already erect.

"No, we don't have time for this. My God, Portia's doing the upstairs windows! She can look right out!"

Silently he closed his hands over her breasts and kissed her hotly on the back of the neck.

"Owen, no!" She turned around.

"Shhh," was all he said, and his unyielding hands moved up under her skirt.

"Owen, are you nuts? Not now."

"Yes," he said. "Now."

And from behind, too. A position he generally didn't like; he preferred to pin her on her back, helpless, and watch her face as he pulsed on top of her.

What had gotten into him?

Maybe, above the clouds, there's a full moon.

Maybe it's . . .

The water lapped with the rhythm of the blues.

. . . the cowboy boots.

She glanced at the yellow windows of the house—windows from which she was now fully, if dimly, visible. Had Portia seen?

And if she had? Lis wondered. Well, so be it. He's *my* husband, after all.

She closed her eyes and was astonished to find herself drowsy —despite the adrenaline that still coursed in her bloodstream, despite the urgency to finish the sandbagging. Well, here's the miracle of the evening. Oh, my God, forget about floods, forget about orgasms out of doors. . . . I think I'm falling asleep.

Lis Atcheson suffered from insomnia. She might go twenty-four hours without sleep. Sometimes thirty, thirty-six hours, spent wholly alert, completely awake. The malady had been with her for years but had grown severe not long after the Indian Leap incident last May. The nightmares would start fifteen or twenty minutes after she'd slipped under—dreams filled with black caverns, blood, eyes that were dead, eyes that begged for mercy, eyes that were cruelly alive. . . .

Like a whipcrack, she'd be awake.

Eventually her heart would slow, the sweat on her temples and neck would evaporate. And she'd lie in bed, a prisoner of consciousness, growing ill with fatigue and teased by hallucinations. Hour after hour after hour. Gazing at the blue-green digital numerals that flicked ever onward. These numbers took on crazy meanings—1:39 seemed snide, the shape of 2:58 was comforting, 4:45 was a barricade; if she didn't cross it asleep she knew she'd lost the battle for that night.

She could recite all sorts of facts about sleep. Einstein needed ten hours a day, Napoleon only five. The record holder for not sleeping is a Californian who was awake for 453 hours. The average person sleeps between seven and a half and eight hours, a tomcat sixteen. There was a fatal type of insomnia, a type of prion disease that destroyed the thalamus region of the brain. Lis owned exactly twenty-two books on sleep disorders and insomnia; sometimes she recited their titles in lieu of counting sheep.

"It's just a way to avoid the nightmares," Lis's doctor had told her. "You have to tell yourself they're just dreams. Try repeating that. 'They're just dreams; they can't hurt me. They're just dreams; they can't hurt me.' "

She did as instructed but the awkwardness of this tongue-twisting mantra tended to waken her even further.

Yet tonight, Lis Atcheson—lying outside, bare-breasted and skirt to her thigh—felt sleep closing in fast. She grew more and more relaxed as she gazed at the greenhouse, the lights glowing ultramarine blue. She heard Owen slam the shovel onto a sandbag with a ring. She saw Portia's shadow in an upstairs bedroom.

Odd images began to dance in her mind. She recognized this as lucid dreaming. She saw faces melting, people becoming dark shapes, vaporous forms, flowers mutating.

Lis pictured a dark-red, a *blood*-red Victorian John Armstrong rose and that was the last image in her mind before she slipped under.

It was perhaps no more than ten seconds later that a branch snapped, loud as a gunshot. Lis, her ruddy hands folded scrupulously on her chest like the effigy of a long-dead saint, sat up, instantly and irrevocably awake, drawing closed her blouse and pulling down her skirt, as she stared at the dark form of the man who appeared from a row of hemlocks and trod forward.

Easing the '79 Chevy pickup off the back road onto Route 236 he goosed the lazy ticking engine until the truck climbed to seventy.

He heard what he diagnosed as an ornery bearing and chose not to think about it further.

Trenton Heck sat nearly reclining, his left foot on the accelerator and his right straight out, resting on the bench under the saggy flesh of a four-year-old male dog, whose face was full of lamentation. This was the way Heck drove—with his leg stretched out, not necessarily with a hound atop it—and he'd bought a vehicle with an automatic transmission and bench seat solely because of this practice.

Exactly thirty-two years older than the dog, Trenton Heck was sometimes referred to as "that skinny guy from Hammond Creek" though if people saw him with his shirt off, revealing muscles formed from a life of hunting, fishing, and odd jobs in rural towns, they'd decide that he wasn't skinny at all. He was *lean*, he was *sinewy*. Only in the past month had his belly started to roll past his waistband. This was due mostly to inactivity though some of it could be traced to chain-drinking Budweisers and to single suppers of twin TV dinners.

Heck tonight massaged a spot on his faded blue jeans under which was a glossy mess of old bullet wound dead center in his right thigh. Four years old (coming up on the anniversary, he reflected), the wound still pulled his muscles taut as cold rubber bands. Heck passed a slow-moving sedan and eased back into his lane. A big plastic Milk Bone swung from the truck's rearview mirror. It looked real and Heck had bought it to perplex the dog though of course it didn't; Emil was a purebred blood.

Heck drove along the highway at a good clip, whistling a tuneless tune between uneven teeth. A roadside sign flashed past and he lifted his foot off the accelerator and braked quickly, causing the hound to slide forward on the vinyl seat, grimacing. Heck eased into the turnoff and drove a quarter mile down a country lane of bad asphalt. He saw lights in the far distance and a few shy stars but mostly felt an overwhelming sense of solitude. He found the deserted roadside stand—a shack from which a farmer had years ago sold cheese and honey. Heck climbed out of the truck, leaving the engine running and the dog antsy on the seat.

Heck's outfit tonight was what he always wore unless the temperature was crackling cold: a black T-shirt under a workshirt under a blue-jean jacket. Covering the curly brown hair that dipped over his ears was a cap emblazoned with the logo of the New York Mets. The cap had been a present from a woman who could recite all the vital statistics of the Flushing Meadow sluggers going back fifteen years (Jill had a great knuckleball herself) but he didn't care for the team and wore the tattered hat only because it was a present from her.

He looked around uneasily and wandered in a slow circle through the dusty parking area. He glanced at the idling truck and concluded that it was too much of a beacon. He shut off the engine and lights. Enveloped in darkness, he resumed his pacing. Rustling sounded nearby. Heck immediately recognized the sound of raccoon's footfalls. Moments later he identified a residue of musk on a skunk's ass fur as the animal passed silently behind him. These creatures weren't a threat, yet as he paced he kept his hand on the black Bakelite ribbed grip of his old automatic pistol, dangling from an even older cowboy holster, complete with rawhide leg thongs.

Clouds filled the sky. The storm was overdue. Rain if you've gotta, he spoke silently though not heavenward, but keep that wind away for another few hours, Lord. I could use some help here and I could use it bad.

A twig snapped behind him, loud, and he turned fast, coming close to drawing down on a conspicuous birch tree. He knew of few animals in the wild that would snap twigs this way; he recalled only a towering moose lumbering along with her calves, and a seven-foot grizzly bear, gazing at Heck hungrily from the amiable haze of his protected-species status.

Maybe it's a drunk deer, he thought, to cheer himself up.

Heck continued to pace. Then lights filled the parking lot and the car arrived. It parked with a leisurely squeal of brakes. Upright as a boot-camp sergeant, the gray-suited officer walked over the damp ground to where Heck stood.

"Don." Heck offered a limp salute.

"Trent. Glad you were free. Good to see you."

"That storm's on its way," Heck said.

"That Emil of yours could scent through a hurricane, I thought."

That may be, he told Haversham, but he wasn't inclined to get himself lightning-struck. "Now, who's the escapee?"

"That psycho they got at Indian Leap last spring. You remember it?"

"Who don't, round here?"

"Snuck off in somebody's body bag tonight." Haversham explained about the escape.

"Crazy maybe but that shows some smarts."

"He's over near Stinson."

"So he drove a ways, this nutzo?"

"Yup. The coroner's boy, the one who was driving's over there now. So's Charlie Fennel and a couple troopers from J. He's got his bitches with him."

The Troop's dogs weren't true trackers but hunting dogs— Labradors—occasionally drafted for scenting. They had fair noses and being spayed bitches they stayed clear of posts and trees and weren't easily led astray. But they did get distracted. Emil was a track-sure dog; when he was on scent he'd walk right over a rabbit sitting in his path and ignore it, and the only sound you'd hear was the rasp of his anxious breath as he charged along the trail. The girls on the other hand were track-happy and spent much of the time quartering with sloppy enthusiasm and yelping. Still, when you were after a dangerous escapee, it was good practice to go with a pack. He asked Haversham what they could use to scent on.

"Skivvies." The captain handed over a plastic bag. Heck was confident that Haversham knew how to handle scent articles. He'd have made sure that the underwear hadn't been laundered recently and that nobody had touched the cloth with their fingers. The trooper added, "He's running mostly naked, near as we can tell."

Heck thought the captain was joking.

"No sir. He's a big fellow, got lots of padding on him. Adler, that doctor at Marsden, he was telling me these schizos don't feel cold like normal people. It's like they're pretty numb. They don't feel pain either. You can hit 'em and they don't even know they're hit."

"Ooo, that's good to know, Don. Tell me, does he fly too?"

Haversham chuckled then added, "They say he's pretty harmless. He does this a lot. Adler says he's escaped from seven hospitals. They always find him. It's like a game for him. The bag he snuck out in? The fellow's it was, was a suicide."

"Harmless? Didn't they read about Indian Leap?" Heck snickered, and nodded down the road toward Marsden hospital. "Who's crazy in there and who isn't?" Heck was suddenly unable to look at Haversham. "Say, over the phone you mentioned five hundred for my fee. And the reward. Ten *thousand*. That right, Don? Ten?"

"Yessir. The fee's from my assistance fund just like normal. The reward's from the state. From Adler's budget. He's pretty anxious to get this fellow."

"I don't suppose he put it in writing?"

"Adler? Nope. But he's really anxious to see this boy caught. You collar him, you'll get your money, Trent. And you're the only civvy on the case. My boys can't take a penny."

"We'll get him."

The captain looked off into the night and seemed to be debating. Finally he said, "Trenton? I know I told you he wasn't dangerous but keep that close to you." Haversham indicated the pistol on Heck's hip. "I gotta tell you—was probably an accident, from what Adler says, but Hrubek might've attacked a couple orderlies. Cracked one of 'em's arm like a toothpick. Could've died if nobody'd found him."

"Well, is he dangerous, or ain't he?" Heck asked.

"All I'm saying is, keep your eye out. Say, what *is* that piece?"

"That old P-38 of mine." Heck patted his holster, remembering in detail the day he handed his Glock service automatic over to this very man, Heck's eyes frozen on the black gun as he turned it in, grip first, clip out, slide locked open. The badge and the ID card followed. Heck had bought the uniform himself so they let him keep that though he had to sign a form that said he'd never wear it in public, and his face was red with anger and shame as he set his name to paper.

"They still sell ammunition for that old thing?"

"Nine-millimeter parabellum is all it is."

Haversham stuck his head through the passenger window and stroked the hound's head. The dog sat insensible and bored, staring at the motion of the captain's gray hair. "All right, Emil, go do us and your master proud. You hear? You go catch us a crazy man. Good boy, good boy." Haversham turned to Heck. "Isn't he a good old boy?"

And Trenton Heck—who'd midwived bitches and nursed pups with eyedroppers and sucked snake venom out of the shoulders of retrievers and sped to vets at ninety mph to save dogs that could be saved and shot them remorselessly with a merciful bullet when they could not, who didn't speak to dogs except to command them—Trenton Heck just nodded at the captain with a cautious smile. "Better be going. 'Fore that track gets cold."

"How the hell did it happen?" Owen barked. "He's a madman. He *can't* escape! Did they leave the son-of-a-bitch door open?"

"Some mix-up of some kind. They were kind of, you know, sketchy on details." Stanley Weber, duly elected sheriff of the Incorporated Village of Ridgeton, turned out to have been the intruder who'd wakened Lis from her brief sleep. He'd passed by without even noticing her, directed by Portia down to the culvert where Owen was working.

His news was far more disturbing than his unexpected arrival.

"My God, Stan," Lis said, "it's a hospital for the criminally insane. Don't they have bars?"

She was remembering: Eyes set deep in the moonish jolly mad face. Teeth yellow. His howling voice. *"Sic semper tyrannis . . .* Lisbone. . . . Hello, Lis-bone!"

"There's no excuse for it." Owen paced angrily. He was a large man, strong in many ways, and he had a temper that scared even Lis. The sheriff crossed his arms defensively and leaned into the anger. "When did it happen?" Owen continued. "Do they know where he's going?"

"Within the last couple hours. I was on the radio." He pointed to his squad car as if trying to lead Owen's fury off track. "I was speaking to Don Haversham. With the state police?" He added significantly, "He's a good man. He's a captain."

"Oh, a captain. My."

Lis found herself staring at the sheriff's feet; in his heavy, dark boots he appeared less a civil servant than a man of combat on a combat mission. A breath of air stirred, reaching damply into her blouse. She watched a dozen leaves fall straight from the branches of a towering maple as if seeking cover before the storm arrived. Lis shivered and realized the kitchen door was ajar. She closed it.

Footsteps sounded suddenly and Lis glanced at the doorway to the living room.

Portia paused then entered the kitchen, still dressed in her thin, sexy outfit, her abundant breasts provocatively defined by the white silken cloth of her blouse. The sheriff nodded at the young woman, who smiled indifferently. The lawman's eyes dipped twice to her chest. Portia's Discman was stuffed into the pocket of the skirt and a single earplug was stuck in one ear. A tinny chunka-chunka sound came from the dangling plug.

"Hrubek's escaped," Lis told her.

"Oh, no." The second earplug was extracted and she flung the wire around her neck the way a doctor wears a stethoscope. The raspy sound of rock music was louder now, shooting from both tiny plugs.

"Say, could you shut that off?" Lis asked, and Portia absently complied.

Lis, Owen and Portia stood on glazed terra-cotta tile as cold as the concrete stoop outside, all in a line, arms crossed. Their formation struck Lis as silly and she broke ranks to fill a kettle. "Coffee or tea, Stanley?"

"No, thankya. He's just wandering around lost, they say. He got away in Stinson, nearly ten miles east of the hospital."

And fifty miles east of where they now stood, Lis thought. Like having a full gas tank or two twenty-dollar bills in your pocket this was a comfort—maybe insubstantial, maybe useless, but a comfort nonetheless.

"So," Portia said, "he's heading away from here."

"Seems to be."

Lis was remembering: The madman bursting to life, hand and foot shackles jingling, his eyes molesting the trial spectators. And she was the person he undressed most eagerly. "Lis-bone, Lis-bone . . ."

Lis had cried then—in June—hearing his hyena-pitched laugh fill the courtroom and she wanted to cry now. She clamped her teeth together and turned to the stove to make a cup of herbal tea. Owen was still firing angry questions at the sheriff. How many men are out looking for him? Do they have dogs? Did he take any weapons? The sheriff endured this cross-examination gamely then responded, "The fact is they're not doing a whole lot about it. It went out as an information bulletin only. Not an escape-assistance request. I myself'd guess they've pretty much cured him. Shocked him, probably, like they do. With those electrode things. He's out wandering around and they'll pick him up—"

Owen waved his hand and started to speak but Lis interrupted. "If nobody's worried about it, Stan, what are you doing here?"

"Well, I come by to ask if you still got that letter. Thought it might give 'em a clue where he's got himself to."

"Letter?" Owen asked.

Lis, however, knew exactly which letter he was referring to. It'd been her first thought this evening when the sheriff had said the word "Marsden."

"I know where it is," she said, and went to get it.

6

Mrs. Lis-bone Atcheson:

I am in this room I can't breathe I can't hear. I am held here unfAIRly and thEY, yes thEy are stopping me from what I MUST DO. This is very Important. they are holding me and have told lles About Me to waShingtOn and the enTIRE worlD. they think that I am dANGERous etc but this is their excUSE and EVErybody beliEVEs it. That is beliEVEs "them". they are very Strong & we Must fear them. they arE eVErywhere.

It is a CONSPIRACY. CON + S + PIRACY.

and I know YOU are in it!!!!

Revenge is mine it is not the LORDS because the LORD knows what I have Done and will not let ME rest. He shoots me in the hEAd every nighT!!! I accept my fATE and YOU who are bEAuTiful mUSt too. Come to me for eternal rest forever.

EVErywhere. forEVEr. rEVEnge.

EVE the woman

COME to ME.

i your lover

Michael Hrubek's penmanship featured green, black and blu ink.

And for her name, and his "signature," red.

The sheriff sucked air between shiny white teeth in a loud,

ritating way. "Does any of this make sense to you?" He addressed the question to Owen.

Lis answered, "It's just babble."

Owen glanced at her then added, "We talked about it when it came but we thought it was a kid's prank."

Lis taught sophomore English at Ridgeton High School.

"I'm a tough grader." She laughed wanly. "I've been on my share of sixteen-year-olds' shit lists."

" 'i your lover.' " The sheriff hitched at his gun belt. He stared at the letter for a moment. "Return address?"

Lis flipped through the manilla folder where she'd filed it—in the *Letters, Miscellaneous* slot. Just past, she now noted, *Last Will and Testament—Owen and Lis*. She found the envelope. There was no return address. The postmark was Gloucester.

"That's nowhere near Marsden," she pointed out.

"Let me make a call." The sheriff glanced at Owen, who nodded at the phone.

As she leaned against the counter, sipping the rose-hip tea, Lis remembered a hot Saturday in September, replanting a bush of hybrid tea roses, lemon yellow. Sweat was running along her nose with a tickle. Owen had been working all day and had just returned. About 6:00 p.m., the sun low and wan. He stood in the doorway, his large shoulders slumped, a piece of paper in his hand. Lis glanced up at him and the plant sank through her fingers, a thorn piercing her skin. Because of the sallow, grave expression on her husband's face she hadn't at first noticed the pain. Lis looked down a second later and saw a sphere of blood on her finger. She set the plant on the ground. Owen handed her this very letter and she took it from him slowly, leaving a bloody fingerprint on the envelope— like an old-time wax seal.

Portia now read it. She shrugged, and announced to Lis, "I've got some stuff with me. Stop by the room, you want. It might relax you."

Lis blinked and forced herself to appear blasé. Only her sister, she reflected from an emotional distance, would offer a joint with one-fifth of the town's constabulary standing nearby (his squad car's bumper proclaiming, *Ridgeton Says NO to Drugs*). This was vintage Portia—playful, cunning, perverse. Oh, Portia—the hip, pale, French-braided younger sister with her Discman and her stream of thin-faced boyfriends. She'd been forced to endure an evening in the country, and she was blowing Lis one of the cold kisses her older sister remembered so well.

Lis did not reply. The young woman shrugged and, with a glance at Owen, wandered out of the kitchen.

The sheriff, who hadn't heard Portia's proposition and probably wouldn't have understood it if he had, hung up the receiver. When he spoke, it was to Owen. "Well . . . The long and the short of it is that she doesn't have anything to worry about."

She? Lis repeated to herself. Was this me? Her face burned and she sensed even old-world Owen shift uncomfortably at the sheriff's patronizing attitude.

"They said it didn't mean nothing. Hrubek's a schizo—they don't do well by people face to face. Too nervous to talk or something. So they write these long letters that're just nonsense mostly and when they do make a threat they're like too scared to act on it."

"The postmark?" Lis asked firmly. "Gloucester."

"Oh, about that. I asked. He may still've sent it. He got sent to this hospital there for some tests the first week in September. It's pretty low-security. He might've slipped away and mailed a letter. But, what I was telling you before, he's headed east, *away* from here."

The sheriff and Lis both looked at Owen, who because he was the largest person in the room and the most grave, seemed to be in charge. "What if he isn't?"

"Hell, he's on foot, Owen. The doctor said there's no way he can drive a car. And who's going to give him a ride, a big crazy like that?"

"I'm just asking you," Owen said, "what if he *isn't* going east. What if he changes him mind and comes here?"

"Here?" the sheriff asked and fell silent.

"I want you to put a man on the house."

"I'm sorry, Owen. No can do. We've got—"

"Stan, this is serious."

"—that storm coming up. It's supposed to be a whopper. And Fred Bertholder's in bed with the flu. Sick as a dog. Whole family has it."

"One man. Just until they catch him."

"Look, even the state boys're spread pretty thin. They're on highway detail mostly because of the—"

"Fucking storm," Owen spat out. He rarely swore in front of people he didn't know well; he considered it a sign of weakness. Lis was momentarily shocked at this lapse—not at the cussing itself but the anger that would be behind it.

"We got our priorities. Come on, don't go looking that way, Owen. I'll check in with Haversham every so often. If there's any change I'll be over here like greased lightning."

Owen walked to the window and looked out over the lake. He was either paralyzed with anger or deep in thought.

"Why don't you go to a hotel for the night?" the sheriff suggested with a cheerfulness that Lis found immensely irritating. "Hey, that way you'll get yourselves a good night's rest and not have to worry 'bout nothing."

"Good night's rest," Lis muttered. "Sure."

"Believe me, folks, you got nothing to worry about." He glanced out the window into the sky, perhaps hoping for a searing streak of lightning to justify his deployment of deputies this evening. "I'll stay on top of it, yessir." The sheriff offered a rueful smile as he stepped to the door.

Only Lis said good night.

Owen paced beside the window, gazing out to the lake. He said matter-of-factly, "I think we ought to do that. A hotel, I mean. We'll get a couple rooms at the Marsden Inn."

A quaint little bed-and-breakfast, lousy (Owen's word) with dried flowers, Shaker furniture, country wreaths and dreadfully sincere paintings of live horses, dead birds and glassy-eyed nineteenth-century children.

"Not exactly the best hideout from a crazy man, would you say?"

"It doesn't sound like he could even get halfway to Ridgeton, let alone find a hotel we're staying at. . . . If he was inclined to find us in the first place. Besides, the Inn's only two miles from here. I don't want to have to go far tonight."

"We need to finish the dam and the taping."

Owen didn't speak for a moment. He asked in a distracted voice, "Where do you think he is?"

"I'm not leaving till we get that levee finished. The sandbags, the—"

Owen's eyes flashed. "Why are you arguing?"

Lis blinked. She'd learned to tolerate his temper. She knew it was usually misdirected. Her husband was angry now, yes, but not at her—at the sheriff. Most times she blustered right back at him. But tonight she didn't raise her voice. On the other hand she wasn't going to back down. "I'm not disagreeing. The hotel's fine. But I'm not leaving until we've got at least another foot's worth of sandbags."

His eyes again looked out onto the lake while Lis's dipped to the letter, resting on the butcher block. Lis smoothed it, then folded the paper. It made a crinkling sound and she thought for some reason of dried skin. She shivered and tossed it onto a stack of bills to be filed.

Lis pulled on her jacket. Was he going to argue, or agree? Unable to anticipate his reaction she felt her stomach twisting into a knot. Cautiously she said, "It shouldn't take more than an hour." Still he said nothing. "You think we can get enough bags piled up by then?"

Owen finally turned from the window and asked what she'd just said.

"Sandbags? Can we stack enough in an hour?"

"An hour? I'm sure we can." His serenity surprised her. "Anyway I don't think it's going to be as bad as they say. You know weathermen around here—they're always sounding false alarms."

The driver downshifted to the lowest of his thirteen gears and nudged the huge White tractor-trailer past the restaurant and into the parking area. He locked the brakes and shut off the diesel, then checked a map, spending more time than he thought normal for a smart man like himself to calculate that he'd be in Bangor by four the next afternoon.

A young man, the driver wore his Dolphins cap backwards and Nike Pumps on his feet. In the Blaupunkt was a grunge tape, backed up by a half dozen rap and hip-hop cassettes (a secret never to be shared with any blood relation). He climbed out of the cab, pausing long enough to glance in the side mirror with discouragement at the constellation of acne on his cheek, then dropped to the ground. He was halfway to the diner when the voice barked, "Hey, John Driver!"

The huge man was suddenly next to him, hovering on legs like tree trunks. The driver stopped, astonished, as he looked up into the glistening round face, the spit-flecked grin, the eyes as excited as a kid's at a ball game.

"Howdy," the driver stammered.

The big man suddenly grew awkward and seemed to look for something to say. "That's quite a machine, it is," he offered though he didn't look toward the truck but kept his eyes fixed downward on the driver.

"Uhn, thanks. You excuse me, I'm pretty beat and I'm gonna get some chow."

"Chow, chow. Sure. It's lucky seven. See. One, two, three, four, five, six . . ." His arm was making a circuit of the vehicles in the parking lot. "Seven." The man adjusted the wool tweed cap that was perched on his bowling ball of a head. He seemed bald and the driver wondered if he was a Nazi skinhead. He said, "Lucky," and laughed too loud.

"Uh-oh. That's eight." The fellow was pointing to another truck just pulling into the lot. His mouth twisted up in a smirking grin. "Always some fucker who ruins it."

"That *does* happen. You bet." The driver decided he could outrun this bozo but was as troubled by the thought of looking like a fool in front of fellow truckers as he was of getting stomped. "Well. Yessir. G' night now." He sidled toward the diner.

The big man's eyes flashed with concern. "Wait wait wait! Are you going east, John Driver?"

The young man looked up into the murky eyes. "That's not truly my name," he said cautiously.

"I'm going to Boston. That's the home of our country. I really have to get to *Boston*."

"I'm sorry but I can't give you a lift. I work for—"

"A lift?" the man asked with great curiosity. "A lift?"

"Uhn, I can't give you a *ride*? You know what I'm saying? I work for a company and they'd fire me I was to do that."

"No such luck, huh? No such luck?"

"A rule, I'm saying."

"But what am I going to *do*?"

"They don't like it too much you try for rides in truck stops?" This wasn't a question but he was too frightened to offer the man a declarative sentence. "You might go up the road a spell and thumb?"

"Up the road and thumb."

"Somebody might pick you up."

"Up the road and thumb. I could do that. Can I get to Boston that way?"

"That intersection up there, see the light? That's 118, turn left, that'd be north. It'll get you to the Interstate and that'll put you in Boston in no time."

"Thank you, John Driver. God bless you. Up the road and thumb."

The big man started through the lot in a muscular, awkward lope. The driver said a short prayer of thanks—both for surviving this encounter and, equally important, for ending up with a good story to tell to his fellow truckers, one that needed hardly any embellishment at all.

Peter Grimes returned to the hospital director's office and sat in a desk chair. Adler asked casually, "He did *what*?" as if resuming a conversation recently interrupted.

"I'm sorry?"

Adler slapped a green file folder. "The nurses' duty report. "Hrubek was *authorized* to be in C Ward. He had access to the *grounds*. He just walked right into the morgue. *That's* how he got there. He just *strolled* into the freezer. Oh, Peter, Peter, Peter . . . This is not good." Adler had conceded the dankness of his office and was now wearing a beige cardigan into whose bottom buttonhole he poked his little finger.

"And I found out why," Grimes announced. "He was part of Dick Kohler's program."

"Oh, for God's sake, not the halfway house?"

"No. Restricted to the grounds here. Milieu Suite and the work program. For some reason he had a job at the farm. Milking cows, or something, I suppose." The assistant gazed out the black window toward the part of the grounds where the hospital's nonprofit farm, operated by volunteers and staffed by patients, spread for some ten acres into the rocky hills.

"Why wasn't any of this in the file?" Adler slapped the folder once again, as if disciplining a puppy.

"I think there're some other files we don't have. I don't know what happened to them. Something funny's going on."

"Did the board recommend Hrubek for the program?" Adler, as member of the Marsden Board of Directors, prayed for one particular answer to this question.

"No," Grimes said.

"Ah."

"Maybe Dick Kohler slipped him in somehow."

" 'Slipped him in'?" Adler pounced. "We have to be very buttoned up about this, my friend. Did you mean that: 'slipped him in'? Think now. Think carefully."

"Well, I don't know. Hrubek was always closely supervised. It's not quite clear who okayed it. The paperwork's sketchy."

"So maybe he wasn't," Adler reflected, " 'slipped in' after all? Maybe some other idiot here dropped the ball."

Grimes wondered if he was being insulted.

The hospital director breathed slowly. "Wait a moment. Kohler's not on staff. Does he have an office here?"

Grimes was surprised Adler didn't know. "Yes, he does. It's part of the arrangement with Framington. We supply facilities for the attendings."

"He's *not* an attending," Adler snapped.

"In a manner of speaking, he is." With the trooper absent, Grimes inexplicably felt bolder.

"I want to find out what the hell is going on here and I want to know in the next hour. Who's the E Ward resident on call?"

"I'm not exactly sure. I think—"

"Peter, you've got to get on top of this," Adler snapped. "Find out who it is and tell him to go home. Tell him to take the evening off."

"Yes. Go *home*? Are you sure?"

"And tell him not to talk to anyone. . . . I'm curious about this woman. . . ." Adler looked for a scrap of paper, found it and handed it to Grimes. "Did Hrubek ever mention her? *Anybody* ever mention her?"

Grimes read the name. "Mrs. Owen Atcheson? No. Who's she?"

"She was at Indian Leap. She testified against Hrubek at the trial. She claims she got a threatening letter from him last September when our little boy was playing with blocks at Gloucester. The sheriff says her husband thinks Hrubek's after her."

"Ridgeton," Grimes mused. "Forty miles west of here. Not a problem."

"Oh?" Adler turned his red eyes on the young doctor. "Good. I'm so relieved. Now tell me why you think it's quote not a problem."

Grimes swallowed and said, "Because most schizophrenics couldn't get three miles on their own, let alone forty."

"Ah," Adler said, sounding like a crotchety old Oxford don. "And with what little qualifiers, dear Grimes, did you shore up your substandard assessment?"

Grimes surrendered. He fell silent and fluffed his crinkly hair.

"A, what if he *isn't* on his own, doctor?" Adler barked. "What if there are co-conspirators, witting or un? And B, what if Hrubek isn't *like* most schizophrenics? How 'bout them apples, doctor? Now, get on it. Find out exactly how the son of a bitch got out."

Grimes had not grown so bold that he failed to say, "Yes, sir." And he said it very quickly.

"If this . . . Hold up a minute there. If this—" Adler gestured, unable or unwilling to give a name to the potential tragedy. "If this becomes a problem . . ."

"How's that?"

"Get Lowe on the phone. I need to have another little talk with him. Oh, and where's Kohler?"

"Kohler? He'll be at the halfway house tonight. He sleeps over on Sunday."

"You think he'll be in for rounds tonight?"

"No. He was here at four-thirty this morning. And after evaluations he went right to the halfway house. And he was dead on his feet *then*. I'm sure he's in bed now."

"Good."

"Should I call him?"

"Call him?" Adler stared at Grimes. "Doctor, really. He's the *last* one we want to know about this. Don't say a word to him. Not . . . a . . . word."

"I just thought—"

"No, you didn't just think. You weren't thinking at all. I mean, for God's sake, do you call up the fucking lamb and say, 'Guess what? Tomorrow's Easter'?"

7

The steam rising from the plastic cup of coffee left a foggy ellipse on the inside of the windshield.

Dr. Richard Kohler, slouching in the front seat of his fifteen-year-old BMW, yawned painfully and lifted the cup. He sipped the bitter liquid and replaced the carton on the dash slightly to the right of where it had been. He vacantly watched a new oval paint itself on the glass, overlapping the one that was now fading.

He was parked in the staff lot of Marsden State Mental Health Facility. The chunky car, half hidden under an anemic hemlock, was pointed at a small, one-story building near the hospital's main structure.

The duty nurse on E Ward, a friend and woman he used to date, had called the halfway house twenty minutes ago. She'd told Kohler about Michael's escape and warned him that Adler was stonewalling. Kohler had flushed his face with icy water, filled a thermos with coffee then run groggily to his car and driven here. He'd pulled into the parking lot and chosen this spot for his stakeout.

He now looked up at the gothic façade of the asylum and saw several lights. One of them, he supposed, was burning in the office of good Dr. Adler.

The wittier orderlies called the two doctors Hatfield and McCoy and that pretty accurately described their relationship. Still, Kohler had some sympathy for the hospital director. In his five years as head of Marsden, Adler had been fighting a losing political and budgetary battle. Most of the state mental hospitals had been closed, replaced by small, community-based treatment centers. But there remained a need for places to house the criminally insane as well as indigent and homeless patients.

Marsden was such a place.

Adler worked hard for his chunk of the state purse, and he made sure that the poor souls in his care were treated kindly and had the best of a bad situation. It was a thankless job and one that Kohler himself would have quit medicine before taking on.

But beyond that, Kohler's sympathy for his colleague stopped. Because he also knew that Adler had a $122,000-a-year job, malpractice premiums and state benefits included, and that for his paycheck he worked at most a forty-hour week. Adler didn't keep up with the current literature, didn't attend institutes or continuing-education sessions, and rarely spoke with patients except to dispense the insincere greetings of an incumbent politician.

Mostly though Kohler resented Adler's running Marsden not as a treatment facility but as combination prison and day-care center. Containment, not improvement, was his goal. Adler argued that it wasn't the state's job to fix people—merely to keep them from hurting themselves or others.

Kohler would respond, "Then whose job is it, *doctor*?"

Adler would snap back, "You give me the money, sir, and I'll start curing."

The two doctors had played oil and water since Kohler first came to Marsden, brandishing court-appointment orders and trying unusual forms of therapy on severely psychotic patients. Then, somehow—no one quite knew how—Kohler had set up the Milieu Program at Marsden. In it, noncriminal patients, mostly schizophrenics, learned to work and socialize with others, with an eye toward moving on to the halfway house outside of Stinson and eventually to apartments or homes of their own.

Adler was just smart enough to recognize that he had a plum deal that he'd have trouble duplicating anywhere in this universe and was accordingly not the least interested in having jive New York doctors rocking his delicate boat with these glitzy forms of treatment. Recently he'd tried to have Kohler removed, claiming that the younger doctor hadn't gone through proper state civil-service channels to get the job at Marsden. But the allegation was tenuous since Kohler drew no salary and was considered an outside contractor. Besides, the patients themselves rose in rebellion when they heard the rumor that they might lose their Dr. Richard. Adler was forced to back down. Kohler continued to work his way into the hospital, ingratiating himself with the full-time staff and cultivating friends among the practical power centers—the nurses, secretaries and orderlies. The animosity between Kohler and Adler flourished.

Many of the doctors at Marsden wondered why Kohler—who could have had a lucrative private practice—brought all this trouble on himself. Indeed, they were perplexed why he'd spend so much time at Marsden in the first place, where he received a small fee for treating patients and where the practice itself was so demanding and frustrating that it drove many physicians out of psychiatry—and some out of medicine altogether.

But Richard Kohler was a man who'd always tested himself. An honors art-history graduate student, he'd abruptly given up that career path at the ripe age of twenty-three to fight his way into, then through, Duke Medical School. Those grueling years were followed by residencies at Columbia Presbyterian and New Haven General then private practice in Manhattan. He worked with inpatient borderline and near-functioning psychotics, then sought out the hardest cases: chronic schizophrenic and bipolar depressives. He battled bureaucratic resistance to get visiting-physician status at Marsden, Framington and other state Bedlams, where he put in twelve-, fifteen-hour days.

It was as if Kohler thrived on the very stress that was his schizophrenic patients' worst enemy.

Early in his career the psychiatrist developed several tricks for combatting anxiety. The most effective was a macabre meditation: visualizing that he was slipping a needle into a prominent vein rising from his arm and drawing out a searing white light, which represented the stress. The technique was remarkably successful (though it usually worked best when accompanied by a glass of Burgundy or a joint).

Tonight, sitting in a car smelling of old leather, oil and antifreeze, he tried his old trick, though without the chemical assist. It had no effect. He tried again, actually closing his eyes, and picturing the mystical procedure in vivid detail. Again, nothing. He sighed and gazed again at the parking lot.

Kohler stiffened and slouched further down into the front seat as a white van, on whose side was painted *Intertec Security Inc.*, appeared and zigzagged slowly through the parking lot, casting its spotlights on suspicious shadows.

Kohler clicked on the penlight he used for neuro exams and returned to the papers in front of him. These sheets represented an exceedingly abridged version of Michael Hrubek's personal history. The records about the young man's life were woefully inadequate; since he was an indigent patient, very few details of his hospitalization and treatment history were available. This was another sin that Kohler couldn't lay at the hospital director's feet. Michael was the type of patient whose files were virtually nonexistent and whose past treatment was largely a mystery. He'd lived on the street so often, been expelled from so many hospitals, and used so many aliases with intake personnel that there was no coherent chronicle of his illness. He also suffered from a particular type of mental disease that left him with a jumbled and confused sense of the past; what paranoid schizophrenics reported was a stew of lies, truth, confessions, hopes, dreams and delusions.

Yet, for someone with Kohler's experience, the file he now scanned allowed him to reconstruct in some detail a portion of

Michael's life. This fragment was startlingly illuminating. He was vaguely familiar with the file, having acquired it four months before, when Michael came under his care. Kohler now wished he'd paid more attention to its contents when he first read it. He wished too that he had more time now to review the material it contained. But having skimmed the pages once, he noticed that the white van had left the parking lot. Richard Kohler set the folder on the BMW's floor.

He started the car and drove over the wet asphalt to the one-story building he'd been watching for the past half hour. He circled behind it and located the back door, which was near a battered green dumpster. He braked to a stop, debated for a moment and then—after wisely clipping on his seatbelt—drove the right front bumper of the auto into the door at what seemed to him a leisurely rate of speed. Still, the impact shattered the wood so violently that the door cracked free of both hinges and flew deep into the darkness inside.

He pulled the Chevy onto the shoulder of Route 236. The battered truck listed hard to the left and an Orange Crush empty rolled against the door. The brakes squealed as the truck stopped.

Trenton Heck pushed the door open and stepped out. The soda can fell clattering to the road's rocky shoulder and Heck stooped painfully and pitched the empty under the seat.

"Come," he said to Emil, who, already aimed down the incline of the seat, relaxed some muscle or another and slid forward then out the door. He landed on the ground and stretched then blinked at the flashing lights of a state-police car across the highway.

Next to the lit-up Dodge cruiser sat another black-and-white, and beside that was a tan county-coroner's meat wagon. Four men looked up as Heck crossed the wide strip of black pebbly asphalt. He led Emil away from the cars—he always got the dog out of the truck as soon as possible at a search scene and kept him far from car engines; exhaust dulls dogs' noses.

"Sit," Heck commanded when they were in a patch of grass upwind from the cars. "Down." Emil did as instructed, even though he eagerly noted the presence of some four-legged ladies nearby.

"Hey, Trenton," one of the men called. He was a large man, large all over, not just the belly—food round, not drink round— and his weight pulled hard at the buttons and pockets of his gray uniform. He was holding back two young female Labrador retrievers, who nosed in the dirt.

"Hiya, Charlie."

"Well, if it ain't the Cadillac of trackers." This, from one of the two young troopers standing on the roadside, a man Heck referred to, though not to his face, as "the Boy." He was a narrow-jawed youngster, six years Heck's junior in age though fifteen in appearance. Trenton Heck's idea of dealing with a budget cutback would have been to fire this kid and keep Heck himself on the force at three-quarters salary. But they hadn't asked his opinion and so the Boy, who though younger had hired on two months before Heck, was still a trooper while Trenton Heck had netted eighty-seven dollars last month carting old washing machines and water softeners to the Hammond Creek dump.

"Hey, Emil," the Boy said.

Heck nodded to him and waved to the other trooper, who called back a greeting.

Charlie Fennel and Heck walked toward the tan hearse, beside which stood a young man in a pale-green jumpsuit.

"Not much of a search party," Heck said to Fennel.

The trooper answered that they were lucky to have what they did. "There's a concert letting out at midnight or so down at the Civic Center. You hear about that?"

"Rock 'n' roll," Heck muttered.

"Uhn. Don sent a buncha troopers over there. They had some boy got shot at the last one."

"Don't they have security guards for that sort of thing?"

"Was a guard who shot the kid."

"Doesn't seem like a brilliant use of taxpayers' money, riding herd on a bunch of youngsters paying to deafen themselves."

Then too, Fennel added, the captain had put a good portion of the troops on highway detail. "He figures what with the storm, they'll be picking 'em off the pavement. Say, I hear there's a reward for catching this crazy."

Heck kept his eyes on the grass in front of him and didn't know what to say.

"Listen," Fennel continued in a whisper, "I heard about your situation, Trenton. I hope you get that money. I'm rooting for you."

"Thanks there, Charlie."

Heck had a curious relationship with Charlie Fennel. The same bullet that had left the shiny star-shaped wound in Heck's right thigh had passed first through Fennel's brother's chest as he crouched beside their patrol car, killing the trooper instantly. Heck supposed that some of the man's living blood had ridden the slug into his own body and that because of that he and Charlie Fennel were blood brothers, once removed. At times Trenton Heck thought that he and Fennel ought to be closer. The more time the men spent in each other's company, however, the less they found they had in common. They occasionally talked about a hunting or fishing trip but the plans came to nothing. It was a secret relief to both of them.

Heck and Fennel now paused beside the coroner's meat wagon. Heck lifted his head and inhaled air fragrant with the decomposition so prominent on damp autumn nights like this. He sniffed the air once more and Fennel looked at him curiously.

"No wood smoke," Heck said in response.

"Nope. There don't seem to be."

"So wherever this Hrubek's got himself to, it wasn't toward a house he could smell."

"You learn that from Emil? Heh."

Heck asked the coroner's attendant, "What happened exactly?"

The young man glanced at Fennel, silently asking permission to answer a civilian. Heck had gotten used to the demise of his own authority. When the attendant received a grunt of approval from Fennel, he explained how Hrubek had escaped then added, "We chased him for a ways."

"Chased him, did you?" Heck couldn't resist needling, "Well, it's not hardly your job to catch him. I wouldn't've blamed you if you'd just hightailed it out of here, to hell with a madman."

"Yeah, well. We didn't. We chased him." The attendant shrugged, young and far above shame.

"All right. Let's get to it." Heck noticed that Fennel had put the tracking harnesses on his dogs some time ago. This had worked them up and confused them. If they weren't immediately going on track, scenting dogs should wear only their regular collars. Heck almost said something to Fennel but didn't. How the trooper ran his dogs was his business; Trenton Heck was no longer a man-tracking instructor.

He took the red nylon harness and quarter-inch nylon track line from his pocket. Emil tensed immediately though he stayed rump-to-ground. Heck hooked him up and wrapped the end of the line around his own left wrist, contrary to the general practice of right-hand grip; drugged up and giddy though this big fellow might be, Heck remembered Haversham's warning and he wanted his shooting hand free. He then took the bag from his other jacket pocket. He opened it, pulling back the plastic from the wad of cotton shorts.

"Jesus," the Boy said, wrinkling his nose. "Dirty Jockeys?"

"Musk is the best," Heck muttered. "Yum . . ." He pushed

the dingy underwear toward the young trooper, who danced away

"Trenton, stop that! They got crazy-man jism on 'em! Keep 'em away!"

Charlie Fennel laughed hard. Heck subdued his own laughte and then called sternly to Emil, "Okay," which meant for the do to stand.

They let Emil and the bitches sniff each other, muzzle and ass as they exchanged their complicated greetings. Then Heck held Hrubek's shorts down toward the ground, taking care not to rub the cloth on the dogs' noses—just letting them get to know a smell that to a human would vanish in an instant, if it was detectable at all.

"Find!" Heck yelled. "Find, Emil!"

The three dogs started shivering and prancing, skittering in circles, noses to the ground. They snorted as they sucked in dust and sour fumes from gasoline or grease and picked out the invisible molecules of one man's odor from a million others.

"Find, find!"

The hound took the lead, straining the line, pulling Heck after him. The other dogs followed. Fennel was a big man but he was being dragged along by two frantic sixty-pound Labradors and he trotted awkwardly beside Heck, who himself struggled to keep up the pace. Soon both men were gasping for breath.

The bitches' noses dropped to the ground sporadically in almost the identical spots on the asphalt of Route 236. They were step-tracking, inhaling at each place Hrubek had put a foot on the ground. Emil tracked differently; he'd scent for a few seconds then raise his head slightly and keep it off the ground for a ways. This was line-tracking, the practice of experienced tracking dogs; continually sniffing on a step-track could exhaust an animal in a couple of hours.

Suddenly Emil veered off the road, south, and started into a field of tall grass and brush, filled with plenty of cover even for a man as large as Hrubek.

"Oh, brother," Heck muttered, surveying the murky heath into which his dog plunged. "Taking the scenic route. Here we go."

Fennel called to the Boy and the other trooper, "Follow along the road. I'll call on the squawker, we need you. And if I call, bring the scattergun."

"He's real big," the coroner's attendant shouted. "I mean, no fooling."

Kohler pulled his BMW out of the Marsden state hospital parking lot and turned onto the long access road that would take him to Route 236. He waved a friendly greeting to a security guard, who was walking quickly toward an alarm bell ringing jarringly in the lot. The guard did not respond.

Although Kohler was a physician and could write prescriptions for any drug that was legally available, Adler had instituted a rule that no controlled substances—narcotics, sedatives, anesthetics— could be dispensed in greater than single-dose quantities without his or Grimes's approval. This edict was issued after a young resident at Marsden was caught supplementing his income by selling Xanax, Miltown and Librium to local high-school students. Kohler had no time to try to bluff his way past the hospital's night pharmacist and found the steel bumper of a German car a much more efficient means than paperwork to requisition what he needed.

As he approached the highway he pulled the car to a stop and examined the fruits of his theft. The hypodermic syringe was unlike most that you'd find in a doctor's office or hospital. It was large, an inch in diameter and five inches long, made of stainless steel around a heavy glass reservoir. The needle mounted to it, protected by a clear plastic guard, was two inches long and unusually thick. Although no one admitted it, least of all the manufacturer, this was actually a livestock syringe. To M.D.s, however, it was marketed as a "heavy-duty model intended for use on patients in agitation- oriented situations."

Sitting beside the instrument were two large bottles of Innovar a general anesthetic Kohler'd picked because of its effectiveness when injected into muscle tissue—unlike most such drugs, which must be injected into the bloodstream. Familiar primarily with psychiatric drugs, Kohler knew little about Innovar other than the prescribed dosages per kilo of body weight and its contraindications. He knew too that he had enough drug to kill several human beings.

One thing he didn't know for certain but that he figured was probably accurate was that by stealing a Class II controlled substance he'd just committed a felony.

Kohler slipped the bottles and the syringe into the rust-colored backpack he carried in lieu of a briefcase then opened a small white envelope. As a bonus he'd also stolen several chlorphentermine capsules, two of which he now popped into his mouth. The doctor put the car in gear and eased forward, hoping that the diet pills would kick in soon and that when they did they'd have the desired effect. Kohler rarely took medicine of any kind and his system sometimes responded in unexpected ways—it was possible that the amphetaminelike drug would paradoxically make him drowsy. Richard Kohler prayed that this didn't happen. Tonight, he desperately needed his thoughts clear.

Tonight, he needed an edge.

An *agitation-oriented situation* indeed.

As he sped out onto Route 236, looking about him in the dark night, Kohler felt overwhelmed and helpless. He wondered if, despite their antagonisms, he should simply have leveled with Adler and enlisted the man's aid. After all, the hospital director too was trying desperately to conceal Michael's escape and to find him as quietly as possible; for once, the two medicos shared a common goal—though their motives were very different. But Kohler decided this would be a foolish, a *disastrous* thing to do, and might jeopardize Kohler's position at Marsden, perhaps even his career itself. Oh, some of Kohler's concern was perhaps paranoia—a junior version of what Michael Hrubek lived with daily. Yet there was a significant difference between Kohler and his patient: Michael was classified a paranoid because he acted as if enemies sought his darkest secrets while in fact his enemies and secrets were imaginary.

In his own case, Kohler reflected as his car accelerated to eighty, they were quite real.

8

Like a quarter horse cutting cattle from a herd, Emil would wheel and swerve, crossing back and forth through brush or over scrub grass until he picked up the scent once more.

The dog found the spot where Hrubek had tangled with the orderlies then returned to the road. Now, he leapt off the asphalt again and charged back into the brush, the Labradors following his lead.

The searchers trotted through this field for a few minutes, heading generally east, away from the hospital, and parallel to Route 236.

At one point as they were making their way through tall, whispering grass, Heck jerked the lead and growled, "Sit!" Emil stopped abruptly. Heck felt him shivering with excitement as if the track line were an electric wire. "Down!" Reluctantly the dog went horizontal. The bitches wouldn't respond to Charlie Fennel's similar command; they kept tugging at their lines. He pulled them back once or twice and shouted several times for them to sit but they wouldn't. Wishing that Fennel, as well as the dogs, would keep quiet, Heck managed to ignore this bad discipline and strode ahead, playing a long black flashlight over the ground.

"Lookit what I turned up," Heck said. He shone the light on a fresh bare footprint in the earth.

"God double damn," Fennel whispered. "That's size thirteen, if it's an inch."

"Well, we *know* he's big." Heck touched the deep indentation made by the ball of a huge foot. "What I'm saying is, he's sprinting."

"Sure, he's *running*. You're right. That Dr. Adler at the hospital said he'd just be wandering around in a daze."

"He's in some damn big hurry. Moving like there's no tomorrow. Come on, we've got a lot of time to make up for. Find, Emil! Find!"

Fennel started the other dogs on the trail, following the footprints, and they ran ahead. But curiously Emil didn't take the lead. He rose on his muscular legs but stayed put. His nose went into the air and he flared his nostrils, swiveling his head from side to side.

"Come on," Fennel called.

Heck was silent. He watched Emil gazing right to left and back once more. The hound turned due south and lifted his head. Heck called to Fennel, "Hold up. Shut your light out."

"What?"

"Just do it!"

With a soft click the two men and three dogs were enveloped in darkness. It occurred to Heck, as it must have to Fennel, that they were totally vulnerable. The madman might be downwind, ten feet away, with a tire iron or broken bottle.

"Come on, Trenton."

"Let's don't be in too big of a hurry here."

Fifty yards north they could see the slow convoy of the squad car and Heck's pickup. Emil paced, his head wagging back and forth in the air. Heck studied him intently.

"What's he doing?" Fennel whispered. "The track's here. Can't he tell?"

"He knows that. There's something else. Airborne scent maybe. It's not as strong as the track scent but there's something there."

It was possible, Heck considered, that Hrubek, huge and sweating, had given off masses of scent, which would eddy and gather here like smoke, remaining for hours on a humid night like this. Emil was probably scenting on the cloud of these molecules. Still,

Heck was reluctant to pull the hound away. He had faith in the cleverness of animals. He'd seen raccoons dexterously unscrew the lids of jam jars and had once watched a cumbersome grizzly bear (the same one that had eyed him so voraciously) carefully poke not just one but two delicate claw holes in the top of a 7-Up can then drink down the soda without spilling a drop. And Emil, in his master's informed opinion, was ten times smarter than any bear.

Heck waited a moment longer but neither heard nor saw anything.

"Come, Emil." He turned and started away.

But Emil would not come.

Heck squinted into the night. There was a faint glow from the sky but most of the moonlight was now obscured by cloud. Come on, boy, he thought, let's get back to work. Our reward money's jogging east at about five miles an hour.

But Emil dropped his nose and pushed into the grass. He quivered. Heck lifted his pistol in front of him and swung aside a thick whip of green and beige shoots. They continued a few feet farther into the maze of grass. It was there that they found what Emil had been seeking.

The dog was no setter but he was as good as pointing at the quarry—a scrap of paper in a plastic Baggie.

Fennel had come up slowly. He put his back to Heck and scanned the grass nervously, his service automatic sweeping left to right. "Bait?"

This had also occurred to Heck. Felons accustomed to being hunted by dogs sometimes leave a pungent article of clothing or spray of urine in a tactical place on the trail. When the tracker and his hound stop to examine the spot, the fugitive attacks from behind. But Heck studied Emil and said, "Don't think so. He was still around, Emil'd smell more of him."

Still, as he picked up the bag, Heck kept his eyes not on the plastic but on the wall of grass surrounding him, and there were several pounds of pressure on the stiff German trigger of his gun. He handed Fennel the bag and they stepped into a clearing, where they could read without fear of immediate attack.

"From a newspaper," the trooper said. "Tore it out. One side's part of an ad for bras, the other's a, hey, lookie . . . A map. Downtown Boston. Historical sites, you know."

"Boston?"

"Yep. We call the highway patrol? Tell 'em to keep the main roads to Massachusetts covered?"

And Heck, who saw his precious ten thousand dollars vanishing before him, said, "Let's hold off for a bit on that. Maybe he left this here to lead us off."

"Naw, Trenton. If he'd've wanted us to find it, he would've left it in the road, not in man-high grass."

"Maybe," Heck said, very discouraged. "But I still think—"

Crack . . .

A fierce noise like a gunshot sounded next to Heck's ear and he swung around, heart pounding, pistol raised. The volume on Charlie Fennel's walkie-talkie had been full on when he received the transmission. Fennel turned down the squelch and volume knobs and palmed the unit. He spoke softly into it. In the distance, on the road, the red and blue roof lights on the Boy's squad car started spinning.

"Fennel here. Go ahead." He lowered his head as he listened.

What *are* they doing? Heck wondered.

Fennel signed off and put the walkie-talkie back on his belt. He said, "Come on. They've found him."

Heck's heart fell. "They *got* him? Oh, damn."

"Well, not quite. He got himself all the way to a truck stop in Watertown—"

"Watertown? That's seven miles from here."

"—and tried to hitch a ride up to, guess where, Boston. The truck driver told him no so Hrubek took off on foot heading north.

We'll drive over there and pick up the trail. Man, I hope he's winded. I myself don't feel like a half-hour run. Don't go looking so sorrowful, Trenton, you'll be a rich man yet. He's not but a half hour away."

Fennel and the bitches bounded back toward the road.

"Come, Emil," Heck called. The hound hesitated just a moment longer and slowly followed his master, clearly reluctant to forsake the grassy fields, damp and cold though they were, for the slippery plastic bench seat of an old, smelly Chevrolet.

When she heard the deliberate footfalls coming up from the basement stairs, the heavy steps, the dull clink of metal, Lis Atcheson understood immediately, and the mood of the night at once turned icy.

Owen walked into the doorway of the greenhouse and looked at his wife, who was pulling more burlap bags from the stack near the lath house.

"Oh, no!" Lis whispered. She shook her head and then sat on a bench made of hard cherry wood. Owen paused then sat beside her, smoothing her hair over her ear the way he did when he explained things to her—business things, estate things, legal things. But no explanation was necessary tonight. For Owen was no longer in his work clothes. He wore a dark-green shirt and matching baggy pants—the outfit he wore under a bright-orange slicker when he went hunting. On his feet were his expensive waterproof boots.

And in his hands, a deer rifle and a pistol.

"You can't do it, Owen."

He set the guns aside. "I just talked to the sheriff again. They've got four men out after him. Only *four* goddamn men! And he's already in Watertown."

"But that's east of here. He's going *away* from us."

"That doesn't matter, Lis. Look how far he's traveled. That's seven or eight miles from where he escaped. On foot. He's not wandering around in a daze at all. He's up to something."

"I don't want you to do this."

"I'm just going to see exactly what they're doing to catch him." He spoke in an austere, assured voice. It was her father's voice. It was a voice that could hypnotize her.

Still, she said, "Don't lie to me, Owen."

And like Andrew L'Auberget, Owen's eyes contracted, hard as a tick's back. He had a faint smile on his face but she didn't believe it for a second. She might very well have been speaking to one of the marble-eyed trophies Owen had nailed up on his den wall, for all the effect her words had on him. She touched his arm and let her fingers linger on the thick cloth. He pressed his hand over hers.

"Don't go," she said. She pulled him to her. She felt a surge of unfocused ardor. It was more than the memory of their liaison earlier. His strength, his gravity, the hunger in his face—they were all immensely seductive. She kissed him hard, open-mouthed. She wondered if the arousal she felt was truly lust, or was rather an attempt to keep him encircled in her arms all this long night until the danger was past.

Whatever her motives might have been, though, the embrace had no effect. He held her for a moment then stepped to the window. She rose and stood behind him. "Why don't you say it? You're going to hunt him down."

She studied her husband's back and the reflection of a face that should, she supposed, be vastly troubled. Yet he seemed very much at peace with himself. "I'm not going to do anything illegal."

"Oh? What do you call murder?"

"Murder?" he whispered harshly, spinning around, and nodding toward the upstairs of the house. "Don't you ever *think* about what you're saying? What if she heard you?"

"Portia isn't going to turn you in. *That's* not the point. The point is you can't just track somebody down and—"

"You forget what happened at Indian Leap," he snapped. "I sometimes think *I* was more upset by it than you were."

She turned away as if slapped.

"Lis . . ." He calmed quickly, wincing at his own outburst. "I'm sorry. I didn't mean that. . . . Look, he's not a human being. He's an animal. You know what he's capable of. *You* more than anybody."

He continued his argument smoothly: "He escaped this time, he could escape again. He got away long enough to mail that letter to you when he was in Gloucester. Next time he's there maybe he'll wander off. And head this way."

"They'll catch him tonight. They'll put him in jail this time."

"If he's still mentally incompetent he goes right back into the hospital. That's the law. Lis, look at the newscasts, they're emptying the hospitals. You hear about it every day. Maybe next year, the year after, they'll just turn him out on the street. And we'd never know when he might show up here. In the yard. In the *bedroom*."

Then the first tears started and she knew that she'd lost the argument. She had probably known it when she first heard his steps on the basement stairs. Owen was not always right, she reflected, but he was perpetually confident. It seemed wholly natural for him to load up the 4x4 with guns and cruise off into the middle of a stormy night to hunt down a psychopath.

"I want you and Portia to go to the Inn. We've done enough sandbagging."

She was shaking her head.

"I'm insisting."

"No! Owen, the water's already up two feet and it hasn't even started to rain here. The part by the dock? Where the creek flows in? We need another foot or two there."

"I finished that part. I added plenty of bags. It's three feet high. If the crest's higher than that, there's nothing we could do anyway."

She spoke coldly. "Fine. Go if you want. Go play soldier. But I'm staying. I still have to tape the greenhouse."

"Forget the greenhouse. We're insured against wind damage."

"I don't *care* about the money. For heaven's sake, those roses are my life. I'd never forgive myself if anything happened to them." She sat again on the bench. Lis had noticed that she commanded less authority standing beside her husband, with him a foot taller. Seated, though much lower, she paradoxically felt more his equal.

"Nothing's going to happen. A few broken windows."

"You heard the report. Eighty-mile-an-hour winds."

Owen sat beside her and gripped her thigh, pressing hard. His elbow was against her breast. Instead of comfort she felt vulnerability, her defenses breached by his proximity.

"I'm not going to argue this," he said evenly. "I don't want to have to worry about you. I want you to go to the Inn. Once they get him—"

"Once *you* get him, you mean."

"Once they get him I'll call you. You two come back to the house and we'll finish the work together."

"Owen, he's going the other way."

His eyes flashed. "Are you trying to deny it? Lis, he's run seven miles in forty-five minutes. He's up to something. Think about it. Why're you being so damn stubborn? There's a killer out there. A psychotic killer! He knows your name and address."

Lis said nothing. She breathed shallowly.

Owen pressed his face against her hair. He whispered, "Don't you remember him? Don't you remember the trial?"

Lis happened to glance up and see on the wall a stone bust of a leering gargoyle. She heard in her memory Hrubek chanting, "Lisbone, Lis-bone, my Eve of betrayal. My pretty Lis-bone."

A cheerful voice filled the room. "Little late for fishing, isn't it, Owen?" Portia stood in the doorway, eyeing his outfit. "The party breaking up?"

Owen stepped away from his wife but he kept his eyes on her.

"I'll pack a few things," Lis said.

"Going somewhere?" her sister asked.

"The Inn," Owen said.

"So soon? I thought that was later on the program. When the crazy man showed up to boogie. Oops, sorry. Was that in bad taste?"

"He's traveled farther than they thought. I'm going to talk to the sheriff about what they're doing to find him. Lis and you're going to a bed-and-breakfast up the road."

"God, he's not coming this way?" Portia asked.

"No, he's going east." Lis looked at her sister. "It'll just be better to spend the night at the Inn."

"Okay by me." Portia shrugged and went to collect her backpack.

Lis rose. Owen squeezed her leg. What, she wondered, does *that* mean? Thanks? I won? I love you? Hand me my guns, woman?

"I won't be long. A few hours, tops. Come lock the door after me."

They walked into the kitchen and he kissed her for a long moment but she could see that his mind was already in the fields and on the roads where his prey wandered. He pocketed the pistol and slung his deer rifle over his shoulder. He then walked outside.

Lis double-locked the door behind him, watching him climb into the truck. She stepped to the window and looked down at the garage. The black Cherokee backed out and paused for a moment. The interior of the truck was dark and she wondered if he was waving to her. She lifted her own hand.

He pulled into the driveway. Of course Owen was right. He knew more about Hrubek than all of the pros did—the troopers, the sheriffs, the doctors. And, what's more, Lis knew too. She knew Hrubek wasn't harmless, that he wasn't wandering around like a dim animal, that he had something on his mind, damaged though it was. She knew these things not as facts but as messages from her heart.

Her cheek pressed against the window for a moment. She backed away and gazed at the uneven, bubble-flecked glass, realizing something she'd never thought of—that these panes had been made two and a half centuries ago. How, Lis wondered, had the fragile glass survived intact all those turbulent years? When she focused again on the yard, the truck's taillights were gone. Yet she continued for a long time to gaze at the shadowy driveway down which the truck had vanished.

Here I am, she thought in disbelief, a pioneer wife, staring into the wilderness after my husband, who's traveling through the night, on his way to kill the man who would kill me.

The lingering dust raised by the vehicles settled and their taillights vanished behind a hill far to the east. The night was still again. Overhead the clouds that swept in from the west obscured a sallow moon, which sat over a rock outcropping above the deserted highway.

There was as yet no hint of storm. No breeze at all. And for a moment this portion of highway was absolutely silent.

Then Michael Hrubek, pulling his precious Irish cap down over his head, pushed aside the grass and walked directly into the middle of Route 236. He replaced his pistol in the backpack.

GET TO

These words swam into his mind and floated there for a moment, doing slow loop-the-loops. He knew they were vitally important but their meaning kept evading him. They vanished and he was left with a prickling reminder of their absence.

What do they *mean*? he wondered. What was he supposed to *do* with them?

He stood on the asphalt and walked in a circle, searching through his confused mind for the answer. What did *GET TO* mean? Filled with a churning dread, he knew that *they* were jamming his thoughts. They: the soldiers who'd just been pursuing him.

Let's think about this.

GET TO

What could it *possibly* mean?

Hrubek again looked east down the highway, the direction in which the soldiers had disappeared. Conspirators! With their dogs on ropes, sniffing and growling. Fuckers! One man in gray, one man in blue. One Confederate soldier. And one Union, the man with the limp. He was the one Hrubek hated the most.

That man was a con-*spirat*-or, a fucking Union soldier.

GET TO

GETTO

Slowly the hatred began to fade as he thought about how he'd fooled them. He'd been only thirty feet away from the soldiers, holding his cocked gun, crouching down in a bowl of dirt high on a ledge of rock above them. They'd eased into the grass and found the bag he'd carefully placed there. Shivering with fear he'd heard their alien voices, heard the wet snorting of the dogs, the rustle of grass.

Hrubek saw the letters again, *GETO*. They floated past, then vanished.

Hrubek recalled the colored lights on the police car starting to spin. A moment later the soldiers returned to the cars and the one who hated him most, the lean fucker in blue, the one with the limp, got into the truck with his dog. They sped off east.

Hrubek crouched down and put his cheek against the damp road. Then he stood up.

"Good night, ladies . . ."

It was coming back to him. *GETO*. He squinted down the highway, westward. He was seeing not the black strip of asphalt but rather the letters, which slowly stopped swirling and began to line up for him. Like good little soldier boys.

GETO 4

Hrubek's mind was filling with thoughts, complicated thoughts, wonderful thoughts. He started walking. "I'm gonna see you cry. . . ."

GETON 4

There!

There it was! He began trotting toward it. The letters were all falling into place.

GETON 47 M

The dogs were gone, the conspirators too. The fucker with the limp, Dr. Richard, the hospital, the orderlies . . . all of his enemies were behind him. He'd fooled them all!

Michael Hrubek searched his soul and found that his fear was under control and that his mission was as lucid as a perfect diamond. He paused and set one of the tiny animal skulls in a nest of grass at the base of the post, muttering a short prayer. He then walked past the green sign that said *RIDGETON 47 MILES*, turned off the road into the cover of brush and began to hurry due west.

9

On her parted lips he rubs the petal of a yellow rose.

His eyes are fixed on hers, two feet away, close enough for him to penetrate the orbit of her perfume, not so close each feels the heat radiating from the other's body in this chill room. She reaches out for him but he motions curtly for her to stop. Her hands acquiesce but then rebelliously reach slowly to her own shoulders and dislodge the satin straps of her nightgown. They fall away and the cream-colored garment drops to her waist. His eyes stray to her breasts but he does not touch her and, as he again commands, she lowers her hands to her sides.

From the green-and-russet tangle of a rosebush, the reigning plant in the darkened greenhouse, he lifts away two more petals. These, pink. He holds them in his large, confident fingers, and lifts them to her eyes, which she closes slowly. She feels the petal skin brush over her lids and continue down her cheek. Again he makes a circuit of her mouth, both petals coursing slowly over her half-open lips.

She wets these lips and tells him playfully that he's destroying one of her prize flowers. But he again shakes his head, insisting on silence. She leans toward him and nearly succeeds in planting a contracted nipple against his forearm but he sways back and their bodies don't touch. A petal caresses her chin then slips from his fingers, spiraling to the slate greenhouse path on which they stand. He snatches another from the shivering bush. Still, her eyes are closed, her hands are at her sides. As he has insisted.

Now, he brushes her earlobes so gently she doesn't at first feel the touch of the flower's skin. He presses the valleys behind her ears and caresses the soft wisps of white-gold hair.

Now, her shoulders, muscled from carrying tubs of earth like that out of which these rosebushes grow.

Now, her throat. Her head tilts back and if she opened her eyes, she'd see a cluster of pale stars awash in the speckled glass. Now, he weakens and kisses her quickly, the petals disappearing from his spreading fingers, which grip her neck and pull her to him. Her breath, matching her desire, rushes inside her, pulling with it his own. She moves her head in a slow circle to increase the pressure of his touch. But he's too fast for her and he dodges away. He stands back again, dropping the crushed petals and tugging more from the thorny stem beside them.

Her eyes still are closed and the anticipation grows unbearable as she awaits the next touch, which occurs on the lower part of her modest breasts, and she seats her teeth as her lips spread in what could be taken for a snarl but is rather evidence of will. The roses move slowly along the arcs of her breasts and she feels too the drag of several of his fingers, a much rougher feel yet equally provocative. . . . Soft and rough. Fingernails, petal flesh. The heat of his touch, the cold of the greenhouse floor on her bare feet.

She feels pressure as slight as a breath. She's astonished that such a large man is capable of such subtle motion. He kisses her again and the sensations from his lips and fingers fire through her.

But he won't hurry. The pressure fades and vanishes and she opens her eyes with a plea for him not to stop. He again closes her eyes and she obeys, listening to a curious ripping sound. Then silence, as her neck and breasts are covered by two huge handsful of petals, which fall away from his hands and trickle to their feet.

He kisses each of her eyes and she takes this as the sign that he wants her to open them. They gaze at each other for a moment and she sees that, no, not all the petals have fallen. One remains. He

*holds it between them, a bright-red oval from a John Armstrong
plant. He opens his mouth and places it on his tongue, like a priest
dispensing host. She desperately works the nightgown over her hips
and reaches for him, enveloping him in her arms, sliding her hands
into the small of his back. He leans forward. Their tongues connect
and as she pulls him down on top of her, they transfer the red petal
back and forth until it disintegrates and they swallow the fragments
as they swallow each other.*

Lis Atcheson remained lost for a moment in this memory then
opened her eyes and gazed out over the flowers in the greenhouse,
listening to the pleasant hiss of spray from the watering system.

"Oh, Owen," she whispered. "Owen . . ."

She set down her packed suitcase and strolled through the damp,
fragrant room, then out the lath-house door to the flagstone patio.
She looked out over the lake.

The black water lapped persistently.

Troubled, she noticed that the level of the lake had risen another
several inches in the last twenty minutes. She glanced to her left,
toward a low-lying portion of the property—the dip in the yard
behind the garage, where Owen had stacked the extra bags. A creek
trickled into the lake there and the marshy shoreline was obscured
with rushes. She couldn't see how well the barrier was holding but
she didn't particularly want to walk down the narrow, slippery path
to find out. Owen was a meticulous—often fanatic—worker and
she guessed that he'd built a solid levee. Her own engineering
efforts, in the center of the yard, looked shoddy. The water was
almost up to the level of the bags she'd dozed upon after she and
Owen had made love; it was only eighteen inches beneath the
top row.

She walked closer to the lake. Above her, no stars. She couldn't
even discern the underside of the clouds; the sky was flat and
smooth, a gray-blue monotone, like the flesh of a shark. Were the

clouds moving or not? Were they a hundred feet in the air, or ten thousand? She couldn't tell.

Vague motion, nearby, startled her. The shell of the large tortoise jerked again as the ungainly creature lumbered toward the lake. Fiercely intent on its goal, the animal scuttled over rocks and roots too high for its reptilian feet, slipping often. Why the urgency? Lis wondered. Was some eerie premonition about the storm prompting the thing to seek the safety of the lake? But what would a tortoise have to fear from the rain? With a loud splash the animal caromed off a willow root and sliced into the water. There, it became a perfect airfoil and cruised eloquently just beneath the surface for a short distance then dove out of sight. Lis watched its wake vanish and the water turn once again to rippling black silk.

She strolled back toward the house, through wide, trellis-covered patches of overturned dirt—her formal garden. She paused before the one rosebush that still retained a number of petals. When she was young, Lis had plotted to dye her hair the copper color of a plant this shade—an Arizona grandiflora—and paid for it with a whipping when her father, in one of his Saturday-morning raids on the girls' room, discovered the Clairol, hidden beneath her mattress.

She clicked a brittle thorn with her nail then lifted away a few dead petals. She rubbed them against her cheek.

The horizon in the west flared brilliantly with a broad gray-green flash. It had vanished by the time her eyes flicked to that portion of the sky.

The petals fell from Lis's hands.

She heard the kitchen door opening then closing. "I'm ready," Portia called. "You have your suitcase?"

Lis walked to the house. Gazing at the yellow windows she said, "Listen, I have to tell you—I've changed my mind."

"You what?"

Lis set her suitcase inside the kitchen door. "I'm going to finish the sandbagging. Taping the greenhouse. It could take an hour or so. I'd really like you to stay too but if you want to leave, I understand. I'll call you a cab."

Emil was sorely tempted by the aroma of grilling burgers and onions but he knew his job and kept his butt planted on the ground.

Trenton Heck himself cast a longing eye toward the truck-stop diner but at the moment the reward money was his main thought and he too ignored the smell of a much-desired cheeseburger. He continued his discussion with the Highway Patrol trooper.

"And he really seemed set on Boston, did he?" Heck asked.

"That's what the driver said. He was babbling about it being the home of our country or something."

Fennel, drawing nearby, said, "He was a history major."

Heck looked up in surprise.

"Yup. That's what I heard."

"He went to *college*?" This made Trenton Heck, with only eleven hours of credits toward an associate degree, feel very bad.

"One year only, before he started to go wacko. But he got himself some A's."

"Well. A's. Damn." Heck pushed aside his personal chagrin and asked the HP trooper if he'd have the truck driver step outside for a minute.

"Uhm, he's gone."

"He's *gone*? Didn't you tell him to wait?"

The trooper shrugged, looking placidly into the civilian's eyes. "It's an escape situation, not an arrest situation. I got his name and address. Figured he didn't need to stay around to be a witness or anything."

Heck muttered to Fennel, "Address isn't going to be real helpful. I mean, what're we supposed to do? Send him a postcard?"

The trooper said, "I asked him a bunch of stuff."

Heck slipped the harness off Emil. The trooper looked even younger than the Boy and would have no seniority over anybody.

The Highway Patrol had a separate budget for salaries and they hardly ever fired anybody. Heck'd had the chance to put in for Highway Patrol when he first joined. But, no, he wanted to fight real crime.

"What was he wearing?"

"Overalls. Boots. Workshirt. Tweed cap."

"No jacket?"

"Didn't seem to be."

"Was he drinking?"

"Well, the driver didn't say. I didn't exactly ask that. Didn't see any need to."

Heck continued, "Was he carrying anything? Bag or weapon. Walking stick?"

The trooper looked uneasily at his notes then at Fennel, who nodded for him to answer the questions. "I don't exactly know."

"Was he threatening?"

"No. Just kind of goofy, the driver said."

Heck grunted in frustration. Then he asked, "Oh, one more thing. Just how big *is* he?"

"The driver said about six five, six six. Three fifty, if he's a pound. WWF wrestler, you know. Legs like a side of beef."

"Side of beef." Heck gazed into the blackness in the east.

Fennel asked him, "Is there enough trail to follow?"

"It's not bad. But I wish it'd rain." Nothing brought out a latent scent better than a gentle mist.

"To hear the weatherman tell it, you're going to get that wish in spades."

Heck hooked up Emil again and refreshed the scent memories of the dogs with Hrubek's shorts. "Find, find!"

Emil took off down the shoulder of the road, Heck paying out the dark-red rope until he felt the twenty-foot knot. Then he followed. Fennel and the retrievers too. But they hadn't gone fifty feet before Emil turned and nosed slowly toward an unlit, dilapidated house squatting in an overgrown yard. A spooky-looking place, with a sagging roof and shingles like old snake scales. In the window was a sign. *Hunting Goods. ETC. Deer dressed and mounted. Pelts bought and sold. Trout too*

"Think he's in there?" The Boy uncomfortably eyed the black windows.

"Hard to say. All that animal work'd confuse even Emil."

Heck and Fennel led the dogs to a cockeyed fencepost and tied them up. The men drew their side arms and simultaneously chambered bullets and put the safeties on. Heck thought, Don't let me get shot again. Oh, please. I got no insurance this time. Though what was behind this prayer wasn't hospital bills of course but the horror of a scalding bullet.

"Trent, you don't have to do this."

"From the sound of this guy, you need everybody you've got."

Conceding, Fennel nodded then motioned the Boy around back. He and Heck walked onto the front porch quietly. Heck looked at Fennel, who shrugged and knocked on the door. There was no answer. Heck leaned forward and looked through a grimy window. He leapt back suddenly. "Jesus! Oh!" His voice clicked into a high register.

Fennel drew down on the window with his Glock. He squinted. Then laughed. Six inches away, through the muddy glass, was the rearing form of a black bear staring out at them, taxidermied into ferocity.

"Goddamn," Heck said reverently. "Son of a bitch, I nearly dampened my pants there."

Fennel pointed to a sign propped in another window. *Closed First Two Weeks of November. Happy huntin'*

"He's telling everybody he's going away? Don't this fellow know about burglaries?"

"He's got himself a watch-bear."

Heck studied the creature with admiration. "That'd be the first thing *I'd* steal."

Then they found the door that Hrubek had kicked in. The men entered cautiously, covering each other. They found the traces of the madman's shopping spree but it was clear he was no longer here. They reholstered their guns and returned outside. Fennel told the Boy to call Haversham and tell him where they were and that Hrubek did in fact seem to be making for Boston.

They were about to continue up the highway when the Boy called, "Hold up a minute, Charlie. There's something here you ought to see."

Heck and Fennel ordered the dogs to sit and then walked around to the back of the building to where the young man was standing, hand on his own pistol. "Look there." He was pointing inside a work shed. There was blood on the ground just inside the doorway.

"Jesus." Out came the Walther again. The safety clicked off.

Heck eased into the shed. The place was chockablock with a thousand odds and ends: hoses, boxes, animal skulls, bones, broken furniture, rusted tools, auto parts.

"Check it out. Over there. We got a 'coon bit the big one."

Fennel shone his light on the limp corpse of a raccoon.

"Think he'd do that? Why?"

"Goddamn," Heck whispered in dismay. He was looking not at the body of the animal, however, but at a narrow beam in the ceiling from which dangled some spring animal traps, toothless but big—the sort that would easily snap the neck of a fox or badger or raccoon.

Or the leg of a dog.

The reason for Heck's dismay wasn't the traps themselves but rather the three empty pegs where, presumably, three other traps had hung until not long ago. Several large bloody bootprints were directly below the pegs.

Heck asked, "Your girls heel?"

"Not when they're on track. Emil?"

"He's slow to, if the scent's fresh. We'll have to tie the lines back and keep 'em next to us. Hell, if he takes to the grass we'll just about have to crawl on our bellies. Hrubek'll be in Boston by the time we get to the county line."

They walked back to the highway and shortened the lines as Heck instructed. He left his pickup at the truck stop with the third deputy, who remained there in case Hrubek wandered back this way. The Boy accompanied Heck and Fennel in his squad car, the headlights dark, just the amber flashers on. The dogs caught a whiff of the scent and started east once more.

"Down the middle of the friggin' road." Fennel laughed nervously. "This boy *is* nuts, that's for damn sure."

But Heck didn't respond. The giddy excitement of earlier in the evening was gone. The night had turned coarse. Their quarry was no longer a big silly fellow, and Trenton Heck felt the same chill he remembered when, four years ago, outside of a neon-lit 7-Eleven, he'd glanced at what he thought was a branch moving in the breeze and saw instead a sphere of muzzle flash and felt a ripping jolt in his leg, as the asphalt leapt up to meet his forehead.

"You think he'd set traps for *dogs*?" Fennel muttered. "Nobody'd do that. Nobody'd hurt a dog."

Heck reached down and held up his hound's right ear, in which was a smooth hole the exact size of a .30-'06 slug. Fennel whistled out his disgust at humankind, and Trenton Heck called, "Find, Emil, find!"

Lis stood in the greenhouse, taping bold X's over the glass that she could remember being glazed into place twenty-five years ago, her mother standing in the construction site, arms crossed, her austere eye on the contractors. Often she frowned because she believed that people wouldn't cheat you if it was obvious that you suspected they were capable of it.

Taping windows as she went, Lis moved slowly around the large room, which was filled with hybrid tea roses in all shades, and grandiflora blushes dotted with the blood-red John Armstrongs, and High Noon yellow climbers twining around an antique trellis. She had large-cluster floribunda Iceberg whites and Fashion corals. A thousand flowers, ten thousand petals.

She preferred the striking shades, the stark colors, especially in the most fragile of flowers.

Recalling the thousands of hours she'd spent here—as a girl, helping her mother, then more recently by herself—she pictured the many times she'd cut back shoots, pruned flowered laterals and snipped away unvigorous stems. Her hands, thorn-pricked and red, would scoop a dormant eye from the budding and peel the bark to make a shield then slide it into the t-cut rootstock, binding the incision with raffia.

Glancing at several recent grafts, she heard a sound behind her and turned to see Portia rummaging through a box on the floor. She was no longer wearing her Manhattan outfit but had finally acknowledged that she was in L. L. Bean country and accepted Lis's offer of jeans, sweater and Topsiders. Lis was overcome with an urge to thank her again for staying. But the girl wasn't interested in gratitude. She seized several rolls of masking tape and disappeared, saying, "Too fucking many windows in this house."

Her footsteps pounded up the stairs, a teenager sprinting to take a phone call.

Lis was suddenly aware of the greenhouse's overhead lights, one bank of which Owen had turned on when he was looking for burlap bags. She now doused them. Lis respected the daily cycle of plants—in the same way that she herself never woke to an alarm if she could avoid it. The rhythm of our bodies, she believed, is linked to our souls' pulse. Plants are no different and in deference to them Lis had installed, in addition to five-hundred-nanometer artificial-sunlight lamps for overcast days, a series of dim blue and green bulbs for nighttime hours. These lights let her flowers sleep—for she believed plants did sleep—while illuminating the greenhouse.

This was what horticulturists call a warm greenhouse. Ruth L'Auberget had scattered archaic heaters around the room but they never worked well. It seemed as if the woman was daunted by technology and had been content to let nature and fate decide whether her roses prospered or died. That wasn't good enough for her daughter. This was after all, Lis reasoned, the computer age, and she had the place outfitted with a microprocessor climate-control system that kept the temperature above sixty-two degrees even on the coldest of nights and operated the automated vents along the roof's peak and roller shades on the south-facing panes (sunlight being as potentially dangerous as frost).

On one side of the thirty-five-by-twenty-foot room were the cuttings, rooted in sand, and the seedlings; on the other were the growing plats for mature bushes, and propagation benches. Soil-warming cables snaked under the cutting area, and hoses, trickle-irrigation pipelines and capillary sand benches provided the water. The connected potting area and lath house were floored in concrete; the greenhouse floor itself was gravel, through which wound a serpentine path of slate—also selected by Lis (to replace the original concrete). The slate was deep green-blue and had been picked by Lis as a reminder of a rose yet to be, the L'Auberget hybrid. This was an ambition of hers—to develop a luminescent teal-colored rose, an All-American Rose Selections designation in her name.

The crossbreeding of this flower had a particular appeal because she'd been told it was impossible; fellow rosarians assured her that the elusive color couldn't be bred. What's more, she was bucking the trend. The current strategy among growers was to cultivate for fragrance and disease resistance. But color and form, now traits in disrepute, were what excited Lis Atcheson. Logically she appreciated the difficulty of the crossbreed. But the irony is that by nature rose lovers have deep romantic streaks and aren't easily discouraged. So, working with a number of yellow varieties and pinks and the Blue Moon hybrid tea, Lis spent hours here grafting and budding as if it were merely a matter of time until she found the evasive color.

From literature, Lis had learned the transcendence of the imagination, which she'd come to believe was God's main prize to us, all things else, even love, being more or less honorable mentions. But from flowers, she learned a better lesson—the persistence of beauty: petals bursting, growing, falling, and curling into dry, colorful flakes.

Roses were more than animate to her; they were virtually human. "Think about it," she'd tell students of hers invited to the greenhouse for informal Saturday-afternoon horticultural lectures. "The history of roses? They migrated west to Europe and America, mostly from the Orient. Their culture? They grow in increasingly sophisticated social clusters. And how about religion? Roses've had as bad a time on *that* subject as we have. They were burned by early Christians because of pagan—excuse the expression—roots. And then what happened? The Pope converted them. Now, ask a Catholic what roses represent—Mary, of course. That's the Mother, by the way, not the prostitute."

Lis's love of flowers began when she was around nine. Skinny and tall, the girl would herd Portia into the huge backyard, where their mother's helper presided. The imported au pair would send the girls on missions to find wildflowers of certain colors, after of course delivering the litany of warnings: the lake, snakes, hornets, bees, abandoned wells, strangers, men with candy, on and on. (The caveats were the product of Andrew L'Auberget; no chubby, carefree Dutch girl could possibly find the world so threatening.)

The speech delivered, paranoia invoked, Jolande would then dole out the assignments. "Leesbonne, a golden flur. Breeng me a gold flur."

Off the children would go.

"Leesbonne, now a red one. A red flur . . . Be careful of that, how you call it, beehive. Poortia, a red one . . ."

The girls would charge off into the woods and return with the blossoms. The daughters would then ask the big girl to trim and wash the bouquet and the trio would deliver the works of art to Ruth L'Auberget, who would nod with approval and thank the girls. She would then tie the blossoms into bright arrangements for the rectory office where she spent her afternoons.

This combination of aesthetics and generosity was irresistible to Lis, and she would sit at the dinner table, too timid to speak, but praying that Mother would report to Father about the flowers—or that talkative Portia would blurt the story to him. Impatient with religion, Andrew L'Auberget only managed to tolerate his wife's involvement in St. John's (it was, the liquor merchant was fast to joke, her only vice). Still, he usually dispensed some backhanded praise. "Ah, very good. Good for you, Lisbonne. And Portia too. You were careful of thorns and wasps?"

His face was stern but Lis believed she heard pleasure in his voice. "Yes, Father."

"And don't run through tall grass. Has our Jolande been careful with you? Broken legs can turn gangrenous very easily. Then off they come. Zip! How about the Reverend Dalcott? He going to snatch you up in a bag and turn you into little Episcopalians?"

"Andrew."

"No, Daddy. He has yellow teeth and his shirt smells funny."

"Portia!"

If he was in a good mood, Father might recite some Robert Burns or John Donne. " '*O my love's like a red, red rose. . . .*' "

Lis harbored a secret belief that the bouquets she'd delivered to her mother had inspired her to build the greenhouse and to start tending roses all year round.

Flowers were what Lis thought about too when her father's mood grew dark and the inevitable willow whip descended on her exposed buttocks. The image of an orange hybrid seemed somehow to anesthetize much of the pain.

Through the mottled windows she now gazed toward the very tree—a black willow—that had sacrificed hundreds of young shoots so that two daughters might grow into proper women. She could see only a vague form, like an image in a dream. It seemed to be just a lighter version of the darkness that filled the yard tonight.

Lis squinted and gazed past the tree. It was then that she saw a curious shape in the water.

What *is* that? she wondered.

Walking outside, she looked again—at a portion of the shoreline a hundred yards from the house. It was a configuration of shapes she'd never noticed. Then she understood—the water had risen so far that it was ganging near the top of the old dam. What she was looking at was a white rowboat that had slipped its moorings and floated to the concrete rim. Half the rocky beach beside the dam was obscured. In thirty years, the water had never been this high. . . . The dam! The thought struck Lis like a slap. She'd forgotten completely about the dam. It was of course the lowest spot on the property. If the lake overflowed, the water would fill the low culvert behind it and flood the yard.

Suddenly from her youth she recalled a sluice gate in the dam, operated by a large wheel. Opening this gate diverted the water to a creek that flowed into the Marsden River a mile or so downstream. She recalled her father's opening the gate once many years ago after a sudden spring thaw. Was it still there? And, if so, did it still work?

Lis walked closer to the house and called, "Portia!"

A second-floor window opened.

"I'm going to the dam."

The young woman nodded and looked up at the sky. "I just heard a bulletin. They're calling it the storm of the decade."

Lis nearly joked that she'd picked a fine night for a visit but thought better of it. Portia eased the window shut and continued her methodical taping. Lis walked cautiously into the culvert that led to the dam and, plunging into darkness, picked her way along the rocky creek bed.

The two Labs suddenly jerked into a frenzy. The trackers simultaneously drew their guns, Heck thumb-cocking his. The men exhaled long as the animal—a raccoon fat on village garbage—jogged away from them, the concentric rings of its tail vanishing into underbrush. The indignant animal reminded Heck of Jill's father, who was a small-town mayor.

Heck, lowering the prominent hammer of his old German pistol, downed Emil and waited while Charlie Fennel futilely scolded the Labs and then refreshed their memory with Hrubek's shorts. As he waited Heck gazed around him at the seemingly endless fields. They'd come five miles from the shack where Hrubek had stolen the traps, and the dogs were still scenting on the asphalt. Heck had never pursued an escapee who stuck so persistently to the road. What seemed like blood-sure stupidity now looked pretty smart: by doing just the opposite of what everybody expected, Hrubek was making damn good time. Heck had a vague thought, which lasted merely a second or two, that somehow, they were making a very bad mistake about this fellow. This impression was punctuated by a shiver that dropped from his neck to his tailbone.

Charlie Fennel's dogs were soon back on the trail and the men hurried along the deserted strip of highway under a sky black as a hole. To stem his own uneasiness Heck leaned over and said, "Know what's coming up this week?"

Fennel grunted.

"St. Hubert's Day. And we're going to be celebrating it."

Fennel hawked and spit in a long arc then said, "Who's we?"

"Emil and me. St. Hubert's Day. He's the patron saint of hunters. St. Hubert hounds—that's what he bred—"

"Who?"

"St. *Hubert*. This is what I'm telling you. He was a monk or something. He bred the dogs that eventually became bloodhounds." Heck nodded at Emil. "That boy goes farther back than I do. Part of St. Hubert's Day is a blessing of the hounds. Aren't you Irish, Charlie? How come you don't know this stuff?"

"Family's from Londonderry."

"You've got those Labs there. We ought to get a priest to bless our dogs. What do you think about that, Charlie? How 'bout over at St. Mary's. Think that priest'd do that for us?" Fennel didn't answer and Heck continued, "You know bloodhounds go back to Mesopotamia?"

"Where the hell's that?"

"Iraq."

"Now *that*," Fennel said, "was a stupid little war."

"I think we should've kept going, tromp, tromp, tromp, all the way to Baghdad."

"I'll second that." Then Fennel laughed.

Heck, grinning, asked, "What's so funny?"

"You're a crazy man after a crazy man, Trenton."

"Say what you will, I think I'm going to find me a priest and get Emil blessed after this is over."

"If he catches the guy."

"No, I think I'll just do it anyway."

The road down which they now pursued Hrubek was a dark country highway, which threaded through a string of small towns and unincorporated portions of the county. If Hrubek had Boston in mind he was taking the long route. But, Heck concluded, it was also the smarter way to travel. Along these roads there'd be hardly any local police, and the houses and traffic would be sparse.

They followed the dogs, still short-lined because of the traps, only three miles east before Hrubek broke away and turned north, onto a small dirt lane. A hundred feet away they found a filthy roadside diner, which looked bleaker yet because of the sloppily taped X's on the windows.

Thinking that Hrubek might be inside, Fennel sent the Boy around back and he and Heck snuck up to the windows of the streamlined, aluminum-sided restaurant. Cautiously they lifted their heads and found themselves gazing straight into the eyes of the cook, waitress and two diners, who, forewarned by the baying Labradors, were staring out the windows.

Heck and Fennel, feeling somewhat foolish, stepped through the door, holstering their guns.

"A posse," the waitress exclaimed, drops of viscous gravy falling from the tilting plate she held.

But, no, nobody here had seen Hrubek, even though to judge by Emil's scenting he'd passed within feet of the window. Without an explanation, or a farewell, the men and the dogs vanished as quickly as they'd come. Emil picked up the scent once more and led them northeast along the dirt road.

Not two hundred yards from the diner they found the spot where Hrubek had taken to the fields. "Hold up," Heck whispered. They stood beside a small grass-filled path—an access road for mowing tractors. The drive darkened as it passed through a dense stand of trees.

Fennel and Heck tied back the track lines until they were shorter than pet-store leads. They found, however, that they didn't need the animals any longer; not more than fifty yards into the woods they heard Hrubek.

Fennel gripped Heck's arm and they stopped short. The Boy

dropped to a crouch. They heard a mad moaning rising from the trees.

Heck was so excited to have found Hrubek that he forgot he was a civilian. He began communicating to Fennel and the Boy with the hand signals law enforcers use when they silently close in on their quarry. Up went his finger to his lips and he pointed toward the source of the sound then motioned Fennel and the Boy forward. Heck bent low to Emil and whispered, "Sit," then, "Down." The dog eased to the ground, obedient but irritated that the game was over for him. Heck loose-tied him to a branch.

"I'll take over from here, you want," Fennel whispered in a casual way but with enough timber to remind Heck who was in charge. Heck was of course willing to yield the role of commander, which was never his in the first place, but no way was he going to miss the hogtying party; he didn't want any argument about the reward money. He nodded toward Fennel and unholstered his Walther.

The Boy, who with his fiery eyes and a big automatic in his fingers didn't look so boyish anymore, circled around to the side, north of the trees, as Fennel had indicated. Heck and Fennel went up the middle of the road. They moved very slowly; they couldn't use their flashlights and the grove was darkly shadowed by the hemlocks, whose branches were dense and lay upon one another like ragged petticoats.

The moaning grew louder. To a man, it chilled their hearts.

When Heck saw the truck—a long semi, parked cockeyed in the shadows—he felt a burst of queasiness, thinking that the moaning was not Hrubek at all but the driver, whom the madman had attacked and gutted. Perhaps he was listening to a sucking chest wound. He and Fennel glanced at each other, exchanging this identical thought in silence, and continued their cautious approach.

Then Heck saw him, an indistinct shape not far away.

Michael Hrubek, so thick around the middle he seemed deformed.

Moaning like a moon-crazed dog.

He lay on the ground, trying to get up. Perhaps he'd fallen and hurt himself, or had been hit by the massive truck.

Maybe he'd heard the Labs and was feigning injury, waiting for his pursuers to get close.

Opposite Heck and Fennel, on the other side of the clearing, the Boy appeared in a crouch. Fennel held up three fingers. The young trooper responded by mimicking it. Then Fennel clicked the safety off his gun and lifted his hand above his head. One finger. Two fingers . . . Three . . . The men jumped into the clearing, three dark pistols pointed forward, three long flashlights pumping their dazzling halogen light onto the massive body of their quarry.

10

"Freeze!"

"All right, don't you move!"

For the love of Mary, Trenton Heck thought, his legs weakening in shock, what's happening here?

The madman, lying on the ground in front of the three lawmen, was shrieking like a bluejay. He suddenly split clean in two, half of him leaping into the air, white as death.

What is going on here? Heck trained the flashlight on the part of the madman that remained on the ground—the part that was now grasping about for something to pull over her ample breasts.

"Shit, son of a bitch!" the man's upper half shouted in an edgy tenor. "What the hell you think you're doing?"

The Boy started laughing first then Fennel joined in and, if Heck hadn't been so upset at losing his reward money, he'd have laughed too. The sight of the skinny man, searching desperately for his shorts, the long condom whipping back and forth as it dangled from his quickly shrunk member . . . Well, it *was* the funniest thing Heck had seen for a month of Sundays.

"Don't hurt me," the woman wailed.

"Son of a bitch," the skinny man growled once more. Heck's humor returned and he whistled the "Dueling Banjos" tune from *Deliverance*.

In a Kentucky-mountain voice Charlie Fennel said, "Naw, I want *him*. He's a purty one."

"Sooo-eee," Heck called. "Here, piggy, piggy, piggy!"

The woman wailed again.

"Oh, shit . . ." The young man fumbled with his pants.

"Calm down now." Fennel shone the light on his badge. "We're state troopers."

"That wasn't funny, I don't care who y'all are. *She* wanted to do it. She picked me up at that diner up the road. It was *her* idea."

The woman had calmed in proportion to the amount of clothing she'd pulled on. "*My* idea? I'll thank you not to make me sound cheap."

"I didn't want——"

"That's your all's business," Fennel said, "but it's *our* business you've had a hitchhiker on the back of your rig for the past ten miles. An escapee."

Heck too understood that this is what had happened and he was angry at himself for not thinking of it sooner. Hrubek had clung to the back bumper guard or loading platform of the truck. That was why the scent had been so weak, and why it had never wavered from the road.

"Jesus, that fellow at the truck stop in Watertown? The big guy? Oh, my everloving Lord!"

"You're *that* truck driver?" Heck asked. "He asked you about going to Boston?"

"Shitabrick, maybe he's still on the rig!"

But the Boy had already circled around and checked out the truck's roof and undercarriage. "He's not here, nope. And the back's padlocked. He must've took off into the fields when the truck stopped."

"Oh, Jesus," the driver whispered reverently, "he's a killer, ain't he? Oh, Jesus, Jesus . . ."

The woman had started crying again. "This is the last time, I swear. Never again."

Fennel asked how long the driver had been there.

"Fifteen minutes, I'd guess."

"You love bunnies hear anything?"

"Nothing, not a single thing," the driver said, eager to please.

"I didn't hear anything either," the woman replied, sniffling, "and I don't like your, you know, attitude."

"Uhn," Fennel responded, then said to the young man, who was buttoning up his shirt, "Now I suggest you get back in that rig and take this lady home and get on your way."

"Take her home? Forget about it."

"You prick," she snapped. "You damn well better."

"I think you ought to do that, son," Heck said.

"Okay. If she don't live too far from here. I've got a load of auto parts I got to get to Bangor by—"

"You prick."

Fennel had checked the bushes around the semi. "No sign of him," he called.

"Well, with the sound these two were making," Heck said, chuckling, "I'd run too. Well, let's get on with it. He can't be more than a half mile from here. We should—"

The Boy said, "Uh, Trenton, I think there's a problem."

Heck looked up to see the young trooper pointing at a small sign that in their silent approach they'd passed but not noticed. Its back was to Heck and Fennel. They strode to it, turned and read.

Welcome to Massachusetts

Heck looked at the scripty green letters and wondered why anybody'd waste a nicely painted sign here on this dim country road, home of madmen, horny truck drivers and loose waitresses. He sighed and looked at Fennel.

"Sorry, Trenton."

"Come on, Charlie."

"We got no jurisdiction here."

"Why, he isn't but a half mile away! He could be two hundred yards from us right now. Hell, he could be watching us from one of those trees over there."

"The law's the law, Trenton. We need to get the Mass troopers in."

"I say let's just go get him."

"We can't cross the state line."

"Hot pursuit," Heck said.

"Won't work. He ain't a felon. Adler said that Hrubek didn't kill that fellow was in the body bag. It was a suicide."

"Come on, Charlie."

"If he ain't so crazy—and it looks like maybe he ain't—and we nab him in Massachusetts, he might sue us for assault or kidnapping. And he could damn well win."

"Not if we get our stories straight."

"Lie, you're saying."

Heck didn't speak for a moment. "All we do is we find him and bring him back. That'd be that."

"Trenton, did you ever falsify a case report?"

"No."

"You ever perjure yourself on the stand?"

"You know I never did."

"Well, you're not wearing a badge now and I know you feel different about those of us who are. But the fact is, we just can't stroll over state lines."

Rising through Heck's prominent anger now was a sudden understanding—that the interest Charlie Fennel and the young trooper had in the search was this: to do their job. Oh, they'd give the pursuit of Michael Hrubek 110 percent and they'd bust their balls and put in all sorts of god-awful overtime and even risk their life. But for that one purpose only: *to do their job.*

Leaving the jurisdiction wasn't their job.

"I'm sorry, Trenton."

"Didn't any of us notify the Mass troopers before," Heck said.

"It'll take 'em a half hour to get the first cars here. Maybe more. If he hops another ride he'll be long, long gone by then."

"Then that's what'll happen," Fennel said. "That's the way it is. . . . I know what the money means to you."

Heck stood with his hands on his narrow hips, looking at the sign for a few moments. Then he nodded slowly. "Let's don't have words over it. You gotta do what you think's right, Charlie."

"I'm pretty sorry about this, Trenton."

"Okay. No hard feelings." He walked back to Emil. "If you two'll excuse us."

"No, Trenton," Fennel said in a firm monotone.

Heck ignored Fennel and continued walking to where Emil was loose-tied to a forsythia whip.

"Trenton . . ."

"*What?*" Heck's voice bristled as he turned.

"I can't let you go by yourself either."

"Don't ride me, Charlie. Just don't do it."

"By yourself? You're a civilian. *You* couldn't argue hot pursuit even if he *was* a felon. You cross that line, it's kidnapping for sure. You could get yourself into a real fix."

"And what if he kills somebody else? You're happy just to let him go."

"There are rules for how this works and I'm going to stick to 'em. And I'm going to see that you do too."

"You're saying you'd stop me?" Heck spat out. "Use that gun? Use that fancy *de*-partmental Glock of yours?"

Fennel was clearly stung by this but he received no apology from Heck, whose fists were balled at his side, as if spoiling for a school-yard fight.

"Don't be stupid, Trenton," Fennel said kindly. "Think about it. That Dr. Adler's a peckerhead to start with. You think he's going to pay you a penny of reward, you snag his boy out of state? You know he'll cheat you if he can. And what if some pansy civil-liberties lawyer gets a hold of you for kidnapping some poor retard. Bang, your ass is hung out to dry."

It wouldn't have hurt so bad, Heck knew, if they hadn't been so close—if he'd gotten a notice that Hrubek was, say, in Florida or Toronto. But they were so *damn* close. . . . Trenton Heck glanced at Fennel then gazed across the empty fields, which seemed white, as if dusted with snow or lime. He saw in the vague, indiscernible distance the shape of a man's back, crouching low as he ran. But as Heck's eyes squinted the back became a shrub and he understood that he was seeing only what his imagination had created.

Without a word to the two men Heck untied his hound and slipped off the harness, replacing it with the jangling ID collar. He said, "Come," and returned to the squad car to wait for the others, Emil trotting along beside.

They didn't notice him for a full minute so he spent that time looking around the shabby office—the cheap desk, the vibrating fluorescent light, the carpet of shocking green, the books with torn jackets or no jackets at all, stacks of recycled manilla folders, the shoddy walls.

Owen Atcheson was himself a homeowner and handy with tools. He recognized that the paneling came from a cheap store and was mounted by cheaper labor. The carpet was stained and the windows were streaked with grease though Owen also observed that the glass in the frames holding the doctor's diplomas was shiny as diamond.

"Excuse me."

The men turned. The one in uniform—this would be Haversham, the captain, the *good man*—pivoted on the heels of his short boots. The other one—whose office this was, a sandy-haired man of about fifty—seemed to have had only two hours of a much-needed sleep. Still, he had keen eyes, which now tersely examined his visitor.

Owen introduced himself then asked, "You're Dr. Adler?"

"I am," said the hospital director, neither polite nor contrary. "What can I do for you?"

The trooper, whose eyes suggested that he remembered the name, surveyed Owen's clothing.

"I live in Ridgeton. It's west of here about—"

"Yes. Ridgeton. I know where it is."

"I'm here about Michael Hrubek."

Adler's eyes flashed with brief alarm. "How'd you find out that he's wandered away?"

"Wandered away?" Owen asked wryly.

"Who exactly are you?"

The trooper spoke up. "It's your wife . . . ?"

"That's right."

Adler nodded. "The woman at the trial? That sheriff called about her a while ago. Some letter Hrubek sent." The doctor squinted, wondering, it seemed, where Owen might fit in the zodiac of the evening.

"You haven't caught him yet?"

"Not quite. You really don't have anything to worry about."

"No? That was a pretty frightening letter your patient sent my wife."

"Well, as I think we explained"—his gaze incorporated Haversham—"to your sheriff, Hrubek is a paranoid schizophrenic. What they write is usually meaningless. There's nothing for you to wor—"

"*Usually* meaningless? Then not *always*. I see. Don't you think there's something to it if he threatened my wife at the trial, then wrote this letter a few months back and here he goes and escapes?"

Adler said, "It's not really your concern, Mr. Atcheson. And we're really quite busy—"

"My wife's safety is my concern." Owen glanced at the doctor's left hand. "It's a man's job to look after his wife. Don't you look after yours?" He noticed with some pleasure that Adler had in this short time grown to dislike him. "Tell me why there are only four men in the search party."

The hospital director's front teeth danced together briefly with several short taps. "The men after him're experienced dog-trackers. More efficient than a dozen troopers just wandering around in the dark."

"He's in Watertown?"

"He was. He seems to be going north. He *is* going north, I should say."

From outside, the sound of hammering boomed. Owen recalled that entering the hospital grounds he'd seen workmen carrying sheets of plywood toward large plate-glass windows in what seemed to be a cafeteria.

"Have they actually spotted him?" Owen asked curtly, and watched the doctor's dislike become active hatred. But Owen was a lawyer; he was used to this.

"I don't think so," Adler said. "But they're very close."

Owen believed posture was a man's most important attribute. He could have hair or no hair, be shaven or stubbled, tall or short, but if he stood up straight he was respected. Now, at attention, he stared down this doctor, who may have believed that Hrubek was harmless but on the other hand *was* here late on Sunday, looking like death itself, with an officer of the state police at his side.

He asked, "He escaped in Stinson?"

Dr. Adler glanced at the far ceiling. He nodded impatiently toward Haversham, who strode to the desk and with a capped Bic pen touched a location on the map. "Here's why your wife's got nothing to worry about. We're tracking him here." He touched a spot near the intersection of Routes 236 and 118. "He escaped . . ." The doctor's eyes bored into Haversham at this choice of word. The captain paused then continued. "He wandered off here, just over the Stinson line."

"And how did he get to Stinson?"

Adler plucked a sentence from inventory and responded quickly, "There was a mix-up. He took another patient's place in a transport van."

Haversham took a moment to detach his gaze from the hospital director's serene face and continued, "Then he eluded two orderlies *here*. In Watertown, *here*, he asked a driver for a ride to Boston. Oh, and he dropped a map of Boston while he was running. He's on Route 118 now."

"Boston? What kind of lead does he have?"

"Just a half hour. And our people are gaining fast. We should have him within twenty minutes."

"Now, if you'll excuse us," Adler said, "we've got some work to do."

Owen had the pleasure of staring the troubled man down once more and said to the state trooper, "I hope you'll do my wife and me the courtesy of keeping the Ridgeton sheriff informed about what's happening here."

"I'll do that, sure."

Nodding to the trooper and ignoring Adler, Owen left the office. He was walking down the dank, murky corridor when the captain stepped into the hall and caught up with him.

" 'Scuse me, sir? A question?"

The trooper was a big man though Owen was bigger and Haversham stepped back a pace so that he wasn't looking up into Owen's eyes at so steep an angle. "You out doing some camping when you heard about this?"

"I'm sorry?"

"The reason I ask is, you're dressed like you've been camping. Or hunting."

"I just threw on some clothes and drove over here."

"All the way from Ridgeton?"

"It's straight down the highway. I'll confess. I didn't obey the posted."

"You might've called." When he received no response the captain continued, "You armed, by any chance?"

Owen asked if Haversham wanted to see his pistol permit.

"That won't be necessary, no. What line of work you in?"

"I'm an attorney."

"Lawyer, huh?" This seemed to please Haversham. "What sort?"

"Corporate mostly."

"The doctor back there, he's got a pretty low opinion of this Hrubek. And I suspect you and your wife do too. Now this fellow may be criminally insane but in the eyes of the law he isn't no dog. He's a human being and if somebody was to shoot him down they'd be guilty of murder just the same as they'd shot a minister. But I don't need to tell you that, being a lawyer and all."

"Let me ask you something, Captain. Have you ever seen Michael Hrubek up close? You ever faced him?"

"I sympathize with you, sir. But I'm telling you, we find him dead somewhere, I personally'll be

peared. He screamed briefly, picked himself up and ran forty feet into the forest, crashing through a line of low brush then dropping onto the ground. A few moments later the green cube of a car drove past slowly and stopped.

A door slammed and a man climbed out. The conspirator walked in a slow circle near the perimeter of the forest. Hrubek curled up on his side. He closed his eyes and prayed that he might fall asleep so that he'd grow invisible.

"Michael!" the man called tentatively, as if undecided whether to shout or whisper. "Are you there?"

Something familiar about the voice.

"Michael, it's me."

Dr. Richard! the stunned patient realized. Dr. Richard Kohler from Marsden!

Or was it? Careful here. Something funny's going on.

"Michael, I want to talk to you. Can you hear me?"

Hrubek opened his eyes and gazed out from between two ferns. It *looked* like Dr. Richard. How did those fuckers *do* it? Hrubek

get off with manslaughter, that'll be the end of your legal practice."

Owen looked back into the calm eyes of the captain, who finally said, "Those are just some things to consider."

"Duly noted, Captain. Good night to you now."

From the corner of his eye Michael Hrubek—running through tall grass—noticed headlights on a service road that paralleled his path along the highway. The car was keeping pace with his speed and he believed it was following him. The vehicle stopped suddenly, made a sharp turn and headed in his direction. "Conspirators!" he crowed. Amid the panic that enveloped him like a cloud of hornets he tripped and fell forward onto the shoulder. Cinders, pebbles and bits of glass embedded themselves in his palms and blood ap-

nervously scooted under a bush. His eyes met... suspiciously as he examined the man, studying the doctor's thin frame, dark-blue suit, black penny loafers and Argyle socks. His backpack the color of old blood. Sure, this looked just like Dr. Richard. Identical! Hrubek gave the conspirator credit for disguising himself so cleverly.

Smart fucker, make no mistake.

"They told me you'd run off. Michael, is that you? I thought I saw you."

The footsteps grew closer, crushing leaves beneath the dainty feet. Hrubek pulled his own backpack to his side. It was heavy and clinked with the sound of metal and chains. He froze at the noise then rummaged inside quietly. At the bottom he found the pistol.

"Michael, I know you're scared. I want to help you."

He aimed the pistol at the shadowy form that approached. He'd shoot the impostor in the head. No, that'd be too merciful. I'll aim for the belly, he thought, and let him die like a battlefield soldier, slowly, with a gut wound from a .54 Minié ball.

. . . for I love the bonnie blue boy who gave his life for me. . . .

The footsteps came closer. The beam from a tiny flashlight swept the ground, lit a patch of grass two feet from his foot, then moved on. Hrubek held the gun close to his face. He smelled oil and metal. As he gazed back into the clearing, a dreadful thought came into his mind: What if this *wasn't* an impostor. Maybe this really *was* Dr. Richard. Maybe *he* was a conspirator too! Maybe he'd been a traitor all along. From the first fucking day they'd met. Four months of betrayal!

"I've been looking all over for you. I want to give you some medicine. It'll make you feel better."

How do you feel better when you're dead? Hrubek responded silently. How does poison make you feel *bet-ter*? If I were a *bettor*, I'd say you were a bad *bet*, you fucker.

The conspirator was ten feet away. Hrubek's right hand began to shake as it gripped the gun, which was pointed directly at the belly of Dr. Richard the betrayer (or John Conspirator the impostor).

"I'm your last chance. There are people who want to hurt you. . . ."

Well, I *knew* that all along. You're telling me something *new*? How'd you like to be in the *news*? CNN can do a story about your blown-up guts. He pulled the hammer back. The click was very soft but inexplicably it released in Hrubek a flood of fear. He began to quiver. The gun slipped from his hand and he remained paralyzed for a long moment. Finally his vision grew blacker than the black forest around him and his mind froze, seated like a hot drill bit in oak.

When he opened his eyes again and was aware of his surroundings, some minutes had passed. The air felt colder, more oppressive, heavy with moisture. The conspirator was gone, his car too. Hrubek found the gun and lowered the hammer carefully, then stowed the weapon in his bag. As he rose to his feet, dazed and discomfited, and started jogging through the night once more, Hrubek wondered whether the entire incident had been just a dream. But he concluded that even if it hadn't been real the apparition was certainly a message from God: to remind him that tonight he could trust no one, not even those who were—or who *pretended* to be—his closest friends on earth.

11

She called it the Berlin Wall.

A six-foot-high stockade fence of gray cedar, surrounding most of the four acres of the L'Auberget estate. Lis now walked along a stretch of this fence on her way to the dam. To enclose the property had cost Andrew L'Auberget eighteen thousand dollars (and they'd been *1968* dollars, no less). But despite the price he was adamant about the barricade. Lis jokingly named it after the German barrier (the reference shared only with Portia and friends, never with her father) though the man's concern hadn't been the Red Peril. Terrorist kidnappings were his main fear.

He'd become convinced that he, as a successful businessman with several European partnerships, was targeted. "God*damn* Basques," he railed. "Goddamn them! And they know all about me." The SDS, the Black Panthers! "I'm in *Who's Who in American Business*. There for the whole world to see! Where I live! My children's names! They could read *your* name, Lisbonne. Remember what I told you about answering the door? Tell me what you'd do if you saw a Negro walking around outside the gate. Tell me!"

The fence, even Lis the naïve child supposed, was easily breachable and less a deterrent to the bad guys than an inconvenience to the family, who had to walk three-quarters of a mile around it if they wanted to go for walks in the woods across Cedar Swamp Road. But like the builders of its namesake, L'Auberget's purpose seemed only partially to keep the enemy out; he also wanted to restrain his own citizenry. "I will not have the children wandering off. They're *girls*, for God's sake!" Lis had often heard this declaration, or variations on it.

As she walked along tonight Lis reflected with some irony that while its German counterpart was now dust, Andrew L'Auberget's cedar folly was still as strong as ever. She noticed too that if the water did overflow the dam, the fence would make a perfect sluice, preventing any flood from spilling off the property into the woods and directing it straight to the house.

She now approached the beach—a small crescent of dark sand. Just beyond was the dam, an old stone-and-cement slab twenty feet high, built around the turn of the century. It was against this wide lip of cement that the white rowboat she'd seen from the house thudded resonantly. Behind the dam was the narrow spillway fed by the overflow; usually dry, tonight it gushed like a Colorado rapid, the water disappearing into the creek that ran beneath the road. The dam was part of the L'Auberget property though it was under the technical control of the state Corps of Engineers, which had been granted an easement to maintain it. Why weren't they here tonight? she wondered.

Lis continued a few feet toward the dam, then stopped, uneasy, reluctant to go further, watching the white jet of water shoot into the creek.

Her hesitation had nothing to do with the safety of the dam or the ragged spume. The only thought on her mind at the moment was the picnic.

Many, many years before: a rare event—a L'Auberget family outing.

That June day had been a mixture of sun and shade, hot and cold. The family strolled from the house to this beach, and hadn't gotten more than ten yards before Father started carping at Portia. "Calm down, quiet down!" The girl was five, even then cheerfully defiant and boisterous. Lis was horrified that because of the girl's rowdiness Father would call off the picnic and she bluntly shushed

her little sister. Portia tried to kick Lis in retaliation and, with a
dark glance from her husband, Mother finally swept up the squirming girl and carried her.

Lis, then eleven, and her father hefted picnic baskets packed by
him so efficiently that she nearly tore muscles under the weight.
Still, the girl didn't complain; she'd endured eight months of her
father's absence while he was in Europe on yet another business
trip and nothing on earth would stop her from walking at his side.
She was thrilled speechless when he complimented her on her
strength.

"How about here?" Father asked, then answered himself. "Yes,
I think so."

It seemed to Lis that he'd developed a minuscule accent in his
recent travels. Portuguese, she supposed. She observed his dark
slacks and white dress shirt buttoned at the neck, without tie, and
short boots. This was hardly American fashion in the nineteen sixties but he'd have nothing to do with Brooks Brothers or Carnaby
Street and remained faithful to the look favored by his Iberian business associates. It wasn't until after he died that Lis and her mother
would laugh that Andrew's style could best be described as post-
immigrant.

That afternoon he'd watched his wife arranging the meal and gave
her strident instructions. The food was cut geometrically, cooked
perfectly, sealed in containers airtight as the NASA capsules that
so fascinated him. Mother set out expensive stainless-steel utensils
and ceramic plates the shade of milky plums.

A Warre's port appeared and they each had a glass, Father asking Mother her opinion of it. He said she had an uneducated palate
and for that reason was worth more than a dozen French somme-
liers. Lis had never heard her mother utter a single negative syllable
about any of the wines in her husband's inventory.

On the day of Lis's birth, Andrew L'Auberget was in Portugal,
where he happened to drop a bottle of Taylor, Fladgate 1879 be-

cause he was so startled by the sharp ringing of his partner's telephone—on the other end of which happened to be his mother-in-law with the news that he was now a father. The story goes that he laughed about the catastrophe and insisted—there, on the phone—that they name Lis after the city in which she'd destroyed seven hundred dollars' worth of port. Two things about this incident had always seemed significant to Lis. The first was the generosity with which he treated the loss.

And second: why wasn't he with his wife at such a time?

That day at the beach, sitting beside the dam, he'd lifted a silver spoon and, against Mother's protests, poured a scant teaspoon down Lis's throat.

"There, Lisbonne, what do you think? That's a 1953. Not renowned, no, but good. What do you think?"

"Andrew, she's eleven! She's too young."

"I like it, Father," Lis said, repulsed by the wine. By way of compliment she added that it tasted like Vick's.

"Cough syrup?" he roared. "Are you mad?"

"She's too *young*." Mother sent Lis out of harm's way and the girls went off to play until lunch was ready.

While Portia sat in a cove of grass and picked flowers, Lis noticed a motion from the state park nearby and stepped closer to explore. A boy of about eighteen stood with a girl several years younger. She was backed against a tree and he was clutching the bark on either side of her shoulders. He would ease forward and kiss her then back away quickly as she wrinkled her nose in mock disgust. He reached suddenly for her chest. Lis was alarmed, thinking that a wasp or bee had landed on her and he was trying to pick it off. She felt an urge to call out to him to leave it alone. They sting when they're scared, she nearly shouted, astonished that a high-school boy wouldn't know this plain fact of nature.

It wasn't of course a bee he was after but the button of her shirt. He undid it and slipped his fingers inside. The girl crinkled her

face again and slapped his knuckles. He withdrew his fingers reluctantly, laughed then kissed her again. The hand crawled back
inside and this time she didn't stop him. Their tongues met outside
their mouths and they kissed hard.

An eerie radiation of warmth consumed Lis. She couldn't tell
from which portion of her body it arose. Maybe her knees. Drawing
some vague conclusions about the spectacle of the two lovers, Lis
cautiously lifted her own hand to her blouse, beneath which was
her swimsuit. She undid buttons, mimicking the young man, and
eased her fingers under her suit as if his hand directed hers. She
probed, with no discernible results at first. Then as she fumbled
the heat seemed to rise from her legs and center somewhere in her
belly.

"Lisbonne!" her father called harshly.

Gasping, she jumped.

"Lisbonne, what are you doing? I *told* you not to wander far!"
He was nearby though apparently he hadn't seen her crime—if a
crime it was. Her heart quivering madly, she began to cry and
dropped to her knees. "Looking for Indian bones," she called in a
shaking voice.

"How horrible," her mother shouted. "Stop that this minute!
Come wash your hands."

"You should respect the remains of the dead, young lady! When
you're dead and laid out, how'd you like someone to molest *your*
grave?"

The girls returned to the picnic blanket, washed and sat down
to the meal, while Father talked about the paste that astronauts
would have to eat on extended space flights. He tried, without success, to explain to Portia what zero gravity meant. Lis was unable
to get down more than a few bites of anything. When they finished
she hurried back to the cleft in the bushes on the pretense of
looking for a dropped comb. The couple was no longer there.

Then came the part of the day that Lis had been dreading. Father took her down to the dark water. He removed his shirt and slacks, beneath which he wore his burgundy trunks. He had a dense body—not strong but with fat distributed evenly, in approximation of muscles.

Her shirt came off, then her culottes, revealing the plain red swimsuit. A thin woman now, Lis was a thinner girl then, but she pulled in her stomach vehemently—not in shame at a belly but hoping, futilely, that it might inflate her chest.

They strode into the cold lake. A championship swimmer in college, Andrew L'Auberget was, he'd told his daughter on a number of occasions, troubled by her fear of the water. He never missed an opportunity to get her into a pool or river or ocean. "It's dangerous, yes. It's far too easy to drown. That's why you must learn to swim, and swim like a fish."

Nervously she flexed her knees, feeling the gracious bed of mud beneath her arched toes. Father made a stern show of these lessons. When he noticed that she was resisting putting her head under water he ordered her to take a breath and pushed her face beneath the waves. Panic finally sent her scrambling upright. As she sputtered and shivered he laughed and told her, "See, that wasn't so bad. Again, for ten seconds. I can do it for two minutes. Two whole minutes without a breath!"

"No, I don't want to!"

"You take that tone, you'll go under for twenty seconds."

She practiced her strokes, beating the water with splayed fingers, which he forced closed into paddles. He supported her and held her buoyant while she swam in place.

"Calm down, girl! Water won't kill you. Calm *down*!"

She rested on his palm, trying to coordinate her legs and arms. Just as she struck a rhythm that approximated a breaststroke, a wave rolled in and lifted her from his hand. For a moment she was actually swimming on her own. Then the crest passed and lowered her once more. But when she drifted back down, she'd moved forward a foot or so and she came to rest with her groin on his fingers. For a tense moment neither father nor daughter moved and—compelled by an urge she understood no better today than then—Lis pressed her legs together, capturing his hand in that spot.

And then she smiled.

Lisbonne L'Auberget looked at her father and gave him a slight smile—not one of seduction or power or pride. Least of all physical pleasure. No, just a smile that sprang spontaneously to her cold, blue lips.

And it was for this transgression, Lis later speculated, rather than the fluke contact of bodies, that she was so ruthlessly punished. The next thing she recalled was being dragged from the water, her arm almost popping from its socket, and being flung to the hard ground, where she lay on her belly, as her father's hand—the same hand that had moments before cradled the most enigmatic part of her body—now rose and fell viciously upon another.

"Don't you ever!" he roared, unwilling to give a name to the offense. "Don't you ever! Don't you ever!" The raw words kept time with the loud slap of his palm upon her wet buttocks. She felt little sting from the powerful blows—her skin was numb from the cold—but the greater pain was in her soul anyway. She cried of course and she cried hardest when she saw her mother start toward her then hesitate. The woman refused to look then turned away, leading her sister from the shore. Portia looked back once with an expression of cold curiosity. They disappeared toward the house.

Nearly thirty years ago. Lis remembered those few minutes perfectly. This very spot. Except for the level of the water and the height of the trees, the place was unchanged. Even the darkness of night was somehow reminiscent of that June. For though the picnic had been at lunchtime, she had no memory of sunlight; she recalled the whole beach being shrouded, as murky as the water in which her father had dunked her.

Tonight, Lis finally managed to push the memory aside and

walked forward slowly over the gray sand of the beach to the dam. The lake was already pouring over a low portion of it—a cracked corner on the side nearest the house. Some of this spillage made its way into the runoff and the creek beyond but much of it was gathering in the culvert that led to the house. She leapt over this flood and walked to the wheel, set into the middle of the dam.

It was a piece of iron two feet in diameter, its spokes in graceful curves like wisteria vines, the foundry name prominently forged in some gothic typeface. The wheel operated a gate, two by three feet, now closed, over which flowed the water that gushed into the spill-way. Opening it all the way would presumably lower the lake by several feet.

Lis took the wheel in both hands and tried to twist it. Rose breeders develop good muscles—from twenty-five-pound bags of loam and manure if not the plants themselves—and Lis strained hard. But the whole mechanism was frozen solid with rust.

She found a rock and pounded on the shaft dully, chipping paint and sending a few sparks flying like miniature meteorites. She tried the wheel again without success then drew back and hammered the mechanism once more, hard. But the rock dipped into the spume of water and was ripped from her hand. It bent back her fingers as it catapulted deep into the culvert. She cried out in pain.

"Lis, you all right?"

She turned and saw Portia climbing cautiously over the slippery limestone rocks. The young woman walked up to the gate.

"The old dam. Still here."

"Yup," Lis said, pressing her stinging fingers. She laughed. "But then where would a dam go? Give me some muscle here, would you?"

They tried the wheel together but it didn't move a millimeter. For five minutes the sisters hammered at the worn gears and the wheel's shaft but were unable to budge the mechanism.

"Been years since anybody opened it, looks like." Portia studied the gate and shook her head. She then gazed at the lake. It stretched away, a huge plain of opaque water at their feet.

"You remember this place?" Lis asked.

"Sure."

"That's where we were going to launch the boat." Lis nodded at the beach.

"Right. Oh, is this it? The same boat?" Portia touched the gunwale of the rowboat.

"That? Of course not. It was that old mahogany sailboat. Father sold it years ago."

"What were we going to do? Run away? Sail someplace? Nantucket?"

"No, England, remember? That's when we'd read books out loud. After lights out. I'd read you some Dickens story. And we were going to live in Mayfair."

"No, it was Sherlock Holmes. I didn't mind them. But Dickens you did solo. That was more than I could take."

"You're right. Baker Street. Mrs. Hudson. I think it was the idea of a housekeeper bringing us tea in the afternoon that we liked best."

"And doing the dishes afterwards. Can you sail to Boston from here?"

"*I* can't sail to the other side of the lake from here."

Portia peered into the water. "I'd forgotten all about the beach. I think one of my dolls drowned here. Barbie. Probably worth a hundred bucks nowadays. And we'd steal Oreos, then sneak down here and eat them. We'd come here all the time." She tried unsuccessfully to skip a stone. "Until the picnic."

"Until the picnic," Lis echoed softly, dipping a hand into the dark water. "This is the first time I've been back."

Portia was astonished. "Since *then*?"

"Yep."

"That was when? Twenty years ago?"

"Try thirty."

Portia shook her head as the number sunk in. The rowboat gave a hard thud and bounced into the dam. She watched it for a moment then said, "It'll go over if we don't do something." Portia eased the boat to the beach and tied it to a sapling. She stepped back, wiping the bits of rotten rope from her hands, and exhaled a fast laugh.

"What?"

"I was thinking. I don't know if I ever asked what happened."

"Happened?" Lis asked.

"That day? The picnic? I'd seen him mad but I'd never seen him *that* mad."

Was it true? Had they never talked about it? Lis's eyes were fixed on the jagged tops of three pines, rising out of the forest; the protruding trees were all different heights and for some reason put her in mind of Calvary. "I don't know," Lis answered. "I sassed him, probably. I don't remember."

"I wish I'd been older. I'd've turned him in."

Lis didn't speak for a moment. "See that?" She pointed to a rock the size of a grapefruit sticking up out of the sand and mud. The water was now an inch away from it. "After he finished spanking me, I crawled over to it. Tried to pick it up. I was going to hit him and push him into the lake."

"You? The girl who never fought back?"

"I remember being on my hands and knees, wondering what it'd be like to be in jail—whether they had separate jails for boys and girls. I didn't want to be in jail with a boy."

"Why didn't you do it?"

After a moment Lis replied, "I couldn't get it out. That's why." Then abruptly she said, "We better get some sandbags here. It looks like we've got about a half hour till it overflows."

Trenton Heck stared into the night sky through the sliding door of his trailer. In front of him, on a red vinyl placemat, sat a plate of tuna salad and rice; at Emil's feet was a bowl filled with Alpo and spinach. Neither had eaten very much.

"Oh, Lord."

The plate got pushed across the table and Heck swiped up a quart bottle of Budweiser, gulping three stiff swallows. He realized that he'd lost his taste for beer as well as his appetite and set the bottle back on the table.

Aside from a glaring light above the table the trailer was dark. He walked over the yellow-and-brown shag carpet to his green easy chair, a Sears "Best," and clicked on the pole lamp. It gave an immediate comfort to the long space. The trailer was large, a three-bedroom model. It was sided in sunlight-yellow aluminum, the windows flanked by black vinyl shingles.

Although Heck had lived here for four and a half years and had accumulated almost everything that a married then divorced man would by rights accumulate in that time, the rooms were not cluttered. Trailer makers are savvy about closets and storage areas; most of Heck's earthly possessions were stowed. Apart from the furniture and lamps the only visible accessories were photographs (family, dogs), trophies (silver-plated men holding pistols in outstretched hands, gold-plated dogs), a half dozen needlepoints that his mother had produced during the period of her chemotherapy (easy sentiments—"Love is where the home is"), cassettes for the stereo (Willie, Waylon, Dwight, Randy, Garth, Bonnie, k.d.,) and a couple of small-bore targets (center-riddled with tight groupings).

Because he was feeling sorry for himself he read the foreclosure notice again. Heck opened the blue-backed paper and laughed bitterly as he thought, Damn, that bank moves fast. The auction was a week from Saturday. Heck had to vacate the Friday before. That part was as unpleasant to read as the next paragraph—the one explaining that the bank was entitled to sue him for the difference between what they made by selling his property in the foreclosure and the amount he still owed.

"Damn!" His palm crashed down. Emil jumped. "God*damn* them! They're taking everything!"

How, he thought bitterly, can I owe *more* than what I bought with the money they lent me? Yet he knew some things about the law and supposed that suing him for this sum was well within their rights as long as they gave him notice.

Trenton Heck knew how fast and bad you could ruin a man's life as long as you gave him notice first.

He figured he could live without the trailer. The worse tragedy—what hurt him like a broken bone—was losing the land. The trailer had always been intended as a temporary residence at best. Heck had bought these acres—half pine forest and half low grass—with some money an aunt had left him. The first time he'd seen the property he knew he had to own it. The thick, fragrant woods giving way to yellow-green hills gently sloped like a young girl's back. A wide stream slicing off the corner of the property, no good for fishing but wonderful just for sitting beside as you listened to the water gush over smooth rocks.

And so he'd bought it. He hadn't asked the advice of his sensible father, or his temperamental fiancée, Jill. He went to the bank, horrified at the thought of depleting a savings account larger than any he'd ever possessed in his life, and put the money down. He walked away from the office of a surly lawyer the owner of four and seven-eighths acres of land that featured no driveway, well or septic tank.

Or a dwelling either.

Unable to afford a house, Heck bought a trailer. He'd allowed Jill a part in *that* decision, and the young waitress—born never to be cheated—had slugged walls and measured closets and interrogated salesmen about BTUs and insulation before insisting that they buy the big one, the fancy one, the *Danger—Wide Load* trailer ("You owe me it, Trenton"). The dealer's men eased the long veicle onto the pinnacle of the prettiest hill on the property, right ext to the spot where he planned to build his dream split-level.

These hopes of construction he believed could be achieved as asily as he'd built his hundred-yard driveway: easing his pickup ack and forth between the trailer and the road fifty times. But the avings he'd planned to replenish never materialized, and therefore either did the house. Finally it came to the point where he could o longer afford the trailer either. When the first overdue notices rrived, Heck recalled to his dismay that the bank had loaned for he trailer on condition it take back a mortgage on the land as vell—all his beautiful acreage.

The same land that as of a week from Saturday was going to be omebody else's.

Heck folded the papers and stuffed them behind a statement from he veterinarian. He walked to the plate-glass picture window, which faced west, the direction the storm would be coming from in just a few hours. In the truck, on the drive back home, he'd heard several announcements about the storm. One of them reported that a twister had cut a swath through a trailer park in a town seventy miles west of here. There'd been no deaths but several injuries and a great deal of damage.

Hearing this newscast, just as he happened to click on the old radio, seemed to Heck a bad omen. Would his trailer survive intact? he wondered, then whispered, "And what the hell does it matter?" He picked up a roll of masking tape and peeled off a long strip. He lay down one long diagonal of an X. He started to do the cross strip, then paused and flung the tape across the room.

Walking into the bedroom he sat on the spongy double bed. He imagined himself explaining this whole matter to Jill—the foreclosure, the lawsuit—although he often grew distracted because when he pictured this conversation he pictured it very explicitly and couldn't help but notice that his ex was wearing a hot-pink peek-aboo nightgown.

Heck continued to speak to her for a few minutes then became embarrassed at the unilateral dialogue. He lay back on the bed, gazing at the roiling clouds, and began another silent conversation—this time not with Jill but with Heck's own father, who at this moment was many miles away, presumably asleep, in a big colonial house that he'd owned for twenty years, no mortgage, free and clear. Trenton Heck was saying to him, It's just for a little while, Dad. Maybe a month or so. It'll help me get my life together. My old room'll be fine. Just fine.

Oh, those words sounded flat. They sounded like the excuses offered by the red-handed burglars and joyriders Heck used to nab. And in response his father glanced down the long nose that Heck was grateful he hadn't inherited and said, "For as long as you like, son, sure," though he was really saying: "I knew all along you couldn't handle it. I knew it when you married that blonde, not a woman like your mother, I *knew.* . . ." The old man didn't tell his son the story about the time he was laid off from the ironworks in '59 then got himself together and started his own dealership and made himself a comfortable living though it was tough. . . . He didn't have to, because the story'd *been* told—a dozen times, a hundred—and was sitting right there, perched in front of their similar but very different faces.

Times aren't what they were, Heck thought as he nodded his flushed thanks. Though he was also thinking, I'm just not like you, Dad, and that's the long and the short of it.

He took a swig of beer he didn't really want and wished that Jill were back. He imagined the two of them packing boxes together, looking forward to a joint move.

A truck horn sounded in the distance, an eerie carrying wail, and he thought of the lonely whippoorwill in the old Hank Williams song.

Oh, come on, he thought, rain like a son of a bitch. Heck loved the sound of the rain on the metal roof of the trailer. Nothing sent him off to sleep better. If I ain't going to get my reward money, at least give me a good night's sleep.

Trenton Heck closed his eyes, and, as he began to doze, he heard the truck's plaintive horn wail once more in the distance.

12

Owen Atcheson knew the harrowing logic of cornered animals and he understood the cold strategy of instinct that flowed like blood through the body of both hunter and prey.

He would stand motionless for hours, in icy marshes, so still that a drake or goose would pulse carelessly thirty feet above his head and die instantly in the shattering explosion from Owen's long ten-gauge. He'd move silently—almost invisibly—inches at a time, along rock faces to ease downwind of a deer and without using a telescopic sight place a .30 slug through the relaxed shoulder and strong heart of the buck.

When he was a boy he'd doggedly follow fox paths and set dull metal traps exactly where the lithe blond animals would pass. He'd smell their musk, he'd see the hint of their passage in the grass and weeds. He'd collect their broken bodies and if one chewed through the stake line he'd track it for miles—not just to recover the trap but to kill the suffering animal, which he did almost ceremoniously; pain, in Owen Atcheson's philosophy, was weakness, but death was strength.

He'd killed men too. Picked them off calmly, efficiently, with his black M-16, the empty bullet casings cartwheeling through the air and ringing as they landed. (For him, the jangle of spent shells had been the most distinctive sound of the war, much more evocative than the oddly quiet cracks of the gunfire itself.) They charged at him like children playing soldier, these men and women, working the long bolts of their ancient guns and he'd picked them off, *ring, ring, ring*.

But Michael Hrubek wasn't an animal driven by instinct. He wasn't a soldier propelled by battle frenzy and love—or fear—of country.

Yet what was he?

Owen Atcheson simply didn't know.

Driving slowly along Route 236 near Stinson, he looked about for a roadside store or gas station that might have a phone. He wanted to call Lis. But this was a deserted part of the county. He could see no lights except those from distant houses clinging to a hilltop miles away. He continued down the road several hundred yards to a place where the shoulder widened. Here he parked the Cherokee and reached into the back. He slipped the bolt out of his deer rifle, pocketing the well-oiled piece of metal. From the glove compartment he took a long black flashlight, a halogen with six D cells in the tube, the lens masked by a piece of shirt cardboard to limit the refraction of the light. Locking the doors he once again checked to see that his pistol was loaded then walked in a zigzag pattern along the shoulder until he found four hyphens of skid marks—where a car had stopped abruptly then sped off just as fast.

Playing the light over the ground he found where Hrubek had jumped from the hearse: the bent grass, the overturned stones, the muddy bare footprints. Owen continued in a slow circle. Why, he wondered, had Hrubek rolled in the grass? Why had he ripped up several handsful of it? To staunch a wound? Was he trying to force himself to vomit? Was it part of a disguise? Camouflage?

What was in his mind?

Six feet from the shoulder was a muddle of prints, many of them Hrubek's, most of them the trackers' bootprints and the dogs' paw-prints. Three animals, he noticed. Here Hrubek had paced for a time then started running east through the grass and brush just beyond the shoulder. Owen followed the trail for a hundred yards then noted that Hrubek had turned off the road, plowing south, aiming for a ridge of hill paralleling the highway fifty feet away.

Owen continued along this track until it simply vanished altogether. Dropping to his knees he scanned the area, wondering if the man was smart enough to deer-walk, an evasion technique used by professional poachers: stepping straight down on the ground, avoiding the most telltale signs of passage (not prints but overturned pebbles, leaves and twigs). But he could find no bent blades of grass—the only evidence most deer-walkers leave behind. He concluded Hrubek had simply backtracked, aborting his southward journey and returning to the path beside the road.

Fifty yards east he found where Hrubek had once again done the same—turned south, walked a short way then backtracked. So, yes, he was moving east but at the same time was drawn to something south of the road. Owen followed this second detour some distance from the highway. He stood in the midst of a field of tall grass and once more saw that the trackers had paused here.

Shutting off the flashlight, he took his pistol from his pocket and waded into the pool of cold darkness that rolled off the rocky hills in front of him and gathered at his feet like snow. He paused here and, against all reason, closed his eyes.

Owen Atcheson tried to rid himself of the hardened, savvy, forty-eight-year-old WASP lawyer inside him. He struggled to become Michael Hrubek, a man consumed by madness. He stood this way, swaying in the darkness, for several minutes.

Nothing.

He could get no sense whatsoever of Hrubek's mind. He opened his eyes, fingering his pistol.

He was about to return to the Cherokee and drive on to the truck stop in Watertown when a thought came to him. What if he was allowing Hrubek too *much* madness? Was it possible that, even if his world was demented, the rules that governed that world were as logical as everyone else's? Adler was fast to talk about mix-ups and doped-up patients ambling off. But step back, Owen told himself. Why, look at what Michael Hrubek's done—he's devised a plan to escape from a hospital for the criminally insane, he's executed it and he's managed to evade professional pursuers. Owen decided it was time to give Hrubek a little more credit.

Returning to the spot where Hrubek's trail ended he placed his feet squarely in the huge muddy indentations left by the madman's feet. With eyes open this time, he found himself looking directly at the crest of the rocky hill. He gazed at it for a moment then walked to the base of the rock. He dabbed his fingers in mud and smeared it on his cheekbones and forehead. From his back pocket he took a navy-blue stocking cap and pulled it over his head. He started to climb.

In five minutes he found what he sought. The nest on the top of the rocks contained broken twigs and grass and the marks of boots. Their indentations were deep—made by someone who'd weigh close to three hundred pounds. And they were fresh. He also found button marks from where the man had lain prone and looked at the highway below, maybe waiting for the trackers and their dogs to leave. Pressed into the mud was a huge handprint above the word *rEVEnge*. Hrubek had been here no more than an hour before. He'd gone east, yes, but only for clothes, perhaps, or to lead his pursuers astray. Then he'd backtracked west along a different route to this outcropping, which he'd spotted on his way east.

The son of a bitch! Owen descended slowly, forcing himself to be careful, despite his exhilaration. He couldn't afford a broken bone now. At the bottom of the rocks he played his flashlight over the ground. He found a small patch of mud nearby and observed bootprints walking away from the rocks—the same prints he'd seen on the top of the cliff. Although they weren't widely spaced, they were toe-heavy, an indication that Hrubek was jogging or walking fast. They led to the road then back south into the fields, where they turned due west.

Following these clear imprints Owen walked for a short way through the grass. He decided that he would make certain that Hrubek was indeed going west then would return to his truck and cruise slowly along the highway, looking for his quarry from the road. Just another ten yards, he decided, and climbed through a notch in a low stone fence, leading to a large field beyond.

It was there that he tripped over the hidden wire and fell, face forward, toward the steel trap.

The big Ottawa Manufacturing coyote trap had been laid brilliantly—in a section of the path with no handholds for arresting falls, just beyond the stone wall so that a searcher couldn't get his other foot to the ground in time to stop his tumble. In an instant Owen dropped the flashlight and covered his face with his left arm, lifting his pistol and firing four .357 magnum rounds at the round trigger plate in a desperate effort to snap it closed before he struck it. The blue-steel device danced under the impact of the powerful slugs. Stones, twigs and hot bits of shattered bullets flew into the air as Owen twisted sideways to let his broad shoulder take the impact of the fall.

When he landed, his head bounced off the closed jaws of the trap and he lay, stunned, feeling the blood on his forehead and fighting down the horrific image of the blue metal straps snapping shut on his face. An instant later he rolled away, assuming that Hrubek had used the trap as Owen himself would have—as a diversion—meant to hold him immobile and in agony while Hrubek attacked from behind. Owen glanced about, huddling beside the fence. When there was no immediate assault he ejected the spent and unfired cartridges then reloaded. He pocketed the two good rounds and scanned the area once more.

Nothing. No sound but a faint wind in the lofty treetops. Owen stood slowly. So the trap had been meant merely to injure a scenting dog. In fury Owen picked up the bullet-dented trap and flung it deep into the field. He found the spent shells and buried them then, by touch, surveyed the damage to his face and shoulder. It was minor.

His anger vanished quickly and Owen Atcheson began to laugh. Not from relief at escaping serious injury. No, it was a laugh of pure pleasure. The trap said to him that Michael Hrubek was a worthy adversary after all—ruthless as well as clever. Owen was never as alive as when he had a strong enemy that he was about to engage—an enemy that might test him.

Hurrying to the Cherokee he started the engine and drove slowly west, staring at the fields to his left. He was so intent on catching sight of his prey that he grazed a road sign with the truck's windshield. Startled by the loud noise he braked quickly and glanced at the sign.

It told him that he was exactly forty-seven miles from home.

Michael Hrubek, crouched down in a stand of grass, caressed his John Worker overalls and wondered about the car at which he stared.

Surely it was a trap. Snipers were probably sighting on it with long-barreled muskets. Snipers in those trees just ahead, waiting for him to sneak up to the sports car. He breathed shallowly and reminded himself not to give away his position.

After he'd passed the *GET TO* sign he'd hurried west through the fields of grass and pumpkin vines, paralleling the dim strip of Route 236. He'd made good time and had stopped only once—to place one of the animal traps beside a stone fence. He'd set a few leaves on top of the metal and hurried on.

Now, Hrubek raised himself up and looked again at the car. He saw no one around it. But still he remained hidden, in the foxhole of grass, waiting, aiming the blade sight of his gun at the trees ahead and looking for any sign of motion. As he smelled the grass a dark memory loomed. He tried his best to ignore it but the image refused to disappear.

Oh, what's that on your head, Mama? What're you wearing there? Mama . . .

Take off that hat, Mama, I don't like it one bit.

Fifteen years ago Michael Hrubek had been a boy both very muscular and very fat, with waddling feet and a long trunk of a neck. One day, playing in the tall grass field behind an old willow tree, he heard: "Michael! Miiii-chael!" His mother walked onto the back porch of the family's trim suburban home in Westbury, Pennsylvania. "Michael, please come here." She wore a broad-brimmed red hat, beneath which her beautiful hair danced like yellow fire in the wind. Even from the distance he could see the dots of her red nails like raw cigarette burns. Her eyes were dark, obscured by the brim of the hat and by the amazing little masks that she dabbed on her eyes from the tubes of mask carrier on her makeup table. She did this, he suspected, to hide from him.

"Honey . . . Come here, I need you." Slowly he stood and walked to her. "I just got home. I didn't have time to stop. I want you to go by the grocery store. I need some things."

"Oh, no," the boy said tragically.

She knew he didn't want to, his mother said. But Mr. and Mrs. Klevan or the Abernathys or the Potters would be here at any minute and she needed milk and coffee. Or something. She *needed* it.

"No, I can't."

Yes, yes, he could. He was her little soldier. He was brave, wasn't he?

He whined, "I don't know about this. There are reasons why I can't do it."

"And mind the change. People short-change you."

"They won't let me cross the street," Michael retorted. "I don't know where it is!"

"Don't worry, honey, I'll give you the instructions," she said soothingly. "I'll write it down."

"I can't."

"Do it for me. Please. Do it quickly."

"I don't know!"

"You're twelve years old. You can do it." Her composure was steadfast.

"No, no, no . . ."

"All you have to do"—her mouth curved into a smile—"is go by the store and get what I need. My brave little soldier boy can do that, can't he?"

But the Klevans or the Milfords or the Pilchers arrived the next minute and his mother didn't get a chance to write down the directions for him. She sent him on his way. Michael, frightened to the point of nausea, a five-dollar bill clutched in a death grip, started out on a journey to the nearby store.

An hour passed and his mother, stewing with mounting concern and anger, received a phone call from the market. Michael had wandered into the store ten minutes before and had caused an incident.

"Your son," the beleaguered manager said, "wants the store."

"He wants the *store*?" she asked, bewildered.

"He said you told him to buy the store. I'm near to calling the police. He touched one of our checkers. Her, you know, chest. She's in a state."

"Oh, for the love of Christ."

She sped to the market.

Michael, shaking with panic, stood in the checkout line. Confronted with the apparent impossibility of doing what he'd been told to do—*Go buy the store*—his conscious thought dissolved and he'd belligerently grabbed the checker's fat arm and thrust the cash into her blouse pocket as she stood, hands at her side, sobbing.

"Take it!" he screamed at her, over and over. "Take the money!"

His mother collected him and when they returned home, she led him straight into the bathroom.

"I'm scared."

"Are you, darling? My little soldier boy's scared? Of what, I wonder."

"Where was I? I don't remember nothing."

" 'Anything.' 'I don't remember anything.' Now get out of those filthy clothes." They were stained with sawdust and dirt; Michael had belly-flopped to the floor, seeking cover, when his mother, eyes blazing beneath her stylish hat, charged through the pneumatic door of the supermarket. "Then I want you to come out and tell my guests you're sorry for what you did. After that you'll go to bed for the day."

"Go to bed?"

"Bed," she snapped.

Okay, he said. Okay, sure.

Was he being punished or comforted? He didn't know. Michael pondered this for a few minutes then sat on the toilet, faced with a new dilemma. His mother had dumped his clothes down the laundry chute. Did she want him to apologize naked? He gazed about the room for something he might wear.

Five minutes later Michael opened the door and stepped out into the living room, wearing his mother's nightgown. "Hello," he said, trooping up to the guests. "I tried to buy the fucking store. I'm sorry." Mr. Abernathy or Monroe stopped speaking in mid-sentence. His wife raised a protective hand to her mouth to stop herself from blurting something regrettable.

But his own mother . . . Why, she was smiling! Michael was astonished. Though her masked eyes were cold she was smiling at him. "Well, here's our pretty little soldier boy," she whispered. "Doesn't Michael look fashionable?"

"I found it behind the door."

"Did you now?" she asked, shaking her head.

Michael smiled. *Fashionable.* He felt pleased with himself and repeated his apology, laughing harshly. "I tried to buy the fucking store!"

The guests, holding the cups that contained tea not coffee and lemon not milk, avoided each other's eyes. Michael's mother rose. "I've changed my mind, Michael. You look so nice why don't you go out and play?"

"Outside?" His smile faded.

"Come along. I want you outside."

"I'd feel funny going outside wearing—"

"No, Michael. Outside."

"But they might see me." He began to cry. "Somebody might see me."

"Now!" she screeched. "Get the fuck outside."

Then she escorted him by the hand, thrusting him out the front door. Two of the neighborhood girls stared at him as he stood on the doorstep in the pale-blue nightgown. They smiled at first but when he began to stare back, muttering to himself, they grew uncomfortable and went inside. Michael turned back to his own front door. He heard the lock click. He looked obliquely through the dirty glass window and saw his mother's face, turning away. Michael walked to the willow tree in the backyard and for the rest of the afternoon huddled by himself in a nest of grass similar to the one in which he sat tonight. Looking for snipers and staring at the car.

As he listened to the rustle of this grass, feeling it caress his skin as it had so long ago, Michael Hrubek remembered much of that day. He didn't, however, remember it with perfect clarity for the very reason that made it so significant in his life—it was his first break with reality, his first psychotic episode. The images of those few hours were altered by his mind and by the intervening years, and were buried beneath other memories, many of which were just as haunting and sorrowful. Tonight, moved by the smell and feel of the grass, he might have delved deeper into that event—

as Dr. Richard had been encouraging him to do—but he'd grown so agitated by now that he could wait no longer. Snipers or no, he had to act. He rose and made his way to the road.

The sports car had apparently broken down earlier in the evening. The hood was up and the windows and doors were locked. A red triangular marker sat in the road near the rear fender. Hrubek wondered if its purpose was to help snipers sight on their target. He sailed it into the brush like a Frisbee.

"MG," he whispered, reading the emblem on the hood. He concluded this meant "My God." Paying no attention to the inside of the car he walked directly to the trunk. A gift! Look at this. A gift from My God! The rack was locked but he simply grabbed the mountain bicycle in both hands and pulled it free. Bits of metal and plastic from the mountings cascaded around him. He set the bicycle on the ground and caressed the tubes and leather and gears and cables. He felt a chill from the metal and enjoyed this sensation very much. He lowered his head to the handlebar and rubbed his cheek on the chrome.

He took a marker from his pocket and wrote on his forearm: *Oh, strANGE aRe the works of GOD. Thank YOU GOD for thIs beautIFul gIFt.* Next to these words he drew a picture of a serpent and one of an apple and wrote the name *EVE.* He licked the name and stepped back, studying his new means of transportation with an uneasy but grateful gaze.

Richard Kohler found himself in an alien world.

He was wearing a wool-blend suit, a silk tie, red-and-green Argyles and a single penny loafer—what other proof did he need, he reflected, that he was no outdoorsman?

Bending forward as far as he dared he pulled his other shoe out of a pool of soupy, methane-laced mud and wiped it on the grass beside him. He stepped back into the wet loafer and continued his journey westward.

Curiously this forest invoked in him a claustrophobia that he'd never felt anywhere else—even in his dark tiny office, where he would often spend fifteen straight hours. His pulse was high, his limbs itched from this fear of confinement and he was having trouble breathing. He also heard noises where no noises should be and his sense of direction was terrible. He was on the verge of admitting to himself that, yes, he was lost. His points of reference—trees, signposts, bushes—were vague and shifty. More often than not, as he walked toward them, they simply vanished; sometimes they turned into grotesque creatures or faces in the process.

Over his shoulder was his ruddy backpack, containing the syringe and drugs, and on his arm was a black London Fog raincoat. He was too hot to wear it and he wondered why on earth he'd brought the coat with him. The radio updates about the impending storm suggested that a helmet and armor would be better protection than gabardine.

Kohler had parked his BMW up the road, a half mile from here, and had made his way through a field into this forest, making slow progress. His leather soles slipped off the damp rocks and he'd fallen twice onto the hard ground. The second time he'd landed on his wrist, nearly spraining it. The vicious thorns of a wild rosebush hooked his pant leg and it took five painful minutes to free himself.

Kohler recognized, though, that he'd been lucky. The nurse who'd alerted him to the escape reported that the young man had run from the hearse in Stinson and had apparently gotten as far as Watertown.

As Kohler had sped in that direction down Route 236, he was certain that he'd sighted Michael in a clearing. The doctor raced to the turnoff, climbed from the car and searched the area. He'd called his patient's name, pleaded with him to show himself, but received no response. Then the doctor had driven off once more. But he hadn't gone far. He pulled off onto a side road and waited. Ten minutes later he believed that he'd seen the same figure hurrying on once more.

Kohler had found no sign of Michael since. Hoping he might stumble across him by chance, the psychiatrist had taken to the wilderness again, heading in the direction in which Michael seemed to be headed—west.

Where are you, Michael?

And why are you out here tonight?

Oh, I've tried so hard to look into your mind. But it's as dark as it ever was. It's as dark as the sky.

He tripped again, on a strand of wire this time, and tore his slacks on a sharp rock, gouging his thigh. He wondered if there was a danger of tetanus. This thought discouraged him—not the risk of disease but the reminder of how much basic medicine he'd forgotten. He wondered if his knowledge of the human brain compensated for the long-forgotten facts of physiology and organic chemistry he once had learned and recited so easily. Then these thoughts faded, for he found the sports car.

There was nothing remarkable about the vehicle itself. He didn't for a minute think that Michael had lifted the hood and tried to hotwire it. His patient would be far too frightened at the thought of driving a car to steal one. No, Kohler was intrigued by something else—a small object resting on the ground behind the rear bumper.

The tiny white skull ironically was the exact shade of the car itself. He stepped closer and picked it up, looking carefully at the delicate bones. A tiny fracture ran through the cheek. Trigeminal, he thought spontaneously, recalling the name of the fifth pair of cranial nerves.

Then the skull teetered on the tips of his fingers for an instant and tumbled with a soft crack onto the trunk of the car, rolling into the dust of the shoulder. Kohler remained completely still as the muzzle of the pistol slid along his skin from his temple to his ear, while a fiercely strong hand reached out and fastened itself to his shoulder.

13

Trenton Heck pointed the Walther up at the turbulent clouds and eased the ribbed hammer down. He put the safety on and slipped the gun back into his holster.

He handed the wallet back to the skinny man, whose hospital identification card and driver's license seemed on the up and up. The poor fellow wasn't quite as pale as when Heck had tapped the muzzle to his head a few minutes before.

But he wasn't any less angry.

Richard Kohler dropped to his knees and unzipped the backpack Heck had tossed onto the grass before frisking him.

"Sorry, sir," Heck said. "Couldn't tell whether you were him or not. Too dark to get a good look, with you crouched down and all."

"You come up on Michael Hrubek that way and he'll panic," Kohler snapped. "I guarantee it." He rummaged inside the pack. Whatever was so precious inside—just a couple of bottles, it looked like—didn't seem to be damaged. Heck wondered if he'd caught himself a tippler.

"And I'll tell you something else." The doctor turned, examining Heck. "Even if you'd shot him, he'd've turned around and broken your neck before he died." Kohler snapped his fingers.

Heck gave a brief laugh. "With a head wound? I don't know about that."

"There's apparently a lot you don't know about him." The doctor rezipped the pack.

Heck supposed he couldn't blame the man for being pissed off but he didn't feel too bad about the ambush. Kohler, it turned out, had been padding down the same path Hrubek must've taken earlier in the evening. In the dark, how was Heck to know the difference? True, the doctor was undoubtedly a lot punier. But then so are all suspects after they turn out not to be suspects.

"What's your interest here exactly, sir?" Heck asked.

Kohler eyed his civvy clothes. "You a cop, or what?"

"Sort of a special deputy." Though this was untrue and he had no more police powers than an average citizen. Still he sensed he needed some authority with this wiry fellow, who looked like he was in the mood to make trouble. Heck repeated his question.

"I'm Michael's doctor."

"Quite a house call you're making tonight." Heck looked over the doctor's suit and penny loafers. "You've did some fine tracking to get yourself all the way here, considering you haven't got dogs."

"I spotted him up the road, headed in this direction. But he got away."

"So he's nearby?"

"I saw him a half hour ago. He can't've gotten that far."

Heck nodded at Emil, whose head was up. "Well, for some reason the scent's vanished. That's got me worried and Emil antsy. We're going to quarter around here, see if we can pick it up."

The tone was meant to discourage company, as was the pace that Heck set. But Kohler kept up with man and dog as they zigzagged across the road and along the fields surrounding it, their feet crunching loudly on leaves and gravel. Heck felt the stiffening of his leg muscles, a warning to go slow. The temperature was still unseasonable but it had dropped in the last half hour and the air was wet with the approaching storm; when he was tired and hadn't slept his leg was prone to seize into agonizing cramps.

"Now that I think about it," Heck said, "you were probably better off tracking him without dogs. He fooled our search party damn good. Led us all in the opposite direction he ended up taking."

Kohler once again—for the fourth time, by Heck's count—glanced at the Walther automatic. The doctor asked, "Led you off? What do you mean?"

Heck explained about the false clue—dropping the clipping that contained the map of Boston.

The doctor was frowning. "I saw Michael in the hospital library yesterday. Tearing clippings out of old newspapers. He'd been reading all morning. He was very absorbed in something."

"That a fact?" Heck muttered, discouraged once again at Hrubek's brainy talents. He continued, "Then he pulled a trick I've only heard about. He pissed on a truck."

"He what?"

"Yep. Took a leak on a tire. Left his scent on it. The truck took off for Maine and the dogs followed it 'stead of going after his footsteps. Not many people'd know about that, let alone psychos."

"That's not exactly," Kohler said coolly, "a word we use."

"My apologies to him," Heck responded with a sour laugh. "Funny thing: I was just falling asleep—you know how this happens sometimes?—and I heard a truck horn. It just come to me—what he'd done. Emil's good but following airborne scent of a man hanging on to a tractor-trailer? Naw, that didn't seem right. For that many miles? I drove back to the truck stop and sure enough picked up his backtrack. That's a trick of the pros. Just like he hid that clipping in the grass. See, I wouldn't've believed it, it'd been lying out in the open. He's clever. He's fooled dogs before, I'll bet."

"No. Impossible. He's never escaped from anything in his life. Not a calculated escape."

Heck looked at Kohler to see if he could spot the lie. But the doctor seemed sincere, and Heck added, "That's not what I heard."

"From who?"

"From my old boss at the state police. Don Haversham. He's the one called me about the search. He said something 'bout seven hospitals your boy'd hightailed it outta."

Kohler was laughing. "Sure. But ask Michael which ones. He'll tell you they were prison hospitals. And when he escaped he was on horseback, dodging musket balls. See what I mean?"

Heck wasn't quite sure that he did. "Musket balls. Heh. We've gotta head through this brush here."

They plunged down a steep dirt path into a valley below. Kohler was soon winded by the arduous trek. When they reached flat ground, he caught his breath and said, "Of course you don't know for certain that he *isn't* headed for Boston."

"How's that?"

"Well, if he was smart enough," the doctor pointed out, "to fool you into thinking he was going east, maybe now he's fooling you into thinking he's going *west*. Double bluff."

Well. This was something Heck hadn't thought about. Sure, why couldn't Hrubek just do the same thing all over again and turn east? Maybe he *did* have Boston in mind. But he thought for a minute and then told Kohler the truth: "That might be but I can't search the whole of the Northeast. All I can do is follow my dog's nose."

Though he was painfully aware that this particular nose presently had no notion of where his prey was.

"Just something to think about," the doctor said.

They followed the path through a valley beside an old quarry. Heck remembered in his youth, a solitary boy, he'd taken an interest in geology. He'd spent many hours pounding with a hammer in a quarry similar to this one, snitching honest quartz, mica and granite rocks for his collection. Tonight, he found himself staring at the tall cliffs, scarred and chopped—the way bone was gouged by a doctor's metal tools. He thought of the X-rays of his shattered leg, showing where the bullet cracked his femur. Why, he'd wondered at the time, as he wondered now, had the goddamn doctor shown him that artwork?

The hound turned abruptly several times, paused then turned again.

"Has he got the track?" Kohler asked, whispering.

"Nope," Heck replied in a conversational voice. "We'll know when he does."

They walked behind Emil as he snaked along the base of the tall yellow-white cliffs around pools of brackish water.

They emerged from the rocky valley and climbed slowly. They found themselves once again back at the disabled MG. Heck was grimacing. "Hell, back to square one."

"Why're you out here by yourself?" Kohler asked, breathing heavily.

"Just am."

"There's a reward for him."

Heck looped the track line for a moment. Finally he said, "How'd you know that?"

"I didn't. But it explains why you're out here by yourself."

"And how 'bout you, doc? If you spotted him, how come you didn't call out the Marines?"

"He panics easily. I can get him back without anybody getting hurt. He knows me. He trusts me."

Emil suddenly stiffened and turned to the forest, tensing. In an instant Heck drew and cocked his pistol. The underbrush shook.

"No!" Kohler shouted, glancing at the gun. He started forward into the bush.

But Heck gripped him by the arm and whispered, "I'd be quiet there, sir. Let's don't give our position away."

There was silence for a moment. Then the muscular doe bounded in a gray-brown arc over a low hedge and vanished.

Heck put the gun away. "You oughta be a little more careful. You're kinda trusting, you know what I mean?" He looked south along the road, where the gray asphalt disappeared into the hills.

Emil'd shown no interest in that direction but Heck thought they ought to try it nonetheless. He started to hold the plastic bag containing Hrubek's shorts down to the dog once more. But Kohler stopped his arm.

"How much?" the doctor asked.

"How's that, sir?" Heck stood.

"How much is the reward?"

Emil was aware that a scent article was dangling over his head and he shivered. Heck closed the bag up again to keep the dog from growing too skittish. He said to the doctor, "That's sort of between me and the people paying it, sir."

"Is that Adler?"

Heck nodded slowly.

"Well," Kohler continued, "he's a colleague. We work together."

"If he's a buddy then how come you don't know 'bout it? The reward?"

Kohler asked, "How much, Mr. Heck?"

"Ten thousand."

"I'll give you twelve."

For a moment Heck watched Emil rock back and forth eager to run. He said to Kohler, "You're joshing."

"Oh, no. I'm quite serious."

Heck snorted a laugh but his face grew hot as he realized that he was looking at a man who could actually write a check for twelve thousand dollars. And probably have some left over afterwards. "Why?"

"Thirteen."

"I'm not bargaining with you. What do you want me to *do* for that kind of money?"

"Go home. Forget about Michael Hrubek."

Heck looked slowly around him. He noticed in the west, far away, a diffuse flash of lightning. It seemed to stretch for a hundred miles. He gazed at the huge expanse of countryside, the muddy horizon against the black sky. He found the view disturbing, for the very reason that this unexpected money was so appealing. How could he possibly find one man in that vast emptiness? Heck laughed to himself. Why did God always drop temptations in front of you when you wanted them the most?

"What's in this for you?" Heck asked again, to stall.

"I just don't want him hurt."

"I'm not going to hurt him. Not necessarily."

"You were about to use that gun."

"Well, if I *had* to I would. But I'm not going to shoot anybody in the back. That's not my way. Wasn't when I was a trooper. Isn't now."

"Michael isn't dangerous. He's not like a bank robber."

"Doesn't matter if he's dangerous like a crazed moose protecting her calves or dangerous like a Mafia hit man. I'm looking out for me and my dog and if that means shooting the man's coming at me with a rock or tire iron so be it."

Kohler gave a little smile that made Heck feel he'd somehow lost a point.

"Look, he's set out traps for dogs. I don't give much quarter to a man like that."

"He did *what*?" The smile vanished from Kohler's face.

"Traps. Spring animal traps."

"No. Michael wouldn't do that."

"Well, you may say that but——"

"Have you seen any?"

"I know he took some. Haven't found any yet."

The doctor didn't speak for a moment. Finally he said, "I think you're being used, Mr. Heck."

"What do you mean by that?" He was ready to take offense but the psychiatrist's voice was suddenly soothing, the voice of someone on his side, trying to help.

"Adler knows that a dog'll make a schizophrenic snap. Chasing someone like Michael is the worst thing in the world for him. A patient like that, cornered? He'll panic. He'll panic *bad*. You'll *have* to shoot him. Adler wants this whole thing wrapped up as smooth as possible. Fourteen thousand."

Lord. Heck squeezed his eyes shut and opened them just in time to see another flash of lightning. At his feet Emil rocked on his paws and had just about had it with this human-conversation stuff.

Take the money and go back home. Call up the bank, feed them a big check. Fourteen'd buy him another nine, ten months. Maybe in that time HQ'd find money to reinstate all the troopers let go in the last three years. Maybe one of the thirty-six security companies that had Heck's résumé would find an opening.

Maybe Jill'd come home with her knuckleball and tip money and her lacy nightgowns.

Fourteen thousand dollars.

Heck sighed. "Well, sir, I understand you're concerned about your patient and all, and I respect that. But there're other people to think about too. I wasn't a trooper for nothing. Emil and me have a chance to capture this fellow. And I'd say it's probably a better shot than you have—even with your talk about double bluffs and all. No offense."

"But he isn't dangerous. That's what nobody understands. You *chasing* him, that's what makes him dangerous."

Heck laughed. "Well, you psychiatrists have your own way of talking, I don't doubt. But those two fellows he almost killed tonight might disagree with you some."

"Killed?" Kohler's eyes flickered, and the doctor seemed as badly shaken as when Heck had pressed the black barrel of the gun against his skin. "What're you talking about?"

"Those orderlies."

"What orderlies?"

"He had the run-in with those two fellows near Stinson. I thought you knew about it. Just after he escaped."

"You know their names?"

"No, sure don't. They were from the hospital. Marsden. That's all I know."

Stepping away from Heck, Kohler wandered to the car. He picked up the small skull. He rubbed it compulsively in his hands.

"So," Heck continued, "I think I gotta turn down your offer."

Kohler stared at the night sky for a moment then turned to Heck. "Just do me a favor. If you find him, don't threaten him. Don't chase him. And whatever you do, for God's sake, don't sic that dog on him."

"I'm not looking at this," Heck said coolly, "like a fox hunt."

Kohler handed him a card. "That's my service. You get close to him, call that number. They'll page me. I'd really appreciate it."

"If I can, I will," Heck said. "That's the best I can say."

Kohler nodded and looked around, orienting himself. "That's 236 down there?"

"Yessir," Trenton Heck said, then leaned against the fender of the car and—with a slight laugh—watched the peculiar sight of this narrow man in a suit and tie, muddy as a ditchdigger, sporting a fine-looking overcoat and a backpack as he strolled down this deserted country road late on a stormy night.

Dr. Ronald Adler's eyes coursed up and down the Marsden County map. "Made it all the way to the state border. Who'd've thought?" He added with neither elation nor interest, "The Massachusetts Highway Patrol should have him within an hour or so. I want a worst-case plan."

"Are you talking about the reward?" Peter Grimes asked.

"Reward?" the director snapped.

"Uhm. What do you mean by worst-case?"

Adler seemed to know exactly but didn't speak for a moment, perhaps out of some vestigial superstition that medical training had not wholly obliterated. "If he kills a trooper when they find him. Or kills anybody else for that matter. *That's* what I mean."

"Okay, that's possible, I suppose," Grimes offered. "Unlikely."

Adler turned his attention back to the E Ward supervisor's reports. "Is all this accurate?"

"Absolutely. I'm sure."

"Hrubek was in the *Milieu Suite*? Kohler was doing *individual* psychoanalysis with him? This delusion therapy he's always boring people with?"

And publishing about in the best professional journals, Grimes reflected. He said, "So it appears."

"NIMH guidelines. We *all* know them. The criteria for individual psychotherapy in schizophrenic patients are that they be young, intelligent, have a past history of achievement. And are more acute than chronic . . . Oh, and that they have some success in a sexual relationship. That's hardly Michael Hrubek."

The assistant came a half breath away from saying, Not unless you call rape a successful relationship. He wondered if Adler would have fired him or laughed.

"A history like his"—Adler riffled pages—"and *still* Kohler puts him in therapy. One way you could view it is that Kohler was *more* than negligent in this whole matter. Let's just take that tack for a minute, shall we? Is that door open? My door there. Close it, why don't you?"

Grimes did, while Adler flipped through one doctor's assessment of Hrubek, in which was recorded the patient's plans to remove this therapist's internal organs with a single bare hand—a process that Hrubek described articulately and, all things considered, with an impressive knowledge of human anatomy.

When Grimes dropped again into his chair, Adler had snapped closed the file and was gazing at the ceiling. His hand dipped into his crotch, where he adjusted something. He said, "You realize what Herr Dr. Kohler has done?"

"He—"

"Do you know the case of Burton Scott Webley? Burton Scott Webley the Third. Or Fourth. I don't recall. Do you know about him? Do they teach you such arcane things in . . . Where did you go to school?"

"Columbia, sir. I'm not familiar with the case, no."

"Co-lum-bi-a," Adler stretched the four syllables out with elastic disdain. "Webley the Third or Fourth. He was a patient in New York. I don't know. Creedmoor perhaps. Or Pilgrim State. Don't let's quibble. No, wait. It was private. Top doctors, like our friend, *Sigmund* Kohler. *Cum laude* sort of doctors. Co-lum-bi-a sort of doctors."

"Got it."

"You see, Kohler has this idea that our mental hospitals are chockablock with van Goghs. Poets and artists. Misunderstood geniuses, vision and madness locked together—the beast with two backs." When he noticed Grimes staring at him blankly, Adler continued, "Webley was a paranoid schizophrenic. Delusional. Monosymptomatic. Twenty-eight years of age. Sound familiar, Grimes? Delusions centered around his family. They were trying to get him, blah, blah, blah. Felt his father and aunt were having an incestuous relationship. Including bouts of televised sodomy. On network TV, if I'm not mistaken. He had a bad episode and threatened the aunt with a pitchfork. Well, he's involuntarily committed. Insulin-shock therapy is all in vogue and his doctors put him into a hundred seventy comas."

"Jesus."

"Then the ECS department third-rails him for six months after his blood sugar becomes an embarrassment. With that much amperage, well, he came out of it rather tattered, as you'd suspect."

"This was when?"

"Hardly matters. A little while after they unplugged him, he sees the senior psychiatrist, who does a new diagnostic. Webley is neat and clean and coherent. And very sharp. Astonishing indeed, considering the SmithKline cocktails he's on. He's polite, he's responsive, he's eager to undergo therapy. The doctor schedules the full battery of tests. Webley takes, and passes, all twenty-five of them. A miracle cure. He'll be written up in the *APA Journal*."

"I can guess what's coming."

"Oh, can you, Grimes?" Adler fixed him with an amused gaze. "Can you *guess* that after he was released, he took a taxi to his aunt's house then raped and dismembered her, looking for the hidden microphone that'd recorded the evidence used to commit him? Can you *guess* that her fifteen-year-old daughter walked into the house as his little search was in progress and that he did the same to her? Any inkling that the only thing that saved the eight-year-old son was that Webley fell asleep amid the girl's viscera? You look sufficiently pale, Grimes.

"But I have to tell you the end of the story. The *shocking* part: it was all *calculated*. Webley had an IQ of 146. After he took himself off his brain candy, he snuck into the library and memorized the correct answers to each of those twenty-five tests and, I submit, honed his delivery pretty fucking well."

"You think Hrubek did the same thing to Kohler? What this Webley did?"

"Yes! Of *course* that's what I mean! Kohler bought a bill of goods. Lock, stock and barrel. Callaghan's death, any *other* deaths tonight—they're ultimately Kohler's fault. *His* fault, Peter."

"Sure. Of course."

"Tell me, what do you think of him? Of Kohler?"

"Pompous little shit."

Adler was pleased to have someone second this sentiment though it reminded him how much he detested Grimes for being such a toady. "I think there's more to it. Why is he being so blind? Kohler's not stupid. Whatever else, he's not stupid. Why?"

"I don't really—"

"Peter, I'd like you to do something for me."

"Look, sir—"

"Some detective work." When the otherwise thin Adler dropped his head to look over the top of his glasses he developed an alarming double chin.

Because it was very late in the evening and he was tired of treading lightly through hospital politics, Peter Grimes chose not to be coy. "I don't think I'd like to do that."

" 'Like to do that'?" Adler snapped. "Don't give me any of your bluster. I want to see fear in your face, young man. You're not union. If I wanted your fucking balls, I'd have them in an instant and a hell of a lot easier than I could castrate those orderlies. Don't you forget that. Now are you listening? Some detective work. Write it down if you can't remember it. Are you ready?" he inquired sarcastically, forgetting for the moment that he was speaking not to an incompetent secretary but to a doctor of medicine.

As man and dog returned to the sports car, Heck grew convinced that Hrubek had hitched a ride or snuck into the back of a repair vehicle that had answered the distress call.

Hiding in trucks for real this time, is he? Heck wondered. He leaned against the car and shivered slightly as a breeze came up.

Oh, man, here I give up almost a year's salary, sounding all grandiose and righteous and look what happens? I lose the trail completely. What would you've done, Jill? Tell me you'd've told him to stuff it too.

But no, Heck knew. Jill would've skedaddled home and tucked Kohler's check in her jewelry box. By now she'd be fast asleep.

In her pink nightgown.

Oh, baby . . .

Then, suddenly, Emil's nose shot into the air and the dog stiffened. He turned north, toward Route 236, and began to trot forward. Heck followed, feeling the line go taut and Emil pick up the pace.

What's going on here?

The breeze blew over them again and Emil began to run.

Glancing down at the asphalt, Heck closed his eyes in disgust. "Goddamn! What was I thinking of? Bicycle!"

Heck commanded Emil to stop then examined the asphalt and found a tread mark leading unsteadily from the car toward the highway. The tread was very wide; the rider could easily weigh three hundred pounds.

The surest clue though was Emil, whose nose was in the air. When a dog raises his nose and switches from trailing ground scent to trailing airborne, it's a good sign that the quarry's on a bike or motorcycle. They'd probably been upwind of the scent until the breeze a moment ago blew a bit of it back in their direction. Emil's ears twitched and he doled his weight from the left paw to the right and back again, ready to run.

Heck was too. Airborne scent is the hardest to track and even a moderate wind will disrupt it. A storm of the sort that was expected would surely obliterate it altogether.

Strapping the thong over his pistol, he wrapped Emil's red lead around his left hand.

"Find, Emil. Find!"

The hound broke from the starting gate and surged down the road. They were on the trail once again.

What's different?

Standing on the edge of the lake not far from the patio, Lis was momentarily disoriented. This place seemed both familiar and foreign. Then she understood why. The lake had risen so high that the shape of the shoreline had changed. What had been a voluptuous outcropping of lawn and reeds was now concave, and a cluster of small rock islands roughly in the shape of the constellation Orion had vanished—completely covered with water.

She turned back to her labors.

The two women hadn't returned to the dam but chose to build the new levee closer to the house, filling and piling sandbags where the culvert met the lawn. Even if the lake were to overflow the dam a line of bags here would, if it held, stop the water from reaching the house. Besides, she decided, they hardly had the time or strength to cart several tons of sand a hundred yards through a rocky culvert slowly filling with water.

Portia filled the bags and Lis dragged or carried them to their impromptu line of defense. As they worked, Lis glanced occasionally at her sister. The rings and crystal necklace were gone and her delicate hands and short, perfect nails—fiery red—were covered by canvas gloves. In place of the black lace headband was a Boston Red Sox cap.

Portia lunged energetically with the shovel, absorbed in the task, scooping huge wads of sand and pitching them into bags. Lis, with years of gardening and landscaping behind her, had always assumed herself the stronger of the two. But she saw now that they were, in strength at least, on par. Thanks, she supposed, to the hours Portia spent on health-club treadmills and racquetball courts. Occasionally the young woman would stop, pull off a glove to see what sort of honorable callus she might be developing, then return to the job. Once, as she gazed out into the forest, Portia twined a strand of hair around her finger and slipped an end into her mouth. Lis had seen her do this earlier in the evening—a nervous habit that she'd perhaps developed recently.

But then, Lis thought, how would I know if she'd picked it up recently or not? She reflected how little she knew of her sister's life. The girl had for all practical purposes left home at eighteen and rarely returned for any length of time. When she had, it was usually for a single night—a Saturday or Sunday dinner—with her current flame in tow. She even spent the majority of holidays elsewhere—usually with boyfriends, sometimes workmates. A Christmas for two in a far-off inn, however romantic, didn't appeal much to Lis. During summer breaks from college Portia would travel with girlfriends, or work at internships in the city. When she'd dropped out of school her junior year, the girl had abandoned her Bronxville apartment and moved to Manhattan. Lis was then working at Ridgeton High School and living in a small rental house in Redding. She'd been hoping that after her sister left Sarah Lawrence, the young woman might come back to the area. But no, Portia smilingly deflected the suggestion, as if it were pure craziness. She added that she *had* to move to New York. It was time for her to "do the city."

Lis remembered wondering what exactly this meant, and why her sister seemed to treat it as an inevitable rite of passage.

What, Lis wondered, was life like when you "did" the city? Did Portia's daytime hours pass quickly or slow? Did she flirt with her boss? Did she gossip? What did she eat for dinner? Where did she buy her laundry soap? Did she snort cocaine at ad-agency parties? Did she have a favorite movie theater? What did she laugh at, *Monty Python* or *Roseanne*? Which newspaper did she read in the morning? Did she sleep only with men?

Lis tried to recall any time in recent years when she and Portia had spoken frequently. During the prelude to their mother's death, she supposed.

Yet even then "frequently" was hardly the word to use.

Seventy-four-year-old Ruth L'Auberget had learned the hopeless diagnosis a year ago August and had immediately taken up the role of Patient—one that, it was no surprise to Lis, her mother seemed born to play. Her monied, Boston *sous*-Society upbringing had taught her to be stoic, her generation to be fatalistic, her husband to expect the worst. The role was, in fact, simply a variation on one that the statuesque, still-eyed woman had been acting for years. A formidable disease had simply replaced a formidable husband (Andrew having by then made his unglamorous exit in the British Air loo).

Until she got sick, the widow L'Auberget had been foundering. A woman in search of a burden. Now, once again, she was in her element.

Buying clothes for a shrinking figure, she chose not the shades she'd always worn—colors that made good backgrounds, beige and taupe and sand—but picked instead the hues of the flowers she grew, reds and yellows and emerald. She wore loud-patterned turbans, not scarves or wigs, and once—to Lis's astonishment—burst into the Chemo Ward announcing to the young nurses, "Hello, dahlings, it's Auntie Mame!"

Only near the very end did she grow sullen and timid—mostly at the thought, it seemed, of an ungainly and therefore embarrassing death. It was during this time that, on morphine, she'd described recent conversations with her husband in such detail that Lis's skin would sting from the goosebumps. Mother only imagined it, Lis recalled thinking—as she'd protested to Owen tonight on the patio.

She'd just imagined it. Of course.

The chills, however, never failed to appear.

Lis had thought that perhaps their mother's illness might bring the sisters closer together. It didn't. Portia spent only slightly more time in Ridgeton during the months of Mrs. L'Auberget's decline than she had before.

Lis was furious at this neglect, and once—when she and her mother had driven into the city for an appointment at Sloan-Kettering—she resolved to confront her sister. Yet Portia preempted her. She'd fixed up one of the bedrooms in the co-op as a homey sickroom and insisted that Lis and Ruth stay with her for several days. She broke dates, took a leave of absence from work and even bought a cookbook of cancer-fighting recipes. Lis still had a vivid, comic memory of the young woman, feet apart, hair in anxious streamers, standing dead center in the tiny kitchen as she slung flour into bowls and vegetables into pans, searching desperately for lost utensils.

So the confrontation was avoided. Yet when Ruth returned home, Portia resumed her distance and in the end the burden of the dying fell on Lis. By now, much had intervened between the sisters, and she'd forgiven Portia for this lapse. Lis was even grateful that only she had been present in the last minutes; it was a time she would rather not have shared. Lis would always remember the curiously muscular touch of her mother's hand on Lis's palm as she finally slipped away. A triplet of squeezes, like a letter in Morse code.

Now Lis suddenly found herself gasping for breath and realized that, in the grip of memory, she'd been working with growing fervor, the pace increasingly desperate. She paused and leaned against the pile of bags, already three-high.

She closed her eyes for a moment and was startled by her sister's voice.

"So." Portia plunged the shovel into the pile of sand with a loud *chunk*. "I guess it's time to ask. Why did you really ask me out?"

14

At her sister's feet Lis counted seven bags, filled, waiting to be piled up on the levee. Portia filled two more and continued, "I didn't have to be here for the estate, right? I could've handled it all in the city. That's what Owen said."

"You haven't been out for a long time. I don't get into the city very much."

"If you mean we don't *see* each other very much, well, that's sure true. But there's something else on your mind, isn't there? Other than sisters socializing."

Lis didn't speak and watched another bag vigorously fill with wet sand.

"What is this," Portia continued, "kiss and make up?"

Lis refused to let herself be stung by the mocking tone. Gripping a bag by the corners she carried it to the culvert and slung it fiercely on top. "Why don't we take five?"

Portia finished filling another bag then planted the shovel and pulled off the gloves, examining a red spot on her index finger. She sat down, beside her sister, on the low wall of bags.

After a moment Lis continued, "I'm thinking of leaving teaching."

Her sister didn't seem surprised. "I never could quite see you as a teacher."

And what exactly *did* she see me as? Lis wondered. She assumed Portia had opinions about her career—and about the rest of her life, for that matter—but couldn't imagine what they might be.

"Teaching's been good to me. I've enjoyed it enough. But I think it's time for a change."

"Well, you're a rich woman now. Live off the fat of the land."

"Well, I'm not going to just quit."

"Why not? Stay home and garden. Watch Oprah and Regis. There're worse lives."

"You know Langdell Nursery?"

"Nope." The young woman squinted, shaking her head. "Oh, wait, that place off 236?"

"We used to go there all the time. With Mother. They'd let us water flowers in the hothouse."

"Vaguely. That's where they had those big bins of onions?"

Lis laughed softly. "Flower bulbs."

"Right. It's still there?"

"It's for sale. The nursery and a landscaping company the family owns."

"Jesus, look." Portia was gazing across the lake into the state park. The water had pushed an old boathouse off its pilings. The ghostly white structure of rotting clapboard dipped slowly into the water.

"The state was going to tear it down." Lis nodded toward the boathouse. "The taxpayers just saved a few dollars, looks like. The nursery, I was saying? . . ." She rubbed her hands together a few times and felt her palms go cold as the nervous sweat evaporated. "I think I'm going to buy the place."

Portia nodded. Again a bit of yellow hair wound between her fingers and the tips of the strands slipped into her mouth. In the muted light, her face seemed particularly pale and her lips black. Had she refreshed her lipstick before coming out here to stack sandbags?

"I need a partner," Lis said slowly. "And I was thinking I'd like it to be you."

Portia laughed. She was a pretty woman and could instantly, as if by turning on a switch, become entirely sensual or charming or cute. Yet she often laughed with a deep breathiness that, Lis felt, instantly killed her appeal. This usually occurred when, as now, she was critical in an obscure way, leaving it to others to deduce their slipups.

Heat bristled at Lis's temples as the blush washed over her face. "I don't know business. Finances, marketing, things like that. You do."

"I'm a media buyer, Lis. I'm not Donald Trump."

"You know more than I do. You're always talking about getting out of advertising. You were thinking about opening a boutique last year."

"Everybody in advertising talks about quitting and opening a boutique. Or a catering company. You and me in business?"

"It's a good deal. Langdell died last year and his wife doesn't want to keep running the place. They're asking three million for everything. The land alone's worth two. Mortgage rates are great now. And Angie said she'd be willing to finance some of it herself, as long as she gets a million and a half at the closing."

"You're serious, aren't you?"

"I need a change, Portia. I love gardens and—"

"No, I think it makes sense for you. I meant, you're serious about *us*. Working together."

"Of course I am. You handle the business and finance, and I handle the product—there, doesn't that sound professional? The 'product'?"

Portia had been staring at the pile of bags she'd filled. She picked one up, carried it to the wall, dropped it into place. "Heavy bastards, aren't they?" she gasped. "Maybe I oughta shovel less."

"I've got a lot of ideas. We'd expand the formal gardens and open a specialty hothouse for roses. We could even have lectures.

Maybe do videos. How to crossbreed. How to start your first garden. You know people in film production. If we work hard, it could really fly."

Portia didn't speak for a minute. "Fact is, I was going to quit anyway after the first of the year. Just stay long enough to get my bonus."

"Really? That's when I was thinking of buying the place. February. Or March."

The young woman added quickly, "No, I mean I was going to take the year off. A couple years maybe. I wasn't going to work at all."

"Oh." Lis straightened one of the sandbags, which teetered between the two women. "And do what?"

"Travel. Club Med it for a while. I wanted to learn how to wind-surf. Demon of the sea."

"Just . . . not do anything?"

"I hear that tone, Mother."

Lis fought down the wave of anger. "No, I'm just surprised."

"Maybe I'll do Europe again. I was poor when I did the back-packing routine. And, God, those trips with Mother and Father? The pits. Señor L'Auberget, fascist tour guide. 'Come on, girls, what the hell're you up to? The Louvre closes in two hours. Portia, don't you dare look back at those boys. . . .' Ha, and you—you were probably the only kid in the history of the world who went to bed without dinner because she bitched about leaving . . . what was that?"

"The sculpture gardens at the Rodin museum," Lis said in a soft voice, laughing wanly at the memory. "A culture victim at seventeen."

After a moment Portia said, "I don't think so, Lis. It wouldn't work."

"For a year. Try it. You could sell out your share if it isn't for you."

"I could also lose the money, couldn't I?"

"Yes, I suppose you could. But I won't let it go under."

"What does Owen think?"

Ah, well, there was that.

"He had some reservations, you could say."

You could also say that it nearly broke up their marriage. Lis began thinking about opening a nursery just before their mother died and it was clear that the sisters would be inheriting a large sum of cash. Owen had wanted to put the money into conservative stocks and invest in his law firm, hiring several attorneys and expanding into new offices. That would be the best return on the investment, he'd told her.

But she was adamant. It was *her* money, and a nursery would be perfect for her. If not the Langdells', then another one somewhere nearby. Always the practical counselor, he rattled off a list of concerns.

"You're crazy, Lis. A nursery? It's seasonal. It's weather-dependent. With landscaping, there're major liability issues. You'll have INS problems with the workers. . . . You want to garden, we'll build another one here. We'll get an architect, we can—"

"I want to *work*, Owen. For heaven's sake, I don't tell you to stay home and read law books for fun."

"You can make a living at law," he'd snapped.

The more he argued, the more insistent she grew.

"Jesus, Lis. At best, you'll probably clear a few thousand a year. You'd make more if you put it in the bank and earned passbook interest."

She flung a *Money* magazine down on the table. "There's an article on profitable businesses. Funeral homes are number one. I don't *want* a funeral home."

"Quit being so damn pigheaded! At least in the bank the money's insured. You're willing to risk it all?"

"Mrs. Langdell showed me the books. They've been profitable for fifteen years."

He grew ominously quiet. "So you've talked to her about it already. Before you came to me?"

After a moment she confessed that she had.

"Don't you think you might've asked first?"

"I didn't commit myself."

"You haven't even got your hands on the money yet and you're pretty fucking eager to throw it away."

"It's my *family's* money, Owen."

Most scripts of domestic confrontation would call for a little parrying at this point. Your money? *Your* money? I supported you when the teachers went on strike. . . . When you lost your big bank client two years ago, it was my salary—a teacher's salary!—that got us through. . . . I'm doing all the estate legal work for free. . . . All those months when we couldn't pay the light bill because you joined the country club . . .

But Owen had done then what Owen did best. He closed his mouth and walked away. He grabbed his old .22 pump rifle and walked out into the woods to plink cans and hunt squirrels and rabbits.

For several hours Lis was left alone with the distant pops of gunshots and the memory of the coldness in his eyes when he'd walked out the door.

And for several hours she wondered if she'd lost her husband.

Yet when he returned he was calm. The last he said about the nursery was, "I'd counsel against it but if you want to go ahead anyway, I'll represent you."

She'd thanked him but it was several days before his moodiness vanished.

Tonight, Lis started to tell her sister some of Owen's concerns but Portia wasn't interested. She simply shook her head. "I don't think so."

After a moment Lis asked, "Why?"

"I'm not ready to leave the city yet."

"You wouldn't have to. I'd do the day-to-day things. We'd get together a couple times a month. You could come out here. Or I could go into the city."

"I really need some time off."

"Think about it, at least. Please?" Lis exclaimed breathlessly to her sister's face, pale and obscure in the darkness.

"No, Lis. I'm sorry."

Angry and hurt, Lis picked up a large sandbag and tossed it onto the edge of the levee. She misjudged the distance though and it tumbled into the lake. "Shit!" she cried, trying to retrieve the bag. But it had slipped deep beneath the surface.

Portia spun some strands of hair once more. Lis stood. Several waves splashed loudly at their feet before Lis asked, "What's the real reason?"

"Lis."

"What if I said I didn't want to buy a nursery. What if I was all hot for a boutique on Madison Avenue?"

Portia's mouth tightened but Lis persisted, "What if I said, Let's start a business where you and I travel around Europe and try out restaurants or rate châteaux? What if I said, Let's start a wind-surfing school?"

"Lis. Please."

"Goddamn it! Is it because of Indian Leap? Tell me?"

Portia spun to face her. "Oh, Jesus, Lis." She said nothing more.

The surface of the lake grew light suddenly, as a huge flash, bile green, filled the western horizon. It vanished behind a slab of thick clouds.

Lis finally said, "We've never talked about it. For six months, we haven't said a *word*. It just sits there between us."

"We better finish up here." Portia seized her shovel. "That was some mean son-of-a-bitch lightning. And it wasn't that far away."

"Please," Lis whispered.

A groan filled the night, and they turned to see the boathouse slide completely off the pilings and into the water. Portia said nothing more and started shoveling once again.

Listening to the *chunk* of the sandbags filling, Lis remained near the shore, gazing out over the lake.

As the boathouse sank, a vague white form appeared in the trees behind it. For a moment, Lis was sure that it was an elderly woman limping slowly toward the lake. Lis blinked and stepped closer to shore. The woman's gait suggested she was ill and in pain.

Then, like the boathouse, the apparition eased off the shore and into the water, where it sank beneath the still, onyx surface. A piece of canvas tied to a cleat on the frame, or a six-mil plastic tarp, Lis supposed. Not a woman at all. Not a ghost.

She'd just imagined it. Of course.

The night Abraham Lincoln died, after spending many hours with a horrid wound in the thick mass of sweat-damp hair, the moon that blossomed out of the clouds in the Eastern part of the United State was blood red.

This freak occurrence, Michael Hrubek had read, was verified by several different sources, one of whom was a farmer in Illinois. Standing in a freshly planted cornfield, 1865, April 15, this man looked up into the radiant evening sky, saw the crimson moon and took off his straw hat out of respect because he knew that a thousand miles away a great life was gone.

There was no moon visible tonight. The sky was overcast and turbulent as Hrubek bicycled unsteadily west along Route 236. It was a painstaking journey. He was now accustomed to the mountain bike and was riding as confidently as a Tour de France racer. Still, whenever a crown of light shone over the road before him or behind, he stopped and vaulted to the ground. He'd lie under cover of brush or tree until the vehicle passed then would leap onto his bike once again, his hammish legs pedaling fast in low gear; he didn't know how to upshift.

A flash of light startled him. He looked across a field and saw a police car patrolling slowly, shining a spotlight on a darkened farmhouse. The light clicked out and the car continued east, away from Hrubek. His anxiety notched up a few degrees as he pedaled on, and he found himself thinking of his first run-in with the police.

Michael Hrubek had been twenty years old and the arrest was for rape.

The young man had been attending a private college in upstate New York, an area pretty enough at the height of a vibrant summer but for most of the year as bleak as the depressed economy in the small city and fields surrounding the campus.

During his first semester Michael had been reclusive and fidgety but he'd done well in his studies, especially in his two courses in American history. Between Thanksgiving and Christmas, however, he grew increasingly anxious. His concentration was poor and he seemed unable to make even the simplest decisions—which class assignment to do first, when to go to lunch, whether it was better to brush his teeth before he urinated or after. He spent hour after hour staring out the window of his room.

He was then nearly as large as he was now, with long curly hair, Neanderthal eyebrows grown together and a round face that paradoxically seemed kind as long as he didn't smile or laugh. When he did, his expression—in fact usually one of bewilderment—appeared to be pure malice. He had no friends.

Michael was therefore surprised, one gray March Sunday, to hear a knock on his door. He hadn't showered for several weeks and had been wearing the same jeans and shirt for nearly a month. No one could remember, he least of all, when he had last cleaned the room. His roommate had long ago escaped to a girlfriend's apartment, a desertion that delighted Michael, who was certain that the student had been taking pictures of him while he slept. On this

Sunday he'd spent two hours hunched over his desk, repeatedly reading T. S. Eliot's "The Love Song of J. Alfred Prufrock." He found this task was like trying to read a block of wood.

"Yo, Mike."

"Who is it?"

The visitors were two students—juniors who lived in the dorm. Michael stood in the open door, gazing at them suspiciously. They smiled their clean-cut smiles and asked how he was doing. Michael stared at them and said nothing.

"Mikey, you're working too hard. Come on. We got a party in the rec room."

"Have something to eat, come on."

"I have to *study*!" he whined.

"Naw, naw, come on. . . . Let's party. You're working too totally hard, man. Have something to eat."

Well, Michael *did* like to eat. He ate three big meals a day and snacked constantly. He also tended to acquiesce to people's requests; if he didn't—if he refused to do what they wanted—his gut erupted with fiery bursts of worry. What would they *think* about him? What would they *say*?

"Maybe."

"Hey, excellent. Party down!"

So Michael reluctantly followed the two young men down the hall toward the dorm's common room, where a loud party was in progress. As they passed a darkened bedroom the juniors paused to let Michael precede them. They suddenly swiveled and pushed him into the room, slamming the door shut and tying it closed.

Michael howled in panic, tugging furiously at the knob. He stumbled, looking unsuccessfully for a light. He stormed to the window, ripped down the shade and was about to break the glass and jump forty feet to the grass lawn when he noticed the room's other occupant. He'd seen her at one or two parties. She was an overweight freshman with a round face and curly hair cut very short. She had thick ankles and wore a dozen bracelets around her pudgy wrists. The girl was passed-out drunk, lying on the bed, skirt up to her waist. She wore no panties. Her hand held a glass that contained the dregs of orange juice and vodka. She had apparently regained consciousness long enough to vomit then passed out again.

Michael leaned close and studied her. Instantly, the sight of her genitals (his first glimpse of female private anatomy) and the smell of liquor and puke sent him into paroxysms of fear. He screamed at the insensible girl, "What are you *doing* to me?" Then he flung himself into the door again and again, the huge noise resounding throughout the dormitory. In the hallway outside, laughter pealed. Michael fell back onto the bed, hyperventilating. Claustrophobia clutched him and sweat flowed from every pore. A moment later his mind mercifully shut down and his vision went black. The next thing he remembered was the cruel grip of two security guards, brutally pulling him to his feet. The now-conscious girl, tugging down her skirt, was screaming. Michael's pants were undone and his limp penis hung out, cut and bloodied by the zipper of his trousers.

Michael recalled nothing of what had happened. The girl claimed she had just gone to bed, having caught the flu. She'd opened her eyes and found Michael spreading her legs and penetrating her violently, despite her desperate protests. Police were called, parents notified. Michael spent the night in jail, under the cautious eye of two very uncomfortable deputies, unprepared for a prisoner who glared at them and threatened to make them "dead fuckers" if they didn't bring him a history book from his room.

The evidence was in conflict. Although there were traces of three different condom lubricants found in and around the girl's vagina, Michael wasn't wearing a condom when the guards captured him nor were any located in the room. The defense lawyer's tack was that the girl herself had lifted Michael's penis from his jeans and alleged rape, rather than admit that she'd taken on a succession of students after drinking herself semiconscious—a theory that, while politically incorrect, might very well have appealed to the jury.

On the other hand there were several purported witnesses to the crime, including the girl herself. Then too Michael had threatened or glared at half the campus at one time or another—particularly women.

But the most damning evidence of all: Michael Hrubek himself —a big, scary boy, more than twice the girl's size, who'd been caught, the prosecutor was only too pleased to point out, with his pants down. Nailing shut his own coffin, Michael grew incoherent after the incident and began to mutter violent epithets. Taking the stand in court would have been a disaster. The lawyer pled him down to one count of sexual assault and he was given probation on condition that he withdraw from school and voluntarily commit himself to a state hospital near his home, where he'd undergo a treatment program for violent sex offenders.

After six months he was discharged from the hospital and returned to his parents' home.

Once he was back in Westbury, reason and madness rapidly began to merge. One day, the autumn after the rape, Michael announced to his mother that he wanted to return to college. He added, "I'm only going to take history. They better let me do that. Oh, and I want to become a priest. I'm not going to study anything else. No math, no English, no al-ge-*bra*! Just fucking forget about it! I'm only going to study *history*."

His bleary-eyed mother, lolling in her unmade bed, her blond hair stiff as straw, laughed in astonishment at his demands. "Go back to college? Are you serious? Look what you did! Do you know what you did to that girl?"

No, Michael *didn't* know what he'd done. He had no idea. All he remembered was some girl lying about him and because of that he'd been forced to abandon his precious history classes. "She's a

fucker! She lied! *Why* can't I go back? Aren't I *fashionable* enough
to go to school? Well, aren't I? Priests are very fashionable. Someday I'll write a *his*-tory about them. They often fuck little boys, you
know."

"Go to your room!" his mother tearfully shouted, and he—a
man in his twenties, a man twice her size—scurried off like a
whipped dog.

Often he'd whine, "Please? I want to go back to *school*!" He
promised to study hard and become one fucker of a priest to make
her happy. He said he'd wear a crown of thorns on his bloody head
and make people rise from their graves.

"Jesus wore thorns because He *rose* from the dead," he explained
one day to her. "That's why roses have thorns."

"I'm going out, Michael," she would cry.

"Are you *go*-ing to run away from me? Where are you *go*-ing?
To al-ge-*bra* class? Are you going to wear a bra while a priest
fucks you?"

His mother left the house. She no longer called him her little
soldier boy. She no longer had nails as red as burning cigarette
embers, and the masks of her eyes often ran in streaks down the
matte skin of her cheeks.

Oh, Mama, what are you wearing? Take that hat off your head.
Take off that crown. All those bloody thorns! I don't like that, not
one bit. Please! I'm sorry for what I said about you and the soldiers.
Please, please, *please*, take that off!

It was an extremely agitated Michael Hrubek who, upon this
damp night in November, bicycled doggedly down Route 236 at
twenty miles an hour, lost in these hard memories—which was why
he didn't hear the police car, dark and silent, until it was within
ten feet of the bike's rear wheel. The lights and siren burst to life.

"Oh God oh God oh God!" Hrubek screamed. Panic exploded
throughout his body.

A voice came over the loudspeaker, jarring as a firecracker. "You there! Stop that bicycle and get off." A spotlight was trained on the back of Hrubek's head.

John Cops! he thought. Agents! FBI! Hrubek coasted to a stop and the deputies stepped from their squad car.

"Just climb off that, young man."

Hrubek swung awkwardly off the bike. The men cautiously approached. One whispered, "He's a mountain. He's huge."

"All right there. Could we see some identification?"

Fucking fucker conspirators, Hrubek thought. Politely he asked, "Are you federal agents?"

"Agents?" One of them chuckled. "No, we're just police officers. From Gunderson."

"Step over here, sir. You have a driver's license?"

Hrubek sat down, his back to the officers, and bowed his head.

The policemen looked at one another, wondering how they might deal with this. Hrubek upped the ante by crying out, "I'm soooo upset! He took everything. He hit me on the head with a rock. *Look* at my hand." He held up his scraped palm. "I've been *look*-ing for help."

They continued forward but stopped a safe distance away. "Somebody attacked you, you say? Are you hurt? If you could just let us see some ID."

"Is it him?" one asked.

"We just want to see some identification, sir. A driver's license. Anything."

"He took my wallet. He took everything."

"You've been robbed?"

"There were several of them. Took my wallet and my watch. That watch," Hrubek reported solemnly, "was a present from my mother. If you'd *watched* the roads better, you might've prevented a serious crime."

"I'm sorry if you've had some misfortune, sir. Could you give us your name and address. . . ."

"John W. Booth is my name."

"Didn't think it was that," one cop said to the other, as if speaking in front of an infant.

"Don't recall. The notice said he's harmless."

"May be, but he's big."

One cop walked closer to Hrubek, who rocked and moaned in mournful tears. "We'd appreciate you standing up, Johnnie, just coming over to the car. People at the hospital're worried about you. We want to take you back there." In a singsong voice he added, "Wouldn't you like to go home? Get some pie and milk maybe? Some nice apple pie?" He stood behind Hrubek, training his flashlight on the man's empty hands then shining it again on the back of the glossy and somewhat blue head.

"Thank you, sir. You know, I would like to be getting back, now that you mention it. I miss the place." Hrubek turned and grinned amiably as he reached up very slowly to shake the officer's hand. The policeman too smiled—in curiosity at the young man's sincere gesture—and gripped Hrubek's meaty fist, realizing too late that the madman was intending to break his wrist. The bone snapped and, shrieking, the officer dropped to his knees, the flashlight falling onto the ground beside him. His partner reached for his gun but Hrubek had already trained the stolen Colt on him.

"Nice try," he announced with damp lips that pulled into a wry smile. "Drop that, drop that!"

The cop did. "Oh, Jesus."

Hrubek took the injured cop's gun from his holster and tossed it away. The man huddled on the ground, cradling his wrist.

"Look, fellow," his partner pled, "you're going to get in nothing but trouble over this."

Hrubek chewed on a fingernail then he looked down at the cops.

"You can't stop me. I can *do* it. I'm *going* to do it, and I'm going to do it quickly!" These words rose like a mad battle cry. He shook a fist above his head.

"Please, young man, put that gun down." The injured policeman's voice broke and his eyes and nose dripped pitifully. "Nothing serious's happened. Nobody's been really hurt yet."

Hrubek turned a triumphant eye on him. He spat out, "Oh, nice *try*, John Cop. But that's where you're wrong. *Everybody's* been hurt. Everybody, everybody, everybody! And it's not over yet."

Owen Atcheson parked his truck along Route 236 next to a large, freshly turned field about seven miles west of the high rock overlook where he'd located Hrubek's nest. As anticipated, he'd found deep indentations of footsteps, indicating Hrubek was moving parallel to the road. From the depth and spacing of the toe prints it was clear he was moving fast, running.

Owen stopped at a closed gas station and used the pay phone to call the Marsden Inn. The clerk told him that Mrs. Atcheson and her sister had called and said they'd be delayed some. They hadn't checked in yet.

"Delayed? Did they say why?"

"No, sir, they didn't. Is there any message?"

Owen debated. He thought of trying to encode a message for her: Tell her the visitor's heading west but she's not to call anyone about it. . . . But there was too much risk that the clerk would be suspicious or get the message wrong.

Owen said, "No, I'll try them at home."

But there was no answer at the house. Just missed them, he thought. He'd call them at the Inn later.

The night was very dark now, the cloud cover complete, the air growing colder, compressing around him. He used his flashlight sparingly, only when he thought he saw a clue and even then lowering the light almost to the ground before clicking it on, to limit the radiation of the light. He then moved on—but slowly, very slowly. Every soldier knows—as between the hunter and the hunted, the prey has the vastly greater advantage.

Owen fell several times, catching his boot on a fence wire or forsythia tendril. He went down hard, always rolling and absorbing the impact with his shoulder and sides, never risking breaking a finger or wrist. He saw no more traps. Only at one point did Owen despair. The trail vanished completely. This happened in a vast grassy field, twenty acres square and bordered on all sides with dense woods. Owen was two hundred yards from Route 236. He stood in the center of this field and looked around him. The field extended through a break in the long line of rocky hills and offered an easy route south toward train tracks and more populated parts of the county. Freight trains came through here regularly and it was conceivable that Hrubek had leapt onto one. Or maybe he'd simply continued through the notch in the hills south toward Boyleston, a town that had both Amtrak and Greyhound stations.

Losing hope, Owen moved aimlessly through the grass, pausing to listen for footsteps, and hearing only owls or distant truck horns or the eerie white noise of an expansive autumn night. After ten minutes of meandering he noticed a glint coming from a line of trees west of him. He headed instinctively toward it. At the grove of maples he went into a crouch and moved slowly through a cluster of saplings until he came to a break in the foliage. With his gun he pushed aside a bough of dew-soaked hemlock, inhaling in surprise as drops of water fell with chill pinpricks on his neck and face.

Walking in slow circles around the old MG, Owen studied the ground. He kicked aside a white animal skull. He recognized it instantly as a ferret's. There were dozens of footprints and tire prints covering the asphalt and the shoulder. Some seemed to be Hrubek's but they were largely obliterated by people who had been here after him. He saw dog prints too and wondered momentarily if the trackers had learned that Hrubek was going west. But there was evidence of only one animal, not the three that he'd seen pursuing Hrubek from the site of his escape.

He circled the car again, weaving over the shoulder and through the bushes nearby. No sign of Hrubek's prints in any direction. Hands on hips, he glanced at the car once more. This time he noticed the bike rack but then he immediately dismissed the idea that Hrubek had stolen a cycle. What kind of escapee, he reasoned, would make a getaway on a bike, riding down open highways?

But wait. . . . Michael Hrubek was a man whose madness had its own logic. A bicycle? Why not? Owen examined the road around the car and found faint tread marks, rather wide ones—either balloon tires or those of a bike ridden by a heavy cyclist. He glanced back at the car. The carrier rack seemed broken as if the bike had been removed by sheer force.

Owen continued to follow the tread marks. At the intersection of this country lane and Route 236 he found where the rider had paused, perhaps debating which way to go.

He was not surprised to find, beside the tread, the clear imprint of Hrubek's boot.

Nor was he surprised to find that the rider had decided to turn west.

15

The house was little more than a shotgun cabin at the end of a dirt-and-rock road winding through this scruffy forest. The BMW squealed to a stop in a rectangle of mud amid discarded auto parts, sheet metal, termite-chewed firewood and oil drums torch-cut as if someone had intended to make a business of manufacturing barbecues but gave up after running out of acetylene, or desire.

Richard Kohler climbed out of the car and walked to the cabin. Rubbing his deep-set red eyes with a scrawny knuckle, he knocked on the screen door. No answer, though he heard the tinny, cluttered sound of a TV from inside. He rapped again, louder.

When the door opened he smelled liquor before he smelled wood smoke, and there was a lot of wood smoke to smell.

"Hello, Stuart."

After a long pause the man responded, "Didn't expect to see you. Guess I might've. Raining yet? It's supposed to be a son-of-a-bitch storm."

"You mind if I come in for a few minutes?"

"My girlfriend, she's out tonight." Stuart Lowe didn't move from the doorway.

"It won't take long."

"Well."

Kohler stepped past the orderly and into the small living room.

The couch was draped with two blankets and had the appearance of a sickbed. It was an odd piece of furniture—bamboo frame, cushions printed with orange and brown and yellow blotches. It reminded Kohler poignantly of Tahiti, where he'd gone on his honeymoon. And where he'd gone after his divorce, which had occurred thirty-three months later. Those two weeks represented his only vacations in the last seven years.

Kohler chose a high-backed chair to sit in. The orderly, no longer in his regulation blue jumpsuit, was now wearing jeans and a T-shirt and white socks without shoes. His arms were covered with bandages, his left eye was blackened, and his forehead and cheeks were flecked with small puncture wounds brown-stained from Betadine. He now sat back on the couch and glanced at the blankets as if he were surprised to find the bedclothes sitting out.

On the TV Jackie Gleason was screaming in a shrill and thoroughly unpleasant way at Audrey Meadows. Lowe muted the program. "They snag him yet?" Lowe asked, glancing at the phone, by which he presumably would already have learned if they'd snagged him.

Kohler told him no.

Lowe nodded and laughed vacantly at Jackie Gleason shaking his fist.

"I want to ask you a few things about what happened," Kohler asked conversationally.

"Not much to tell."

"Still."

"How'd you hear about it? Adler wanted it kept quiet."

"I've got my spies," Kohler said, and did not smile. "What happened?"

"Uh-hum. Well, we seen him and we run after him. But it was pretty dark. It was *damn* dark. He must've knowed the lay of the land pretty good and he jumped over this ravine but we fell into it."

Lowe closed his mouth and once more examined the screen, on which an automobile commercial now played. "Look at all that writing on there. Giving all that financing crap. Who can read that in three seconds? That's stupid, they do that."

The room wasn't shabby so much as dim. The prints on the walls weren't bad seascapes but they were dusky. The carpet was gray, as were the blankets that Lowe was pretending he hadn't been wrapped in five minutes before.

"How you feeling?"

"Nothing broke. Sore, but not like Frank. He took the worst of it."

"What'd Adler say to you?"

Lowe found some serviceable words and submitted them. Nothing much. Wanted to know how Lowe was feeling. Where Hrubek seemed to be going. "Truth be told, he wasn't real happy we dropped the ball in the first place and he got loose."

Across the bottom of the TV screen ran a banner announcing that a tornado had touched down in Morristown, killing two people. The National Weather Service, the streaming type reported, had extended the tornado and flash-flood warnings until 3:00 a.m. Both men stared at these words intently and both men forget them almost as soon as the bulletin ended.

"When you found him tonight, did Michael say anything?"

"Can't hardly recall. I think something about us wearing clothes and him not. Maybe something else. I don't know. I was never so scared in my life."

Kohler said, "Frank Jessup was telling me about Michael's meds."

"*Frank* knows about that? I didn't think he did. Wait, maybe I mentioned it to him."

The doctor nodded at the screen. "Art Carney's my favorite."

"He's a funny one, sure is. I like Alice. She knows what she's about."

"Frank wasn't sure how long Michael'd been cheeking them. He said two days."

"Two?" Lowe shook his head. "Where'd he hear that? Try five."

"I think they want to keep it quiet."

Lowe began to relax. "That's what Adler told me. It's not *my* business. I mean, with . . ." The comfort vanished instantly and Kohler noticed Lowe's hand seeking the satin strip on the blanket beside him. "And I just spilled the beans, didn't I? Oh, fuck," he spat out, bitterly discouraged at how easily his mind had been picked.

"I had to know, Stu. I'm his doctor. It's my job to know."

"And it's my job, period. And I'm gonna lose it. Shit. Why'd you trick me?"

Kohler wasn't giving any thought to Lowe's employment. He felt his skin crackling with shock at this confirmation of his hunch. In his last session before the escape, yesterday, Michael Hrubek had looked Kohler in the eye and had *lied* about the Thorazine. He'd said he was taking all his meds and the dosage was working well. Three thousand milligrams! And the patient had given it up purposefully and lied about doing so after he'd been off the pills for five days. And he'd lied very well. Unlike psychopaths, schizophrenic patients are rarely duplicitous in such calculating ways.

"You've got to come clean, Stu. Hrubek's a time bomb. I don't think Adler understands that. Or if he does he doesn't much care." Kohler added soothingly, "You know Michael better than most of the *doctors* at Marsden. You've got to help me."

"I got to keep my job is what I've got to do. I'm making twenty-one thousand a year and spending twenty-two. Adler'll have my nuts for what I told you already."

"Ron Adler isn't God."

"I'm not saying anything else."

"Okay, Stuart, you gonna help me, or do I have to make some phone calls?"

"Fuck." A can of beer flew from the big hand into the gray wall and with a spray of foam fell gushing onto the dingy shag carpet. It was suddenly vitally important for Stuart Lowe to tend the embers of his fire. He leapt up and pitched three fresh logs onto the heap of the dying flames. A gorgeous cascade of orange sparks bounced to the hearth. Lowe returned to the couch and said nothing for a moment. Kohler believed this meant that he accepted the terms of the agreement, which was of course no agreement at all. The signal of surrender was the soft pop as the TV was shut off.

"Did he stockpile all the Thorazine or flush it? You have any idea?"

"We found it. He stockpiled it."

"How much?"

Lowe said resignedly, "Five full days. Thirty-two hundred a day. This'll be the sixth."

"When you saw him tonight, was there any indication of what he had in mind?"

"He was just standing there in the buff, looking at us like he was surprised. But he wasn't surprised at all."

"What do you mean?"

"Nothing," Lowe spat out. "I don't mean a fucking thing."

"Tell me what he said. Exactly."

"Didn't *Frank* tell you? You already talked to him." He looked at Kohler bitterly to see if he had been as big a fool as he thought. The doctor had no choice but to oblige. "Frank's still recovering from surgery. He won't be conscious till morning."

"Jesus Christ."

"*What* did Michael say? Come on, Stu."

"Something about a death. He had a death to go to. I don't know. Maybe he meant a funeral or graveyard. I was pretty shook, you know. I was trying to fight him off Frank."

Kohler didn't respond and the orderly continued, "With those rubber things they give us."

"The truncheons?"

"I tried. I was trying to get him upside the head but he don't feel no pain. You know that."

"That's one thing about Michael," Kohler agreed, observing what a sorrowful liar Lowe was and feeling pity for this man, who'd obviously abandoned his partner to die a terrible death.

"That's all I heard. Then Michael grabbed away the club and come after me. . . ."

"Now tell me what Adler really said to you."

Lowe exhaled air through puffed-out cheeks. He finally said, "I wasn't supposed to say nothing about the meds. To nobody. And he wanted to know if Michael'd said anything about that lady in Ridgeton. He sent her a note or something."

"What lady?"

"Some broad at his trial, I don't know. Adler asked me if Michael'd ever mentioned her."

"Did he?"

"Not to me he didn't."

"What about this note?"

"I don't know nothing about it. Adler said to keep quiet about that too."

"When did he send it to her?"

"How the fuck should I know?"

"What's this woman's name?"

"You're going to ruin me, aren't you? I didn't get your patient back and you're going to fuck me over. Why don't you just admit it?"

"What's her *name*, Stu?"

"Liz something. Wait. Liz Atcheson, I think."

"Is there anything else you can tell me?"

"No," Lowe blurted so quickly all Kohler could do was fill the ensuing silence with his serene, unyielding gaze. The orderly finally said miserably, "Well, the wire."

"Wire?"

"I told Adler and Grimes and they made me swear I wouldn't say anything. Oh, Jesus . . . What a time I've had."

Kohler didn't move. His red, stinging eyes gazed at Lowe, who said *sotto voce*, as if Ronald Adler were making this a threesome, "We didn't fall."

"Tell me, Stu. *Tell* me."

"We could've jumped over that ravine easy. But Michael strung a trip wire for us. He knew we were coming. Strung a piece of fishline or bell wire and led us over it."

Kohler was dumbfounded. "What are you saying?"

"What am I saying?" Lowe blurted furiously. "Aren't you listening? Aren't you *listening*? I'm saying your patient may be off his brain candy and may be a schizo but he was fucking clever enough to lead us into a *trap*. And he damn near killed both of us." The orderly sealed his testimony by clicking the television back on and slouched into the couch, refusing to say anything more.

Passing over the Gunderson town line Trenton Heck braked deftly with his left foot as he skidded around a deer that stepped into the road and stopped to see what a collision with a one-ton pickup might do to her.

He eased back into the right lane and continued caroming down Route 236. He was driving like a teenager and he knew it, even taking the extreme measure of strapping a very unhappy Emil into the passenger seat with the blue canvas seatbelt, which the hound immediately began to chew through. Behind the truck swirled a wake of dust and bleached autumn leaves.

"Stop," Heck barked over the roar of the engine, knowing that "Don't chew," let alone "Leave that seatbelt be," would register in Emil's mind as mere human grunts, worth ignoring. The familiar command was pointless, however, and Heck let the matter go. "Good fellow," Heck said in a rare moment of sentiment, and reached over to scratch the big head, which slipped away in irritation.

"Damn," he muttered, "I'm doing it again." He realized that the hound's evasive maneuver reminded him of the way Jill had dodged away from his embrace the day after she'd served him with papers.

Got to stop thinking about that girl, he now ordered.

But of course he didn't.

"Mental cruelty and abandonment," Heck had read after the process server left. He hadn't even comprehended at first what these documents were. Abandonment? He thought they meant Jill herself was being sued for leaving the scene of an accident. She was a terrible driver. Then like a firecracker going off inside him he understood. Heck had been little good for anything for the month after that. It seemed that all he did was work with Emil and spend hours debating the separation with Jill—or rather with Jill's picture, since by then she'd moved out. Sitting on the bed where they'd romped so friskily he tried to recall her arguments. It seemed that he hadn't upheld his end of a vague bargain that had been made the morning following one particularly romantic, playful night. Their seventh date. At sunrise he'd found her plowing through his kitchen cabinets, looking for the Bisquick mix, and he'd interrupted the frenzied search to blurt a proposal. Jill had squealed and in her eagerness to hug him dropped a bag of flour. It detonated with a large white mushroom cloud. With happiness in her eyes and a little-girl pout on her lips, she cried, talking at curious length about the home that had been denied her all her life.

The marriage had been a stormy union, Heck was the first to admit. When you were on Jill's side, heaven's gate opened up and she rained her good nature on you and if you were her man there were plenty of other rewards. But if you didn't share her opinion or—good luck—if you opposed her, then the flesh over her cheekbones tightened and her tongue somehow contracted and she commenced to take you down.

Trenton Heck in fact had not been all that certain about getting married. Unreasonably, he was disappointed at having a fiancée with one syllable in her name. And when Jill grew angry—he couldn't always predict when this would happen—she became a tiny fireball. Her eyebrows knit and her voice grew husky, like the tone he believed hookers took when confronting obnoxious clients. She would mope aggressively if he said they couldn't afford a pair of high-heeled green shoes dusted with sequins, or a microwave with a revolving carousel.

"You're icky to me, Trenton. And I don't like it one bit."

"Jill, honey, baby . . ."

But the fact remained that she was a woman who'd leap into his arms at unexpected times, even at the mall, and kiss his ear wetly. She would smile with her entire face when he came home and talk nonstop about some silliness in a way that made the whole evening seem to him like good crystal and silver. And he could never forget the way she'd wake suddenly in the middle of the night, roll over on top of him, and drive her head into his collarbone, humping with so much energy that he fought hard not to move for fear it would be over too fast.

Slowly though the pouts began to outnumber the smiles and humps. The money, which was like a lubricant between their spirits, grew sparse when he was denied a raise and the mortgage on the trailer was adjusted upward. Heck began to like Jill's waitress friends and their husbands less and less; there was much drinking in that group and more silliness than seemed normal for people in their thirties. These were clues and he supposed he'd been aware of them all along. But when he finally understood that she really *meant* mental cruelty and abandonment—*his* mental cruelty and *his* abandonment—it knocked the wind clean out of him.

Exactly twenty-two months ago, at nine-forty-eight one Saturday night, Jill let slam the aluminum door of their trailer for the last time and went to live by herself in Dillon. The ultimate insult was that she moved into a mobile-home park. "Why didn't you just stay with *me*?" he blurted. "I thought you left because you wanted a house."

"Oh, Trent," she moaned hopelessly, "you don't understand nothing, do you? Not . . . a . . . thing."

"Well, you're in a trailer park, for God's sake!"

"Trent!"

"What'd I say?"

So Jill left to live in a mobile home somehow better than the one that Trenton Heck could offer her and once there, he supposed, entertain men friends. Billy Mosler, Heck's truck-driving buddy from next door, seemed relieved at the breakup. "Trenton, she wasn't for you. I'm not going to say anything bad about Jill because that's not my way—"

Watch it, you prick, Heck thought, eyeing his friend belligerently.

"—but she was too dippy for you. Bad choice in a woman. Don't look at me that way. You can do better."

"But I *loved* her," Heck said, his anger sadly tamed by a memory of Jill making him a lunch of egg salad one autumn afternoon. "Oh, damn, I'm whining, aren't I? Damn."

"You didn't *love* her," Billy Mosler said sagely. "You were *in love* with her. Or, *in lust* with her, more like. See the difference?"

Watch it, prick. Heck recovered enough to begin glaring once more.

The worst of the sting wore off after a few months though still he mourned. He drove past her restaurant a hundred times and would call her often to talk to her about the few things they could still talk about, which was not much. Many times he got her answering machine. What the hell does a waitress need an answering machine for, he brooded, except to take men's phone calls? He grew despairing when the machine picked up on the second ring, which meant that someone had called before him. Heck saw his ex-wife all over the county. At Kmart, at picnics, driving in cars he didn't recognize, in Jo-Jo's steakhouse, in liquor-store parking lots as she hiked her skirt up to adjust her slip, rolled at the waist to compensate for her being four foot eleven.

There weren't this many Jills in the universe but Trenton Heck saw them just the same.

Tonight, his ex-wife fading very reluctantly from his mind, Heck turned off the highway. Emil stirred with relief as the truck braked to a fast stop and the evil seatbelt came off. His master then hooked up the harness and track line and together they bounded off down the road.

Emil easily picked up Hrubek's scent and trotted down the highway, mimicking more or less the bicycle's passage. Because they were on the asphalt with good visibility, Heck saw no need to keep the hound short-lined; Hrubek wouldn't be setting traps on the surface of the road. They made good time, coursing past abandoned shacks and farms and lowlands and pumpkin fields. Still, after passing two intersections—and verifying that the madman was continuing west on Route 236—Heck ordered Emil back to the truck. Because of the bicycle, which Hrubek could pedal at fifteen or twenty miles an hour, Heck continued to drop-track—driving for several miles then stopping just long enough to let Emil make sure they were still on scent. For a diligent dog like Emil to follow a bicyclist was certainly possible—especially on a damp night like this—but doing so would exhaust him quickly. Then too Heck, with his damaged leg, was hardly up for a twenty-mile run after a man on wheels.

As he drove, scanning the road before him for a bicycle reflector or Hrubek's back, Trenton Heck thought about the meeting with Richard Kohler. He recalled the doctor's slight scowl when Heck had rejected his offer. This reinforced Heck's fear that maybe he'd blown it bad, that he'd chosen exactly the opposite from what a smart person would've picked. He often had trouble choosing the sensible thing, the thing everybody else just *knew* was best. The thing that *both* Jill and his father would appraise and say, "Damn good choice, boy."

He supposed in some ways it *was* crazy to turn down that money. But when he actually pictured taking the check, folding it up, going home—no, no, he just couldn't have done it. Maybe God hadn't made him like Emil, doling out to him a singular, remarkable knack. But Trenton Heck felt in his heart that if he had any purpose at all, it was to spend his hours tracking behind his dog through wilderness just like this. Even if he never found Hrubek tonight, even if he never caught a *glimpse* of him, being here *had* to be better than sitting in front of the tube with a quart of beer in his hand and Emil fidgeting on the back deck.

What troubled Heck more than turning down Kohler's offer was altogether different, maybe something more dangerous. If it was really his goal to catch Hrubek before he hurt someone, then why didn't he just call Don Haversham and tell him that Hrubek had changed direction? Heck was in Gunderson now and would be coming up on Cloverton soon. Both towns had police departments and, despite the storm, probably a few men to spare for a roadblock. Calling Haversham, he thought, was the prudent thing to do, the proper procedure. It promised the least risk to everyone.

But of course if the local police or troopers caught Hrubek, Adler would surely balk at paying Heck the ten thousand.

So, steeped in guilt and uneasiness, Heck pressed the stiff accelerator with his left foot and continued after his prey, speeding west in secret and under cover of the night—just like, he laughed grimly, Michael Hrubek himself.

He was twenty-two miles from Ridgeton when the idea of an automobile slipped into his mind and rooted there.

A car'd be so much *nicer* than a bicycle, so much more *fashionable*. Hrubek had mastered pedaling and now found the bike a frustrating way to travel. It flicked sideways when it hit rocks and there were long stretches of inclines that required him to ride so slowly that he could have walked faster. His teeth ached from the air he sucked into his lungs with the effort of low-gear pedaling. When he hit a bump the heavy animal traps bounced and jabbed him in the kidney. But more than anger at the bike, Hrubek simply felt the *desire* for a car. He believed he had the confidence to drive. He'd fooled the orderlies and whipped the cops and tricked all the fucker conspirators who were after him.

And now he wanted a car.

He recalled the time he'd pumped a tank of gas for Dr. Anne when she'd driven Hrubek and several other patients to a bookstore in a mall near Trevor Hill Psychiatric Hospital. Knowing—and compulsively reciting—the statistics on auto fatalities on American highways, he was terrified at the thought of the drive but reluctantly agreed to go along. The psychiatrist asked him to sit in the front seat. When they stopped at the gas station, she asked, "Michael, will you help me fill up the tank?"

"Noooo."

"Please?"

"Not on your life. It's not safe and it's not fashionable."

"Let's do it together."

"Who knows what comes out of those pumps?"

"Come on, Michael. Get out of the car."

"Nice try."

But he *did* it—opening the tank door, unscrewing the lid, turning on the pump, squeezing the nozzle handle. Dr. Anne thanked Hrubek for his help and, glowing with pride, he climbed back into the front seat, snapping his belt on without her telling him to do so. On their next outing she let him drive the gray Mercedes through the hospital parking lot, arousing the envy of the patients and the amusement—and awe—of several doctors and nurses.

Yep, he now decided, the bike's got to go.

He coasted to the bottom of a long hill, where he stopped at a darkened gas station, its windows spattered with mud and grease. What had caught his interest was an old lime-green Datsun parked beside the air pump. Hrubek climbed off the bicycle. The car's door was unlocked. He sat in the driver's seat, smelling oil and mold. He practiced driving. He was very tense at first then relaxed and gradually remembered what he knew about cars. He moved the steering wheel. He put the gearshift lever in D. He practiced pushing the accelerator and the brake.

He looked down at the wheel pedestal and saw a key in the ignition. He turned it. Silence. He climbed out. He supposed the car might need a battery or maybe gasoline. He opened the hood and found that what the car needed, however, was an engine. Some fucker had stolen it, he observed, and slammed the hood closed.

Can't trust anybody.

Hrubek walked to the front of the store and looked in. A soda machine, a snack machine, a wire tray holding boxes of doughnuts and pastries. Twinkies. He liked Twinkies. He muttered a line he had once heard on TV: "A wholesome snack." Repeating this phrase over and over he walked to the back of the station. "Be smart," he whispered. "Use the back door." He hoped there was an engine lying around inside. Could he install it himself in the green car? he wondered. You probably just plugged them into the engine compartment. (Hrubek knew all about plugs; because the electrical appliances in his parents' house contained listening devices or cameras, Michael had settled into the daily routine of unplugging them every morning. The VCR in the Hrubek household was perpetually flashing 12:00).

He strode to the back door of the gas station and knocked out the glass in the window then undid the deadbolt. He walked inside and perused the place. He found no ready-to-mount auto engines, which was an immense disappointment though this setback was largely mitigated by the doughnuts on the rack by the door. He immediately ate an entire package and put another in his backpack.

Taste That Beats the Others Cold promised the torn and faded poster taped to the ancient Pepsi machine in the front of the store. He easily ripped open its door and pulled out two bottles of soda. He had forgotten all about glass containers—in mental hospitals you get soda in plastic cups or not at all. He popped the cap off with his teeth and, sitting down, he began to drink.

In five minutes the parking lot outside turned silver, then white. This attracted Hrubek's attention and he rose, walking to the greasy glass to determine the source of the light. A glistening metallic-blue 4x4 truck pulled into the driveway. The door opened and the driver climbed out. She was a pretty woman with frothy blond hair. To a phone pole beside the air pump she taped a poster advertising a church auction to be held tomorrow night.

"Will they auction their *memorabilia*?" Hrubek whispered. "Will they sell their memory-*labia*? Will the priest stick his finger in your *pussy*?" He glanced inside the truck. The woman's passenger was a teenage girl, her daughter, it seemed. He continued, speaking now in a conversational tone, addressing the girl. "Oh, you're very beautiful. Do you like al-ge-*bra*? Are you wearing one over your tits? Did you know that ninety-nine percent of schizophrenics have big cocks? The *cock* crowed when Jesus got betrayed—just like Eve. Say, is the priest going to stick his *snake* in you? You may know that as a serpent."

The driver returned to the truck. Oh, she looks beautiful, Hrubek thought, and couldn't decide whom he liked best, mother or daughter. The 4x4 turned back onto the highway and a moment later pulled into a driveway or side road a hundred yards west on Route 236. It vanished. He stood for a long moment at the window, then blew hot breath onto the cold glass in front of him, leaving a large white circle of condensation, in the center of which he drew a very good likeness of an apple, complete with leaves and stem and pierced by what appeared to be a worm hole.

Their Maginot Line, four feet high, was starkly illuminated by another sudden flash of distant lightning.

The women, both exhausted, stepped back from their handiwork as they waited for thunder that never sounded.

Portia said, "We oughta break a bottle of champagne over it." She leaned heavily on the shovel.

"Might not hold."

"Fucking well better." The water in the culvert leading to the dam was already six inches high.

"Let's finish taping the greenhouse and get out of here."

They stowed the tools and Lis pulled a battered tarp over the depleted pile of sand. She still felt hurt by Portia's rebuff earlier but, as they strolled back to the house like two oil-workers at day's end, Lis nonetheless had a sudden urge to put her arm around her sister's shoulders. Yet she hesitated. She could picture the contact but not the effect and that was enough to stop the gesture. Lis recalled bussing cheeks with relatives on holidays, she recalled handshakes, she recalled palms on buttocks.

That was the extent of physical contact in the L'Auberget family.

Lis heard a clatter not far away. The wind had pushed over a set of aluminum beach chairs beside the garage. She told her sister she was going to put them away and started down the hill. Portia headed up to the house.

Pausing in the driveway, Lis felt a sharp gust of wind—an outrider of the storm. Ripples swept across the surface of the lake and a corner of the tarp covering the sand snapped like a gunshot. Then calm returned, as if the breeze were a shiver passing through a body.

In the silence that followed she heard the car.

The tires crunched on the glistening white stone chips that she and Owen had spread in the driveway last summer during a heat spell. She'd feared then for their hearts under the scalding sun and insisted that they finish the job after dusk. Lis Atcheson knew that the visitor tonight was driving over fragments of premium marble from a quarry somewhere in New England. But for some reason the thought came to her that the sound was of wheels on crushed bone and once there the horrid image would not leave.

The car moved urgently through the stand of pines through which the serpentine driveway ran. It pulled into the parking area, paused then headed toward her. Blinded by the beams, she couldn't identify the vehicle, which stopped a dozen yards away.

Lis stood with arms crossed, her feet separated, frozen like a schoolgirl playing statue. For a long moment neither she nor the driver moved. She faced the car, whose engine was still running, lights on. Finally, before uneasiness became fear, she cleared her throat and walked forward into piercing shafts of white light.

16

"They haven't caught him yet?"

Lis motioned with her hand toward the back door and Richard Kohler preceded her into the kitchen.

"No, I'm afraid not." He stepped to the counter and set a small backpack on the butcher block. He seemed quite possessive about it. His thin face was alarmingly pale.

"Lis, there's a car—"

Portia walked into the doorway and paused, glancing at Kohler. Lis introduced them.

"*Portia?*" Kohler repeated. "Don't hear that name much nowadays."

She shrugged and neither sister said a word about the burdens of being the daughter of a man utterly devoted to the business of fortified wine.

"I'm going to tape the west windows. In the parlor. That's where it'll hit worst."

"You're right. We forgot to do those. Thanks."

When she left, Lis turned to the doctor. "I don't have much time. As soon as we're finished here, we're going to a hotel for the evening." She added pointedly, "Because of Hrubek."

It was the moment when he'd tell her there was nothing to worry about, the moment when he'd laugh and say that his patient was harmless as a puppy. He didn't.

What he said was, "That's probably not a bad idea."

On the other hand he didn't seem particularly alarmed or suggest that they get the hell out of the house immediately and flee for safety.

"Do they know where he is?"

"Not exactly, no."

"But he *is* going away from here? East?"

"I saw one of the men tracking him not too long ago. He's still east of the hospital but it looks like he may have gone east and then turned around."

"He's coming west?"

"I'd say he's more likely wandering in circles. He isn't as disabled as some people are making him out to be, but I don't think he'd be able to get this far."

"What exactly can I do for you, doctor? I'd like to be out of here in twenty minutes or so."

"I'm worried about Michael. I'd like to find him before the police do. Not many people know how to handle a patient like him. He could hurt himself or somebody else if they try to arrest him like any other prisoner."

"Well, what can *I* do?"

"I understand he sent you a letter not long ago."

"In September."

"It had to do with the . . . incident last May?"

"It doesn't seem to have to do with anything. It's mostly gibberish."

Kohler lifted his eyes but not his head and stared directly at her. "Mrs. Atcheson, I need to know about Indian Leap. Will you help me?"

Six large water spots were evident on the counter beside the sink. Lis lifted a sponge and rubbed them away.

"You see, I'm Michael's attending psychiatrist. But I frankly don't have a clue about what's going on in his mind tonight. What happened last May was very . . . significant in his life."

"Significant?" she repeated, appalled at the word.

"I don't mean to downplay the tragedy."

"Well, what exactly can I tell you?"

"I've read some newspaper stories. I have a few files. But Marsden hospital's practically broke. We have very sketchy records. I don't even have a transcript of his trial."

This struck her as the epitome of bureaucratic nonsense, and she said so.

"Transcripts cost two dollars a page," he explained. "Michael's would have cost six thousand dollars. The state can't afford it."

"It seems to be just common sense to spend money like that."

He gestured in concession.

"I really don't think there's time." She nodded outside. "My sister and I have hotel reservations. And the storm . . ."

"It won't take long." He curled two fingers of his right hand around two fingers of his left, and Lis pictured the gangly teenage Richard Kohler asking a pretty girl to dance.

"The fact is, I'd rather not talk about it."

"Yes, of course . . ." Kohler hesitated and seemed to be examining her. "But you have to understand my perspective. It's important that I find him quickly. If he wanders up to someone's house . . . If he gets scared and panics. People could get hurt. Inadvertently."

Lis stood silent, looking down at the ruddy tile floor.

"*That's* what I'm concerned about, you see. Getting him back before there's an . . . accident. And, I have to tell you, there *is* a chance he's on his way here. Very slight, but it is a possibility. If you help me I might be able to prevent that."

After a long moment Lis said, "Cream and sugar?"

Kohler blinked.

"You've glanced at the coffee maker three times in the last minute."

He laughed. "I've been trying my best to stay awake."

"I'll give you twenty minutes, doctor. Not a minute more."

"Thank you very much," he said sincerely.

She stepped to the cupboard.

"Hope it's no trouble." His eyes were hungrily fixed to the can of Maxwell House.

"Can I ask a question?"

"Please."

"Could you fall asleep now?" Lis asked.

"I beg your pardon?"

"If you were home now would you be able to fall asleep?"

"At home? Yes. In my car, yes. On your front lawn. On your kitchen floor. Anytime, anyplace."

She wagged her head at this miracle and watched the pot fill with black liquid. Impulsively she decided to have a cup too. "I won't be asleep before eleven tomorrow night, whatever happens tonight."

"Insomnia?" he asked.

A condition on which she was an expert, she explained. Warm milk, hot baths, cold showers, hypnosis, self-hypnosis, valerian roots, biofeedback, medication. "You name it, I've tried it."

"In my practice I work with patients' dreams a lot. But I've never done much with sleep disorders."

She doctored her coffee with milk. Kohler took his black. "Let's go in here," she said.

With their thin mugs of steaming coffee in hand they walked into the greenhouse, at the far end of which was an alcove. As they sat in the deep wrought-iron chairs, the doctor looked about the room and offered a compliment, which because it had to do only with square footage and neatness meant he knew nothing of, and cared little for, flowers. He sat with his legs together, body forward, making his thin form that much thinner. He took loud sips, and she knew he was a man accustomed to dining quickly and alone. Then he set the cup down and took a pad and gold pen from his jacket pocket.

Lis asked, "Then you have no idea where he's going tonight?"

"No. He may not either, not consciously. That's the thing about Michael—you can't take him literally. To understand him you have to look behind what he says. That note he sent you, for instance; were certain letters capitalized?"

"Yes. That was one of the eeriest things about it."

"Michael does that. He sees relationships between things that to us don't exist. Could I see it?"

She found it in the kitchen and returned to the greenhouse. Kohler was standing, holding a small ceramic picture frame.

"Your father?"

"I'm told there's a resemblance."

"Some, yes. Eyes and chin. He was, I'd guess . . . a professor?"

"More of a closet scholar." The picture had been taken two days after he'd returned from Jerez, and Andrew L'Auberget was shown here climbing into the front seat of the Cadillac for the drive back to the airport. Young Lis had clicked the shutter as she stood shaded by her mother's protruding belly, inside of which her sister floated oblivious to the tearful farewell. "He was a businessman but he really wanted to teach. He talked about it many times. He would've made a brilliant scholar."

"Are you a professor?"

"Teacher. Sophomore English. And you?" she asked. "I understand medicine runs in the genes."

"Oh, it does. My father was a doctor." Kohler laughed. "Of course he wanted me to be an art historian. That was his dream. Then he grudgingly consented to medical school. On condition that I study surgery."

"But that wasn't for you?"

"Nope. All I wanted was to be a psychiatrist. Fought him tooth and nail. He said if you become a shrink, it'll chew you up, make you miserable, make you crazy and kill you."

"So," Lis said, "he was a psychiatrist."

"That he was."

"Did it kill him?"

"Nope. He retired to Florida."

"About which, I won't comment," she said. He smiled. Lis added, "Why?"

"How's that?"

"Why psychiatry?"

"I wanted to work with schizophrenics."

"I'd think you'd make more money putting rich people on the couch. Why'd you specialize in that?"

He smiled again. "Actually, it was my mother's illness. Say, is that the letter there?"

He took it in his short, feminine fingers and read it quickly. She could detect no reaction. "Look at this: '. . . *they are holding me and have told lIes About Me to waShingtOn and the enTIRE worlD.*' See what he's really saying?"

"No, I'm afraid I don't."

"Look at the capitalized letters. 'I AM SO TIRED.' "

The encoded message sent a chill through her.

"There are a lot of layers of meaning in Michael's world. 'Revenge' contains the name 'Eve.' " He scanned the paper carefully. " 'Revenge,' 'eve,' 'betrayal.' "

He shook his head then set the letter aside and turned his hard eyes on her. She suddenly grew ill at ease. And when he said, "Tell me about Indian Leap," a full minute passed before she began to speak.

Heading northeast from Ridgeton, Route 116 winds slowly through the best and the worst parts of the state: picturesque dairy and horse farms, then small but splendid patches of hardwood forests, then finally a cluster of tired mid-size towns studded with abandoned factories that the banks and receivers can't give away. Just past one of these failed cities, Pickford, is a five-hundred-acre sprawl of rock bluffs and pine forest.

Indian Leap State Park is bisected by a lazy S-shaped canyon, which extends for half a mile from the parking lot off 116 to Rocky Point Beach, a deceptive name for what's nothing more than a bleak rock revetment on a gray, man-made lake about one mile by two in size. Rising from the forest not far from the beach is what the State Park Service, still overly generous, calls a "peak," though it's really just a flat-topped summit six hundred feet high.

These rocks have their ghosts. In 1758 a small band of Mohegans, trapped on the side of this mountain, jumped to their deaths rather than be captured by rival Pequots. The women flung their screaming children before them then leapt to the rocks below with their men. Lis could still recall in perfect detail the bad, earnest illustration in her fifth-grade textbook of a squaw, looking more like Veronica Lake than a princess of the Mohican Confederacy, reaching for her tearful child as they were about to sail into the air. The first time she'd come here, a skinny wan girl, Lis walked these trails close to tears, thinking of the sorrow—whole families flying through the air. Even now, thirty years later, sitting across from Kohler, she felt the chill horror the story had evoked in her childhood.

Six months ago, on May 1, the Atchesons and the Gillespies—a couple they knew from the country club—planned a picnic at Indian Leap. Accompanying them were Portia and a former student of Lis's, Claire Sutherland.

The morning of the outing—it was a Sunday—had begun awkwardly. Just as Lis and Owen were about to leave, he got a call from his firm and learned that he had to go into the office for several hours. Lis was used to his zealot's schedule but was irritated that he acquiesced today. He'd worked almost every Sunday since early

...pring. The couple fought about it—genteelly at first, then more ...ngrily. Owen prevailed, though he promised he'd meet them at the ...ark no later than one-thirty or two.

"I didn't realize until later how lucky it was that he won that ...rgument," she told Kohler softly. "If he hadn't gone into work . . . ...t's funny how fate works."

She continued with her story. Portia, Claire and Lis rode with ...orothy and Robert Gillespie in their Land Cruiser. It was a pleas...ant two-hour drive to the park. But as soon as they arrived, Lis ...egan to feel uneasy, as if they were being watched. Walking to ...he lodge house to use the phone she believed she saw, in a distant ...cluster of bushes, someone looking at her. Because she had the ...mpression that there was something of recognition in the face, ...which she took to be a man's, she believed for an instant that it ...was Owen, who'd changed his mind and decided not to work after ...all. But the face vanished into the bushes and when she called her ...husband's office, he answered the phone.

"You haven't left yet?" she asked, disappointed. It was then ...noon; he wouldn't be there before two.

"Fifteen minutes, I'll be on my way," he announced. "Are you ...there yet?"

"We just got here. I'm at the gift store."

"Oh"—Owen laughed—"get me one of those little pine out...houses. I'll give it to Charlie for making me come in today."

She was irritated but agreed to, and they hung up. Lis went into ...the store to buy the souvenir. When she stepped outside a moment ...later and rejoined the others at the entrance to the park, she ...glanced over her shoulder. She believed she saw the man staring ...again, studying the five of them. She was so startled she dropped ...the wooden outhouse. When she picked it up and looked back ...again, whoever it might have been was gone.

...was someone to whom Lis could confide sins ...urth level of hell.

...thy, Lis recalled, who'd heard that the weather ... supposed to be particularly beautiful and had

...spring of data). They never became ...clothes (about

...laire?"

...d, the girl had been in Lis's English class her ...e was intensely shy, with a pale, heart-shaped ...ebody," Lis explained, "you hoped wouldn't be...because it seemed there was no way she could

...was. Seeing her on the first day of class, several ...truck immediately by the girl's ethereal face, ...licate fingers. Teachers peg students instantly,

Kohler asked her about the others on the picnic.

"Robert and Dorothy? We met them at the club about a year ago."

The foursome had coincidentally picked adjacent poolside tables. They became friends by default, being about the only childless couples over thirty in the place. This mutual freedom broke the ice and they gradually got to know each other.

Owen and Lis were initially no match socially for their friends. Not yet inheritors of the L'Auberget fortune, the Atchesons lived in a small split-level in Hanbury, a grim industrial town ten miles west of Ridgeton. In fact the country-club membership itself, which Owen had insisted on so that he might court potential clients, was far too expensive for them, and many nights they'd eaten sandwiches or soup for dinner because they had virtually no cash in the bank. Robert, on the other hand, made buckets of money selling hotel communications systems. Owen, a lawyer in a small firm with small clients, masked his chagrin under careful smiles but Lis could see bitter jealousy when the Gillespies pulled up in front of the Atchesons' tacky house in Robert's new forest-green Jag or Dorothy's Merc.

There was the matter of temperament too: Robert had lived in Pacific Heights and on Michigan Avenue, and spent several years in Europe. ("No, no, I kid you not! It was Tourette sur Loup. Ever hear of it? A medieval city in the mountains northwest of Nice, and what do we find in the town square? A cross-dressing festival. Really! Tell 'em, Dot!")

He seemed ten years younger than his forty-one and you couldn't help but feel the tug of his boyish enthusiasm. With Robert, all the world was a sales prospect and you w[...] be hawke[...] Owen had more substance but he [...] too. He didn't like taking second [...] charmer who resembled JFK in b[...]

But then last March, when R[...]

and Lis had felt an immediate fondness for Claire. She'd made an effort to stay in touch as the girl made her way through her junior then senior years. Lis rarely singled out any youngsters from school; only on one or two other occasions had she maintained relationships with students, or former students, outside of class. She generally kept her distance, aware of the power she had over these young people. When she wore light-colored blouses she noticed boys' eyes

when [...] that her mother wo[...] while their cheeks [...] grew red

that her mother [...] invite her along.

That May 1 the picnickers set up camp [...] Portia left immediately for a run—an improvised 10K [...] winding canyons. She runs marathons, Lis told Kohler

"So do I," the doctor said.

Lis laughed, astonished, as ever, that people actually engaged in this sport for fun.

"We sat on the beach for a while, Dorothy, Robert, Claire and I. Watching the boats. You know, just chatting and drinking soda and beer."

They had been there for about a half hour when Dorothy and Robert began to argue.

Dorothy had left Lis's book in the truck. "*Hamlet*," she explained. She'd been preparing for final exams and had carted along a well-read and annotated volume. "I had my hands full with picnic things and Dorothy said she'd get the book. But it had slipped her mind." Lis had told her not to worry; she wasn't in the mood to work anyway. But Robert leapt up and said he'd get it. Then Dorothy made some sour comment about his doing anything for anybody in a skirt. It was supposed to be a joke, Lis supposed, but it fell flat—since she'd managed to insult both Lis and Robert at the same time.

"Robert asked her what she meant by that. Dorothy waved her hand and said, 'Just go get the fucking book, why don't you?' Something like that. Then she told him he ought to jog all the way to the parking lot. 'Work off some of that fat. Look, he's getting tits.' "

Lis was embarrassed for Claire's sake. Robert jogged off angrily and Dorothy sullenly returned to her magazine.

Lis had pulled off her shorts and unbuttoned her workshirt, beneath which she wore a bikini. She lay back on a warm rock and closed her eyes, trying not to go to sleep (daytime naps are taboo for insomniacs). Claire, with whom Robert had struck up an immediate friendship en route to the beach, had seemed the most anxious of anyone for him to return. After he'd been gone a half hour, she stood and said she was going to look for him. Lis had watched the girl as she strolled toward the towering, weathered rocks. Repulsive and fascinating, the cliffs seemed hard as polished bone. They reminded her of the yellow skull sitting on the lab table in the school's biology classroom.

Lis noticed Claire standing in the mouth of the canyon about a quarter mile from the beach. Then she vanished.

"And I thought suddenly," Lis told Kohler, "where is everyone? What's going on? I felt very concerned. I picked up my purse and started toward the place where I'd seen Claire disappear." Then she saw a flash of color ahead of her. She believed it was yellow, the color of Claire's shorts, and leaving Dorothy behind she hurried into the canyon. Lis was perhaps a hundred yards into the ravine when she found the blood.

"Blood?"

It was right outside a cave. The entrance had been chained off at one time but the post holding the chain had been pulled out of the ground and flung aside. No way, she thought, was she going inside. But she knelt down and looked into the passageway. The air was chill and it smelled of wet stone and clay and mold.

Then she felt a shadow over her. A huge man appeared just feet away, standing behind her.

"Michael?" Kohler asked.

Lis nodded.

Hrubek started howling like an animal. Holding a bloody rock, he looked right at her and screamed, "*Sic semper tyrannis!*"

Richard Kohler held up a thin hand, indicating for her to wait. He made his first notation of the evening.

"You didn't think of going to find a park ranger?" Kohler asked.

Lis suddenly grew angry. Why had he asked her this? It was the sort of question the lawyers had asked, and the police. Did I think of looking for a ranger? Well, for God's sake, wouldn't we *always* do it differently if we could? Wouldn't we recast our whole *lives*? That's why time doesn't reverse, of course—to keep us sane.

"I thought about it, yes. But I don't know, I just panicked. I ran into the cave."

Inside, it wasn't completely dark. Thirty, forty feet above her, shafts of pale light streamed inside.

The walls rose straight up to an arched roof full of stalactites. Lis, breathless and frightened, leaned against a wall to steady herself. A high-pitched moaning of some sort filled the air. It was like wind over a reed, like someone imitating an oboe. Terrible! She looked at the trail at her feet and saw more blood.

Then Hrubek slipped through the cave opening. Lis turned and raced down the path. No idea where she was going, not really thinking, she simply ran. Once out of the main chamber she fled down a long corridor, about eight feet high. Hrubek was somewhere behind her. As she ran she noticed the tunnel was growing smaller. By now it had shrunk to six feet, and the sides were closing in. Once she slammed into a rock, cutting her forehead and leaving a scar that still remained. By then the chamber had narrowed down to five feet and she was running crouched over. Then, four feet. Soon she was crawling.

Ahead of her the tunnel grew even smaller though on the other side of a very narrow opening it seemed to widen and grow brighter. But escaping that way would mean crawling through a tunnel that was no more than twelve or so inches high. With Hrubek right behind her.

"The thought of being, well, exposed to him like that. I mean, wearing just my swimsuit . . . I couldn't do it. I turned to my left and crawled through a larger entrance."

It was black, completely black, but she felt cool air circulating and assumed it was a large space. She climbed inside, feeling her way along the smooth floor. Looking back she could see the entrance—it was slightly lighter than the surrounding walls. Slowly it darkened then grew less dark again, and she heard a hissing sound. He was in this small cave with her. She lay flat on the ground and bit a finger to keep silent while she sobbed.

"You have no idea what noise is until you've been in a place like that. I was sure my heartbeat or the sound of blood in my ears would give me away. I think I could hear my own tears falling on the floor of the cave."

All the while Hrubek was shuffling around her. He passed her, no more than five feet away. Then he paused and sniffed the air and muttered, "There's a woman in here. I can smell her pussy."

Lis ran. She couldn't bear it any longer. "I scrambled to the opening and turned back down the narrow corridor, the way I'd come. That is, I thought I did. But somehow I took a wrong turn."

In one sense it was lucky. The light was better here and the roof of the cave high. She saw discarded cigarettes and beer cans—which led her to believe she was heading toward an exit. She kept moving toward the light.

"Then I felt a breeze stirring and way up ahead I heard running water. I ran toward it as fast as I could. Then I turned the corner. That's where I found the body." She gazed through the misty windows into the yard, now filled with a blustery wind. "I didn't recognize it at first. There was too much blood."

17

Robert Gillespie lay on the cave floor.

"He was twisted like a rag doll and had a huge gash in his head. But he wasn't dead."

She'd taken Robert's hand and leaned close, urging him to keep breathing. She'd get help, she said. But then she heard footsteps. Ten feet away Hrubek stood staring at them. He was smiling cynically, muttering.

"He was talking," Lis told Kohler, "about conspirators."

Stumbling backwards Lis landed on her purse. Inside, she felt a knife. She'd packed it for the picnic, she explained, wrapping it in a paper towel and placing it in her bag so no one would reach blindly into the picnic basket and cut themselves. She pulled it out now and ripped the towel away from the blade—it was very sharp, a Chicago Cutlery, nine inches long. She pointed it at Hrubek and told him to keep back. But he just kept walking at her, saying, "*Sic semper tyrannis!*" again and again. Her nerve broke. She dropped the knife and ran.

"That was the knife that he used?" Kohler asked. "I remember reading that the victim was stabbed as well as beaten. Sexually mutilated too."

After a moment Lis answered, "Robert was badly hurt but he probably could've survived. According to the evidence at the trial they think he would've recovered from the rock blows. He died from the stabbing." She paused. "And the mutilation? Yes, Hrubek stabbed Robert in the groin. A number of times."

Only fifty feet away Lis found the exit and scrabbled through it. She collapsed on the ground and caught her breath. Then she headed into the canyon. But after running only a dozen yards she pulled up with a fierce cramp in her side. Hrubek was twenty or thirty feet behind her. He was saying, "Come here. You're a very beautiful woman but what's that on your hair? I don't like your hair that way. What's that on your *head*?" She'd gotten some of Robert's blood on her hair. This upset Hrubek. He was very angry. She supposed that he was worried it was evidence. "What did you do to yourself?" he called. "That's not *fashionable*. You shouldn't've done that!"

He stepped toward her and she dropped to her knees, rolling under a jutting overhang about a foot and a half high. It went back into the rock maybe six feet and there she wedged herself, shivering in the cold and fighting the panic from confinement. As she stared at the path, his feet appeared. He wore shoes. Huge ones. Wingtips. This astonished her. For some reason she expected him to be barefoot, with long yellow toenails. She wondered if he'd killed a man for the shoes. Then he bent down and lay on his belly.

" 'Nice try,' he kept saying. 'Come on out here. You're Eve, aren't you? Beautiful lady. Ought to shave that fucking hair off.' "

She wedged herself as far back as she could, her face pressing into the rock. When he groped for her, she screamed and the piercing sound of her own voice stunned her ears. He screamed too, crying at her to shut up. He grunted and tried again to grab her. With a huge effort he jammed his arm forward. The tip of his middle finger eased against her thigh. Those were the only parts of their bodies close enough to touch. Lis felt the feathery trail of his callused skin move toward her knee. The sensation was like a burn and it remained, searing, even when Hrubek stood and vanished.

Lis lay, whimpering and fighting the grip of claustrophobia. Where was he? she wondered. Did she dare leave? It'd been a half hour since she'd disappeared from the beach. She knew Owen wouldn't have arrived yet but Portia and Dorothy might've come looking for her. Claire too would be somewhere nearby.

Outside she noticed rain beginning to spatter on the stone path.

"I started to push myself out. Then I heard two things. One was Hrubek's voice. He was very close and talking to himself. The other sound was thunder."

It shook the ground. She was worried that the rock above her might shift and trap her where she lay. But this fear was soon replaced by a more immediate one—that she would drown. Huge gushes of water suddenly flowed down the arroyo and the cave began to fill.

She eased closer to the opening. If Hrubek had reached in again, he could have grabbed her easily. Her head was sideways—the only way it would fit into the narrow space—and she was twisting her mouth upward, desperately gasping for air. Soon, filthy water was surging around her face, flowing over her lips. She spat it out and started choking. More thunder, more torrents of water, tumbling over the stone. She pushed toward the opening but couldn't make headway. Fighting the rush of water she finally got far enough through the current to fling her hand outside the cave. Blindly, she gripped a rock and pulled herself toward it.

"Then the rock moved. It wasn't a rock at all but a shoe. I pulled back quickly but a huge hand grabbed me by the wrist and tugged me out." Lis looked away from Kohler. "My swimsuit snagged on a rock and tore open."

She was half-naked. But she had no choice—she couldn't stay in the cave any longer. She remembered thinking she wished that she had the courage to choose to die by drowning rather than be raped and murdered by the madman. As she was drawn out of the cave, her mind was filled with images of Hrubek's huge hands prodding her breasts and reaching between her legs. She began to cry.

Then a man's voice said, "It's all right, ma'am, it's all right. What's the matter?"

She collapsed into the arms of the park ranger.

Leaning against the rock in the torrential rain she told him about Robert and Hrubek. He began asking questions but Lis couldn't concentrate. All she could hear was a horrid keening that filled the air. It seemed to come from earth itself, resonating from the rocks, stretching out thinner and thinner, impossibly thin, an unsustainable note that nonetheless refused to stop. " 'What *is* that?' I asked. 'Make it stop. Oh, for God's sake.' "

And soon it did, Lis explained to the psychiatrist.

For, as Lis found out just moments later from another ranger, an underground stream, swollen with rain, had overflowed into the cave where Lis had found Robert's body—the cave where Claire had been all along. The sound had been the girl's wail for help that had been stifled by the rising waters in which she'd drowned.

Stopping the truck abruptly and extinguishing the lights, Owen Atcheson gazed about him, surveying this dismal stretch of deserted road.

He slipped the pistol out of his pocket and stepped into the clearing, playing his flashlight on the dusty shoulder. Hrubek's bike had been laid or had fallen on its side and there were footprints around it. Several of these he recognized as the madman's boots but the others weren't familiar to him. It was clear that at one point Hrubek had sat on the ground—the sides of his heels made deep cut marks and his hams wide indentations in the dirt of the highway's shoulder.

He couldn't make any sense of what'd happened here. He noticed the bicycle treads led on again, continuing west down Route 236, yet still he studied the turnoff carefully, trying to get a clearer idea of how Hrubek's mind worked. He saw a grassy access road nearby:

a path disappearing into the forest. A number of tire treads led toward it, some fresh.

Beyond this was a long road descending through trees, bushes, tall grass, vines, mist. Where the path flattened out again and vanished into the murky shadows of the forest was a car, sitting cock-eyed in the brush. Owen shone his flashlight toward it but the distance was too great for illumination; all he saw was a vague image of the vehicle. He deduced it was an abandoned hulk because it appeared to be two-tone; Detroit had stopped making those a long time ago. He didn't bother to explore the vehicle further but returned to the road and drove slowly west, checking every hundred yards or so for the weaving bike tread.

And pondering again the biggest problem of the evening.

His was no moral dilemma. Oh, Owen Atcheson had absolutely no ethical difficulty with walking right up to Hrubek and putting a bullet into his forehead. No, it was simply practical, one that Haversham had reminded him of in Adler's office: how could he kill Michael Hrubek without ending up disbarred and in jail himself.

If Hrubek had been a convicted felon, Owen would have an easier time of it. Fleeing felons could legally be shot in the back (Owen now squinted as he recited from cold memory the rules in the state Penal Code). But Hrubek was *not* a felon. Although the jury found that he had in fact killed Robert Gillespie, the verdict that was entered was not guilty by reason of insanity.

This meant that there were only two justifiable ways to kill Hrubek. First, to be attacked by him in a place from which Owen couldn't reasonably escape: an enclosed room, a blocked tunnel, a bridge. Second, to catch Hrubek in the Atcheson house, where Owen could legally shoot him without provocation and have nothing but an inconvenient trip to police HQ to show for it. And possibly not even that.

One of these scenarios would have to be engineered. But he was still too far from his prey to figure out exactly how. No, there was nothing to do now but continue on, driving slowly through the misty night, amid this troubled uncertainty—not of purpose, but of means. He gave in to the mood of combat, thinking purely of the mechanics of the kill: Which shot would be the most effective? Which gun should he use? How far would a man of Hrubek's size be able to run with a mortal wound? (Like a cape buffalo or bear, a frighteningly long way, he guessed.) Was Hrubek himself stalking his pursuers? Was he even now laying another steel-jawed trap? Or something more deadly? From his military days, Owen knew the huge variety of booby traps that can be created out of gasoline, naphtha, fertilizer, nails, tools, lumber, wire.

He was considering these matters when he passed an old roadside gas station and general store, closed and dark. He slowed and studied the road carefully. The station had apparently attracted Hrubek too; the bike treads turned into the driveway. Owen pulled the truck past the lot and stopped very slowly to keep the damp brakes from squealing. He took his pistol from his pocket and, verifying that he still had the rifle bolt with him, climbed out of the truck.

He noticed in the front of the building, near one of the pumps, a box of doughnuts, half-empty. It seemed a little too prominent— as if it'd been left here to lure pursuers into a trap—and when Owen walked to the back of the building he walked very quietly. Yes, the window was broken and the deadbolt unlatched. He inhaled slowly, to steady himself, then pushed the door open—fast, to keep the hinges from squealing—and stepped inside and moved immediately out of the doorway.

Standing still, he let his eyes grow accustomed to the gloom. His mouth was open wide—a soldier's trick to mute a loud inhalation should he be startled. When he heard nothing for five full minutes, he walked in a crouch among the shelves filled with auto parts and greasy cartons.

Foot by foot, Owen covered the back room of the store and found no evidence of Hrubek. Through the open doorway and smeared glass beyond he saw the highway. A car drove past and the light flooded around him, creating a thousand shadows that flipped from left to right, coalescing then spreading out again into darkness. The headlights had dimmed his night vision and he waited five minutes until he could see well enough to continue.

Owen found another empty doughnut carton. Powdered sugar and cinnamon were scattered on the floor. He made his way toward the narrow doorway that opened onto the front room. He stopped suddenly, listening to a rumbling. It grew louder. Lights flickered outside, outlining the old-time gas pumps. A burping explosion from a truck's exhaust stack filled the air as the driver revved the engine to upshift coming off the long incline of the highway. The truck thundered past.

Owen partially closed his eyes to protect them from the light.

That was when he felt, more than saw, the movement. He opened his eyes in alarm and gazed at the dark shape swinging into the doorway. Before it reached him he leapt backwards. But he misjudged and tripped over a metal table, falling backwards and dropping his gun. His head struck the steel edge on the way down and he lay on the concrete floor, stunned, while the shadowy form of his assailant filled the doorway, not more than three feet from him.

Beckoning, the glossy truck sat like a blue jewel in the driveway.

"That'll take me to Ridgeton in no time at all. Make no mistake, no time at all."

O beautiful truck, I could sit upon your seat while the priest's beautiful daughter sits upon his cock. . . .

From the old gas station Hrubek had cycled to the long gravel driveway down which had vanished the 4x4 that contained the woman and her daughter. He couldn't see any lights and guessed that their house must be a half mile or more from the highway.

He'd slowly trudged through the field beside the driveway, pausing to take the last trap from his canvas bag and place it under some strands of tall grass. He continued on, carrying the bicycle with him, thinking, What a truck that is! Why would I go *by* a *bi*-cycle store to *buy* a fucking *bi*-cycle when I can drive a truck?

He had paused, taken the rear wheel in both hands and eased his shoulders back. Like a discus thrower he spun around twice and sent the bike flying through the air; it fell into a clump of plants thirty feet away. He was disappointed it didn't explode on impact, though he had no idea why it should. He continued up the driveway, thinking less about the truck than the woman's beautiful hair. That's what intrigued him the most. He supposed she had breasts, he supposed she had a pussy, he supposed she had masks on her eyes. But what captivated him so was her hair. It reminded him of his own hair before he cut it all off. When had he done that? Tonight? No, last year. And why? He couldn't remember. Microphones probably.

Hrubek had walked a half mile until he came to the place where he now stood—the driveway beside the house. "Now be smart," he told himself gravely. By this he meant: there'd be a husband. A woman with such soft hair and a delicate face wouldn't live alone. She'd be married to a big man with cold eyes—a conspirator, like the limping fucker with the dog.

He crouched and walked closer, hiding in a stand of juniper, the dew soaking through his overalls. He looked at the three-story colonial. The lights were golden, the trim garden was filled with Indian cornstalks and fat pumpkins on runners, the house itself was solid, symmetrical, plumb-even, a picture-book place, its red front door decorated with a dried-flower wreath.

He turned away and studied the shiny truck in the driveway. Next to it was a sporty yellow motorcycle. He vaguely remembered that he'd ridden a cycle several times at college and recalled being thrilled, as well as terrified, by the sensation. The cycle looked very nice, bright and springy. But the truck had captivated him first and it continued to possess his heart.

Hrubek walked up to the house and, standing in the side yard, he peered through a window. He tasted bitter paint where his lips pressed against the sill. Through a thick screen and thicker glass he could see the kitchen. There she was! The woman with the beautiful hair. Yes, she *was* beautiful. Much prettier than she'd seemed at the gas station. Tight blue jeans, a white silky blouse . . . And hair cascading to her shoulders—no hats for her, just tangles of soft, blond hair. The daughter was heavier and wore a thick sweatshirt with the sleeves drooping over her hands. A third woman in the room was dark and her face was tight and sultry. Hrubek didn't like her at all. The women vanished from sight for a moment. The kitchen door opened. The mother and daughter were carrying boxes out of the house. "Last load," the woman said. "Be back soon."

In a high edgy voice the girl said, "Mom, I'm tired."

"It's the church auction. And you volunteered to help."

"Mom," she repeated hopelessly.

Hrubek thought, Don't whine, you little fucker.

He heard a ringing. He squinted into the darkness of the driveway. Oh, no! The keys to the truck! *His* truck! They were taking it away. He stood and tensed to leap into the driveway. As he watched them load the boxes into the back of the truck, he rocked back and forth, willing himself to act.

"See you later, Mattie."

"Bye," the dark woman called and returned to the kitchen. Through the window Hrubek saw her pick up the phone. The pretty woman and her daughter the whiny little shit climbed into the truck. Hrubek couldn't move; if he stepped out of hiding, the woman on the phone would call for help. The engine started. Overcome by a burst of anxiety, Hrubek nearly leapt forward but he restrained himself and closed his eyes, squinting furiously until his head screamed with pain and he regained control. He hunkered down beneath a holly bush, whose leaves were sharp as knives.

The truck rolled past him, crunching gravel. When it was past he stepped away from the house and watched it disappear, and neither the mother nor daughter heard Hrubek's anguished hiss of rage.

With a resounding thud he kicked the motorcycle's fender. He gazed at the cycle for a moment then continued to the back door of the house. Quietly he opened the screen and looked through the small window high in the back door. The dark-complected woman, still on the phone, was gesturing broadly and shaking her head as she talked. This made Hrubek think she'd be a screamer. On the stove was a tea kettle just starting to steam over a high flame. As he silently twisted the knob back and forth, checking that the door was not locked, Hrubek thought, She's having tea, that means she isn't about to leave and won't be expected anywhere soon.

Hrubek congratulated himself on this smart thinking and he continued to act smart—he didn't open the door and step into the kitchen until the woman had hung up and walked across the kitchen to the stove, far away from the phone.

Owen Atcheson, his ear numb from striking the table leg as he fell, scrabbled away from the door, and unable to find his gun grabbed a soda bottle lying nearby. He cracked it hard against the floor and held the shard like a knife. He crouched and made himself ready for attack.

The assailant didn't move.

Owen waited a moment longer. Finally he stood. Owen grabbed his pistol from the floor. When he heard no breathing and saw no other motion, he flicked on the light switch.

Taste T

Beats t

Others C

In fury Owen kicked shut the door of the old Pepsi machine. "Jesus," he spat out. The lock had been broken—by Hrubek undoubtedly—and the door, dislodged by the semi as it rumbled past, had swung open into the doorway. His anger was so great he nearly put a bullet through the navel of the bikini-clad girl on the old, faded poster taped to the door. He jammed the gun into his pocket and trotted outside to his truck.

Only a few hundred feet west he found the tread again, turning into a private road or driveway of a residence. He couldn't see a house from the road and, observing the length of the drive and the size of the property, guessed that the family was wealthy. Horse ranchers maybe. He looked back at the ground and noted that Hrubek had left the drive and was traveling through the brush. Making his way silently on the patches of dirt. Owen followed the madman's clear path. A flash in the distant west caught his eye. Lightning.

Attempting to circle in front of Hrubek, he made his way west from the driveway into the field of tall, flesh-colored grass and moved south. From here he was able to see, a quarter mile away, a stately house. Although it was late, there were many lights on, giving a homey glow to the place.

But that impression vanished when Owen noticed a single unsettling token—the kitchen door was wide open, sending a shaft of bone-white light onto the gravel driveway, as if someone had fled quickly from the house.

Or maybe, Owen reflected, had *entered* quickly. And was still inside.

18

One who loves flowers and literature can't doubt the existence of God. The lesson He's got for us, though, probably isn't so hot. We see miracles daily, that's true. On the other hand God's got the universe to mind and doesn't have much time for passengers on colliding trains, kids dragged to death behind buses, and dear friends murdered by a madman in a state park.

"That," Lis explained to Richard Kohler, "was the thought I just couldn't get out of my mind. For months after the murder I repeated it to practically everyone I met. I'm sure they thought I was totally mad."

Kohler nodded her bit of theology politely aside and frowned sympathetically. "You lost two friends at the same time. How terrible. I didn't know about the girl's death."

Lis was silent for a long moment. Finally she said, "No, it wasn't featured in the news about the trial. Her death was considered accidental."

"May I ask . . . ?"

Lis glanced at him inquiringly.

"Did you hear anyone call for help?"

"How do you mean?"

"Claire, I'm thinking of. Before you saw Michael and ran into the cave, did you hear her scream?"

When Lis didn't respond, Kohler added, "It just seems that with Michael chasing her down the path . . . I mean, he *was* chasing her, wasn't he?"

Lis couldn't guess the purpose of his questions. After a moment she said, "I didn't hear anything. There weren't any screams."

"Why would she go into the cave in the first place?"

"I don't know."

"It's curious, isn't it? You'd think with Michael after her, she'd continue running down the canyon. A cave is the last place I'd want to be with Michael chasing me."

She was testy. "I can't speak for her. Obviously."

"I'm just wondering. Later, did you think about it? A young girl, being chased by a huge man like Michael. I would've thought she'd scream at some point."

"Maybe she did. Maybe I didn't hear her. I don't really—"

"It was close to where you were looking for her though, wasn't it?" Kohler persisted. "From the way you described it, I—"

"It was *close* to where I was, yes, but . . ." She felt cross-examined and forced herself to be calm. "I don't know. Maybe I blocked it out. Maybe she did scream, and I don't remember it. That's possible, isn't it?"

"Oh, sure. Post-trauma stress. Very possible."

"Well, then."

Kohler said something, perhaps by way of apology, but Lis didn't hear. She was thinking: Claire. My poor Claire. And pictured the girl's pale eyes, the hair that tumbled over her shoulders like water, the white mouth that needed lipstick the girl was too bashful to apply.

She had grieved for Robert, yes, but it was the girl's death that hurt her the deepest. She hadn't known that she could be so attached to a youngster. Lis had always felt a certain uneasiness around children, even her students. She rarely put it that way and tended to think of her and Owen's childlessness as circumstance. But the truth was, she just hadn't wanted a son or daughter. She couldn't picture the Atcheson family on a picnic, austere Owen cradling an infant Andy, she herself dropping a line of formula onto her wrist to test the temperature. Baby showers. Strollers. PTA meetings. Embarrassing conversations about the facts of life . . .

But about Claire Lis felt differently. Claire she'd sought out. Lis viewed the girl through a rare crack in the wall of distant time and saw in the student's eyes and halting manners the effigy of another thin, shy girl from years before. A child whose father was both intimate and hating, and whose mother dared to be truly present only when her man was not. Lis could not refuse the covert pleas for help—like the times the girl stayed after class to ask intelligent if calculated questions about Jacobean drama, or happened—too coincidentally—to find herself walking beside her teacher on the deserted riverside behind the school.

Lis was again picturing Claire's face when she realized that the psychiatrist was asking her a question. He wanted to know about the trial.

"The trial?" she repeated softly. "Well, I got to the courthouse early . . ."

"Just you?"

"I refused to let Owen come with me. It's hard to explain but I wanted to keep what happened at Indian Leap as separate as possible from my home. Owen spent the day with Dorothy. After all, *she* was the widow. She needed comforting more than I."

Inside the courtroom, when Lis first saw Hrubek—it'd been five and a half weeks since the murder—he looked smaller than she recalled. He was pale, sickly. He squinted at her and his mouth twisted into an eerie smile. As she walked down the aisle Lis tried to keep her eyes on the prosecutor, a young woman with a mass of flyaway hair. She'd been prepping Lis all week for the court appearance. Lis sat behind her but in full view of Hrubek. His hands were manacled in front of him and he lifted them as far as he could then simply stared at her, his lips moving compulsively.

"God, it was eerie."

"That's just dyskinesia," Kohler explained. "It's a condition caused by antipsychotic drugs."

"Whatever, it was scary as hell. When he spoke he almost gave me a heart attack. He jumped up and said, 'Conspiracy!' And 'Revenge,' or something. I don't remember exactly."

Apparently these outbursts had happened before because everyone, including the judge, ignored him. As she walked past he grew very calm and asked her in a conversational tone if she knew where he was on the night of April 14 at 10:30 p.m.

"April *14*?"

"That's right."

"And the murder was May 1, wasn't it?"

"Yes."

"Did April 14 mean anything to you?"

She shook her head. A small notation went into Kohler's book. "Please go on."

"Hrubek said, 'I was murdering somebody. . . .' I'm not quoting exactly. Something like, 'I was murdering somebody. The moon rose blood red and ever since that day I have been the victim of a conspiracy—' "

"Lincoln's assassination!" Kohler looked at her with raised eyebrows.

"I'm sorry?"

"Didn't it happen in mid-April?"

"I think it *was* around then, yes."

Another notation.

With disdain Lis observed the brief smile that crossed Kohler's lips then she continued, "He was saying, 'I've been implanted with tracking and listening devices. I've been tortured.' Sometimes he was incoherent, sometimes he sounded like a doctor or lawyer."

Lis was the main prosecution witness. She swore her oath then settled in a huge wooden chair. On its seat was a crocheted cushion and she wondered if it had been made by the wife of the grizzled, slouching judge. "The prosecutor asked me to tell the court what happened that day. And I did."

Her testimony seemed to take an eternity. She later learned she was in the spotlight for all of eight minutes.

She was dreading cross-examination by the defense attorney. But she wasn't called. Hrubek's lawyer said simply, "No questions," and she spent the next several hours in the gallery.

"All I could do was stare at the plastic bags that contained the rock stained with Robert's blood, and the kitchen knife. I sat in the back of the courtroom with Tad. . . ." Kohler lifted an inquiring eyebrow. "He's a former student of mine. He does work for me around the yard and greenhouse. I told everybody I knew not to attend the trial. But Tad ignored me. He was there all day long, cheerful and smiling. We sat together."

Before she testified, the young man found her in the corridor outside and handed her a paper bag. Inside was a yellow rose. He'd trimmed the thorns and cut the stem back, wrapped it in wet paper towels. Lis had cried and kissed him on the cheek.

"Was it a long trial?" Kohler asked.

Not really, she explained. The defense lawyer didn't dispute the fact that Hrubek had killed Robert. He relied on the insanity defense—Hrubek lacked the mental state to understand that his acts were criminal. Under the M'Naghten rule, Lis relayed to Kohler what she'd learned during the jury instruction, the death becomes an act of God. The lawyer didn't even put Hrubek on the stand. He offered medical reports and depositions, which were read out loud by a clerk. This all had to do with Hrubek's inability to appreciate the consequences of his actions.

All that time the madman had sat at the defense table, hunched over, twining his dirty hair between blunt fingers, laughing and muttering, filling sheet after sheet of foolscap with tiny frantic characters and lines. She hadn't paid any attention to these doodlings then but understood later that he hadn't been as crazy as it appeared—this was undoubtedly how he'd recorded her name and address.

A verdict of not guilty by reason of diminished capacity was entered. Under Section 403 of the Mental Health Law, Hrubek would be classified as dangerously insane and would be incarcerated indefinitely in a state hospital, to be re-evaluated annually.

"I left the courthouse. Then—"

"And what about the incident," Kohler asked, palms meeting as if he were clapping in slow motion, "with the chair?"

"Chair?"

"He jumped up on a chair or table."

Ah, yes. That.

The courtroom began to empty. Suddenly a huge voice rose over the murmuring of the spectators and press. Michael Hrubek was shouting. He threw a bailiff to the ground and climbed onto his chair. The manacles clanked and he lifted his arms over his head. He began screaming. His eyes met Lis's for a moment and she froze. Guards subdued Hrubek, and a bailiff hustled her out of the courtroom.

"What did he say?"

"Say?"

"When he was on the chair. Did he shout anything?"

"I think he was just howling. Like an animal."

"The article said he shouted, 'You're the Eve of betrayal.' "

"Could be."

"You don't remember?"

"No. I don't."

Kohler was shaking his head. "Michael had therapy sessions with me. Three times a week. During one he said, 'Betrayal, betrayal. Oh, she's *courting* disaster. She sat in that *court*, and now she's *courting* disaster. All that betrayal. Eve's the one.' When I asked him what he meant, he became agitated. As if he'd let an important secret slip. He wouldn't talk about it. He's mentioned betrayal several times since then. You have any thoughts on what it might mean?"

"No. I don't. I'm sorry."

"And afterwards?"

"After the trial?" Lis sipped the strong coffee. "Well, I took a trip to hell."

After the publicity faded and Hrubek was committed in Marsden, Lis resumed the life she'd led before the tragedy. At first her routine seemed largely unchanged—teaching summer school, spending Sundays at the country club with Owen, visiting friends, tending the garden. She was perhaps the last person to notice that her life was unraveling.

Occasionally she'd skip a shower. She'd forget the names of guests attending her own cocktail parties. She might happen to glance down as she walked through the corridors of the school and find that she was wearing mismatched shoes. She'd teach Dryden instead of the scheduled Pope and berate students for failing to read material she'd never assigned. Sometimes in lectures and in conversations she found herself gazing at embarrassed, perplexed faces and could only wonder what on earth she'd just uttered.

"It was as if I was sleepwalking."

She withdrew into her greenhouse and mourned.

Owen, patient initially, grew tired of Lis's torpor and absent-mindedness and they began to fight. He spent more time on business trips. She stayed home more and more frequently, venturing outside only for her classes. Her sleep problems grew worse: it was not unusual for her to remain awake for twenty-four hours straight.

Adding to Lis's difficulty was Dorothy, who stepped as brusquely into widowhood as she slipped into the front seat of her Mercedes SL. She was gaunt and pale and didn't smile for two months. Yet she functioned, and functioned quite well. Owen several times held her out as an example of someone who took tragedy in stride. "Well, I'm not *like* her, Owen. I never have been. I'm sorry."

When Dorothy sold her house and moved to the Jersey shore in July, it was not she but Lis who cried during their farewell lunch.

Lis's life became school and her greenhouse, where she would snip plants and wander like a lost child over the slate path, her face occasionally damp as the leaves of a plantain lily.

But gradually she improved. She took Prozac for a time, which made her jaw quiver and fingers tremble and infused her dreams with spectacular effects. It also aggravated the insomnia. She switched to Pamelor, which was gentler.

And then, one day, she simply stopped taking the pills and hung up her housecoat.

"I can't tell you what happened. Or when exactly. But I suddenly just knew it was time to get on with my life. And I did."

"I'd had some clues that Michael's delusion involves American history," Kohler told her. "Particularly the Civil War . . . 'Sic semper tyrannis'—that's what Booth shouted after he shot Lincoln."

" 'Thus ever to tyrants.' " Lis the schoolteacher added, "It's also the state motto of Virginia."

"And the April 14 reference. The assassination."

"What does Lincoln have to do with anything?"

Kohler shook his head. "Michael's been very reluctant to talk to me about his delusions. Only hints, cryptic phrases. He didn't trust me."

"Even you, his doctor?"

"*Especially* me, his doctor. That's the nature of his illness. He's paranoid. He's always accusing me of trying to get information out of him for the FBI or Secret Service. He has a core delusion but I can't get to the bottom of it. I suppose it centers on the Civil War, Lincoln's death, conspirators. Or some event he associates with the assassination. I don't know."

"Why's his delusion so important?"

"Because it's central to his illness. It explains to him why every day is so unbearably hard. A schizophrenic's life," Kohler lectured, "is a search for meaning."

And whose isn't? Lis wondered.

"It's a very controversial matter right now," the doctor said, adding that he himself was considered a bit of a renegade. She thought he was a little too smug with this characterization of himself. "Schizophrenia is a physical illness. Just like cancer or appendicitis. You have to treat it with drugs. No one disputes that. But I differ from most of my colleagues in thinking that you can also treat schizophrenic patients very effectively with psychotherapy."

"I can't really imagine Hrubek lying on a couch talking about his childhood."

"Neither could Freud. He said schizophrenic patients shouldn't be treated with psychoanalysis. Most psychiatrists agree. The current treatment is to get them on brain candy—that's how the cynics among us refer to their medication—and force them to accept reality, teach them to order in restaurants and do their own laundry then turn them loose. And it's true—extended analysis, with the patient on the couch, that's wrong for people like Michael. But certain types of psycho*therapy* work very well. Seriously ill patients can learn to function at a very high level.

"Most psychiatrists think that schizophrenic patients ramble incoherently, that their delusions are meaningless. I think that almost everything they say is meaning*ful*. The more we try to translate their words into *our* way of thinking, yes, the more pointless those words are. But if we try to grasp their *metaphoric* meaning, then doors open up. Take a Napoleon, okay? That's the popular image of a schizophrenic. I won't try to convince a patient that he isn't

Napoleon. And I wouldn't just pat him on the head and say, "*Bonjour*," when I pass him in the hall. I'd try to find out *why* he thinks he's the emperor of France. Nine times out of ten there's a reason. And once I know that, I can start to unlock doors. I've had remarkable results with patients—and some of them are a lot sicker than Michael." He added bitterly, "I was *just* getting inside him, I was almost there . . . When this happened."

"You make him sound innocent."

"He *is* innocent. That's the perfect word for him."

She thought angrily, Oh, isn't the good doctor used to people buying his bill of goods? The malleable patients who nod their damaged heads and shuffle off to obey. The sorrowful families pecking through his pompous words for comfort like birds for seed. Young, terrified interns and nurses. "How on earth," she asked, "can you *romanticize* him? He's just a set of muscles free to do whatever he wants. He's a machine run amok."

"Not at all. Michael's tormented by the inability to achieve what he thinks he can become. That conflict shows itself as what we call madness. To him, his delusions are merciful explanations for why he can't be like the rest of the world."

"You seem to be saying his disease isn't anybody's fault." She waved her arm at the clouds speeding past. "Well, neither are tornadoes but we'd stop them if we could. We should *stop* Hrubek. Somebody should . . . lock him up and throw away the key." She'd come a split second away from saying, track him down and shoot him. "He's just a psychopath!"

"No, he isn't. That's a very different diagnosis from schizophrenia. Psychopaths adapt well to society. They seem normal—they have jobs and families—but they're completely detached from morality and emotion. *They're* evil. A psychopath would kill you because you took his parking place or wouldn't give him ten dollars. And he wouldn't think twice about it. Michael would only kill for the same reasons you would—self-defense, for instance."

"Please, doctor. Michael's harmless? Is *that* what you're telling me?"

"No, of course not. But . . ." Kohler's voice faded. "I'm sorry. I've upset you."

After a moment Lis said, "No. We see things differently, that's all." But she said it quite coolly.

"It's late. I've used up my twenty minutes." He rose and walked toward the kitchen. When they approached the back door, he asked, "One thing I'm still curious about. Why would he associate you with betrayal? 'The Eve of betrayal.' 'Revenge.' 'Forever.' Why?"

"Well, I suppose because I testified against him." She lifted her palms at the simplicity of this deduction.

"You think that's it?"

"I suppose. I really don't know."

Kohler nodded and fell silent. A moment later his mind made another of its odd leaps, punctuated by a stab at his pale scalp with a nervous finger. "There's a car lot outside of town, isn't there?"

She thought she'd misheard him. "A car lot? What did you say?"

"Cars. A dealership."

"Well, yes. But . . ."

"I'm thinking of the big one. All lit up. A Ford dealership."

"Klepperman's Ford, that's right."

"Where is it exactly?"

"Half mile outside of town. On Route 236. Just over the hills east of town. Why?"

"Just curious."

She waited for an explanation but none came and it was clear that the interview, or interrogation, or whatever it had been, was over. Kohler cleared his throat and thanked her. She was grateful he was leaving; the visit had angered her. But she was confused too. What had he learned that was so helpful?

And what had he not told her?

Outside, walking to his car, they both looked up at the thick clouds. The wind was fierce now and whipped her hair in an irritating way, flinging it into her face.

"Doctor?" Lis stopped him, touching his bony upper arm. "Tell me, what are the odds that he's on his way here?"

Kohler continued to gaze at the clouds. "The odds? The *odds* are that they'll find him soon, and even if not, that he'd never make it this far alone. But if you want my opinion I think you should go to that hotel you mentioned."

He glanced at her for a moment then it was clear that his thoughts were elsewhere, maybe wandering with his terrified, mad patient through brush and forests, lost on highways, sitting in a deserted cabin somewhere. As she watched him walk to his car, she pushed aside her anger for a moment and saw Kohler for the ambitious young physician that he was, and tough and devoted. And undoubtedly damn smart too. But she sensed something else about him and was unable for a few moments to fathom exactly what that might be. His car had disappeared down the long driveway before she understood. Dr. Richard Kohler, Lis decided, was a very worried man.

The ambulance and the police car arrived simultaneously, their urgent lights painting the underside of the trees with peculiar metallic illumination. The brakes squealed and the yard was filled with uniformed men and women, equipment, stretchers, electric boxes dotted with lights and buttons. The medics trotted toward the large colonial house. The police too, holstering their long flashlights as they ran.

Owen Atcheson sat on the back steps beside the kitchen door, which was still open. His head was in his hands as he watched the medics run toward the doorway. One said to him, "You called 911? Reported a woman was attacked?"

He nodded.

"Where is she?"

"In the kitchen," Owen said, exhaustion and discouragement thick in his voice. "But you can take your time."

"How's that?"

"I said there's no rush. The only place she's going tonight is the morgue."

Spirits of the Dead

19

"Who is it? Not Mary Haddon? Jesus, not their *daughter*?"

"No, that's not her."

"That's not Mary?"

"*Look* at her, for God's sake! It's not Mary."

But nobody wanted to look. They'd look at the wall calendar, the Post-it notes, the shattered teacup, the scraps of paper clinging to the avocado-colored refrigerator door under fruit-shaped magnets. They'd look everywhere but at the terrible creature tied with bell wire to the maple captain's chair. The senior medic walked carefully into the room, minding the huge slick of blood on the tile floor. He bent down and studied the intricately tied knots. Her head, loosened by the deep cut to her throat, lolled backwards, and her blouse was pulled open. The awkward letters cut into her skin were stark against her blue-white chest.

"Fucking mess," one of the young cops said.

"Hey, let's don't have any of that talk here," a plainclothes detective said. "Check out the house. All the bedrooms."

"I think Joe and Mary're over at the church. The charity auction's tomorrow and he's chairman. I heard they're working late. Oh, I hope their daughter's with them. Man, I hope that."

"Well, call 'em up or get a car over there. Let's get on with this."

One cop entered and looked at the corpse. "Lord, that's Mattie! Mattie Selwyn. She's the Haddons' housekeeper. I know her brother."

The nervous banter continued. "Oh, this is a bad thing. What's

that in her lap, that little white thing? . . . Jesus, some kind of skull
or something. A badger?"

"Why tonight?" a deputy lamented. "Storm'll be here any time.
Already had a twister in Morristown. Couple people died. You
hear? Man—"

Owen stood in the doorway and looked again at the carnage. He
shook his head.

"You the one who called us, sir?" the detective asked, running
his hand through his salt-and-pepper hair.

Owen nodded and wiped sweat from his face. After calling 911
he'd glanced into a window and seen on his face the mud smeared
on his cheekbones and forehead to mask the glossiness of his skin.
He had washed his face before the police arrived. Still, his hand-
kerchief now came away from his forehead dirty and he supposed
he looked a mess. He explained about Hrubek's escape, the bicycle,
following him here. The detective said, "Yessir, we had a notice
about that runaway. But we thought he was heading east."

"I *told* them he wasn't," Owen said heatedly. "I *told* them he'd
turn west. They wouldn't listen. Nobody took this thing seriously
from the start. And now look. . . ."

"We also heard he was harmless," the detective said bitterly,
staring at the body. Then he glanced at Owen. "What's your role
in this exactly?"

He told them that he'd come out to see what the state police
were doing to capture the escapee, who appeared to have a grudge
against his wife. As he spoke he realized that the story *was* out-
landish and he was neither surprised nor offended when the officer
asked, "Could I see some ID, please?"

Owen handed over his driver's license and his attorney's regis-
tration card.

"You don't mind if we confirm this?"

"Not at all."

The detective picked up the phone and called his office. A moment later he nodded and hung up. He walked back to Owen and returned the ID. "Are you armed, sir?"

"Yes."

"I assume you have a firearm permit, Mr. Atcheson?"

"I do, yes. And four years of combat experience." He said this because the detective was about his age and had a serenity in the face of butchery like this that comes from only one thing—surviving firefights. The detective squinted a bit of reluctant camaraderie into his face.

One cop stuck his head into the foyer and, his wide eyes on the dead woman, said to the detective, "Found something, Bob. We got motorcycle tracks. They look fresh."

The detective asked Owen, "Yours?"

"No."

The cop continued, "Only, the helmet's still on the ground. It seemed—"

The policeman who'd identified the housekeeper called from the living room, "That helmet? Was hers, Mattie's. She drove a Honda. Yellow one, I think."

The detective called, "Where do the tracks head?"

"They go behind the garage, down a path then out over to 106. They turn south."

Owen asked, "To 106? That's the road to Boyleston."

"Sure is. He was to head down 106 on a motorcycle, he'd be there in forty, fifty minutes."

"Boyleston's the closest Amtrak station, isn't it?"

The detective nodded. "That's right. Notice we got said he was making for Massachusetts. They were thinking he'd gone on foot but, sure, he could take the train. Maybe he doubled back. Like a feint, you know."

"That makes sense to me."

The detective barked an order to a uniformed sergeant, telling him to notify the Boyleston police about the murder and to send two of their own cars south on 106. Immediately. As the cops turned back to the body and busied themselves with fingerprints and crime-scene photos, Owen stepped outside and strolled around the property, looking for tracks. He studied the estate's rolling pastures, a horse stable and several small barns that had been converted into garages.

"You see anything?" the detective called to him.

"Nope."

"Say, Mr. Atcheson, we'll need a statement from you. And I'm sure Attorney Franks, our prosecutor, will be wanting to talk to you."

"In the morning, I'd be happy to."

"I—"

"In the morning," Owen said evenly.

The officer kept eye contact for a moment then chased to his wallet for a business card, which he handed to Owen. "You'll call me then? Nine a.m. sharp?"

Owen said he would.

The detective, tours of duty aside, looked Owen up and down. "I understand what you're going through, sir. I myself might be inclined to head off after him this minute, I was in your position. But my advice is for you to stay out of this whole thing."

Owen merely nodded and gazed south toward the ruddy haze of lights that would be Boyleston. He stepped aside as the medics brought the woman's body out of the door. He stared at it, seeing not so much the dark-green bag as, in his mind's eye, the bloody black strokes of the letters that had been cut into her chest.

The words they spelled were *forEVEr rEVEnge*

He lost the scent on the outskirts of Cloverton.

Emil was once again quartering, zigzagging across the asphalt, his master in tow, looking for a trail he simply couldn't find. Even

Trenton Heck, who supported his dogs 110 percent, was having an uneasy time of it.

The big obedience problem with tracking was that you never knew exactly what was in the dog's mind. Maybe just as you lowered the scent article to his nose, the hound got a whiff of deer and with the shout of "Find!" he'd bounded off in pursuit of a big buck who'd trotted nearby hours ago. The hound would be doing exactly what he believed he'd been ordered to do, and woe to the handler who failed to slip him a Bac'n Treat just the same as if he'd treed the escaping convict. Yet Heck replayed the evening and didn't see how Emil could be mistaken. Come on, boy, he thought fervently. I got faith in you. Let's do it.

Emil started toward a water-filled ditch but Heck ordered him back. It occurred to him that a man who'd lay traps would also poison water though Heck was more worried about natural contamination. It was his rule to let dogs drink only water from home. (When his fellow troopers would snicker at this and mutter, "Evian," or "Perrier," he'd tell them, "Fine, boys, just go to Mexico yourselves sometime and drink from the tap. See how you enjoy it. For your hound, anyplace that ain't home could be Mexico.") Tonight he took a jar from the truck and gave Emil a long drink. The hound lapped greedily. They started on the trail again.

Far distant in the west, lightning flashed in mute bands at the horizon, and a misty rain had started falling. This, Heck supposed, was what had ruined the scent. Earlier he'd been welcoming the rain but that was when Hrubek was on foot. The madman was now on a bicycle and they were following a very different type of trail. Dogs detect three different scents—body scent in the air, body scent pressed into the ground, and track scent, which is a combination of crushed vegetation and smells released by whatever the prey might step on. Rain intensifies and freshens the latter two. But add a hard rain to airborne scent on asphalt—which is chock-full of chemicals that foul dogs' noses—and you've got the worst possible combination to track over.

"Come on, why don't you get off that damn bike?" Heck muttered. "Can't you hoof it? Like a normal escapee?"

Emil slowed and looked around him. A bad sign. *I got you for your nose, boy, not your eyes. Hell, I can see better'n you.*

The hound slowly strolled off the road and into a field. His leg on fire, Heck led the dog along a grid search pattern, loping in huge squares over the ground, moving slowly under the guidance of the flashlight for fear of the steel traps. Emil paused for long moments, sniffing the ground then lifting his nose. Then he ambled off and repeated the process. As Heck watched the hound his sense of futility grew.

Then Heck felt a tug on the track line and he looked down with hope in his heart. But immediately the line went slack, as Emil gave up on the false lead and returned to nosing about in the ground, breathing in all the aromas of the countryside and searching in vain for a scent that, for all Heck knew, might have vanished forever.

Michael Hrubek's father was a grayish, somber man who had, over the years, grown dazed by the disintegration of his family. Rather than avoiding home, however, as another man might have done, he dutifully returned every evening from the clothing store in which he was the formal-wear manager.

And he returned quickly—as if afraid that in his absence some new pestilence might be threatening to destroy whatever normalcy remained in his house.

Once home though he spent the tedious hours before bed largely ignoring the chaos around him. For diversion he took to reading psychology books for lay people and excerpts from *The Book of Common Prayer* and—when neither proved to be much of a palliative—watching television, specifically travel and talk shows.

Michael was then in his mid-twenties and had largely given up his hopes of returning to college. He spent most of his time at home with his parents. Hrubek senior, attempting to keep his son happy and, more to the point, out of everyone's hair, would bring Michael comic books, games, Revell models of Civil War weaponry. His son invariably received these gifts with suspicion. He'd cart them to the upstairs bathroom, subject them to a *pro forma* dunking to short out sensors and microphones then stow the dripping boxes in his closet.

"Michael, look: Candyland. How 'bout a game later, son? After supper?"

"Candyland? Candyland? Do you know *anybody* who plays Candyland? Have you ever met a single person in the fucking *world* who plays Candyland? I'm going upstairs and taking a bath."

For his part, Michael avoided his father as he avoided everyone else. His rare forays outside the house were motivated by pathetic missions. He once spent a month looking for a rabbi who would convert him to Judaism and he devoted three fervent weeks to hounding an anxious Armed Forces recruitment officer, who couldn't shake the young man even after explaining a dozen times that there was no longer a Union Army. He took a commuter train to Philadelphia, where he stalked an attractive black newscaster and once cornered her on the street, demanding to know if she was a slave and if she enjoyed pornographic films. She got a restraining order that the police seemed eager to enforce with whatever vigor was necessary but Michael soon forgot about her.

On Saturday mornings his father would make a big pancake breakfast and the family would eat amid such ranting from Michael that his parents eventually tuned out the noise. Michael's mother, most likely still in her nightgown, would pick at her food until she could face the plate no longer. She would rise slowly, put on lipstick, because that's what proper ladies did after meals, and after spending several frantic minutes looking for the *TV Guide* or the remote control, she would return to bed and click on the set. His father did the dishes then took Michael to a doctor whose small office was above an ice-cream parlor on Main Street. All that Michael remembered about this man was that with almost every sentence he said, "Michael."

"Michael, what I'd like to do today is for you to tell me what some of your earliest memories are. Can you do that, Michael? An example would be: Christmas with your family. Christmas morning, Michael, the very first time—"

"I don't know, fucker. I can't remember, fucker. I don't know anything about Christmas, fucker, so why do you keep asking me?"

Michael said "fucker" even more often than the doctor said "Michael."

He stopped seeing this psychiatrist after his father's insurance company refused to reimburse the family for any more visits. He spent more and more time in his room, sometimes reading history, sometimes wearing his mother's clothing, sometimes screaming out the windows at people who walked past. The Hrubeks' pale-blue home became a renowned house of terror among the children of Westbury, Pennsylvania.

This was his life for the years following his expulsion from college—living at home, going on his mad sorties, dunking toys, eating junk food, reading history, watching television.

It was around his twenty-fifth birthday, in April, that Michael withdrew into his room and stopped talking to anyone. One month later he tried to burn down the house to stop the voices that came from his mother's bedroom. The following Saturday Hrubek senior dressed his son in an ill-fitting suit and took him, along with three books, a change of underwear and a toothbrush, to a state mental hospital in New York. He lied about state residency, and had the boy admitted to the facility under an involuntary-commitment order intended to last for seventy-two hours.

His father hugged Michael and told him the hospital would stabilize his condition and make him well enough to live at home. "I'll have to think about that," a frowning Michael responded, not knowing that those would be the last words ever spoken between father and son.

Upon his return to Westbury, the depleted man sold the house at a loss and moved to the Midwest, where his family had come from years before.

After six weeks the hospital's Third-Party Payments Section gave up trying to track down his father, and Michael became a guest of the state.

This hospital was bleak—an institutional desert, where the long hours were broken only by Pill Time and Meal Time and Shock Time. At this point in his illness, however, Michael was more evasive than aggressive and didn't need electroconvulsive-shock treatment. His pills calmed him down and he spent the days sitting placidly in his room until his butt grew sore then he'd stand and stare out the windows barred by wire lattice that dangled with tiny streamers of greasy dust.

Once a week he would talk to a doctor.

"You have to take your meds. . . . Are you taking them? Good. You see, we're aiming to get you to the point where you're aware, I'm speaking of a conscious awareness, that your concerns are a function of your illness not of the reality around you. . . ."

Michael would grunt disagreeably and remind himself to keep a suspicious eye on the fellow.

After six weeks in the hospital Michael Hrubek was diagnosed as mildly schizophrenic, nonviolent, possibly paranoid, and was among eighty-seven similar patients released when the hospital closed one of its wings due to budget cutbacks.

Because Third-Party Payments had never informed Discharge that the location of Michael's father was unknown, the release notice was sent to a fictitious address in Valhalla, New York. On the day Michael was discharged an orderly parked him on a bench in the waiting room and told him to wait for a family member to pick him up. Four hours later Michael told the duty nurse that he was going to say goodbye to one of the groundskeepers. Instead, he wandered unchallenged through the front gate—thus beginning a lengthy and harrowing journey that would lead him to cities throughout the Eastern Seaboard, to hospitals of varying degrees of renown and infamy, to idyllic Trevor Hill Psychiatric and his beloved and betraying Dr. Anne, to the snakepit of Cooperstown, to the deaths at Indian Leap, to Marsden State Mental Health Facility, to Dr. Richard . . . and finally—after so many miles and so very many lifetimes—to the astonishing place in which Michael found himself tonight: the driver's seat of a black, thirty-year-old Cadillac Coupe de Ville, speeding not toward Boyleston at all, but straight down Route 236 west to Ridgeton, which was now less than twenty miles away. As he drove, musical words flew from his lips:

"Cadillac, hard tack . . . Hard tack, horseback . . . Soldier boys, gray and blue . . ."

His hands left a residue of sweat on the white steering wheel and he kept repeating to himself which pedal was the accelerator and which was the brake. He'd sometimes find himself easing over the center line and in panic forget which lane he was supposed to be in. Then, remembering, he'd forget how to steer back into the proper lane and would drive English-style for some distance before gradually returning to the right.

On and on he drove, a steady forty miles an hour in a fifty-five zone. He swallowed and moaned often and muttered to himself, and he wanted nothing so much as to fall onto the smooth plain of the upholstered seat, cover his head and fall fast asleep. But he didn't. No, Michael remained as upright as a soldier on guard duty, looking straight into the darkness where the guns of his enemy waited.

His eyes left the asphalt only once, to glance at the sign that said, *RIDGETON 17 MILES*, then returned to the highway. With pleasure he inhaled the sweet smell of the heater that blasted air into his face. The memories he'd had this November evening, Michael thought with a burst of rare perception, had traveled as far as he had. And he thought now about an afternoon long ago, sitting in the library of one of his hospitals, singing a song that he himself had written. He recalled that he'd sung it over and over until the librarian asked him to stop and then he sang it in his head, silently mouthing the words.

Now, ensconced in his luxurious black car, he once again sang it and he sang it loud.

> *"Hard tack, horseback, the Capital's asleep.*
> *The soldier boys are crying. Somewhere a woman weeps.*
> *Hard tack, the moon's back, and bloody in the sky.*
> *I'm going to the graveyard, where the body lies. . . ."*

Michael points the black nose of the car down a long hill and feels the gradual, smooth acceleration of the engine. Unexpectedly though, despite the glory of newfound speed, despite his immense pride at mastering this machine that a year ago would have paralyzed him with terror, Michael Hrubek begins to cry.

He gulps hot air into his lungs, fueling the sobbing, and feels the moisture on his wide cheeks. His throat stings.

Why am I crying? Michael wonders, barely conscious that he *is* crying.

He really has no idea. But somewhere deep in his mind is the answer that he cries for man's genius in making this exquisite automobile. He cries for all the miles he's traveled tonight. And for the vague memory of a woman wearing a very unfashionable hat on her otherwise perfect head.

For the past dead and for those soon to be.

And he cries for what is surely sitting above the thickening storm clouds over his car right now—a moon blood red.

I'm going to the graveyard, where the body lies. . . .

Lis was taping the top row of windows in the greenhouse when the storm finally hit.

Her face was inches from the glass as she was reaching out to lay a strip on a hard-to-reach pane. Suddenly a slash of rain cracked against the window. She twisted away, dropping the tape, thinking for an instant that someone had flung a handful of gravel at the panes. She nearly tumbled backwards off the ladder.

She climbed down and retrieved the masking tape, surveying the sky. Worried that a window might shatter into her face if she continued to tape, Lis again considered leaving—now. But the north windows, those facing the storm, were still to be done.

Ten minutes, she decided. She'd allow herself that.

Climbing up once again she thought about Kohler's advising her to leave. Yet she felt no extreme urgency. He hadn't seemed particularly concerned on her behalf. Besides, she reasoned, the Ridgeton sheriff would certainly have called if he'd learned that Hrubek was headed for town.

As she laid the X's on the squares of glass, her eyes fell on the lake and the forest. Beyond them, barely visible in the rain, was a huge expanse of countryside—a muddy horizon of fields and woods and rocks disappearing into the black windy sky. The sweep of terrain seemed so limitless, so perfectly able to contain the infection of Michael Hrubek, that it was foolish to think that he might even get close to Ridgeton. The vastness of the landscape would protect her husband too; how could either man possibly find the other?

And where was Owen at this moment?

In her heart she believed he'd be back soon. Perhaps even before she and Portia left for the Inn. Returning empty-handed, angry and frustrated—because he'd missed his chance to play soldier.

And because he had lost an opportunity to do penance.

Oh, Lis had understood that from the start. She knew that his errand tonight had a tacit purpose. It was part of a complicated debt he seemed to feel he owed his wife.

And perhaps he did, she reflected. For Owen had spent much of last year in the company of another woman.

He'd met her at a legal continuing-education conference. She was a trust-and-estates lawyer, thirty-seven years old, divorced with two children. He offered these facts as proof of the virtue of his infidelity; no young, gum-snapping bimbo for *him*.

Yale-educated.

Cum laude.

"Do you think I give a *fuck* about her credentials?" Lis had shouted.

When she'd first seen a MasterCard receipt for a hotel in Atlantic City, dated the weekend he was supposed to be in Ohio on business, she was devastated. Never before a victim of adultery, Lis hadn't realized that illicit sex is only a part of the infidelity game. There's illicit affection too, and she wasn't sure which hurt the worst.

Why, bedding the bitch in Trump's Palace, her highly educated thighs squeezing Owen's, flicking tongues, shared spit, exposed nipples and cock and cleft . . . Those were bad enough. But Lis was almost more stung by the thought of their joined palms, romantic walks on the turbulent Jersey beach, the two of them sitting on a bench and Owen sharing his most private thoughts.

Stern Owen! Her *quiet* Owen.

Owen from whose mouth *she* had to pry words.

Much of this was speculation of course (he'd learned his lesson and volunteered nothing more after blurting out the woman's CV).

But the thought alone of an intimacy deeper than sex was horrifying to Lis and her fury at their furtive conversations and entwined fingers grew beyond all reasonable proportion. For weeks after his confession she was racked by a sensation that she might at any moment erupt in madness—anytime, anywhere.

By the time she confronted him, the affair was over, he said. He'd taken his wife's head in his long hands, stroking her hair, jiggling the earrings he'd given her (during the height of his infidelity, Lis had noted with ire, and that night pitched the jewelry out). The woman had asked him to leave Lis, Owen said, and marry her. He refused, they fought and the affair ended bitterly.

After the initial, cataclysmic weeks following this confession, after the long nights of silence, after those funereal Sunday mornings, after an intolerable Thanksgiving, they began to discuss the matter as couples do—tactically, then obliquely, then reasonably. Lis now had only vague memories of the conversations. You're too demanding. You're too strict. You're too quiet. You're too reclusive. You're not interested in what I do. You have to loosen up sexually. You come on like a rapist. You never complained. . . . Yes but you scare me sometimes I can't tell what you're thinking yes but you're so stubborn yes but . . .

The second-person pronoun occurs never so often as in the aftermath of infidelity.

Finally they decided to consider divorce and went their separate ways for a time. During this period Lis finally admitted to herself that the affair was no surprise. Not really. Owen's having an attorney for a lover, well, *that* was a shock, yes. He didn't fare well with strong women. To hear him tell it, his best relationship prior to Lis had been with a young Vietnamese woman in Saigon during the war. He was tactfully reluctant to go into many details but he described her glowingly as sensitive and demure. It took Lis some translating, and prying, to figure out that this meant she was subservient and complacent and she spoke very little English.

That's a relationship? she wondered, unnerved to find that this was the sort of woman her husband had sought out. Still, there seemed to be something more to the liaison. Something dark. Owen wouldn't go into the details and Lis was left to speculate. Maybe he had accidentally wounded her and stayed with her out of loyalty, slipping her stolen rations and medicines and nursing her to health. Maybe her father was a Viet Cong whom Owen had killed. Plagued with guilt, he'd offered some reparation and fallen in love.

This all seemed far too romantic, operatic even, for Owen Atcheson, and she ultimately attributed the affair to youthful lust, and his fond memories of it to the revisionist ego of a middle-aged man. But there was no denying that a servile young thing had a certain appeal to him. The greatest friction between them—and his worst flares of temper—arose when she opposed him. She could rattle off a hundred examples—buying the nursery, urging him to be more of a sexual partner, suggesting they see a therapist when the marriage hit rough spots, traveling less.

And yet, ironically, his domineering side did have a certain appeal to Lis. As troubling as this was, she couldn't deny it. She still recalled seeing him for the first time. She was in her mid-thirties, an age at which most Ridgeton women were sensible mothers several times over. Lis had attended a town-council meeting, where Owen was representing a building developer seeking a P&Z variance. Stern and unyielding, Owen Atcheson stood at the podium and comfortably withstood the assault of wrathful citizens. Lis stayed long after her own minor ministerial proceeding and watched him play the king's knight. She was captivated by his cold articulation and, watching him grip the podium with his large hands, actually found herself aroused.

She engineered a chance meeting in the parking lot afterwards, suggesting they exchange phone numbers. "Who knows? Maybe I'll need a good lawyer someday."

One week later he asked her to dinner and she accepted at once.

On the first date he showed up scrubbed and trimmed, wearing a blue blazer and khaki slacks, carrying a dozen roses. Owen ordered for her, picked up the check discreetly, held open every door she walked through and capped the evening with a chaste kiss after escorting her to the door.

He did everything by the book and she felt absolutely nothing for him.

He didn't call her afterwards and—despite a brief sting to the ego—she decided she was relieved not to hear from him. She went out with several other men casually, thinking no more about the austere Owen Atcheson. Then one Saturday, six months later, they ran into each other in a store on Main Street. He claimed he'd been meaning to call but had been traveling extensively. Why, Lis had wondered, did men think this made you feel better, explaining how much they'd *wanted* to call but had not?

As she and Owen stood awkwardly at the counter of Ace Hardware, he glanced down at the white plastic tubing she was buying. It was for her garden, she explained. Did she need any help installing it? When she hesitated he looked into her eyes and said he didn't have many talents but there were a few things he was very good at. Plumbing was one.

"All right," she said.

They returned to the small bungalow she was renting. With Owen supervising, together they hooked up the irrigation system in half an hour. When the work was finished, he walked to the spigot, beckoning her to follow. He took her hand and placed it on the knob then enfolded her fingers with his. "Shall we?" he asked, and turned the faucet on full as he lifted her chin with his free hand and kissed her hard on the mouth.

They spent the rest of the afternoon in Lis's brass bed, not even bothering to climb beneath the blue gingham covers, their dirty work-clothes strewn about them on the stairs and floor.

They were married eight months later.

Throughout their six years together Lis had frequent doubts about their future yet she'd never thought that infidelity would end the marriage; more likely, she believed, one of them would just pack and leave—maybe after, in a fit of temper, he finally delivered one of the slaps he'd come close to inflicting on her in the past. Or after she'd insisted, no, no compromises, that he choose between her and another weekend at the office.

So his affair was a sobering event. She was, at first, fully ready to divorce him and start life on her own. Initially this had a great appeal to her. But Lis Atcheson was not at heart an angry woman and as the weeks went by she found she needed to remind herself to be indignant about the affair. This equilibrium made the idea of living alone again less attractive. Besides, he was excruciatingly contrite, which gave her a curious power over him—the only upper hand she'd ever attained in the marriage.

A practical matter too: Ruth L'Auberget, who'd been ill with cancer throughout this time, finally passed away, and the daughters were heirs to a complicated estate. Lis, with no interest in financial matters, found herself relying more and more on Owen. Business and money were, after all, aspects of his profession and as he became involved in managing the estate the couple grew close once again.

Their life became easier. Lis bought the 4x4. As agreed among the sisters and Ruth L'Auberget, Lis and Owen moved into the Ridgeton house with its dream greenhouse and Portia received the co-op. Owen bought suits from Brooks Brothers and fancy shotguns. He went deep-sea fishing in Florida and hunting in Canada. And he continued to take business trips, often overnight. But Lis believed his pledge of fidelity. Besides, she reasoned, Owen clearly liked being wealthy, and the money, stock and house were all in Lis's name.

So when, tonight—after they'd learned of Hrubek's escape—Owen had stood before her, armed with his black guns, Lis had looked past his grim mouth and the consuming hunt lust in his eyes and had seen a husband trying the only way he could to fix a love altered by his own carelessness.

Well, bless you, Owen, for your errand tonight, Lis thought, taping the last of the windows. Your efforts are appreciated. But hurry home now, won't you?

The wind was rising. It drove a whip of rain across the roof and north side of the greenhouse with such a clatter than Lis gasped.

It was time to leave.

"Portia! Let's go."

"I've got a couple more to do," she called from upstairs.

"Leave 'em."

The woman appeared a minute later. Lis studied her for a moment and was surprised to see that in these country clothes, so atypical of Portia, the sisters looked very much alike.

"What?" Portia asked, noting Lis's gaze.

"Nothing. You ready?" Lis handed her a yellow rain slicker and pulled her own on.

Portia slung her backpack over one shoulder. Lifting her small Crouch & Fitzgerald suitcase Lis nodded toward the door. They walked outside into the rain that now was falling steadily. A sudden gust ripped the baseball cap from Portia's head. She shouted in surprise and ran to retrieve the hat while her sister double-locked the back door, and they stepped along the soggy path to the edge of the parking area.

Lis turned to look back at the house. With the windows barred by X's of tape, and the old, warping shingles, the colonial had a battle-weary air, as if it squatted in the middle of a no-man's-land. Her eyes were on the greenhouse when she heard her sister ask, "What *is* that?"

Lis spun around. "My God."

Spreading out before them was a field of mud and water, nearly a foot deep, covering much of the driveway and filling the garage.

They waded through the chill, slimy water and gazed at the lake. It wasn't their levee that had given way; it was the sandbags by the dock—the ones that Owen had assured Lis he'd stacked high and solid. The rising lake had pushed them over and the water was backing into the creek behind the garage. Amid eddies and whirlpools, the stream was filling the yard.

"What do we do?" Portia shouted. Her voice was harsh and unsettling; despite the quick-moving current, the flood was virtually silent.

There wasn't much they *could* do, Lis decided. The water was flowing in through a twenty-foot gap—too large for the two of them to dam. Besides, the garage was in a low-lying area of the property. If the level of the lake didn't rise much more, the house and most of the driveway would be safe.

She said, "We leave is what we do."

"Fine with me."

They waded into the garage and climbed into the Acura. Lis slipped the key into the ignition. She paused superstitiously—concerned that the flood had shorted out the battery or ruined the starter. She looked at Portia then turned the key. The engine kicked to life and purred smoothly. Backing out carefully, Lis eased the car through the flood up the incline of the driveway.

They were nearly out of the dark pool surrounding the garage when the car shuddered and the front wheels, the drive wheels, dug through the gravel and into the slick mud below, where they spun uselessly, as if they rested in ruts of ice.

This, Lis recalled, had been her second concern.

He eased his BMW around the curve on Route 236 and sped out of Ridgeton through the cutting rain.

Richard Kohler now descended through the hills and swept to the right, heading due east once again. There it was. Perfect. Just perfect! He laughed out loud, thinking that the scene was far more impressive than he'd remembered. He pulled into the back of the lot, parked and shut the engine off. He unzipped his backpack, extracting Michael Hrubek's file—the one he'd started to read earlier that evening.

This battered folio had been penned by sixty-five-year-old Dr. Anne Weinfeldt Muller, a staff psychiatrist at Trevor Hill Psychiatric Hospital.

Trevor Hill was a renowned private facility in the southern part of the state. Michael had been Anne Muller's patient for merely five months but her insights into his plight, and his improvement under her care, were inspiring. It was, Kohler reflected, a true tragedy that no one would ever know how effective Muller's treatment of Michael Hrubek might have been.

Like Kohler, Anne Muller divided her time among various hospitals and happened to have come across Michael at a small state facility where she worked with severe schizophrenics. Impressed by his intelligence and struck by his unusual delusions, she campaigned to pry open the doors of expensive Trevor Hill and have Michael admitted as a *pro bono* patient. The hospital administrators—preferring patients that were more "mainstream" than Michael (that is, able to pay their bills)—had resisted her efforts at first but had finally acquiesced, largely because of her own prestige and talent and pigheaded manner.

His first day had been spent in a restraint camisole. Then he'd calmed and the feared garment had come off. Kohler glanced again at Muller's notes, jotted in the first week of the young man's commitment:

Pt. is hostile & suspicious. Afraid of being struck. ("You hit me on the head, you're one dead fucker, make no mistake.") No apparent visual hallucinations, some auditory . . . Motor activity is extreme restraint at times necessary. . . . Affect flat or inappropriate (Pt. began sobbing when noticed book of Ameri-

can history; later Pt. laughed when asked about maternal grandmother and said she was "one dead fucker") . . . Cognitive functioning good but flights of ideas indicate purely random thinking at times. . . .

Although the many state hospitals in which Michael had been committed undoubtedly blended together into a grim stew of memories, Trevor Hill might very well have stood out pleasantly in his mind. In state facilities, patients wore filthy clothing and sat in drab rooms with blunt crayons or Play-Doh for entertainment. Many of the men and women had the indentations of lobotomies on the crowns of their heads and were regularly third-railed by electroconvulsive-shock technicians or sent into insulin comas. But Trevor Hill was different. There were far more orderlies and doctors per patient than in the state hospitals, the library was full of books, wards were sunny and windows unbarred, the grounds landscaped with trim paths and gardens, and rec rooms stocked with learning toys and games. ECS was used occasionally but medication was the major tool of treatment.

Yet, as with all schizophrenic patients, getting the right drug and dosage for Michael was a major task. One young resident at Trevor Hill had naïvely asked him what medicines he'd taken in the past and the patient answered like a diligent medical student. "Oh, lithium. Generally, chlorpromazine and its derivatives are contraindicated for me. I'm a schizophrenic—make no mistake about that—but a big component of my disease is manic-depression. You may know that as bipolar depression. So, lithium has generally been my drug of choice."

The impressed resident prescribed lithium and under the drug's effect Michael went berserk. He threw the ward's television through a window, leapt out after it and got halfway through the main gate before being tackled by three burly orderlies.

After this incident Dr. Muller took over treatment personally. She put Michael on a loading dose of Haldol—a dosage larger than he would ultimately need but intended to stabilize him fast. He improved immediately. Then began the fine tuning, balancing the drugs' effectiveness against the side effects of weight gain, dry mouth, the uncontrollable moving of the lips that antipsychotic drugs cause, the nausea. His regimen included, at various times, Thorazine, Stelazine, Mellaril, Moban, Haldol, and Prolixin. Thirty milligrams of this, one hundred of that, up it to two hundred, no, better mix it. Eighteen hundred of Thorazine, no, go higher, switch to Haldol, ninety milligrams of it, well, that's the same as forty-five hundred of Thorazine, too high, how's his dyskinesia? Okay, back to Stelazine . . .

Muller finally settled on what Kohler himself found worked best with Michael: high levels of Thorazine. Michael's treatment consisted of this workhorse drug and his therapy with Dr. Anne. She met with him every Tuesday and Friday. And what was distinctive about his sessions with this psychiatrist was that unlike so many of his doctors in the past she *listened* to what he had to say.

"You've said a couple of times now, Michael, that you're worried about what's 'ahead.' Do you mean your immediate future?"

"I never said that," he snapped.

"Did you mean something ahead of you in the hallway? Was someone upsetting you?"

"I never said a word like that. Someone's making up things about me. The government's usually to blame, the fuckers. I don't want to talk about it."

"Do you mean 'a head,' like someone's head, a skull?"

He blinked and muttered, "I can't go into it."

"If it's not the head maybe you mean someone's face? Whose?"

"I can't fucking go into it! You're going to have to use truth serum on me if you want that information. I'll bet you have already. You may know that as scopolamine." He fell silent, a smirk upon his face.

The therapy was no more sophisticated than this. Like Kohler, Anne Muller never tried to dissuade Michael of his delusions. She dug into them, trying to learn what was inside her patient. He resisted with the resilience of a captured spy.

But after four months Michael's paranoid and contrary nature suddenly vanished. Muller herself grew suspicious—she'd come to recognize that Michael had a calculating streak in him. He grew increasingly cheerful and giddy. Then she learned from the orderlies that he'd taken to stealing clothes from the laundry room. She assumed that his apparently improved temperament was a ruse to shift suspicion about the theft.

Yet before Muller could confront him, Michael began to deliver the loot to her. First, two mismatched socks. He handed them to her with the bashful smile of a boy with a crush. She returned the articles to their owners and told Michael not to steal anymore. He grew very grave and told her he was "unable at this time to make a commitment of that magnitude."

Important principles were involved, he continued. "Very important."

Apparently so, for the next week, she received five T-shirts and more socks. "I'm giving these clothes to you," he announced in a whisper, then walked away abruptly as if late for a train. The gift-giving went on for several weeks. Muller was far less concerned about the thefts themselves than understanding what Michael's behavior meant.

Then, when she was lying in bed at three in the morning, the epiphany occurred. She sat up, stunned.

In the course of a long, disjointed therapy session that day, Michael had lowered his voice and, eyes averted, whispered, "The reason is, I want to get my *clothes* to you. Don't tell anyone. It's very risky. You have no idea *how* risky."

Clothes to you. *Close* to you. I want to get close to you. Muller bolted from her bed and drove immediately to her office, where she

dictated a lengthy report that began with a subdued introductio
tantamount to a psychiatrist's shout of joy:

*Major breakthrough yesterday. Pt. expressed desire for emo-
tional connection with Dr., accompanied by animated affect.*

As the treatment continued, Michael's paranoia diminished further. The thefts stopped. He grew more sociable and cheerful and
he required less medication than before. He enjoyed his group-
therapy sessions and looked forward to outings that had previously
terrified him. He started doing chores around the hospital, helping
out the library and gardening staffs. Michael, Muller reported, had
even driven her car several times.

Kohler now looked up from the report and gazed across the gritty
parking lot. Lightning flashed in the west. Then he read the final
entry in the file, written in a hand other than Anne Muller's. He
found he could picture the scene upon which these notes were
based only too well:

*Michael lies on his bed, looking through a history book, when a
doctor comes into his room. He sits on the bed and smiles at the
patient, inquiring about the book. Michael immediately stiffens. Little
sparks of his paranoia begin to burn.*

"Who're you, what do you want?"

"I'm Dr. Klein. . . . Michael, I'm afraid I have to tell you that
Dr. Muller is sick."

"Sick? Dr. Anne is sick?"

"I'm afraid she's not going to be meeting with you."

Michael doesn't know what to say. "Tomorrow?" *he manages to
blurt, wondering what this man has done with his doctor and friend.*
"Will I see her tomorrow?"

"No, she's not coming back to the hospital."

"She left me?"

"Actually, Michael, she didn't leave you. She left all of us. She passed away last night. Do you know what it means, 'passed away'?"

"It means some fucker shot her in the head," he answers in an ominous whisper. "Was it you?"

"She had a heart attack."

Michael blinks a number of times, trying to comprehend this. Finally a bitter smile snaps onto the patient's face. "She left me." He begins nodding, as if relieved to hear long-anticipated bad news.

"Your new doctor is Stanley Williams," the man continues soothingly. "He's an excellent psychiatrist. He trained at Harvard and he worked at NIMH. That's the National Institutes for Mental Health. How's that for credentials, Michael? Very sharp fellow, you'll be pleased to know. He's going to—"

The doctor manages to dodge the chair, which splinters against the wall with the sound of a gunshot. He leaps into the corridor. The heavy oak door restrains Michael for about ten seconds then he finishes kicking his way into the hall and storms through the hospital to find his Dr. Anne. He breaks the arm of an orderly who tries to subdue him and they finally net him like an animal, a nineteenth-century technique that had been used at Trevor Hill only once since it opened.

One week later, his advocate and therapist dead, Michael Hrubek and his sole material possessions—toothbrush, clothes and several books of American history—were shipped to a state mental hospital.

His life was once again about to become an endless stream of Pill Time and Meal Time and Shock Time. And it would have too, except that after sitting in the hospital's intake waiting room for two hours, temporarily forgotten about, he grew agitated and strolled out the front door. He waved goodbye to a number of patients and orderlies he'd never met and continued through the gate, never to return.

Dr. Richard Kohler noted that the date of that disappearance had been exactly fourteen months ago; the next official record about Michael Hrubek was an arrest report written by the unsteady hand of a trooper at Indian Leap State Park on the afternoon of May 1.

The psychiatrist set aside Anne Muller's file and picked up the small notebook filled with the jottings he had made at Lis Atcheson's house. But before he read he stared for a moment outside at the drops of thick rain that rattled on the windshield, and he wondered just how much longer he'd have to wait.

21

"Where'd you find this?"

Under the bed, up a tree, in between Mona the Moaner's legs . . .

Peter Grimes didn't respond and to his great relief the hospital director seemed to forget the question.

"My God. He's been talking to DMH for *three months*? Three fucking months! And look at all of this. Look!" Adler seemed almost more astonished at the volume of paperwork that Richard Kohler had generated than by the contents of those papers.

Grimes noticed that his boss was touching the sheets rather gingerly, as if afraid of getting his fingerprints on them. This was perhaps Grimes's imagination but it made the young doctor extremely uncomfortable—largely because it seemed like an excellent idea, one he wished had occurred to him earlier, before he'd left the evidence of his identity imprinted all over the documents.

Adler looked up, his thoughts hovering, and to keep him from asking again where the papers had come from, Grimes read from the sheet that happened to be face up in front of the two men. " 'Dear Dr. Kohler: Further to your proposal dated September 30 of this year, we are pleased to inform you that the Finance Division of the State Department of Mental Health has provisionally agreed to fund a program for inpatient treatment of severely psychotic individuals according to the guidelines you have set forth in the aforementioned proposal. . . .' "

"God*damn* him," Adler interjected with such vehemence that Grimes was afraid to stop reading.

" 'A preliminary budget of 1.7 million dollars covering the firs year's financial needs for your program has been provisionally approved. As agreed, funding will come from existing allocations to the state mental-health hospital system, in order to bypass the necessity of a public referendum,' "

But stop he did when Adler muttered "bypass" as if it were an obscenity and snatched away the sheet to read the final paragraph himself. " 'This is to confirm that your proposal is conditioned upon approval by the Board of Physicians of the State Department of Mental Health, following your final presentation of the six case studies and verbatims upon which your proposal was based (Allenton, Grosz, Hrubek, McMillan, Green, Yvenesky). A representative of the Board will contact you directly regarding times for oral presentations of those case studies. . . .' "

Adler slammed the paper to the desk and Grimes decided that, while his fingerprint paranoia was perhaps misplaced, the hospital director should be somewhat more careful. If Kohler noticed damaged pages he might complain of a suspected theft—to which, Grimes was painfully aware, there'd been a witness. A half hour before, the assistant had summoned an irritable Slavic janitor to open the door of Kohler's office. Not a seasoned burglar, Grimes had neglected to send him away and had failed to notice that the squat man planted himself on the threshold to watch with amusement the young doctor's heist from start to finish.

"Our *money*. He's getting our money, on top of everything else! And, look at this. Look at it, Grimes. He's using *our* patients to fuck us! He's selling us out—our patients, our money—for *his* program."

Adler grabbed the phone and made a call.

As he gazed out the window, Grimes considered Kohler's scheme and he was both shocked and impressed. Kohler had used Michael Hrubek as a shining example of how his combination of drugs, delusion therapy and milieu resocialization treatment could produce dramatic improvements in chronic, dangerous schizophrenic patients. The Department of Mental Health had agreed to give Kohler a great deal of money and let him create a little fiefdom—carved out of Marsden hospital itself, at Adler's expense no less. But of course if Hrubek wasn't captured quietly, if he injured or killed someone, the DMH Board of Physicians would abort Kohler's plan as unworkable and dangerous.

Still, it was an admirable scheme, Grimes thought, and he regretted playing a part in the downfall of a talented man, one who probably would've been a better choice to hitch his star to—if of course Kohler's career had survived this evening. Which it surely would not.

The rain spattered the greasy windows. A huge wail of wind ended in a crash of plate glass from somewhere in the courtyard below. Several other patients had joined Patient 223-81 and a chorus of frightened wailing filled the halls. Grimes looked absently out the window and tried to avoid thinking about the effect on patients if a tornado touched down nearby.

Adler slammed down the phone and looked at him. "He's not at the halfway house. Some son of a bitch tipped him off."

"Who, Kohler?"

"He got a call a couple hours ago. He's *out* there. He's after Hrubek right now."

"By himself?"

"He *has* to go by himself. He has to get Hrubek to come back like a quiet little lamb. Then he'll claim he simply walked up to him and asked him to come home. And the son of a bitch will. *After* Kohler hits him with a taser or a tranquilizer gun . . . Shit! The break-in."

"I'm sorry?" the assistant asked cautiously.

"Security said somebody broke into the pharmacy tonight."

"Right. Well, they said it was a car accident, looked like. We won't know till morning if anything's missing."

"Oh, something's missing, you can bet on it. That son of a bitch lifted a tranquilizer gun. He's going to . . ." Adler spat out, "Jesus, he's going to make Hrubek look like the fucking little puppy *I've* said he is all along. Jesus Lord."

Grimes impersonated a fish again, chewing water urgently, and wondered aloud what they might do next.

"I want to be ready to pre-empt the press. If this . . ." He tried out several words for size before saying, "If this situation becomes critical—"

"If it's a worst case."

"Yes, if it's worst-case, we'll have to go public immediately. I want a release. Write it up—"

"A press release?"

"What *else* would I mean? Can you draft one up? Subject, verb. Subject, verb. That too much for you? And let's go over it, you and me. Say that, unbeknownst to staff, no, say unbeknownst to *administrators* and *officials*, a private physician with privileges here gave Hrubek access to all wards, which allowed him to escape. Say 'with privileges'; don't say 'attending.' Let's confuse the morons. Then say that this was in defiance—"

"Defiance?"

"—of clear instructions that any transfer of Section 403 patients must be approved by the office of the director before they go into any milieu, group, or off-ward therapy."

Instructions, yes, well, his assistant stammered. But there *were* no instructions to that effect, were there? Oh, it made sense, yes. There probably *should* be, yes. But at the moment there were none.

"The memo," Adler said impatiently. "Don't you remember? The 1978 memo?"

Grimes glanced out the window. Adler was referring to a directive that required notice to the director's office before criminally insane patients could be moved into medium- or low-security wings, even temporarily—if, for instance, the showers on E Ward weren't work-

*g. While this *was* a rule, yes, it was observed only by the most Grimes allowed himself the diagnosis) anal-retentive of the doctors *t* Marsden.

"This seems a little . . ." Now words evaded Assistant Grimes.

"And put a copy in here. What's the matter?"

"I just . . . The issue isn't really access, is it?"

"Well, what *is* the issue?" Adler said this with a sneer in his *oice* and Grimes had an urge to call him a schoolmarm, which *:ertainly* would have cost him his job faster than jokes about rape.

"Kohler doing delusion therapy. *That's* what set Hrubek off. *That's* what we can hang him with."

This was, Adler reflected, a good point. Hrubek's roaming the *halls* near the morgue was essentially the *orderlies'* fault. They *missed* his medicine stockpile and they were careless with Cal-*laghan's* body. But Kohler's sin, as Grimes accurately pointed out, *was* far more serious. He had somehow awakened Hrubek's *desire* *to* escape. The means *were* largely irrelevant. Those fantasies ought to have been tucked away inside Hrubek, tucked away very deeply—or, better yet, behaviorially conditioned out of him. Say what you might, electrodes and food could turns rats into quite model animals. Why, witness young Grimes. . . .

Still, the hospital director assessed, Kohler's errors would be tough to sell to the public—simple people who would want simple answers in the event that Hrubek knifed a trooper to death or raped a girl. He thanked Grimes for his insight and then added, "Let's just lay the access issue at our friend's feet, shall we? By the time it's all sorted out, he'll be everybody's whipping boy, and no one'll really care exactly what he did."

And his assistant, pleased to have been patted on the head, nod-ded instantly.

"Don't be too specific. We have to massage the facts. Say, be-cause of his involvement in Kohler's program Hrubek was free to get into the freezer, the morgue and the loading dock. None of the other Section 403 criminally insane have that access. That's true isn't it?"

It was, Grimes confirmed.

"*But for* his involvement in the program he never would've escaped. *Sine qua non.*"

"You want me to say that?"

"Well, not '*sine qua non*,' obviously. You know what I'm saying? You get the picture? And don't use Kohler's name. Not at first. Make it sound like we're concerned about, you know . . ."

"His reputation?"

"Good. Yes, his reputation."

The only mechanic answering the phone tonight was in Roenville, about fifteen miles west on Route 236. The man chuckled and answered that sure he had a truck but it'd be four or five hours before he could get somebody over to Ridgeton.

"Already got three roads out in this part of the county alone. And my men're getting a wreck off Putnam Valley Highway. Injuries. Mess of 'em. Hell of a night. Just one hell of a night. So, you wanna go on the list?"

Lis said, "That's okay," and hung up. She then called the Ridgeton Sheriff's Department.

"Why, hello, Mrs. Atcheson," the dispatcher answered respectfully. The woman's daughter was in Lis's class; parents tended to address her as formally as their children did. "How you weatherin' the storm tonight? So to speak. Ha. It's something, isn't it?"

"We're getting by. Say, Peg, is Stan around?"

"Nup, not a soul here. Everybody's out. Even Fred Bertholder, and he's got the flu like nobody oughta have. And they didn't cancel that rock concert like they oughta've. Can you believe that? A lotta youngsters got stranded. What a mess."

"Have you heard anything from Marsden hospital, about Hrubek?"

"Who'd that be?"

"That man who escaped tonight."

"Oh, him. You know, Stan called the state police about that just 'fore he went out. He's in Massachusetts."

"Hrubek? In Massachusetts?"

"Yes'm."

"You're sure?"

"They tracked him to the state line then our boys had to call off the search. Handed it over to the Mass troopers. They're top-notch at finding people even though they don't have any sense of humor. That's what Stan says."

"Have they . . . ? Have they found him?"

"I don't know. The storm'll hit there in an hour, hour and a half, so I don't suppose a drugged-up psycho's a real high priority but that's me speaking not them. They might not take to madmen from out of state. Being so serious and all. You know, Mrs. Atcheson, been meaning to speak to you about that C-minus Amy got."

"Could we talk about it next week, Peg?"

"Absolutely. It's just that Irv coached her like a demon, and he reads all the time. Knows his literature, and I don't mean just schlock either. He read *Last of the Mohicans* even before it was a movie."

"Next week?"

"Absolutely. Good night to you, Mrs. Atcheson."

She hung up and wandered out to Portia, who stood sipping a Coke on a small screened-in porch off the kitchen. They didn't use the place much for entertaining. The sun never reached it, and the view of the yard and lake was all but cut off by a tall growth of juniper.

"This is pretty," her sister commented, running her hand along an elaborate railing of mahogany, carved in the shapes of flowers, vines and leaves. The wind blew an aerated mist of icy rain toward the house and the women stepped back suddenly.

"That's right, you haven't seen it."

Lis had noticed the balustrade at an upstate demolition site and knew at once that she had to have it. In one of her brashest moments she'd laid quick, cold dollars into the ponderous hands of the wrecking-crew captain. It was probably an illicit deal, for he turned his back as she dragged off the delicate sculpture, which she then spent another two thousand dollars incorporating into the railing here.

Friends wondered why such a beautiful piece of woodwork accented a dark, out-of-the-way porch like this. But the carving had one frequent admirer: Lis herself spent many nights here, bedded down in a chaise longue she'd commandeered for the times when the insomnia was particularly bad. The porch was open on three sides. If there was wind the breezes flowed over her as she lay beneath the blankets and if there was rain the sound was hypnotic. Even when Owen was away on business, she'd often come down here. She supposed it was risky, being alone and so exposed to the night. Yet the game of finding sleep is a crucible of trade-offs and an insomniac can't afford the luxury of separating slumber and vulnerability.

"I heard," Portia said. "No tow truck?"

"Nope."

"Can we walk?"

"Two miles? In this rain and wind?" Lis laughed. "Rather not."

"What about Hrubek?"

"Supposedly in Massachusetts."

"So why don't we just sit it out? Get a fire going and tell ghost stories?"

If only they'd left twenty minutes sooner . . . Angrily Lis remembered Kohler. If he hadn't stopped by, they'd be at the Inn by now. She felt a chill thinking that it was as if Michael Hrubek had sent an agent to detain her.

Portia asked, "Well? We're staying?"

Overhead the wind sliced through the treetops with a hissing sound—the noise electric trains make—of motion not propulsion. The rain pounded the soaked earth.

"No," Lis said finally, "we're leaving. Let's get some shovels and dig out the car."

Animals are far easier than humans to pursue for long distances, for three reasons: They eat whenever they're hungry. They don't control elimination of wastes. They have limited options for loco-motion.

The world at large, Trenton Heck reflected, may have considered Michael Hrubek an animal but so far his journey west had all the trappings of a trip by a damn clever human being.

Heck was in despair. The driving rain had virtually erased all the airborne scent and he could find no other evidence of Hrubek's trail. Emil had quartered again and again over the highway and surrounding fields for an hour and had found nothing.

But now, just outside of Cloverton, Heck found that the madman had lapsed momentarily. His animal's impulse to eat had overcome his need for evasion.

At first Heck didn't think anything of the Hostess doughnut box lying in the driveway of the old gas station. Then he noticed it wasn't empty. This said to him that it couldn't have been there more than a half hour. No self-respecting raccoon, he concluded, would let pastry sit uneaten for longer than that.

As Heck and Emil walked up to the box, the dog immediately tensed. Heck knew this had nothing to do with a canine fondness for sugar and grease, and he scanned the ground carefully. There! Hrubek's bootprints, just visible on the concrete apron near the pumps. All right! His heart thudded at this good luck. Just west of the station Heck found a tread mark in the dirt beside the highway. For some reason Hrubek was now keeping to the shoulder and in the rain it was easy to follow the tread by sight. Heck and Emil returned to the truck and drove west. He saw that the track continued only for another hundred yards or so then cut suddenly across the highway, aiming directly for a long driveway or private road.

Heck stopped the truck and got Emil harnessed up, once again short-lined because of Heck's fear of the traps. He picked up the scent immediately and together man and dog crashed through brush, the hound in heaven—his coat glistening with misty rain, his lungs filling with great gulps of cool air, his familiar master beside him, his simple dog's mind and solid body doing what God had created them for.

As they ran, Heck remembered another dog who loved fields, Sally Dodgeson's St. Anne—Emil's predecessor.

Sal was a smarter dog than Emil and with a faster gait and lither step. Those last two qualities, however, had been her downfall; she developed the curse of large working dogs, hip dysplasia. Heck retired her early and spent the bulk of his—and Jill's—sparse savings on operations. The surgery was not successful and it was a terrible thing to watch Sal, a young invalid, staring at the fields she'd loved to run through. Often she made pathetic attempts to escape and Heck would have to go retrieve the struggling animal, carrying her in his arms, his heart as broken as hers. The condition and the pain that accompanied it grew worse.

On the last visit to the vet Heck himself took the syringe from the doctor and injected the lethal dosage. Oh, it was a hard thing to do, and he wept, but Trenton Heck would let no stranger put down a dog of his.

When he returned home, Jill asked, too improvidently for his taste, "Would you cry for me that way?"

Heck was stung but he told her the truth and said of course he would. But the timing of his response was somehow off and Jill got huffy. She went out that night with her girlfriends, a batch of fun-loving waitresses, and he mourned alone, which was his preference anyway. The next morning at seven, Jill having returned just three hours before, Heck arose by himself and went to the breeder to talk about bloodhound pups.

Heck had used a classic dog-handler's trick to pick Emil out of a litter of five mournful-looking, irresistibly adorable bloodhound puppies. The breeder set up a piece of quarter-inch plywood next to the pen where the young pups were playing. In the middle of the board was a tiny hole. Heck crept up to the wood sheet and, unseen by the litter, watched through the hole as they rolled and nipped and tried out their long legs. In a few minutes one of the puppies lifted his head with a spark of curiosity in his eyes—a glint clearly visible despite the folds of skin that nearly obscured them. He tilted his head back and looked around then stumbled toward the hole behind which was Trenton Heck's right eye. The dog sniffed the alien scent for two minutes before becoming bored and returning to romp with his sorrowful-faced brothers and sisters.

The next day Heck did the same thing and again the ungainly puppy, tripping over his huge ears and paws, was drawn to investigate—while his siblings slept or played, oblivious to the intruder. When, the next week, the dog passed the scent test three for three, Trenton Heck stood, scooped up the dog and, one-handed, wrote a very large check to the breeder.

When Emil was twelve months old, the training started. Heck used only inductive training—dispensing rewards, never punishing. During the first six months of this work Heck's slacks stank of the meaty dog treats. Then he weaned the dog off food and onto praise as a reward tool. The training was a thousand times harder on Heck than on Emil, who had only to learn what commands to obey and to grasp how those words related to using his nose to do what it wanted to anyway.

Heck on the other hand had to make sure the training remained fun. Smart dogs like Emil get bored easily and Heck was forced to devise ways to keep the scenting interesting but feasible. Knowing when to stop for the day, figuring out when Emil was frustrated or horny or in a bad mood—those were his tasks. He had to pick scent articles that were challenging but not impossible (a scrap of leather was too easy; Bic pens and Jill's trashy romance novels too hard).

Heck, who at the time had a full-time trooper job and a wife who ate up much of his time, would rise at 4:00 a.m. to train his hound—a hardship for him but not for Emil, who woke immediately and joyously, knowing he was on his way to the fields. Oh, Trenton Heck worked. He knew the old tracking adage: "If you're not handling the dog right, it's your fault. If the dog's not tracking right, it's your fault."

But Emil did track right. He had a remarkable nose—one of the few, in his vet's estimation, that were two or three million times more sensitive than a human nose. He learned fast and the hound so exploited his nature that Heck, whose marriage was rocky and whose job was going nowhere, occasionally felt bad watching this astonishing dog and lamented that he himself had no consuming skill or drive to match Emil's.

After six months of training, Emil could follow a mile-and-a-half trail in record time, shaming the German shepherds that were the troop's unofficial trackers. By age two Emil had his American Kennel Club TD classification and a month later Heck took him up to Ontario, where he was awarded his Tracking Dog Excellent certification by pursuing a stranger over a thousand-yard trail that was five hours old, never hesitating on the turns or the cross-tracks meant to confuse the hound. After the TDE rating Emil more or less joined Haversham's troop, to which Heck was assigned, though the state technically had no budget for dogs. The troop did, however, spring for membership (dog and man) in the National Police Bloodhound Association, which two years ago gave Emil the famed Cleopatra Award for finding a lost boy who'd fallen into the Marsden River and been swept downstream in a heavy current, after which he'd wandered deep into a state park. The trail, through water, marsh, cornfields and forest, was 158 hours old—a record for the state.

Heck had taken to reading a lot about bloodhounds and believed that Emil was the descendant (spiritual, there being no true lineage) of the greatest of all tracking bloodhounds, Nick Carter, who was run by Captain Volney Mullikin down in Kentucky at the turn of the century, a dog credited with more than 650 finds resulting in criminal convictions.

Emil himself had put a fair number of people behind bars. Much tracking work involves trailing suspects from crime scenes or linking weapons or loot to defendants. Emil, because of his AKC papers and his solid history of tracking, was a permitted "witness," though he appeared on the stand through his spokesman, one Trenton Heck. Most of the dog's assignments, however, involved locating escapees like Michael Hrubek.

Tonight in fact it was the anticipated triumph in tracking down the psycho and earning Heck his reward that preoccupied him as they pushed through the brush. He should have had his mind on what he was doing though for he didn't see the spring trap until Emil stepped right onto it.

"No!" he cried, jerking back hard on the line, pulling the hound off balance. "Oh, no! What'd I do?" But Emil had already fallen sideways onto the large Ottawa Manufacturing trap. He yelped in pain.

"Oh, Jesus, Emil . . ." Heck dropped to his knees over the animal, thinking about splints and the emergency vet clinics, frighteningly aware that he had no bandages or tourniquets to staunch the flow of blood from a severed vein or artery. As he reached for his dog, however, his trooper instincts took over and realized that the trap might be a diversion.

He's waiting for me, it's a trick!

Heck flicked rain from his eyes, lifting the Walther, and spun about, wondering from which direction the madman would come charging at him. He paused momentarily, debated and when he heard nothing turned back to Emil. He'd have to risk an attack; he wasn't going to leave the dog unattended. Holstering the gun he reached for Emil, Heck's hands shaking and his heart only now beginning to pulse quickly in the aftermath of the fright. But the dog suddenly shook himself snootily and stood upright, unharmed.

What had happened? Heck gazed at the animal, who, as far as he could tell, had landed square on the burnished trigger plate of the trap.

Then he understood—the jaws had been sprung *before* Emil stepped on the trigger.

"Oh, Lord." He gripped the dog around his neck and hugged him hard. "Lord." The dog eased back and shook his head, embarrassment now piled on top of his indignation.

Heck crouched down and examined the trap. It was identical to those at the shop on Route 118. Hrubek obviously had set it. But how had it been sprung? There were two possibilities, Heck supposed. First, that a small animal, its head lower than the steel jaws, had bounded onto the trigger and set it off. The second possibility was that someone had come by, seen the trap and popped it with a stick or rock. This, Heck decided, was the likely explanation—because next to the trap he saw several bootprints in the mud. One set was Hrubek's. But someone else had been here as well. He looked closely at the prints and his heart plummeted.

"Oh, damn!" he whispered bitterly.

He recognized the sole. He'd seen these prints—of expensive L. L. Bean outdoorsman's boots—earlier in the evening, not far from the overhang where he and Emil had picked up Hrubek's westward trail, miles back.

So I've got some competition here.

Who is it? he wondered. A plainclothes trooper or cop maybe. Or more likely—and more troubling—a bounty hunter like Heck himself, seeking the reward money. Heck thought of Adler. Had he sent an orderly to find the patient? Was the hospital director playing a game of ends against the middle?

With the stake being Heck's reward money?

He rose and, clutching his gun, examined the two men's tracks carefully. Hrubek had continued south along the private road. The other tracker was coming *from* that direction and heading back toward Route 236. He'd done so after Hrubek—some of his prints covered the madman's—and he'd been running, as if he'd learned where Hrubek was headed and was in pursuit. Heck followed the L. L. Bean prints to the highway and found where the man had stopped and studied a tread mark, left recently by a heavy car. The tracker had then sprinted to the shoulder of Route 236, where he'd climbed into a vehicle and hurried west, spinning his wheels furiously. From the tread marks it was clear that the man was driving a truck with four-wheel drive.

The scene told him that Michael Hrubek had got himself a vehicle and was probably just minutes ahead of this other pursuer.

Heck looked around the turbulent night sky and saw a distant flash of silent lightning. He wiped the rain from his face. He debated for a long moment and finally concluded he had no choice. Even Emil couldn't track prey inside a moving car. Heck would speed west down the highway, relying on luck to reveal some sign of the prey's whereabouts.

"I'll leave the belt off, Emil," Heck said, leading the dog into the pickup. "But you sit tight. We're gonna waste some fuel here."

The hound sank down on Heck's outstretched leg, and as the truck sped onto the highway with a gassy roar, closed his droopy eyelids and dozed off.

22

Seven miles outside of Cloverton, along Route 236, Owen spotted the car parked by the roadside near a stand of evergreens.

Oh, you smart son of a bitch!

He drove past the old Cadillac then abruptly slowed and turned off the road, parking the truck in a cluster of juniper and hemlock.

He'd gambled, and he'd won.

About time, he thought. I'm due for a little luck.

Walking over the grounds at the murder site in Cloverton, Owen had noticed that two of the small barns near the house contained antique autos. He'd slipped inside and looked under the blue Wolf car covers to find an old '50 Pontiac Chief, a Hudson, a purple Studebaker. In one building, a stall was empty, and the car cover was dropped in a heap on the floor—the only disorder in the entire barn. His inclination was to dismiss the possibility of Hrubek's stealing such an obvious getaway car. But, remembering the bicycle, Owen yielded to his instincts and, after a brief search of the ground, he found recent tread marks of a heavy auto leading from the barn, down the driveway and then west on Route 236. Without a word to the Cloverton police he'd left the house and sped not to Boyleston but after the old car.

Now he climbed from the truck and walked back toward the Cadillac, the sound of his passage obscured by the steady rain and sharp slashes of wind. He paused and squinted into the night. Sixty, seventy feet away a large form stood with his back to Owen, urinating on a bush. The man's bald head was tilted back as he looked up into the sky, staring at the rain. He seemed to be singing or chanting softly.

Owen crouched down, slipping his pistol from his belt. He considered what to do next. When it had seemed that Hrubek was heading for the house in Ridgeton, Owen had planned simply to follow him there and then slip into the house ahead of him. If the madman broke in, Owen would simply shoot him. Maybe he'd slip a knife or crowbar into the man's hand—to make a tidier scene for the prosecutor. But now Hrubek had a car and it occurred to Owen that maybe Ridgeton wasn't his destination after all. Maybe he really would turn south and make for Boyleston. Or simply keep going on 236 and drive to New York, or even further west.

Besides, here was his quarry, defenseless, unsuspecting, alone —an opportunity Owen might not have again, wherever Hrubek was ultimately headed.

He made his decision: better to take the man now.

But what about the Cadillac? He could leave his truck here, dump the body in the trunk of the old car then drive it to Ridgeton himself. Once there he'd lug the body inside the house and—

But, no, of course not. The blood. The .357 hollow points would cause a lot of damage. Some forensic technician was sure to examine the Cadillac's trunk.

After a moment of debate Owen concluded that he'd simply leave the car here. Hrubek was crazy. He'd become scared of driving and had abandoned it, continuing on foot to Ridgeton. It occurred to him too that he probably shouldn't kill Hrubek here—the coroner might be able to determine that he'd died an hour or so before Owen claimed he had.

He decided that he'd just immobilize Hrubek now—shoot him in the upper arm and in the leg. Owen would lug him into the back of the Cherokee and drive on to Ridgeton.

And there the patient would be found, in the Atchesons' kitchen. Owen would be sitting in the living room, staring numbly out the window, staggered by the tragedy of it all—having fired two shots to try to stop him and finally a third, a lethal, bullet, when the big man would not heed Owen's orders to halt.

The blood in the Cherokee? Well, that was a risk. But he'd park it behind the garage. There'd be no reason for any investigators to see it, let alone have a forensic team go through the truck.

He analyzed the plan in detail, deciding that, yes, it was chancy but the risks were acceptable.

Cocking the pistol he made his way closer to the looming shape of Hrubek, who'd now finished his business and was staring up at the turbulent sky, listening to the sharp hiss of the wind in the tips of the pine trees and letting the rain fall into his face.

Owen got no further than five steps toward his prey before he heard the distinctive double snap of a pump shotgun and saw the policeman aim the muzzle at his chest.

"On the ground, freeze!" the young man's trembling voice called.

"What are you doing?" Owen cried.

"Freeze! Drop your gun! Drop that gun!"

Then Hrubek was running, a thick dark mass fleeing toward the Cadillac.

"I'm not going to tell you again!" the cop's voice was high with panic.

"You fucking idiot," Owen yelled, his temper flaring. He stepped toward the cop.

The trooper lifted the shotgun higher. Owen froze and dropped the Smith & Wesson. "Okay, okay!"

The sound of the Cadillac firing to life filled the clearing. As the car sped past them, the trooper glanced in shock at the sound. Owen easily shoved the shotgun muzzle to the side and drove his right fist into the side of the trooper's face. The young man dropped like deadweight and Owen was on him in a minute, slugging the trooper again and again, anger exploding within him. Gasping, he finally managed to control himself and looked down at the bloody face of the unconscious cop.

"Fuck," he spat bitterly.

The sudden crack sounded some yards behind him. It seemed like a gunshot and Owen dropped into a crouch, snatching up his pistol. He heard nothing else other than the wind and the drumming of the rain. The distant horizon lit up for a moment with huge sheets of lightning.

He turned back to the cop and handcuffed the man's wrists behind his back. He then stripped off the regulation patent-leather belt and bound the officer's feet. He stared in disgust for a moment, wondering if the trooper had gotten a good look at him. Probably not, he concluded. It was too dark; he himself hadn't seen the cop's face at all. He'd most likely figure that Hrubek himself had attacked him.

Owen ran back to his truck. He closed his eyes and slammed his fist on the hood. "No!" he shouted at the wet, breezy sky. "No!"

The left front tire was flat.

He bent down and noted that the bullet that had torn through the rubber was from a medium-caliber pistol. A .38 or 9mm probably. As he hurried to get the jack and spare, he realized that in all his plans for this evening this was something that he'd never considered—that Hrubek might be inclined to defend himself.

With a gun.

They stood side by side, holding long-handled shovels, and dug like oyster fishermen beneath the brown water for their crop of gravel. Their arms were in agony from filling and lugging the sandbags earlier in the evening and they could now lift only small scoops of the marble chips, which they then poured around the sunken tires of the car for traction.

Their hair now dark, their faces glossy with the rain, they lifted mound after mound of gravel and listened with some comfort to the murmuring of the car's engine. From the radio drifted classical music, interrupted by occasional news broadcasts, which seemed to have no relation to reality. One FM announcer—sedated by the sound of his own voice—came on the air and reported that the storm front should hit the area in an hour or two.

"Jesus Christ," Portia shouted over the pouring rain, "doesn't he have a window?"

Apart from this, they worked silently.

This is mad, Lis thought, as the wind slung a gallon of rain into her face. Nuts.

Yet for some reason it felt oddly natural to be standing in calf-high water beside her sister, wielding these heavy oak-handled tools. There used to be a large garden on this part of the property—before Father decided to build the garage and had the earth plowed under. For several seasons the L'Auberget girls grew vegetables here. Lis supposed that they might have stood in these very spots, raking up weeds or whacking the firm black dirt with hoes. She remembered stapling seed packets to tongue depressors and sticking them into the earth where they'd planted the seeds the envelopes contained.

"That'll show the plants what to look like, so they'll know how to grow," Lis had explained to Portia, who, being four, bought this logic momentarily. They'd laughed about it afterwards and for some years vegetable pinups had been a private joke between them.

Lis wondered now if Portia too recalled the garden. Maybe, if she did, she would take the memory as proof that going into business with her sister might not be as improbable as it seemed.

"Let's try it," she called through the rain, nodding toward the car.

Portia climbed in and, with Lis pushing, eased her foot delicately to the gas. The car budged an inch or two. But it sank down into the mud almost immediately. Portia shook her head and got out. "I could feel it. We're close. Just a little more."

The rain pours as they resume shoveling.

Lis glances toward her sister and sees her starkly outlined against a flare of lightning in the west. She finds herself thinking not about gravel or mud or Japanese cars but about this young woman. About how Portia moved to a tough town, how she learned to talk tough and to gaze back at you sultry and defiant, wearing her costumes, her miniskirts and tulle and nose rings, how she glories in the role of the urbane femme lover.

And yet . . . Lis has her doubts. . . .

Tonight, for instance, Portia didn't really seem at ease until she discarded the frou-frou clothes, ditched the weird jewelry and pulled on baggy jeans and a high-necked sweater.

And the boyfriends? . . . Stu, Randy, Lee, a hundred others. For all her talk of independence, Portia often seems no more than a reflection of the man she is, or isn't, with—precisely the type of obsolete, noxious relationship that she enthusiastically denounces. The fact is she never really *likes* these excessively handsome, bedroom-eyed boys very much. When they leave her—as they invariably do—she mourns briefly then heads out to catch herself a fresh one.

And so Lisbonne Atcheson is left to wonder, as she has frequently, who her sister really is. Is she truly the stranger she seems?

Lis just doesn't know. But she's decided to find out. If not through the nursery business, then in some other way. For a thought occurred to her recently—not long after Indian Leap, in fact. A thought she just can't shake: that the only way the dark heritage of the L'Aubergets can be redeemed—*if* it can be redeemed at all— is through the two surviving members of the family.

These two, together.

She can't say exactly why she wants this reconciliation. But nonetheless Lis feels, inexplicably, that this is something she must try. As a student told her last week, after she caught him cheating, "Hey, you play the odds."

They sling more gravel, as the rain falls heavily in thick dashes through the car's white headlight beams. Then the stuffy announcer fades in to tell his listeners that coming up next will be Handel's *Water Music*. He's apparently oblivious to the joke, and moves on to other news, while the sisters look at each other for an instant, and laugh, then return to their task.

The Cadillac raced down the highway amid the sticky rush of thick tires on wet asphalt and the hum of the grand engine's eight calm cylinders.

Michael Hrubek was still anxious from the run-in with the conspirators twenty minutes before. The fuckers! He'd escaped, yes, but his hands quivered violently and his heart pounded. His mind kept slipping off track, and he'd forget where he was and what he was doing. The echo of the gun's loud crack, the memory of the feel as it jumped in his hand, were prominent in his thoughts.

"*Cadillac*," he sang frantically, "*hard tack, sic semper tyran-ak . . . Dr. Anne, won't you come back?*"

After the death of Dr. Anne Muller, Michael began to wander. He occasionally spent time in state hospitals but lived mostly on the street, surviving on cheese sandwiches from social workers and scrounging through dumpsters outside restaurants. He was ravaged by anxiety and paranoia though the latter condition had a positive consequence: fearing drugs, all of which he believed to be poisonous, he remained uninfected by AIDS, hepatitis and other serious illnesses.

After several months in the Northeast he meandered south to Washington, D.C., intending to apologize for his past crimes to Andrew Johnson, Ulysses S. Grant or the current President, whomever he met first. He managed to get to the White House gate and knocked on the door of the guard's station.

"It's vital that I talk to you about this assassination business, John Guard. It's *vital*!"

Picked up, bang, by the Secret Service.

"That was stupid," he told himself glumly as he waited in an interrogation room somewhere in the Treasury Department. "Shouldn't've done that."

But he wasn't tortured as he'd expected. He was simply asked a series of what he called mind-messing questions and released after two hours. He knew that during the session the agents had somehow planted a tracking device in his body and he threw himself in the reflecting pool of the Washington Monument to short out the battery. He felt better after this dip and moved into Arlington National Cemetery, where he lived for a month.

Finally he grew bored with the capital and wandered back north, looking for his father. After a month of sporadic searching Michael believed he found his family's house in an old neighborhood of Philadelphia. He walked through the unlocked front door to see if anyone was home. Someone was, though it turned out to be not his father but the wife of a police detective.

Picked up, bang, for that one too.

Released the next day he hiked all the way to Gettysburg and lay in the middle of the battlefield, howling in shame for his role in ending the life of the greatest President the United States had ever known.

Picked up, bang.

Phillie, Newark, Princeton, New York, White Plains, Bridgeport, Hartford.

That was Michael's life: hospitals and the street. He slept in boxes, he bathed in rivers when he bathed, and he wandered purposefully. Every day was an intense experience. He saw truths with a piercing clarity. There were truths everywhere! Raw and painful truths. In red cars zipping down the street, in the motion of a tugboat easing into a slip, in the part of a teenage boy's hair, in a symmetrical display of watches in a jewelry-store window. He considered each of these revelations, always wondering if it might ease the burden of his anxiety and fear.

Did it *say* something to him? Did it offer solace?

Michael met people in his wanderings and they sometimes took to him. If he was clean and was wearing clothing recently given to him by a priest or social worker, someone might sit beside him on a park bench as he read a book. With a Penguin Classic in your hand, you were easily forgiven rumpled clothes and a short stubble of beard. Like any businessman out on a fine Sunday afternoon, Michael would cross his legs, revealing sockless ankles in brown loafers. He'd smile and nod and, avoiding the subjects of murder, rape and the Secret Service, talk only about what he saw in front of him: sparrows bathing in spring dust, trees, children playing flag football. He had conversations with men who might have been chief executives of huge corporations.

This nomadic life finally came to an unpleasant end in January of this year when he was arrested and charged with breaking into a store in a small, affluent town fifty miles south of Ridgeton. He'd shattered the window and torn apart a female mannequin. He was examined by a court-appointed psychiatrist, who believed there were sexual overtones to the vandalism and declared him violently psychotic. Giving his name as Michael W. Booth he was involuntarily committed and sent to Cooperstown State Mental Hospital.

There, even before an intake diagnostic interview, Michael was shuttled into the Hard Ward.

Still in a restraint camisole he was deposited in a cold, dark room, where he remained for three hours before the door opened and a man entered. A man bigger even than Michael himself.

"Who're you?" Michael challenged. "Are you John Wilkes Orderly? Do you work for the government? I've been to Washington, D.C., the capital of this great country. Who the *hell* do you—"

"Shut the fuck up." John Orderly slammed him into the wall and then shoved him to the floor. "Don't scream, don't shout, don't talk back. Just shut the fuck up and relax."

Michael had shut the fuck up but he hadn't relaxed. *Nobody* relaxed at Cooperstown. This was a place where patients simply gave up, surrendering to their madness. Michael spent much time sitting by himself, looking out windows, jiggling his legs with nervous energy, repeatedly muttering a single song—"Old Folks at Home." The staff psychologist who spent about seven minutes a week with Michael never pursued this compulsion but if he had he'd have found that the old Stephen Foster song contained the line "Oh, darkie, how my heart is yearning," which to Michael referred not to a slave but to darkness, specifically night. Night brought the hope of sleep, and sleep was the only time when he was at peace in this terrible place.

Cooperstown—where nurses would put two women patients in a room together with a single, oiled Coke bottle and watch from the door.

Cooperstown—where John Orderly would bend Michael over the tin washbasin and press into him again and again, the pain crying up through his ass into his jaw and face, the cold metal of the orderly's keys bouncing on the patient's thigh and matching the rhythm of his thrusts.

Cooperstown—where Michael slipped far, far from reality and came to believe with certainty that he was living in the time of the Civil War. In his month on the Hard Ward Michael had access to only one book. It was about reincarnation and after reading it a dozen times, he understood how he could in fact be John Wilkes Booth. He carried Booth's soul around with him! The spirit had flown from the old wounded body and circled for a hundred years. It alighted upon the head of Michael's mother just as the baby struggled out of her, leaving the red marks on her stomach that she had told him were his fault but not to worry about.

Yes, within him was the soul of Mr. John Wilkes Booth, a fair actor but a damn good killer.

One day in March of this year, John Orderly took Michael by the arm and pushed him into Suzie's room. He slammed the door shut and aimed the video camera through the window.

They were alone, Michael and this twenty-four-year-old patient, on whose pretty face was only one blemish—a tiny indentation of scar in the middle of her forehead. Suzie looked at Michael carefully with her sunken eyes. She was someone whose only earthly power was in knowing what was expected of her. She observed that Michael was a man and immediately hiked her skirt over bulging thighs. Down went her panties and she rolled onto her hands and knees.

And Michael, knowing that John Orderly was just outside the door, also knew what to do—exactly the same. Pants down, on his hands and knees. Here they remained, butts bare to the world, while John Orderly fled down the hallway when a doctor unexpectedly happened by. The psychiatrist glanced inside the room and opened the door. He inquired what the patients were doing.

Michael answered, "Waiting for John Orderly. I'm ready for him and so is she. Make no mistake. Like all men of medicine, John Orderly's got a very big cock."

"Oh, my God."

The investigation resulted in the dismissal of five orderlies, two nurses and two doctors from Cooperstown. Michael, however, never learned John Orderly's fate because as one of the most victimized patients he was immediately transferred out of the Hard Ward into the voluntary-commitment section of the hospital. "Due to stabilization of his condition," the report said. "Prognosis for improvement: fair to good." In fact Michael was far sicker than when he'd been admitted but the administrators wanted to isolate him from the questioning reporters and state mental-health examiners who descended on the hospital to investigate what one newspaper dubbed "Psycho Ward Atrocities."

Reforms were instituted, the reporters went elsewhere for their stories, and Cooperstown fell from the public eye—just as Michael himself was largely forgotten within the halls of the hospital.

A month after the scandal he was still a resident of the Cooperstown Soft Ward. One weekend he found himself unusually agitated. On Saturday evening the anxiety increased to massive proportions and he began to feel the walls of his room closing in on him. Breathing grew difficult. He suspected the Secret Service was behind this; agents frequently bombarded him with beams that electrified his nerves.

Michael didn't know that his anxiety was due not to the federal government but to something much simpler: his medication instructions had been misplaced and he'd received no Haldol for four days.

Finally in desperation he decided to find the one person in his recent memory who might help him. He had, he recalled, accused Dr. Anne of being a conspirator and had even announced on hundreds of occasions that he was happy she was dead. He decided that the only way to find relief was to retract his cruel pronouncements and apologize to her. He spent the night plotting his escape from Cooperstown, a plan that involved diversionary fires and costumes and disguises. The elaborate scheme proved unnecessary, however, because on Sunday morning he simply dressed in jeans and a T-shirt and walked out the front gate of the hospital, right past a guard unaware that he was a Hard Ward patient in the Soft Ward wing.

Michael had no idea exactly where Dr. Anne might be. But he knew Trevor Hill was in the southern part of the state and that was the direction in which he started to jog that spring morning. Soon he became lost in a tangle of country roads and the more lost he became, the greater was his anxiety. Panic crawled over his skin like hives. At times he took to sprinting, as if fear were an animal snapping at his heels. Other times he hid in bushes until he felt unseen pursuers pass him by. Once, he summoned up his courage and climbed onto the back of a flatbed truck, on which he rode for an hour, hiding under the canvas tarps, until the driver stopped at a roadside diner. Noticing that there were four trucks parked in the lot and fearing this very unlucky number, Michael leapt off and escaped down a nearby country lane.

Around noon he found himself in the middle of a large parking lot. He paused, caught his breath and walked through the lot toward a row of trees, nauseous with anxiety. He ran through the lot and disappeared into the bushes just beyond the large wooden sign. He glanced at the words that were carved into it as if by a huge wood-burning iron.

Welcome to Indian Leap State Park

Michael Hrubek thought of that day now, six months later, as he steered his black Cadillac over the crest of a hill on Route 236. He saw before him a long smooth straightaway sailing into a distance filled with flashes of lightning and the soft glow of lights that perhaps were those of Ridgeton. He cringed as rain clattered on the roof and windshield.

"Betrayal," he muttered. Then he repeated the word, bellowing. He was scalded with anxiety. "Eve of betrayal! Fuckers!"

In an instant his pulse rate leapt to 175 and sweat sprung from his pores. His teeth clattered like galloping hooves on concrete. His mind snapped shut. He forgot *GET TO*, he forgot Lis-bone, he forgot Eve, the conspirators and Dr. Anne and Dr. Richard. . . . He forgot everything but the icy clutch of fear.

His hands quavered on the steering wheel. He gazed at the Cadillac's hood with shock—as if he'd suddenly awakened and found himself riding a rampaging bull.

I'll fight this, he thought. God, please help me fight this! He lowered his head and chewed on his inner cheek. He tasted blood. I *will* fight it!

And for a very brief moment he did.

For a very brief moment he gripped the ivory wheel firmly and forced the car back into the right lane of the highway.

For this brief moment Michael Hrubek was not a maladroit lunatic, a host holding an ancient killer's soul. He was not driven by unbearable guilt. Abraham Lincoln was merely a great, sad figure from history whose face graced copper pennies, and Michael himself was just a big, strong, young man filled with much promise, driving a gaudy old car down a country road, scared to death, yes, but more or less in charge of himself.

And then this delusion vanished.

He could fight it no longer. He lost all conception of the controls and it was the pedal on the right upon which he stamped his huge foot in an effort to stop the skid. He covered his eyes, howled a plea for help and kept his foot to the floorboard as the car disappeared into a low stand of juniper and began turning over and over and over.

23

You've got this thing to do ahead of you. . . .

Owen Atcheson remembered his platoon lieutenant looking steel-eyed and crazed from hits of local funnydust but sounding calm as a college professor. "You've got this thing ahead of you, and you've got to go out and meet it. . . ."

Owen and three others Marines more often than not rolled their eyes at this pep talk. But, inspired by it nonetheless, they then clipped on their gear and blackened their faces and disappeared into the jungle to cut the throats of thin soldiers or murder politicians with silenced pistols or rig gelignite and C4 satchel charges.

Owen thought of those times now—as he stood on the ridge of a hill, looking at the antique Cadillac that sat upright, its roof half-staved in and windows spidered with fractures, one parking lamp the only light that had survived the crash. He opened the cylinder of his gun. He'd owned revolvers all his life and, fastidious about safety, had always kept the chamber under the hammer empty. He now loaded a sixth shell into the gun and swung the cylinder closed. He started toward the car. The incline was steep and Owen needed one hand to steady himself as he climbed down to a low hedge.

He felt a stunning exhilaration and told himself that he shouldn't be enjoying this so much. The thrill diminished when he recalled that Hrubek was armed and saw that there was no way to approach the car under cover. It had crashed through a line of juniper and tumbled for thirty feet into the center of a grassy clearing.

The rain wasn't heavy and the wind was subdued; his approach would be noisy. And Hrubek—assuming his injuries hadn't prevented him from doing so—had also had plenty of time to establish a defensive position. Owen considered tactics for a moment then decided not to bother with a cautious approach. He clutched the gun hard, inhaled long then ran at top speed, ready to aim and shoot from a tumbling position. As he sped across the grass, a primitive howl bubbled in his throat and he suppressed the urge to let this grow into the Marines' battle cry.

He charged the car straight on and slid into the grass like a runner stealing home, ending up behind the rear bumper. The muddy leaves scattered by his run settled around him and he looked about frantically. The rear windshield was less obscured than the others but he still was unable to tell if Hrubek was inside. He crouched, using the trunk as cover, and looked behind the car.

Nothing.

He moved toward the rear door. . . .

Underneath!

Owen dropped to his stomach with a grunt and aimed the gun under the car. A shattered pipe hung like an arm and startled him but Hrubek wasn't hiding there. He stood and breathed deeply several times then switched his gun to his left hand and yanked the car's right rear door open.

Empty. The Cadillac held no evidence of Michael Hrubek other than a smell of animallike musk and sweat and fragments of shattered animal skulls—like the one Hrubek had left on the woman's lap in the house in Cloverton. The keys were in the ignition.

Owen stood and looked around him. The spongy leaves had left no footprints and there was no sign of blood or other trail. Owen stepped behind the Cadillac and turned his back to it as he scanned the vast forest, damp and gray and dark. His heart fell. He knew how hard it was to track on wet leaves and through dark woods. And after an accident this bad Hrubek might be disoriented or stunned and could wander pointlessly in any direction. He might—

The trunk!

Owen cocked the gun and spun on his heels, aiming at the broad dented plain of metal—a perfect hiding place. The trunk was secured by a keyhole button but—since the Caddie was an older car—it did not automatically lock. Owen approached. He touched the cold chrome latch, pushed it in. The mechanism snapped open. He pulled the lid up and leapt back.

The spacious trunk had ample room for someone as large as Michael Hrubek. But it did not in fact contain him.

Owen turned toward the forest and in a crouch ran to the closest opening in the tall fence of brush and trees. In an instant he was swallowed up by the cold darkness around him. He shone his shielded flashlight on the ground in a slow U pattern. After ten minutes he found two of Hrubek's bootprints. They led deeper into the forest. He smelled pine in the damp air. The psycho might have headed out of the deciduous trees and Owen would find a clear trail in pine needles. He had proceeded only thirty feet when he heard a thud and a snap nearby—a careless footstep, it seemed.

He aimed his pistol toward the sound.

Owen gauged his footsteps perfectly and placed them on foliage-free ground, making no noise as he moved. He crouched, pistol in front of him, and stepped onto the bed of fragrant needles.

The man was sitting on a fallen tree trunk and massaging his outstretched leg, as if taking a break on a Sunday-afternoon hike.

"Looks like we just missed him," the lanky man in a New York Mets cap said to Owen, looking up without a trace of surprise in his face. "So you're the other bounty hunter. Guess we got a few things to talk about."

The woman was thirty-six years old and had lived in this prim little bungalow all her life, the past six of those years, after her mother's death, alone. She hadn't seen her father since the day the old man got his other daughter pregnant, was arrested for it and taken away. One week after the trial the sister too moved away.

The woman's life consisted of filling cartons with electronic circuit boards that did something she had no desire to understand, of lunch with one or two fellow workers, sewing, and—for entertainment—church and the newspaper on the day of rest, and television on the other six.

The house was an island of caution and simplicity in a grassy clearing carved out of what had been one of the oldest forests in the Northeast. The half acre of grass was almost a perfect circle and was marred only by a rusted hull of a pickup that would never go anywhere under its own power and a doorless refrigerator her father had been meaning to cart to the dump one Saturday morning ten years ago when he chose instead to pay a visit to his daughter's bedroom.

Blonde, thin and fragile, the woman had a plain face and a good figure though on the rare occasions when she and a few girlfriends went to the rocky beach at Indian Leap or the riverside at Klamath Falls, she would wear a high-necked swimsuit that she'd bought mail-order so she wouldn't have to try it on in a store. She dated some—mostly men she met at church—though she rarely enjoyed the outings and had recently started to think of herself, with some comfort, as a spinster.

Tonight she'd just finished preparing a bedtime snack of Jell-O with mandarin oranges and a cup of hot milk, when she heard the noise in the yard. She walked to the window and saw nothing other than blowing leaves and rain then returned to the maple dining table.

She sat down, said grace and put her napkin in her lap then lifted a spoonful of Jell-O as she opened *TV Guide*.

The knocking on the front door seemed to shake the whole house. The spoon fell to the table and the gelatin cube wobbled off her lap then escaped onto the floor. She stood abruptly and shouted, "Yes, who is it?"

"I'm hurt. I had an accident. Can you help me?"

It was a man's voice.

She hesitated, walked to the front door, hesitated again then opened it as far as the chain allowed. The big fellow was bent over, clutching his arm. He seemed like a working man.

"Who are you?"

"I was driving by and my car, she rolled over and over. Oh, I'm hurt. Please let me in."

No way on God's green earth, thank you very much. "I'll call an ambulance, you wait right there."

The woman closed the door and deadbolted it then went to the table that held the rotary-dial phone. She picked it up. She banged the button down several times and when the silence continued said, "Oh, dear."

It was then that she realized the sound she'd heard a few moments before was coming from the place where the phone line ran into the house. This thought stayed with her only a moment though because Michael Hrubek had grown tired of waiting outside and kicked open the door. Huge and wet, he walked into the living room and said, "Nice try. But your phone, it doesn't work. I could've told you that."

Standing beneath a cluster of thick pine trees, which offered some shelter from the streaming rain, Owen asked how Trenton Heck happened to find the Cadillac.

"I followed his track to Cloverton. That's where I picked up your prints and tire tread. I saw you headed west. Then I saw the Jeep parked up there and figured it might belong to you. My dog picked up Hrubek's scent right away beside the Caddie."

"Did the detective have any more news?"

"How's that?"

"I don't recall his name." Owen patted his pockets for the card he had been given. "The detective in Cloverton. At the house where he killed that woman?"

"*What?*" Heck blurted.

"You didn't know? Didn't you stop at the house?"

"I didn't see a house. I hightailed it west as soon as I saw your prints."

To a troubled Trenton Heck, Owen explained about the killing, the terrible butchery in Cloverton. He then told him about the antique cars stowed in a barn. "I figured he'd try to lead us off track with that motorcycle. He drove it south a few hundred yards and dumped it in a marsh somewhere to fool everybody, I'd guess. Then he took the Cadillac and came here. That man is too damn smart."

Heck asked, "What's your interest in all this?"

Owen stooped down and retied his boots, which were muddy and scuffed but looked as expensive as Heck had guessed they'd be. The tall man stood and said, "Was my friend he killed at Indian Leap. And my wife saw him do it."

Heck nodded, thinking that this put a whole new spin on the evening. "Tell you what, let me get my dog. He stays and keeps quiet when he's told but mostly it addles him." He walked off into the woods, glancing at the signposts of bushes and trees for direction.

"You're quiet when you move," Owen said, impressed. "You hunt?"

"A bit." Heck chuckled.

They found Emil sitting nervously, shifting weight from paw to paw. He calmed as soon as he saw his master.

Owen asked, "Purebred blood?"

"Edouard Montague of Longstreet the Third. He's as pure as they come."

"Quite a name."

"That's what he came with but it wouldn't do of course, not

around here. So I call him Emil and he answers to it. If he ever mates a pure bitch I'll have to put his full name on the papers but till then it's our secret."

Walking back to the clearing beside Heck, Owen asked, "How'd you follow the scent if he was on a bicycle?"

"That's nothing for Emil. Hell, he's gone through a foot of snow in a blizzard. So you think maybe he's after your wife?"

"I don't really know. But it's too dangerous to leave in the hands of cops who don't know what they're doing."

This rankled Heck and he said, "You got your state troopers on the case, you know."

"Well, a lot of mistakes've been made, I should tell you." Owen glanced at Heck's pistol. "You mentioned a bounty. You're a professional tracker?"

"I hire out my dog, yep."

"How much's the reward?"

Hot-faced, eyes fixed on the dark forest, Heck said, "Ten thousand dollars." He spoke emphatically, as if making clear to Owen that even if he was just a hired hand he wasn't coming cheap.

"Well then," Owen said, "let's go catch this psycho and make you some money. What do you say?"

"Yessir."

Heck roused Emil with Hrubek's scent and off they went through the woods. The track was easy to follow now, with abundant ground scent in the moist forest. The dog's excitement and the uncanny atmosphere of the woods at night urged them forward in a kind of dazed ecstasy, and they could do nothing but give in to this lust. They crashed through the brush. Hrubek could've heard them coming from a hundred yards away but there was nothing to be done about it. They couldn't have both stealth and speed, and they chose the latter.

     •   •   •

Michael watched her carefully, irritated that she was crying so much. It made him very anxious. The blonde woman didn't speak. All the points of her face—her nose and chin and cheekbones—were red from the silent tears. She quivered and shredded a paper napkin between her fingers while Michael paced. "I had to take down your telephone. Stop that crying. The line's sure to be tapped anyway."

"What," she sobbed, "are you going to do to me?"

He walked through the living room, his huge muddy feet pounding on the boards. "This is a nice place. Stop crying! I like your eyes. You don't have masks on them. Where did you get it? The *house*, I'm speaking of."

She glanced at the small cap on his head. "What are you—?" He repeated his question sharply and she stammered, "My mama died and she left it to me. I've got a sister. It's half hers." As if he intended to steal it, she added, "We own it free and clear."

Michael lifted the Irish cap by the brim, courteously tipping it to her. He rubbed his hand over his smooth head. In the bright light a residue of the blue ink was still visible. He saw her staring at the cap as he replaced it. He smiled. "Fashionable, isn't it?"

"I'm sorry?"

He frowned. "My hat. *Fashionable*. Isn't it?"

"Yes," she exclaimed. "Very. Extremely."

"My car rolled over and over and over. She was a good car while she lasted." He walked closer and examined her body. He thought it was strange that although she was a woman she didn't frighten him. Maybe because she was so frail. He could lift her with one hand and could snap her neck as easily as he had the raccoon's earlier in the evening. What's that smell? Oh, it's woman. The smell of woman. This brought back an indistinct and troubling memory. He felt darkness around him, claustrophobia, fear. Rocks and water. Bad people. What was it? His anxiety notched up a few degrees.

He also found he had a fierce erection. He sat down so that she wouldn't notice.

The wind slammed against the windows and the sound of the rain grew louder. The clatter of muskets, he thought. Lead balls cracking apart a thousand heads . . . He covered his ears at this unnerving sound. After a moment he realized that she was staring at him.

"People are after me," he said.

"You're a *convict*?" she whispered. "You escaped from the prison over in Hamlin?"

"Nice try. Don't expect to get anything out of me. You know too much as it is."

She shivered as he leaned forward and stroked her fine hair. "That's nice," he muttered. "And you're not wearing a fucking hat. Good . . . Good."

"Don't hurt me please. I'll give you money. Anything . . ."

"Give me a penny."

"I have some savings. About three thousand but it's in the bank. You could meet me there at nine tomorrow. You're welcome to—"

Michael roared, "A *penny*!"

She dug frantically into her purse. He looked over her shoulder. "You don't have a microphone in there? A panic button or anything?"

She looked mystified then whispered, "No. I'm getting you the penny like you asked."

Guilty, Michael said, "Well, you can't be too careful."

He held out his massive hands and she dropped the coin into his palm. He held it up behind her head. "What seven-letter word is on the penny?"

"I don't know."

"Guess," he said petulantly.

She wrung her hands together. "*E Pluribus Unum*. In God We Trust. Legal Tender. No. United States. Oh, God, I can't think!" Then, *sotto voce*, she began murmuring the Lord's Prayer.

"It's right behind seven-letter Abraham Lincoln." Without looking at the coin he said, "The word is right *behind* him, seven letters, like the barrel of a gun pointed at his head."

He poked her scalp with a blunt finger. She closed her eyes and whispered, "I don't know."

Michael said, " 'Liberty.' " He dropped the penny on the floor. "I'm pretty hungry. What's to eat?"

She stopped crying. "You're hungry?" She gazed at the kitchen. "I have some roast beef, some vegetarian chili. . . . You're welcome to it."

He walked to the table and sat down, easing into the chair. He delicately opened a paper napkin. It covered only a part of his huge lap.

She asked, "Can I stand up?"

"How can you get me dinner if you don't stand up?"

She hurtled into the kitchen and busied herself preparing a plate while Michael sang, " 'For I love the bonnie blue gal who gave her heart to me.' " He played with the pepper mill. " 'Her arms, her arms, are where I want to be! . . .' "

She returned, setting a tray in front of him. Michael roared, " 'For I love the bonnie blue gal who gave—' " He stopped abruptly, picked up the fork and cut a piece off the beef. This, together with a portion of Jell-O, he put on the pink saucer and placed it in front of her.

She glanced at the food then looked inquiringly at him.

"I want *you* to eat that!" he said.

"I've already . . . Oh, you think it's poison."

"I don't *think* it's poison," he sneered. "I don't *think* there's a posse outside that window. I don't *think* you're a Pinkerton agent. But you can't be too *careful*. Now come on. Quit being a shit."

She ate. Then she smiled and went blank-faced again. He studied her for a moment and set his fork down. "Do you have some milk?"

"Milk? I have low-fat is all. Is that all right?"

"Some *milk*!" he blared, and she jumped to get it. When she returned he'd already started to eat. He drank the glass down, taking with it a mouthful of food. "I used to work in a dairy."

"Well, yes." She nodded politely. "That must be a nice place to work."

"It was very nice. Dr. Richard got me the job."

"Who is he?"

"He was my father."

"Your father was a doctor?"

"Well," he scoffed, "I don't mean a father like *that*."

"No," she agreed quickly, seeing the darkness fall over his face. He stopped eating. She told him she liked his tweed cap. He touched it and smiled. "I like it too. I have hair but I cut it off."

"Why did you do that?"

"I can't tell you."

"No, don't tell me anything you don't want to."

"If I don't *want* to, I won't. You don't have to give me permission."

"I wasn't giving you permission. I didn't mean to sound like I was. You can do whatever you want."

"Don't I know it." Michael cleaned his plate.

"Would you like some more?"

"Milk. I'd like more milk." When she was in the kitchen he added, "Please."

As he took the tall glass from her he intoned in an FM disc jockey's voice, "A wholesome snack."

She barked a laugh and he smiled. As he poured the milk down she asked, "What are you doing?"

"I'm drinking milk," he answered with exasperation.

"No. I mean, what are you doing out tonight? There's supposed to be a storm like we haven't seen in a donkey's age."

"What's a donkey's age?" He squinted.

She stared at him with a vacant face. "Uhm, now that you ask, I don't exactly know. It means for a long time."

"Is it like an *expression*? Is it like a *cliché*?"

"I guess so."

He stared down, his eyes as empty and filmy as the glass in his hand. "Did you know that 'anger' is five-sixths of 'danger'?"

"No, I didn't. But it surely is. How about that?"

"So there."

She broke the very dense silence by asking, "What did you do in the dairy?"

Michael's erection had not gone away. His penis hurt and this was beginning to anger him. He reached into his pocket and squeezed himself then stood and walked to the window. He said, "What's the biggest town near here that has a train station?"

"Well, Boyleston, I suppose. It's south about forty, fifty miles."

"How would I get there?"

"Go west to 315. It'll take you right there. That becomes Hubert Street and it goes right past the train station. Amtrak."

"In no time at all?"

"No time at all," she agreed. "Why are you going there?"

"I told you," he snapped. "I can't say!"

Her hands went into her lap.

Michael began rummaging through his backpack. "I'm sorry, I'm very sorry," he said to her. But he uttered these words, then repeated them, with such deep longing that it was clear he was apologizing not for being curt but rather for something else—something he was *about* to do, something far graver than bad manners. He sat down beside her, his thigh pressing hard against hers, and as she cried, he set a small white animal skull in her lap and, very gently, began stroking her hair.

Under clouds so fast and turbulent they seemed like special effects from a science-fiction movie, Portia L'Auberget inhaled the scents of decaying leaves and the musky lake. Several feet away her sister lifted the shovel and dropped a huge pile of gravel around the front wheels of the stranded car.

The young woman flexed her hands. They stung and she supposed the skin was starting to blister from the wet gloves. Her muscles were on fire. Her head ached from the pounding rain.

And she was troubled by something else, a vague thought—something other than the storm. At first she wondered if it might be the escape. Yet she'd never really believed that someone like Michael Hrubek could make it all the way to Ridgeton from the mental hospital, certainly not on a night like this.

No, some nebulous memory kept rising up disturbingly then vanishing. It seemed that it had something to do with this portion of the yard. She was picturing . . . what was it? Plants? Had there been a garden here of some sort? Ah, yes. It *was* here. The old vegetable garden.

Then she remembered Tom Wheeler.

How old had they been? Twelve or thirteen probably, both of them. One fall afternoon—maybe November, like tonight—the skinny red-haired boy had shown up in the yard. Portia strolled outside and they sat on the back steps. She managed simultaneously to both ignore and converse with him, teasing mercilessly. Finally he suggested that they go to the state park. "Why?" she asked. "I dunno," he responded. "Hang out, you know. Got the new Jefferson Airplane." He nodded lethargically at an eight-track-tape player at his feet. She told him no, she didn't want to, but a moment later she disappeared into the house and returned with a blanket.

He started for the state park.

"Uh-uh," Portia announced. "This way."

And led him to the vegetable garden. Here she spread the blanket in partial view of the house and lay down, kicking off her Keds and stretching sumptuously. But somebody might see, he protested.

Somebody could be watching right now! She placed his hand on her breast and he stopped worrying about voyeurs. Portia lay on her back, surrounded by slug-chewed pumpkins and short blond cornstalks. Tommy beside her, covering her hot mouth with his; she had to breathe for long stretches through her nose. She now recalled smelling this same scent of wet, late fall. Drowsy flies strafed them. Finally, confusing him by not protesting, she allowed his pale, freckled hand to pass the elastic barrier. He glanced at the windows of the house then jabbed with a shaking finger, leaving inside her a glow of pain and on her bare hip a large wet spot that matched the one spreading across the front of his dungarees.

They lay awkwardly, side by side, for a few minutes then he suddenly whispered, "I think there's somebody there."

Though he'd said that only to escape and he rose quickly and vanished down the driveway. Hearing the resonant guitar licks fade, Portia grew dizzy as she watched the thick clouds pass overhead and wondered about the mysteries of bodies. She spent a long time unsuccessfully trying to convince herself to feel bad that he'd fled.

Portia now realized, with a twist in her belly, that it was not this memory of speedy Tommy Wheeler at all that was so troubling. It was Indian Leap.

She had almost not accompanied her sister and brother-in-law on the picnic. She had no interest in the out-of-doors, no interest in state parks—especially the park to which she'd been dragged by teachers on tedious field trips and in which she later spent hours gazing at treetops, as she lay beneath boyfriends, or friends of boyfriends, or sometimes strangers.

No, it was essentially a decision by default. She was fed up with the quiet anxiety of solo life in Manhattan: The dinners of turkey sandwiches and cole slaw. The companionship of rented movies. The tired come-ons in bars and at parties, delivered as if the men actually thought she hadn't heard it all a thousand times before.

Socializing with lean, ponytailed girlfriends who'd discard you in an instant if doing so moved them an inch closer to a Better Job or an Available Man.

So, on that May 1, she'd reluctantly packed bagels and lox and cream cheese and magazines and bikini and sunscreen. She endured the surly rent-a-car clerk, she endured the traffic, she endured the tense company of the poor, shy Claire. She suffered through all the stress of a day in the country. Yet there was one aspect of the trip that didn't require enduring. Robert Gillespie, Portia thought at first, was hardly a catch. As she sat in the back of his 4x4 with Lis and Claire, en route to Indian Leap, she reviewed his ledger and came up mostly with debits: only marginally cute, fifteen pounds overweight, too smooth, too pompous, too talkative, a wife who was a complete cipher.

There was, Portia realized, no logical basis for finding him irresistible. But irresistible he was. While Lis had dozed in the back of the truck and while dull Dorothy liberally applied her oh-puh-leaze red nail polish, Robert deluged Portia with questions. Where did she live, did she like the city, did she know this or that restaurant, did she like her job? It was all a come-on. Of course it was. But still . . . And his liquid eyes danced with excitement as they talked. Portia recalled thinking helplessly, Oh, it's true: seduce my mind and my body will follow.

By the time they arrived at the park, Portia L'Auberget was his for the asking.

As they walked along the path from the parking lot to the car, he glanced at her running shoes and discreetly asked—in a way that was both intimate and lighthearted—if they might take a run together.

She responded, "Maybe."

He took this to mean yes. "Let me leave before you," he whispered. "Then I'll meet you near the old cave. Give me ten minutes. Then follow me."

"Maybe."

When they got to the beach she appraised her power over him and decided not to abdicate a single bit of it. She did a few fast stretches then jogged away first, blatantly ignoring him. She ran a half mile to the secluded gully he'd mentioned. Past the cave was a stand of pine trees, beneath which was an inviting nest of soft needles, some green, some ruddy. Portia sat on a nearby rock, wondering if he'd join her. Maybe he'd retaliate for her defiance by remaining with his wife and Lis. She'd certainly have more respect for him if he did. Yet Portia L'Auberget had no particular desire, or need, to respect men, especially men like Robert Gillespie, and decided he fucking well better show; she'd make his day miserable if he didn't. She examined the small clearing, which was gloomy and shadowed by the steep walls of pale rock rising on either side of the trees. Overhead the sky had turned heavily overcast. Much less romantic, she reflected, than a Club Med beach in Curaçao or Nassau. On the other hand there were no condoms littering the ground here.

She scooted from the rock to the needle bed, separated from sight of the clearing by a tall line of bushes and young hemlocks. A half hour passed, then forty minutes, and finally Robert came jogging toward her. He caught his breath and earned many points by not saying a word to Portia about disregarding his instructions. He was studying his chest, pouting.

She laughed. "What?"

"My wife says I'm getting tits."

Portia pulled off her T-shirt and sports bra. "Let's compare."

They rolled back under the pine trees. Robert kissed her firmly, stroking her bare nipples with the backs of his hands. He closed his fingers around hers and placed them on her breasts. She began fondling herself while his tongue slid down to her navel then continued to her thighs and knees. He remained there, teasing, until Portia finally seized his head in both hands and directed it firmly between her legs. Her thighs rose as her head pressed back hard into the pine bed, needles fixing themselves in her sweat-damp hair. Staring through half-closed lids at the speeding clouds she gasped for breath. He rolled on top of her, and their mouths met hard, brutally. He had just entwined her legs around his waist and was thrusting into her savagely when a branch snapped near their heads.

Claire walked out of a stand of trees and stopped, frozen, six feet from them. Her hand rose to her mouth in shock.

"Oh, my God," Portia shouted.

"Claire, honey . . ." Robert began, as he rolled to his knees.

Claire, speechless, stared at his groin. Portia remembered thinking, My God, she's eighteen. This can't be her first hard-on.

It took a moment for Robert to recover some wits and he looked frantically for his shirt or shorts. As the girl's eyes remained fixed on him, Portia watched the young blonde. This curious à trois voyeurism aroused her all the more. Robert grabbed his shirt and wrapped the knit garment about his waist, abashed and grinning. Portia didn't move. Then Claire choked a sob and turned, running past the cave and back up the path.

"Oh, shit," Robert muttered.

"Don't worry."

"*What?*"

"Oh, don't take it so seriously. Every teenager gets a shock at some point. I'll talk to her."

"She's just a kid."

"Forget her," Portia said offhandedly, then whispered, "Come on over here."

"She's going—"

"She's not going to say anything. Hmm, what's that? You're still interested. I can tell."

"Jesus, what if she tells Lis?"

"Come on," she urged breathlessly. "Don't stop now. Fuck me!"

"I think we ought to get back."

Portia dropped to her knees and pulled his shirt away, taking him deep into her mouth.

"No," Robert whispered.

He was standing, head back, eyes closed, shuddering uncontrollably and gasping when Lis stepped into the clearing.

Claire must have run into her almost immediately and Lis had either learned, or deduced, what had happened. She stood above the half-naked couple and stared down at them. "Portia!" she raged. "How could you?" Her expression of horror matched Robert's perfectly.

The young woman stood and wiped her face with her bra. She turned to face her sister and with detachment watched Lis's throat grow remarkably red as the tendons rose and her jaw quivered. Robert pulled up his running shorts, looking around again for his shirt. He seemed incapable of speaking. Portia refused to act like a caught schoolgirl. "How could you?" Lis gripped her arm but Portia stepped away abruptly. Meeting her sister's furious gaze she dressed slowly then, saying nothing, left Lis and Robert in the clearing.

Portia walked back to the beach, where Dorothy was starting to pack up; the temperature had dropped and it was clearly going to rain. She looked at Portia and seemed to sense something was wrong but said nothing. The wind picked up and the two women hurried to gather up the picnic baskets and blankets, carting them to the truck. They made one more trip back to the beach, looking for their companions. Then the downpour began.

Moments later sirens filled the park and police and medics arrived. It was in a rain-drenched intersection of two canyons that Portia met her sister, red-eyed and muddy and disheveled, looking like a madwoman, being led by two tall rangers out of a flooded arroyo.

Portia had stepped toward her. "Lis! What—?"

The slap was oddly quiet but so powerful it brought Portia down on one knee. She cried out in pain and shock. Neither woman moved, and Lis's hand remained frozen in the air as they stared at each other for a long moment. A shocked ranger helped Portia to her feet and explained about the deaths.

"Oh, no!" Portia cried.

"Oh, no!" Lis mimicked with bitter scorn then stepped forward, pushed the ranger aside and put her mouth close to her sister's ear. In a rasping whisper she said, "*You* killed that girl, you fucking whore."

Portia faced her sister. Her eyes grew as cold as the wet rocks around them. "Goodbye, Lis."

And goodbye it had been. Apart from a few brief, stilted phone conversations, those words had been virtually the last communication between the sisters until tonight.

Indian Leap. It was the first thing in Portia's mind when Lis had invited her here this evening—just as it had reared in her thoughts when the subject of the nursery was raised, and, for that matter, every time Portia had thought of moving back to Ridgeton, which —though she'd never confess it to Lis—she'd considered frequently in the past few years.

Indian Leap . . .

Oh, Lis, Portia thought, don't you see? *That's* what dooms the L'Auberget sisters, and always will. Not the tragedy, not the deaths, not the bitter words or the months of silence afterwards, but the past that led us to that pine bed, the past that's certain to keep leading us to places just as terrible again and again and again.

The past, with all its spirits of the dead.

Portia now looked at her sister, ten feet away, as Lis put aside the shovel and waded toward the front seat of the car.

The sisters' eyes met.

Lis frowned, troubled by Portia's expression. "What is it?" she asked.

But just then a low whistle squealed from the car's grille. The engine choked, and kicked hard several times as the fan blade slapped water. Then with a shudder it died, leaving the night filled only with the sounds of the wind, the rain and the lilting music of a clever baroque composer.

24

"Well, I didn't go for help because it's over a half mile to the neighbors and if you've listened to the radio you *know* what kind of storm it's supposed to be. I mean, doesn't it make *sense*?"

The words fired from the pale mouth of the petite blonde. She'd stopped crying but was pouring down brandy from a dusty bottle in a medicinal way. "And anyway," she said to Trenton Heck, "he told me not to and if you ever saw him you'd *do* what he told you. Oh, my Lord. All I kept thinking was, Lucky me, lucky me, I had communion today."

Owen Atcheson returned from the side yard to the house's tiny living room, where Heck and the fragile woman stood.

"Lucky me," she whispered and tossed down a belt of liquor. She started to cry again.

"He just pulled one wire out," Owen reported. He lifted the receiver. "I got it working."

"He's got my car. It's a beige Subaru station wagon. An '89. Apologized about ten times. 'I'm sorry I'm sorry I'm sorry. . . .' Phew." Her tears stopped. "That's what I mean when I call him strange. Well, you can imagine. Asked me for the keys and of course I gave them. Then off he went, squatting behind the wheel. Missed the drive completely but found the road. Guess I'll write that vehicle off."

Owen grimaced. "If we'd gone that way he would've come right to us."

Heck looked again at the tiny skull, resting on the paper towel in which she'd handed it to him, unwilling to touch the bone itself.

"Well," the woman continued, "you can find him on 315."

"How's that?"

"He's going to Boyleston. Route 315."

"He said that?"

"He asked me about the nearest town with a train station. I told him Boyleston. He asked me how to get there. And then asked me for fifty dollars for a train ticket. I gave it to him. And a little more."

Heck stared at the phone for a minute. Can't keep it a secret anymore, he thought. Not with Hrubek killing one woman and terrorizing another. He sighed and sucked air through bent teeth. Very conspicuous in Heck's mind now was the thought that if he'd called Haversham like he'd thought of doing—after figuring out that Hrubek was heading west—they might've caught him before he got to that house in Cloverton. All law enforcers, Heck too, had inventories of times when their mistakes and failings had gotten other people hurt—times that occasionally returned hard and kept them from sleeping, and sometimes did worse than that. Though he was removed from the sorrow at the moment, he supposed that that woman's death would be the most prominent in his personal store of those events, and he could only guess how bad it would later come back to him.

Now though he wanted only one thing—to see this fellow caught—and he snatched up the receiver. He placed a call to the local sheriff and reported Hrubek's theft of the Subaru and where he seemed to be going. He turned to the woman. "Sheriff says he'll send somebody out to the house to take you to a friend's or relative's, ma'am. If you want."

"Tell him yes, please."

Heck relayed this information to the sheriff. When he hung up, Owen took the phone and called the Marsden Inn and was surprised to find that Lis and Portia still hadn't checked in. Frowning, he called the house. Lis picked up on the third ring.

"Lis, what are you doing there?"

"Owen? Where are you?"

"I'm in Fredericks. I tried to call you before. I thought you'd left. What're you doing there? You were supposed to be at the Inn an hour ago."

A momentary hollowness on the line. He heard her calling, "It's Owen." What was going on? Through the line he heard a roll of thunder. Lis came back on and explained that she and Portia had stayed to build up the sandbags. "The dam was overflowing. We could've lost the house."

"Are you all right?"

"We're fine. But the car's stuck in the driveway. The rain's terrible. We can't get out. There're no tow trucks. What are you doing in Fredericks?"

"I've been following Hrubek west."

"West! He *did* turn around."

"Lis, I have to tell you . . . He killed someone."

"No!"

"A woman in Cloverton."

"He's coming here?"

"No, it doesn't look like it. He's going to Boyleston. To get a train out of state, I'd guess."

"What should we do?"

He paused. "I'm not going after him, Lis. I'm coming home."

He heard her exhale a sigh. "Thank you, honey."

"Stay in the house. Lock the doors. I'm only fifteen minutes away. . . . Lis?"

"Yes?"

He paused. "I'll be there soon."

Heck and Owen said goodbye to the woman and hurried out into the rain, buffeted by the terrible wind. They followed the driveway to the dim road that led back to the highway.

Owen glanced at Heck, who was trudging along morosely.

"You're thinking about your reward?"

"I have to say I am. They'll probably get him in Boyleston for sure. But I *had* to call and tell them. I'm not going to risk anybody else getting hurt."

Owen thought for a moment. "You're still due that money, I'd say."

"Well, the hospital's gonna have a different opinion on that, I'll guarantee you."

"Tell you what, Heck, you burn on down that highway to Boyleston, and if you get him first, fine. If not, we'll sue the hospital for your money and I'll handle the case myself."

"You a lawyer?"

Owen nodded. "Won't charge you a penny."

"You'd do that for me?"

"Surely would."

Heck was embarrassed at Owen's generosity and after a moment he shook the lawyer's hand warmly. They continued in silence to the clearing where the ruined Cadillac sat.

"Okay, Emil and I'll head south here. It's a beige Subaru we're looking for, right? Let's hope he doesn't drive Japanese any better'n he drives Detroit. Okay, let's do it." On impulse he added, "Say, after this's over with, let's stay in touch, you and me. What do you say? Do some fishing?"

"Hey, that's a fine idea by me, Heck. Happy hunting to you."

Heck and Emil limped, and trotted, back to the battered Chevy pickup fifty yards down the road. They climbed in. Heck started up the rattling engine, then sped through the fierce rain toward Route 315, his left foot on the accelerator and an eye on his modest prize.

The sign revolved slowly in the turbulent night sky.

Dr. Richard Kohler looked toward the flashes of light in the west and laughed out loud at the metaphor that occurred to him.

Wasn't this how Mary Shelley's doctor had animated his creature? Lightning?

The psychiatrist now recalled very clearly the first meeting with the patient who would play the monster to Kohler's Frankenstein. Four months ago, two weeks after the Indian Leap trial and Michael's incarceration in Marsden, Kohler—overcome with morbid and professional fascination—had walked slowly into Marsden's grim, high-security E Ward and looked down at the huge, hunched form of Michael Hrubek, glaring up from beneath his dark eyebrows.

"How are you, Michael?" Kohler asked.

"They're lis-ten-ing. Sometimes you have to keep your mind a complete blank. Have you ever done that? Do you know how *hard* it is? That's the basis of Transcendental Meditation. You may know that as TM. Make your mind a complete blank, doctor. Try it."

"I don't think I can."

"If I hit you with that chair your mind'd be a *complete* blank. But the downside is that you'd be a dead fucker."

Michael had then closed his mouth and said nothing more for several days.

Marsden was a state hospital, like Cooperstown, and offered only a few dismal activity rooms. But Kohler had finagled a special suite for patients in his program. It was not luxurious. The rooms were drafty and cold and the walls were painted an unsettling milky green. But at least those in the Milieu Suite—so named because Kohler's goal was to ease the patients here gradually back into normal society—were separated from the hospital's sicker patients and this special status alone gave them a sense of dignity. They also had learning toys and books and art supplies—even the dangerous and officially forbidden pencils. Art and expression were encouraged and the walls were graced by the graffiti of paintings, drawings and poems created by the patients.

In August Richard Kohler commenced a campaign to get Michael into the Milieu Suite. He chose the young man because he was smart, because he seemed to wish to improve, and because he had killed. To resocialize (one did not *cure*) a patient like Michael Hrubek would be the ultimate validation of Kohler's delusion-therapy techniques. But more than precious DMH funding, more than professional prestige, Kohler saw a chance to help a man who suffered and who suffered terribly. Michael wasn't like the many schizophrenic patients who were oblivious to their conditions. No, Michael was the most tragic of victims; he was just well enough to imagine what a normal life might be like and was tormented daily by the gap between who he was and who he so desperately wanted to be. Exactly the sort of patient Kohler wished most to work with.

Not that Michael leapt at the chance to join the psychiatrist's program.

"No fucking way, you fucker!"

Paranoid and suspicious, Michael refused to have anything to do with the Suite, or Kohler, or anyone else at Marsden for that matter. He sat in the corner of his room, muttering to himself and suspiciously eyeing doctors and patients alike. But Kohler persisted. He simply wouldn't leave the young man alone. Their first month together—and they saw each other daily—they argued bitterly. Michael would rant and scream, convinced Kohler was a conspirator like the others. The doctor would parry with questions about Michael's fantasies, trying to break him down.

Finally, tuckered out by Kohler's aggressiveness and by massive dosages of medicine, Michael reluctantly agreed to join his program. He was gradually introduced to other patients, first one on one, then in larger groups. To get the young patient to talk about his past and his delusions, Kohler would bribe him with history books, filching them from the library at Framington hospital because the collection at Marsden was almost nonexistent. In their individual sessions Kohler kept pushing the young man, turning up the emotional heat and forcing him to spend time with other patients, probing into his delusions and dreams.

"Michael, who's Eve?"

"Oh, yeah, right. Like I'm going to tell *you*. Forget about it."

"What did you mean by 'I want to stay ahead of the blue uniforms'?"

"Time for bed. Lights out. Nighty-night, doctor."

So it went.

One cold, wet day six weeks ago, Michael was in Marsden's secluded exercise area, walking laps under the surly eyes of the guards. He gazed through the chain-link fence at the bleak, muddy New England farm on the hospital grounds. Like most schizophrenics Michael suffered from blunted affect—hampered display of emotion. But that day he was suddenly swept up by the bleak and sorrowful scenery and started to cry. "I was feeling sorry for the poor damp cows," Michael later told Kohler. "Their eyes were broken. God should do something for them. They'll have a hard time."

"Their eyes were broken, Michael? What do you mean?"

"The poor cows. They'll never be the same. Good for them, bad for them. It's so obvious. Their eyes are *broken*. Don't you understand?"

The flash came to Kohler like an ECS jolt. "You mean," he whispered, struggling to control his excitement, "you're saying the *ice* is broken."

With this backhanded message—like the one about getting close to Dr. Anne Muller—Michael was trying to express his inmost feelings. In this case, that something about his life had changed fundamentally. He shrugged and began to cry in front of his therapist—not in fear but out of sorrow. "I feel so *bad* for them." Gradually he calmed. "It seems like a difficult life to be a farmer. But maybe it's one that'd suit me."

"Would you be interested," Kohler asked, his heart racing, "in working on that farm?"

"The farm?"

"The work program. Here at the hospital."

"*Are you mad?*" Michael shouted. "I'd get kicked in the head and killed. Don't be a stupid fucker!"

It took two weeks of constant pressure to talk Michael into the job—far longer, in fact, than it took Kohler to gin up the paperwork to arrange the transfer. Michael was technically an untouchable at Marsden because he was a Section 403 commitment. But there is no easier mark than state bureaucracy. Because Kohler's voluminous documentation referred to "Patient 458-94," rather than "Michael Hrubek," and because the supervisors of vastly overcrowded E Ward were delighted to get rid of another patient, Hrubek was easily stamped, approved, vetted and blessed. He was assigned simple tasks on the farm, which produced dairy products for the hospital and sold what little surplus there was at local markets. At first he was suspicious of his supervisors. Yet he never once had a panic attack. He showed up for work on time and was usually the last to leave. Eventually he settled into the job—shoveling manure, lugging sledgehammers, fence stretchers and staples from fencepost to fencepost, carting milk pails. The only times you'd suspect he wasn't your average farm boy was when he'd use white fence paint on Herefords to even up markings he found unpleasant or scary.

Still, as soon as he was told not to paint the cows, he shamefacedly complied.

Michael Hrubek, who'd never in his life earned a penny of his own money, was suddenly making $3.80 an hour. He was having dinner in the hospital cafeteria with friends and washing dishes afterwards, he was writing a long poem about the Battle of Bull Run, and he was an integral part of Kohler's delusion-therapy program, not to mention the cover boy of his proposal to the State Department of Mental Health.

And now, Kohler reflected sorrowfully, he was a dangerous escapee.

Oh, where are you, Michael, with your broken eyes?

One thing he was convinced of: Michael was en route to Ridgeton. The visit with Lis Atcheson had been doubly helpful. Partly for what it revealed about Michael's delusion. But also for what it revealed about *her*. She'd lied to him, that was clear. He'd tried to deduce exactly where her story about Indian Leap deviated from the truth. But she seemed to be a woman used to living with secrets, with feelings unexpressed, passions hidden, and so he hadn't been able to spot the lie. Yet Kohler felt that whatever she wasn't telling him was significant—very likely significant enough to prod Michael out of the haze of his deluded but secure life and urge him to make this terrifying journey through the night.

Oh, yes, he was on his way to Ridgeton.

And here waiting for him, huddled in the driving rain, was Richard Kohler, a man willing to bribe bounty hunters with thousands of dollars he could scarcely afford, to troop through hostile wilderness, to track down and meet his edgy and dangerous patient all by himself and spirit him back to the hospital—for Michael's sake and the sake of the thousands of other patients Kohler hoped to treat during his lifetime.

The doctor now gazed over the spacious parking lot and drew his black overcoat about him in a futile effort to ward off the heavy rain and gusts of wind. He opened his backpack and lifted out the sturdy metal syringe then filled the reservoir with a large dosage of anesthetic. He flicked the bubbles to the top and fired a small spurt into the air to expel them. Then he leaned back, his face pelted with rain, and he looked up once more at the perpetual motion of the sign above his head.

25

"Look at this!"

A mile down the road Michael rounded a curve and barked a sudden laugh. He calmly recalled which pedal was the brake and he pressed it gently, slowing to ten miles an hour.

"Look!" He leaned forward, his head almost to the windshield, and gazed into the sky, filled with rain that reflected red, white and blue lights in a million spatters.

"Oh, God, what could this *mean*?" His skin hummed with emotion and upon his face a vast grin was spreading. Michael pulled onto the shoulder and stopped the Subaru. He stepped out into the rain and, as if in a trance, began walking through the parking lot, his John Worker boots scraping on the asphalt. He paused at the base of the shrine and stood with his hands clasped before him, reverently, staring up into the sky. He dug into his backpack and observed that he had two skulls left. He selected the one in worse condition—it was cracked in several places—and set it at the base of the sign.

The voice came from nearby. "Hello, Michael."

The young man wasn't startled in the least. "Hello, Dr. Richard."

The thin man sat on the hood of a white car, one of fifty, all in a row. Doesn't he look small, doesn't he look wet? Michael thought, reminded once again of the raccoon he'd killed earlier in the evening. Such little things, both of them.

Dr. Richard scooted off the Taurus. Michael glanced at him but his eyes were drawn irresistibly to the radiant sign revolving above their heads.

Michael ignored the middle portion of the sign, noting only that the word *MERCURY* was bloody red. What he stared at were the two words in blue, Union-soldier blue: On the top, *FORD*. On the bottom, *LINCOLN*.

"That's where you killed him, isn't it, Michael? The theater?"

This is surely a miracle. Oh, God in your infinite brilliance . . .

"Ford . . . Lincoln . . . Ford's Theater . . . Yessir, I sure did. Make no mistake. I snuck into the presidential box at ten-thirty on April 14, the year of our Lord eighteen hundred and sixty-five. It was Good Friday. I came up behind him and put a bullet into his head. The President didn't die right away but lingered until the next day. He linnnnn-gered."

"You yelled, '*Sic semper tyrannis*.'"

"They've been after me ever since." Michael looked at his doctor. No, he was no impostor. It was truly Dr. Richard. You look tired, doctor, Michael thought. I'm awake and you're asleep. What do you make of that? He gazed up at the sign again.

"I want to help you."

Michael chuckled.

"I'd like you to come back with me to the hospital."

"That's nuts, Dr. Richard. I just *left* there. Why would I want to go back?"

"Because you'll be safe. There are people looking for you, people who want to hurt you."

Michael snapped, "*I've* been telling you that for months."

"That's true, you have." The doctor laughed.

Michael took the pistol from his pocket. Dr. Richard's eyes flicked down momentarily but returned immediately to his patient's. "Michael, I've done a lot for you. I got you the job on the farm. You like that job, don't you? You like to work with the cows, I know you do."

The pistol was warm. It was comfortable in his hand. It was, he thought, quite *fashionable*. "I've been wondering if—wouldn't this be strange—if this was the same gun I'd used."

"To shoot Lincoln?"

"The very same gun. That would have a special *meaning*. That would make a lot of *sense*. Do you like the *scent* of blood, Dr. Richard? When do you think a soul makes the a-*scent* to heaven? Do you think souls linnnnger on earth a while?"

Why is he stepping closer to me? Michael wondered. When he's this close, it's easier to read my mind.

"I wouldn't know."

Michael held the pistol close to his face, smelling the metal. "But how do you explain that it was just there for me? This gun. It was just *there* in the store. The store with the heads."

A shudder ran through Michael Hrubek.

"What heads?"

"All the little heads. White and smooth. Beautiful little white heads."

"Those skulls?" Dr. Richard nodded toward the sign pole.

Michael blinked but said nothing.

"So you shot Lincoln, did you, Michael?"

"Sure did. I was willing and *abe*-le."

"Why didn't you ever tell me about it? In any of our sessions?"

Michael's stomach twisted with unbridled anxiety. "It was . . ."

"Why?"

Fear prickled at his neck. Between rapid breaths, Michael answered, "It was too terrible. I did a terrible thing. *Terrible*! He was such a great man. And look what I did! It was . . . It hurts! Don't fucking ask me any more."

"What," Dr. Richard asked gently, "was so terrible about it? What was too terrible to tell me?"

"Many things. Too numerous to go into."

"Tell me about one."

"No."

"Just pick one thing and tell me, Michael."

"No."

"Please. Now. Quick."

"No!" What's this fucker up to?

"Yes, Michael. Tell me." For an instant the thin doctor's eyes grew fierce and commanding. He ordered, "Now! Tell me!"

"The moon," Michael blurted. "It . . ."

"What about the moon?"

"It rose bloody red. The moon is a sheet of blood. Eve is wrapped in the sheet."

"Who's Eve, Michael?"

"Nice try, fucker. Don't expect me to say anything more." Michael swallowed and looked around nervously.

"Where did the blood come from?"

"The moon. Ha, just kidding."

"Where, Michael? Where did the blood come from? Where?!"

In a whisper: "From . . . their head."

"*Whose* head, Michael?" Dr. Richard said, then shouted, "Tell me! Whose head?"

Michael began to speak then he smiled grimly and snarled, "Don't try to trick me, fucker. *His* head. His, his, his head. Abraham Lincoln's head. The sixteenth President of the United States' head. The rail-splitter from Illinois's head. *That's* who I meant. I put a fucker of a bullet in his head."

"Is that what you mean when you'd say 'ahead,' Michael? You were talking about somebody who got hurt in the head? Who? Who *else* got hurt, besides Lincoln?"

Michael blinked, and sizzled in panic. "Seward, you're thinking of! Secretary of State. But he got *stabbed*! If you're going to trick me, get your facts straight. He didn't enjoy the evening much either, by the way."

"But someone else got *shot*, didn't they?"

"No!"

"Think, Michael. Think back. You can tell me."

"No!" He pressed his hands over his ears. "No, no, no!"

"Where did all that blood come from? Blood everywhere!" Dr. Richard whispered. He leaned forward. "So much blood. Enough blood to cover the moon. Sheets and sheets of it."

Enough blood to cover the sheet . . .

Michael cried, "There was so *much* of it."

"Who else, Michael? Who else got shot? Please tell me."

"I *tell* you, you *tele*graph the CIA and the Secret Service!"

"It'll be our secret, Michael. I won't tell another living soul."

"Will you tell a *dead* soul?" he roared, throwing his head back and raving into the pouring rain. "*They're* the ones we have to worry about! All the *dead* souls! *That's* where the danger is!"

"Who, Michael? Tell me."

"I . . ."

Oh, what's that on your head? What's that you're wearing? Daddy'll be home soon. Daddy'll make her take it off.

Her beautiful head, all ruined. No, no!

"Michael, talk to me! Why are you crying?" Dr. Richard gripped his arm. "What are you thinking?"

He's thinking: I came into the house. I'd been in the backyard doing many important things. I came into the house and there she was, and there were no masks on her eyes and her fingernails weren't burning. There she was in the bedroom, wearing the same nightgown she'd worn for days and days and days. Very *fashionable*. The *very* thing to wear to go by the store to buy the store. The *very* thing to wear when you're holding a gun, this *very* gun. John Wilkes Booth had given it to her.

"Michael! What's the matter? Look at me! What are you thinking?"

He's thinking: Booth must have been her lover and he gave her this gun—to protect her from dead Union *sold*iers. But she *sold* me out. She betrayed me!

"Did you say betrayal? I can't hear you. You're muttering. What are you saying, Michael?"

She held the gun in her hand. She was lying in bed in her nightgown. She sat up when I came into the doorway and she said . . . She said . . . She said, "Oh, you."

Michael heard her words tonight, as he'd heard them a million times before—spoken not in surprise or contempt or supplication but out of infinite disappointment.

He's thinking: And then she kissed her gold hair with the lips of the gun, and blood flew high as the moon and covered her head like a red glistening hat. It covered the sheets.

Oh, you . . . Oh, you . . .

Michael had stood in the doorway of her bedroom as he watched the blond hair grow dark under the crimson hat. Then he leaned down and touched her quivering hand awkwardly, the first physical contact between mother and son in years. Her unfocused eyes grew dark as eclipses, her forked fingers shuddered once and relaxed and then slowly lost whatever warmth they'd once held, though Michael let go long, long before her flesh grew cold.

"The beautiful head . . ."

"*Whose*, Michael?"

Then the memories vanished, as if a switch had been shut off. The tears stopped and Michael found himself gazing down at Dr. Richard, who was now only a foot or so from him.

"Who?" said the doctor desperately.

"Nice try," Michael said, cheerfully sarcastic. "But I don't think so."

Dr. Richard closed his eyes for a moment. His lips tightened then he sighed. "Okay, Michael. Okay." He fell silent for a moment then said, "How 'bout we drive back to the hospital together? I've got the BMW. We talked about going for a ride sometime. You said you'd like that. You said a BMW was one fucker of a car."

"Fucker of a *Nazi* car," Michael corrected.

"Let's go, come on."

"Oh, but I can't, Dr. Richard. I'm going to pay a little visit to Lis-bone. Oh, that was bad, what happened there. I've got some evening up to do."

"Why, Michael? Why?"

"She's the Eve of betrayal," he answered as if it were self-evident.

Dr. Richard's face slowly relaxed. He looked away for a long moment. Then his face brightened—every bit of his face except his eyes, Michael noticed. "Hey, you've got a car too. I'm impressed, Michael."

"It's not like a Cadillac," he sneered.

"Look over there," the doctor said casually. "At that row of cars. All those *Lincolns*. Row after row of *Lincolns*."

"That's interesting, Dr. Richard," Michael said agreeably, studying not the cars but his doctor's face. "But what's more interesting is why you've been hiding your hand behind you all night, you fucker!"

"God, no!" The doctor's left cross thudded harmlessly into the huge chest, as Michael ripped the syringe from the narrow fingers.

"What've we got *here*? This is shiny, oh, this is pretty. You've got a present for me? Oh, I know all about you! You came out all by yourself to stick me in the back and turn me over to the conspirators. So nobody'd know about me, nobody'd know about Dr. Richard's little secret who ran away. Don't tell the world until you're ready. Right? Stick me in the back then stick me in a crash bag, you fucker?"

"No! Don't do this!"

Michael leaned forward. "*Oh, you . . .*" he whispered, and moved the long needle with its razor-sharp beveled edge even with the doctor's eyes. It moved closer and closer, passing inches from his face as the man's thin muscles struggled uselessly against Michael' overwhelming strength.

"Please, no!"

The needle turned directly toward the doctor and started towar his chest.

"No!"

Then, with a skill that came from years of careful observation Michael eased the needle deep into the doctor's skin and injected the drug.

From Dr. Richard's lips came a mournful wail, which seemed not to be a cry of pain but appeared to come rather from a deeper sort of anguish—the sound perhaps of a man realizing that the last image in his thoughts as he died would be the look of betrayal upon the face of someone that he had, in a way, loved.

"How far away was he?" Portia asked.

"Fredericks. It's only eight or nine miles from here. But the roads're bound to be terrible."

They had changed clothes and shared the hair dryer. Lis stood in the kitchen window and saw, through the rain, a dot of light reflecting on the lake, a mile away. The house of their closest neighbor—a couple Owen and Lis knew casually. They were young, married only six months. The woman was very much a hausfrau and on several occasions had talked to Lis breathlessly and with queasy candor about wifedom. She asked many questions and watched with squinting eyes, her elbows on a vinyl placemat, as Lis awkwardly dished out advice about relationships. For heaven's sake, Lis thought, how would *I* know if you should have sex with your husband even if you've got the flu? As if there were rules about such things.

"You're all packed?" Portia asked.

"Packed? Nightgown, toothbrush, underwear. It'll be about a six-

...our stay. God, what I want is a hot bath. They might even catch ...im before Owen gets here. Hey, I need a drink. Brandy?"

"Tastes like soap."

"Acquired taste, granted. Grand Marnier?"

"More my style." ·

Lis poured two glasses and wandered into the doorway of the greenhouse.

"We make a good dam. It's still holding."

A huge burst of wind shook the windows. It howled through the open vents, loud enough to obscure conversation. The leafless trees whipped back and forth and whitecaps broke on the surface of the lake. Lis said that she'd never seen the water this turbulent. A huge streak of lightning split the sky to the west and the floor seemed to drop beneath their feet when the thunder rolled over the house.

"Let's retreat. To the living room?"

Lis was happy to agree.

They sat in silence for a moment. Lis avoided her sister's eyes and glanced instead at a cluster of photographs on the end table. Pictures from their childhoods: Portia, sassy and sexy. Lis, studious and vigilant and, well, plain. Tall, stern Andrew, complete with anachronistic mustache and ubiquitous white shirt. And gracious Mother with her uplifted matriarchal jaw, her eyes commanding everyone except her husband, in whose presence she was timid.

"Portia," Lis said slowly, eyes now on the frames, not the photographs, "I'd like to talk to you about something."

Her sister looked toward her. "The nursery business?"

"No," Lis finally answered. "It's about Indian Leap. What happened there. Between us, I mean. Not the murder. You don't want to talk about it, I know. But will you just listen to what I have to say?"

Portia was silent. She licked the sweet liquor from the rim of her glass and waited.

Lis sighed. "I never wanted to see you again after that day."

"You must've figured that was how I felt too. Since we *haven't* seen each other."

"I've felt so guilty."

"I don't want an apology."

"Hitting you, saying the things I said . . . I was out of control. I've never been that way before. Never in my life. I was everything I always prayed I'd never be."

"You had a good teacher." Portia tapped the photo of their father. "Got your right hook from him, it felt like."

Lis didn't smile; she felt ill with shame and anger. She looked now for signs of forgiveness, softening. But Portia merely sat hugging her glass and staring—almost bored, it seemed—into the greenhouse. The eerie moaning of the wind continued.

Absently, Lis said, "I went to the Dairy Queen the other day. Remember it?"

"They're still around? I haven't been inside one for years."

"No, remember. There *is* no inside."

"That's right. Sure."

Lis pictured them as young girls, with their Dutch bodyguard Jolande, buying the soft vanilla cones at a little screen window and sitting on a sticky picnic bench beside the parking lot. During the day bees hovered, and at night moths and beetles died fast, brilliant deaths as they flew into the mesmerizing purple glow of the bug zapper.

"We'd get the cherry coatings," the younger sister squinted as she recalled.

"And the ice cream was always melting and running down the cone. It was always a race—trying to lick it off before it got to our hands."

"Sure, I remember."

They fell silent, as the whine from the wind grew more piercing. Lis walked to the greenhouse and closed the vent tightly. The sound waned but didn't cease completely. When she returned she said,

I never mentioned it to you, Portia, but I had an affair last spring, nd there are some things I have to tell you about it."

He cruises at seventy miles an hour, the tach on the dash edging ed on the uphill grades, the engine a tortured whine. Owen Atcheson passes the Sav-Mor, now closed, the plate glass taped with uge X's, as if instead of a fall storm a hurricane is anticipated. Then he speeds past a housing development, and beyond that, the Ford dealership, the blue and red sign turning like a lighthouse beacon slowly in the sky.

Then Route 236 begins to curve through the hills that border Ridgeton—the hills that are also part of the same geologic glitch that, two hours away, rises high above the stone valley of Indian Leap, where Robert Gillespie had died broken and bloody.

Owen slows to take these turns then speeds again to fifty, hurrying through the red light at the intersection of 116. The road now rises along the crest of a long hill and he catches a glimpse of water thirty feet below him, off to the right. From the dark creek rise the spindly black legs of the old Boston, Hartford & New York railroad trestle. He slows for the road's only hairpin turn and lifts his foot off the brake to accelerate onto the long straightaway that will take him into downtown Ridgeton.

The beige Subaru seems to drift leisurely from the cleft of bushes where it was hidden, pointed nose out. Owen sees, however, that the car's rear wheels spin furiously, shooting mud and water behind them, and the import is actually moving at a good clip. In the instant before the huge hollow bang, he thinks he might escape, so close do the vehicles approach without striking. Then the car hits the Cherokee solidly amidships with a terrible jolt that twists Owen's neck badly. Pain explodes in his face with a burst of yellow light.

The Subaru stops short of the cliff's edge as the truck eases over the side. It teeters for what seems an eternity, giving Owen Atcheson plenty of time to see the face of Michael Hrubek, a mere six feet away. He's grinning madly, pounding on the wheel, and shouting as he tries frantically, it seems, to make himself heard. Owen stares back but never does figure out what the message might be because just then the truck lurches forward and starts its plunge toward the creek far below.

26

Portia laughed shortly and asked with astonishment, "You? An affair?"

The older sister's eyes were fixed on the sheets of gray rain that cascaded down the windows.

"Me. Wouldn't've guessed, would you?"

There, Lis thought. I've done it. The first time I've confessed. To anyone. There's lightning nearby but so far it hasn't struck me dead.

"You never said anything." Portia was clearly amused. "I had no clue."

"I was afraid, I guess. That Owen would find out. You know him. That temper of his."

"Why would I tell Owen?"

"I didn't think you would. It just seemed to me that the more people who knew, the more the chance word would get out." She paused. "Well, there's something else too. . . . I was ashamed. I was afraid of what you'd think."

"Me? Why on earth?"

"An affair isn't anything to be proud of."

"Were you just fucking? Or were you in love?"

Lis was offended, yet Portia's question seemed motivated merely by curiosity. "No, no, no. It wasn't just physical. We *were* in love. I really don't know why I didn't tell you before. I should have. There've been too many secrets between us." She glanced at her sister. "Owen had an affair too."

The young woman nodded knowingly. Lis was horrified that Portia had somehow learned this already. But, no, it turned out that she'd simply pegged Owen as a man with a wandering eye.

This offended Lis too. "Well, it was only one time," she said defensively.

"Frankly, Lis, I'm surprised you waited as long as you did to find somebody."

"How can you say that?" Lis retorted. "I'm not the sort . . ." Her voice faded.

"Not like *me*?" her sister asked wryly.

"I mean that I wasn't *looking* for anyone. We were trying to work it out, Owen and me. He'd given up the woman he was seeing and we were making a conscious effort—"

"Conscious effort."

Lis listened for mockery and believed she heard none. She continued doggedly, "—an *effort* to keep our marriage together. The affair . . . just happened."

She'd begun the liaison at an awkward time, right in the middle of the terrible sequence of last winter: Owen's affair, the slow death of her mother, her increased discontent with teaching, taking over the estate. . . . The worst *possible* time, she thought, then reflected: As if there's a convenient moment for cataclysm.

Lis's affair, unlike the tidy Hollywood version that she imagined Owen's to have been, had tormented her mercilessly. It would've been far easier, she told herself, if she'd been able to separate the dick from the soul. But she couldn't and so of course she fell in love—as her paramour did with her. At first, Lis admitted, she was partly drawn to her lover out of retaliation. It was petty, yes, but there it was—she wanted to get even with Owen. Besides, she found, she simply couldn't control herself. The affair was all-consuming.

Portia asked, "It's over now?"

"Yes, it's over."

"Well, what's the big deal?"

"Oh," Lis said bitterly, "but it is a *big deal*. I haven't told you everything."

Lis opened her mouth to speak and for an unbearable moment she was about to confess everything. She truly believed that she was going to blurt out every scathing fact.

And she probably would have if the car hadn't arrived just then.

Portia turned from her sister and looked out the kitchen window toward the driveway.

"Owen!" Lis stared out the window, both overjoyed at his arrival and bitterly disappointed that the conversation with her sister was being interrupted.

They walked into the kitchen and peered through the sheets of rain.

"No, I don't think it's him," her sister said slowly. They watched the headlights make their snaking way along the driveway. Lis counted the flares as the beams hit the orange reflectors along the route. Portia was right. Although she couldn't make out the vehicle clearly through the bushes and trees, it was light-colored; Owen's Cherokee truck was black as a gun barrel.

Lis flung open the kitchen door and looked out through the dazzling rain.

It was a police car. A young deputy climbed out. He glanced at the Acura sitting in the middle of the flood and ran into the kitchen, flicking rainwater from his face in an effeminate way. He was round with the tautness of recent fat and had the face of a man on an unexpected assignment.

"Lis." He pulled his hat off. "I'm sorry to have to tell you this. We just found Owen's truck at the bottom of a ravine."

"Oh, God!" Lis's hands flew to her eyes and she pressed hard, as if they stung with smoke.

"He'd been run into—by that fellow Hrubek, looks like. The psycho. Knocked him off the road. Seemed to be a ambush."

"No! Hrubek's going to Boyleston. You're wrong!"

"Well, he ain't going to Boyleston in the car he was driving. Front end's mashed in."

Lis turned instinctively toward where her purse lay on the counter. "How badly hurt is he? I have to go to him."

"We don't know. Can't find him. Or Hrubek either."

"Where did it happen?" Portia asked.

"By the old railroad trestle. Near downtown."

"Downtown *where*?" Lis snapped.

His fat mouth fell silent. Perhaps he suspected her of hysteria. He said, "Well, downtown Ridgeton."

No more than three miles from where they stood.

The wreck wasn't too bad, the deputy explained. "We think Hrubek took off and Owen's after him."

"Or, Owen's running, with Hrubek after *him*."

"We thought of that too. The sheriff and Tom Scalon are out looking for them. All the phones in this part of town're out. Stan had me drive over to tell you. He's thinking you oughta leave. Till they find him. But your car's outta commission, looks like."

Lis didn't respond. Portia told him that they couldn't get a tow truck.

"Believe you'll need more'n a tow for that particular vehicle." He nodded toward the sunken Acura. "Anyway, I'll take you. Just get your stuff together."

"Owen . . ." Lis looked around her, scanning the woods in vain.

"I'm thinking," the deputy said, "we oughta get a move on."

"I'm not going *anywhere* until we find my husband."

Perhaps she sounded ferocious, for the deputy added cautiously, "I understand how you feel. . . . But I don't exactly know there's a lot you can do here but fret. And I'll—"

"I'm not going anywhere," she said slowly. "You understand?"

He looked at Portia, who gave no response. Finally he said, "Have it your way, Lis. That's your business. But Stanley said to make sure you're okay. I better call him and tell him you don't want to leave." He waited a moment more, as if this might intimidate her into leaving. When she turned away he walked out into the rain once more and climbed into the front seat of the cruiser to make the radio call.

"Lis," Portia protested. "There's nothing we can do."

"Go sit in the car with him if you want. Or have him take you to the Inn. I'm sorry, but I'm not leaving."

Portia glanced outside, at a tree bending under a furious gust of wind. "No, I'll stay."

"Go lock the windows. I'll check the doors."

Before he'd left, Owen had deadbolted the front door. Lis now fixed the security chain, thinking momentarily how tiny the brass links seemed compared with the manacles that had gripped Hrubek's hands at trial. She then locked and chained the door off the kitchen utility room. She wondered if Owen had remembered the lath-house door—the only way one could enter or leave the greenhouse from the outside. She walked toward it but paused halfway. She noticed a large rose plant—a Chrysler Imperial hybrid cultivated into a tree. Last year, one week after Owen confessed his affair, he had bought her this plant. It was the only one he'd ever purchased without her guidance. On the day of rest after owning up to Ms. Trollop, Esq., he appeared with the massive scarlet rosebush in the back of his truck. At the time Lis nearly pitched it out. Then she decided not to. The plant owed its reprieve to a passage from a class assignment in *Hamlet*, which her students were then studying.

Cut off even in the blossoms of my sin . . . No reckoning made, but sent to my account, with all my imperfections on my head.

The coincidence was too great to dismiss—this combination of literature, horticulture and real-life drama. So what could Lis do but resist the urge to destroy it? She rooted the damn thing and wondered if the plant would survive. It of course proved to be one of her hardier specimens.

Lis stepped forward and cradled the flower. It was a paradox of her love for plants that her gardener's hands had toughened so much that she could no longer feel the delicacy of petals. She brushed the backs of her hands over the blossoms, then started once again toward the door. She'd taken only a few steps when she saw vague motion from outside.

Walking cautiously to a window, thick with condensation and the sheets of rain, she wiped the glass with her sleeve and saw to her shock the indistinct form of a tall man standing near the house. Hands on his hips, he was trying to find the front door, it appeared. He wasn't the young deputy. Maybe, she thought, another officer had accompanied him, though this fellow didn't seem to be in uniform.

He noticed the side door that led into the utility room and walked to it, oblivious to the downpour. He knocked politely, like a man picking up a date. Lis walked cautiously to the door, and looked out through the curtain. Although she didn't recognize him he had such a pleasant, innocent face, and looked so completely wet, that she let him in.

"Evening, ma'am. You must be Mrs. Atcheson." He wiped his lanky hand on his pants, leaving it just as wet as before, and offered it to her. "Sorry to trouble you. My name's—"

But he didn't have the chance to complete the introduction just then because a large bloodhound pushed his way uninvited into the greenhouse and started to shake himself enthusiastically, showering them both with a million drops of rain.

Owen Atcheson, lying half in and half out of the chill creek, slowly came to. He sat up, praying that he wouldn't faint again.

After the Cherokee had stopped tumbling, Owen hadn't waited for Hrubek to come leaping down the hill after him. He'd examined his left shoulder and felt the indentation where the bone ought to be. He'd made certain his pistol and ammunition were in his pocket and flung the bolt of the deer rifle far into the dark creek, exhaling at the astonishing pain caused by this slight effort.

Then he'd struggled to his feet and run clumsily through the stream, putting distance between himself and the truck.

Two hundred yards into the forest that surrounded downtown Ridgeton he'd stopped and rolled onto his back, lying against a flat rock softened by an old growth of moss. He'd slipped a length of oak branch into his mouth and chewed down hard, gripping his left biceps with his right hand. With excruciating concentration he had forced himself to relax and slowly, slowly manipulated the bone, eyes closed, breathing staccato bursts and sending his teeth deep into the wood. Suddenly, with a pop, the shoulder had reseated itself in the cuff. He cried out softly as the amazing pain made him vomit and then he fainted and slid into the creek.

Now, his eyes open, he crawled to the shore and lay on his side. He allowed himself no more than five minutes of recuperation before standing up. He removed his belt and tightly bound his left arm to his side. The temporary sling increased the pain but would safeguard against a catastrophic jolt of agony that might make him faint again. He lifted his head and breathed deeply. The rain was falling steadily now and the wind whipped into his face. He threw his head back and inhaled the wet air. After a few moments he began to struggle through the woods, slowly making his way north, around downtown Ridgeton. He didn't want Hrubek to find him of course but neither did he wish to be spotted by anyone else—least of all a meddling sheriff or deputy. After a torturous mile he came to the intersection of North Street and Cedar Swamp Road. He found a pay phone and lifted the receiver. He was not surprised to hear only silence.

Driving north on Cedar Swamp was the only way to reach their address. It was possible to approach the house from the opposite direction but only after driving around two hundred acres of state park and into a different township then back south once again. Hrubek had rammed him so hard the Subaru was surely useless; the psycho would now be on foot too. If the Atcheson property was his destination, he'd have to come this way.

Despite the delay to reset his shoulder Owen doubted that Hrubek had preceded him here. Unfamiliar with the area the man would first need to find a map. Then he'd have to orient himself and find the correct streets, many of which were not clearly marked.

Owen struggled into the intersection cautiously—a soldier on advance patrol, sighting out ambush and fire zones, high ground, backfields, perimeters. He saw a drainage ditch and a corrugated metal pipe, four feet wide. A good hidey-hole, he thought, falling easily into combat-speak. He pictured Hrubek loping cautiously down the middle of the road then Owen himself stepping out, silently, coming up behind with the pistol at his side.

The rain was cool and fragrant with the scents of a deep autumn. Owen inhaled this liquid air deeply then slipped down into the icy water that filled the ditch, guarding his damaged arm. But he was no longer faint and was able to ignore the worst of the pain. As he moved in his military crouch, he recited to himself the profile of kill areas: chest head abdomen groin, chest head abdomen groin. . . . He repeated this gruesome mantra again and again as around him the rain grew fiercer.

Lis Atcheson escorted the man into the kitchen and handed him a towel. She decided that in the baseball cap, with the curly hair dipping toward his shoulders, he looked very much like the backhoe operator who'd dug the trench for their new septic tank last year. He stood with one hip cocked in a stiff way that made her wonder if he had fallen and injured it. He looked mussed enough, she thought, to have taken a tumble recently.

"I'm from over in Hammond Creek? East of here?" Trenton Heck spoke as if no one had ever heard of Hammond Creek—a town with which she wasn't in fact familiar.

Lis introduced Portia, who glanced at Heck in a dismissing way. With a juvenile grin Heck waited for an explanation of the exotic name. "Like the car," he laughed. The young woman offered nothing but her hand, and that unsmilingly.

The young officer was in the squad car, trying to get an update on Hrubek's whereabouts.

"Mr. Heck—" Lis began.

"Trenton. Or Trent," he said good-naturedly, laughing. "Mr. Heck, ha."

"Would you like something?"

He declined a beer but guzzled a can of Coke in less than thirty seconds then leaned against the kitchen island, looking out the windows in an analytical, self-assured way that made Lis wonder if he was an undercover policeman. But, no, he explained, he was more of a consultant. When he told her how Hrubek had led the trackers astray then doubled back, Lis shook her head knowingly. "He's no fool at all."

"Nup."

"I thought he was supposed to be crazy," said Portia, who was rubbing the dog's head with an enthusiasm the hound did not share.

"Well, he is that. But he's a clever son of a gun is what he is too."

Lis asked how he happened to come here.

"I met your husband over in Fredericks. We found this woman. Hrubek told her he was headed for Boyleston. So I went that way and your husband was going to keep on coming this way. The deputy tells me they think Hrubek drove him off the road."

"We don't know where he is. We don't know where *either* of them are. Why'd you change your mind and come this way?"

It was something he just felt, Heck explained. He was halfway to Boyleston when he decided that Hrubek was leading them off track again. "He'd been too, you know, methodical about moving west and trying to throw us off or stop us. He even set out traps for Emil here."

"No!"

"Surely did. I was thinking, he's been clever up till now and there's no reason for him to stop being clever."

"But why didn't you just call the police?"

He was suddenly awkward; she thought he was blushing. Eyes fixed on the window, he gave the women his account, which contained not a single period or comma, all about a reward and his being laid off and having been a state trooper for nearly but not quite ten years and a recession and a trailer that was about to be foreclosed on.

Heck then asked about Owen.

"There're men out looking for him. The sheriff and another deputy."

"I'm sure he'll be okay," Heck said. "He seems to know what he's about. Was in the service, I'll bet."

"Two tours of duty," Lis said distractedly, gazing outside.

Heck, paying no attention to the sisters, dropped to his knees and began drying the dog with paper towels in a wholly absorbed, methodical way, even blotting the inside of his collar and wiping the gaps between his stubby claws. He went through the same ritual as he dried his pistol. Watching this, Lis understood immediately that Trenton Heck was both simpler and sharper than she, and she resolved to take him more seriously than she'd been inclined to.

The deputy returned and squeegeed the water from his cheeks with thick fingers.

"Stanley tells me he notified the troopers about Owen's truck. They're passing that info along to some fellow in the state police named Haversham—"

"He's in charge of the search, sure. My old boss," Trenton Heck said. He seemed not to like this news. Because, Lis supposed, he was not keen on losing or sharing his reward. He added, "He'll probably send a Tactical Services squad—"

"What's that?" the deputy asked.

"Don't you know? Like SWAT."

"No fooling?" The deputy was impressed.

Heck continued, "They'll be here in forty minutes, I'd guess. Maybe a little longer."

"Why don't they send them by helicopter?"

"*Helicopter?*" Heck snorted.

Lis looked past the others for a moment as a sheet of lightning canopied the sky. She felt the thunder in her chest. The deputy was asking her something but she didn't hear a word of it and when she left the room she was running. Portia stepped after her and, alarmed, called, "Lis, are you all right? What is it?"

But Lis was by then taking the stairs two at a time.

In the bedroom she found the Colt Woodsman, a thin .22 automatic pistol that Owen kept beside the bed. He'd insisted that she learn to use it and had made her fire the pistol a dozen times into a paper target tacked to a pile of rotten wood behind the garage. She'd done so, dutiful and nervous, her hand jerking unartfully with every shot. She hadn't touched it since then, perhaps three or four years ago.

She hefted the gun now and noted that, unlike rose petals, the checkered grip and metal of this long pistol left strong sensations upon her callused hands.

The pistol disappeared into her pocket. She walked slowly to the window. The immense blackness outside it—lacking any reference point—hypnotized her and drew her forward. Like a sleepwalker she approached the glass, three feet, two, compelled to find something visible on the other side of the blue-green panes—a branch, an owl, a cloud, the verdigris Pegasus weather vane atop the garage, *anything* that would make the darkness less infinite and permanent. Lightning lit the flooded driveway. She recalled waving goodbye to her husband. She realized with a shock that that gesture might have been the last communication between them ever, and, worse, perhaps one that he had not even seen.

She gazed into the night. Where are you, Owen? Where? Lis knew he was near. For she'd by now realized that, injured or not, he was making his way back to the house, trying to get Hrubek onto their property and complete his mission—to kill him and make it look like self-defense. They could be a mile from the house, or fifty yards away. It was only a matter of time.

Another bolt of lightning streaked from the sky and hit nearby. Lis gasped, stepping back, as the thunder rattled the badly glazed eighteenth-century panes. The storm now came forward like a wave, a wall of indifferent water a thousand feet high. It sped frantically across the lake, whose surface was oddly illuminated as if the globules of rain emitted radiation when they collided with the dark water.

A huge growl of thunder enveloped the house, finishing with a sharp whipcrack. Lis hurried downstairs. She pulled her rain slicker from a hook and said, "I'm going outside. I'm going to find my husband."

On April 15, 1865, Doctor Samuel A. Mudd splinted John Wilkes Booth's leg and put him to bed in one of the cots that served as a small infirmary in his home office.

Dr. Mudd had an idea who his patient was and what he'd done the night before but the doctor chose not to ride to town and report Booth to the authorities because his wife was afraid to be left alone with the eerie, feverish man and begged him not to go. Mudd got arrested as part of the conspiracy to assassinate Lincoln and came one vote from being hanged. He was finally released from prison but he died a ruined man.

Michael Hrubek, now reflecting on Mudd's ordeal, thought: He had a woman to thank for that. Just goes to show.

He also thought a doctor might not be a bad idea right at the moment. His wrist burned wildly; it had slammed into the steering wheel when he drove his car into the conspirator's truck. It didn't hurt much but the forearm was glossy, swollen nearly double. From fingers to elbow it was a log of flesh.

As he walked through the rain, however, he grew too excited to worry about his injuries.

For Michael Hrubek was in Oz.

The town of Ridgeton was magical to him. It was the end of his quest. It was the Promised Land and he looked at every strip of pale November grass and every rain-spattered parking meter and mailbox with respect. The storm had darkened most of downtown and the only lights were battery-driven exit and emergency signs.

The red rectangles of light added to the mythic quality of the place.

Standing in a booth, he flipped through a soggy phone book and found what he sought. He recited a prayer of gratitude then turned to the map in the front of the book and located Cedar Swamp Road.

Stepping back into the rain Michael hurried north. He passed darkened businesses—a liquor store, a toy store, a pizza restaurant, a Christian Science reading room. Wait. A *scientific* Jesus Our Lord bless us? Jesus Cry-ist was a physic-ist. Cry-ist was a chem-ist. He laughed at this thought then moved on, catching ghostly images of himself in the plate-glass windows. Some of them were protected by wrinkled sheets of amber plastic. Some were painted black and were undoubtedly used for surveillance. (Michael knew all about one-way mirrors, which could be purchased for $49.95 from Redding Science Supply Company, plus shipping, no COD orders please.)

" 'Good night, ladies,' " he sang as he splashed through a torrent of water in the gutters. " 'Good night, ladies . . .' "

The street ended at a three-way intersection. Michael stopped cold and his heart suddenly began to crawl with panic.

Oh, God, which way? Right or left? Cedar Swamp is one way but it is *not* the other. Which? Left or right?

"Which *way*?" he bellowed.

Michael understood that if he turned one direction he would get to 43 Cedar Swamp Road and if he turned the other he would not. He looked at the signpost and blinked. And in the very small portion of a second it took to close and open his eyelids, his rational mind seized like an overheated engine. It simply stopped.

Explosions of fear surged through him, so intense that they were visible: black and yellow and orange sparks popped through the streets, caroming off the windows and wet sidewalks. He began a fearful keening and his jaw shook. He sank to his knees, pummeled by voices—the voices of old Abe, of the dying soldiers, of the conspirators. . . .

"Dr. Anne," he moaned, "why did you *leave* me? Dr. Anne! I'm so afraid. I don't know what to do! What should I do?"

Michael hugs the signpost as if it's his only source of blood and oxygen and he cries in panic, searching his pockets for the pistol. He must kill himself. He has no choice. The panic is too great. Unbearable terror cascades over him. One bullet in the head, like old Abe, and it'll all be over. He no longer cares about his quest, about betrayal, about Eve, about Lis-bone and revenge. He must end this terrible fear. The gun is here, he can feel its weight, but his hand is shaking too badly to reach into his pocket.

Finally he rips the wool and slips his hand inside the rent cloth, feeling the harsh grip of the pistol.

"I . . . can't . . . STAND . . . IT! OH, PLEASE!"

He cocks the gun.

The brilliant light swept across his closed eyes, filing his vision with bloody illumination. A voice was speaking, saying words he couldn't hear. He relaxed his grip on the gun. His head jerked upright and Michael realized that someone was talking to him, not Dr. Anne or the deceased President of the United States or conspirators or good Dr. Mudd.

The voice was that of a scrawny man in his late fifties, sticking his face out of a car window not three feet from where Michael huddled. He apparently hadn't seen the gun, which Michael now slipped back into his pocket.

"Say, you all right, young man?"

"I . . ."

"You hurt yourself?"

"My car," he mumbled. "My car . . ."

The gray and skinny man was driving a battered old Jeep with a scabby canvas top and vinyl sheets for windows. "You had an accident? And you couldn't find a phone that worked. Sure, sure. They're mostly all out. 'Causa the storm. How bad you hurt?"

Michael breathed deeply several times. The panic diminished.

"Not bad but my car's in a state. She wasn't that good. Not like the old Cadillac."

"No. Well. Come on, I'll ride you over to the hospital. You should get looked at."

"No, no, I'm fine. But I'm turned around. You know where Cedar Swamp is? Cedar Swamp Road, I mean."

"Sure I do. You live there?"

"People I'm suppose to see. I'm late. And they'll be worried."

"Well, I'll drive you over."

"You'd do that for me?"

"I think I ought to be taking you to the emergency room what with that wrist of yours."

"No, just get me to my friends. There's a doctor there. Dr. Mudd, you know him?"

"Don't believe I do, no."

"He's a good doctor."

"Well, that's good. Because that wrist is pretty surely broken."

"Give me a ride"—Michael stood up slowly—"and I'll be your friend till your dying day."

The men hesitated for an uncomfortable moment, then said, "Uh-huh . . . Well, hop in. Only mind the door. You're a tall one."

"Owen's trying to make it back here to the house," Lis explained. "I'm sure of it. And I think Hrubek's chasing him."

"Why wouldn't he just go to the station house?" the deputy asked.

"He's worried about us being here, I'm sure," Lis said. She said nothing about the real reason that Owen wouldn't go to the police.

"I don't know," the deputy said. "I mean, Stan told me—"

"Look, there's nothing to talk about," Lis said. "I'm going out there."

The deputy objected uneasily, "Well, Lis . . ."

Portia again echoed his thoughts. "Lis, there's nothing *you* can do."

Heck took off his pitiful baseball cap and scratched his head. When he replaced the hat, he left a forelock of curly hair dipping toward his right eye. He was studying her. "You testified at his trial?"

Lis looked back at him. "I was the chief prosecution witness."

He was nodding slowly. Finally he said, "I arrested me a fair number of men and testified at their trials. None of them ever came after me."

Lis looked into Heck's eyes, which immediately fled to an old Shaker chair. She said, "You were lucky, then, weren't you?"

"That I was. But it's pretty, you know, rare for an escapee to come after somebody. Usually they just hightail it out of the state."

He seemed to want a response but she gave none other than, "Well, Michael Hrubek probably isn't your typical escapee."

"No argument from me there." Heck didn't continue his line of thought.

Lifting the bright rain slicker from the hook by the door Lis said to her sister, "You stay here. If Owen gets back before I do, honk the horn."

Portia nodded.

"Uhn, ma'am?"

Lis glanced at Heck.

"That might make you a bit, you know, obvious, don't you think?"

"How's that?"

"The, uhn, yellow."

"Oh, I didn't think about that."

Heck lifted away the sou'wester and hung it up. Lis reached for her dark bomber jacket but Heck held up a hand. "Tell you what. I'm thinking let's don't any of us go tripping over our own tails here. I know how you feel and everything, him being your husband

and all. But I'm speaking as somebody's done this sort of thing before. I get paid to track people. Let me go out there by myself. No, let me finish. I'll go out and look for your husband and if he's anywhere nearby I'll stand a chance of finding him. Probably a sight better than you. And not only, if you're wandering around out there too, it'll just distract me." His voice was taut, anticipating Lis's protest.

She guessed his essential motive was the reward. Yet what he said was true. And even if Lis happened to find her husband, she wondered how persuasive she would be in urging him to give up the hunt for Hrubek and return home. He hadn't listened to her before; why would he now?

"Okay, Trenton," Lis said.

"What I think we should do is I'll go out in the woods, toward the front gate. He could climb the fence, of course, but I'll risk that. He won't be swimming the lake, not in this wind. That's for sure."

Heck then glanced at the deputy. "I'd say you stay closer to the house. Like a second line of defense. Somewhere near here."

The deputy's interest was rekindled. He'd done his duty and what more could he say to an ornery woman of the house? Now he had allies and might see some action and glory after all. "I'll back the car into the bushes over there," he said excitedly. "How'd that be? I can see the whole of the yard and he won't catch a glimpse of me."

Heck told him that was good idea then said to Lis, "I know your husband's a hunter. Now, you might not feel too comfortable with side arms but you think maybe you could turn one up for yourself?"

Lis took perverse glee in lifting the pistol from her pocket. She held it, muzzle down, finger outside the trigger guard—just as Owen had solemnly instructed her. Portia was appalled. The deputy guffawed. But Trenton Heck merely nodded with satisfaction as if one more item had been crossed off a checklist. "I'll leave Emil with you here. Storm's too fierce even for him. Keep him by you. He's not an attack dog but he's big and he'll make a bushel of noise if someone was to come by uninvited."

"I don't have anything darker that'll fit," Lis said, nodding at the sou'westers.

"That's okay. I'm pretty impervious to water. But I'll take a Baggie for my gun. It's an old German Walther and rusts easy."

He slipped the pistol into a bag and tied the end closed, returning the gun to his cowboy holster. He gazed outside and stretched his leg out for a moment, wincing. She supposed that whatever was wrong with his thigh wouldn't be helped by the rain. The pain seemed quite severe.

The deputy went outside to the car though not before he'd unsnapped the thong of his automatic and circled his fingers around the grip several times like a bad actor in a bad western. Lis heard the car start. He backed into the bushes halfway between the garage and the house. He could turn on his spotlights and illuminate the entire backyard from where he was parked.

Trenton turned to her and spoke in a low voice. "You know how to use that weapon, I'll bet, but I don't suppose you ever *did* use it, not in a situation like this." He didn't wait for confirmation but continued, "What I'd like you to do is shut all the lights out in the house. Sit yourselves away from the windows. I'll keep my eye on the property as best I can. Flick the lights if you need me and I'll come running."

Then without a word to either woman, or his dog, he vanished into the sheets of rain. Lis closed the door behind him.

"Jesus, Lis," Portia whispered but there were so many things she might be shocked by that her sister had no idea to what she was referring.

Thoughts of his wife are long gone from Dr. Ronald Adler's mind. The way she tastes, the arc of her thigh, her skin's texture, the smell of her hair—memories that so occupied him earlier in the evening are wholly absent now.

For Captain Haversham called him not long ago with the news.

"Cloverton," the trooper growled. "Hrubek just killed a woman. The lid's off it now, doc."

"Oh, my God." Adler closed his eyes and his heart seemed to fibrillate as he was lanced with the mad thought that Hrubek had committed this crime solely for the purpose of betraying him. He held the phone in quivering hands and heard the trooper explain with ill-concealed fury how Hrubek had murdered a woman and carved her up, then stolen a motorcycle to escape to Boyleston.

"A *motorcycle*. Carved her up?"

"Cut words on her boobs. And two cops in Gunderson are missing. They were cruising down Route 236 and called in with a report on him. Last we heard. We're sure he's killed 'em and dumped the bodies somewhere. Low-security? Harmless? Jesus *Christ*, man. What were you *thinking* of? I'll be in your office in a half hour." The phone went dead.

Adler is now on his way back to his office from the hospital's cafeteria, where he had taken Haversham's dismaying call and where he had then sat, numb, for the next thirty minutes. But the doctor isn't making very good progress.

Alone in the dark hallway he pauses and spends a moment considering the chain reaction of miraculous physiology that's now causing his neck hair to stir, his eyes to water, and his genitals to contract alarmingly. And although he's thinking about the vagus nerve and adrenaline release and synaptic uptake, what's most salient in his mind is how fucking scared he is.

The corridor is 130 feet long. Twenty doors open off it and all but the last one—his—are closed and dark. Every other bulb in the overhead fixtures has been removed as an economy measure and of those remaining most are burnt out. Three corridors also lead off this one. They too are dark as graves.

Adler looks down the dark hallway and wonders, Why aren't I walking?

He's left the elevator alcove and he knows that Haversham is waiting impatiently in his office. Yet here the doctor stands frozen with fear. His arms are weak, his legs too. He squints away an unfunny apparition—a huge pale form that has stuck its head out of a corridor nearby and darted back into hiding.

The patient's ghostly wailing is displaced by the howl of the wind. It reverberates in Adler's chest, and he thinks, All right. Enough. Please.

Adler walks five paces. Again he stops—on the pretext of flipping through a file he carries.

It is at this moment that he is struck by the sudden awareness that Michael Hrubek has returned to kill him.

That there's no logic to this mission doesn't lessen Adler's growing panic one bit. He gasps as the elevator, summoned from below, grinds downward. He hears a patient somewhere utter a guttural moan of infinite, inexpressible sorrow. As this sound strokes his neck, he places one foot before the other and doggedly starts walking.

No, no—Michael Hrubek has no need to kill him. Michael Hrubek doesn't even *know* him personally. Michael Hrubek couldn't have made the journey back to the hospital in this short time, even if he *did* feel like eviscerating the director.

Dr. Ronald Adler the veteran of the state mental-health-hospital system, Dr. Ronald Adler the fair-to-middlin' graduate of a provincial medical school—these Dr. Ronald Adlers believe that he's probably safe.

Yet the man whose head was entwined between his wife's fragrant legs earlier in the night, the man who mediates board-meeting conflicts far better than he cures madness, the man who now pads down this murky, stone hallway—*these* Ronald Adlers are paralyzed by the sound of his own gritty footsteps.

Please, don't let me die.

His office now seems miles away, and he gazes at the white trapezoid of light falling onto the concrete from his open doorway. He continues on, passing one of the arterial corridors, and exhales a fast astonished laugh at his inability to turn and look down it. If he does he will see a Technicolor film clip of Michael Hrubek reaching into Adler's mouth. The hospital director cannot purge from his thoughts the passages of Hrubek's transcripts he read earlier in the evening. He recalls in particular detail the patient's lively discussion of locating and rupturing a spleen.

Enough. Please!

Adler passes by the corridor safely but a new worry intrudes—that he'll lose control of his bladder. He's insanely furious at his wife—for gripping his cock earlier in the evening and unwittingly putting in mind the now-consuming fear of incontinence. He must urinate. He absolutely *must*. But the men's room is a lengthy way down the corridor he now approaches. The restrooms are dark this time of night. He considers pissing against the wall.

I don't want to die.

He hears footsteps. No, yes? Whose are they?

The ghosts of one woman and two troopers.

What's that *sound*?

Hah, they're his own feet. Or perhaps not. He pictures the urinal. He turns toward it and begins to walk through the dim hall, and as he does a thought comes to mind: that Michael Hrubek's escape tugs at everything he's ever done wrong as a doctor. The escape is the crib sheets that accompanied him into organic-chemistry exams, it's the charts he misplaced, the misprescribed medications, the aneurysms he forgot to inquire about before dispensing large dosages of Nardil. The madman's escape is like lifting a twenty-pound line and watching rise from a murky pond some diseased fish snagged by your hook, bloated and near death—a prize you regret ever seeking, a token you wish would forever go away.

"Listen to me, you son of a bitch," Haversham growled, after he hung up the telephone. His audience—the hospital director and a glazed-eyed Peter Grimes—stared at him numbly. A grating rain fell heavily on the windows of Adler's office. The wind screamed.

"We just got ourselves another notice," Haversham continued. "This one's from Ridgeton. Seems there's a report somebody crashed into a truck and drove it off the road. Both drivers disappeared into the woods. The truck got hit was registered to Owen Atcheson."

"Owen—?"

"The husband of that woman testified against Hrubek. The fellow who was here before."

So now, maybe four dead.

"They know for a fact it was Hrubek who did it?"

"They *think*. They don't *know*. That's what we need you for."

"Oh, Jesus," Adler muttered. He touched his eyes and pushed until he heard soft pops of pressure beneath the lids. "Four dead," he whispered.

"It's up to you, doc. We need to know where to put our resources."

What was he talking about? Resources?

"No cuddly-pup psychocrap. I want a straight answer. We've had two reports—Boyleston and Amtrak, or Ridgeton and that woman testified against him. Where's he headed?"

Adler gazed at him blankly.

"I think they want to know where to send their men, sir," Grimes explained delicately.

"That's the problem, yeah. Two reports. They don't jibe. Nobody knows jack shit for certain."

Adler looked from his assistant to the tall cowboy of a trooper and thought: Sleep deprivation, that's my problem. "Well, the Ridgeton sheriff has men he can send, doesn't he?"

"Sure he does. Only they got but four in the whole of the department. They sent somebody out to the house so the woman's safe. But I need to know where to deploy. We gotta *catch* this boy! I got four Tactical Services troopers ready to go. The rest of the men won't be available for close to an hour. Where should I send the van? It's your call."

"*Me?* I don't know the facts," Adler blurted. "I need *facts.* I mean, are they sure Hrubek hit Atcheson? Where did he get a car? Was he actually *sighted* on the motorcycle? We can't decide anything until we know that. And—"

"You've got all the facts there are," Haversham muttered, gazing steel-eyed at the doctor. "This boy's been in your care here for four months. Whatever you know about him is all you got to go on."

"Ask Dick Kohler. *He's* Hrubek's doctor."

"We would. But we don't know where he is and he ain't answering his pager."

Adler looked up as if to ask, Why me? He leaned forward and pressed his palms together. He chewed compulsively on a red index finger.

Boyleston . . .

The doctor's finger left his mouth and traced along the same map on which earlier in the evening he had plotted Michael Hrubek's capture and Richard Kohler's downfall.

Ridgeton . . .

Suddenly his face began to bristle, and nothing in this mad universe was as important to Dr. Ronald Adler as capturing his errant patient. Capturing him alive if possible but if not then putting him on a slab with his meaty toe tagged for burial in potter's field, lying cold and blue and still.

Oh, let this night be over, he prayed. Let me slip back home and lie against the hot breasts of my wife, let me find sleep under the thick comforters, let this night end with no more deaths.

Adler ripped open Hrubek's file and leafed frantically through the sheets. They spun out and scattered on his desk. He began to read.

Hrubek, Adler considered, displays classic paranoid-schizophrenic symptoms—thought content illogical, flights of ideas, loose association, pressure of speech and increased motor activities typical of manic episodes, blunted and inappropriate affect. . . .

"No, no, no!" Adler spat out in a whisper, garnering troubled glances from the two men nearby. What, he raged to himself, do these words *mean*? What is Hrubek *doing*? What is *driving* him?

Who *is* Michael Hrubek?

Adler spun his desk chair and gazed out the rain spattered window.

Item: Hrubek suffers from auditory hallucinations and his speech is a typical schizophrenic's word salad. He might have told that truck driver, "Boston," meaning to say, "Boyleston."

Item: Revenge, the purported reason for going to Ridgeton, is a common element of paranoid-schizophrenic delusions.

Item: A schizophrenic would shun the circuitous path of getting to Boyleston via Cloverton.

Item: Amtrak runs through Boyleston. Train travel has a far lower stress factor than air travel, and accordingly would be preferred by a psychotic.

Item: Despite being off Thorazine, he *is* driving a vehicle. Thus Hrubek has, through will or miracle, tamed his anxiety and might make the more arduous and complicated journey south to Boyleston rather than the logistically simpler trip to Ridgeton.

Item: With all his tricks tonight, his false clues and cleverness, Hrubek was displaying astonishing cognitive functionality. He could easily be setting up a feint to Ridgeton, intending all along to go to Boyleston.

Item: But on the other hand he might be *so* high-functioning that he was double-feinting—appearing to head for Ridgeton when that town was in fact his destination.

Item: He's capable of unmotivated murder.

Item: Some of his delusions have to do with United States history politics and government agencies. And several times in his therapy sessions he mentioned Washington, D.C.—a place he could get to via Amtrak.

Item: He has a hatred of women, and he has a rape conviction. He threatened the Atcheson woman several months ago.

Item: He has a fear of confrontation.

Item: He cheeked his medicine, in anticipation of this evening, indicating a long-thought-out plot.

Item . . . *Item* . . . *Item* . . .

A thousand facts cascaded though the doctor's sumptuous mind. Dosages of Haldol and Stelazine, intake-interview observations, milieu-therapy encounters, verbatims of his delusional ramblings, psychopharmacologists' and social workers' reports . . . Adler spun back to confront the files, spearing some sheets of paper beneath his narrow fingers and clutching others randomly. He looked at a page of transcript but he saw instead Michael Hrubek's face—eyes that revealed no ebullience or lethargy, no affection or contempt, no trust or doubt.

Adler sat very still for a moment. Suddenly, he looked up at the lined, exhausted face of the state trooper and spoke what he devoutly believed to be the truth. "Hrubek's making for the train station. He's going to Washington, D.C. Send your troopers to Boyleston. Now!"

The two sisters went about their tasks, combing the house, shutting out lights. They walked in silence, jumping at the noise when there was thunder and at the shadows when there was not. Finally, the house was lit only by ambient light from outside and a few blue up-lamps in the greenhouse, which Lis had left on for the comfort of the faint illumination; she reckoned they'd be invisible from the outside. Shadows fluttered on the walls and floors. Together, they returned to the kitchen and sat side by side on a bench, facing an army of pine and birch trees through the rain-swept backyard.

Five minutes of quiet passed, the rain battering the greenhouse, the wind screaming through the holes and cracks in the old house. Finally Lis was no longer able to keep from speaking. "Portia, there's something I started to tell you tonight."

"Earlier?"

"The affair," Lis whispered discreetly, as if Owen were in the next room.

"I don't know if this is the time—"

Lis touched her sister's knee. "This thing's been between us too long. I can't stand it anymore."

"*What*'s between us? Lis, this isn't really the time to have a talk. For heaven's sake."

"I *have* to talk to you."

"Later."

"No, now!" Lis said heatedly. "Now! If I don't do it now, I may never."

"And why's it so important?"

"Because you have to understand why I said those terrible things to you. And I have to know something from you too. Look at me. Look!"

"Okay, you told me you were seeing somebody. So what? What does Indian Leap have to do with it?"

"Oh, Portia . . ."

Lis must have unknowingly inhaled a huge lungful of air; her chest stung suddenly and she lowered her forehead to her drawn-up knees to ease the pain. In the turbulent silence that flowed between them Lis felt the pain drift away and she lifted her head again to face her sister. As she was about to speak, a faint, not unpleasant roll of thunder filled the room and as it did Portia's eyes narrowed with understanding. She said, "Oh, no."

"Yes," Lis said. "Yes. My lover was Robert Gillespie."

28

"So how long you known the Atchesons?"

The Jeep driver had a narrow face and gray wattles running down his throat. He downshifted the old vehicle and nursed it up a hill north of downtown Ridgeton, exhaust popping and the gears in agony. The big man next to him was studying the shifting with more interest than the driver thought natural.

"Years and years I've known them," he said. "Many years."

"I know Owen," the driver said. "Talked to him a few times. We run into each other at Ace Hardware some. A decent sort. For a lawyer."

"A hundred years, I'd guess."

"Pardon me?"

"Lis-bone especially."

"I didn't think she pronounced it that way. But you know 'em better'n me, I'd guess." The Jeep bounded over a rough spot of road. "You're lucky I come by. Nobody's out on the streets tonight because of the storm. Those weathermen with their toupees and funny names, they said it's going to be a pisser of a storm but naw it's just a little rain is all it is."

The big man didn't respond.

The Jeep hissed past the intersection of Cedar Swamp and North Street and for a moment the driver thought that he saw someone turn quickly, startled by their passage, and drop over the side of a small hill near the drainage ditch. Simultaneously the sky filled with a huge sphere of lightning and shadows danced every which way. A branch fell nearby. The driver put the apparition down to a freak arrangement of lights and fog and rain. He sped up and followed the winding, uneven course of Cedar Swamp. "Shameful on the part of the county. When're they going to get around and do it up right? Put some new asphalt along here? This road's mostly mud and twigs."

"Mud and twigs," the big man fired back. "Mud and twigs."

I believe I may've made a mistake here. "What happened to your car?"

"Mud and twigs maybe, something *you* seem to know a lot about."

When his rider added nothing more, the driver said, "Ahn."

"She slipped out from under me on a slick road. She went and twisted. Rolled over and over."

"What about the police?"

"They're busy elsewhere. Two of them. Two young men. I was particularly sorry about them. Poor Gunderson boys. But I had no choice."

Never again, the driver thought. Never ever again, rain or no rain, cracked wrist bone or no.

The big man stared intently at the trees then with great concentration unlocked and relocked his door seven times. He asked, "You ever been in the army?"

What's the best answer to give? The driver said, "Did a tour, yessir. Was stationed in—"

"Army intelligence?"

"Nope. I was a GI."

The big man frowned. "What's *that*?"

"Government Issue. A dogface. Combat infantryman."

"A GI."

"Yessir."

"GI, GI. *Gee, I* wonder if you know where Abraham Lincoln was shot."

"Uhm."

"In the head. Or during a play. They're *both* right answers."

"I knew that, sure." Oh, brother, what've I done to myself here? "Quite a storm after all. I stand corrected. Glad I got four-wheel drive."

"Four-wheel drive," the man said. "Yes. What *is* that exactly? What *is* four-wheel drive?"

"You don't know that?" The driver blurted a laugh. "Everybody knows what four-wheel drive is." The big man turned to him with a malevolent glare and the driver rubbed the back of his hand across a stubbled cheek, adding, "That was most probably a joke."

"Nice try," the man snapped, leaning across the gearshift, placing his round face very close to the driver's. "But if somebody was *away* in a different *country* for a long time, isn't it possible that they might not know what four-wheel drive is?"

"Put that way, it's more'n possible."

"What if somebody from *1865*, for instance, just showed up now? Are you saying it's not *possible* that they might not know what four-wheel drive is?"

"More'n possible," he repeated miserably. "You know, I'm thinking we should really stop by that hospital. Get your arm looked at."

The big man wiped his face with his stubby peasant fingers, yellow as his teeth, and then took from his pocket a blue-black pistol. He lifted it to his face and smelled it then licked the barrel.

"Ah," the driver whispered and began to pray.

"Take me to the Atchesons' place," the man bellowed. "Take me there now and use all of those damn four-wheeled drivers of yours!"

Several miles up the road the driver pulled the Jeep to a stop, bladder loose and hands quivering. I'll never forgive myself for doing this to the Atchesons, he thought, but this's the way it's gotta be. "That there's the driveway."

"Nice try but I don't see the sign."

"There it is. There! Underneath that rose on the mailbox. See the name? Are you going to kill me?"

"You get out of this car and I want to make it so it won't work anymore."

"The Jeep?"

"Yes. I want to make it so it won't work."

"Okay, I can do that. Let's both get out. Only I'm asking you not to hurt me."

"You ever have a mind to go to Washington?"

"D.C. you're speaking of?"

"Of course D.C.! Who gives a *shit* about Seattle?"

"No, no! Never have. I swear."

"Good. Show me how to dismember this truck."

"You take off the distributor cap and pitch it away. This thing'll never start."

"Do that."

The driver opened the blunt hood of the car and ripped the cap off. It sailed into the woods. He looked completely forlorn. The rain matted his hair and ran into the deep grooves of his face. The big man turned to him. "Now, you think I'm stupid. You're trying reverse psychology. You say you don't *want* to go to Washington hoping I'll say go there? Is that right?"

The man choked. "That's about right, sir."

"Well, I want you to run. You run all the way to Washington, D.C., and tell them that revenge is here."

"Are you going to shoot me in the back?"

"You tell them that."

"Are you going to—"

"RUN!"

He ran, never looking back, believing that he'd die before he got ten feet. Then before he got twenty. Then fifty. Running through the streams of rain, waiting for death. He never turned and so he never saw the big man, holding the pistol high in front of him like a nineteenth-century Pinkerton detective, stalk slowly down the driveway of gravel and mud.

Lis stared at the young woman's face. Even in the dark she could clearly see silver dots of reflection in her eyes. Yet Lis would have turned on all the lights in the kitchen, risked attracting a hundred Michael Hrubeks, to witness her sister's expression at this moment, to see if her words were lies or the truth.

"Tell me honestly, Portia. Did you know about us, Robert and me? Before you . . . made love with him."

Either way I lose, she thought. Either her lover had betrayed her. Or her lover *and* her sister. Still, she had to know the answer.

"Oh, Lis, of course not. I wouldn't do that to you. Didn't you know that?"

"No! How *could* I know. You're my sister but . . . No, I *didn't* know." Lis wiped tears, looking down. "I thought he might have told you, and you, well, you just decided to go ahead anyway."

"No, of course he didn't."

Lis's heart hadn't beat this hard since she'd been in the cave at Indian Leap, fleeing from her mad pursuer. "I didn't know. All these months, I just didn't know."

"Believe me, Lis. Think about it. Why would Robert say anything? He wanted to get laid. He wasn't going to spoil it by confessing that he was my sister's lover."

"When I saw the two of you there together . . ." She closed her eyes and massaged her temple. "And tonight, when you were flirting with Owen . . ."

"Lis."

"Weren't you?"

Portia's lips pressed together tightly. Finally she said, "I flirt, sure. It doesn't mean I want somebody. If Robert'd told me about

you two, I'd've said no. Men look at me. It's a power I have. Sometimes I think it's *all* I have."

"Oh, Portia. It was Robert of course I was so angry with. Not
you. I wanted to hit *him*. I wanted to kill . . ." Her voice faded. "I
felt so betrayed. Claire died because of him. After she saw you two,
she was so upset she ran off and got lost in the cave."

"Half the guys I go out with are Roberts. You can spot 'em a
mile away. Lis, he was all wrong for you."

"No! It's not what you think. It wasn't just a fling. We were
equals, Robert and me. Dorothy was dragging him down. They hated
each other. They fought all the time. And Owen? He doesn't love
me the same way. Not at all. I could feel it. After being with Robert,
all I felt was the absence of Owen's love. The night before the
picnic, that Saturday night . . . Owen was working late in Hartford.
And Robert came over."

"Lis—"

"Let me finish. Owen called and said he wouldn't be home before
two or three. Robert and I made love in the greenhouse. We were
there for hours. He'd pull the petals off flowers and he'd touch me
with them—" Lis closed her eyes and lowered her head once more
to her knees. "And then he proposed."

"Proposed?" From Portia's lips popped her breathy laugh. "He
asked you to *marry* him?"

"He and Dorothy had been unhappy for a long time. She'd been
cheating on him for several years. He wanted to marry me."

"And you said no, right?"

"And," Lis whispered, "I said no."

Portia shook her head. "So he was pissed at you. And when I
turned my big hazel eyes on him in the truck, he jumped at the
bait. Oh, brother, did I put my foot in it, or what?"

"I didn't want to *end* it with him. I just couldn't leave Owen. I
wasn't ready to. He'd given up that woman for me. I thought I
should try to make it work."

"Mistake, Lis. Mis-take. Why didn't you go for it? My God, it may've been your only chance to dump the last of the family."

Lis shook her head, confused. "You?"

"No, no! Owen. You should've done it years ago."

"What do you mean, last of the family?"

Portia laughed. "Doesn't Owen remind you just a little of Father?"

"Oh, don't be crazy. There's no comparison. Why, look what he's doing tonight." She waved at the window. "He's out there for me."

"Owen's a despot, Lis. Just like Father."

"No! He's a good man. He's solid. He *does* love me. In his way."

"Well, Father put a roof over our heads. You call that love?" Portia had grown angry. "You call it love when somebody says, 'You didn't clean up very well this week' or 'How dare you wear that low-cut blouse'? Then lifts up your skirt and leaves those darling little welts on you? The willow tree's still in the backyard, I see. If I'd moved here, that's the first thing that would've gone. I'd've chopped that son of a bitch to the ground in ten seconds flat.

"Tell me, Lis, how did *you* explain the marks in gym class? You probably changed into your uniform with your back to the locker. *I* told everybody I had an older lover who tied me up and jerked off while he whipped me. Oh, don't look so horrified. You talk about love. . . . *Love?* For Christ's sake, if we grew up in such normal circumstances, how come you hide away in this Neverland and why'm I the easiest fuck on East Seventy-second Street?"

Lis buried her head in her arms, the tears streamed.

Her sister said, "Lis, I'm sorry." She laughed. "Look what being back here does. It makes me crazy. I've had more of a dose of family than I can deal with. I knew I shouldn't have come on the picnic. I shouldn't've come tonight."

Lis touched her sister's knee, observing that Portia was once more wearing her gaudy silver rings, and the flecked crystal, like a huge grain of salt, again hung from her neck. A moment passed and Portia lowered her hand onto her sister's toughened, ruddy fingers but offered no pressure and soon withdrew it.

Then Lis too took back her hand and looked out the window, staring at the rain snaking down the glass. Finally she stood up. "There's something I have to do. I'll be back in a minute."

"Do?"

"I'll be right back."

"You're going outside?" Portia sounded frightened, mystified.

"The padlock on the basement door. I have to see about it."

"No, Lis. Don't. I'm sure Owen checked it."

"I don't think so."

Portia shook her head and watched Lis take the gun from her pocket and awkwardly pull the slide to put a bullet in the chamber. "Lis . . ."

"What?"

"Nothing. I . . . Nothing."

Carefully pointing the muzzle toward the floor, Lis dons the bomber jacket. She pauses at the back door, looking back. The old house is dark, this house three stories high and filled with flowers and books and the spirits of many dead. She thinks how odd it is that we're awed by our mortality only during the small moments—when we think of painted fingernails, or a passage of music, or the proximity of sleeping bodies—never at mean, ruthless times like these. She flicks off the safety catch of the gun and feels no fear whatsoever as she steps into the rain-drenched yard.

Owen Atcheson, every inch of his skin wet, in agony, ducked against the muddy embankment of the drainage ditch and cringed like a child as a shaft of lightning engulfed the sky above him. The thunder shook his teeth and sent spasms of pain through his left arm.

After all this, he thought, please don't let me get electrocuted.

He looked along Cedar Swamp Road, down which the Jeep had

vanished five minutes before, sending rooster tails of dirty rain into the air behind it. He'd recognized it as Will McCaffrey's. He supposed the old coot had worked overtime at the mill and was finally heading home.

Owen sank back into the dirty, foaming water. This unpleasantness didn't bother him. On hunting trips, he'd endured leeches, mosquitoes and temperatures of 110 degrees and 30 below. Tonight, he carried only his pistol and twenty rounds of ammunition; on other occasions he'd borne not only his weapons but an eighty-pound pack and, more than once, the body of a fallen comrade as well.

These hardships he could cope with. Far more troubling was the question—where the hell was his prey?

Owen surveyed the terrain for the dozenth time. Yes, he supposed, it'd be possible for Hrubek to avoid the road completely and reach the house through the forest. But that would require a compass and hours of time, and would force him to swim the lake or skirt the shore, which was thickly overgrown and virtually impassable. Besides, Hrubek had shown a strong preference for roads— as if his impeded mind believed that people could be connected only via asphalt or concrete.

Roads, Owen reflected. Cars . . .

The Jeep . . .

McCaffrey, he recalled, didn't live north of town. His bungalow was on the west side. He'd have no need or occasion to take Cedar Swamp, certainly not to reach his house. The only reason someone who didn't live near here would come this way was to take the shortcut to the mall in Chilton. And there sure weren't any stores open there this time of night.

Owen looked up the dark, rain-swept road for a moment then struggled from the water and began the agonizing run to his wife and his home.

29

Trenton Heck slowly climbed the face of the huge rock shelf that cut the Atcheson property in two.

The surface was slick with rain but slipperiness was not the greatest impediment to his twenty-foot climb; rather, Heck's disobedient leg made for very slow progress. He was as exhausted as he was drenched by the time he reached the summit and collapsed on the rocky plain. He caught his breath while he massaged his thigh and scanned the driveway and forest below him. He saw nothing but the mesmerizing flutter of leaves as the rain poured down. After resting for a moment he rose slowly and in a crouch eased along the crest of this hill, parallel to the vague white strip of driveway in the shallow valley below. He made his way slowly from the house toward Cedar Swamp Road—keen to spot Hrubek, yes, but even more eager to find Owen, a man with whom Heck felt considerable kinship. And a man maybe weaponless, maybe injured.

As he moved cautiously toward the road, he found himself thinking about Lis Atcheson. He kept returning to the question that had occurred to him on the hectic drive here after he'd abandoned his journey to Boyleston. Limping into cover behind a tall oak tree for a futile inspection of the rain-drenched panorama beneath him, he wondered again: why exactly was Michael Hrubek after her?

Of course the fellow was maybe completely mad, Heck allowed. Lord knew, enough people seemed to think so. But if Heck understood right, Hrubek'd need one hell of a motive to go through with a trip like this—a journey that clearly terrified him. It'd be like Heck himself standing up and with full intent walking right toward someone threatening to shoot him in the leg again.

Why would a man bring that kind of heartache on himself?

Lis testifying against him? Naw, there had to be more to it. It was true, as he'd told her, that convicts rarely make matters worse for themselves by hurting witnesses.

The only time . . .

Well, usually the only time they carried out threats was when the witness had lied. But why would she've done that?

These musings were interrupted by something Heck saw in the distance: a large cube of faint blue light. It was in the direction of the house. He made his way closer and squinted through the rain. The lights of the greenhouse. She must have forgotten to turn them off. The radiance was, he thought, an unfortunate beacon but there was nothing to be done about it now.

Lightning flared through the forest and Heck was jarred by the encompassing blast of thunder. The lightning troubled him—not from fear of a hit but because he couldn't afford to be light-blinded. Also, a nearby strike would make him, if even for a fraction of a second, as sharp a target as if he'd been flare-lit.

Thunder sounded again.

Or *was* it thunder? The sound was more of a crack than a boom. And now that he thought about it, the noise seemed to have come from the driveway of the Atcheson place. Alarmed, he looked toward the house again for Lis's summoning signal but no lights flashed.

Through the plastic bag he thumbed the old Walther nervously and stalked toward Cedar Swamp Road, surveying the dense forest around him—with its mulchy, cluttered carpet of downed foliage. In this tangle he saw a dozen shadows that clearly resembled the man he sought. Then he forgot about the thunder that resembled a gunshot and grew depressed. The task of finding either Owen or Hrubek suddenly seemed hopeless.

"Oh, man," Heck muttered. Here he'd turned down Kohler's bribe, he'd helped get a woman killed, and he could just *hear* Adler saying, Oh, no, sorry Mr. Heck, it really was Tactical Services that caught Hrubek.

But here's a hundred bucks for your trouble.

"Damn."

Five minutes later he was engaged in a conversation with Jill about his troubles when he saw out of the corner of his eye a flash of light coming from the direction of the house. He stepped forward quickly, thinking at first that it was a summons from Lis. But then he stopped and, squinting through the rain, noted how remarkable it was that light would reflect so vibrantly off a bald, blue-tinted head.

Michael Hrubek was not fifty feet away.

The madman was oblivious to Heck and hiding in a stand of bushes overlooking the garage.

Lord, he's a monster, Heck thought, his face burning at the first sight of his quarry. He trained the Walther, still in the Baggie, on the man's back. He flicked up the thumb safety and, walking as silently as he could, closed the distance between them. When he was thirty feet away Heck took a deep breath and called, "Hrubek!"

The big man jumped and barked out a frightened, pathetic cry. He looked back through the streaming rain toward Heck, his eyes scanning the darkness.

"I want you to lie down on the ground. Do it. I got a gun here."

Okay, Heck thought, he's going to run. You going to shoot him or not? Decide now. Otherwise you chase him.

Hrubek's eyes darted and his tongue appeared, circling his open lips. He seemed like a confused bear, rearing in fright.

Heck decided. Shoot. Park one in his leg.

Hrubek ran.

Heck fired twice. The bullets kicked up leaves behind the fleeing figure, who was covering ground like a wide receiver, dodging trees and crashing over saplings, falling, scrabbling through leaves then leaping to his feet again. He howled in fear. Heck pursued in a fast lope. Though Hrubek carried nearly twice Heck's weight, he set a furious pace and kept his distance for a long ways. But slowly Heck began to gain.

Then suddenly he cried out at a searing eruption of agony. A cramp seized his game leg from calf to hip. Heck dropped to his side, his leg out straight, twitching, muscles hard as oak. He contorted desperately, trying to find a position that would ease the pain. Slowly it subsided on its own, leaving him exhausted and breathless. When he sat up and looked around him Hrubek was gone.

Heck rolled upright and stood, gasping. He scooped up his gun and hurried along the low ridge near where Hrubek had disappeared. Orienting himself, he located the house, a hundred yards away. Through the rain he saw a thousand trees and ten thousand shadows, any one of which might be hiding his prey.

As he started toward the house, hurrying as fast as he dared on the trembling leg, Heck heard the gunshot not more than ten feet behind him. At the same time he felt, with more shock than pain, the tug of the bullet as it tore through his back. "Oh," he gasped. He staggered a few steps, wondering why no one had ever suggested that Hrubek might have a gun. He dropped his pistol and looked down at the pucker of his workshirt where the hot bit of metal had exited.

"Oh, no. Damn."

Dimly, in his mind's eye, Trenton Heck saw his ex-wife Jill in her freshly pressed waitress uniform. Then, as in his actual life, she vanished from him quickly, as if she had far more important matters to attend to, and he dropped to his knees, falling forward and beginning an endless tumble down the hill of slick leaves.

"Lis!" Portia called, as her sister returned to the kitchen and hung up the bomber jacket, shaking the water out of her hair.

Glancing at Portia she locked the door then turned and stared into the backyard, which was just a blur in the heavy rain.

"That noise," Portia blurted.

"What noise?"

"Didn't you *hear* it?" The younger sister paced, and wrung her hands compulsively. "It seemed . . . I mean, it wasn't thunder. I thought there were gunshots. I was worried—where *were* you?"

"I had trouble getting through the mud to the basement door. It was locked after all. Waste of time."

Portia said, "Maybe we should tell the deputy." Lightning struck nearby and she jumped at the thunder. "Shit. I *hate* this."

It was fifty or sixty feet to the police car. Lis stood at the door and waved but received no response from the deputy. Portia said, "He can't see you. Let's go tell him. With the rain he might not've heard anything. All right, don't look at me that way. I'm *scared*. What do you expect? I'm so fucking scared."

Lis hesitated then nodded. She put on the jacket again and a black rain hat that was Owen's—more for camouflage than to protect her drenched hair. Portia pulled on the baseball cap and a navy-blue windbreaker—useless against the rain but less conspicuous than the slicker. Then Lis flung open the door. Portia stepped outside and Lis followed, clutching the gun in her pocket. They were immediately overwhelmed by the storm. They leaned into the torrent of rain and wind and struggled toward the car. Halfway there Lis's hat vanished toward the turbulent lake.

It was from this direction—the lake—that the figure suddenly appeared. He grabbed Lis around the shoulders and they fell together into the saturated mud of one of her rose gardens. The fall emptied her lungs and she bent double, gasping for breath, unable to call for help. His full weight was on her, pinning her to the ground. She yanked at the pistol but the rear lip of the receiver caught in the cloth of her pocket.

Portia turned and saw the assailant. She screamed and made a dash for the police car, as Lis kicked him away. She succeeded only in sliding through a muddy trench and catching herself, in an ungainly sitting position, on the thorny stalk of a blossomless Prospero rose shrub. She was held immobile as the man, his head lowered like an animal's, crawled through the muck after her, muttering eerie sounds. Lis ripped the pocket flap open and pulled the Colt from it. She placed the black muzzle against his head just as Trenton Heck looked up and said, "Help me."

"Oh, my God."

"I'm . . . Can you help me?"

"Portia!" she shouted, pocketing the automatic once again. "It's Trenton. He's hurt. Get the deputy. Tell him."

The young woman stood at the door of the patrol car.

"It's *Trenton*," Lis shouted over the wind and rain. "Tell the deputy!"

But Portia didn't move. She stepped back from the car and began to scream. Lis ripped her jacket from the rosebush and crawled away from Heck. Lis approached her sister cautiously, frowning. Smoke poured from the front seat of the cruiser. Portia pressed her hands over her face then fell to her knees, gagging. A moment later she vomited violently.

When the deputy had been shot—point-blank in the face—the cigarette he held fell into his lap and started his uniform smoldering.

"Oh, no," Portia was crying, "no, no . . ."

Lis pushed her sister aside then scooped up mud and patted out the embers. She too gagged at the smell of burnt cloth, hair and skin.

"The radio!" Portia screamed. She stood, wiping her mouth, and shouted the word twice more before Lis understood. But only a curly black wire protruded from the dash; the handset had been torn off. Lis bent to the deputy once more though there was nothing to be done. He was pasty and cold. Lis stepped away and glanced at the Acura. The water was up to the windows now and had filled the car, covering the cellular phone inside.

Together, the women stumbled through the mud to where Trenton Heck lay on his side. They managed to get him to his feet and struggled toward the back door. The rain pelted their faces and stung; it lay on them heavily like a dozen wet blankets. Halfway to the house a huge gust of wind slapped them from behind and Portia slipped into a trench of mud, pulling unconscious Heck after her. It took long, agonizing minutes to get him out of the soggy yard and to the kitchen. Portia collapsed in the open doorway.

"No, don't stop here. Get him inside."

"I have to rest," Portia gasped.

"Come on, *you're* the runner. You got the stamina genes in the family."

"Jesus."

The women dragged him into the living room and laid him on the couch.

Emil joined them but apparently the hound had no sixth sense of disaster. He sniffed once at his master's boot and went back to the corner he'd commandeered, where he flopped down and closed his eyes. Portia locked the door and turned on a small lamp in the living room. Lis pulled Heck's workshirt open.

"Oh, my God—a bullethole." Portia's voice was high with shock. "Get something! I don't know. A towel."

Lis walked into the kitchen. As she pulled a handful of paper towels off the roll she heard a noise outside—faint at first then growing until it rivaled the howl of the wind. Her heart froze, for the sound reminded her of Claire's final keening, emanating up through the ground from the caves of Indian Leap. Dazed by this terrible memory and her present fear Lis stumbled to the door and stared out. She saw nothing but rain and wind-bent foliage, and it was a moment before she realized that the sound was Michael Hrubek's unearthly cry, calling from nowhere and from everywhere, "Lis-bone, Lis-bone, Lis-bone . . ."

Trenton Heck lapsed into and out of consciousness. Lis tried to find his pulse and couldn't, though when she rested her head on his chest his heart seemed to beat stridently.

"Can you hear me?" she shouted.

Like a sleepwalker he muttered unearthly sounds. He hardly responded to what must have been excruciating pain when Lis pressed the towels firmly against the ragged black-bordered hole in his stomach.

Portia sat in the corner of the living room, her arms folded around her knees, her head down. Lis stood and walked past her. Standing in the dark kitchen she looked out over the yard, and saw no sign of Hrubek, who had ceased calling to her. Still, the macabre sound of his voice, chanting her name, resonated in her mind. She felt tainted, abused. Oh, please, she thought, despairing. Just leave me alone. Please.

For a long moment Lis stood at the window. Then she turned to her sister. "Portia."

The woman looked at her and began shaking her head. "No."

"Put this on." Lis handed her the bomber jacket.

"Oh, Lis, no."

"You're going for help."

"I can't."

"Yes, you can."

"I'm not going out there."

"You know where the sheriff's department is. It's on—"

"The car's stuck."

"You're going to take the deputy's."

Portia gasped. "No. *He's* in it."

"Yes, you are."

"I'm not going. No. Don't ask."

"A left out the drive. A mile and a half down Cedar Swamp you come to North Street. Another left, then drive about six miles. The sheriff's on the right side of the road. Cedar Swamp'll be washed out, parts of it. You'll have to go slow till you get to town."

"No!" Portia's face was awash with tears.

With fingers white from the rain and red from a man's blood Lis seized her sister's shoulders. "I'm going to put you in the car and you're going to drive to the sheriff's."

Portia's eyes flicked to the crimson stains on the sweater. Her voice cracked as she said, "You're getting his—"

"Portia."

"—*blood* on me! No!"

Lis pulled the blue-black gun from her pocket and held it in front of her sister's astonished face. "Don't say another word. You're going to climb into that car and get the fuck out of here! Now let's go!"

She grabbed Portia by the collar and thrust her out into the rain.

With their arms around each other's shoulders, they stumbled toward the car. The ground was so marshy that it took them five minutes to get to the cruiser. The muddy water that surrounded the garage now was approaching the bend in the driveway, four feet deep. Soon the deputy's car too would be submerged.

Once, they lost their balance and fell into the muck. Lis's knee stuck in the ooze and Portia actually had to pull her out with both hands. Foot by foot they made their way through the grimy sluice of water toward the car.

Twenty feet to go.

"I can't look," Portia whispered.

Lis left her at the edge of the driveway and struggled to the squad car by herself. The rain was still heavy but there seemed to be a faint illumination from somewhere in the sky—though it was too early for dawn. Perhaps, Lis thought, her eyes had simply gotten used to the darkness. All her senses seemed honed, like an animal's. She was attuned to the falling temperature, the smells of rain, smoke and compost, the slickness of the mud and pages of wet leaves beneath her. She was poised to attack anyone who might slip into the field of this blood radar.

Reaching for the door handle she looked back at her sister. What is that? she wondered, looking over Portia's shoulder. A dozen yards away a large cloud seemed to form, slowly growing blacker than the surrounding haze of rain. It floated forward unsteadily in their direction.

And finally stepped clearly into view. Michael Hrubek waded toward them, one arm outstretched, the other dangling, apparently injured. In the damaged hand hung a pistol, dwarfed by his fingers.

He was staring directly at Portia.

"Lis-bone . . . Lis-bone . . ."

The young woman spun around and screamed, falling backwards into the mud.

Lis froze. Oh, my God! He thinks she's me!

Hrubek reached toward her. "Eve . . ."

Lifting the dark Colt Woodsman with both her hands Lis pulled the trigger, once, twice, more perhaps. She yanked the sharp tongue of metal so hard she nearly broke her finger. The bullets zipped into the night, missing Hrubek by inches.

He howled and, covering his ears, fled into the brush. Lis ran to her sister and pulled her to the car.

Portia was limp with fear, her head lolling. Lis thrust the gun at her. She took it and stared at the black barrel while Lis reached into the police car, grabbing the beefy deputy by the shoulders. With a huge effort Lis pulled him out of the car and dropped him irreverently into the mud then reached inside and started the engine. She snatched the Colt away from Portia, who started to back away. Lis closed her tough hands on her sister's arms and shoved her into the front seat. Easing into the pool of blood, Portia cringed as if the liquid seared her thighs. She was sobbing, quaking. Lis slammed the door. "Go."

"I . . . Get his legs . . . Get his legs out!" Portia wailed, gesturing down at the deputy, whose knees were directly in front of the rear tires.

"Go!" Lis shouted and reached through the window, pulling on the headlights and dropping the gearshift into drive. As the car jerked forward, the side mirror knocked into Lis. She slipped on a layer of wet pulverized leaves and fell to the swampy ground. Slowly the police car drove over the deputy and into the driveway. Portia gunned the engine. With a panicked spray of mud and marble chips the car sped forward. It vanished, sashaying down the long driveway, sending up plumes of dark water in its wake.

Lis clambered to her feet, blinded for a moment—the rear tires of the squad car had sprayed her with mud. She leaned back, letting the downpour clean her face, flushing her eyes. When she could see once more, she noticed that Michael Hrubek was wading toward her again, cautiously, churning through the water, already halfway across the yard.

Lis slapped her side. The gun was gone. When she'd fallen, it had slipped out of her torn pocket. She dropped to her knees and patted the sticky ooze around her but couldn't find the pistol. "Where?" she cried. "Where?" Hrubek was just thirty feet away, advancing slowly through the waist-high flood surrounding the garage. Finally she could wait no longer and fled into the house, slamming the door behind her.

She double-locked it and from a wooden block took a long carving knife. She turned to face the door.

But he was gone.

Stepping cautiously to the window she surveyed the backyard carefully. She couldn't see him anywhere. She stepped away from the glass, fearing that he might suddenly pop into view.

Where? *Where?*

His absence was almost as frightening as watching him stalk toward her.

Hurrying from the kitchen into the living room, she knelt and checked on Trenton Heck. He was still unconscious but his breathing was steady. Lis stood and gazed around the room, her eyes looking at but not really seeing her family's pictures, the porcelain-bird collection, the Quixote memorabilia her father had brought back from Iberia, the chintz furniture, the overwrought paintings.

A crash outside. Breaking glass. Hrubek was circling the house. A shadow fell across a living-room window then vanished. A moment later his silhouette darkened another curtain and moved on. An unbearable minute of silence. Suddenly a huge kick shook the front door. She gasped. Another kick slammed into the wood. A panel broke with a resounding crack. He kicked it again but the wood held. She saw Hrubek's bulk move past the narrow doorside window.

Her head swiveled slowly, following his circuit of the house. She heard him rip open the toolshed door then slam it shut.

Silence.

A fist rapped on a bottle-glass window in the far guest room. The pane broke but she heard nothing else and guessed the windows were too high and the lattice too solid for Hrubek to climb through.

Silence again.

Then he howled and pounded on a wall, ripping cedar shakes from the side of the house.

As she scanned the rooms, her eyes fell on the basement door. My God, she thought suddenly. Owen's guns. His collection was downstairs. She'd get one of his shotguns.

Yet as she took a step toward the basement she heard a crash from outside. Then more—powerful blows that seemed to shake the foundation of the house. Wood splintered. And with a huge bellow Hrubek kicked his way through the outside basement entrance. The padlock on the door had stopped him for all of thirty seconds. His feet scraped on the concrete floor. A moment later the stairs began to creak, the stairs leading up to the hallway in which she stood.

Oh, Christ . . .

The door to the basement was deadbolted but the fixture was thin brass, more cosmetic than substantial. She looked for something with which to wedge the door closed. Just as the knob started to turn, she lifted a heavy oak dining-room chair and shoved it into hallway, wedging the door shut.

The knob turned sharply. She leapt back, wondering if he could still shatter the door, just kick his way in. But he didn't. After a minute of playing with the knob—almost timidly—he started back down the stairs. The blanket of silence returned, broken by an eerie laughter and the sound of his feet scraping on the basement floor. He muttered words she couldn't hear. After five minutes, even these stopped. Was he still there? Would he set the house afire? What was he doing?

She heard no other sound from downstairs. Or from outside either, other than the steady patter of rain. Michael Hrubek had vanished again. Holding the knife in one hand and leading Heck's hound with the other, Lis Atcheson walked into the greenhouse and sat in a dark corner to wait.

The rain clattered like marbles on the greenhouse roof. Portia'd been gone twenty minutes. It was only eight miles or so to the

Sheriff's Department but the road might now be completely impassable. It could take her an hour or more to get through. Yet as the time passed and she heard nothing more of Hrubek, she began to relax. She even let herself wonder if maybe, just maybe, he'd fled. She felt a glow of euphoria and reflected that perhaps this was all that comfort ever was: believing that we're safe despite the clear and unobvious dangers from which we're protected by nothing more than single-strength glass.

She found herself wondering about Owen. She refused to think the worst. No, no. He was fine. With so much flooding he'd probably ducked into a garage or house to wait out the worst of the storm. She looked up at the black sky above her head and uttered a short prayer for dawn—exactly the opposite of what she usually prayed for, lying in bed, trying so desperately to sleep.

A prayer for light, for morning, for rampaging red and blue and white lights atop approaching cars.

She smelled a rose, whose scent now wafted past her face. Only twenty minutes more. Or nineteen. Or fifteen. Help will be here by then. Surely Michael Hrubek was lost in the forest. Surely he'd fallen and broken his leg.

Lis scratched the dog's ears. "It's all right, your master'll be all right," she said to him as he tilted his head. Lis put her arm around the drooping shoulders. The poor thing. He was as nervous as she —his ears were quivering and his neck was a knot of muscle. Lis eased back and looked at him, the folds of skin and bored-looking eyes. His nose was in the air and his nostrils began twitching. She smiled. "You like roses too, boy? Do you?"

He stood. His shoulder muscles tensed.

An unearthly growl rumbled from deep in his throat.

"Oh, my Lord," Lis cried. "No!"

He sniffed the air hard, his legs eager, his head lifting and falling. He began to walk quickly back and forth over the floor. Lis leapt to her feet and grabbed the knife, looking around her at the misted glass of the greenhouse. She couldn't see through it. Where was he?

Where?

"Stop it," she shouted to the dog, who continued to pace, sniffing the air, growing more and more frantic. Her palms were suddenly slick with cold sweat and she wiped them and gripped the handle of the knife once again.

"Stop it! He's *gone!* He's not here anymore. Stop howling!" She was turning in circles, looking for an enemy only the dog could detect. The growling became a bay, a banshee's wail, ricocheting off every inch of window.

"Oh, please!" she begged. "Stop!"

And he did.

Silently the hound spun around and ran straight to the lath-house door—the one Lis recalled she'd been on her way to check when Heck had arrived.

The door that she'd forgotten completely about.

The door that now burst open and struck the hound in his ribs, knocking him down, stunned. Michael Hrubek stepped into the greenhouse. He stood, dripping and huge and muddy, in the center of the concrete floor. His head swiveled, taking in the gargoyles, the flowers, the mists—all the details—as if he were on a garden-club tour. In his hand was the muddy pistol. Seeing Lis, he called her name in an astonished whisper and his mouth hardened into a smile—a smile that arose from neither irony nor triumph nor even mad humor, but was instead reminiscent of an expression one might find upon the faces of the dead.

31

Standing before her, he was so much larger than she remembered.

At the trial he'd seemed small, a dense bole of evil. Here, now, he filled the large greenhouse, expanding to touch every wall, the gravel floor, the peaked roof. He wiped rain from his eyes. "Lis-bone. Do you remember me?"

"Please . . ." she whispered. The narcotic of fear flooded through her and stilled her voice.

"I've traveled very far, Lis-bone. I fooled them all. I fooled them pretty good. Make no mistake."

She stepped back several feet.

"You told them I killed that man. R-O-B-E-R-T. Six letters in his name. You lied. . . ."

"Don't hurt me. Please."

A fierce growling came from the hound, who was standing tall and tense behind Michael. The flesh of the dog's mouth was drawn back from his ardent yellow teeth. Michael looked down and reached for him as if the dog were a stuffed toy. The hound dodged the hand and sank its teeth into Michael's swollen left forearm. Lis thought he'd scream in agony but the huge man seemed not to feel the bite at all. He lifted the dog by its teeth and dragged him to a large storage closet. He pulled the slavering jaw from his arm and threw the animal inside, slamming the door.

Oblivious to the gleaming razor-sharp knife in her hand Michael turned to Lis. Why bother? He can't feel pain, he's huge, he has a gun. . . . Still, she held the knife firmly in her hand and it was pointed directly at his heart.

"Lis-bone. You were in court. You were part of that betrayal."

"I *had* to be in court. I had no choice. They *make* you be a witness. You understand that, don't you? I didn't mean you any harm."

"Harm?" He sounded exasperated. "Harm? There's harm all *around* you! How could you *miss* it? The fuckers are everywhere!"

Trying to stall him she said sympathetically, "You must be tired."

Ignoring this he said, "I have to tell you something. Before we get down to it."

Down to it.

A chill ran from her neck to her thighs.

"Now *listen* carefully. I can't speak loudly because this room is sure to be bugged. You may know that as sur*veil*lance, where they watch you from behind *veils* or masks or TV screens. Are you *listening*? Good."

He began a lecture, frantic yet passionless. "Justice cures betrayal," he said. "I killed someone. I admit it. It wasn't a fashionable thing to do and I know now it wasn't smart." He squinted, as if trying to recall his text. "True, it was not what *you* think of as killing. But that doesn't excuse me. It doesn't excuse anybody. *Anybody!*" He frowned and glanced at words written in red ink on his hand. They had bled, like old tattoos.

The monologue continued, his subject betrayal and revenge, and he paced the greenhouse floor, occasionally turning his back on Lis. At one point she almost leapt forward and plunged the blade into his back. But he turned quickly, as if suspicious of her, and continued to speak.

With its faint blue-green lights the room seemed far removed from this time and place. It reminded her of a scene from a book she'd read years ago, perhaps the first novel of her childhood. *Twenty Thousand Leagues Under the Sea*. It seemed, in her own numb dementia, that they stood not in a rural greenhouse but in a Victorian submarine and that she was an innocent harpooner, watching the mad captain rant while the dark ocean passed over and around them.

Michael talked about cows and Christian Scientists and women who hid behind unfashionable hats. He mourned the loss of a beloved black car. Several times he mentioned a Dr. Anne and, scowling, a Dr. Richard. Was that, she wondered, Kohler?

Then he wheeled toward her. "I wrote you a letter. And you never answered it."

"But you didn't put a return address on it. And you didn't sign it. How would I know who it was from?"

"Nice try," he snapped. "But you *knew* I sent it."

His eyes were so piercing she said at once, "I knew, yes. I'm sorry."

"*They* kept you from writing, didn't they?"

"Well—"

"The spirits. The con-*spirat*-ors."

She nodded and he rambled on. He seemed to think her given name had seven letters in it. This pleased him enormously and she was terrified that he'd find some correspondence or a bill that would reveal the extra letter and he'd kill her for this deceit.

"And now it's time," he said solemnly, and Lis shivered again.

He pulled his backpack off and set it beside him. Then he undid his overalls, pulling them down over his massive thighs. The fly of his boxer shorts parted and, stunned, she saw a dark stubby penis, semi-erect.

Oh, God . . .

Lis gripped the knife, waiting for him to put down the pistol and pull his engorged prick free. She'd leap the instant he did.

But Michael never let go of the gun. His left hand, the damaged one, was deep within his stained and filthy underwear, as if exciting himself further. But after a moment, when he removed his fingers,

she saw he was holding a small plastic bag. The opening had bee
tied shut with a piece of string and he squinted like an absorbe
child as he carefully untied it with his good hand. He paused t
pull his overalls up once more and with some frustration reclippe
the straps.

He pulled from the bag a piece of newspaper. It was damp an
tattered. He held it out like a tray and on it he reverently place
a tiny perfect animal skull, which he'd taken from his backpack
When she didn't touch either of these, he smiled knowingly at he
caution and laid them on the table beside her. He opened and
smoothed the newspaper clipping then pushed it halfway to her
stepping back like a retriever that had just deposited a shot quail
at a hunter's foot.

His hands were at his side, the gun muzzle down. Lis planned
her assault. She would slip closer and aim for his eyes. What a
horrible thought! But she had to act. Now was the time. She tightened her grip and glanced at the clipping. It was a local newspaper's account of the murder trial, the margins filled with the minute
scrawl of his handwriting. Bits of words, pictures, stars, arrows—a
good freehand drawing of what seemed to be the presidential seal.
A silhouette of Abraham Lincoln. American flags. These all surrounded a photograph Lis recognized: her own grainy black-and-
white image, taken as she walked down the courthouse steps toward
the car after the verdict.

She and Michael were now six feet apart. She casually stepped
closer, lifting the clipping, tilting her head toward it as she pretended to read. Her eyes were on the gun in his hand. She smelled
his foul odor, she heard his labored breathing.

"There's so *much* betrayal," he whispered.

She gripped the knife. His eyes! Aim for the eyes. Do it. Do it!
Left eye, then right. Then roll beneath a table. Do it! Don't hesitate.
She eased her weight forward, ready to leap.

"So much betrayal," he said, and flecks of his spittle pelted her face. She didn't back away. He looked down at the gun and transferred it to his good hand. Lis's grip tightened on the knife. She was incapable of praying but many thoughts filled her mind: Of her father. And mother. Oh, and please, Owen, I hope you're alive. Our love was perhaps damaged but at least, at times, it *was* love. And Portia I love you too—even if we'll never become what I hoped we might.

"All right," Michael Hrubek said. He turned the gun over in his palm and offered it to her, grip first. "All right," he repeated gently. She was too afraid to take her eyes from the pistol for more than an instant but in that brief glance at his face she saw the abundant tears that streamed down his cheeks. "Do it now," he said with a choked voice, "do it quickly."

Lis did not move.

"Here," he insisted, and thrust the gun into her hand. She dropped the clipping. It spun to the floor like a leaf. Michael knelt at her feet and lowered his head in a primitive signal of supplication. He pointed to the back of his head and said, "Here. Do it here."

It's a trick! she thought madly. It *must* be.

"Do it quickly."

She set the knife on the table and held the gun loosely. "Michael . . ." His first name was cold in her mouth. It was like tasting sand. "Michael, what do you want?"

"I'll pay for the betrayal with my life. Do it now, do it quickly."

She whispered, "You didn't come here to kill me?"

"Why, I'd no more kill you than hurt that dog in there." He laughed, nodding toward the supply closet.

Lis spoke without thinking. "But you set traps for dogs!"

He twisted his mouth up wryly. "I put the traps down to slow up the conspirators, sure. That was just a smart thing to do. But they weren't *set*. They were sprung already. I'd never hurt a dog. Dogs are God's creatures and live in pure innocence."

She was shocked. Why, his whole journey this evening mean
nothing. A man who'd kill people and revere dogs. Michael had
traveled all these miles to play out some macabre, pointless fantasy

"You see," he offered, "what people say about Eve isn't true
She was a *victim*. Just like me. A victim of the devil, in her case.
Government conspirators, in mine. How can you *blame* someone
who's been *betrayed*? You can't! It wouldn't be *fair*! Eve was persecuted, and so am I. Aren't we alike, you and me? Isn't it just
amazing, Lis-bone?" He laughed.

"Michael," she said, her voice quivering, "will you do something
for me?"

He looked up, his face as sad as the hound's.

"I'm going to ask you to come upstairs with me."

"No, no, no . . . We can't *wait*. You have to do it. You have to!
That's what I've come for." He was weeping. "It was so terrible and
hard. I've come so far. . . . Please, it's time for me to go to sleep."
He nodded at the gun. "I'm so tired."

"A favor for me. Just for a little while."

"No, no . . . They're all *around* us. You don't understand how
dangerous it is. I'm so *tired* of being awake."

"For me?" she begged.

"I don't think I can."

"You'll be safe there. I'll make sure you're safe."

Their eyes met and remained locked for a long moment. Whatever Michael saw in hers, Lis never guessed. "Poor Eve," he said
slowly. Then he nodded. "If I go there, for you"—he looked at the
gun—"then you'll do it and do it quickly?"

"Yes, if you still want me to."

"I'll go upstairs for you, Lis-bone."

"Follow me, Michael. It's this way."

She didn't want to turn her back on him, yet she felt that some
fragile fiber of trust—spun from madness perhaps but real to him
—existed between them. She wouldn't risk breaking it. She led the

way, making no quick gestures and saying nothing. Climbing the narrow stairs she directed him to one of the spare bedrooms. Because Owen kept confidential legal files here, a strong Medeco lock secured the door. She opened the door and he walked inside. Lis clicked on the light and told Michael to sit in a rocking chair. It had been Mrs. L'Auberget's and was in fact the chair she'd died in, leaning forward expectantly and squeezing Lis's hand three times. He went to the chair and sat. She told him kindly, "I'm going to lock the door, Michael. I'll be back soon. Why don't you close your eyes and rest?"

He didn't answer but examined the chair with approval and began to rock. Then he lowered his lids as she'd suggested and lay his head against the teal-green afghan that covered the chair back. The rocking ceased. Lis closed the door silently and locked it and walked back to the greenhouse. She stood in the exact center of the room for a long time before the swarm of emotions surrounded her.

Another line from Shakespeare slipped into her thoughts. *"No beast so fierce but knows pity."*

"Oh, my God!" Lis whispered. "My God . . ."

She dropped to her knees and began to sob.

Ten minutes later Lis was wiping Trenton Heck's sweaty forehead. He seemed to be hallucinating and she had no idea if bathing his face helped at all. She squeezed a sponge over his skin and wiped away the effluence in a delicate and superstitious way. She was standing up to get more water when she heard a sound at the door. She walked into the kitchen, wondering why she hadn't heard the sheriff's cars arrive or seen their lights. But it wasn't the police. Lis cried out and ran to the door to let Owen inside. Gaunt and muddy, he stumbled into the kitchen, his arm bound to his side with his belt.

"You're hurt!" she cried.

They embraced briefly then he turned, gasping, and gazed outside, surveying the yard like a soldier. Pulling his pistol from his pocket he said, "I'm all right. It's just my shoulder. But, Christ, Lis—the deputy! Outside. He's dead!"

"I know. I know. . . . It was horrible! Michael shot him."

Leaning against the doorjamb he gazed into the night. "I had to run all the way from North Street. He snuck past me."

"He's upstairs."

"We've got to get away from the windows. . . . What?"

"He's upstairs," she repeated, stroking her husband's muddy cheek.

Owen stared at his wife. "Hrubek?"

She held up Michael's filthy gun and handed it to him. Owen shifted his gaze from Lis's haggard face to the pistol.

"This is *his*? . . . What's going on?" He laughed shortly, then his smile faded as she told him the story.

"He wasn't going to kill you? But why did he *come* here?"

As she fell against Owen's chest once more, mindful of his shoulder, she said, "His brain's gone completely. He wanted to sacrifice himself for me, I think. I don't really know. I don't think he does either."

"Where's Portia?"

"She's gone for help. She should've been here by now so I guess the car got stuck."

"The roads are mostly out in the north part of town. She'll probably have to walk."

Lis told him about Trenton Heck.

"That's his truck outside, sure. Last I heard he was going to Boyleston."

"Bad luck for him he didn't," she said. "I don't know if he's going to make it. Could you look at him?"

Owen did, examining the unconscious man with expert hands. He knew a lot about wounds from his military service. "He's in hock. He needs plasma or blood. There's nothing I can do for him."

He looked around. "Where is he? Hrubek?"

"I locked him in the small bedroom upstairs, the storeroom."

"And he just *walked* up there?"

"Like a puppy . . . Oh!" Her hand flew to her mouth. Lis went to the closet and set free Trenton Heck's dog. He was not pleased at the confinement but strode out unhurt.

She hugged Owen again then walked into the greenhouse, picking up the newspaper clipping. She read, *The BETRAYER hIdeS as the crusher of heADs. i AM to be sacrificed to save POOR EVE*

She exhaled in repulsion at the madman's macabre words. "Owen, you should see this." Lis glanced up and saw her husband studying Michael's pistol. He flipped the cylinder open and was counting how many bullets were inside. Then he did something whose purpose she couldn't understand. He pulled on his leather shooting gloves and wiped the gun with the soft cloth.

"Owen, what are you doing? . . . Honey?"

He didn't respond but continued this task methodically.

It was then that Lis realized he still intended to kill Michael Hrubek.

"No, you can't! Oh, no . . ."

Owen didn't look up from the gun. He spun the cylinder slowly so that, she supposed, a bullet was aligned under the hammer. With a loud click the gun snapped shut.

Lis pled, "He wasn't going to hurt me. He came here to *protect* me. His mind's gone, Owen. It's *gone*. You can't kill him!"

Owen stood very still for a moment, lost in thought.

"Don't do it! I won't let you. Owen? . . . Oh, God!"

A ragged white flash of light enveloped his hand and all the panes of the greenhouse rattled at once. Lis threw her palm toward her face in a mad effort to deflect the bullet, which narrowly missed her cheekbone and snipped a lock of her tangled hair as it streaked no more than an inch from her left ear.

32

She fell to the floor, toppling a small yellow rose shrub, and lay on the teal slate, her ear ringing, smelling her own burnt hair.

"Are you mad?" she shouted. "Owen, it's me! It's *me*!"

As he lifted the gun once more, there was a blur of motion, a brown streak. The dog's teeth struck Owen's injured arm just as they had Michael's. But her husband, not numb to the pain, cried out. The pistol flew from his hand and clattered behind him.

Then he was frantically kicking the dog, hammering on its solid shoulder with his good fist. The hound yelped in pain and fled out the lath-house door, which Owen slammed shut.

Lis leapt for the pistol but Owen intercepted her, grabbing her wrist and throwing her to the rocky floor. She rolled, opening patches of skin on her elbow and cheek. She lay for a moment, gasping, too shocked to cry or say a word. As she climbed to her feet, her husband walked slowly toward the pistol.

My *husband*, she thought.

My own husband! The man I've lain with the majority of nights for the past six years, the man by whom I would've borne children had circumstances been different, the man with whom I've shared so many secrets . . .

Many secrets, yes.

But not all.

As she ran into the living room, then down the basement stairs, she caught a glimpse of him standing, gun in hand, looking toward her—his quarry—with a piercing, assured stare.

His gaze was cold and for her money the madness in Michael Hrubek's eyes was twice as human as this predatory gaze.

Poor Eve.

No light. None. The cracks in the wall are large enough to admit air. They're large enough to bleed brown rain, which here falls not from the sky but from the saturated earth and stone of the house's foundation. If the time were two hours later, perhaps the uneven wall would admit the diffuse light of dawn. But now there's nothing but darkness.

The scuffling sounds outside the door.

He's coming. Lis lowers her head to her drawn-up knees. The wound on her cheek stings. Her torn elbows too. She makes herself impossibly small, condensing her body, and in doing so exposing wounds she didn't know she had. Her thigh, the ball of her ankle.

A huge kick against the wooden door.

She sobs silently at the jolt, which is like a blow to her chest. It seems to send her flying into the stone wall behind her and her mind reels from the crash. In the hallway outside Owen says nothing. Was the blow one of frustration or was it an attempt to reach her? The door is locked, true, but perhaps he doesn't know it can be locked from the inside. Perhaps he believes the room is empty, perhaps he'll leave. He'll flee in his black Jeep, he'll escape through the night to Canada or Mexico. . . .

But, no, he doesn't—though he seems satisfied that she's not inside this tiny storeroom and moves on elsewhere in the rambling basement to check other rooms and the root cellar. His footsteps fade.

For ten minutes she has huddled here, furious with herself for choosing to hide rather than flee from the house. Halfway to the outside basement door—the one Michael had kicked open—she'd paused, thinking, No, he'll be waiting in the yard. He can outrun me. He'll shoot me in the back. . . . Lis then turned and ran to this old room in the depths of the basement, easing the door shut behind her, locking it with a key only she knows about. A key she hasn't touched for twenty-five years.

Why, Owen? *Why* are you doing this? It's as if he's somehow caught a virus from Michael and is raging in a fever of madness.

Another crash, on the wall opposite, as he kicks in another door. She hears his feet again.

The room's dimensions are no more than six by four and the ceiling is only chest-high. It reminds her of the cavern at Indian Leap, the black one, where Michael had whispered that he could smell her. Lis thinks too of the times as a girl when she huddled in this same space, then filled with coal, while Andrew L'Auberget was in the backyard stripping a willow branch. Then she'd hear *his* footsteps too as he came for his daughter. Lis read *Anne Frank: Diary of a Young Girl* a dozen times when she was young and although she understands the futility of concealment she always hid.

But Father found her.

Father hurt her doubly when she'd tried to escape from him.

Still, she made this castle keep as defensible as she might—stockpiling crackers and water and a knife and flinging all but one of the green brass keys to the ancient lock into the lake, hiding the remaining one on a nail inside, above the door.

But the mice got the crackers, the water evaporated, a cousin's child found the knife and took it home with him.

And the key proved irrelevant for when Father said open the door she opened it.

Metal sounds on concrete and rings as it falls. Owen grunts as he retrieves the crowbar. Lis cries silently, and lowers her head. She finds in her hand the clipping—Michael's macabre gift, spookier to her than the skull. As the blows begin, she clutches the newsprint desperately. She hears a grunt of effort, silence for the length of time it takes the metal to traverse the passageway outside then a resounding crash. The oak begins to shatter. Yet her room, so far, is inviolable. It's the old boiler room next door that Owen is assaulting. Of course . . . That room has a head-high window. He'd be thinking that she would logically pick the room that offers an exit. But no—smart Lis, Lis the teacher, Lis the scholar after her father's own heart, has cleverly chosen the room without an escape route.

Another crash, and another. A dozen more. The wood shrieks as nails are extracted. A huge crack. His footsteps recede. He's looked inside and seen that she isn't there and that the window is still covered with dusty plywood.

She hears nothing. Lis realizes that she can see again. A tiny shaft of light bleeds into the room around her through a crack in the thin wall shared with the boiler room. Her eyes grow accustomed to the illumination and she peers out, seeing nothing. She cannot hear her husband and she is left alone in this cell with the spirit of her father, a dozen pounds of ancient anthracite, and the clipping, which she now understand holds the explanation as to why she is about to die.

The BETRAYER hIdeS as the crusher of heADs. i AM to be sacrificed to save POOR EVE

The paper is smeared and disintegrating. But she's able to read most of Michael's handwriting.

. . . heADs. i AM . . .

AD . . . AM

ADAM

These sentences, circled, are connected by lines resembling blood veins to the photo accompanying the article. The person they point to, however, is not Lis. They extend to the left of the photograph and converge upon the man who holds open the car door for her.

The BETRAYER hIdeS as the crusher of heADs. i AM to be sacrificed . . .

Michael's inked lines encircle Owen.

The BETRAYER IS ADAM.

Is this the purpose of Michael's journey tonight? Has he come here as an angel of warning, not of revenge? She opens the clipping fully. It is stamped, *Library Marsden State Mental Health Facility.*

Think now. . . .

Michael saw the article in the hospital, perhaps long after the trial. Perhaps in September—just before he sent his note to her. She tried to recall his words. . . . Eve of betrayal. Perhaps his message was not that she was the *betrayer* but rather the *betrayed.*

Perhaps . . .

Yes, yes! Michael's role at Indian Leap was that of witness, not murderer.

"Lis," Owen says calmly. "I know you're down here somewhere. It's useless, you know."

She folds the clipping and sets it on the floor. Perhaps the police will find it in the investigation that will follow. Perhaps the owner of this house fifty years from now will notice the clipping and wonder about its meaning and the people depicted in the photo before tossing it out or giving it to his daughter for a scrapbook. More likely, Owen will comb the house and tidily dispose of it, like every other clue.

He is, after all, meticulous in his work.

No more prayers for dawn. The storm rages and the sky outside is as dark as the hole in which she hides. There are no whipsawing lines of colored lights filling the night. Owen's grisly task will take only seconds: a bullet into her with Michael's gun then one for the madman with his own. . . . Owen would be found sobbing on the floor, clutching Lis's body, raging at the same police who'd ignored him when he begged for protection of his wife.

She hears his footsteps on the gritty corridor outside.

And then, the same as with her father, Lisbonne rises to her feet and, dutifully and with a minimum of fuss, unlocks the door then pulls it gratingly aside.

"Here I am," she says, just as she used to.

Ten feet away Owen holds the crowbar. He's somewhat surprised to see her appear from this direction and he seems, if anything, disappointed that he was careless enough to let his enemy get behind him. She says to him softly, "Whatever you want, Owen. But not here. In the greenhouse." And before he can speak, she has turned her back to him and started up the stairs.

33

He whispers, "You thought I'd never find out."

Lis backs into a rosebush and senses a thorn easing into her thigh. She feels little pain, she hardly hears the rain pummeling the glass roof above them.

"How pathetic of you, Lis. How pathetic. Sneaking into hotels. Strolling on the beach . . ." He shook his head. "Don't look so shocked. Of course I knew. Almost from the beginning."

Her throat clogs with fear and her eyes dip momentarily shut. "And that's why you're doing this? Because *I* had an affair? My God, you—"

"Whore!" He lunges forward and strikes her in the face. She falls to the ground. "My wife. *My* wife!"

"But *you* were seeing someone!"

"That gives you license to cheat? That's not the law in any jurisdiction that I know of."

Lightning flashes though it's now in the east. The heart of the storm has passed over them.

"I fell in love with him," she cries. "I didn't plan on it. Why, you and I spent months talking about divorce."

"Oh, of course," he says in a snide voice, "that excuses you."

"Robert loved me. You didn't."

"Robert was interested in anything in a skirt."

"No!"

"He fucked half of the women in Ridgeton. A few of the men too probably—"

"That's a lie! I loved him. I won't have you . . ."

But through these protests another thought rises into her mind. She considers months and dates. She considers their reconciliation after Owen's affair—just around the time Mrs. L'Auberget was diagnosed as terminally ill. She considers his resistance to buying the nursery. Her tears slow and she looks at him coldly. "It's something else, isn't it? It's not just that I was seeing Robert."

The estate. Of course. Her millions.

"You and Robert talked about getting married," Owen says, "you talked about divorcing me, cutting me out of everything."

"You talk like it's money *you* earned. It was my father's. And I've always been more than generous. I . . . Wait. How did you know Robert and I talked about getting married?"

"We knew."

Stunned by a blow sharper than his palm a moment before, Lis understands. *We* knew. "Dorothy?"

Owen wasn't seeing a lawyer at all. *Dorothy* was his lover. Was and still is. Obedient Dorothy. They planned Lis's death all along. For Owen's insane pride and for the money. Charming, careless Robert had perhaps left some evidence of the affair around the Gillespie household, or perhaps had simply not stopped talking when he should have.

"Who do you think called the day of the picnic to get me into work? That wasn't my secretary. Oh, Lis, you were so blind."

"You were at the park after all. I *thought* I saw you."

"I stopped at the office and had my calls forwarded from there to the phone in the Acura. I was at the park fifteen minutes before you. I followed you to the beach."

And he waited.

Dorothy forgot Lis's copy of *Hamlet* intentionally, thinking that she'd go back to the truck alone for it. Owen would be waiting for her.

But it was Robert, not Lis, who went after the book, hoping to meet Portia. Robert must have wandered past Owen, who attacked him at the mouth of the cave. Bleeding badly, Robert had run inside and Owen had pursued him. Claire must have heard Robert's calls for help and followed.

And it would have been Owen who found the knife Lis had dropped near Robert's body.

"The mutilation! Why, you bastard!"

"Let the punishment fit the crime."

"Michael never hurt Robert?"

"Hurt him? The son of a bitch tried to save him! He was crying, he was saying, 'I'll get that blood off your head, don't worry, don't worry.' Some crap like that."

"And you've been waiting for something like this. . . ." She laughs, looking around her at the night. "You didn't go out there to kill him at all. You went to *bring* him here! You were going to let him . . . let him finish the job tonight!"

"At first I thought that was why he escaped—to come after you. Then I tracked him to Cloverton. He—"

"That woman . . . Oh, Owen . . ."

"No, he didn't hurt her. He just tied her up so she couldn't reach the phone. I found her in the kitchen. He'd been muttering to her that he was on his way to Ridgeton to save someone named Lisbonne from her Adam."

"*You* did it?" she whispers. "You killed her?"

"I didn't *plan* it. It wasn't *supposed* to be this way! I made it look as if he'd done it. I dumped her motorcycle in a river. The cops thought he was going to Boyleston but I knew he was headed this way."

Of course he did. He knew all along that Michael had a motive for coming to Ridgeton—to find the woman who'd lied about him in court.

"And you shot Trenton. And the deputy outside!"

He grows eerily calm now. "It got out of hand. It started simple and it got out of hand."

"Owen, please, listen to me. Listen." She hears in her voice the same desperate but soothing tone with which she'd addressed Michael a half hour before. "If you want the money, for God's sake, you can have it."

But looking at his face, she knows that the money isn't the point at all. She thinks of her conversation with Richard Kohler. Michael might be mad, yes, but at least his demented world is incorruptibly just.

It's her *husband* who's the psychopath; he's the one immune to mercy.

Lis realizes now that he must have begun planning her death from the very beginning of the evening—when he first heard about Michael's escape. Making a scene about the sheriff's putting men here, insisting she go to the Inn—they were just efforts to make him look innocent. Why, after he murdered Michael, he'd have rung up Lis at the Inn and told her to return. All's safe, my love. Come home. But he'd be waiting for her. For her and . . .

"Oh, God," she whispers.

Portia too.

She realizes that he must have intended to kill her as well.

"No!" Her wail fills the greenhouse. "No!"

And she does the very thing she'd left her basement hideout for, the very thing she prayed for strength to do but never believed herself capable of until this instant—she turns, picks up the kitchen knife from the table behind her and swings the blade at him with all her strength.

She's aimed for his neck but instead hits his cheek. His head bounces back from the impact of the metal. The gun flies from his hand. He blinks in shock.

Blood appears instantly, sheets of blood covering his head like a crimson veil.

For an instant they stand motionless, staring at one another, their thoughts as frozen as their bodies. Neither breathes.

Then with the howl of a combat soldier Owen leaps for her. She falls to the ground, dropping the knife, holding her hands over her face to ward off his maniacal pummeling. She takes a stunning strike on her jaw. Her vision crinkles momentarily to black. She drives her fist into his left shoulder. His cries are like an animal's as he leans away, clutching the tormented joint.

But he recovers quickly and renews the assault, his fury overpowering her. She's no match for his strength or weight, even with the wound on his face and a damaged arm. Soon she's on her back, her shoulders and neck lacerated by bits of gravel. His hand is on her throat, squeezing hard. The lights of the greenhouse, blue and green, dim lights all, grow dimmer as her lungs beg for oxygen they can't have. Her hands flail toward his hugely bloody face. They strike only air then fall to the ground. A dust of blackness fills her eyes. She says something to him, words he cannot possibly hear, words she herself does not understand.

In her last moment of consciousness a small shadow forms at some distant focal point—part of her brain dying, she thinks. This shadow grows from a tiny mass to an encompassing darkness that hangs in the air, a wad of black storm cloud. Then the glass roof directly above the struggling couple disintegrates into a million shards, and bits of wood and glass envelop the hurtling shadow like bubbles of air following a high diver into water.

The massive body lands sideways, unbalanced, half on Owen, half on a tall Imperial rose tree, whose thorns dig deep parallel scratches like musical-staff lines along Michael's cheek and arm. He sobs in panic from the twenty-foot leap—a terror that for anyone would be overwhelming and for him must be beyond comprehension.

A long boomerang of glass slits Lis's neck. She rolls sideways away from the struggling men and huddles, covering the wound with a shaking hand.

Through the gaping hole in the glass roof a light mist falls and a few swirling leaves descend. Bulbs shatter under the cold moisture from the sky and the room is suddenly immersed in blue darkness. Then a sound fills the air, a sound that Lis believes at first is the rejuvenated storm. But, no, she realizes that it's the howling of a human voice inflected with madness—though whether it's Michael's or Owen's or perhaps even her own, Lis Atcheson will never know.

Here, in this storm-tossed yard, the vigilant and serious sheriff's deputies dispersed doggedly, combing the house and grounds.

Here the medics, directed first to pale Trenton Heck, took his vital signs and determined that he hadn't lost a critical quantity of blood. Here the same medics stitched and dressed Lis's own sliced neck, a dramatic but unserious wound, whose scar would be with her, she guessed, for the rest of her days.

And here Portia was flying into her sister's arms. Embracing her hard, Lis smelled shampoo and sweat and felt one of the young woman's silver hoop earrings tap against her lips. They hugged for a full minute and when Lis stepped away it was the younger of the two sisters who was crying.

A mud-spattered state-police car arrived, its rooftop speaker already turned to the receiving channel and stuttering with broadcasts, all of which were related to the cleanup efforts following the storm. A tall, gray-haired man stepped out of the car. Lis thought he resembled a cowboy.

"Mrs. Atcheson?" he called.

She caught his eye and he started for her but then paused halfway through the muddy yard to gaze with undisguised surprise, then concern, at Trenton Heck, lying on a gurney. He was barely conscious. The two men said a few words to each other before the medics carted the lanky tracker off to an ambulance.

Don Haversham approached her and asked if she felt like answering a few questions.

"I suppose."

As they were talking, a doctor emerged from one of the ambulances and put a butterfly bandage on the cut on Lis's arm then retreated, saying only, "Hardly a scratch. Wash it."

"No stitches?"

"Nup. That bump on your head, that'll go away in a day or two. Don't worry."

Unaware that she had a bump on her head she said she wasn't worried. She turned back to Haversham and spoke with him for the better part of half an hour.

"Oh, listen," she asked, after she'd finished her account, "could you get in touch with a Dr. Kohler at Marsden hospital?"

"Kohler?" Haversham squinted. "He's disappeared. We were trying to find him."

"Hey, would that be a *Richard* Kohler?" The Ridgeton sheriff had overheard them.

"That's him," Lis said.

"Well," the sheriff responded, "fella of that name was found drunk an hour ago. At Klepperman's Ford."

"Drunk?"

"Sleeping off a bad one on the hood of a Mark IV Lincoln Continental. To top it off, had a raincoat laid over him like a blanket and this skull, looked like a badger or skunk or something, sitting on his chest. No, I'm not fooling. If that ain't peculiar I don't know what is."

"Drunk?" Lis repeated.

"He'll be okay. He was pretty groggy so we got him in a holding cell at the station. Lucky for him he was *on* the car and not driving it, or he could kiss that license *good*-bye."

This hardly seemed like Kohler. But nothing would have surprised her tonight.

She led Haversham and another deputy into the house and coaxed Michael outside. Together they walked him to an ambulance.

"Looks like that's a broken arm *and* ankle," the astonished medic said. "And I'd throw in a couple cracked ribs too. But he don't seem to feel a thing."

The deputies stared at the patient with fear and awe, as if he were the mythical progeny of Jack the Ripper and Lizzie Borden. Michael, upon Lis's solemn promise that it was not poison, consented to a shot of sedative and allowed his own wounds to be cleaned though only after Lis asked the medic to dab antiseptic on her wrist to prove it was not acid. Michael sat in the back of the ambulance, hands together, staring down at the floor, and said not a word of farewell to anyone. He seemed to be humming as the doors closed.

Then Owen, battered but conscious, was taken away.

As was the horrible rag-doll body of the poor young deputy, his blood, all of it, lost in his squad car and in a bed of muddy zinnias.

The ambulances left, then the squad cars, and Lis stood next to Portia in the kitchen, the two sisters finally alone. She looked at the younger woman for a moment, examining the bewilderment on her face. Perhaps it was shock, Lis pondered, though more likely a virulent strain of curiosity, for Portia suddenly began asking questions. Although Lis was looking directly at her, she didn't hear a single one of them.

Nor did she ask Portia to repeat herself. Instead, smiling ambiguously, she squeezed her sister's arm and walked outside, alone, into the blue monotone of dawn, heading away from the house toward the lake. The bloodhound caught up with her and trotted alongside. When she stopped at the far edge of the patio, near the wall of sandbags the sisters had raised, the dog flopped onto the muddy ground. Lis herself sat on the levee and gazed at the gun-metal water of the lake.

The cold front was now upon Ridgeton and the trees creaked with incipient ice. A million jettisoned leaves covered the ground like the scales of a giant animal. They'd glisten later in the sun, brilliant and rare, if there was a sun. Lis gazed at broken branches and shattered windows and shingles of wood and of asphalt yanked from the house. The heavens had rampaged, true. But apart from a waterlogged car the damage was mostly superficial. This was the case with storms around here; they didn't cause much harm beyond dousing lights, stripping trees, flooding lawns and making the good citizens feel temporarily humble. The greenhouse, for instance, had seen several howling tempests and had never been damaged until tonight—and even then it'd taken a huge madman to inflict the harm.

Lis sat for ten minutes, shivering, her breath floating from her lips like faint wraiths. Then she rose to her feet. The hound too stood and looked at her in anticipation, which, she supposed, meant he'd like something to eat. She scratched his head and walked to the house over the damp grass, and he followed.

Epilogue

The blossoms of the floribunda are complicated.

This is a twentieth-century rose plant, and the one that Lis Atcheson now trimmed, a shockingly white Iceberg, was a hearty specimen that spilled in profusion into the entryway of her greenhouse. Visitors often admired the blossoms and if she was to enter it in competition she was confident that it would be a blue-ribbon rose.

Today, as she cut back the shoots, she wore a dress that was patterned in dark-green paisley, the shade of a lizard at midnight. The dress was appropriately somber but it wasn't black; she was on her way to a sentencing hearing, not a funeral.

Although the results would make her a widow of sorts, Lis was not in mourning.

Against his lawyer's recommendation Owen rejected a plea bargain—even after Dorothy turned state's witness in exchange for a manslaughter charge. Owen insisted that he could beat the rap by pleading insanity. An expert witness, a psychiatrist, took the stand and in a long-winded monologue characterized Owen as a pure sociopath. This diagnosis, however, apparently didn't have the same allure to juries that Michael's illness did. After a lengthy trial Owen was convicted of first-degree murder on the first ballot.

Last week Lis signed the contract to purchase Langdell's Nursery and that same day she gave notice to the high school; at the end of the spring semester her twelve-year bout as an English teacher would officially end.

Surprising her older sister, Portia had asked for the nursery's P&L statements and balance sheet, which she'd then shown to her current boyfriend—Eric or Edward, Lis couldn't recall. An investment banker, he'd seemed impressed with the company and recommended that Portia buy into the deal while she still could. The young woman had spent several days considering the proposition then waffled in a big way and declared that she wanted more time to think about it. She'd promised Lis an answer when she returned from the Caribbean, where she planned to spend February and March.

Portia had spent the night and would be accompanying Lis to the hearing today. Following Owen's arrest, the young woman had stayed for three weeks in the Ridgeton house, helping Lis clean and repair. But a week after the indictments were handed up, Lis decided that she wanted to be on her own again and insisted that her sister return to New York. At the train station Portia suddenly turned to her. "Listen, why don't you move into the co-op with me?" Lis was touched by the offer although it was clear that the majority of Portia's heart voted against it.

But the city was hardly for Lis and she declined.

Cranking closed the upper vanes of the greenhouse today, shutting out the winter air, Lis had this thought: We face death in many ways and most are hardly as dramatic as finding the ghosts of our dead ancestors in greenhouses or learning that it's your husband who's traveled miles to slice your thin throat as you lie drowsing in bed. Reflecting on these subtler confrontations with mortality, Lis thought of her sister and she understood that Portia wasn't being perverse or cruel all those long years of separation. Nothing so premeditated as that. There was a simpler point to her escape from the family: she did what she had to.

Too many willow switches, too many lectures, too many still-as-death Sunday dinners.

And who knew? Maybe old man L'Auberget changed his tune

after Lis's fateful swimming lesson, and climbed into the sack with Portia when she was twelve or thirteen. She, after all, was the pretty one.

There was a time when this thought would have been madness and seething heresy. But madness had since come to roost in Lis's own backyard and if the night of the storm—the delicate euphemism the sisters had settled upon—taught her anything it was that there are only real two heresies: lies and our willing acceptance of them.

Trenton Heck would also be at the hearing today. He had an interest in this case beyond justice. Before being removed as director of Marsden hospital by the Department of Mental Health, Dr. Ronald Adler had reneged on the reward Heck felt he was due. Adler's successor could find no moral, let alone legal, reason to pay over the money, which Adler apparently had no authority to pledge in the first place. And so with a certain reluctant desperation Heck sued Owen for shooting him in the back.

The insurance company wouldn't pay off for such malfeasance and Heck was horrified to find that suing Owen ultimately meant suing Lis. He immediately offered to withdraw the case but Lis told him that he more than anyone deserved to profit from this tragedy and over her exasperated lawyer's objections wrote him a check for far more than he asked.

There was, Lis understood, no reasonable connection between the two of them, Trenton Heck and herself, yet in some ways she felt they were stations along the same route. Still, when he asked her out to dinner last week, she declined. It was true that he needed something in his life other than a mobile home and a dog. But she doubted that it was for her to provide whatever that might be.

One person who wouldn't be at the hearing was Michael Hrubek.

On Thanksgiving, at the patient's shy request, Lis had paid him a visit at the Framington State Mental Health Facility, where he was once again under the care of Richard Kohler. Michael at first had been peeved that Lis, as an agent of God, refused to take his life in exchange for that of a nineteenth-century President. But he had apparently come to accept that saving her was part of a complicated spiritual bargain that only he understood and had acquiesced to remaining on this good earth for the time being.

Michael himself had an upcoming trial—for the murder of a fellow prisoner during his escape from Marsden. The evidence clearly suggested that the man's death was a suicide and the case was going forward only because Michael's escape made fools of the hospital and the police. Michael, his attorney assured Lis, would emerge from the trial not only innocent but with a better public image than that of the prosecutor, who, at least one editorial pointed out, ought to have better things to worry about than the death of Bobby Ray Callaghan, an institutionalized killer.

There were other charges too. Auto theft, breaking and entering, assault and the intentional confinement of two extremely unhappy Gunderson police officers in their squad-car trunk, one of them with an extremely painful broken wrist. Michael was admittedly the perpetrator. But he probably would serve no time in prison, the lawyer reported. All he need do was tell the judge the truth—that he was simply evading Pinkerton agents pursuing him for Abraham Lincoln's assassination—and, bang, he'd be out of the lockup and back into his hospital room in no time.

Michael Hrubek was a good example of using history to your own advantage.

Lis now pulled on her coat and called to her sister that it was time to leave. They were taking two cars; after the hearing she was planning to spend an hour or two at Framington.

She'd been back to the hospital several times since Thanksgiving. She was still somewhat wary about seeing him. But she'd found that when sitting across from Michael, sometimes in the company of Richard Kohler, sometimes not, she got an indefinable pleasure from his company. When she entered the room, he took her hand with a delicacy and awe that sometimes moved her nearly to tears. She would like to understand the immensely complex matrix of his emotions. She'd like to understand why he undertook his quest to save her, of all people, and why—even though it was rooted in madness—that journey touched her so.

But those were questions beyond Lis Atcheson, and she was content simply to sit with him in a lounge overlooking the snowy fields and drink coffee and soda from plastic cups while they talked about dairy cows or the state of American politics or insomnia—a problem, it seemed, they both suffered from.

With dancing eyes, Michael would listen carefully to what she had to say then lean forward, sometimes touching her arm for emphasis, and offer his thoughts—some of them illuminating, some preposterous, but always delivered as if he were speaking God's own truths.

And who's to say, Lis sometimes thought, that he isn't?